DONZALO'S DESTINY

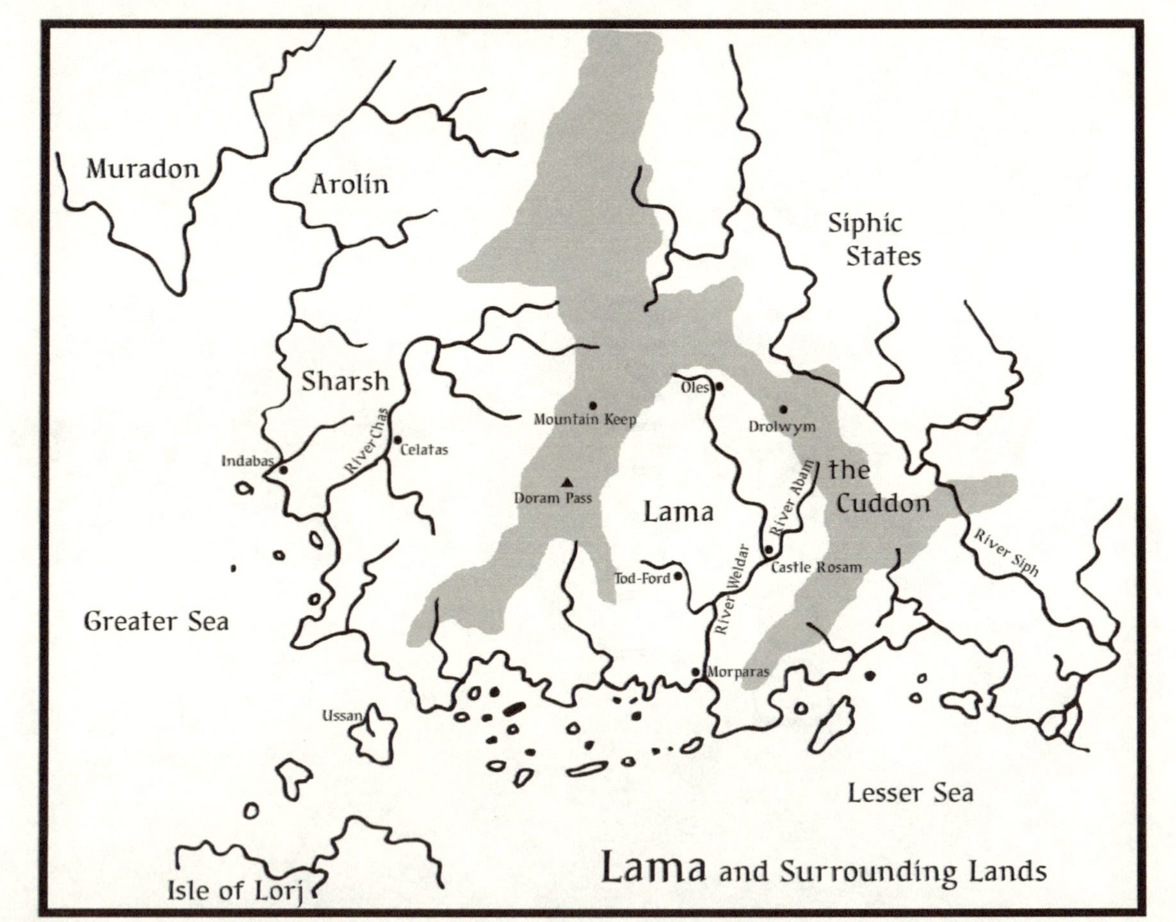

Muradon
Arolin
Siphic States
Sharsh
Oles
Mountain Keep
Drolwym
Indabas
River Chas
Celatas
the Cuddon
Doram Pass
Lama
River Abain
River Siph
River Weldar
Castle Rosam
Greater Sea
Tod-Ford
Morparas
Ussan
Lesser Sea
Isle of Lorj
Lama and Surrounding Lands

Donzalo's Destiny

Stephen Brooke

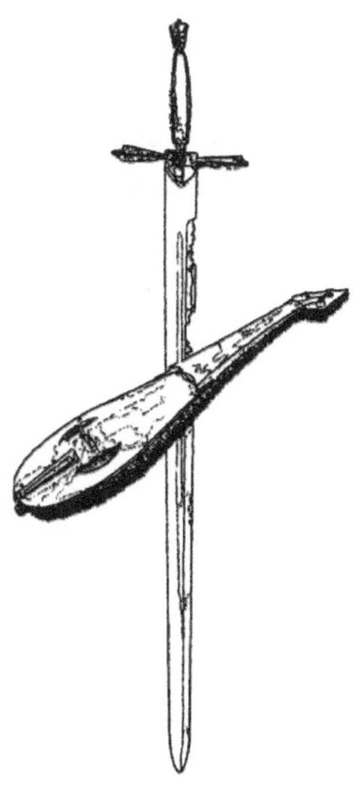

Arachis Press 2016

He knew now with certainty what he had suspected:
Donzalo would be not an ordinary man but a man of destiny.

Donzalo's Destiny
©2016 Stephen Brooke

ISBN 978-1-937745-37-0

Arachis Press
4803 Peanut Road
Graceville, FL 32440
http://arachispress.com

This volume includes the text of the four previously published novels that make up the tale of *Donzalo's Destiny*
  The Song of the Sword
  The Shadow of Asak
  The Sign of the Arrow
  The Hand of the Sorcerer

Book I
The Song of the Sword

Of Sons: the First Tale

1

Tall mountains, tall battlements and a tall man upon them — here, on the border of his realm, Lareth looked to the East. Odd, he mused, that he be in this place. Odd and ironic, for only a generation earlier his father had wrested this land and this castle from old Duke Paren. Now, joined by marriage to that same family, he awaited word making their alliance more permanent. The East would be opened for trade, opened, perhaps, for expansion.

From the battlements, the king had watched his messenger ride in. This arrival meant a report at last, be it good or bad: at worst, the death of his daughter in childbirth. Well loved and youngest of his children, Lareth had regretted the necessity of her marriage to that Eastern clod. Yet that was ever the fate of princesses, to wed where policy best was served.

But now the news, of whatever sort, would be known for here approached the man, escorted by Lord Radal.

"Your highness, the messenger," announced the dark nobleman. A travel-worn knight dropped to one knee before his king.

"Speak."

"Sire, the best of tidings: the Lady Lomela has given birth to a son. Both she and the baby were healthy when I departed Castle Rosam."

The king smiled, but his look of concern remained.

"Excellent news. We thank you — Sir Blen, isn't it? You must be quite weary after such a journey. Go find yourself a meal and a bed.

"Lord Radal, remain please. I have matters to discuss with you."

Radal tossed the man a small purse and dismissed him with a nod. He stood, awaiting his king's word, in the shadow of the stone arches.

Lareth turned from his adviser, looking again to the East.

"Now must we heed the Oracle. Its warning was clear enough."

"Too clear to ignore, my king."

"And Cars is ever a true oracle. You know we cannot change what is to be, Radal."

"Yet, sire, we must try."

"We must try. Yes, we must try." The king spoke quietly now, almost to himself. "There can be no threat to the child nor to his future.

"So we act," he announced, his decision made. "You will be our ambassador, Radal. Take the usual gifts to the parents and the family, and take whom and what you need to remove the danger."

Again gazing eastward, he paused a moment. "Our grandson shall be heir to Borrago, despite the pronouncements of Cars. Go now."

Lord Radal bowed and left his king, brooding still upon the battlements.

Another castle, another man. From his seat at the high table, Count Borrago surveyed the feasters filling his hall. It was large, the Great Hall his father had built, yet it overflowed. Then, with the air of a thoroughly satisfied man, he leaned back and addressed his brother.

"Events could not have turned out better, eh? Our alliance with Sharsh is firmly cemented and I have an heir."

"It's good that your boy settled down and fathered a legitimate son at last," answered the burly Paren, a man given to plain speech.

"Indeed. There are enough bastards about this place. Bolos has been chasing chamber maids and serving wenches since he had legs to run on."

His eyes fell on his younger son, seated at a side table where he listened intently to the tales of a group of travelers. "I sometimes wish Donzalo would run after a woman or two."

"You always judge him too harshly. I would be pleased that he is not like his brother. And he dotes on the child, already."

"I'm glad of that. He and Bolos have never gotten along. Perhaps the baby will bring them closer."

Sir Paren considered this a moment. "I rather doubt it," he said, looking up at the massive ceiling beams, hewn of oak from the forests near his own manor. "Bolos seems to have little interest in his offspring, or in his wife for that matter. I hear he has scarce touched her since their wedding night."

"Apparently, they touched enough," chuckled Borrago. "It's a shame, though, that he and Lomela don't seem to care for each other. I fear she thinks him a complete lout."

"You must admit he can be."

"Yes, and she can put on her airs as well as any other western lady. Then she turns around to become a giggling girl, which is just as bad!"

"Well, that's youth for you. I certainly put up with enough from you when we were boys. And," Paren, ever tolerant, continued with a smile, "she is very young yet. No older than Donzalo."

"Both their heads are filled with the same childish romantic nonsense. There's too much of this Sharshite chivalry about."

"It's the way of the times, Borri. Even quite sensible and serious fighting men try to act the gallant these days.

"Now what's this commotion over by the doors?"

Borrago straightened up to take a look. "Another arrival, I suppose. Go see who it is, will you?"

"No need. Here they come. Ah, they're from Sharsh."

"A rather uncouth assemblage, sir."

Radal glanced at his youthful aide. "The most powerful Eastern nobles are here." His tone was even, matter-of-fact, that of patient teacher to pupil. "They are not to be sneered at."

"The count rises to greet you, my lord. He shows great respect."

"Also his shortness. He stands so as not to be dwarfed by those seated around him, especially his bear of a brother. Remain with the gifts and keep your silence."

The Sharshite lord, a tall, dark, lean man, his stylishly embroidered black tunic gray with the dust of the road, approached the dais to make a deep and graceful bow.

"To his grace, Borrago, Count Rosam, greetings from his royal highness, and your faithful brother, Lareth. I bear the best wishes and congratulations of Sharsh's king and people for Lord Bolos and Lady Lomela at the birth of a son, and gifts for the child." He waved the aide forward. "Here be —"

The count broke in. "It is custom here to present the gifts on the naming day. That will be two days hence, sir."

Radal nodded and gestured for his man to withdraw. "Then, my lord, may I present myself?"

"By all means," spoke Borrago, settling back into his chair. He knew this man, though, and his reputation. Why might such an envoy come to him?

Showing no signs of being disconcerted by the count's direct manner, the Sharshite continued. "I am Radal, Knight and Lord Councilor of Sharsh. In the name of King Lareth, and acting as his personal ambassador, I bid good health to you, my lord, and to all this company, and humbly request your hospitality."

Neither failed to note the stir Radal's name had created among those present. Borrago suspected that the man enjoyed his notoriety.

"Welcome, Lord Radal, to County Rosam and the free lands of Lama." Borrago could not resist pointing out that he and his guests recognized no overlord. Nor did he — nor Radal, for that matter — fail to appreciate the political advantages to be gained by mentioning it before his peers. Too many had concerns about this apparent alliance with Sharsh.

"And welcome to our celebration. But, surely, you are worn with travel. Sir Paren, will you see to our guests?" The look he gave his brother clearly said, "I do not trust this fellow. Keep an eye on him."

The envoy bowed, the ghost of a smile on his thin clean-shaven face. "We thank you for your hospitality, your grace."

"Feel free to join us once you have settled in, Lord Radal," invited the count. "If you are too tired, my brother will have something sent from the kitchens."

"I fear, my lord, fatigue will prevent our presence."

"Until the morrow, then. We ride to the hunt early, should you wish to accompany us. For now, I bid you good night."

"This way, sir," said Paren, and led Sharsh's delegation from the hall.

2

"You didn't return last night."

"By the time I finished with the Sharshites, I was in need of sleep." Paren smiled and added, with an air of mock apology. "You know I'm not as young as I used to be."

"Ha. You could never keep up with me."

"I never wanted to."

"Thank you for attending to them. Any problems?" queried the count. "I see none chose to ride with us this morning."

"It would have been surprising if they had; the way from Sharsh is long and weary, and they rode fast and hard. I am astonished they managed to get a delegation here at all before the naming ceremony.

"Ah the hounds have a scent." Paren shielded his eyes and looked toward his brother's pack.

"Another coyote, no doubt. Let the others ride ahead; I would talk with you."

The knight reined in his horse, a sturdy mount of Anian lineage, bred for the hunt and the hills. Trotting beside his brother, he spoke. "This Radal's presence concerns you?"

"Yes, Parri. It makes no sense for such a man to serve as ambassador." He shook his head. "No sense at all."

"Because of his position?" asked Paren. "Or because of his, uh, reputation?"

"Because of the effect his reputation might create here. Lareth must feel he has some strong reason to risk offending me and the other nobles."

"He fears someone. Why else send an assassin?"

"More than an assassin — a sorcerer."

"I do not trust those who deal in magic."

"Nor do I," agreed Borrago. "But by all accounts he is loyal to his king."

Paren was silent for a moment. "You do not think he would strike at you?"

"At this time? Lareth is not a fool."

"No. Perhaps he only seeks to safeguard the child."

"Perhaps. Some of our guests are, indeed, less than reputable. Did Lord Radal ask after any of them?"

"Not by name. He seemed more interested in the family." Paren raised his head. "It sounds like the chase is on."

The brothers galloped to the top of a ridge. Below was the hunt, in full pursuit of their prey.

"A prairie wolf, isn't it?" asked the count, pointing into the broad, shallow valley.

"Aye. I haven't seen one here in years," answered Paren. "Your hounds have no experience with such prey. You may lose some."

"Can you make out that horseman in the lead? I know your eyes are better than mine."

"Guesare."

"The Cuddonian? He's a bold one." Borrago's tone expressed admiration.

Paren chuckled. "But one of those less than reputable fellows you mentioned."

"True. Let's ride to the kill."

This was the heartland of County Rosam, a patchwork of farm and forest spread upon the rolling hills. The two noblemen angled down the slope to intercept the hunting party.

"The wolf has turned to fight," called Paren, "yet none of your pack has courage enough to close with him."

"They were bred for intelligence," the count retorted.

"Look. Guesare has arrived."

They watched the hunter approach the snarling, harried wolf, ringed by baying hounds. He passed at full gallop, loosing an arrow from the saddle.

"He handles a bow like an Easterner."

"The wolf is down. Now my pack is on it!"

The brothers, and the rest of the hunt, had caught up with the Cuddonian. Dismounting, the master of hounds beat his charges back from their kill.

"A huge beast, my lord," he reported to Borrago.

"Is the skin worth saving?"

"I think not, sir. 'Tis badly torn."

"It was your kill, young Guesare. Do you want a trophy?"

"Dispose of it as you will, Cousin," answered the young man, lounging in his saddle. "I have many such at home."

The count raised an eyebrow, then nodded. "Take the head, Master Saj, and let the hounds have the rest." He wheeled his horse. "Gentlemen, you may continue the hunt without me. Sir Paren and I return to the keep."

"What kin is Guesare to us? A third cousin?"

"I believe so. It's difficult to keep Mother's family sorted out."

"He seems half an Anian."

"Some nobles of the Cuddon do have Ani blood. None in his line, though, as far as I know. Of course," Paren admitted, "there are many things I don't know. He doesn't look Ani, anyway."

The count and his brother were riding up a winding dirt road to Castle Rosam, pasture land on either side. On the highest point of a ridge, overlooking the River Weldar, stood the keep. Less than two miles below, the Weldar was joined by the waters of the Abam. It was one of the most important sites, strategically and economically, in all of Lama.

"His familiarity with me borders on contempt."

"In the marches, we are accustomed to that."

Paren looked wistfully down at River Abam. More than twenty leagues up its stream lay his home, a simple but well fortified manor near the borders of the Cuddon. At heart, he was a farmer, and ill at ease with the politics of Castle Rosam.

"It's good to have you here, Parri, and the Lady Thara, too. We miss a woman's touch in this pile of stones."

"You have Mother." Paren's smile was full of mischief. "Isn't she the mistress of the manor?"

"She's more interested in entertaining young minstrels than running a household."

"I don't suppose Lomela's any help?"

"The girl has been very careful not to assert herself, but she will, in time. I've been watching her build a loyal circle." Borrago gave his brother a meaningful look. "She's very much her father's daughter."

"Bolos will need such a woman by his side."

"If he will listen to her."

They passed through the last of three concentric stone walls, each higher than the one before, to enter the keep. Built on a leveled hilltop, most of the structures here — the great hall, barracks, stables — were of wood. In the center, however, rose a stone tower, Castle Rosam's last line of defense.

Dismounting, Paren gestured toward a trebuchet standing in one corner of the spacious yard. "Why do you have that antique here?"

"That's Donzalo's toy," laughed the count. "He can lob a stone right into the river. Well," he continued, "most of the time. I must admit it's cheaper than playing with a cannon."

"Does he still have some notion of us starting our own foundry?"

"Yes. The boy is a dreamer. Here, lad, take care of our horses." Borrago handed the reins to a groom. "We won't need them again this day."

Perdos and Percos were ill at ease.

"What if we were seen?" asked the older brother.

"Someone might suspect," added Percos, the younger.

"Many visitors have called here," the Lord Radal assured them, "and with so many coming and going all through this keep, none will make special note of you."

"We've been keeping our eyes open, sir," said Perdos. "Do you want a report?"

Radal managed to conceal his contempt. "Later, perhaps." These thugs were useless as spies. What he needed now was muscle. "Do you know young Donzalo?"

"Donzalo?"

"He's not important."

"We've been getting close to Bolos."

"Hmm. What does he think of his brother?"

"He holds him a weakling."

"Yes." Percos nodded his head. "Bolos bullies the boy."

"And what is your opinion?"

The two looked at each other. "I've never thought about it," Percos admitted.

"Me, neither," agreed Perdos.

"But he seems a decent enough young fellow."

"Harmless."

Radal openly sneered. "I need him truly harmless. Can you make him so?"

"Here?" wondered Perdos. "In his father's own manse?"

"Most accidents do occur at home," Percos pointed out.

Perdos gave the Sharshite what he thought a shrewd look. "Pruning the family tree, eh?"

"You might say so, but don't. It is none of your affair."

"It shouldn't be difficult to get the boy alone. He is trusting and keeps no personal retainers about him."

"Over the wall, you think?" Percos asked.

"He might fall into a cistern," suggested Perdos.

"Whatever," interrupted Lord Radal, "but nothing too subtle. It must seem an obvious accident. Any death," he pointed out, "is bound to draw suspicion to me."

"Ah." Percos had an insight. "Otherwise, you'd just poison the lad and be done with it."

The Sharshite was amused. "There is hope for you two. Gold, also, when you are successful." And a life of blackmail later, thought Radal. It would be useful to have these fools in Bolos's inner circle.

"You may leave me now."

"Good afternoon, Grandmother. Lomela? They let you out of bed?"

"I let myself out of bed. It's been near two weeks! My attendants would have kept me there forever. I think they fully expected me to nurse the child, too!" The young mother grimaced. "But the Lady Vibola rescued me and found a wet-nurse."

"Grandmother, you spoil her. Father would not approve."

"Borrago has picked up too many peasant ways in this land," spoke the old woman, from her seat near the fire. It was early spring, and still cool. "Unlike his father, who was a true gentleman of Sharsh." She looked up at the tall, gawky young man. "Come sit by me, Donzalo."

"You speak of the Count Ros, my lady?" inquired Lomela. "What was he like?"

"I wish you would call me Grandmother."

"Very well, my Lady Grandmother," she impishly replied.

"Behave," warned Donzalo, "or we shall start addressing you as 'Princess.'"

"Saucy boy. You should learn your place." The Lady Lomela tossed back her long, wavy hair. She was young and spirited, and knew she was attractive, though no great beauty. "I would know of the man if my son is to be his namesake."

"Ros was the youngest of old Duke Paren's four sons. The other three died in battle against your grandfather's forces." Lady Vibola nodded toward the girl. "But Ros had been sent to aid in the struggle against the Ani here in the East."

"Did the duke die, too?" asked Lomela. "There is disagreement among the histories I have read."

"No, he escaped the taking of his keep. Paren stayed here a time after that." She stopped for a moment, lost in her memories. "An ugly, bandy-legged, little fellow he was," she continued, "with a great, bristling mustache. Borrago rather favors him."

"Didn't he go east?" prompted Donzalo.

"Don't interrupt," Lomela told him.

"He traveled to the Siphic city-states and became a condotierre. Re-married and raised an whole other family there, I understand.

"Ros looked little like his father. He was tall and handsome and very gallant." The old woman let her gaze linger on Donzalo for a moment. He seemed so much like his grandfather. "But a man, still," she mused, "with all the good and ill that brings."

Lomela was suddenly serious. "Was your marriage arranged?"

"He sought my hand. Oh, there were politics involved, to be sure, in its winning. My parents had many doubts as to this adventurer who'd come calling." The old woman smiled. "I helped them make up their minds."

"A minstrel should tell your tale!" Lomela decided. "Let's put one on it."

"None here are good enough," objected Donzalo." Our court does not attract talent."

"I think we may have just the man among our guests," stated Lady Vibola. "I shall invite him to join us later."

3

The naming ceremony takes place tomorrow morning, my lord," Radal's aide informed him. "Feasting in the evening."

"No other celebrations?"

"It is considered a holy occasion, sir, to be kept solemnly. There will be a tourney and fair the next day."

"They do follow the Kamation rites?"

"Largely, sir. They seem a zealous people."

"They are a fanatical people."

"My lord?" The young man was puzzled.

"Their religion and their fight for independence have so intertwined that they see themselves as a holy nation, surrounded by infidels. The years of Anian domination saw to that."

The aide pondered his words. "My lord, doesn't that make them, well, dangerous?"

Radal laughed. "It does, indeed. That, my boy, is why we are here." The nobleman paused a moment. "We should have known when the gift-giving takes place."

The younger man nodded cautiously.

"But that is more my fault than yours. We both were forced to leave Sharsh too hurriedly." Radal's voice took on a serious note. "There is a lesson for both of us there." His eyes returned to the dispatches spread before him.

"Yes, my lord. Will you have further need?"

"I think not. You've some place to go?" He glanced up. "A girl, perhaps?"

"An invitation from the Lady Lomela. You know, my lord, we were friends at court."

"Of course. It got you this assignment."

"Yes, my lord, I was aware of that." Slightly embarrassed, the aide went on. "She wants to introduce me to her circle. The count's younger son will be there, and some minstrel from the east."

"Guesare?" The envoy took sudden interest. That name had occasionally popped up in his dispatches, often linked to questionable occurrences.

"I believe that's the name, sir."

"Go. But later, Jobareth, I want a full report on your evening. Do you understand?"

"Yes, sir."

Radal smiled to himself. He could not have asked for a better spy than this trusting young fellow.

"Bolos drinks much too heavily. Can't you say something to him, dear?"

"He is far past listening to his old uncle."

"Aunt Thara! Uncle Paren!" Donzalo was hastening after them, down the covered walkway that led toward their suite.

"What is it, child?" asked Lady Thara.

"Some of us are getting together in Grandmother's chambers. You are both invited." He paused for breath. "The Lady Lomela will be there, and a new minstrel."

"Oh, Donni, you know I'm not at ease at such gatherings."

"I think we will be retiring, boy."

"You're welcome if you decide to join us." Donzalo was disappointed, though this response had not been unexpected. "Good evening, Aunt Thara." He nodded toward Paren. "Uncle." The young man turned abruptly and hurried away.

"Are you certain you don't want to go?" Paren asked his wife. "You love music."

"Not in your mother's company. I couldn't take an evening of her looking down her nose at me."

"She never understood why I loved a plump little peasant girl." He hugged her. "And I still do."

"Donni's a sweet boy," Thara remarked. "It — it pleases me to think our son might have grown to be like him."

For a moment, both savored the bitter-sweet taste of memory.

"Hmm, yes," spoke Paren. "He will be our heir, I suppose, and reeve of the manor when I am gone. We should have him come stay with us."

"He could be your squire."

"Donzalo would learn little of knighthood at my side."

"But much of running a manor."

"I'll speak to Borri." He smiled at his wife. "It would do us all good."

"Here he comes."

"Act natural, now."

"Good evening, my lord."

Donzalo laughed. "No lord am I."

"Fool," Percos admonished his brother. "It is Master Donzalo."

"A lordling, then, and just as good. Lad, will you have a drink with us?"

"Why do you not drink with my brother?" asked the bemused youth. "Are you not his friends?"

"Lord Bolos dove too deeply into his cups and will not come up till the morn," the younger brother explained. "Won't you join us? We've, um, a full keg downstairs."

"Near the cistern," snickered Perdos.

"I thank you, no. I am expected by the Lady Vibola."

"Let the old woman wait. We have an excellent wine."

"From Sharsh," Perdos added.

"Yes, Sharsh — and a very good vintage," his brother agreed.

"Twenty-two."

"Twenty-two? That's not any good," objected Percos.

"Oh, of course. Twenty-three, 'tis. I had forgotten."

"I haven't the time, gentlemen." Donzalo brushed past them. "And I would thank you to speak more respectfully of my grandmother." He quickly vanished around a corner.

"You certainly ruined that. Vintage of Twenty-two, indeed!"

"It was all your fault. You insulted his granny."

"What do we do now?"

"Grab him after his party."

"And throw him over the wall!"

Perdos thought briefly. "We should have masks. Someone might see us."

"Let's go get them. And let's sample that wine, too."

"Idiot."

"What have you there, Jobareth?"

"A book, my lady. I thought to bring a gift for our hostess."

"She can not read." Lomela looked the slim volume over. "Not your poetry? You've had it printed?"

"There are three presses operating now in the capital, and the cost of printing keeps going down. Soon, everybody will be able to publish a book."

"I do not think Lady Vibola would understand your poems. She would not even understand the courtly language in which they are couched." She took his arm and confided "I read to her often, and her tastes run to the most lurid of romances.

"Come, let me present you. You might as well bring the book." She led the young Sharshite across the room, to where her grandmother-in-law reposed on a centrally placed divan.

"Lady Vibola, this is Master Jobareth Nafal, a gentleman of Sharsh and aide to the Lord Radal."

"My lady." He bent to kiss her hand. The older woman gave the younger an impish look.

"I like this one, Lomela. What have you there, young sir?"

"It's a book of his poems," the girl told her, taking it from his hands. "I shall read them to you later, but I must warn you that they are dreadful."

"Why doesn't the gentleman read some for us?"

Lomela feigned horror. "Oh, Grandmother," she moaned, "don't encourage him!"

"I would be honored, my lady."

"But not now, I think," said the older woman, smiling benevolently. "Lomela will want you to meet her friends."

Lady Vibola's suite of rooms, of paneled pine and draped with tapestries, were the largest private quarters in Castle Rosam. She had appropriated them after the count's wife had died and he moved into a small, spartan space in the tower. Her friends and favorites could gather here, as they had this evening.

Some of those attending were regular visitors, residents of castle or town. Other were guests, come for the naming celebration. Lomela introduced her friend around the room.

"Here's Donzalo, arriving at last," she told him.

"He's a tall one," commented the Sharshite.

"Yes," agreed Lomela. "I suspect he'll fill out and look like his uncle in a few years."

"By the way, my lady, please don't introduce me as 'Master.' It's 'Lector' since I finished at the university."

"Very well," the young woman laughed. "Donzalo will be jealous; his father would not permit him to study abroad." She showed sudden, rather exaggerated, puzzlement. "He's coming over. Now which of you should I present to the other? He's of the more noble family, but you have found a title and position."

Jobareth gave her a suspicious look. "I feel you are poking fun at me, Lady Lomela. But, truly, in his home he takes precedence." Nafal was well-schooled in protocol.

"Very well." She turned to her brother-in-law. "Master Donzalo Rosam, may I introduce Lector Jobareth Nafal?"

"Pleased." He extended his hand but looked at Lomela. "My lady, how is the baby?"

"He is fine, Donzalo, and well cared for, or I would not be here." Her voice took on a note of exasperation. "My servants thought it most frivolous to leave the child on the eve of his naming day."

"That's not surprising, Lomela, I mean, my lady." He turned back toward her friend. "Lector, huh? We must talk later. Very pleased to meet you — I should pay my respects to Grandmother."

"Yes, pleased." An amused Jobareth watched the gawky Laman leave, pushing his way through the crowded room.

"Donzalo can be terribly rude at times but he means nothing by it. Please like him." Lomela sounded anxious.

Nafal nodded. "I already do. And I know the type well; the university is full of them. Including," he laughed, "most of the professors."

More seriously, he noted, "You like him a great deal."

Lomela seemed slightly flustered. "He's the only one in this dismal place with any culture," she replied, "the only one I can — talk with." She was finding it hard to put into words. "Oh, he's the only one here who understands me."

"Then he's a better man than I, my lady. I have always found you quite baffling."

"Humph. I've been around Lamans long enough to see through your courtly banter, Jobareth. Come, the minstrel is about to play."

4

Donzalo's long legs carried him along the western rampart. Behind him scurried two tall figures, heads covered with black cloths, eyes peering through ill-cut holes.

Though not the shortest way to his rooms, it kept him out of the mud and stench and noise of a lower route. And he liked the view here, high above the river and town. The boy longed to pass down the Weldar some day, to the great port Morparas and its university.

As he paused a moment, refreshing this dream, his shadows rushed him.

"Get his legs!" barked one, clamping a hand over the struggling Donzalo's mouth.

"Ow! He kicked me," complained the other. "Got him now."

"Over the wall with him!"

On three sides of Castle Rosam, the hill rose gradually and wide grassy spaces were left between the three concentric walls. Here, it stood steep and the lower battlements were little more than catwalks above a cliff face. He would fall a very long way.

Another figure suddenly joined them. Unlike their intended victim, this was a man who knew how to fight, and fight well. One assailant dropped from a blow to the face. The other let Donzalo loose and attempted to grapple with the newcomer, only to meet hard fists, two to his midsection, one — lower. So, that quickly, it was ended. Doubled over, he and his partner fled.

"Guesare!" the youth choked out.

"If my rebec is damaged, I shall be most unhappy," stated the minstrel, removing the instrument from its bag.

"Wh — what happened?"

"It seems, young kinsman, those ruffians meant to assassinate you." He looked his rebec over. "And nearly succeeded. But neither you nor my instrument," he decided, putting it away, "appears harmed."

"I thank you, sir." Donzalo was puzzled. "Why would anyone wish to kill me? I mean, I am nobody. Even I know that."

"You are third in line to the title of count. That makes you someone." The Cuddonian's mood became sober. "Let's get you to your quarters. I think we need to talk, you and I."

Jobareth knew better than to question his master about the two men — one limping — he passed outside their rooms. He hoped only to slip in unnoticed and find his bed.

Luck was not with him. "Tell me of your evening," ordered Lord Radal, "before sleep softens the memories."

"My lord, it was but a gathering of the more, um, sophisticated Lamans. Something of a welcome diversion in this dour land."

"The Lady Lomela is at the center of this group?"

"Near the center, sir. The count's mother holds that place, but the princess will, I think, be her heir."

Radal nodded. "Who made up the guests? Be thorough."

"A number were of the merchant class, my lord, either residing in the town or travelers who do business there. They are often more cultured than the nobles in Lama."

"Travel broadens one."

"Yes, sir. There was a sprinkling of noble visitors, some from the Cuddon. The Lady Vibola's family springs from those hills, I am told. Also, members of the local nobility, mostly young. They seem to revolve around the Lady Lomela."

The councilor considered this. "Not surprising," he said, almost to himself, and then asked, "what of the count's younger son? Donzalo."

"Oddly, sir," reported the aide, "most of his friends are townspeople. His interests are too scholarly, perhaps, for Laman noblemen."

"Then he holds little influence?"

"On the contrary, my lord. He seems Lady Lomela's closest friend in this place. Further, his circle includes many who may not be noble but have considerable wealth."

"Ah. There was a minstrel, you say?"

"More than one, sir. Two mediocre fellows currently at residence in the castle, and Lady Vibola's cousin."

"This Guesare of whom I have heard so much."

"Yes, my lord. His work is excellent, if somewhat old-fashioned. He insists on rhyming his lines and is somewhat free in his meter."

The Sharshite lord permitted himself a small smile. "He is, I understand, quite a fighting man."

"So they say, my lord, though he struck me as a bit frivolous. And, um —"

Radal noted his reluctance. "Continue."

"Well, I think he made a pass at me. Sir."

The nobleman openly laughed. "Feel flattered, Jobareth. That will be all." He looked down at his papers as his aide left.

Too bad, he thought, that this young fellow didn't share the Cuddonian's tastes. It would make him an even more useful spy.

"The king has gotten it into his head that you are a threat."

"Me? Why would Lareth think such a thing?"

"There is an explanation, and I may give it to you, in time. For now, I offer you my protection."

"There is an explanation for that, too, I suppose?" Donzalo's voice held more than a trace of sarcasm.

"Indeed there is, lad. Let us just say that my friends are Sharsh's enemies."

"That would include many people."

The Cuddonian smiled amiably. "Yes, it would." He stroked his curling, golden beard and looked about the young man's quarters. "You should be safe for the moment, but there will be other attempts. Lareth is not one to give up, nor is Radal."

"The ambassador? Oh, of course," Donzalo realized. "That is why he is here."

"You catch on quickly." The minstrel gave an approving nod. "His henchmen having failed, and you now being warned, he may act directly. And Lord Radal is a very dangerous man."

"They say he has skill in the black arts."

"They speak truth. I think, my boy, I should stick close to you from now on."

"Do you wish to stay here, tonight?" Donzalo's invitation came hesitantly. He occupied two small, cluttered rooms.

"I must go, but keep your door barred till morning. A thought," he added. "You might cultivate the envoy's young aide."

"Jobareth?"

"Aye. I doubt he is involved in any of this, yet he may prove a source of information. My own attempt to befriend him went awry." Guesare laughed ruefully. "I — misjudged the fellow."

"What of my assailants? I have suspicions as to their identity."

"As do I. Leave that for the morrow."

5

"Master Donzalo."

"Lector. Need help?"

"What place should the ambassador take in this procession?"

"I'm not sure." The young Laman had been assisting Sir Paren in his attempts at organization. "Uncle, where do you want Sharsh?"

Paren turned to them. "Lord Radal represents the child's grandfather. He should be up front with the family." He looked at Jobareth. "You could stay close behind him."

"I'll be a couple of rows back, too. Walk with me," suggested Donzalo, "and we can keep each other from being bored."

"Thank you, sirs. Uh, do you think this attire suitable?" He wore sober gray, a long Sharshite tunic, his sash minimally embroidered in white and yellow. "I confess, I did not expect so many bright colors this morning."

"You'll see more when we reach the town. We are not perpetually somber here."

"Gray is always appropriate," Paren felt. "Simple and unassuming."

"But you might suggest that Lord Radal not wear his accustomed black," added Donzalo, with a laugh. "It is spring, after all!"

"Yes, certainly. Good day, sirs." The Sharshite hurried away.

"I doubt Radal even owns anything that isn't black."

"He is very dark, himself," replied the knight. "I understand there's Southern blood in his family."

"His father was a mercenary from Lorj who rose high in Sharsh. Lomela told me that." Donzalo was struck by a sudden thought. "I wonder if the Wisest was so dark."

"I don't know, boy. Not all Lorjam are." Paren returned to his task. "Ho, there, where *are* you taking that cart?"

"Everyone walks?"

"Yes, my lord. It is considered more respectful."

"Very well," sighed Radal. "Let us be thankful the weather is still cool."

"Those who do not go on foot will be borne on litters. Perhaps, sir, I could arrange one."

"No, Jobareth, I shall walk. However, I will not wear a colorful costume."

"I did not — think you would, my lord," replied the aide, "but felt I should mention it to you." He sounded unsure.

"You acted correctly. I have hopes for you, young man."

"Hopes, sir?"

"There should be a permanent ambassador here. Not you, Nafal," he hastened to add. "You haven't enough age." Lord Radal placed his hand on the young man's shoulder, the long, dark fingers unadorned save his ring of office. "Some bland diplomat to hold the title, with you doing the real work — and reporting to me."

"The assignment would not be unwelcome, my lord," was Jobareth's thoughtful response. "This place is not nearly so bad as I feared."

"There are far worse posts, and it would be for but a while. We might as well go."

Although Castle Rosam had a chapel, most of the naming ceremony was to be held in the local temple, just above the town. Following a general blessing, they would proceed down to it.

First came the litter bearing Lady Lomela, all in white and rose, and her son, flanked by Bolos and a priest. Radal took his place in the second rank, beside Borrago and the Lady Vibola's litter. Behind them were Sir Paren, his wife — who had disdained a litter — and Donzalo. The count's son motioned for Jobareth to join him.

"Is it correct for me to be up here?"

"If anyone notices you, they'll just assume you have some role. Like the litter bearers." Donzalo waved his arm in their direction. "Or the bodyguards right behind us."

The Sharshite glanced at the four well-armed retainers. Further back, was a large group of kinsmen and noble guests, Guesare the minstrel among them.

"Lord Radal has the right to have a man nearby," Paren assured him. "Now hush during the blessing."

The priest spoke a few words, making the sign of the arrow over them, and they began their slow descent to the temple.

Guesare was always an observant man and today he was particularly attentive. Yet he could not find the two faces for which he searched. No doubt, he told himself, they rode down earlier rather than join the procession.

Ahead of him, he could see young Donzalo, leaning to whisper to Radal's aide. The Sharshite was nearly a head shorter than the two Laman men; he seemed a gray mouse beside his brightly clad companions. The minstrel knew this to be illusion. Jobareth was every bit as tall as he, and a well-knit youth, though slender.

Further forward, strode the unmistakable figure of Lord Radal. Guesare was a man of passions. The passion he felt for Radal was hate. He felt it strongly; he felt it more deeply than any hate he had ever known. It was a hate for all that was his opposite, for the cold and cunning soul inhabiting that dark body.

As the procession wound down the hill and out the lowest gate, folk from the countryside began to line the road. These joined them, falling in at the rear. Most were tenant farmers. Serfdom might have disappeared from Lama after the expulsion of the Ani, but the land was still in the hands of the nobles.

Guesare, coming from a society of small freeholders, disapproved. Still, he recognized that different circumstances created different ways. This was a good, rich, peaceful country, unlike his native Cuddon.

Now, the road curved, allowing town and river to be seen. Where Abam joined Weldar stood the largest settlement in Lama, north of

Morparas. That great port — a free city, though in the Anian sphere — dwarfed any town of the hinterland.

Through the trees, the minstrel caught a glimpse of the temple roof. They were nearly there.

"Your master wore black," whispered Donzalo. "We thought he would."

"The Lord Radal is very careful to maintain the image he has created. For the same reason, I think, he chose not to use a litter." A certain admiration colored the Sharshite's speech. "He pushes himself harder than men half his age."

Donzalo seemed disappointed. "Then the black is but for effect? He doesn't truly prefer it?"

"All he does is well calculated. Radal would have gone naked today, if he thought it to his advantage."

"You are a perceptive fellow, Lector Nafal. The envoy is fortunate to have you."

"That, too, is calculated, I am sure. But," Jobareth laughed, "I have not yet figured it out."

As they went along, the Laman pointed out such local points of interest as existed — often apologetically. At last, they stood before the temple.

"I suppose it is not much compared to those in Sharsh," said Donzalo of the modest sandstone stoa.

"You'd better stay here," Paren suggested. "We must take part in the ceremony."

Jobareth remained by the litters, while the family advanced. On the steps waited the hierophant, a small balding man in robes of red and white. The crowd spread to form a rough arc around them, as priest and parents, Lomela carrying the baby, climbed the short stairway.

Turning at the top, the hierophant led them through a brief ritual of question and response. Then, he marked the boy with ash from the sacred flame, touching shoulders and brow.

"Behold," he announced to those gathered, "Ros!"

Bolos held the child up before them. The crowd erupted in cheers; the babe erupted in tears.

Able to relax now, Donzalo took a look around. Soon, he spotted the two men he sought, one with his eye swollen shut.

Guesare had made his way to his side. "I see them, too."

"Perdos and Percos. I suspected as much."

"You know them?"

"Hangers-on of my brother. Could — could he have aught to do with this?" The idea sickened him.

"It seems unlikely. Have you plans for this afternoon?"

"None. The Ladies Lomela and Vibola will be taking the baby home to rest, while my father and brother remain here, receiving townspeople. I thought perhaps to show the Sharshite around."

They strolled to the spot where Jobareth had stationed himself. "We intend to amuse ourselves in town, Lector. Would you care to join us?" invited the minstrel.

"I thank you, sirs, but no. Lord Radal and I return to the castle. His sergeant has brought down horses for us."

"Ah, then we shall see you this evening, no doubt." Guesare spoke lightly, as if amused by some private jest. "We bid you farewell, young sir, and send our greetings to your master."

6

"If we come upon your attackers, pay them no heed."

"I am not completely witless, Cousin," came Donzalo's good-natured reply.

"No, you are not. Some, I think, judge you too lightly. That," the minstrel emphasized, "is to your advantage."

"You have a plan?"

"We wait for tonight's feast. I want witnesses." Guesare almost slipped on a patch of clay. "Damn this mud." He wiped a spatter from his boldly patterned kilt.

Spring rains had saturated the ground, turning the roadway to mire. Many of those who had gathered at the temple now followed it into town.

"They wouldn't pick a quarrel with us here, would they? Even they should have learned their lesson last night."

"I take it you do not think much of their abilities. Keep in mind," Guesare pointed out, "they almost ended your life."

Sheepishly, the young man agreed and changed the subject. "How does our little county compare to the rest of the world?"

"Why Master Donzalo, to a yokel from the Cuddon, County Rosam is quite impressive, and your town far exceeds anything we have at home."

The Laman persisted. "Your travels are legendary. Tell me of Morparas."

"Many of your friends visit there."

"Yes, but they see it through merchants' eyes, not a poet's."

"Morparas. Big, yes, and dirty, and an evil odor arises from the bay. In many ways, it is but a larger version of this town. It has the same temporary look about it, like the inhabitants might tear it all down one day and start over."

"Have you seen the university?"

"I even sat through some lectures, seeking to improve my Muram."

"I had hoped to study there." Donzalo paused in thought a moment, then decided, "I still do."

"There are better schools in the Siphic cities, or even Sharsh. But," the bard declared, "the great university at Lanlaz is superior to them all."

"In Lorj? You've been to Lorj?" The name of that exotic island evoked wonder — it lay not so distant yet it seemed to be on the other side of the world.

"I have. A pleasant land, though uncomfortably hot. One should visit only during the winter." They had stopped before an inn. "What say you to some ale?"

"What *is* he talking about?"

The Lady Lomela looked up from her reading. "I warned you, Grandmother. That sort of thing is stylish in Sharsh, these days. At least," she asserted, smiling, "among young men with too much education."

"Humph. Then I'm glad Donzalo was not allowed to study abroad."

"Your grandson has more interest in cannons than cantos. He might learn many things of value — to him and to his family."

"I suppose it would do the boy good to get out of this backwater for a while." Vibola gave the girl a knowing look. "But we'd both miss him, eh?"

"Yes, Grandmother." Lomela lowered her head again. "Let me find something more interesting." She leafed through the pages. "Here. This one even rhymes."

"Praise be to Kamat."

"It's titled 'In Love's Service,'" she announced gravely, and began to read.

Though oft I wear Love's livery,
No mistress of mine shall she be.

Of Love's bonds I will be free
To sup on life and have my fill,
To take my pleasures where I will;
I'll remain my own man still.

The Lady Vibola sniffed, but said nothing.

So if Love's praises I may sing,
Know that my words mean not a thing;
They are birds that take to wing.
They bear sweet songs to whom they might,
And, leaving naught to mark their flight,
Are away and out of sight.

"He fancies himself quite the gallant."

"I would not take his words too seriously, Grandmother. They are but poetic conceit. There's more."

I'll stay not long in Love's service,
Only a while, to have her kiss.
Then I'll go, rememb'ring this:
She welcomes back all former men,
However long it may have been,
Come to share her gifts again.

She gently shut the book of poems, saying, "That last part, I think, seems forced."

"How like a man," harrumphed the old woman, "to tell himself his infidelity bears no cost."

"My lady, you are much too cynical. Jobareth is not at all that way, really."

"Ah, but he'd like to be."

Lomela broke into gay laughter. "Perhaps we all would, Grandmother." The expression on her oval face then grew quite serious. "Are men truly so fickle?"

"Of course not, girl. I once met one I suspected of being faithful," chuckled Lady Vibola. "No, some men can be true — my Paren, for example. I never understood why he loved Thara, but he did and does still. Even after their son died, he would not hear of divorcing her and taking a younger wife. He said he would rather have Thara than an heir."

"You are not always kind to the Lady Thara." Lomela was a king's daughter and not afraid to express herself.

"I try to be, my dear, but there's a willful old woman in me who sometimes won't behave." She did not sound overly repentant. "That's enough of your friend's poetry; read to me from the *Tales of Borm* a while, will you?"

The town had no name; it was simply the town. Travelers might refer to it as Ros-town, particularly those who hailed from one of the other, smaller towns along the Weldar. For most, though, "the town" sufficed.

It was built of wood, this town. Wood was abundant; wood was cheap. Wood did not offend suspicious noblemen.

Donzalo and Guesare ambled down one of the winding, muddy streets. It would lead them, in time, to the river. They had no business at the river, but it was as good a destination as any.

"It takes a good deal of ale to fill you up," commented the Cuddonian.

"I am a larger than normal container," responded his young companion.

"That you are. You could be a formidable fighting man," Guesare told him, "if you wished."

"I do not wish. I am a scholar."

"You may find you have no choice."

Donzalo sighed and walked on a way. "I've been hearing this all my life. 'Remember your birth,' people tell me. 'Think of your duty.'"

"It is the way to which you were born."

"It is a dying way. Power is passing out of our hands, sir, and into those of merchants and tradesmen."

The minstrel considered this novel concept. "As in the Siphic League?"

"Or Sharsh. There the old aristocracy is being squeezed out by the king on one side and the newly wealthy on the other."

"There may be something to that. Such ideas would not endear you to your family."

"I have learned not to speak of them. My father expects me to settle into the life of a landed gentleman, like Uncle Paren. And Bolos thinks I belong in a religious order. However," Donzalo chuckled, "I am not prepared for celibacy."

"That does not seem to bother many priests but I see you would take such vows seriously," observed Guesare. "Even so, religion upholds tradition. You would not fit in there."

"What of you, kinsman? How came you to your calling?"

"There is little choice for a younger son in the Cuddon. Many become mercenaries; I became a minstrel." He added, in explanation, "I do not take discipline well."

"The river is still high." They had reached the banks of the Weldar. "A fortnight ago, we would have been standing knee-deep here."

"It is a mighty flood. Only the Siph is greater."

"Even a small stream might carry one elsewhere," mused Donzalo. "But now, our legs should carry us back to the castle."

"Yes, and we'd best attach ourselves to a group. It would not be wise to be on the road alone."

"My lord?"

"What is it, Nafal?"

"May I ask, sir, how much longer we remain here?"

"Through the morrow, at least. Hand me my sash, will you? No, the one with the purple embroidery." Radal tied it about his lean waist. "What thought you of today's ceremony?"

"Terribly boring, sir. These Lamans know nothing of theater."

"They scorn pageantry. You walked beside young Donzalo."

"Yes, my lord."

"Tell me of your conversation."

"It rambled to many subjects. Uh, including you, sir."

"That, I expect."

Indeed, thought Jobareth. Here was a man who did understand theater.

"The Laman told me much of this land. He was also rather interested in my experiences at the university. His desire to go abroad is considerable." The young man hesitated before daring to make a suggestion. "Perhaps, sir, it would be advantageous to have him study in Sharsh."

"Perhaps."

Seeing that Radal had no further comment, he went on "Also, my lord, we spoke of the Lady Lomela. I think he has great affection for her."

"As do you."

The aide swallowed. "As do I, my lord."

"The lady has a talent for attracting loyalty." For once, the Sharshite's smile seemed genuine. "Not unlike her father."

Jobareth knew when to remain silent. Lord Radal's unwavering allegiance to the king was renowned, as was the tale behind it.

"You'd better dress, Nafal. I expect you at the feast, tonight. Make sure the naming gifts are at hand and then feel free to enjoy yourself."

7

Bolos, when he chose, could display the courtly manners expected of him. Even when he drank too much — which was often — the in-grained habits of a noble upbringing carried him through.

Borrago's heir was neither a particularly good nor a particularly bad man, just as he was neither particularly tall nor short, clever nor dull. He was an ordinary sort of fellow who found it all too easy to indulge his appetites. It told in his thick waist and red face, in his blurred and blood-shot eyes. Already, he was into his cups.

Jobareth Nafal greeted his master at the door of the great hall.

"Yon lordling will drink himself to an early death," Lord Radal whispered to his aide. "We must be prepared when it comes."

"Yes, my lord. Sir Paren asks when we wish to present. Sharsh can be first, if you desire, or just before the final gift. That would be the Count Borrago's."

"What do you think?"

Jobareth had already considered this problem. "First, sir. We need not invite comparisons with the count."

"Let it be so." The envoy was approving. "You have the makings of a true diplomat."

"Thank you, my lord. Your seat is at the high table."

"Of course."

"Yes, of course, sir. No one is being announced but there should be an attendant around. Here he is now, my lord." A servitor had approached them. "You will show the ambassador to his place?"

"This way, my lord," said the man. With a Laman's typical disregard for ceremony, he started away.

"Hold a moment," requested Radal. In a low voice, he asked Jobareth "Where will you be?"

"Some of Lady Lomela's friends asked me to sit with them, sir. That will be on your — left, about half-way down the hall."

"Try to keep an eye on the Cuddonian minstrel. Don't worry if you can't; it's not overly important. Report to me in the morning." He turned to the attendant. "Lead on."

Tonight, little Ros had the place of honor, propped up in an ornately carved crib for all to see. To his right sat his father and, beyond him, Borrago. His mother was to the left and to her left, Lord Radal, as representative of her father.

Bolos made a short speech welcoming the guests. He was not yet too far gone for that. Soon he would be, now that his duty was done.

So was the baby's. He had made his appearance and, after a few minutes, his nurse carried him away.

Radal felt a hand upon his left arm.

"Is not that tunic terribly uncomfortable, my lord?"

His garment was long, heavy, and stiff with embroidery. It might be normal wear for formal occasions in Sharsh, but he saw that most of the other guests wore knee-length tunics, or kilts in the Cuddonian style.

"Indeed it is, Countess Vibola."

The old woman's smile was radiant. "Hardly anyone remembers that is still my title." She tipped her head "So why wear it?"

"It is what a well-dressed gentleman of Sharsh dons for such an affair." He shrugged in mock resignation. "I have no choice, my lady."

"My husband never wore such a get-up, and he was as fine a gentleman of Sharsh as any."

He found this elderly noblewoman's bluntness somewhat disconcerting. "Both times and fashions change, madame."

"But not for the better."

"Lady Vibola, are you pestering the ambassador?" chided a voice at his other elbow.

"My lady," protested the Sharshite lord, "it is a pleasure to converse with two such fascinating and lovely companions."

The women exchanged incredulous looks.

"I have known Lord Radal all my life. Don't be taken in by his smooth manner," warned Lomela. "His daughter was my playmate. How fares the Lady Fachalana, sir?"

"As rebellious and troublesome as ever, I fear. She refuses every suitor, my lady, and fancies herself an actress."

"Does she wear black, too?" inquired Vibola, all pretend innocence.

Lady Lomela choked back her laughter. "Hush. There is an entertainment."

It was the first of several. Acrobats, musicians, even an itinerant company of players had found their way to Castle Rosam. One of the resident bards presented a preposterous poem in honor of the occasion. The other, not to be outdone, droned through an interminable saga of the first Ros.

Lady Lomela leaned forward to address Vibola. "Why isn't Sir Guesare performing this evening, my lady?"

"He excused himself, claiming some pressing, private need."

Donzalo, seated beyond his grandmother, kept his eyes on Lord Radal, but the envoy betrayed neither interest nor emotion. He noted the boy, however, and smiled inwardly.

"This is going on forever. When will the gifting begin?"

"Next," Paren told his brother. "I sent the word to your steward."

Thanks to his loud voice, Saj, Master of Hounds, at times served also as herald. Now, he announced the origin of each gift and servants brought it forth.

Sharsh's presents, though showy, seemed small; they had been carried swiftly, and from a distance, on horseback. A richly worked golden cup and an ornate pistol were displayed.

"The gunne is made in Sharsh," whispered Paren. "Pretty, but not to be compared with those from the Siphics."

Borrago nodded his agreement. "Have you seen that pair Guesare carries?"

A procession of lesser offerings followed, the gifts of Laman noblemen; the wealthy commoners had been received earlier in the day. Presents ranged from weapons to furniture to jewelry and even a puppy.

"Every boy needs a dog," announced its somewhat tipsy donor.

"Wake up, Bolos." The count nudged his son. "My gift is coming."

A handsome saddle, suited to a pony, came forth, and a skillfully painted wooden horse, as well.

"Until the boy's old enough to ride," the proud grandfather informed his heir, but Bolos had again dozed off.

"I'll give the thank you speech," sighed Borrago.

Radal's aide had quickly grown bored. These young nobles were a shallow lot, with their gossip and talk of fashions. He found himself watching Guesare.

The minstrel was seated not far from Jobareth. He, too, seemed to be watching someone. The Sharshite soon recognized that the object of Guesare's interest was the two men he had passed outside his quarters.

Turning to one of his companions, he asked, "Know you those two gentlemen?" He nodded in their direction. "The two big fellows."

The plump young man looked up from his plate. "No gentlemen those," he replied, wiping his fingers fastidiously, "though someone saw fit to confer knighthood on them. They belong to the garrison here — part of Sir Bolos's private guard. Brother Grippo, do you remember yon ruffians' names? Bolos's bullies over there."

"Perdos and Percos," answered his tablemate, who wore the robe of an acolyte. "Scum from the northern marches."

"Yes, of course. Bad sorts. Best stay away from them, Lector."

"Good advice. I thank you, sirs." Nafal sipped his wine. "This is not bad stuff. A local vintage?" The young man knew wines, for his family had made its fortune in their trade.

"Surely it doesn't compare with the wines of Sharsh!" objected the fat Laman.

"Sharsh produces its share of swill, but it doesn't find its way across the mountains to you."

Something was going on. The last gifts had been presented and guests began moving about the hall.

He sipped again. "I'd imagine that your summers are too hot to produce truly great wines. Now in Arolin — " From the corner of his eye, he saw Guesare approach the two knights.

"Ah, you will excuse me, gentlemen. I must attend to some business for my master." He rose abruptly and moved closer to the minstrel.

With easy insolence, the Cuddonian looked Perdos over. "What happened to this pretty face?"

"My brother, uh, fell and hurt himself."

"Brothers, eh? Are you certain you are not half-brothers?"

Percos scratched his head. "What's he mean by that?"

"You fool! He insulted Mother!"

As he grasped the meaning of Guesare's words, Percos reddened. "Hey, you don't even know our mother!"

"I know her reputation. All Lama knows her reputation."

The inebriated knight was not difficult to provoke. "I demand satisfaction!" he bellowed in the bard's smirking face.

"Then meet me on the field of honor."

"Tomorrow!" seethed Percos.

"Nay, the tourney is tomorrow." Master Saj had stepped between them. "If you must duel, let it be the next day."

"We know now the nature of Guesare's personal business," stated Lady Vibola.

"But what," asked Lomela, "Could he possibly have to do with those two?"

"He was responsible for Perdos's face," Donzalo informed them. He escorted the two women to his grandmother's rooms. "There was an — incident last night."

"That sounds intriguing. Will you come in and tell us about it?"

"Indeed I will, my lady. The minstrel asked me to remain with you until he arrived."

Donzalo opened the heavy oak door for them and they entered, passing into one of the smaller chambers. There, Lady Vibola's most recent maidservant — none lasted long with her — helped her to her seat by the fire.

"Your ambassador is charming," the old woman observed, settling herself. She smoothed her deep crimson gown and tossed aside the shawl she had worn against the coolness of the evening air.

"He would cut your throat — or mine — in an instant if he felt it in the interests of Sharsh."

"I would never doubt it."

"Yet," Lady Lomela admitted, "he can be charming, though you know it all is but a game with him — and he knows that you know." She turned to Donzalo. "What game does Lord Radal play with you?"

"With me, my lady?"

"I saw you watching him," she accused, "as I saw him carefully ignoring you."

The young man sighed. "You are better schooled in intrigue than I, Lomela."

"What is going on, Donni?" asked his grandmother.

"It seems the Lady Lomela's father wants me dead." Donzalo tried to speak as calmly, as matter-of-factly, as possible, ignoring the fear growing within him. This was more than a game.

Lomela, although surprised, readily accepted his statement. "But why?"

"I know not the whole story." A knocking came at the door. "That will be Guesare; I'll let him tell it."

8

"Was it safe for you to come here by yourself?" Lomela asked, when Guesare finished his tale.

"They would not dare attack me after our public quarrel. That's one reason I provoked it."

"The Lord Radal might," she warned. "He would care little if suspicion fell on two such minions."

"True, but he will wait a while, I think, before risking direct action." The Cuddonian turned to Donzalo. "Young sir, will you serve as my squire tomorrow?"

"Me, Guesare?" came the confused reply. "You mean at the tournament?"

"Perdos would like to get a crack at me before I duel his brother. If I enter the joust, he most certainly will as well, in hopes of doing me harm."

"I'm honored, sir, but I know little of the, uh, knightly arts." He didn't say so, but Donzalo thought the tournament terribly old-fashioned.

"It matters not; I seek chiefly to keep you nearby," explained the minstrel, becoming quite serious. "Henceforth, for your safety, we should remain close."

Lady Vibola spoke up. "Why don't you two stay here tonight? I have far more room than I need. But don't," she chuckled, "tell your father that, Donzalo."

"Should we tell him any of the rest of this?" wondered the young man.

"In time," Guesare answered. "No point in doing so, now."

"Yes," agreed Lomela. "He'd probably go straight to Radal in his anger."

"And we have no solid proof," the minstrel pointed out. "There is naught more to be done." He reached for his rebec. "How about a song?"

"I like this little hill." The ambassador pointed toward a grassy piece of land beside the road. "What think you of it as the site of our embassy?"

"It seems an excellent location." Radal must have made note of it the previous day. "We would have one built, sir?"

"Eventually, and it would be your job to see it done. At first, though, you'll need to find lodging in the town."

"Not in the castle, my lord?"

"No. We are a powerful and independent nation, not just another little county or city-state. The Lamans must be reminded of that fact."

"Yes, certainly, sir," Jobareth answered, and then made bold to add, "and it gives us a certain privacy."

Lord Radal nodded. "Indeed. I expect you to make as many contacts in the town as in the castle. Anyone," he emphasized, "no matter how mean, can prove useful."

The Sharshites accompanied a party riding down from Castle Rosam. "This is a different road," observed the ambassador, as they turned to the right.

"It takes us around the town, my lord. The tourney is to the north." The aide shaded his eyes. "I can see the pennants and tents of the fair from here."

"I fear this day will be wasted," sighed Radal, "but we depart in the morning. Be certain all is ready."

"Yes, my lord." So they would not stay for the duel. Jobareth thought that odd, as his master had shown considerable interest in the situation. "Will it be early, sir?"

"I hope so. If I finish our business with the count today, we can leave well before the dawn."

A level field beside the Weldar had long served as Borrago's fair ground. In the summer, it found constant use; this was a center of trade for all of Lama. But such crowds as gathered now were unusual so early in the year.

Even the well-traveled Cuddonian was impressed.

"You should be here at mid-summer," Donzalo told him. "It's said to be the largest fair in the world."

"The world is very wide. Yet, I admit I have never seen larger." Guesare gazed across a sea of tents and booths. "The taxes must overflow your father's coffers."

"There is an income from rents and river tolls, and more to be made, indirectly, by the fostering of trade in our lands. It has been my dream to establish greater manufacture here." There was passion in the young man's voice. "We depend too much on imports."

They had come to an open space, with box seats along one side. "Now this must be the site of our tourney."

"Do you intend to joust on that horse?" Guesare straddled his rugged pony of the Cuddon.

"Nay. I have been lent a charger by one of my kinsmen." The minstrel laughed. "He hopes to fill his pockets wagering on me."

The river edged the field to the west and the seating spread along the other side. Pavilions stood at either end, for the use of the contestants.

"No one in the boxes yet," noted Donzalo. "Not many spectators at all."

"'Tis early. Let's find the heralds and get ourselves sorted out."

A succession of diversions filled the morning: shooting competitions with both bow and gunne, races, displays of horsemanship, even wrestling matches. The knightly events would be held in the afternoon.

Radal found himself bored. The count would not grant him the few minutes needed for a serious discussion, and only one contest held interest for the noble of Sharsh. He waited impatiently for the jousting.

Briefly, Lord Radal had considered risking magic last night. Better, he decided, to wait; the truly effective spells required time and concentration. If Perdos failed against the Cuddonian, he would call upon his powers tonight. If Guesare fell, leaving young Donzalo unprotected, more ordinary agents might be employed.

Borrago, notoriously tight with his money, provided no lunch. It was necessary to send young Jobareth among the vendors. He returned with meat — pork, they assumed — smothered in spicy sauce, and a sort of fried cake popular in Lama. Both Sharshites found the fare indigestible.

Then began the joust. Full armor was a rarity here, and specialized tilting armor, unknown. The combatants wore what plate or mail they possessed, and wrapped themselves and their steeds in heavy quilting. With blunt lances, that usually sufficed.

"Sit beside me, Nafal," requested the envoy. "Put away your tablet; no more dictation today." Radal had kept them both busy all morning with the reading and answering of dispatches.

The aide took a seat by his master.

"Do you follow the joust, boy?"

"Not really, my lord. It seems dated."

"I suppose it is. Still, a lancer can be a deadly fighting man."

"No doubt, sir, but I would not care to charge massed musketry."

"In this part of the world, the gunne is less of a factor in war."

The younger man nodded. That will change, he thought to himself.

Aloud, he commented, "You are well known as an enthusiast, my lord."

"Ah, a shift in focus, and very tactfully done, too," approved Lord Radal. "I was never much in the lists, myself, but I squired for King Lareth when I was young — Prince Lareth, then."

Jobareth knew this story: a youthful Radal, snubbed by the old aristocracy of Sharsh, had become Lareth's protégé. The two's destinies had been intertwined almost from the start.

"Despite the crudities of this tournament, we may see some very good performances today." The ambassador's interest seemed genuine. "They take their tilting seriously here in Lama."

9

"Our Sharshites finally seem to be paying attention."

"Lord Radal is a great patron of the tourney," Lomela told her husband. "Have you any favorites?"

"My man Perdos is handy with the lance."

"Sir Guesare is said to be quite skillful, as well. I think it likely they will meet before the day is done."

Bolos scowled. "I hope Perdos unhorses that Eastern show-off."

"He probably hopes to do more than just unhorse the man."

"Oh, yes, the duel." He frowned at his wife. "My brother talks to you. Why would he choose to squire for the Cuddonian? Is it to spite me?"

"They have become friends. That's all, I'm sure."

"I know what sort of friendship this Guesare prefers. I have long suspected Donzalo of being the same."

Lomela smiled at the absurdity of his idea. "I think not, Bolos, I think not."

The first two entrants stood ready at either end of the field. These Lamans might not have had the steeds and armor of noble Western jousters, but they knew their business well. As they hurtled forward, paths separated by a low fence, their lances were aimed squarely at each other's shield.

"A clean strike," Lomela commented.

"And neither unhorsed." Bolos sounded disappointed. "Some wine, my lady?" he queried, filling his goblet from a jug. "Damn, I'm out."

"That's all right, my lord husband. Perhaps later."

Bolos motioned to an attendant as the jousters prepared for another pass. This time, one went down into the mud.

"All you need do is stand here with a spare lance. Hand me up my shield now, will you?" requested Guesare. "And move those steps out of the way." The knight had used them to mount his tall charger.

"Here you go, sir. Good luck!" Donzalo watched the dashing Cuddonian gallop onto the field and rein his tall, dappled steed in dramatically. Guesare knew how to play to a crowd. Then, becoming serious, the knight turned to the work at hand. He quickly disposed of his opponent, knocking him from the saddle in one pass, and returned to his novice squire. Donzalo took shield and lance, brought the wooden steps, and helped him dismount.

"Too easy," Guesare remarked.

"You should meet Perdos in the fourth round," the young Laman told him. "If you both make it that far," he added.

"Barring bad luck, we shall. The man showed ability in his first match. What he lacks in technique, he makes up in strength."

Twice more, both knights readily unhorsed those they met. Only four contestants remained.

Donzalo expressed his concerns. "The scoundrel will not fight cleanly, I fear."

"Nor shall I," came the Easterner's retort. "But neither of us will be so blatant as to commit a foul. At least, not right away."

The other pair was to go first. Donzalo pointed out one knight, well-mounted, well-armored.

"That is Sorsen, son of Count Orgelo. He has quite a reputation as a fighter."

"I know of him, and of the count. Both staunchly anti-Sharsh."

"Their borders lie too close to the mountains."

Guesare nodded. "What of this other lad? One of your father's men, isn't he?"

"Copago, his master of arms — and my half-brother, by rumor."

"Indeed?" The minstrel raised his eyebrows. "That is one I had not heard."

"My father was discreet. Sir Copago dearly dislikes Perdos and would welcome the chance to face him."

"I shall do my best to disappoint the fellow. If not," he laughed, "perhaps I can soften up his opponent for him."

"Do not count Sorsen out. He is certainly the better equipped."

"But less skilled at tilting. His experience has been in more practical forms of combat."

Sir Sorsen was impressive. He could not match the flamboyance of Guesare but, rather, his appearance tended toward the imposing. The tall nobleman wore a closed helm, black, as was his armor. Black, too, was the fiery steed he straddled. Both were bedecked in his colors of blue and white.

At the other end of the field waited Copago. The man was short and muscular, more resembling Count Borrago than either of his legitimate heirs. Though not as well accoutered as his foe, Copago's position had enabled him to find adequate, if mismatched, armor, as well as his choice of the count's warhorses.

The herald — not Master Saj, but a professional of the tournaments, resplendent in dark blue cloak and turban — gave the signal to charge. In one pass it was over. Sorsen lay flat on his back.

"Perfectly struck!" exclaimed Lord Radal.

"Is the — yes, Sir Sorsen is rising. The crowd cheers him, my lord."

"He seems unhurt." The ambassador had a sour look about him; he did not share the people's affection for Sorsen. "I would not mind seeing harm come to Orgelo's boy," he admitted, "but not in the tourney, of course."

Jobareth had doubts as to his master's sincerity. Radal, he suspected, was trying to maintain his image as an even-handed patron of the tournament.

Sorsen saluted the crowd, and gave a short bow to his vanquisher before leaving the field.

"I know Count Orgelo leads the opposition to Sharsh," said the aide. "Do you consider him that much of a threat, sir?"

"Yes, but let us not discuss politics now. I have particular interest in the next match-up."

Jobareth looked to the neighboring box and chuckled. "My lord, the Lady Lomela attempts to waken her husband. They must have concerns of their own about its outcome."

"Backing opposite sides, I imagine," mused the envoy. "As are we? What say you to a wager, young sir?"

"I say only a fool wagers with his master, my lord."

"We wager every time we speak, Nafal. You have played the game well, so far."

True enough, thought the young Sharshite. But where he risked his career, Radal gambled for larger stakes. "Thank you, sir," he replied, suddenly leery of saying too much.

The older man smiled with what seemed to be true warmth. "Remember, my boy, it is but a game. Now, do you think this Cuddonian popinjay truly has a chance?"

"There is more to him, my lord, than his manner would suggest. We have seen that on the field today."

"He depends over much on natural talent. The Laman may not possess the most polished of technique, but he is a solid performer."

"Yes, sir, he seems a hard man to unhorse."

"Exactly. If each strikes dead-center on his opponent's shield, Sir Perdos should have the better of it."

"But Guesare will avoid that, won't he, my lord?" asked Jobareth. He had but the sketchiest understanding of jousting strategy.

"He will try. It's a classic contest: finesse versus strength."

The two adversaries moved into position. Neither seemed to hold an advantage in armor or mount. At a sign from the herald, they hurtled toward each other.

10

Copago knew he was not well liked. His manner could be brusque, even harsh. He was too demanding for some. Others resented what they saw as favoritism shown to him by the count. But Copago knew also he had earned what he had achieved and that he demanded more from himself than anyone else. As for his manner, that couldn't be helped; it was who he was.

He stood now, watching the contest between Guesare and Perdos. His brother, acting as his squire, stood beside him. Both knew they were half-brothers. Neither had ever mentioned it.

"These two want to hurt each other," commented the younger man.

"There seems to be enmity between them. You know of the duel?"

"Indeed, yes. I was there when the Cuddonian provoked it. Oddly enough," he continued, "the young Sharshite aide seemed to be expecting something of the sort."

"It's politics, then." The master of arms spat the words out. "You are fortunate, Grippo, to be entering the priesthood, beyond all this."

"And you are naive, brother, to think there is no intrigue in the temple. They're set for a second run."

"Let's see if Guesare aims high on the shield again."

"He hopes to wear down his opponent? Render his shield arm useless?"

"Or, at least, tire it. It's a risky tactic; he must avoid the brunt of Perdos's attack."

The combatants came together. For the second time, Guesare managed to send his enemy's weapon glancing away with minimal impact. His own strike, again high, caused the Laman's buckler to fly upward. Its edge caught Perdos in the face, opening a cut above his eye.

Copago whistled. "That was pretty."

"I trust you are not referring to the Northerner's face," joked his brother. Grippo was as light-hearted as his sibling was sober.

The knight gave him a smile, but quickly became serious once more. "Whichever of these two succeeds," he stated, "may be in no shape to face me."

As Donzalo moved forward to tend Guesare, the herald approached them, his expression stern.

"I warn you, sir, we will tolerate no deliberate attempts to injure your adversary."

The knight nodded. "Certainly, Herald." He threw his spear to the ground. "Donzalo, my lance has split. Hand me up a new one."

The man rode to Perdos to issue the same message.

"This time," Guesare confided, "I aim low."

Donzalo's look expressed his confusion. What was the Cuddonian attempting?

"He thinks my tactic is to attack his arm. I look to catch him off-balance."

Once more, the two thundered toward each other. This time, Guesare did catch his opponent off-balance. But Perdos caught him squarely, as well, and both men went to the ground.

A crew of attendants immediately filled the field, catching the horses, picking up the shattered lances, and helping the jousters to their feet. Donzalo remained at his post, for that was the custom, and waited anxiously.

Neither was incapacitated; there would be another round.

"Perdos must be growing frustrated. I expect him to disregard the rules on this pass," said Guesare. "There's the herald; time to mount up."

Donzalo understood. These men were not concerned with winning. They wished only to hurt each other. He helped the minstrel up the steps and onto his steed; he could feel that the man was starting to stiffen up.

"I shall try to finish him," Guesare continued, from the saddle. "This may be my best opportunity."

"Why doesn't that idiot finish him?" grumbled Bolos.

"We shall see a winner this time, I feel certain," Lady Lomela told him, "or else a disqualification."

"Oh?" Her husband turned to her in interest. "You anticipate a foul?"

"By one or both," she replied. "They are beyond caring."

"I must have you along the next time I lay a bet," Bolos declared, half-serious, half-mocking. "I did not realize that you were so knowledgeable."

"There is much, my lord husband, that you do not know about me."

For a moment, he sat in silence. "Yes, I have neglected you." He looked again at his wife. "You think me a drunken clod."

"You think yourself one, Bolos," she answered, "and you must decide whether you are."

Bolos said nothing. Lomela was uncertain whether the man pondered her words or was merely confused by them. At last, she chose to break the awkward silence.

"They stand ready."

"Yes." The nobleman unsteadily poured another goblet of wine, red drops splattering his already stained tunic. "Now we shall see."

Again, the jousters rushed forward. Their lances were held steady, though Perdos's shield drooped noticeably. Suddenly, his point went low — low enough to be considered a foul. It seemed that he meant to slip under his opponent's shield in hopes of striking hip or leg, or, failing that, horse.

But Guesare was still too quick, too agile. He maneuvered shield and steed sufficiently to catch the tip and send it sliding harmlessly away. His own lance impacted the top of Perdos's sagging shield, then smashed into his shoulder.

Perdos fell; the Cuddonian rode on to the cheers of the crowd.

Bolos regarded his wife with new admiration. "You guessed right, my lady."

"Everyone knew the two disliked each other," she replied modestly. They watched Perdos struggle to his feet, his left arm hanging limp. "I think your man is hurt."

"Might be a broken arm."

"Or collar bone."

"Either way," concluded Bolos, "he'll find it hard to second his brother tomorrow."

"If the Easterner has any sense, he will forfeit the final match."

"Yes, my lord," agreed Jobareth. "He has accomplished what he intended."

"Exactly. And he has the morrow to consider." Not that I will permit him to reach his duel, Radal told himself. The man must be dealt with tonight — and the boy, as well.

On the field, preparations had been made for the last match. The master of arms now waited, his fiery charger stamping impatiently. A few moments later, Guesare mounted up and rode forward to deafening applause.

Radal laughed scornfully. "He needs play to the rabble. The man is a fool."

Or wishes us to think he is, thought the aide. There was plotting here, he knew, to which he was not privy.

The crowd cheered wildly as the tilters came together to touch lances in a gesture of respect, then galloped back to their posts. There, they whirled to face each other, and, at the herald's mark, charged.

Despite the lack of armor and fine horses, despite the lack of pomp and show, all knew that these two were the equals of any jouster out of Sharsh, and that this contest was very much as exciting as any held before the court of King Lareth. Lances level, shields steady, they crashed into their opponents.

Both men reeled, but neither fell.

As they returned to their starting points, however, Guesare slumped in the saddle. The herald immediately rode to him. After conferring briefly, he went to the center of the field and signaled that Copago was the winner.

"He cannot continue!" exclaimed Radal. "He has forfeited."

"Do you think it a serious injury, my lord?" inquired Jobareth.

The ambassador shrugged. "Let us pray it is not." He mouthed the words, but obviously did not mean them. Why, his aide wondered, was Radal not bothering to conceal his feelings?

"Ah, the count is motioning to me. At last, I can conclude my business with him."

11

Donzalo was concerned. "Should I fetch a doctor?"

"No, lad," whispered Guesare, leaning on his friend's arm. "I am un-injured. This is all for show." Grimacing, he gripped his midsection. "Let them believe I've cracked a few ribs."

"You feigned your hurt?" The young man's eyes traveled to Sir Copago, receiving the accolades of the crowd.

"There seemed no need to take on yon champion again. Honor was served and chances are he would have unhorsed me, anyway," he informed his companion. "Why risk harm with tomorrow's doings hanging over us?"

"But you felt it worthwhile to take one pass?" wondered Donzalo. "Just so our enemies would think you injured?"

"And also think me foolhardy. Which, perhaps, I am. I could not bear to withdraw without making at least one run at the fellow." Guesare regarded his erstwhile opponent with unconcealed admiration. "He is very good, you know. Is he a friend?"

"He is no enemy. His devotion to duty leaves him room for few friends, but we do share, um, certain interests."

An attendant approached them. "Shall I send for a litter, Master Donzalo?"

"Yes, thank you. We wish to depart for the castle at once."

Guesare watched the man hurry away. "All the servants seem to like you," he mused. "That's a good sign. Shared interests, you say?"

"In armaments, fortifications, that sort of thing. He helped me get that old trebuchet into operation."

"A useful man to have on your side, Donzalo."

"I have a side?"

"So the ambassador's taking his leave of us?"

"Yes. He plans to depart tonight."

"None too soon for me, Borri."

The count nodded his agreement. "When will you be going?"

"There is no great hurry," Paren told him, "though I miss the peace of my home."

"Peace on the edge of the Cuddon? Those hills team with wild men and wild beasts," protested Borrago, "and other beings, more dangerous."

"Oh, those don't bother us. The occasional troll wanders down, but they're not much trouble. Some are downright friendly."

The two rode on without speaking. Their entourage followed at a discreet distance.

After a time, Paren brought up a subject that had been on his mind. "Have you thought on my offer yet? Will you let Donzalo come home with us?"

"If he's willing, I am. Did you speak to him?"

"I wanted to hear from you first."

"He may be less than enthusiastic," warned Borrago. "The boy has never shown any interest in farming."

"Let's call it a short visit, a month or two, and see if it can be stretched into autumn," his brother suggested. "Once he gets there, he may find much to divert him."

"He'll probably want to rebuild your walls," chuckled the count, "or dam up the Abam."

"I've been considering doing that. He gave me the idea last year."

"Would it work?"

"I think so. If nothing else, I'd have a place to go fishing. That project would keep him happy for a while."

"It might be just the lure to get him there," Borrago felt. "I trust you will do your best to school him in running a manor."

"And in the obligations of his station. With luck, he'll be ready for knighthood when he returns."

"Donzalo needs to get away from the influences of this place. I don't like him spending all his time with merchants and minstrels." The count looked up. "Here's the last gate. Let's talk further tonight."

The way from the Sharshites' quarters to those of Lady Lomela was not long. Long enough, though, for Jobareth to have time to think. Now he hesitated outside her door.

Why had she invited him here to a private dinner? Was it only to say farewell or something more? Such questions might not have occurred to him two days earlier.

And what was his master's purpose? He had locked himself in his room with orders that he remain undisturbed. Radal's grim look had told his aide that he did not seek rest.

Jobareth knew that this mission involved more than simply presenting gifts or studying the diplomatic situation. There was plotting here he could not hope to comprehend.

He rapped lightly on the door. It was a plain affair, unadorned pine, as was much of this place. A plump middle-aged woman opened to him.

"Why, Mistress Traspa," said he in surprise. "I did not know you were in Lama."

"Someone has to care for my lady among these savages," replied the dowdy maid. "Come on in, boy."

For a moment, Jobareth considered telling her it was "Lector," but he realized Lomela's loyal servant would always think of him as a boy. She had known him too long.

"Will, uh, anyone else be joining us?" he asked her. A note of anxiety had slipped into his voice; too much was going on.

The maid thought she understood his nervousness. "You mean the husband? I can count the nights he has spent in my lady's rooms on one hand. And, then," she confided, "He mostly was too drunk to do more than pass out."

"But surely he visits? Takes meals with her?"

Traspa shook her head. "Not Bolos. I guess he sees all he wants of her and she doesn't complain about his lack of attention. Give me your cloak, young master, and I'll tell the lady you're here."

He handed the garment to her. "Doesn't anyone come here?"

"Our Lomela does most of her socializing elsewhere. A few lady friends call. And Donzalo — the count's younger son."

"I know him."

She nodded. "He drops by frequently. In fact, he and that minstrel were here earlier." The maid went into the next room.

Lomela occupied a small suite, a floor above the great hall. Though not as spacious as Lady Vibola's quarters, the rooms were lighter and less stuffy, being on a corner. It was certainly an improvement over the windowless dungeon assigned to the visitors from Sharsh.

"The baby will stay in his nurse's room all night, my lady," Traspa was telling the princess as they entered. "Shall I attend you?" She suspected that her mistress would desire privacy.

"No, thank you. Someone will be coming up from the kitchen. Why don't you go down there and find that cook you're forever making eyes at?"

"My lady! I merely admire his culinary skills," objected a blushing Traspa. "Though any man who can prepare such delightful desserts will find a soft spot in my heart." Having hurriedly wrapped herself in a shawl, she paused at the door to promise, "I'll tell them to send your meal up at once."

"Come with me, Jobareth," requested Lomela. "Did you know this is the only room in the castle with a balcony? Not," she added, "that there's anything worth seeing from it." They stepped out onto a small platform overlooking the main gate.

"Lady Vibola and her count occupied these rooms. He added this whole wing when they married. I wonder how many times she saw him pass through that gate." She sighed. "And one time, he didn't return. The lady continued to live here until Borrago's wife died."

"You seem in a somber mood, my lady."

"Yes." Lomela brightened, yet seemed wistful still. "It must be this balcony. But I can speak to you out here with assurance of not being overheard."

Then, another change of mood: the young woman became serious. "Sir Guesare was not sure I should trust you. You are my friend?" She raised her questioning green eyes to his.

"Always, my lady."

"I need a friend. Listen well, Jobareth, and do not disappoint me."

12

This was a risk, Radal knew. There would be suspicion; indeed, many would feel certain that his hand was involved. So be it.

There had been one bit of fortune. Guesare had chosen to spend the night in Donzalo's quarters. The minstrel would seem the target of this attack and the boy no more than an unfortunate bystander. Suspicion might even be directed toward Perdos and Percos.

In any event, best he be gone before the deed was discovered. Spies enough remained behind to keep him informed, Traspa not the least of them. It was Lomela's maid who had told him of Donzalo's whereabouts and had brought hairs from the boy's head, essential for this spell. He had done well to recruit her, before ever she left Sharsh — all the more since Traspa believed she served the interests of her mistress.

Such magics as he would raise tonight were no slight undertaking. They would require all his strength and all his concentration. The guard posted at his door had the strictest of orders; no one would be allowed to interrupt, no matter what the emergency.

The Sharshite opened a small cask, ebony bound with iron, and removed a skull. A grim smile touched his lips as he looked upon all that remained of his instructor in the black arts, a mighty mage in his day. A man into whom he had slipped a knife when the time was right.

Radal raised the relic high. "Asak!" he cried. "Asak! Asak!"

Jobareth hurried back to his room, carrying far too many thoughts. At least, he now had a much clearer understanding of his master's motivations. But why, he wondered, was young Donzalo considered a threat? Neither he nor Lomela could find a reason there.

Yet it seemed that she withheld some secret, something she was not ready to share. Having known the princess most of his life, he also knew her moods, her thoughts, her ways.

For Jobareth Nafal loved Lomela. From his first visit to the royal court, he had adored her. He had been five, she, three, and they had grown up together, princess and bookish boy, playing in the gardens of King Lareth. There in the shade of the arbored roses, she had first kissed him. There they had kissed farewell, more than a year ago.

He had reached the envoy's chambers. At the door was posted a guard, as usual. This, however, was not any guard but the sergeant of the small troop that had accompanied them to Lama, Radal's most trusted man-at-arms. Jobareth nodded and hastened by. The fellow always made him uncomfortable. He had heard tales of Sergeant Sojel's habits, his cruelty to both men and women. The soldier ignored him, with an impassiveness almost insolent. Sojel held the young scholar in very low regard and made no attempt to hide it.

As he passed, Nafal could not help but note the cold green lights that flickered from below his master's door. He had never before witnessed Radal's infamous magics but knew instinctively that there were spells being cast behind that locked and guarded slab of oak. He shivered despite himself, aware that Sojel would mark his reactions and sneer, as he continued down the hall.

In his own small room at last, the Sharshite began the sorting through of this evening's events. Of one thing he was certain: he had chosen the side of Lomela — and Donzalo — over that of Radal and the king. It was a dangerous choice. It was the only choice.

"You are a fool," Jobareth Nafal told himself. "You have no business playing such games." Having decided that, he began to prepare for departure. His master wished to take leave of this place in a few hours.

Guesare had not been allotted the best of quarters. He had, in fact, been given a bed in the stables, a space shared with sundry other visitors of lesser rank. Now he and his gear were settled in Donzalo's rooms.

"You know, boy," he had confided, "that people will talk. I have a, uh, certain reputation." For once, the minstrel seemed somewhat unsure.

Donzalo found that amusing. He also fleetingly wondered why the man should be concerned about his reputation. "It will only confirm my brother's suspicions. I have no fear of such gossip." He spread his arms. "Make yourself at home. There's not much to the place."

The young noble spoke truthfully. He occupied two small untidy rooms against the west wall, above the barracks. The rear wall of his sleeping chamber was the stone castle wall itself; the rest was built of sturdy oak. This was one of the oldest sections of Keep Rosam, built, in fact, when the place was still in Anian hands.

"I'll spread my blanket here among your books." Guesare gazed admiringly at the collection lining the walls. "You must have the largest library north of Morparas."

His host did not bother to conceal his pride. "I think so. I certainly have more in this room than are found in the entire rest of the castle. Here, look." He pulled down a volume. "This was brought across the Central Sea."

The bard puzzled over the strange script for a moment. "Can you read this?" he asked.

"It seems to be a dialect of Muram. But," continued Donzalo, "it also appears to be the same text as this." A small tattered book was passed to Guesare.

"A treasure!" exclaimed the Cuddonian. He looked up at the lad with narrowed eyes. "Know you what this is?"

"I know it is very ancient. I also know it to be a treatise on magic."

His guest nodded. "Indeed, quite ancient. This particular volume would seem to be from Lorj. No?"

"Yes." Donzalo crouched beside the minstrel and turned pages in the book. "Here," he said, pointing. "Coradean, some six hundred years ago."

"Ah. But this other text is far, far older. Thousands of years, I would think."

"You know of such things?"

"I have a smattering of knowledge. With enemies such as Radal it is needed. Oh," Guesare added, "the white magics only, I assure you."

"The priests assure us that all magic is black."

"Their own rites are white magic by another name. I must study these someday," he remarked, returning the volumes to Donzalo. "Not tonight. I've a duel to fight on the morrow and should rest."

Radal was not an old man, but the powerful magics take their toll. He seemed now aged far beyond his years, his face become a skull to match that of his long-dead mentor. Slowly, he replaced that old object of power in its cask, closed the small grimoire he carried ever on his person, and sagged into a chair.

I have done what I can, he told himself. There was no way to tell whether his spells had achieved his desired ends. That news should reach him in Sharsh, soon enough.

Now, he had no time to rest. He could take elixirs; they would give him the strength for the hurried return to his king. He rose and cracked the door.

Good. His faithful dog Sojel still stood guard.

"Sergeant." The stolid soldier turned attentively to his master. "We leave as soon as possible. Make things ready."

"Yes, my lord."

"And send Nafal to me."

"The rebec is not a difficult instrument."

"Easier than the harp?" asked Donzalo. He had been listening to his guest's idle strumming.

"Oh, aye, much easier. At least," continued the minstrel, "for the sort of thing I do. I should use a bow, of course, but I keep losing them. Now my friend, Oder — " He stopped, as if suddenly aware of what he had said.

"Oder. An Anian name."

"Yes. I shouldn't admit to having such friends in the heart of Lama."

The boy shrugged. "It is no concern of mine. But I would be cautious of announcing it outside these walls."

He has prejudices but tries to overcome them, thought Guesare. His casual reference to the hated Easterners had been dropped into their conversation to learn just this. He had suspected the boy to be open but it was good to be certain he would not reject the Ani unthinkingly.

"I shall be careful," he announced. "Oder, as I was saying, is a true master of the instrument. He can — what is it?"

Donzalo was staring into the corner. There, a circle of cold light was floating, growing, a ghastly, green halo.

At its center lay a hole into the darkest of hells.

13

"Quickly, lad, span and prime my pistols. They're already loaded." Guesare slid his heavy saber from its scabbard. "Hurry now!"

Donzalo drew forth the matched pair of wheel-locks, holstered on the minstrel's worn saddle. He had handled the handsome weapons admiringly earlier in the evening. The young Laman might be no fighter but fine craftsmanship and all things mechanical fascinated him. He measured out gunpowder for each and wound their springs.

"What is that?" he asked his companion. The circle continued to expand.

"A gateway. I doubt not that evil lies on its far side."

"Here are your pistols. Can't we get away?" Donzalo eyed the heavy door.

"It will be targeted to one of us. Most likely, you." The minstrel shook his head. "And will follow where'er you run."

"Best then I arm myself." The younger man stepped into his bedchamber, returning with a heavy spiked mace. "This needs little skill." He laughed nervously, then looked again to the door. "Even if this thing will indeed pursue me, might we not better face it in the open? With perhaps some help?"

He stepped forward and attempted to lift the bar. "It — it will not move." He struggled with the wooden beam. Donzalo believed in logic. His belief had let him down.

"You knew it would not," he accused.

"I suspected it would not. Radal is thorough. Stand ready!"

Something was stirring within the portal, now nearly a yard wide.

"My lord?"

"Come in, Nafal. We leave at once. Is all prepared?"

"Yes, my lord. Are you well, sir?" Jobareth was shocked by the man's appearance. "I mean, can you travel?"

"I must, so I can. Have you heard of anything unusual happening this night?"

"Here, sir? No, it has been as quiet as ever."

"Dead quiet, I hope." Radal smiled a brief, mirthless smile at his private joke. "Let's go. Bring the diplomatic bag."

The way was thankfully short. In the courtyard awaited Sergeant Sojel and his troop, horses and baggage ready. Sir Paren also stood there to give them an official goodbye, as well as to keep an official eye on them.

Although he wondered at the Sharshites' midnight departure, the knight was more than happy to see them go.

Slowly, stiffly, but by his own power, the envoy mounted. His young aide once started forward to help but a look from Sojel quickly warned him away. Radal would not allow himself to show weakness. The sergeant knew this, admired this: a godless man, he worshiped only his master.

Then they rode forth, silently, through the gates of Castle Rosam. Taking one last look back, Jobareth Nafal was certain that he glimpsed the Lady Lomela, watching from her balcony.

An eye. A pointed snout. The gleam of sharp teeth. Animals, several of them, but none that Donzalo had seen outside of nightmares.

"'Tis Jov's own fortune that you spied the light when you did," whispered his companion. "Had we been sleeping there would have been no chance."

"Do you know what they are?"

"Wart dogs."

The name brought forth a vague memory in the Laman's mind; he had read something, sometime. Of course, the hounds of Asak, God of Death. Bred in the mountains of Asa-Zad by that deity's priests.

"Weren't they exterminated when Asa-Zad fell?"

"I doubt these beasts were raised in this world at all. They may well come straight from Asak's realm." Guesare lifted a pistol. "I'll try to kill two before they come through. If there be time, reload for me."

There was no time; the beasts rushed forward at the first shot. One never made it through the gateway. Another fell dead just inside the room.

They *are* dogs, thought Donzalo with brief surprise. Then he was swinging a mace with all the power inherent in his over-sized frame. Fortunately, his chambers had high ceilings, allowing a full motion; he had chosen them for their headroom.

He brought the weapon down on the powerful gibbous shoulders of the first misshapen beast to reach him, barely avoiding the curving tusks. Donzalo did not fail to note, despite his immediate concern with survival, that the entire pack had come toward him, not the minstrel.

He also did not fail to note that a blow to the shoulders was not overly effective — too much muscle there. The head made a better target.

Guesare fell upon the creatures with saber and abandonment, wisely cutting at their legs. A hamstrung wart dog posed little danger. One by one, in silence, the death god's pack bounded into the room. They began to form a ring around their intended victim, keeping just beyond reach of his deadly mace.

Fortunate it had been that Donzalo had picked up the unused weapon, when sorting through the armory with Copago one day. He had never thought to use it as more than a wall hanging.

"Back to back!" called Guesare.

Donzalo complied. "How many?" he gasped over his shoulder.

"Thirteen, of course," laughed the bard. "Four of them down."

The room was small and cramped; that was to the advantage of the men. They could not be effectively rushed by the entire pack. Indeed, the hounds barely had room to maneuver.

Donzalo saw his chance, lunged forward, and shattered the jaws of one.

"So you're a fighting man after all!" exclaimed Guesare.

"Not if I can help it," he grunted in reply. "Aah!"

A hound had slashed his leg with its tusks. Not without taking a saber in its side for its effort.

"My bedchamber! We can defend the doorway."

"Yes," the Cuddonian agreed. "Let's — "

"Go!" shouted Donzalo.

Swinging his weapon wildly, he cleared the way.

"No one seems to know how badly this minstrel is hurt."

"The Sharshite seemed to think he might not show at all," Perdos told his brother. "I got the impression he had his own plans for the fellow."

"I hope not. I want to kill him myself."

"I care not who kills him." He took another gulp from his tankard. "As long as he is dead."

Percos nodded. His brother might never again use his shattered arm, now in a sling. "Wouldn't it be better to lie down or something?"

"This damned arm hurts too much unless I sit. Pour me another, will you?"

"Sure. No more for me — want to be sharp in the morning."

"Good thinking, kid, you'd best get some sleep. But I intend to get as drunk as possible."

"Not too drunk, Dos," grinned the younger brother as he rose, "or you'll miss my skewering of the dog."

Donzalo bled; it made his boot soggy and most uncomfortable. The throbbing torture of the wound itself he attempted to ignore. He could not ignore the stiffening of his leg.

He stood ready now behind the minstrel, who defended the narrow doorway. Massive mace firmly in a two-handed grip, Donzalo was prepared to brain any beast that got past Guesare's sword.

It seemed an impasse. The wart dogs would lunge and snarl, but kept themselves away from that deadly blade. The Cuddonian knew he would tire soon. He knew also that Radal's spells would expire before long. Would he be able to last? Would he be able to withstand the inevitable charge?

For they would charge; their mission in this world meant more than their lives. They hungered for the blood and flesh and soul of Donzalo Rosam.

There was no door to shut against them — only a curtain had separated the rooms. Nor was there any furniture of convenient size to block the way. Their strength and their weapons would have to serve.

Then, suddenly, the pack stopped and withdrew, gathering themselves in silent menace. Seven remained standing; an eighth, entrails spilling on the floor, attempted to crawl forward to join its comrades.

"The rush is about to come," warned Guesare.

"Let it!"

14

"Radal and his entourage are gone," reported Paren. "Good riddance."

"You must be more practical, brother. Sharsh is our ally now."

"An ally I would never trust."

Borrago chuckled. "That is true of all allies. Lareth will certainly stand watching. Still," he continued, "our courses run together for the time."

He looked toward the door. There stood the master of arms, concern evident on his hawk-like visage.

"What is it, Copago?"

"Sir, there may be a problem with your son — Donzalo, that is." The soldier strode into the room to give his account. "A servant reported odd sounds coming from his chambers. When we investigated, it sounded like a struggle was taking place."

"Did you enter?" Borrago rose to his feet immediately, heading for the door.

"We could get no answer from within." He seemed perplexed. "The way was barred and our attempt to force it was without success."

"Wasn't Guesare with him, Paren?"

"Yes," replied the tall knight, hurrying down the hall on the heels of his brother. "I would expect no foul play from him."

"He might well be the target of such," interjected Copago.

"By Kamat, why couldn't that minstrel leave my boy alone?"

The silence of his adversaries disconcerted Guesare. A single snarl might make them seem more real, more capable of being vanquished.

Behind him, Donzalo assessed their foes. The bard would kill one, perhaps two, before he went down beneath their weight. Then the remainder into the small bedchamber; that would not do. He bent to speak into his companion's ear.

Guesare nodded agreement. As the first of the pack charged forward, he ducked beneath its leap. The younger man's club took it full aside the head, which nearly parted company with the hairless, nodose body. As quickly, the Cuddonian rose and ran this saber through the second in line.

Alas, he could not withdraw it from the beast's body. Seeing his predicament, Donzalo passed him the long recurved knife he normally bore on his belt; he was a nobleman and expected to carry a blade of some sort. For Guesare it was practically a short sword, with a full foot of edge.

At any rate, it was a far more effective armament than the dainty poniard at his own waist.

For a moment, only, the pack had been tangled in, and delayed by, its own dead. Now the remaining five came on. The first fell upon the min-strel, bearing both to the floor. Massive slobbering jaws snapped in the man's face as he disemboweled it.

Holding the mace like a battering ram, Donzalo charged the remain-ing dogs, crashing through them and into the other room. Though none were seriously harmed, their attack had been broken, scattered, and a young giant now stood among them, swinging his deadly spiked weapon.

One fell, its forelegs shattered; another took a blow that cost it an eye and made it wobble briefly. Yet it came on, its one instinct to taste the blood of the Laman. A blood-soaked Guesare struggled from beneath the mass of his dying attacker to behold the boy become of a sudden the man.

And he knew now with certainty what he had suspected: Donzalo would be not an ordinary man but a man of destiny.

"This way, sir."
"What? Donni changed his quarters?"

"He moved last year," answered Copago. "He's above the barracks now."

"My old rooms," added Paren.

"Oh, the high ceilings. Of course." Borrago again took the lead, with quick, purposeful strides.

A knot of soldiers waited at the barred door. "What report?" barked the master of arms.

"There is still commotion inside," answered their sergeant. "We heard no speech," he continued, laying his hand on the heavy oak door, "and we can not force this with the strength of our shoulders. I sent for a ram."

"Not much room to use one," Paren pointed out.

"Axes!" commanded Borrago. "Chop that door to splinters."

Copago nodded. "Go." The sergeant motioned for two of his men to follow and hurried off.

"I do not like this, my lord." The master of arms gestured toward the entrance. "Not at all. This door should not be so difficult to break down. I know the lad has only a light bar on it."

"You and I," Paren said to him, nodding in its direction. "Maybe with my weight we can budge it."

"Very well, sir. On three!"

At the count, the two men slammed their shoulders into the door, which literally flew from its hinges. Copago and Paren sprawled atop the fallen panel.

"Hello, Uncle," came the cheerful greeting of Donzalo. He was seated in a battered chair, foot propped upon the most hideous creature the knight had ever beheld. "Hello, Master Copago."

Borrago stepped around his brother's prone form. "Are you alright, boy? And what, by all the ice in hell, is that — are these?" he asked, surveying the bodies that littered the room.

"These were a parting gift from Sharsh," spoke a weary and blood-stained Guesare, rising from a corner, "which we must discuss. But first, Cousin, this brave lad needs a physician."

"The wound is not bad, sire," reported Doctor Heragos. He pulled at the thin tuft of beard adorning his chin. "But I know not what poisons might lie in yon jaws." The young man, recently come from a Siphic school, shook his head at the sight of the gruesome corpses, now piled to one side of the chamber.

"All I can do is wash it thoroughly with brandywine and stitch it up."

"There is a healing virtue to brandywine?" queried Guesare, always a man of curiosities and interests.

"Not truly, sir, any strong liquor seems to prevent the growth of poisons. The potent drink the peasants here make from corn should work quite as well."

"Ah," Paren observed, "just as it will preserve fruit and such."

"Then Bolos need never fear poisoning," laughed Donzalo. "Ow!" The doctor was vigorously cleansing his hurt.

"My lord, we'd best dispose of these carcasses," Copago pointed out.

"Far from the keep," suggested the minstrel, "and buried deep. Hmm, I must remember that rhyme." He looked to his erstwhile comrade in arms. "I intend to immortalize our battle, my friend.

"Kinsman Borrago, your younger son is a warrior true."

"So I see," answered the count, "so I see. You have done well yourself — Cousin."

Donzalo was gritting his teeth and ignoring Heragos, now busy with needle and thread. "Guesare must fight again in a few hours," he reminded the group.

"Yes," exclaimed Borrago, "I'd forgotten! Physician, see to this man when you finish there." His voice became stern, his eyes narrowed in reproof. "I expect an explanation of all this when you finish your duel, young fellow," he told the bard. Then he chuckled. "So be sure you win!"

"Wake up, Brother."

"What? Damn, my arm! Don't shake me like that!"

"It's dawn. Time to go."

"Is Jak here?"

"Right here," announced the man in question, a burly, balding soldier. "Ready to be his second."

"Good, let's go. Any word on the Cuddonian?"

"There was some sort of commotion," Jak reported, "but I saw the dog a short time ago. Looked tired."

"Did he seem hurt?" asked Percos.

The soldier shook his head.

Grumbled Perdos, "Too bad."

"It's okay, Dos, I'll hurt him good," his brother promised. The trio headed for the castle gate; all duels must be held outside the triple ring of walls.

"Anyone know if the boss is coming?" asked Jak.

"Bolos? I doubt it." Percos spat. "He doesn't give the shit in his bowels about any of us."

"No lord does, Cos. We just take their money and do our job."

The younger brother nodded. "As long as it suits us."

"Aye."

Jak looked from the one to the other as they strolled through the second gateway. "You two are a hard lot, aren't you? I like the young lord."

Perdos snickered. "Like him all you like, but don't trust him."

"Third gate is still closed," said Percos. "We'll have to wait."

"Ho, sluggards," called his brother to the soldiers manning the wall, "why didn't you open at dawn?"

"Count's orders," their leader announced. "Something's going on up at the keep."

15

"I could order this duel be canceled," the count told Guesare, "or postponed."

"It must be now, if ever. I should be away and so should your son. He is not safe remaining here. And," continued the minstrel, "I do not wish to leave a dangerous and vengeful enemy behind."

"You do not think that these Northerners were involved in last night's doings? If they had aught to do with it, I'll hang them from the walls."

"No, Cousin, though I've no doubt they are in the pay of Sharsh. 'Twould raise awkward questions if you acted against them directly. Best I slay one; that sends a more subtle message."

Borrago smoothed his mustache, a habit when he became thoughtful. "Yes, it is best that I not acknowledge the attack openly. But, damn it, Guesare, they almost killed my boy! And you too." He looked at his kinsman questioningly as they rode down toward the outer wall. "Which of you was the intended target, I know not."

"I will tell all after this business, if I can. But should I fail today, get the lad to some safe place. 'Twas he Lareth wants gone." He glanced ahead, spying the trio standing at the gate. "My opponent awaits us."

"Copago!" called the count over his shoulder. "Go tell Sergeant Ubos to open up." The master of arms galloped ahead, leaving a pair of his most trusted men to guard their master. Paren had remained at the keep, left the task of quietly disposing of twelve deceased wart dogs.

Donzalo, despite his objections, had also stayed behind, resting in well-guarded safety.

Out they rode, now, through the open gateway and into the green countryside, into a fresh spring morning. Borrago ignored the three men on foot as he passed.

"What's up here, lads?" rasped Jak. "Why is the count with yon minstrel?"

"They're kinsmen," came Perdos's nonchalant answer.

"Everyone knows that," added Percos.

But the look the two brothers exchanged betrayed their nervousness. "We've been found out," the younger man whispered.

"Maybe so. Play it cool."

They followed the mounted contingent to a field not far from the gates, a bit of pasture that had long served as dueling ground. The two groups stopped a short distance apart.

Jak stepped forward to fulfill his duties as second. Copago did the same. The two men spoke briefly but Percos could not make out the words. Instead, he found himself listening to a mocking bird on the far side of the meadow.

For a moment, he thought he heard his name in its song.

"Wake up, fool," hissed his brother. "Here comes the count's bastard."

Solemnly, Copago announced, "Guesare sends his greetings and his defiance. Draw your sword and may Kamat be with you."

Borrago loved his natural son, an indiscretion of his youth, every bit as much as his legitimate children, yet he always had difficulty showing the affection he felt for Copago. His pride, however, was obvious.

The two stood now, side by side, the younger man a mirror of the older.

"I pray Guesare's injuries do not prove his undoing here."

"He received none yesterday, sir."

The count raised an eyebrow. "Indeed?"

"The minstrel faked his hurts. He could have faced me for another tilt."

"Not the action of a gentleman, eh?"

"I would have done the same, my lord."

"As would I, Copago, as would I. He did not seem to take any harm during last night's adventure."

The master of arms shook his head. "No, sir, but he is bound to be sore and tired from both that affair and the jousting. Percos seems fresh."

The combatants approached each other, swords at the ready. Guesare held his saber. A longer straight sword was in the hands of his opponent.

"So," mused Borrago, "Guesare's speed will suffer. One of his main assets."

"And his stamina, sir. He might normally have hoped to wear his man down."

"Yes. He will need to be bold."

The duelists circled cautiously, neither risking an attack. Guesare seemed to move slowly, painfully.

"The sly trickster! He's still acting the wounded man."

"Yes," agreed Copago, "but it will give him only one chance to surprise his foe."

"The longer he can wait, the better it will work," observed the count. "Who is this?" A horseman approached.

"It is your son, my lord."

A bleary-eyed Bolos cantered up. He remained astride his mount, watching the fight.

Encouraged by his opponent's apparent condition, Percos took the initiative. The bard backed slowly away from his onslaught.

"Guesare can not do that for long," Borrago stated.

Guesare did not need to. The larger man, veteran and victor of many such combats, allowed his confidence to become over-confidence. He aimed a sweeping two-handed blow, knowing his strength should overwhelm an injured opponent. And in doing so, Percos left an opening, so brief an opening, yet all the Cuddonian required. Then, as in the case of most duels, it was quickly over.

The body of Percos slid from the saber that had pierced his chest. As he died, on that fine spring morn, he again heard the mocking bird sing his name.

◆

With an oath, Perdos slipped his dagger form its sheath.

"Hold there," growled Jak, grasping his arm. "Do not be a fool."

Bolos alit beside them and gave Jak an approving nod. "We'd best gather up yon unfortunate. Use my horse."

As a brooding Perdos watched, he and the stolid soldier loaded the corpse onto his steed, covering it over with the tattered and stained cloak Percos had shrugged off a few minutes earlier. Jak led it off toward the castle. "Come along, man," said Bolos, putting a hand on the bereaved brother's shoulder. "There is no more to be done."

"Not now," spat Perdos, giving Guesare a look of hatred. "Not now," he repeated, the words almost a whisper, and followed his brother home.

The bard was calmly cleaning his blade. Guesare was a man of moods. The earlier elation had given way a great weariness, a let-down now that this affair had reached its anticlimactic end. He mumbled a short prayer for the soul of Percos and meant it.

Slowly, the minstrel returned to the others. "My Lord Cousin," said he, addressing Borrago, "I ask for your patience. I will tell you all I know, but now I fear I need sleep."

16

"It is decided, then," declared the count. "Donzalo will go to live with his uncle for now." Paren nodded his agreement.

"And Guesare will accompany him. I do not understand your involvement in this, Cousin, nor fully the reasons Lareth wishes my boy dead. But I thank you for your aid."

"I think, my lord, that I am attaching myself to a rising star." Borrago seemed amused by the minstrel's new-found respectfulness to him — and to his son. "The young man needs learn much. Between us, your brother and I can teach him well."

For the first time in this council, Bolos spoke. "It amazes me that this whole affair was going on under my unsuspecting nose." He gave a rueful laugh. "I was in my cups far too much of the time.

"It also seems I have greatly underestimated you, Brother," the nobleman told Donzalo, "as well as my wife. Are you sure she is to be trusted?"

"As much as anyone in this room," the younger man averred. He sat to one side, his wounded leg propped on a stool. "And her friend, Nafal, too — I believe."

"Very well. Perdos has already told me he is leaving my service. I will need not dismiss him.

"He will neither forget nor forgive you, minstrel." From his manner of address, it seemed that Bolos still felt a certain distaste for the Cuddonian.

Guesare shrugged. "So be it. I will deal with that scum when the time comes.

"And when, sir," he asked Borrago," will the time come for us to depart?"

"Give the boy some time to heal and prepare himself. A week."

"Guesare says he will give me the full explanation once we are on the road. I think — " Donzalo hesitated. "I think it is something he does not wish you to know."

"There are those things we do not wish him to know," replied a smiling Lomela. They looked out over the courtyard, as the evening breeze toyed with the lady's auburn hair.

The young man returned the smile. "We all have our secrets."

"I will miss you, Donni. Is the leg truly healed?"

"Yes, Lomela, and we must go on the morrow. I will miss you as well, my princess."

"I have dismissed Traspa for the night. Stay with me."

By mid-morn, they were leagues from the keep. Donzalo rode silently by Guesare's side, a short distance behind his aunt and uncle. His thoughts were many but foremost was the knightly bard's promised explanation. He could contain himself no longer.

"Sir?"

Guesare gave a small smile. "You await my story."

Not certain whether this was a question, Donzalo nodded.

"You have heard of the oracle at Cars." He paused briefly; again his companion nodded.

"In Lorj," he said.

"Yes. The oracle is never wrong — ambiguous at times, as oracles are wont to be, but never wrong. Before the birth of your nephew, King Lareth sent a secret envoy to Cars, to pay the price and ask his question."

"Uh, Guesare, how do you know of this? I mean, if it was secret?"

"I have friends who are well rewarded to learn such things. Nations other than Sharsh employ agents.

"Anyway, the question was this: 'What future awaits the first born of Lomela?' 'Twas worded thus because Bolos already had several bastards. One must be careful of such things when questioning an oracle.

"The reply Lareth received may not have directly answered his query, yet it was straightforward enough. Cars prophesied that the son of Donzalo would rule in Lama."

Guesare rode on in silence, allowing the boy to think about this a while. Then he spoke.

"Now such a statement could be interpreted many ways. Your son, perhaps, could be a vassal of young Ros, holding lands in feality, or you might win yourself new holdings in the East, or even marry into some other landed family. But, taking the worst view, he saw you as a threat to his grandson's future. After all, the question had been about the babe.

"The fool! He went seeking the future, only to reject what he found. He must need make the attempt, even knowing that it would fail, and try to remove you."

Unexpectedly, Donzalo smiled, then suppressed a giggle.

"That is not the response I expected from you," said the minstrel, puzzled.

"It is only that I understand the oracle."

Guesare waited for him to explain.

"You see, Lomela and Bolos didn't really like each other very much. My brother is somewhat older than his wife and, I think, prefers women of a coarser sort. And then, he was often gone from Castle Rosam, and Lomela and I found ourselves together a great deal and became close and so — "

"So? Ah!" he exclaimed, in sudden enlightenment. "So Ros is your son and will someday rule as the oracle predicts." The Easterner broke into laughter, but sobered suddenly.

"Does Bolos know this?"

"I am sure he has no suspicions. My brother has trouble keeping track of whom he bedded when, especially if he has been drinking."

"This does not change the danger to you, boy. Old King Lareth still wants your blood." Guesare reflected a moment. "It does change your situation with regards to me and my friends. Yet I think you will be useful, even so, perhaps even more than before. Be that as it may, I am not the sort to abandon one I have promised aid."

"Then you intend to remain?"

"Indeed, I shall. I've not only duty but friendship to hold me. Let's ride, Donni; it is a long road ahead."

Of Roads: the Second Tale

1

Morparas stank; it reeked of refuse and tide flats, of fish and of fires burning on ten thousand hearths. The stench did not trouble Sojel. He liked this town with its fleshpots and taverns, as much as he liked any place in his world.

The man across the table from him he despised as a fool.

"You're from Mura, aren't you?" asked his companion. He only nodded. He had no intention of telling this fellow why he had left his home.

Perdos shrugged his broad shoulders, one rising higher than the other. It wasn't hard for him to guess that Sojel had worn out his welcome in most of the places he had been. Let the saturnine sergeant keep his silence. He did not care for this knife-blade of a man anyway.

"Any new orders from your master?" he asked.

"None. He sought only a report."

"Humph. I do wish he'd let me act. I would dearly love to skewer that minstrel."

Sojel's sneer told of his contempt for the Laman's abilities. "You did poorly enough the last time you tried. Wait for orders."

"I'm sick of waiting!" Perdos was as quick to anger as ever. "I care naught for the boy nor for your wizard. If he does not say to act soon I'll do it myself."

"The chance will come. Bide your time, man, and keep up the watch." The sergeant drained his tankard. "I need a woman. What say we find a couple?"

"The best idea I've heard this evening. Don't mistreat yours," he warned the soldier. "I don't need any trouble here."

"Finesse! Finesse!" scolded Guesare. "Do not depend so much on your strength."

Paren chuckled. "The lad is already a far better swordsman than I."

"Perhaps you should have some lessons as well, Uncle."

"One over-sized pupil is quite enough! What news, Sir Paren?" The knight had watched their practice patiently but his desire to interrupt had been obvious.

"You are to be an uncle again, Donni. The Lady Lomela is with child."

The bard and his protege exchanged a meaningful look. "Um, good news, Uncle Paren. Any word on my brother?" asked Donazalo.

"Your father seems very pleased with Bolos these days. He drinks far less and apparently takes his husbandly duties seriously."

"That is well," commented Guesare, absently stroking his golden beard. "'Twill soon be winter; we'd best be making plans."

Donzalo shrugged off his jack-coat. "I want to see my home," he declared. "Harvest Feast comes soon."

"Celebrate with your aunt and me, boy. I don't like the idea of you being on the road, even with Sir Guesare's skills to protect you." Paren's concern, and his love for his nephew, was plain. "There have been too many reports of strangers skulking about lately."

"I have seen them, myself," said the minstrel, "and have little doubt that they are here to spy on Donzalo, perhaps to do him mischief. He well might be safer wintering at Castle Rosam. Or," he added, "in the Cuddon."

"Your home?" The young man was surprised.

"Aye. We celebrate the Yule properly in the hills!"

"Well," spoke Paren, "I'll have to give this some thought. Tonight we will speak further on it." He turned abruptly and strode away, leaving the two in their sheep pen turned fencing ground.

"Your uncle does not wish to see you go." Guesare turned to his young friend and spoke in a low and serious voice. "I thought the princess wrote to you."

"Yes, frequently. She never mentioned this."

"The child is your brother's?"

"I do not know."

"Hello, Jobo."

"My Lady Fachalana." Jobareth turned toward a shadowed bench.

"My lady?" asked the young woman, rising to her full and considerable height. "Why so formal?"

"In the home of your father, it seems wise."

Fachalana was of an age with Nafal and, by any standards, striking. "You were never so in the past. I thought you liked me," she teased, her expression thoroughly theatrical.

"Certainly, my lady," he replied, but sounded quite uncertain.

"Ah, but you've always had the hots for Lomela." His blush brought a gentle and only slightly mocking, laugh. "Don't deny it, Jobo."

"Yes," he admitted, "but she has married, as princesses must. She knew her duty. And," the young diplomat added, "I knew mine."

Fachalana laughed again and tossed back the black hair she allowed to fall free upon her shoulders. "And I don't? I'll marry if and when I please, and not to suit my father's ambitions." A sly and somewhat wicked smile found its way to her face. "I wonder what he would think of you as a choice."

"I think, my lady," said he, falling into a pattern of easy banter, "that the Lord Radal would applaud any choice now."

"Nicely parried! Did you know," she asked, changing the direction of their conversation, "that I have been studying the sword?"

"No more acting?"

"Oh, yes. I wanted to use a blade convincingly on stage. However, I must admit that I enjoy fencing." The young noblewoman continued with genuine pride. "I can best most of the other students. I have educated more than one well-bred boy!"

"I do not doubt it, Lana. You always threw yourself into whatever you chose to do."

"Are you on your way to Father?"

"Yes. He called for my presence. I know not why."

"He plans to travel to the East," she confided.

"To Lama?"

"Only to the mountains." A dramatic pause was necessary; they often were in Fachalana's speech. "But you will go further."

"Then an embassy is being sent at last," mused Jobareth. "You seem to know a great deal."

"I pay attention." The serious and the jesting mingled themselves in her voice. "You would do well to cultivate me, Jobo."

"Indeed. Yet it seems, alas, that I shall soon be far away." It was his turn to tease.

"Behave yourself or I won't tell you who the ambassador is to be."

Nafal gave a nonchalant shrug. "I'm sure your father will let me know, soon enough."

"Well then, I shall beat the great Lord Radal!" the impatient Fachalana declared. Then she leaned close and whispered, "Lord Doufan."

A picture of an affable, middle-aged courtier came to his mind. "Very much the nonentity he promised. I'd best go, Lana. It is not good to keep your father waiting." He kissed her hand. "Thank you, my lady."

"You're very welcome, Jobareth. I do like you, you know, and wish you weren't going off to live with those barbarians." Her tone changed from the wistful to the impish. "Use the time to write a play for me — if Lomela doesn't keep you too busy."

"I will miss Donni," admitted Thara, "but six months is a long stay. He should at least visit his home."

Paren nodded his agreement. "I fear for his safety on the road. There is too much that needs my attention here or I would accompany them."

"You know fully well, husband mine, that I can run this manor without you."

These were the words he had hoped to hear. The knight valued his wife's approval. "I suppose I could make it there and back in a week."

"Take a fortnight — and do not include your time on the road in that! If you stay long enough he may decide to return with you."

He absently toyed with his cup. "I'll ask Borri to mention that idea to him. Still, once the boy is home, it may be the safest place for him to winter. I can't see him going off to the Cuddon!"

"It might not hurt Donni to travel some come the spring. Guesare seems an able protector."

"Aye. I'll miss him as well. Never thought to be saying that!" He chuckled. "I think a certain stable boy will miss him too."

"Perhaps we should be grateful he has such tastes. The last minstrel to stay here left half the serving maids with child." The Lady Thara had no problem being blunt. "Donzalo hasn't shown interest in any of the women here, has he?"

"Not that I've noticed. I think, my dear," he told her with a wink, "he takes after his old uncle and is waiting for the right one to come along."

2

"Ah, Blen. Enter!"

"Sire." The knight, who had hesitated at the doorway, stepped forward and bowed to his king.

Lareth regarded the man a moment. Sir Blen seemed a person of little significance, quiet and unassuming, yet he had served well as a courier some three years now, often in dangerous circumstances. The king motioned him to a seat and noted his awkwardness in accepting it.

"You are not comfortable around your king." He smiled thinly and added, "Nor around people in general, are you?" Lareth did not wait on an answer. "But on your own, you are a quite capable fellow. I have seen the reports."

"Um — thank you, Sire." Blen most certainly was uncomfortable.

"And most have, therefore, underestimated you. Even my Lord Radal." He was briefly amused by the man's reaction to that name. "You should, on the merits of your deeds, have seen advancement long before."

"I have no complaints, Highness," the knight blurted. "I like my position. I like being on the road."

"I'm sure you do, but you can hide there no longer. I have plans for you, Sir Blen. Plans, indeed! Come, walk with me."

The King of Sharsh stepped out through a stone archway, onto the eastward-facing battlements, the very spot where this man had brought him news some six months earlier. "Can you be loyal to me, Blen? To me and to none other?"

"Yes, Sire. To — to whom else could I be loyal?"

"You might be surprised at how divided ones loyalties can be."

"Not mine, my king. I am yours entirely." Blen certainly meant it, at least at that moment of enthusiasm.

"Then I call on you to take on a new post in my service. You will accompany my delegation to County Rosam, not as courier but as master of arms." Lareth gazed in the direction of that Laman court. "You know the area and the people. You know how to take care of yourself. Now," he continued, "I ask you to care for my envoys as well."

"I am honored, your Highness. Am I then, um, under the orders of Lord Doufan?"

"In name, Doufan is in charge. In fact, his secretary Nafal will probably run things. This," stated the king, "is why I need a man such as you there, one who will answer directly to me rather than being a creature of Radal.

"I trust the loyalty and motives of Lord Radal, but not always his methods and secrecy. And I believe Jobareth Nafal to be a decent young fellow. My daughter certainly does." He smiled at the thought, remembering the happy days when Lomela was a girl, playing with Jobareth in his gardens. How courtly the boy had tried to be, and how he had tried so to please his princess! Then the king continued. "I must trust you to keep an eye on things, to report to me privately what you see and what you think. Everything. Do you understand?"

"Yes, Sire." He paused a moment. "I am to be your spy."

"Just be who you already are, Sir Blen — a man no one notices but who notices everything."

"Tell me, Guesare, do you think I should grow a mustache?"

"'Twould make that great nose of yours seem all the larger," opined the minstrel. "Go for the full beard, my boy."

"And look like Uncle Paren? I think not!"

"Well, you've a good start there. Will you shave it all off when we reach the keep?"

Donzalo rubbed at his bristling chin. "I suppose it would be best. It is not the style. Not," he continued, looking at his companion's curling whiskers, "among those in my circle back home, anyway."

"Merchants who ape the court fashions of Sharsh."

The younger man nodded. "It is important to them to appear sophisticated. They are new to their power and know not whether they are nobles or tradesmen."

"Hmmph. I'd set them straight." Guesare had both a nobleman's and an artist's disdain for merchants.

Donazalo was quiet for a few moments, looking about him as they rode on. There was a taste of autumn in the air and most of the trees had begun to turn. Here they were coming out of a patch of forest and into more open farmland. It would not be far now to home.

"Speaking of appearances," he said, "do you think our escort will show itself?"

"Oh, you noted them, did you? Three men, I think."

"So did I count them. The tallest one might be our old friend Perdos."

"Only spies, I assume." The minstrel showed no concern. "If they meant mischief it would have happened before now, when there was more cover. And we do outnumber them." He glanced back at their companions, Paren and a pair of men-at-arms. Donzalo's uncle had been unwilling to spare more men from his manor at harvest time.

"I suspect that Perdos would love to send an arrow your direction."

"And I suspect he has orders otherwise," replied Guesare. "We'll be at Castle Rosam by nightfall and it will no longer matter."

Jobareth shut the heavy iron-bound door behind him.

"We are ready, then?" asked Sir Blen, who had apparently been waiting for him in the hall.

"Yes, Blen." The young man had decided to regard and treat this knight as an equal, as they officially shared a second-in-command status, and Blen had chosen to respond in kind. It would make things easier for both. "We can ride in the morning."

His companion nodded as they started down the hallway. "Any last minute changes, Lector?"

"None. We but went over a few details." He gave his companion a sideways glance. "You know, Sir Blen, my master does not know quite what to make of you. It is unusual enough for him to be taken by surprise, as he was by your appointment." He stopped and looked squarely at the man. "But he does not know who you are. I think he paid you no attention until the king named you.

"And that," he chuckled, "is a puzzle as well."

"Shh," warned Blen, placing his hand on the younger man's shoulder. Striding toward them was Lord Radal's man, Sojel. He passed them wordlessly, not deigning to glance in their direction.

"No puzzle about him," said the knight. "He's on his way to get his own orders from your master."

Jobareth nodded. "Let us be hope those orders take him the way opposite of ours."

"Agreed. Indeed, I would wish that they take him straight to hell."

3

The outer wall of Castle Rosam, that portion nearest the first gate, was an earthen berm, surmounted by low stone walls. In the days of Borrago's childhood, there had been a wooden palisade but the count had, stone by stone, strengthened his walls as he had increased his wealth and power. Further down the ramparts on each side, where the hill grew steeper, the walls became all stone, eventually merging with the natural rock cliffs.

"What a fine day it is, Uncle!" Donzalo urged his mount forward and galloped through the open timber gate.

"It is a fine day," said Guesare to Paren, as they followed more sedately. "A fine autumn day and a fine day to return home. I've been thinking of my own home, lately."

The older man only nodded. He was already starting to miss his wife and manor.

"Where is the boy headed?" wondered the minstrel. For better defensibility, the gates of the three walls did not line up. After passing through the outer entrance, one had to turn to his right and go some distance laterally before reaching the second.

And, having passed that gate, one need turn back to the left and follow the path to the main portal into the castle itself. Donzalo, however, was heading straight ahead to the wall.

"The boy's in a hurry," laughed Paren. "They will let him down a ladder and he'll be home before we pass the second gate."

Already, a wooden ladder was being lowered; it was always kept at that spot on the walls for those in a hurry.

"Someone will come down to get Donni's horse. Oh, no need. It has decided to come with us." The riderless steed cantered up to them, where one of Paren's men took hold of its halter.

The lawn between the two outer walls was fairly broad. Outsiders were allowed into this area — but no further — to sell to those within the keep and, too, tents would rise here when the keep overflowed with guests. Mostly, though, it was used for training and sport. As the party approached the second gate and its iron portcullis, set between two towers in the rough stone wall, a voice rang out.

"Hail, Sir Paren! The count awaits you. How went the journey?"

Paren looked up to where Copago leaned out over the wall. "Well enough, Sir Copago, and hail to you. Is there any news I should know?"

"Nay, sir, it has been a quiet season. We do expect a delegation from Sharsh soon."

The knight exchanged a telling look with Guesare and, with a wave, rode on through the gateway.

Sojel was not easy on horses. He pushed them as he pushed his underlings, as he pushed himself. He had ridden hard through the night, the cold mountain night, beneath a hunters' moon, while behind him, even as it was setting, the official delegation to the court of Count Ros had prepared to depart. Now, fresh horse after fresh horse, day and night, he had pulled far ahead of them, catching a snatch of sleep in the saddle, ever speeding eastward.

Ahead, lay the rendezvous to which his master had dispatched him.

Never a man given to deep thoughts, Sojel neither knew nor cared about the reasons for his orders. They were his orders; that was enough.

Still, his mind wandered into many strange places as he rode. Most were locales we would not wish to visit. He also thought upon the envoys he was leaving ever further behind. Who was this Blen, anyway? Sojel recognized that the man disliked him and fully returned the sentiment. He and young Nafal had best not get between him and his task.

As the horizon before him began to dimly foretell another dawn, he passed from the hill country and, soon, turned aside from the main road into a wood. The river, and Ros-town beyond it, were not far further down that road, but his destination lay near at hand.

"Who goes there?" a voice barked from the darkness.

"Your master, dog," he curtly replied.

"Ah, Sergeant. You made good time, sir."

Sojel only grunted in reply, swinging down from his steed and handing the reins to the man. "Are all within?"

"Aye, sir."

"See that my horse is well rubbed down." Sojel might use his tools hard but he also knew to take good care of them, after. He turned to a hut hidden away in this grove, a hint of light coming from around its door. More light than he would have permitted, had he been here earlier. Now it mattered little.

A rough-looking group awaited him inside, three men including the Laman, Perdos. All were awake and huddled about a small fire pit, the smoke of which passed out through a hole in the cobweb-shrouded ceiling.

Or mostly passed out — the hut itself reeked of it and the filth of the occupants. Sojel addressed them. "We have orders. Gather 'round."

"Should we call in Van?" asked one, a moon-faced scoundrel. His moon-face included more than a few craters.

"Nay, he is tending my horse." Vanob was the one man here in whom Sojel put any trust whatsoever, being one of his soldiers rather than a common ruffian like these three. He could fill him in later, if need be.

"The time is come," said Sojel, "to remove the young lordling Donzalo, now he is returned to his father's keep. You," he nodded toward Perdos, "will have to sit it out. You are too well known around Borrago's holdings."

The Laman scowled but said nothing. After all, he thought, I care nothing about the boy. There will be a chance at that Cuddonian when this business is done.

"Asak made you two for this sort of thing anyway," he told the others. "Now here's the plan."

Donzalo bounded up the stairs, his long legs taking two or three risers at a time. He would see his father later; time enough for that! Right now, he had other affairs to attend. Yet, as he reached the door to Lady Vibola's room, he paused, suddenly uncertain.

A waylaid page had assured him the Lady Lomela was with his grandmother. But would she want to see him? Perhaps he should have waited, cleaned off the dust of the road, seen his father. Oh, well. He shrugged and knocked at the panel.

He did not know the serving girl who answered and she, apparently, did not know who he was. Fresh from the farm, Donzalo thought to himself, and getting a quick education from Grandmother.

"You may tell the Lady Vibola that her grandson is calling."

"Oh, is that Donni? Let him in, silly girl!"

He smiled at her as she opened wide the door and took his travel-soiled cloak. Life is probably hard enough for her as it is, the young man thought, and it never hurts one to be pleasant. He couldn't help note that she was rather pretty, too, being, as we just mentioned, a young man.

"Welcome home," spoke Lomela, who sat beside the old woman. "We have both missed you."

Donzalo now noted the changes in both these women. Lomela was only obviously pregnant to one who already knew. Five months, perhaps, he thought. Not mine.

It was the Lady Vibola whose appearance jarred him. She looked far older, far less the vibrant matriarch he had left two seasons ago. "Grandmother." He knelt down to embrace and kiss her. "I have very much missed you." He looked up and gave the younger woman a smile. "You too, of course, my Lady Lomela."

And suddenly found tears in his eyes.

4

The troop was small that rode from Mountain Keep that early morning. Along with its two leaders came a pair of attendants and four soldiers, all former comrades of Blen in the eastern command. Their mission was only to pave the way for the ambassador, Lord Doufan, who would follow in the spring.

Unlike the man who had, unknown to them, preceded their group down this road, Sir Blen and Lector Jobareth Nafal were in no hurry. There was no urgency to their work and it was fine autumn weather, dry and cool. Blen looked back at the castle.

"You are a scholar," he said to his companion, "where I know only the tales told in barracks and bars."

Jobareth nodded, though he suspected that the knight was more knowledgeable than he was admitting.

"This castle back here, it belonged to the Rosam at one time, didn't it?"

"Hmm, well, they weren't called the Rosam then, in that Count Ros was son to the man who ruled there. But yes, it was that family."

Blen looked at him expectantly and Nafal, who had no objections to lecturing, took his cue. "Back in the days of the short-lived Anian occupation of Sharsh, an adventurer, or freedom fighter, some might say," both men smiled at that, knowing what they did of politics, "set himself up as an independent power in the mountains. That was Paren, who styled himself a duke."

"The father of Ros."

"Right. He had three other sons, all of whom died in battle, but Ros had been sent eastward to Lama to seek out allies. Instead, he married into them. Actually," continued the lector, "there were daughters as well, who married into the Sharshite nobility. Their descendants are now a part of the court."

"Despite the fact that Lareth's father murdered most of the family," mused the knight.

"King Greneth had only succeeded in driving the Ani out and could not permit this independent power to sit on his border. Moreover, Paren had taken a wife from the old royalty and could well have challenged him for the throne.

"It was treachery that undid Duke Paren, a traitor who opened a gate for the king's men. They slew the three sons but the old man himself escaped into the east. And since," he concluded, "the keep has been a bulwark of Sharsh, defending the main mountain pass in this region and the eastern border."

"That means," said Blen, with a sudden insight, "that Count Borrago and his clan have not only a claim on the Mountain Keep and its surrounds, but also on the throne itself." He whistled softly. "This, I did not know."

"I'm sure King Lareth knows it very well," replied Jobareth Nafal.

"It looks like storm weather moving in," observed Sir Paren.

Borrago only nodded absently but Guesare looked to the grey northern horizon. "It's already to the upper Cuddon, I'd say. There might even be snow."

"Far too early for that here." Paren, none the less, looked a bit worried. His manor was on his mind, as often before and, no doubt, many times to come.

They were gathered atop the tower that stood at the center of Castle Rosam. Borrago liked to sit up here, the highest point in the keep, and think on things. Now, it seemed as good a place as any to hold a council, as long as the threatening weather held off.

His sons were here — the two legitimate ones — and Paren and Guesare. He had considered including his other son. He had even considered the Lady Lomela, yet still had reservations as to her loyalties. Best to keep it to these five, felt Borrago. Let others in later, if need be.

"How do we greet the delegation from Sharsh," he asked the group, "considering what happened the last time one was here?" Borrago looked directly at Donzalo.

"I count Jobareth Nafal a friend," his son replied, "and would welcome him as such."

"And that is, of course, good diplomacy," added Guesare, with the slightest of shrugs.

"Have we any idea who is accompanying the young lector?" asked Paren, ever quick to get to practical questions.

"Yes, Brother. Do you recall the courier Blen?"

Paren nodded. "A decent fellow, seemingly," he allowed.

"He's to be their master of arms and would, I assume, have the running of the household. We could do far worse than having him and Nafal here. Naturally," Borrago continued, "we can assume a spy among their retinue."

"Only one?" quipped Guesare.

Bolos had been pacing the weathered plank floor. "How," he asked, speaking up at last, "can we act as if nothing occurred? We all know the Sharshites want my brother dead. I say turn them away!"

"What is that cliché, Guesare? Keep your friends close and your enemies closer?"

"That's it, Cousin Borrago. But not close enough to slip a knife into one, I would hope."

Bolos harrumphed. "The only harmless enemy is a dead one."

"We can't kill all of Sharsh, Bolos." Paren shook his head. "Best to pretend that what everyone knows happened, didn't. At least for now."

The other three murmured their agreement and Bolos shrugged in acquiescence.

"So," continued the count, "our other business: what do we do with Donzalo now?"

"Donzalo has his own ideas about that," stated the person in question.

"Why don't you come back to the manor with me?" asked Paren. "There's more to do and learn and you may well be reeve there when I am gone. Assuming, " he bowed toward Bolos, "the count at that time so wishes."

"Don't assume you'll outlive me, Parri," growled his older brother. "I'm not sure it's safer for him than right here."

"The walls of Castle Rosam were no defense last time," Guesare reminded them. "But then, neither would be Sir Paren's keep. By the way, my lord," he turned toward the knight and hesitated slightly before speaking, "I took the liberty of leaving a few charms of protection behind, just in case someone attempted magics while we were gone."

Paren looked askance at the minstrel, but only for a moment. "Perhaps that is well. I thank you for protecting the Lady Thara."

Guesare nodded. "They would be useless against the sort of attack Radal unleashed here but they might block smaller evils."

"Is it possible to ward this castle?" asked Bolos.

"Again, only against small magics. Yet, truly, it is unlikely that a powerful sorcerer would get close enough to do harm now that we are on the guard. Certainly, we wouldn't let Radal through the gates again!"

Donzalo laughed. "So all I have to do is lock myself in this tower for the rest of my life."

"That would work," came Guesare's dry reply. "You are at risk if you venture out far, into the countryside or the town, and more from ordinary assassins than from sorcery."

"Ah, well, 'tis good then, my friend, that you taught me how to use a sword."

"I wish you had arrived in time for the Autumn Feast! It is so solemn and dreary here compared to the celebrations in Sharsh."

"The equinox is considered a holy day, Lomela, all about the balance between light and dark. You have been here long enough and seen enough of our Kamatian ways to know that." Donzalo leaned back and looked about the familiar yet seemingly new room. Wasn't it much the same, really, the balcony, the faded tapestries, the young woman, as lovely as ever he remembered her? Yet he sensed it had changed.

"And you also know we celebrate Harvest Feast with a great deal of enthusiasm!"

"Oh, you Lamans are like children at Harvest Feast, with your masks and ghost stories and your feasting and dancing all night."

"Not so much dancing for you this year."

The princess sobered. "It is Bolos's, of course."

Donzalos nodded.

"He has become — better. Oh, he is still Bolos but I think all that happened this spring past awakened something in him. I have tried," she continued, staring at the floor before lifting her eyes to her companion, "to be a good wife to him."

"His drinking?"

"He gave up completely!" laughed Lomela. "He drinks only some brew of burnt barley that he learned of from our Siphic doctor."

Donzalo thought upon these things for a while. "It's all to the good, isn't it?" he finally said.

"I think so," replied the girl he had loved.

The cool air blew in from the balcony. There was touch of dampness to it, a harbinger of the cold coming.

"Damn this rain!"

"That's Laman weather for you, Lector. I've traveled this road in worse."

"Is it bad in winter, Blen?" Jobareth readjusted the soggy cloak he had pulled over his head.

"Not much snow this far south. That's why the Mountain Keep is where it is — it's the northernmost pass that remains open all winter." He thought a moment, then added, "Most winters."

"Ha, depending on what happens most times has often gotten people into trouble."

"Indeed. Most of the time!" Both men laughed. They had been cool when they met but had grown to like and even depend on each other. Weeks together on the road may do that — or create enemies.

"Without this mud we'd have been inside, before a fire by now."

"Ho, here is the turning of the road." He gestured to the men to follow him. "We'll find your fire shortly."

A few minutes later, the party stood before Castle Rosam's outermost gate.

5

Two men slid along a back street of Ros-town. "It's right up here," said the shorter of the pair.

His companion turned a round, pock-marked face to him. "What good will this do us?"

"The young Laman is likely to visit sooner or later. It's our best chance of catching him on the streets. Unless," he spat into the mud, "you want to risk waiting around the castle for him to come out."

"Good enough. He's a friend of the envoy, eh?"

"Yeah. I heard they arrived last night. Staying at the castle now but they'll move in down here in a day or two. There is the place." They had reached the end of an alley and he gestured to a large two-storied house on the far side of the street.

"Nice digs."

The shorter man, a dark broadly built fellow, nodded. "One of us will have to keep watch here from now on."

"Not from right now," replied the other, with a grin. "We can wait till someone moves in over there, right? Let's go grab an ale."

"Only one, though. We need to stay sharp."

"Of course. I'm not new to this business."

"So, my father is finished with you?"

"He is, friend Donzalo. Considering all that occurred last time I visited, he was surprisingly cordial."

"The count knows I consider you an ally."

Jobareth made a slight grimace at the use of the word. "An ally — I suppose so, for now, and ever a friend. But I have loyalties to my king," he paused, "and to his daughter. If our ends diverge, I will choose them, you know."

"None to Radal?"

"Only so far as he serves my king. I feel no personal loyalty to the man."

"As long as you put your loyalty to Lomela above that to Lareth, we will have no quarrels." Donzalo changed subject and tone. "How has it been with you this past six-month, Lector?"

"The existence of a very junior diplomat largely consists of copying out dispatches or taking dictation. At least, in the capital there are theaters to help break the boredom."

"We hear tales of the parties and fetes of the noble families, not to mention the royal court. Aren't you invited to those?"

"I am not noble, Donzalo. I am of a family of wine merchants." Jobareth laughed. "Although my grandfather could buy and sell most of the noblemen. Indeed, perhaps he already has, considering how much money he has lent them." Turning more serious, he continued. "I have always been welcome in the King's home, as my family's money has often been put in his service.

"And, someday, if I rise in the diplomatic corps, I may well be awarded a title. I will never be a member of the old aristocracy, however, and they will always snub me."

"Few noble families here go back more than three generations," mused Donzalo. "They were leaders in the wars against the Ani who became the new rulers when things settled down."

"One could say the same about our Sharsh royals," replied Jobareth. "Well, here we are. Shall I knock?"

"In a moment. You should know that my grandmother has not been well. She is an old woman, after all, but I never noticed it so much until my return."

Jobareth nodded. He had lost both his grandmothers in recent years. He turned and lightly rapped on the door.

Donzalo was slightly surprised, and perhaps even a bit pleased, that the same maid answered as on his last visit.

With mock solemnity, he proclaimed, "Lector Jobareth Nafal and Master Donzalo Rosam most humbly request audience with the Lady Vibola." The girl blushed and giggled at this, which pleased the young man even more. Jobareth glanced at her and, for a moment, thought he might know her from somewhere else.

Then she pulled open wide the door for their admittance. The Countess seemed in better health and spirits than when last Donzalo had seen her, but still showed her age. Jobareth stepped forward and, bowing, kissed her hand. "My Lady Vibola."

"Oh, you're the young gallant with the book of poems. I remember you, sir! Why have you not come visit me for so long?" she added in a slightly peevish tone.

"Only duties abroad could keep me from your presence, my lady."

Vibola looked to the Lady Lomela, seated nearby. "Well, I couldn't rattle him. You were right, Granddaughter." Then both burst into laughter.

"Grandmother is up to her old tricks," Donzalo confided to his companion.

With a gracious smile, Jobareth turned to the princess. "My Lady Lomela. *You* remember, don't you?"

In answer, she rose to her feet and embraced her childhood friend. "I, too, wish you could have visited sooner."

"Well, my ladies, you will be putting up with me all winter, it seems. I may reside in the town but I shall spend much time here.

"Oh," he said, reaching into his pouch, "and I have a new book of poetry for you."

Two horses, two riders. On a dark and barely discernible pathway through the woods, Perdos and Sojel met.

"What news?" asked the Laman.

"None."

Perdos, by this time, knew better than to be offended by Sojel's taciturnity. This did not mean that he despised the man any the less.

"Then why are we meeting?"

"My men may or may not succeed in their mission. That is none of your concern. I need you to keep an eye on Paren's keep and the road between it and Castle Rosam."

"In case things do not go well." Perdos had learned to read between this Muram's lines.

Sojel stared impassively at the man he considered his underling. Perdos, of course, thought himself no such thing. He spoke. "There is always that chance."

Then, in a gesture uncharacteristic for him, he went on. "It might give you a shot at your Cuddonian too. If the boy is dead, we no longer care what you do to his protector — but until he is, we will not allow you to interfere and bungle. Now keep a sharp lookout. I'll send Vanob along to you for a report. Meet him here in a week."

With that, the soldier turned his mount and rode away, disappearing into the darkened woods.

"It seems a decent enough place." Blen turned to the agent who had taken this house for them. "Bigger than we need right now, of course." But, he thought, when Doufan and the entire delegation arrives it may prove insufficient. "How far are we from the river?"

The agent fully understood why the knight asked this. "More than a hundred yards, sir. No flood waters reach this far."

"Then, Master Marmoyo, why is it raised up so high?" asked Jobareth. The wooden structure was practically on stilts.

"Um, I should say they don't reach this far most years. There are always exceptions."

The Sharshites laughed at their private joke.

"Most years will do, my good man. We expect flood waters in Rostown. Lector Jobareth," Blen asked his co-commander, "have you any objections to the house?"

"None. I was mostly concerned with it having an impressive front in a prestigious neighborhood. If there be such here. We can start moving in immediately."

"We'll need furnishings. Perhaps you can help us with that," Blen said, addressing the agent.

"Of course, sirs, of course. And I should say that this is as good a street as any in town and close to the largest lending houses."

"We shall prepare a list for you." He turned from the man and in a lowered voice asked, "Say, Jobareth, have you noticed the lurker across the street?"

"I can't say that I did. You are a more observant man than I." He glanced toward the opposite alley but saw no one. "Do you suspect trouble?"

"Possibly just a curious neighbor. Possibly something more. It's hard to tell," he said dryly, "most of the time."

6

"So, they celebrate tomorrow, a harvest feast of some sort." Moon-face was explaining something to his partner, as they sat in a darkened corner of the ale-house, hidden from the eyes of a handful of patrons. Neither used proper names, being old to their game of espionage and murder, and wishing to leave no traces of themselves.

"We had harvest feasts back home," replied his comrade. "I think they have them about everywhere."

"But here they make something more of it. And they wear masks."

"Masks?" The idea of lawfully going disguised appealed to both.

"Aye. If our target comes down to celebrate, we can do our job and get out without anyone seeing our faces."

The shorter man nodded, then had a thought. "Ah, but what if Do — er, the target wears a mask as well?" He had nearly forgotten to leave all names out of the business. No one need overhear them mention the young Rosam.

"Are you jesting?" asked his round-faced companion. "He stands head and shoulders above just about everyone else in town! Besides," he confided, "our spy in the castle can point him out."

"You are joining us, Master Grippo?"

The young acolyte sprawled in a comfortable chair, his white robe — for only priests added red to their raiments — thrown open to reveal the costume of a jester. "I would not miss it. Harvest Feast is my favorite time of year."

Guesare gave forth a grunt of obvious disapproval. "Our minstrel," observed Donzalo, "is a player in a perpetual masque. To attend ours is rather redundant."

"Yet attend I shall, to keep an eye on you. I disapprove of you going into town, especially on such a night as this. As does," he observed, "your father."

Donzalo looked momentarily uncomfortable, knowing he should exercise more prudence. But he wanted out of this castle! It had been bad enough having a pair of guardsmen follow him about all summer.

"There will be a group of us," Grippo pointed out. "If we stick together, who would give us any trouble?" He was quite unaware of the plot against Donzalo, of course, and of much that had happened six months earlier.

"Ha! I would trust myself to the protection of Guesare far sooner than that crowd of foppish bloods."

The minstrel gave him a small bow. "Yet there is safety in numbers," he said.

Donzalo replied, with a shrug, "I don't intend to stay with them, anyway. We are going to the Sharshites's new place and will introduce Lector Nafal to the delights of Harvest Feast."

"Very well," spoke Guesare. "So Grippo here and some of his friends will accompany us down? A few men will help to discourage trouble, fops or not."

"A few women too, Sir Guesare," the acolyte said. "Everyone enjoys dressing up for the festival."

"Yes, and I have invited a guest of my own," added Donzalo.

"Now are you sure you won't be needing me, my lady?"

"I shall be fine, Traspa. I would have joined you had it not been," she put one hand to her belly, "for this."

"Ah, yes, Lady Lomela. I remember how you danced a year ago!" Traspa became uncharacteristically introspective for a moment. Something had been nagging at her for a while — ever since that boy Donzalo had returned, in fact. She would have to talk to her mistress later.

But now it was time for gaiety. "And you shall dance again, next year," she declared.

"That is up to the gods and my husband," replied Lomela. The thought of pregnancies — and their cause — led her to a moment of silence as well. "Have you a costume?" she asked, after her short reverie.

Elsewhere, another lady and her maid also conversed, but with much less amity.

"Should a young girl like you be out with that crowd?"

"Oh, my lady, Mistress Traspa is going along."

"Hmm, she seems somewhat sensible." opined the Lady Vibola. "Despite her dalliances with the kitchen staff."

"Food, I think, is more her weakness than men, my lady."

Vibola looked closely at her maid. This girl had more to her than she had first realized. "Posena," she said, "my grandson invited you, didn't he?"

"Yes, my lady." The girl prettily blushed but the older woman wasn't convinced completely of her innocence. She knew that there had come a tension between Donni and Lomela and that a woman with her wits about her might take advantage of it. The boy, at times, seemed a lost soul and Vibola wasn't the only one who could see that.

"Do not take advantage of him. Do you understand me?"

Posena nodded. "Yes, my lady." But she may or may not have meant it.

"It is a bother to take horses down with us," explained one of the young revelers. "The walk is not that far, anyway."

"It won't hurt you any to walk, Cousin," chided Donzalo. Guesare had not been pleased to find that they were traveling shanks' mare.

"Not on the way down," he admitted, "but coming back may be another question."

"No one goes home until morning!" laughed another of their companions. The minstrel recognized her as daughter to one of the knights in Borrago's retinue. "Except for poor Brother Grippo," she continued.

"He has to be at his early services." She made a face at the unfortunate acolyte.

"All of you forget that the morrow is a holy day, albeit a minor one."

"Yes, the Feast of Family. It is observed in the Cuddon, as well, even if we don't follow your Kamatian ways. But we do not have this carnival the night before."

"Then that is your loss, Sir Guesare! What good is solemnity without some festivity to balance it?" The crowd murmured their approval. There were at least twenty of them, of varied station, and they had already started down the path toward town.

"Come and walk with us, Posena," called Donzalo. "You, as well, Mistress Traspa."

"Nay, young sir, I shall walk with Hendel here." She was hanging on the arm of a burly, bearded man in monk's robes. He was, of course, no monk but a pastry chef, costumed for the masque. "You go join them, girl," she told Posena, giving her a little push. "We can do fine without you." Traspa gave her companion a wink.

Soon, they were mingling with other groups on the road, some from the countryside, others come down separately from the castle. Many carried lanterns, carved fancifully from gourds or rutabagas, and others sang gaily. Posena walked demurely at Donzalo's side, not too close, yet closer than to anyone else. Behind their backs were many smiles.

7

"By Jov!" swore Guesare. "This be quite some party."

"That it is," agreed Jobareth, who stood beside his guests on the high porch of his new dwelling. Below them, the town blazed and blared in celebration.

"A warning, Sir Guesare," spoke Grippo, low and seriously. "It would be best not to use the names of the old gods, even in oaths. Some here may take it wrong." He had chosen to accompany Donzalo's group, parting ways with his young companions from the keep.

"Jov is still venerated in Sharsh," Jobareth pointed out. "You Kamatians are not so bold there."

"Your master, Radal, is of our way, isn't he? Even if he follows the Darkness rather than the One Truth." Grippo looked uncertain as to whether he should say more but wine and fellowship had loosened his tongue. "I do believe that there is one all-powerful God and it matters little what we choose to call him."

Jobareth looked out into the night for a moment and then asked, "Can you tell me, Master Grippo, why this all-powerful deity of yours allows evil to exist?"

"Because, my friend," replied the acolyte with a small smile, "evil is also all-powerful."

"Is this what the priests teach?" interjected Donzalo.

"Some of them," Guesare said. "I've heard such theology in Lorj. Here, I suspect, it smacks of heresy."

"Perhaps," agreed Brother Grippo. "So I usually keep such thoughts to myself."

Jobareth seemed intrigued by this concept. Ever the scholar, and somewhat a skeptic, he asked, "Then what *is* evil? Another god?"

The acolyte sighed. "I have read much on it and thought much on it. I would say evil is not a thing but, rather, the absence of good." He paused to gather together his thoughts. "And good — or God or Kamat or whatever name we choose — is the only reality. Good and evil are being and non-being, existence and the void.

"Can Being exist without emptiness?" he asked. "What would it fill? Nor, for that matter, could emptiness exist — if I might speak of the existence of that which does not actually exist — without Being to define it."

Guesare nodded. "All well and good, Brother, but I have seen the work of Asak and know that it is more than real."

Grippo had an answer. "Asak embodies that part of Being which strives to return to the Void, to become nothing. It has taken form, even though it hates its form and its existence — all existence."

Posena had moved close to Donzalo and was hanging on his arm. Now she looked up at him. "I do not like this talk, Master Donzalo. It gives me shivers."

"And I as well," he replied. "Let us join the celebration, friends!"

Blen had not mingled with the guests of the diplomat, but he had kept his eyes and ears open. They had told him there was potential to this group of young people, even if they did not recognize it themselves. This was the sort of thing his king had sent him here to learn — not state secrets or military movements so much as who might move events, be it now or later.

He watched the party fade into the carnival lights and turned back to his duties. This house still needed much work. Marmoyo had scrounged some satisfactory furnishings, and the men had settled in. The soldiers were now barracked in a large rear room, which had probably been intended for dining. He himself had taken a space scarce longer than his own body, a pantry off the main room, as his quarters. It would allow him to be close to all that went on.

Jobareth, of course, had a bedroom upstairs, and the two servants were there as well. For now, meals came from a nearby inn.

Not that any of it mattered much. Their primary mission was to have a new embassy built above the town. Could it be readied in time for the ambassador's arrival? Blen doubted it. Not in the upcoming winter weather.

But they could choose the location — Jobareth said there was already a likely spot — and make preparations. Much of that would be Blen's task, as the young envoy would have to spend time on his diplomatic duties.

Jobareth Nafal seemed so young. Yet, Blen reminded himself, he was not much older. A soldier at sixteen, knighted before he turned twenty, he scarcely remembered ever feeling truly young.

For a moment, he wondered if he could slip on a mask and join the crowd without. No, he shook his head. It is too late for that.

Ever since he began shooting up to his current height, Donzalo had worn the same Harvest Feast costume: a tree. His reasoning for the choice? A tall man and a short man look the same wrapped inside a tree trunk. It was the best disguise.

Except that, by now, everyone knew who was in the tree.

So, for once, the young nobleman chose new costuming. He was advised in doing this, as well, by Guesare, who had pointed out the difficulties of wielding a sword while encased in wood. His guise was barely a costume at all, only festive robes and a half-mask, but Posena had told him it looked quite elegant.

That was enough for Donzalo. In fact, he had the tailor, already beleaguered at this season of year, immediately take time to make up a similar outfit for the girl.

The two of them wandered the carnival streets and it did not take long for them to go on hand in hand, ever more oblivious of their companions — jester Grippo, Jobareth as mock soldier in a bristling false beard, Guesare deigning to don a black half-mask and no more.

From a passing vendor, he bought them prani, the sugary, nut-filled candy that was known to every Laman child. Posena seemed oddly unfamiliar with it but downed hers with relish, regardless. Then she pulled his head down to her, pressed her sweetened lips to his. Her blond hair fell back, behind her pale, shapely shoulders.

Why, she looks like an Anian, thought Donzalo. Then he thought more. An Anian wouldn't know about prani.

"Who are you, truly?" he whispered to her.

"A friend," she whispered back.

Donzalo straightened himself and looked about. He did not see his companions; indeed, he didn't see anyone at all. They stood in the darkness at the mouth of some warehouse alley, shielded from the lights and festivities on the streets.

"Oh, watch out, my lord!" she suddenly cried. From deeper in the shadowed alley emerged two man-shadows, swords in hands. For a moment, it seemed she would stand by him. Then she broke and ran for the lights, barely slipping by one man who had moved to block Donzalo's exit, noticing only his round face, half-hidden behind a scarf.

Guesare turned to see a breathless girl running toward him. "Quickly," she gasped out. "Quickly, my lords! They — will — kill him."

Damn! How did we get separated? the minstrel asked himself. He knew this carnival was a bad idea.

Posena was running back the other way now and he followed her, Grippo and Jobareth not far behind. An alley opened to their left and from it came the sounds of metal on metal.

And in it stood Donzalo, calmly dueling with a short, powerfully-built, and decidedly skillful swordsman. In the mud, near them, lay a taller man, split open from gullet to bowels, the latter spilling out onto the clay. A scarf partly concealed his countenance.

Guesare bounded forward and the would-be assassin backed toward the darkness. Too late — Donzalo's sword flicked out and caught him even as he turned to bolt.

"Well, my large student has passed his final exam, I would say." The Cuddonian looked at the two dead men. "Still, it is fortunate that Posena was able to run and warn us."

Donzalo looked about. "Where is she?"

The girl had disappeared completely.

8

One masked figure whispered to another, then slipped away to rejoin the festival.

By Asak's hell, thought the other, whose costume was no more than a kerchief across his lower face, another plot gone awry. Who'd have thought the young Laman so capable?

And who was that girl with him?

But that was none of his concern. A courier must be dispatched immediately to the mountains with this news. He would ride himself, thought Sojel, but there was too much to do here, men to gather for his fall-back plan.

Sojel and his master always had a fall-back plan.

"I am sure she is Ani," stated Donzalo.

Guesare seemed perplexed and, for once, was quite speechless. He only shook his head.

"The question," Jobareth said, "is whether she intended you good or harm." He remembered now, too, how her appearance had seemed to touch at some memory in him. The Sharshite wondered about that but felt it best he say nothing.

The minstrel found his tongue. "If she meant ill for the boy, she would not have run to us."

The others nodded in agreement. "And," he continued, "even if she is Anian she need not be in the employ of the Empire. Spies will serve any master who pays well."

"Then a spy, you think?" asked Jobarth.

Donzalo replied to the question. "I would think so. Why else run away? She knew I had found her out."

With some reluctance, Guesare said, "Do you think we should inform the count, Donni? He could send soldiers out to search for her."

"Let her go. She did no harm and will not return."

The Cuddonian seemed relieved by the answer. "Probably so, probably so."

"Well, that's that. Are you gentlemen spending the night or heading back to the castle?"

"I must go, Lector," responded Brother Grippo. "I thank you for your hospitality."

"Any time, sir. I would hope to discuss philosophy with you at greater length, some day."

"Then I shall accompany good Grippo," said Donzalo. "And Guesare will accompany us, of course, as he feels obligated to protect me."

"Do not become arrogant, " returned the minstrel, dryly. "The next time two skilled assassins attack you, luck may not be on your side."

Count Borrago did hear of the events that befell his son; it was inevitable that the town constables would report them. Of Posena, however, none made any mention. Donzalo chose to lie to his grandmother, telling her that her maid had been called home for a family death. His grandmother did not believe a word of it.

And she did not like her new maid one bit.

In a different room, Lomela was listening to her own maid.

"It was a dreadful fight, my lady! They say Donzalo was attacked by a half-dozen men and chopped them to pieces!"

The princess, despite herself — and knowing the story exaggerated — felt proud of her Donni, for there was still a place in her heart where he dwelt. "And Lady Vibola's maid was nowhere to be found?"

"No, my lady. Maybe they murdered the poor girl." The thought suddenly possessed her and Traspa heaved a great sob and fell to her knees. "Oh, my Lomela, there is so much wickedness in this world!"

She looked up to her mistress with teary eyes. "And I have done wickedness too. Forgive me, my lady!"

"Why, what are you talking about, Traspa? Come here and sit beside me."

"It — it was that Radal." The older woman slid onto the edge of Lomela's couch and, reaching out, took her hands. "He made me do it!"

Lomela suddenly felt chill. "The Lord Radal has much to answer for." She spoke calmly. "Tell me of this, Traspa."

"It was he that had me spy on you and young Donzalo. He had me tell him things, bring him things. Oh lady, he said I was protecting you." Now the maid truly began to wail.

The princess pulled Traspa to her, wrapped her in her arms. "My dear, I know you would do me no harm. And I think now you know that Donni would not, either. Whatever that evil man had you do," she stared straight ahead, her face set in a bitter mask, "is more than forgiven."

Now her expression softened. "And Traspa," she said, raising the woman's head so she might look into her eyes, "from now on, serve only me."

"Yes, my lady, yes. You are my princess!" She began to sob again, head pressed against Lomela's bosom.

"Ah, yes, Traspa," the girl whispered, "there is much wickedness in this world."

Guesare was puzzled. An Anian spy in Castle Rosam? Well, that was not so strange; what was strange was that he would not know of it.

But then, there could be all sorts of spies here, or in the town. Some of them perhaps in Anian employ — though the Empire would be unlikely to send anyone of Ani birth here — or from any of a dozen or more other nations or city-states. Posena was a puzzle.

Not so much because she was a spy but because she had attached herself to Donzalo. To protect him? To corrupt him? Ah, for all he knew, she was no more than an adventuress looking to find herself a noble lover.

Such thoughts accompanied him all the way to the door of the Great Hall. Today was the Feast of the Family, the second day of Harvest

Feast, and the only one on which people actually feasted. Tomorrow, the Feast of the Dead, was given to fasting. Guesare had always preferred feasting to fasting.

He entered, and bowed toward the dais where Borrago and his family sat. Immediately, it registered on him that the Lady Vibola was not taking part. He felt a fleeting pang and felt as well that he should write an ode on the brevity of human life. Or, better yet, he could just go visit the old lady.

Borrago lifted a hand in greeting and went back to his conversation with his brother.

The hall was rather empty, actually. Oh, of course, only the family. There would be no guests, no diplomats, no retainers. A server showed him to a table not far from the count's.

Donzalo plunked himself down across from him. "Hail, Kinsman." The young fellow leaned back and stated, "And I am proud to call you such on the Feast of the Family."

"And I, you, Cousin Donzalo. So where's the food?"

"First comes the blessing of the hearth."

"Oh. We don't make a big thing of that in the Cuddon. For the head of the household, it is his first act of the day."

"Remember, we have priests here, Guesare. We have to give them something to do."

The minstrel smiled and nodded. "It's not that we don't have priests back home, you know. Not your Kamatians though — the old gods are still loved there." He paused. "And feared, as well."

"I do find it interesting that you hold to much the same pantheon as they do in Sharsh, despite all of Lama lying between you."

"We must be a related people, don't you think?" asked Guesare. "We even look somewhat alike."

"Here is the hierophant. We'll be eating soon."

The high priest entered, in robes of red and white — the more red, the higher the position in the hierarchy. Two priests of lesser rank attended him and, behind them, a pair of acolytes. "Hey, there's Grippo," whispered Donzalo.

Guesare nodded benignly. "That boy will be moving up in the world. If he isn't drowned as a heretic first."

The hearth, which was actually quite small, and more ceremonial than practical, had been thoroughly cleaned. Now the Hierophant opened his gilded jar and spread holy ash upon it, blessing it and the household for another year.

Then with a bow, the priest and his retinue exited.

"Probably wants to get home to dinner," confided Donzalo.

"What family has a celibate priest?" queried the Cuddonian.

"Oh, the whole of the priesthood is considered his family, once a man is ordained. That must lead to a rather crowded table," he chuckled.

"Here comes our food," announced Guesare. "In the Cuddon, again, things are different. Most of the priests are married. And," he added, "we have priestesses as well. They are not known for their celibacy."

Servers came around with platters and bowls, filled with the fruits of the harvest and the hunt. There were sundry fowl, and beef and venison heaped up. Sweet Potatoes and maize were stacked, and bowls of light and dark gravies, and more fruits than Guesare could put a name to. He realized that he had neglected some aspects of his self-education.

"Very well," he admitted with an exasperated — and certainly, exaggerated — tone. "The Cuddon can not match this."

"And you brag so on the Yule celebration there!"

"This feast marks the half-way point between equinox and Yule. Six weeks or so — you really should come celebrate with us, my boy."

"Ha, you didn't even want me to go into town yet you think I should ride into those wild hills?"

"You might be far safer in said hills. Think on it, Donzalo. Think on it."

9

"I need a full account of what has happened," said Count Borrago. He turned to his scribe. "You may leave. Have those papers ready for me to sign." The man bowed and departed wordlessly.

Across the table from Borrago sat his youngest son. "Just from you to me," he said. "No one else is here."

Donzalo gulped. It was not that he couldn't handle himself, but he missed having the support, moral or otherwise, of Guesare or Paren. "There's not much to it, Father," he began.

The count held up his hand. "We shall see. First though, I must say I am proud that you handled yourself so well. I — I long underestimated you, my son.

"Now, let's start from the start. You left here with a group."

"Yes, sir. There were several of us, to some of whom I'm not sure I could put names. But I was actually going down with Guesare and Grippo."

"And a serving girl, I hear."

The young man nodded a reply. "I did invite Grandmother's maid to accompany us. Oh, and Mistress Traspa was with her." He tried to sound nonchalant.

"I know. Mistress Traspa was the one who told me about the girl."

"Oh. Anyway, sir, we all went down to the celebration but I and Grippo and Guesare stopped by the house the Sharshites are renting."

"With the girl."

"Yes. with the girl. Who is, truly, the person you're interested in, right?"

The Count only smiled.

"All I can say is she ran off after the fight. And that she didn't seem to have anything to do with the assassins being there." Donzalo was not going to mention his suspicions of her being Ani. He spread his arms in a gesture of puzzlement. "Maybe she was just scared by all that happened and decided to go back to the farm."

"We both doubt that, Son."

"Or maybe she was a spy. Who knows? She's gone."

"She might not have been if I'd known of her right away. But you felt you owed her a debt, didn't you?" The count rose. "That's all right. She did run for help so I understand how you feel. I do wish we'd had the chance to find out who she was."

Donzalo rose now as well.

"Donni," continued his father, "we must decide soon where you will winter. Less than a fortnight here and you're already battling assassins. This is not good."

"I know, Father." The younger man bowed and left.

Borrago rose and walked to the slit of a window in this tower room. It was still light out. What if he went to see his other family on this day? Copago had a wife at home, and a pretty little daughter. His granddaughter. Would he be welcome?

Ah, he had papers to go over. Let them feast in peace and not be bothered by an old man.

Perdos waited beneath a massive oak, one of the wide-spreading oaks of the South, that overhung the road. It was time again for his weekly rendezvous with Vanob.

And here came the man, astride his gray nag. Perdos rose and held up his hand in greeting.

"What report?" asked the man.

"As usual," replied Perdos. "Nothing. Nothing passes on this forsaken road for days on end."

"That time of the year," shrugged Vanob. "I do have some news for your ears. Let's sit. I'm road-worn."

Both settled beneath the tree and the soldier pulled out a leather-covered flask, took a gulp, and offered it to Perdos. He sampled it — fierce corn liquor.

"Pretty potent stuff," said his companion. "The peasant folk around these parts brew it."

Perdos laughed at that. "I drank plenty enough of it down at Castle Rosam. So what is this news you bear?"

With something resembling a smirk, Vanob spoke. "The sergeant's assassins failed him. That so-called boy has apparently turned into a swordsman and cut them to ribbons." He spat onto the dry leaves. "So much for his plotting."

Perdos saw that this man loathed Sojel as much as he. But then, who didn't?

"This means," continued Vanob, "that young Donzalo and his uncle may be passing back up this road soon to winter quarters. You'll need to keep a sharp lookout."

Perdos nodded. "Will I have more men to help? We may be able to set an ambush."

"Sojel himself will be coming soon with all the men he needs. Unless," he sneered, "he has once again underestimated his opponents."

"My Lady Lomela, this was among the dispatches I received yesterday." Jobareth held out an envelope to the princess. He knew its author's hand by the scrawl of an address.

As did Lomela. "Why, it's a letter from Fachalana." She tore it open. "Oh, her spelling is dreadful!"

"That was unlikely to change."

"Um-huh. Let me — hmm, yes — yes. Well, she does tell me to take good care of you, Jobo. She says she may find herself in sudden need of a husband."

The diplomat groaned.

"Hmm. Ah, wishes for a safe pregnancy — asking after my son — the usual pleasantries. And — well, this is odd. She asks about Donzalo. How might she have heard of him? She wouldn't — no, she wouldn't be part to her father's schemes, would she?"

"I would not think so, my lady." Jobareth asserted, coming to stand next to her. A knock came on the door, solid and rapid. "And speaking of Donzalo, that is most certainly he."

"Well then, make yourself useful and let him in. Do you think Traspa can do everything around here?"

It was indeed Donzalo, and Guesare as well. Both affected nonchalance — the minstrel better achieving it — but there was an air of the serious about them. "My lady," Donzalo came forward in greeting and lightly embraced Lomela. "Lector." He nodded a greeting to her companion.

Guesare gave a graceful bow to the pair and settled into a chair near the door.

"Well," began Donzalo, "it seems that I will be off again soon."

"Oh, Donni, already?"

"Yes. Pretty much everyone is in agreement on it — my father, my uncle, my shadow over there." He nodded toward the minstrel. "And I, as well. I can't just sit here in the castle all winter. I need to do something!"

"Not long ago you might have been content to read through the winter," the girl reminded him. "And visit with me and your grandmother."

"We all change." This came from Jobareth.

"I would that we didn't," replied the princess. "I would that we could be as we were." She, of a sudden, began to sob.

It was the Sharshite, not Donzalo, who put his arm around her in comfort. She raised her moist eyes to the young Laman. "When will you leave?"

"In two days, most likely." He gave Jobareth a look, as if undecided to continue in his presence. With a shrug, he continued. "You might as well know all this too, Lector.

"We will head back to my uncle's keep, giving out the word that I intend to winter there, but along the road Guesare and I shall part company with Sir Paren and head to the Cuddon. It is to be hoped that none will know where I am."

He looked to Traspa, busying herself on the far side of the room, but no doubt listening to everything. "Make sure this does not leave the room, Mistress Traspa. No gossiping in the kitchen."

"Traspa may be trusted," Lomela assured him. But the look she gave her maid was full of unspoken warning.

Traspa trembled slightly and spoke. "My mouth will be shut as tight as your father's purse, young lord!" She took a step forward and looked up into Donzalo's face. "And I beg your forgiveness for any harm I may have done before."

He pulled her into the embrace of his long arms. "All I ask of you, Traspa, is that you take good care of your lady while I am gone."

Blen and Jobareth, accompanied by a single soldier, trotted up the castle road.

"Here's the spot," said the envoy, pointing out a hill that overlooked their path. "Lord Radal picked it out when we were here in the spring."

"Nice piece of land," observed Blen. "Who owns it?"

"All the land about here, strictly speaking, belongs to the count. Even that under the house we currently rent. We would have to work out a lease with him and his agents before we could build."

"Will he want us so close to the castle?" asked Blen and then, laughing, answered himself. "Of course, he would be able to keep a better eye on us here."

"I know that he would prefer we stay in his keep rather than build an embassy. Both Lord Radal and the king are set against that idea. Hence, our current abode."

"It is an excellent location," the knight said and, dismounting, began to walk up the slope. Jobareth likewise alit from his horse to join him. The soldier came forward to hold their steeds.

"We would be about half-way between castle and town here," Jobareth informed him, "and near where the road to the great market splits away."

Blen nodded. "The view from up here is very good." They stood atop the rising, looking down toward the town and river. "I'm sure your master recognized that one could keep a watch on the road from here." He turned back toward the horses and their man below. "Not bad for defense, either, if need came."

"Let us hope it does not." Jobareth started his descent. "I shall approach Count Borrago on the morrow."

"You spend much time in his keep." It was a statement, flat and neutral.

"And no doubt will spend much more. It is part of the job. Still," he continued, "I enjoy the company there."

"The princess."

"Yes, and her friends as well. Young Donzalo is an interesting fellow."

Blen smiled inwardly to hear this youth describe Donazalo as "young," but then realized that he did hold two or three years advantage over the lordling. It was not unlike the difference between himself and Jobareth.

"I hear that he is leaving us."

The diplomat recognized that the knight was fishing for information. They might be partners, they might even be friends — though that still remained uncertain — but he knew that each had his own agenda, his own masters.

They had reached the horses. Jobareth swung up into the saddle and spoke loudly enough that the man holding his bridle might hear as well — he knew that at least one member of their retinue must be a spy for someone. "Yes, he is headed back to Sir Paren's manor for the winter. We'll see no more of Donzalo till spring."

10

So that's done, Radal told himself, as he watched the messenger bearing orders to his minion, Sojel, disappear down the shadowed hallway. But there is much more.

He turned back into his room, only to gather the necessary items — a book, a brazier, misshapen jars, the cask containing his greatest object of power — and then began to ascend into one of the soaring towers of Mountain Keep. Another magic, another spell that might bring him close to Asak's dark door, but must be accomplished.

All understood that this was the sorcerer's chamber, here high in this tower. No others came nor went. He shut the massive door, all of brass and ebony of the southern islands, behind him, turning an intricate key in its lock.

Sojel would be readying himself back in County Rosam, following the failure of his assassination plot, gathering his men to watch the road, perhaps even find the opportunity to attack the traveling Lamans. His sergeant had a larger force at his disposal now, a formidable troop, but that guaranteed nothing. Lord Radal had other servants to whom he could turn.

He laid out his magical objects before him, methodically, precisely. A breath before beginning; relax, he told himself. For a moment, he let his mind wander. Why was he doing this? Why did he continue to seek that boy's death?

And what if they had chosen to befriend him rather attempt his assassination? Ah well, that caravel had long sailed.

So far as he knew, Donzalo as yet had no son. That had lessened the urgency, led him to be cautious in his approach. And then, there was that gnawing conviction in him that it was all pointless. The oracle had spoken, hadn't it? He shrugged and set to work.

"I shall send the Rupa," he whispered to himself. "Yes."

Count Borrago was no fool. He therefore dispatched a dozen of his most battle-seasoned men to accompany Paren's small retinue on the road. The morning of their departure dawned clear and cold.

Donzalo breathed in the crisp air. "A year past, I might have been out gathering nuts on such a day."

"I have consumed more than a few pecans since our arrival here," said Guesare. "They do not grow so well nor plentifully in the Cuddon. But we do have filberts aplenty, thickets in the hollows of the hills."

"It's a dry country, isn't it?"

"Not terribly so. The soil is poor, for the most part, which gives the land the look of desert to those who don't know it. Much of what grows is scrubby. None of these huge oaks you have here." Guesare's tone had become, for a moment, wistful. "It's my home. I love the high hills where only the wild grasses grow. In the spring," he continued, "ah, in the spring they are ablaze with flowers. Who would give up such for trees?"

"A man who loves nuts, obviously," replied Donzalo.

"Indeed, young friend, indeed. And a man who can not stay put in one place."

The tall young man suddenly stood in his stirrups and reached an overhanging limb. "Here's one nut at least," he said, displaying the brown oblong he had plucked. "Now I can say I've gone gathering this year."

"That's no pecan," said the minstrel, looking at the nut in Donzalo's open palm.

"No, a wild hickory. Hard to shell and not much meat inside, but I'll keep it anyway. A last memento of my home." He tucked it into his belt pouch.

In a lowered voice, he asked, "How soon do we split away?"

"This first night, I think, would be best, with the cover of darkness. Paren will let the guard know of the plan before we leave — your father gave him a letter for the captain — and continue to his manor as if nothing happened."

The Cuddonian looked up to the sky, suddenly. "What is it, Sir Guesare?" asked his companion.

"I don't know. I thought I felt a presence — up there." He gestured toward the heavens. "And I did not like what I felt."

Seventeen men, Perdos counted. Sojel had best bring an army if he intended to waylay these Lamans while they traveled. He urged his mount forward; if he hurried on the back trails he knew, he could ride ahead of the party and meet the sergeant and his men by morning. Would they attack knowing these odds?

He doubted it. There would be other opportunities after these soldiers had returned to Castle Rosam, when Paren's people would become less watchful, confident of their safety in their own keep.

If Sojel had any sense he would not let them catch a glimpse of him at this point in the game.

Night was come but a half-waned moon would soon provide enough light for him to make his way, even on these overhung paths through the woods. What if he just turned around right now, wondered Perdos, and sent an arrow towards that Cuddonian? Why should he care about the Sharshites and their schemes?

Best he keep to the set course for now. Opportunities would come. Forward rode Perdos, and eastward into the night.

"How long have you been on that beard, Donni?" It was an idle question, as the pair quietly threaded their way through the trees, leading their mounts.

"I stopped shaving the day we decided on this action. That makes this the, uh, third morning." He scratched at his bristling chin. "Or is it the fourth?"

"It is going to be a prodigious growth. None will recognize you."

"That was my thought, and that I might as well look like I belonged in the Cuddon." Donzalo rubbed his bristling chin. "Do you think we can ride now?"

"I believe so." Guesare glanced upward. "I wish that we had less moon, though."

"We both know it was better to go now than to wait a week or two."

"Oh, aye. I but grumble. Let's mount up."

"The moon may be of little concern shortly. Do you feel that southern wind?"

The wind was indeed building from the south. It felt moist and warm.

"Another autumn storm comes. Well, it will give us more cover."

"And slow us," said Donzalo. "How long yet is our way to the Cuddon?"

"Now that we have crossed the river, and if we held to this due eastward course, not much further than the one to your uncle's house." They had forded the Abam earlier that night, before the moon rose high. "But that," continued the minstrel, "would bring us only to the borders and no guarantee of safety. My home lies well north, in the upper Cuddon."

Within an hour, the moon was playing hide-and-seek behind the scuttling clouds. The country they crossed was rising, as well, and the way becoming more difficult.

"I will not chance a road yet," stated Guesare. "We can not be certain that our departure was not observed."

It had not been. Paren's company broke camp the next morning as if there were no change and set off up the road.

The road was become a lonely place, now as the year wound down. Many of the trees showed their naked, barren branches and the fallen leaves drifted across the pathway. But it was good weather and they were making good time; they should reach the manor by the morrow.

Twenty-some leagues lay between that manor and Castle Rosam. Borrago's holdings were too far-flung, some said, and he should keep his brother closer.

Borrago trusted that brother to hold his border there, near the edge of the Cuddon, and to keep trade safe along River Abam. Not so much *on* the river, as much of its length was unnavigable, with shoals and falls aplenty, though some quantities of timber did come down its flow. The count's own patrols passed back and forth on this road, but rarely beyond Paren's keep.

"Captain," called Paren, "any report?"

Two scouts, sent ahead, had returned. "None, sir. No travelers, no tracks."

Paren nodded, as the commander continued. "But we both know someone is out there. All we can do is keep our eyes open and our swords ready."

"And let us hope this rain holds off," said Paren, glancing toward the gray skies, "so we may also keep our powder dry."

The first thing Lareth noted was how worn, how tired, his old comrade seemed. Magics again, he thought to himself. They will surely kill him and send him to one of the hells from which he now draws power. Where went that eager youngster he had taken under his wing, years agone?

"Here, sit, my friend. Bring wine," he ordered the attendant. The king took a chair opposite his councilor.

"You have taken measures, haven't you? No, don't tell me what. I neither need nor want to know."

Radal drank deeply of the cup he was brought. "I have done all I can, my king. All I can for now."

"Then that must be enough," responded Lareth. He gestured to a stack of dispatches. "Much has been going on in Lama."

This brought a grimacing smile to Radal's weary visage. "There is always much going on in Lama. Sometimes, I think we should just leave them on their side of the mountains and stay on our own."

"Were it only the Lamans, I might agree, Radal."

"Of course, of course." The sorcerer drained his cup. "The Coradeans and Partanacans both have their ambitions in Lama. Even the Ani, though no longer so much a threat."

"And in the mean time, I have to deal with the Mura on our northern border. They would like nothing better than a chance to reclaim Arolin from us. Ah, Radal, we should be old men enjoying our golden years."

"You, at least, are a grandfather, my king, and several times over. No such luck for me. Where is that attendant?" He held out his cup, steeling himself so only a slight tremor shook his hand, as the servitor came forward to refill it.

"Though, you know what, Lareth? My wayward Fachalana seems to have become interested in young Nafal. I may see her married yet!"

"That," replied the king, raising his own cup, "is something I will drink to."

11

"Afternoon is the best time for such doings," whispered Vanob. "Our sergeant knows the riders will be tired and sleepy."

But still too many and too wary for us to attack, thought Perdos. "We shall see," he said to his companion. Van seemed a solid fellow but the Laman did not forget for a moment that he was Sojel's man, body and soul.

They were in two parties, on either side of the road. A well-equipped troop, too, most with bows, a pair carrying matchlock muskets. These latter had dismounted, the better to aim their fire. Perdos had counted eighteen of them. Nineteen, if he included himself, which he did not particularly wish to do. They might be a formidable force to some but they did not match the professional soldiers coming up the road. Why, he himself could take on any two of them without likelihood of harm, bad arm and all.

"They come. Pass the word," came from the man to his left. He whispered the same to Vanob. Would Sojel order the attack?

He did not. The passing column of well-armed, well-armored men, shields all turned outward, was too daunting for ruffians accustomed to sure victory and the ambush of the helpless. The thud of their horses' hooves diminished into the distance.

Perdos smiled thinly. It had been as was to be expected. But there was something unexpected as well — he had counted the passing men and come up with only fifteen.

"That is a marvelous tale, my dear! I so wish I could have been there."

"I do not believe you could ever pull off the role of serving girl, Lana."

"It's true. I'll never be the actress you are."

"Nor have you the proper look. But I was not actress enough or the young gallant would never have recognized me as a fraud," replied the young woman. "I wonder if I should have dyed my hair."

"Oh, no, Maresta, you did right to remain blond. One mistake with the dye and you might have been given away — and you would have needed to keep dying it regularly. That's not easy for a servant in a castle."

"Especially one attending the Lady Vibola!" laughed the other. "Though I rather liked the old lady. She had integrity."

"The word that has leaked out is that they think you are an Anian spy," Fachalana told her. "That news arrived before you."

"It is a very long journey, even by the southern route. Did you learn of it from snooping in your father's papers?"

"No need. There are at least half a dozen young aides who fall over each other to whisper secrets to me."

Maresta smiled knowingly. "My Ani blood does show up rather boldly." She shook back her blond locks. "That is both a blessing and a curse when it comes to the stage."

"Oh, you were made to play villains, Maresta. Make the best of it!"

The young actress sighed. "Would that I had not played villain for brave Donzalo."

"Rain is bad enough. Is this typical Cuddon weather?"

Donzalo and Guesare pushed on through the sleet. "I am afraid so," responded the minstrel. "Be thankful we're on a road now. I wouldn't want to be crossing rough country in this."

The Laman thoroughly agreed with this. The last several days of cross-country travel, many of them rainy, had become increasingly difficult. "Does this road actually lead somewhere?"

"Aye, boy, it does. Follow it another hundred leagues and half that again and you can take a bath in River Siph."

"I'd rather have my bath in a tub of hot water, before a fire. Any such near us?"

"I fear not. Oh, there be cots about here, but no place we would expect welcome."

Though Guesare spoke nonchalantly, Donzalo suspected there might be more than a few places in the wide world where the minstrel would not expect welcome.

"Well then," he asked, "how far and how long till we reach hospitality?"

"Seriously, my lad, I do not think we should make our presence known anywhere in this land until we are safely with my clan."

He paused. "Not only for fear of spies but for those who inhabit this land. There are many old feuds simmering in the Cuddon. And then, there are the Other Folk."

"I think this may be letting up," observed Donzalo, facing into the freezing wind. "The Others, eh? Trolls?"

"Aye, and various creatures of their kind. Most harmless, most willing to avoid us, but a dangerous folk, none the less." He also faced into the storm. "I think you're right. It may be clear by morning. And very cold.

"There is a place not far ahead where we may stop the night."

"Shelter?"

"Of a sort," laughed the Cuddonian.

The shelter of a sort consisted of an open log lean-to at the crossing of two roadways. "We will turn north here in the morning," said Guesare. "First a fire and some rest."

A fire already burned before the hut, the single figure of a man silhouetted against its flame. As they approached, he rose to turn and greet them.

"This, Donzalo, is my friend Oder."

Home! A weary Paren swung down from his horse and took a moment to look about. All in order, all as it should be. He felt weariness flow away from him. He had done what he could for his nephew and now it was time and enough to return to his duties here.

The Lady Thara burst from the door, and ran to embrace him. "Oh," she exclaimed, peering past his massive middle, "you have brought so many guests with you! Is — is Donni here?"

"No, my wife. Our Donzalo must ride other roads this winter and warm himself before other hearths. His destiny is no longer in our hands.

"But, yes, I have brought a fair number of hungry fellows with me. They shall remain here a few days before returning to Borrago."

Her eyes were full of questions.

"All will be explained," he told her, "sooner or later. Let me see to the men's barracking now and you see if you can prepare a large enough feast to fill them all."

The captain came up to stand beside him. "I believe I need a wife, Sir Paren."

"Well, you can't have mine," replied the reeve. "But there are plenty of other possibilities around this place. You'll be here a week. Make use of it!"

"Perhaps I shall, sir. I would that we could remain longer. I am certain that there was an armed band somewhere in those woods."

"As am I. Send out your patrols but if nothing is found, follow my brother's orders and return home."

The soldier nodded. "The count has ordered extra men on the road all winter. We won't forget you are up here."

"There is a fellow here, sir, walked right into camp. Says he was sent to see you — even knew you by name."

Sojel rose. "I expected someone. A messenger, it is?"

"I think not," replied Vanob. "He looks — well, I'm not sure how he looks."

"Bring him. No, wait, I'll go to him. Where has that Perdos gotten to? I haven't seen him around camp."

"I can't say I have either, Sergeant." The man rubbed his chin. "He rode out a bit after we made camp but I don't think he came back. Figured you'd sent him off to scout again."

"Deserted," spat the saturnine soldier. "He was never one of us, anyway — good riddance, I say. Where is this stranger?"

A somewhat plump individual, long beard spilling over long robes, stood between two guards. He bowed, with surprising grace, to Sojel. "Sir," said he, "I am Sabatare the Mage."

Sojel but stared at him, saying nothing, but enjoying the man's growing unease.

"I — I am your fellow servant of — of the great — "

"Stop, fool," barked the sergeant. "Never mention his name before such as these." He swung his arm, indicating the band of scoundrels he commanded.

"Of course," replied the wizard, his face grown red. "Where — ?"

"Come with me."

He led the way past the pickets and then turned to appraise the man, looking him thoroughly up and down, the luxuriant beard, the thick middle, the soft hands. The robe, he suspected, would be spotless on a day of less inclement weather.

"You're Cuddonian, aren't you? And a wizard of sorts." Sojel practically sneered; he knew well what a real wizard looked like.

"My Lord —" He looked about before uttering the name. "Radal has ordered me to give you assistance."

"Ordered you? How? When? No messengers have reached me."

"Our master has messengers who travel far faster than men and horses, but only other mages can understand them. He sent one such to me last night."

Sojel nodded grimly. He knew his master used such at times. Then, another thought came to him. "He knows of what occurs here? Have you been reporting to him?"

"Not I, good sir," replied the wizard. "Not I." He leaned forward and whispered, as if in confidence, "He has sent the Rupa."

The sergeant had no idea what that might be. "Explain," he ordered. That was how one learned what was needed.

"It is a demon, a great flying shape like unto a bird. But not a bird," he added, barely murmuring, "not a bird at all.

"It has been observing the party of Lamans from a distance and reported their safe arrival to our master. Acting on what he heard from it, he sent his message to me."

"This Rupa came to you?"

"Oh, no sir!" The very idea obviously frightened the man. "Only one of his ordinary couriers, a little spirit of the winds. Just beholding the Rupa closely," he shivered, "might well tear the soul from a man's body and send it shrieking into hell."

"Humph. Well, tell me how you are supposed to help me with our problem."

12

An Anian! For a moment, a chill went though Donzalo and not a chill from the harsh north wind. Oh, he had seen Anian delegations at his father's court and even the occasional merchant come upriver from Morparas. But this was an Ani warrior, the villain of an hundred and more Laman folk tales, the savages who had looted and raped their way across his land scant generations earlier.

He shook the feeling off. That was another time and this was another man and a friend of Guesare, as well. He stepped forward to take the Ani's hand. Oder was blond, not surprisingly, far paler than a typical Laman or even those of Sharshite blood. And Donzalo found himself troubled by a seeming familiarity in the man's face. He looked like someone he knew, somehow.

"Greetings, young lord," said the warrior, with barely a discernible trace of accent. "And greetings to you, my beloved one." He opened his arms to Guesare.

Now Donzalo knew all about Guesare's proclivities yet he found himself slightly shocked to see the passion of the men's embrace. Oder winked at him over Guesare's shoulder. "This Cuddonian has ever been the sentimental one. Yet I wager he forgot all about me when we were apart."

Which Donazalo knew for the truth. "Let us get you two out of the weather," continued the Anian. "I've a warm fire and a pot of stew."

Sated with Oder's highly seasoned pottage and with their cloaks spread before the fire to dry, the world seemed almost halfway normal again to Donzalo. But this Anian —

He turned to the man and bluntly asked, "Are you a spy?"

Oder considered the question. "I can see how one might call me that. But Guesare here, now he is a true spy."

"'Tis true," admitted the Cuddonian. "but I only report to this Anian fellow. He took advantage of my innocence, long ago, and led me on this path!"

"It was he that corrupted me," protested Oder, "and seduced me to boot!"

Donzalo sighed. "How can I expect truth from a pair of minstrels? Why, making things up is your trade."

"But we are very good at it, one must admit." Donzalo wasn't sure which said it and knew it didn't matter. He was falling asleep and intended no other thoughts to intrude.

It was too late to find the trail, Perdos knew, and impossible in this weather anyway. Which night did the pair slip away? That would depend on where they were headed, he realized, and they could be headed anywhere.

No, not anywhere. They wouldn't head toward Sharsh, so probably not to the west. South to Morparas, perhaps? The city was crawling with spies and hoodlums who would blithely turn them in for the price of a beer. Maybe to Tod-ford, though. Count Orgelo would be glad to harbor anyone Sharsh sought to harm — and use them for his own ends.

But no, Borrago would never agree to sending his son there.

Over the hills to the Siphic lands? Dangerous. But then, the minstrel came from those hills. Might they choose to hide there? Perdos exhaled slowly. A curse came to his lips. Of course. They were in the Cuddon and there was no way he, an outsider, was going to go searching through those hills for them. Best find some place to hole up for the winter and wait. They would come down to Lama again, sooner or later.

She was waiting, perched half inside the window. Red, she was, as rust, or as vermilion — no, like the hibiscus that used to grow by his mother's window — and her wings spread like pools of fresh blood, or was it —

"None of your tricks," Radal ordered, raising his hand in rebuke. She settled down, returning to one form, one subdued color, the color of old claret. "Report."

"Maaaaneeee meeeeeen. Maaaaneeee speeeears! Aaaall hooome noooow." She stared at the wizard with eyes as blank as an old statue's. "Preeeeteeee meeeen. Ooone fooor Ruuupaaa?"

"If you fulfill your task, why not?" He very much enjoyed the thought of Guesare being carried off to service this creature in the far mountains where she nested. "So my force was not able to ambush them on the road." The Rupa nodded gravely.

"Well, we must crack the egg of Sir Paren's keep, it would seem. And you shall help, my lady of the crags!"

Still had Radal a clutch of hairs from the head of Donzalo, the work of the unwitting Traspa. From them, and from magic, he conjured forth an image of the boy before them. "This is he you must destroy, Rupa, to reclaim your freedom. Look well upon him and know him."

She stared, her impassive, almost beautiful, face giving no evidence of her thoughts. "Ruuuuupaaa gooooo!" she suddenly cried and launched herself from the parapet, winging eastward.

It was a wizened, waist-high creature that stood at the mage's side. Sojel had seen many things, evil things and some of them of his own doing, yet he shivered at the presence of an Other. Sabatare seemed to have grown more confident, regaining his poise now that he could flaunt his prowess in his own field.

With a bow of respect to his companion, the wizard excused himself — or so it seemed, for Sojel did not understand the tongue he spoke — and stepped forward. "I have gathered some, ah, helpers for our cause. This be their leader." He indicated the small man-creature behind him with a movement of his head. "A kobold. The Folk do not give out their names so best you simply address him as 'sir.'"

So that is a kobold, thought the sergeant to himself. Not so scary once you get used to it.

"It is — what? A chief of their tribe?"

"No, no, my good sir. He is not unlike you, leader of a band. There be outlaws among the Others as surely as there be among men."

"Ah!" Knowing that made the little fellow seem even less strange. "How many does he command?"

"Perhaps a dozen. Some of his sort, an ogre — which is but an overgrown kobold, to be honest — a few trolls. Not that formidable a group but they can bolster your own men. And some," he added, lowering his voice as though imparting secrets, "know a bit of the minor magics."

"Well, keep them under control. If magic is needed, we depend on you." He looked the kobold up and down. "It looks tough enough, despite its stature."

The pair walked to where the fay awaited them. It — no, he — turned his face up, tilting it quizzically to stare at the sergeant. A long nose jutted from the thin, hairless face. Hairless everywhere, noted Sojel, as the little man went quite naked. Sabatare jabbered something at him.

This time, the soldier caught a few words and recognized that the pair were speaking some sort of pidgeon, cobbled together of Laman, Cuddonian, and who knew what else. Old Laman, that is, not the dialect of Muram used in most of the south these days.

It might be advantageous to learn some of this patois. Later. There were other tasks at hand.

"The detail from Borrago's castle is preparing to return home, it seems. We should be able to mount an attack in a few days." Sojel knew that the longer he waited, the less wary Paren's people would become. But not too long — winter was coming and he couldn't hold this band together forever. Nor would these Others be likely to wait. "So be prepared."

"Yes, Sergeant. I have, um, other news."

"Spit it out, man."

"Our master is sending the Rupa to join the attack." His small companion looked up at him in unmistakable fear at the mention of that name. "It has but one mission, to find and destroy this Donzalo person. It will not aid our assault but only seek its target. I would make sure," he warned, "that none get in its way."

"Stay, Madin."

The scribe settled himself back onto his stool. "I may have need of your pen," said Borrago.

The door stood ajar to this, the count's private chamber. It was a small room, one floor up, in the keep's central tower. Above it lay Borrago's own spartan quarters, with a narrow staircase connecting the two.

"Come in," he called. The Sharshite envoy, Jobareth Nafal, entered, followed closely by Sir Blen. Borrago remained uncertain on just what this man's status was — in public, he was reserved, at times barely noticeable, and seemed no more than an aide to Nafal. All the intelligence gathered by the count's agents, however, suggested that the two were equal in footing when it came to decisions.

The charade continued in their appearances today. The envoy was formally attired in a long Sharshite tunic, boldly colored green and white, and heavily embroidered. His companion was drab and could pass for a common soldier. Which he may well have been, once, surmised Borrago.

Formalities exchanged, the count went straight to the business at hand. Waving his guests to a pair of high-backed chairs, he settled back in his own and spoke. "So, you Sharshites want to build an embassy on my land, eh?"

"Yes, my lord," answered Jobareth. "If the chosen location is amenable to you."

"It's a nice piece of land," Borrago said, "but a bit far from town. Wouldn't you prefer to be down there?" I'd prefer them on the other side of the mountains, he told himself.

Blen spoke up for the first time. "We felt that a location closer to your seat might be the better choice, sir."

"Maybe so." And perhaps it is better than actually having them in the keep, although young Nafal spends most of his time here anyway. "I have no objections.

"Now, as to the price," he continued with a smile.

"Sharsh is quite willing to pay any fair rent on the land, my lord," stated Jobareth. "We would hope to reach an agreement swiftly and begin building."

"I have had a lease drawn up." Borrago beckoned his scribe, who brought the document forward. Giving a quick last moment glance, for the Count was ever a meticulous man of business, he slid it forward across the table.

Jobareth read it with growing astonishment and wordlessly passed it to his companion. The knight only smiled lightly and handed it back with a nod. "You are most generous, my lord," said the envoy.

"Yes, it is my greatest failing," Borrago agreed, though not without the hint of a wink. "I have no need of Sharsh's money for that bit of land but I do want you to fix your residence and stay there. Hence, my terms."

"Despite your gracious terms," said Blen, "it will still need to be approved by someone back home. I think," he continued, with a glance at Nafal, "that they will readily agree to the price you ask."

"Oh, well, if one basket of groundnuts a year is too much, we can always renegotiate," the count replied. "So, sign the paper, if you will and we'll be done here."

Jobareth took the pen offered by Madin, the scribe, and scrawled a signature, and then again on a second copy. He handed it on to Blen, who did the same. So they *are* equal in this, thought Borrago.

The envoy then pulled out an official seal, the small sort a man of either diplomacy or business might carry on his person, inked it and stamped the documents. The secretary came forward and did the same with the count's seal and signed as well, as witness.

"I trust we can come up with the sufficient quantity of nuts for the next hundred years," Jobareth stated. "I should hate for my country to default on its obligations."

Then the young man changed course. "And with that out of the way, I will ask you to indulge me for a few moments more, my lord."

Borrago looked up from the freshly signed documents before him and then handed one back over to the Sharshites. "Yes?"

"Is there news of your son, sir? Donzalo, that is."

"Of course. I know you've little interest in the other one. Although," he added, "as a diplomat, perhaps you should.

"I received a messenger but this morning, newly returned from my brother's manor. All have arrived without incident. They even managed to stay ahead of most of the bad weather."

Jobareth knew that Donzalo would not have been with the party that arrived with Paren and Borrago knew that he knew. This was a fact to which Blen was not privy so the two must need watch their words.

"Ah, sir, then please send my greetings and best wishes to your brother and your son. It is good to know that there were no difficulties."

The Sharshites rose and took their leave. Outside the door, Blen said, "I should bear that document to Sharsh myself."

Jobareth was surprised. "It is a long journey," he protested, "and certainly not the best time of year to undertake it."

"I know, Jobareth. There are other reasons I should return as well, and those I may not tell you."

The younger man nodded. "Each of us has his secrets. Try to be back by the Yule."

13

The road had not been so bad, at first. Frozen mud is not the kindest of pavings, and the horses often seemed about to lose their footing on the slippery surface. Finally, the three travelers dismounted and led their animals.

Alas, under the bright clear sky, the frozen mud soon became just mud, sucking at the feet of all six. The road led over ever steeper hills, slowing them further. "Never fear, boy," Guesare told Donzalo, "we'll make it home by the Yule."

"If we don't starve first," grumbled the Laman.

"Oder is an excellent huntsman," the minstrel assured him, "and we've money enough on us to buy provisions, if need come."

"I thought we were avoiding those who dwell here."

"Not so much now. There are larger villages ahead where traveling strangers are welcome enough. Even," he nodded toward their companion, "the odd Anian."

Said Anian responded. "Still, we shall wish to remain as inconspicuous as is possible." He looked Donzalo up and down. "And to do so, we had better get this overgrown boy into some Cuddonian garments. He's recognizable enough as it is."

"None of my kilts would fit him, I fear," stated Guesare. "Not without showing too much of what shouldn't show."

"They are far too garish, anyway," Oder said. "We should get him outfitted soon, before he is seen."

"I'll slip into the next village by myself and buy something for him. A good length of cloth will do — that's all a kilt is anyway — and then there will be no wondering as to why I might be purchasing over-sized garments.

"I know of a good camp spot not far ahead. What say we put an end to this day's travel?"

The spot was, in fact, a shallow cave, little more than a depression in a rock wall, not far off the road, and sheltered in a small hollow, with a spring-fed stream trickling by. Its flow might well have been frozen earlier that morning.

Fire and food soon returned a semblance of cheer to the weary travelers.

"What say you bring out your rebec, friend?" said Guesare to the Anian.

"If you do the same," responded Oder.

For a few minutes, the two men exchanged random bits of music and brought their instruments into tune with each other. Or close to it.

"Here is a song of the Cuddon you should know," Guesare told Donzalo. "Oder and I often play it."

"'The Song of the Sword?'" asked Oder. "'Tis an Anian song, my friend."

"So you would like to believe," responded the Cuddonian. "In truth," he said, addressing Donzalo, "there must be hundreds of different verses bards have created over the years and no one knows where and when it started."

"Nor in what language, for that matter," said Oder, who put bow to his instrument and began to sing a plaintive yet forceful melody. His voice was surprisingly high and clear.

The song of the shining sword, I sing,
The song of a bird with a bright steel wing;
I sing of blows that make blades ring,
The life it has, the death it will bring.

Guesare took his turn on a second verse. As was his wont, he strummed rather than bowing the rebec.

My tales of time-lost battles I tell,
The sieges where great cities fell;
Of men who fought bravely and well,

The many souls sent down to hell.

The Cuddonian's singing was more emotional, less exact, than that of Oder, and he pitched his voice an octave lower. Donzalo recognized his technique as typical of the minstrels he had known. Oder took his turn.

To music made by clashing shields,
The sword sings over many fields;
A scythe Death unrelenting wields:
Men's lives, the crop his reaping yields.

"Is that one of yours?" asked Guesare.
"Nay, I heard it a while back on the northern borders. A bit of a mouthful isn't it?" Oder went on to sing another verse.

I watch by the light of a blood-red moon,
Where broken ramparts rise in ruin;
The cold wind carries a song of doom
As armies march to the ancient tune.

"Oh, that's different!" exclaimed Guesare. "Here's one of mine."

Before the sword, each nation falls;
It overthrows their high-built walls.
Barbarians plunder Tesra's halls;
The mighty end their days as thralls.

"Who is Tesra?" broke in Oder, lowering his bow.
"Rather, 'what is Tesra?'" Guesare answered. "Or perhaps more properly, 'where is Tesra?' You know of Tesra, don't you, Donni?"

"The legendary city of Tesra across the Central Sea. It ruled a great empire before the Mura took it." He pondered a moment. "And supposedly it was home to a race of mighty sorcerers."

Oder smiled. "Not so mighty if they let the Mura take their city."

"They were much fallen by then," said the Cuddonian. "So say the books, anyway."

He continued. "The books, or some of them, also say they were not truly a race of magicians, only very long lived. A people able to see their plans through. Whereas we may do well to see tomorrow."

"You try too hard to be literary," said Oder, pulling bow once again across his rebec. He threw back his long blond hair and raised his voice, and at that moment Donzalo realized of whom the man reminded him.

The sword cares naught for prideful powers
That gather wealth and build high towers.
It throws them down as mankind cowers;
They lie forgotten beneath the flowers.

"You have outdone me once again," remarked Guesare.

Things seemed quiet enough but Paren was uneasy.

He had watched Borrago's soldiers ride away. Their captain had done so with a too-obvious twinge of regret, as he left behind a woman to whom he had become somewhat attached over these past few days. He will certainly make other opportunities to visit here, the reeve told himself, especially if the patrols were to be increased along their road. It would be good to have such a man in his household, if he — and the widow Tiana — could woo him from his brother's service.

Did their enemies know that Donzalo was not here? Surely there were spies, if not worse, out there, and all this pretense must eventually be discovered. He could only hope his nephew be far enough away by then.

There was much to do on this manor before winter truly set in, the last of the harvest to get into storage, barns to repair, firewood to lay in. Best he back to his duties and put his trust, as always, to Kamat and to his sword.

The ferry slowly made its way across the Weldar, toward a fog-hidden western bank. Beyond it, Rosam holdings extended some distance and then various small-holders as the wide Laman valley rose toward the mountains. In those mountains lay Blen's destination, the end of a near two hundred league journey.

It would be a grueling ride, accomplished in less than half the time of his travel here with Nafal. Changes of horses would be posted regularly along his route, but there was no replacement for the rider.

He looked up the river. He could come back that way — a relatively short trip due east from the Mountain Keep would bring him to Oles on the upper Weldar and boats aplenty that could provide a leisurely passage down to Ros-town. Ah, if only he had the time for such a luxury!

It might not be a good season of year for that anyway. There would be ice on the river up there. Blen wished to dally no more than a day or two in the mountains, to deliver his documents to the proper diplomats and to closet with the king, who had sent word that he would be there for a few brief days.

Indeed, he might actually make it back to County Rosam by the Yule. He had no better place to celebrate it, after all.

There were men in the fields, and women too. Some were gathering in straw, the stubble left from the harvest. Some were in the barns and the yards, with brooms or with shovels. Children went about their chores or played hide-and-seek among the corn shocks. Some were moving animals from one field to another, or into pens, small eager dogs assisting.

None saw those who were creeping up on them.

Small wizened man-like forms crawled forward, their naked bodies daubed with paint. A misshapen creature, nigh as tall as a man but half again as broad, trundled through the forest's edge, a massive club in its grasp. And further behind, stocky, hairy little gray-skinned men, large of ear and of foot, whispered to each other, building up their resolve.

Elsewhere — on the other side of the manor, to be exact — men on horseback also waited.

Sojel blew his whistle, a loud shrill blast. He had been longing to put his lips to it for weeks, a signal for the death-dealing and cruelties that he loved. The motley mix of Others sprang forward and Sojel's men burst from the cover of the trees.

Some of Paren's folk turned and ran. Others turned to defend themselves with whatever was at hand. A pitchfork here, a pruning bill there; these were not a helpless people but the sturdy folk of a somewhat lawless frontier. Soldiers flew to their weapons, sword and lance and bow. A flash came from the ramparts of Paren's modest keep, followed by the thunder of a musket. One of the soldiers pitched from his horse.

The musketeer, naturally, was astonished he hit anything at such a range. He grinned and reloaded, hoping luck would again guide his shot. Then he felt a shadow pass over him.

Up he looked, where something moved before the sun. A great bird of some sort? He turned back to the loading of his matchlock.

Some of the reeve's garrison were on guard; some were out on patrol. Others were asleep. All were well tested veterans and more than a match for the rabble Sojel commanded, if they could ready themselves quickly, keep their attackers from capitalizing on the advantage of their surprise attack.

"It has come," Paren stated, matter-of-factly, to his master of arms. He had remained cautious, ready, continuing to expect some action, sooner or later.

"Shall we ride against them, sir?" asked the soldier.

"Only those who are already in saddle. The rest needed to fall back and protect the gates. Get my people to safety before all else!"

The man nodded curtly and rushed to carry out his orders.

And far above, the Rupa circled, seeking the one she had been sent to destroy. He was not there. Wider the demon circled, and wider, searching. Higher she climbed, until the keep was no more than a crumb on the wide plate of the world.

Then she turned and sped north.

14

Hendel did not know why he was being called before the count. Had something gone awry in last night's dessert? Into the great hall he was led, where Borrago reposed in his high seat, the Lady Vibola to one side, the Lady Lomela to the other. All the faces here were stern, the nobles and the master of arms who stood below them.

This was serious. His portly frame shook as he realized that his secrets were secret no longer.

Borrago leaned back and took a long look at the cook, his distaste evident. Then he rose. "Hendel of Pora, I name you a spy."

The man fell to his knees in fear.

"I have my mother, the Lady Vibola, to thank for finding you out; aye, the Lady Lomela as well. And now I have this," He held up a slip of paper which Hendel knew to be one of the messages he had passed, "thanks to their vigilance."

"Shame on you," cried the older woman, unable to contain herself. "You have used Mistress Traspa to become privy to our secrets!"

"She trusted in you," said the Lady Lomela from the count's other side. "She loved you, I think. That is a great betrayal."

"Hear my judgment," spoke Borrago. "Some would say you have done no great harm. Passed along a bit of gossip, an overheard confidence. For these I would have had you flogged from my lands. But I believe too that you betrayed my son and set murderers upon him; for this you should hang from my walls in the morning."

Hendel cringed in his terror, his bulk practically sinking into the stone floor.

"But," he went on, "my ladies have asked for clemency. Not for your miserable soul but for sake of our poor Traspa. You will leave and never again enter County Rosam on penalty of death. You shall tell Mistress Traspa that you must return to your homeland and duty will keep you there. And if you ever deal with another Sharshite, I shall command Sir

Copago to hunt you down and return with your head." Copago, standing at attention before his father, smiled grimly.

"Now go and be outside my walls by sundown or you shall be thrown over them."

The two guards grasped the one-time maker of delightful desserts beneath his arms, heaved him up to stand quaking before his judge, and marched him out the door.

"Ah," sighed Borrago. "He really should have hung."

"No doubt, my son," said Vibola. "He could have been offed quietly and Mistress Traspa would never have known."

"Grandmother!" chided Lady Lomela.

"Just how did you two come to suspect the man?" asked Borrago, holding up his cup to summon a server holding a wine jug. "Do you want any, my ladies?"

Lomela began. "I had told the Lady Vibola of how Traspa unwittingly revealed things she shouldn't have. But Grandmother," she smiled at the Countess, "thought there might be more to it."

"I am a most untrusting old woman," stated Lady Vibola, taking the wine cup that had been brought to her. "This had better be your good stuff, Borri."

"So I kept watch," Lady Lomela continued. "It was not difficult. When she was not with me, Mistress Traspa was almost certain to be with that traitor."

"And we warned you to keep an eye on him and that was that," concluded Lady Vibola. She shook her head. "Poor trusting Traspa. But I'll drink to her loyalty," she said, and drained her cup.

"What do you think?" the one minstrel asked the other.

"He'll pass as Cuddonian if he keeps his mouth shut," the other replied.

"We rarely come this large," said Guesare, "but he has the proper look."

"I know I called your kilts gaudy, Brother — and I apologize — but you needn't have gone so far in the opposite direction."

"'Twas the only suitable cloth in town. I think it becomes the boy."

The 'boy' spoke. "It looks like a horse blanket."

"And it is," admitted Guesare. "I felt that gray plaid would look as good on you as on any steed."

Donzalo scrutinized his friend's face. "I know you enjoy your jests, Cousin, but I also know the purchase of a horse blanket was less likely to draw attention than any other sort of cloth.

"And speaking of cousins, what will be our relationship when we reach your home?"

"Not long ago I might have introduced you as who you are, my cousin Donzalo from Lama." He shook his head. "Perhaps not such a good idea, now."

"He could be an apprentice," suggested Oder.

"An apprentice who can neither play nor sing?"

"And how do you know that?" asked Donzalo.

"I heard you once when you drank too much," said the Cuddonian, "and thought you were alone. I was, um, with someone in the barn at your uncle's when you wandered in, bellowing."

Oder chuckled. "We have the better part of the day left. Let's be on the road."

Guesare looked up. "I feel something. A presence. The same as on the day we left Castle Rosam, Donni. Remember?"

The three looked out across the hills, drab in their late autumn cover, and to the misted horizons and to the cloudless sky. "There," cried Oder, pointing.

A speck, a mote, sometimes disappearing in the glare of midday sun. But growing, slowly, larger and larger.

"A bird?" wondered Donzalo.

"No," said Oder. "A dragon, maybe, though I've never seen one this far from the Lofty Mountains."

While they stood and peered upward, Guesare was charging his pistols.

Fachalana paced back and forth. She did so dramatically and found herself comparing the different ways she strode across the room.

"Ah," she sighed. "I am the worst of frauds."

For a moment, she stared at herself in the full-length mirror. Fachalana had many full-length mirrors. She struck a stance and drew the saber that hung at her hip. Then, with an oath such as young ladies of breeding should not use, she threw the sword to the floor.

Would that she could go somewhere, anywhere, and truly use a sword. Not fencing practice with a shriveled old master who cared more for grace of movement than deadliness. She dreamed of crossing the mountains to Lama, as she had sent her friend Maresta.

"She may be a good spy but I would be one who acted!" she exclaimed, retrieving her sword from where she thrown it a moment before. She flourished it and laughed.

"Yes, the Lady Fachalana is a terrible fraud!"

"They've managed to close the gate!"

This was what Sojel had hoped to prevent. There had been a desperate battle before the gates, Paren and his guard charging like madmen to give his people time to reach safety. He did not care about those who were outside, a dozen or so of whom lay dead, and the rest fled to hide. The young Laman must be within those walls. Would Radal's demon help them dig him out?

His purpose here, he knew, was more to provide a distraction so this Rupa might act unhindered, but he would dearly like to take that keep, to sate all his lusts upon its inhabitants, to range through it with his sword until none were left alive.

He noticed a troll gnawing one of the bodies. Not one of his men — not that it mattered.

"What can you do about this, Mage?"

"There are spells," answered the wizard. "I prepared myself for just this eventuality."

Sabatare positioned himself well away from the keep, but on a slight rise so he might see the better. He surveyed the erstwhile battlefield, nodded to himself, and, raising his staff, began to weave an enchantment. Sojel watched him from where he directed his men.

"Bar sunai! Bar sunai set!" he commanded loudly. Nothing happened. The kobold leader at his side looked up at him, questions in his beady, deep-set eyes.

Then the mage lowered his staff, his face betraying his consternation. "I am blocked!"

A wizard, maybe a stronger one than he, had placed a spell here.

The little Other placed a hand upon his staff, to lend his magic to that of the mage. As one, they raised the rod and their arms and Sabatare called upon the strongest demon he dared to aid him. "Sebuchax! Sebuchax! Bar sunai set!" It seemed like a great wind rushed against the castle but the gate barely shivered, much less burst.

"It is no use," Sabatare moaned. "The protective spell is too well placed."

"Damned, useless hedge-wizard," growled Sojel.

The mage shrugged. "He who placed that charm is a gifted enchanter. 'Tis a simple bit of work but he imbued it with great strength. His strength, whomever he may be."

Arrows continued to fly from the battlements, and an occasional musket shot, mostly falling harmless, but Sojel saw a troll stumble.

"I think, sir," continued Sabatare, "that it is all moot anyway. I saw the Rupa circle yon keep and then fly far away. Your Donzalo must not be within."

"Now you tell me, idiot?"

"The trolls are running away!" called one of his men. The rest of the Other Folk broke and ran, following them.

"Fall back," he called. There was no more to do here and no reason to do it. He should report all this to his master, and soon.

But before quitting the battlefield, he ran his saber through Sabatare's chest and had the satisfaction of watching him gasp out his life. That's one thing done right today, anyway, Sergeant Sojel said to himself.

15

Oder sprang forward to prepare his own pistols. "Help me with the bows," Guesare called, laying aside his readied brace. He and Donzalo quickly nocked the two powerful recurved weapons, and set the quivers up. Last, the young Laman pulled a small pistol of his own from his pouch and began winding its spring.

"The biggest man here has the smallest gunne!" laughed Oder. To Guesare, he said, "Arrows first, you think?"

"Yes, and then all together with the pistols!"

"What is it?" asked Donzalo, almost in a whisper as the great, red, winged shape glided down.

"The Rupa, I fear," came the reply.

Oder swore an oath in his native tongue. It was the first time Donzalo had heard him use it.

Now, the thing swooped toward them. Was it a bird? No — or was it? And how large? It seemed hard to tell where it started and ended. "Don't be dazzled by it," cried Guesare. "That form serves to spread its terror but it must become solid to do us harm."

The two bowmen drew their strings back to their cheekbones, arrows in readiness. "Wait for it — " Suddenly, the Rupa seemed to coalesce, as if a lens were brought to focus. Both men loosed arrows and immediately reached for their pistols. Five shots rang out, almost as one. Did they have any effect on the creature?

None that they could see, yet it hissed and veered away. The minstrels took up their bows and reached for fresh arrows but Donzalo, in a moment of sudden inspiration, leaped upward, forward, all his lanky body and long arms reaching out, and threw his heavy saber toward the Rupa's wing. It shrieked, and tumbled in the air.

"Go after its wings," he cried, "and ground it!"

They could see now that their adversary was not so much bird as bat, and that Donzalo's blade had torn the membrane of one wing. They could see also that 'it' was she, her body a deformed caricature of a woman's.

She reverted now to her nebulous form, shifting colors and shapes that might dazzle and ensorcel an unwary man. It became difficult to tell exactly where she was at any moment, seeming to be on all sides at once. "This could drive one mad," gasped Oder.

"Many men have become so," came Guesare's retort. "The Rupa entraps men for her own use, normally. This one has been sent to kill!"

The three stood, back to back to back, ready for her attack. It would come but would they still be sane enough to withstand it? Look away and she might take form instantly, killing claws at ones throat before he knew what happened. Fix ones eyes upon the Rupa and go mad, sooner or later.

But Donzalo thought he saw a faltering, an unevenness, in her mesmerizing flight. She was limping!

"She is hurt," he said. "She won't be able to keep this up."

Guesare immediately saw. "It takes away from the power of her dance. And look, the ichor on the ground must be hers."

"Can we outlast her?" wondered the Laman.

"We must, boy," responded Oder.

And then she took form, a little above them, intending to pounce — to pounce upon Donzalo, of course, as she had no orders about the other two. Still, it might be nice to take a man or two back to her nest, back to her sisters in the wild high crags.

Again, she had misjudged the young man's reach, or perhaps her strength had been oh so slightly sapped. He leapt into the air, slashing with all his strength. Down she went, her wing torn. Oder immediately swung and half-severed the other

The Rupa crouched, hissing. She tried to move, to start her hypnotic spell anew, but managed no better than a trembling double-image. "Weeel meeen keeeel meeee?" she wailed. "Ruuupaa liiiiike preeeteeee meeeen." She folded her wings and wept.

Oder and Donzalo stepped back, uncertain. Not Guesare; he swung his sword without hesitation, decapitating the demon-woman. They stared for a moment at the head that lay upon the withered grass, at once repellent and somehow beautiful.

"She would have died here anyway, without the use of her wings," the Cuddonian pointed out.

"He left so sudden-like, my lady. I wonder if he loved me at all!"

"Who is to say, my dear Traspa? There are other cooks in the kitchen, you know."

"Indeed, my lady." The maid sniffled and then smiled. "And more than one of them has tried to get me away from that Hendel!"

"And anyone of them perhaps just as good!" declared Lomela.

"True, my lady, but none have his way with cake."

"Tell me," said the Lady Lomela, approaching the question cautiously, "did Hendel ever ask about where Master Donzalo was headed on his recent journey?"

"Why, yes he did. But I only told him that he was going to stay with his uncle. I can keep a secret, my princess!"

"That is good, Traspa. Considering how he ran off, you were wise not to trust him."

"'Twas none of his business anyway! He always snooped too much and gossiped too much about his betters."

"So I have heard, my dear, so I have heard."

In a small room in the theater district of Celatas, Sharsh's capital city, a young woman put pen to paper.

"Dearest brother," she wrote, "I am returned to Sharsh after my escapades in Lama."

That sounds good, she thought, and pushed back the blond locks that had fallen forward as she wrote. Maybe I *should* dye this. Hmm.

"It is regrettable that my cover was uncovered." She giggled as she wrote this, then went back to strike it out. "It is regrettable that my disguise was penetrated." Oh, I might not have minded Donzalo penetrating — no, don't think such things, young lady! "Yet it is fortunate that I helped prevent your person of interest from being skewered."

She thought for a moment, leaning forward on the tiny dressing table that served as desk, before starting again. "And it was indeed fortunate that my service here could coincide with your needs there. I never expected that attaching myself to the Lady F. might be so rewarding." And frequently frustrating. "Imagine her paying me to carry out her spy missions when I am already spying on her!

"I will be here at least through the winter. It is no time for travel and there is always work on the stage in this city, even if the provincial theaters do close down. And then, F. is always good for a little cash, if I'm short."

"I will continue to ply her for information and send that in my more formal reports. She does tell me much about her father's doings, and those of the diplomatic corps, in general. But she is restless and may not continue to be so reliable a source."

"Trusting all is well with you and that your tangled webs have netted a few flies."

She signed, "Your dearest sister, A."

That should do, she told herself. Then she thought of her handsome brother, when last she saw him. She must travel east again, soon. There was much out there that was important to her.

"I will soon take leave of you," Oder told them, as they sat their horses, looking northward. Guesare had known that but always preferred to make no mention of subjects he found unpleasant. "It has been good to ride with you, young Donzalo.

"And now must I be the Anian spy-master," he went on. "The Empire has an interest in you. We won't deny that. We know of the prophecy and we know of Lareth's intentions toward you. You may or may not be useful to us, politically, but we are always glad to thwart Sharsh.

"That is why we sent Guesare to you."

That minstrel had a slightly sheepish expression.

"So, are the Ani better than Sharsh?" asked Donzalo. "Why should I trust you?" He knew well the history of the Anian occupation of his homeland.

"Our empire is grown old," said Oder. "We will never again come pouring over the mountains to conquer, as we did when we were savages fresh from the steppes. Now, we only hope to contain the ambitions of our neighbors."

"In other words," said Guesare, "a Lama free of Sharshite influence is to Anian advantage."

Oder nodded. "To the point, my brother, and quite true."

"Very well, that's out of the way," said Donzalo. "How much further to your home, Cousin?"

"Three or four days journey now, if the weather holds."

"Then let us ride." As the three urged their mounts forward, Guesare pulled forth his rebec and strummed a chord.

Oh, I shall sing the song of the sword,
Of that which ever is man's lord;
A song arising from discord,
For we march still to the song of the sword.

Book II
The Shadow of Asak

Of Knights: the Third Tale

1

"When I told my father of your recent exploits, he was more than willing to confer knighthood on you."

"I hope you did not exaggerate too much." Donzalo lazed by the fireplace, seemingly half-asleep, with his long legs stretched out before him.

"There was no need, my boy. Even without them, he would have accepted my vouching for you and you are certainly old enough." Guesare paused. "Just how old are you, anyway?"

"I turned twenty while we were on the road."

"Why, you should have said something!"

"Oh? And might you have stopped to bake me a cake?"

"I would have crafted you a birthday ode," sniffed the minstrel. His companion, knowing Guesare's moods well by this time, recognized that it was but a show of mock indignation.

"In truth," admitted Donzalo, "I lost track of the days while we journeyed and would not have known quite when it fell."

"Then we could celebrate right now. And I will certainly compose something for your dubbing."

"There has been celebration enough since we arrived. It seems you Cuddonians have naught more to do with your time than spend it in endless feasting!"

"'Tis that time of year. Truly, though, young Donzalo, in this weather what else is there to do but eat and drink and sing? And," Guesare continued, "we are not yet to the Yuletide. Then shall you see some true feasting!"

The younger man nodded, somewhat absently. "So that will be the day I am knighted?"

"Indeed. First thing in the morning — what better time than at the birth of a new year?" The bard smiled broadly and stroked his curling, golden beard. "Alas, you shall have to fast the day before and then keep vigil in a frigid temple. There are definite advantages to receiving ones spurs during the warmer months."

"Then I'd best fortify myself this fortnight and be prepared," replied Donzalo. "How about another pitcher of wine?"

Lord Radal looked eastward from his sanctuary, high in a dark stone tower of the Mountain Keep. He had waited long for the return of his servant-demon, the Rupa. He had called to her across the leagues but there came no answer.

Nor was the mage Sabatare to be found by the elemental spirits he had sent searching. Things must have gone very much wrong.

Radal was frustrated. This was unusual for a man so accustomed to being in control of both his own self and the world around him. Every effort to separate Donzalo from his life, to remove the threat he presented, had fallen short.

For this, the sorcerer blamed himself. He had consistently underestimated the abilities of his enemies. True, he was at a disadvantage attempting to operate at such a distance, using what tools were available. Perhaps it was time he took care of the young Rosam personally.

Ah, but was this undertaking destined for failure? If so, he was all the more a fool and all the more to be blamed for continuing. Radal drew his robe of sable around him and turned from the parapet. Night was cold here, high in the pass between Sharsh and Lama.

He had seen Sir Blen ride in as the shadows of the mountains crept down across the castle. Reporting to the king — Lord Radal did not like being left out of that conversation. Perhaps he should have his own talk with this Blen before the man returned into the east.

Perdos had caught sight of the fire from some distance. Dismounting, he led his horse quietly toward the light, one hand on the sword loosened in its scabbard. Whoever camped ahead was being none too cautious, caring neither about their flames being seen nor their voices being heard.

Drawing closer, he recognized the two men sprawled by the blaze as members of Sojel's band. He could not put names to them. He did not care. They passed a wine-skin back and forth.

Beyond them huddled a naked woman, shivering against the cold.

"Ho, the camp!" called the tall Laman, remaining hidden in the darkness of the woods.

The two stumbled to their feet at the greeting. "Who goes?" barked the shorter of the two, a paunchy fellow with a red, ulcered nose. The other had his sword out and was holding it unsteadily before him.

"One of your companions in arms." The knight decided to gamble on their ignorance and stepped forward. "It is I, Perdos."

The two looked at him a moment, unsure as to why this man should be here. Then the taller shrugged and lowered his sword. "Come have a drink, man. Where have you been? We thought you long gone."

"Oh, the sergeant, um, sent me to scout to the north. How went your raid?"

"Badly," spat the other. "No loot for us and Sojel didn't get what he was looking for either." He squinted at Perdos. "Are you heading to report to the sergeant?"

Perdos nodded. "Well then," continued the man, "you can come with us in the morning. He left us behind to keep an eye on the keep while he withdrew with the rest of our band." He leered at their captive and wiped his nose. "We found this one in the woods. Ran away when we attacked, I reckon, and she's given us a bit of entertainment while we waited around here."

His companion grinned widely, displaying a mouth full of black teeth. "We can have some more fun with her tonight before we have to get rid of her," he said. "But wine first."

The knight tied his horse to a branch and squatted by the fire with the two ruffians. The woman, half-hidden in the shadows, stared at him, eyes filled with overwhelming despair. Perdos took the proffered wine-skin but did not drink deeply before passing it back.

"Where are you meeting the company?" he asked.

"Our rendezvous is west of here," replied the paunchy fellow, "that high hill near the second ford. You know the spot." Perdos gave a barely perceptible nod. "I figure the sergeant will disband us and send us on our ways. No booty and the cold of winter coming. That's hard." Rising to his feet, he took a long pull on the wine and passed it to the other. "I want some of that," he slurred, stumbling toward their captive and pulling up his kilt.

The taller man snickered. "You can have a turn when we're through," he told Perdos and turned toward his companion who was lowering himself onto the bound, struggling woman. Then, he spoke no more but gurgled his life out, throat slit. The other barely had time to come to his feet, his eyes darting wildly in search of a weapon, before a dagger plunged into his gut. He slid off the weapon to writhe a few seconds and then lay still.

The woman cringed as Perdos approached, bloody blade in hand. "Hold still, girl," he ordered, as he cut the bonds from her wrists. "I'll do you no harm."

Hard man though Perdos might be, and mercenary, he had still a code of honor. For a moment, before remembering it, there had been temptation to join in the sport of these rogues. I'm a knight, he told himself, and I'll be damned if I'll become like these two.

He threw one of the men's blankets to the woman. "I'll remove this carrion," he told her, "and then I'll have to figure out what to do with you."

As much as it was possible for a king to like those who served him, Lareth liked Blen. He even trusted him, for the most part. This was a man who could serve his son well — he should bring the two together, when these affairs in Lama were more settled. After all, neither he nor Lord Radal would last forever.

He had listened to the knight's report, asking few questions. There was little need for them.

"Well done." The king lifted a bronze hand-bell from his desk and rang for a servant. "Bring us wine," he ordered. The man bowed and wordlessly left the room. "Blen, join me by the fire."

The two settled into high-backed wooden chairs as Lareth's man returned, bearing a pitcher and two chased goblets. "Leave it," said Lareth. The silent servitor placed the wine between them and slipped from the room, carefully closing the massive door behind him. "Will you pour, Sir Blen?" asked the king.

"How soon do you wish to return to Lama?" the monarch queried, taking the cup Blen offered him. "You are certainly welcome to remain here a while and throw off your road weariness."

"I had hoped, your highness, to return to Castle Rosam before the Yule. That does not leave me much time to travel."

"I know how quickly you can make that journey, Blen, with fresh horses along the way. Your days of service as a courier have not been forgotten." Lareth smiled, remembering the man's reluctance to leave that post. "Still, there is no point in pushing yourself needlessly."

"Then, sire, I shall start back tomorrow. If you have no further need of me here." Blen sipped his wine. It was a fine Arolin red, the best he had tasted in many months.

"Very well. Continue as you have and send regular dispatches to me. We shall not see each other again for some time, while you remain busy preparing for the arrival of our ambassador. Young Nafal must come to us in the spring and fetch Lord Doufan.

"This will be the third embassy of Sharsh in Lama. We have long had a presence in Oles and, more recently, Morparas. Both of those cities are doors to the East but the Rosam are the key to Lama itself."

"Yes, highness, they are a balance to the power of Orgelo in County Arvaram."

Lareth gave him an approving nod. "Do not underestimate this Doufan when he arrives. In some ways, he is not unlike you, Blen, a man of discretion and quiet capability. But he is also an opportunist with no great loyalty to any man or party."

The king put down his cup. "I shall leave on the morrow, as well, back to Celatas. A king must occasionally visit his capital. As well," he sighed, "as his family."

2

Donzalo was not quite sure whether the name Drolwym referred to this shabby keep or to the lands surrounding it. Maybe both, he mused. The keep of Drolwym rambled along a ridge, walls laid out with no apparent sense of design, towers jutting where they would.

The Thane of Drolwym, Guesare's father, had paid his guest little attention since they had ridden in, weary from their long journey up the backbone of the Cuddon. That was apparently to change, for the call had come to attend Vantare in his chambers.

"Father was giving you time to recuperate, that's all," claimed Guesare. "Don't be put off if he seems unfriendly. It's just his way."

They ascended a stair of rough-hewn timber, darkened with age. "Then, good Guesare, I take it son and father are unalike?" Donzalo spoke half-jestingly.

The minstrel stopped climbing and turned to his tall companion. "Quite unalike, Donzalo. But the thane is a good man. Better than his son, maybe." He began to climb again and the two spoke no more until they stood outside Vantare's door.

A huge man waited by the entry. "Brother Guesare!" he bellowed and embraced the bard in a bear hug.

"Ourru," gasped Guesare, when his brother released him. "This is our kinsman Donzalo, from Lama. A Rosam," he added as further explanation.

"Welcome, Cousin!" The large Cuddonian embraced the young man as he had Guesare. The two were of near equal size, Donzalo a little taller, Ourru thicker. Both had heavy black beards, though Ourru's was much the longer.

"Ha," laughed Guesare, "you look like a member of the family, Donzalo!"

"He does indeed! Now you will have a fifth burly brother, little Guesare." Ourru roared at his own joke. "Father awaits you. Go on in."

As they entered the room, Donzalo whispered a question to Guesare. "You have four brothers?"

"Aye. Half-brothers." He stepped forward. "Greetings, Father. I've brought our cousin Donzalo."

Having just met his large son, Donzalo was surprised that the man who stood before them was of quite ordinary size. His beard was white but he stood erect and steady. Steady, too, were the bright green eyes beneath his bushing brows.

"Welcome, Master Donzalo." The old man's salutation was formal and grave, with a trace of the Cuddon's accent to it. "Know, young kinsman, that I have dispatched a messenger to your family to tell them you arrived safely. Your father had sent word to watch for you." Then he softened. "How is my cousin, the Lady Vibola?"

"She was — well, when I left."

The thane had noted his momentary hesitation. "Ah, but growing old. We were young together." He sighed. "She was as an older sister to me.

"But we can speak of such things some other time." The thane became serious again. "You know that the news is bound to get out eventually that you are here."

"Yes, my lord."

"Don't address me as lord. We don't do that in the Cuddon."

"The peasantry would hang us from the nearest tree if we put on such airs," said Guesare. "If they could find a large enough tree in these hills."

Vantare glanced at his son with an expression that mingled amusement and exasperation. Donzalo could see that this somewhat dour nobleman and his carefree offspring might well have had their moments of discord.

"Sir, then?" he asked.

"Aye, that will do." The thane looked the young Laman up and down. "My son tells me you are both a fighting man and a scholar. More importantly, he tells me you are someone who may be trusted. I trust that you will live up to your vows when I make you a knight."

The old man turned from them without further word. Guesare took Donzalo's sleeve and led him quietly from the room.

Perdos had become a more sober man since the death of his brother. He had always had a streak of common sense — more so than the late Percos. It had been his temper that often got him into trouble.

On realizing that Guesare and Donzalo were fled to the Cuddon, where he dare not follow, Perdos had decided to travel south, find a place to hole up for the winter. He'd money enough to keep him in some out-of-the-way inn. He could wait.

That was when he had come on Sojel's men. Now, he led the pair's horses along with his own, and their captive, this diminutive, olive-skinned woman, walked silently beside him. They approached the out-lying fields of Sir Paren's manor.

"Have you a husband, woman?" he asked, maybe a bit too brusquely. She nodded in reply. "Well, he need not know any of what happened to you. Just tell him you wandered about lost for a while and found your way home."

She seemed to think on this for a few moments, before venturing to look up at his impassive face. "You won't be coming to the keep, sir?"

"No. There is not good blood between your master and me. That is as that is." He shrugged, the one shoulder rising higher than the other. "But you should tell Sir Paren of what truly happened. He needs to know what's going on in his lands. Also," he added, his voice lower, the words coming slowly and with care, "let him know that Perdos — he knows the name — had nothing to do with the attack and has no quarrel with him or his family." Which was mostly true, Perdos told himself.

She dropped to her knees before him. "I thank you, Sir Perdos." Wrapping her arms around his legs, she began to sob.

"Enough of that." He lifted the woman to her feet. She stood no taller than his chest. "We are near enough the manor that you can find your way. And I must be on my own."

Perdos turned from her, mounted his horse and rode south.

"It is rumored that this theater is haunted," claimed the blond woman.

"My father says there are no such thing as ghosts. I tend to take his word on these matters," replied her taller, darker companion.

"Really, my Lady Fachalana? I thought he had regular business dealings with spirits!"

"They are as solid as you and I, but exist in worlds other than our own. Or so I have gleaned from his books when I had a chance to peek into them."

"I'm not sure but that I should be disappointed." She looked around the empty hall. "Oh well, what do you think of the place?"

"It will do, Maresta. Let's go see the dressing rooms. You know," said Fachalana, "there is no reason why you couldn't move in here. Why spend money on rent when we have this place?"

We have this place? thought the actress. How long would that *we* last if I crossed her? And, of course, she thinks I could keep an eye on it for her, as well as be constantly available to cater to her whims. Maresta knew her patroness well. Still, she realized it would not be a bad idea.

"Why indeed?" she answered aloud. "We will have to have workmen in. I see the need for repairs, here and there."

Fachalana nodded, not really paying attention. She was seeing herself on this now-empty stage, playing the heroine before a packed house. "I must have Jobo write me a play," she said, to no one in particular.

"Jobo, my lady?"

"Oh, Jobareth Nafal, my friend since childhood. He's a writer, you know, when he isn't an errand boy for Father."

The blond woman knew the name well and that she must be careful to avoid the man. "He isn't in town, is he?" she asked. "You know I met him while I was spying for you in Lama. He would recognize me, I am quite sure."

"No, he is still off in Lama being a diplomat. I don't know when he will be back here again." Maresta let out a slow breath of relief. "Maybe in the spring.

"But my father will be here soon! He and the king are returning to court."

"Ah, then we had best get this place into operation, my lady. There may be a royal command performance in our future!"

There were ways into the Mountain Keep where one might enter without drawing attention. The correct password, a little-traversed passageway, and Sojel was at the door of his master's chambers. He did not hesitate to rap, using a specific pattern of knocks that would identify him.

Lord Radal himself answered and motioned him into the room. The tall man, wrapped in an unadorned black robe, did not seem surprised to see his minion. Sojel suspected that sentries had spied him riding up the valley but with a sorcerer, one could never be sure.

"So, I assume your mission failed." Sojel swallowed. It was to be expected that Radal would know that.

"Yes, my lord. It was — well, a fiasco. Nothing went right."

"Tell me of it." The mage sat by a window, open despite the cold, and listened to Sojel's report without speaking. He remained silent for a while after his man was done.

"What of Sabatare?" he asked abruptly.

"That useless wizard? He was slain while fleeing." Which was true, as far as it went — no need for Sojel to mention that he had personally put a sword through him.

Radal suspected there was more to it than his sergeant chose to reveal but it did not matter. "And the Rupa flew away. Too bad you don't know which direction." There was a barely-concealed note of accusation in his voice. "Did you see any sign of the minstrel?"

Sojel considered the question for a moment. "No, my lord, I can't say that I did. Huh, he wasn't at the keep either, then, or he would have joined in the battle."

"Yes. Whatever else one may say of him, he is a fighting man and would have been in the fray. He has slipped away and taken the boy somewhere else." Sojel, for a moment, wanted to tell his master that Donzalo was far from being a boy anymore but knew to keep his mouth shut. Discretion had always been one of his strong points. "The Cuddon," stated Radal. "Yes."

He rose from his seat. "That is no place for you to go in the mid-winter but I have other servants there." Lord Radal sighed. "I shall be in the tower all this night. Go rest. I shall need you in the morning.

"I must accompany the king back to Celatas."

3

"So that's the tale," finished Sir Paren.

Captain Corgos shook his head. "I should have remained longer, sir."

"That was not to be helped," replied the reeve. "At any rate, it is all over. Now what," he continued, "do you make of our Erlana's tale?"

The captain took a draught of his dark beer. "I would certainly agree it was best that her husband and the rest of your people not know what truly befell her. But Perdos —" He shook his head. "That is a puzzler."

"I know little of the man. Only that he left Castle Rosam under a very heavy cloud of suspicions." Paren would not mention what he actually knew of the deadly events of those few days in the spring. That was knowledge for the family only.

"He was one of Bolos's private retainers. We didn't actually serve together," said Corgos. "Same with his brother, may Kamat keep him." He made the sign of the arrow and continued. "Percos was a real hothead."

Paren nodded. "And it got him killed."

"Yes. Both of them had tempers. That, and being none too bright, was their main failing. One could wonder, though, just what he was doing in those woods when he found your Erlana."

"I have no doubt that he was somehow involved with those who attacked us. But it's true that no one saw him here and we always knew that his quarrel was with the minstrel Guesare."

"The one who slew his brother." It all made sense to Corgos now. "Ah, so it's a vendetta."

"Perhaps that is his only involvement," agreed Sir Paren, "and I'm willing to give him a pass for rescuing the girl. I might not kill Sir Perdos on sight but I would most certainly escort him from my lands.

"Now, have you given thought to joining my service here? My master of arms is leaving me and I would have you take his place."

"I am sworn to patrol the roads for your brother this winter."

"Then we shall be seeing you here from time to time. Mistress Tiana will approve of that — though she would more approve a permanent stay." Paren laughed to see the seasoned soldier blush at his words. "I shall ask you again, come spring. And, if possible, try to make one of your visits here fall on the Yuletide."

◆

"Are your other brothers as large as Ourru?" asked Donzalo.

"Much larger," replied Guesare, solemnly. Then he laughed, unable to help himself. "Nay, he is the biggest of the bunch. But they are all, indeed, large men. One could certainly guess that you are all related."

"Not very closely," objected the Laman.

"Hmm, third cousins, once removed. Close enough, it seems, for it to show."

"Very well, Guesare. Half-brothers, you said?"

"Yes. My mother was the thane's second wife. I've a pair of half-sisters as well. I must admit that they are also on the large side."

The two had settled at a table in the kitchens. On the tabletop near them slept a large gray cat. There were many cats in Drolwym Keep.

Donzalo remembered something he had read of Cuddonian customs. "None of them will be thane, will they?"

"That's right. The title is inherited through the female line. I've a cousin about here somewhere who will be the next thane."

"The son of your father's oldest sister." Donzalo thought he had that right. "It seems an odd custom to us in Lama."

"But there is never any question of paternity, in that it doesn't matter. And there are far odder customs." Guesare chuckled at a sudden thought. "Perhaps you would like to be Anian and have many wives."

"Perhaps so," agreed the young Laman, quite seriously, "if they all looked like Posena."

"Ah, Donni, it is not wise to fall in love with an Ani spy." The minstrel shook his head, his expression rueful. "I know from experience."

Donzalo sat quietly a few moments, listening to those seated around them. Most were household retainers of some sort or another, maids, grooms, men-at-arms. They spoke in a mix of accented Muram and the native Cuddonian tongue, occasionally switching from one to the other mid-sentence.

"I should learn Cuddonish," he told Guesare. "Will you teach me?"

"Krevod," replied the minstrel. "Our language is Krevod. Your first lesson."

"Oh, yes, of course. Cuddon is a word from my own Muram." Donzalo chuckled softly. "Not a very flattering one, either, is it?"

"Wasteland. But we wear the name with pride."

Blen had not hurried. There would be hardship enough, soon, when he was on the road to Castle Rosam, so why not stay abed this morning, enjoy a leisurely breakfast?

Mid-morning found him readying his steed in the stables of the Mountain Keep. All about him was noise and activity, as the king's entourage prepared for their own journey. He expected to be off first, headed the direction opposite.

"Sir Blen," came a voice from behind him. It was a voice he recognized well. "Have you a moment?"

"My Lord Radal," he said, turning, "I always have time for the king's councilor." Behind the sorcerer stood his henchman, Sojel. As ever, that man appeared inscrutable yet exuded malice.

"I have some dispatches here for Nafal," said Radal. "Nothing very important but they might as well travel with you." It was no more than an excuse for this meeting but both men pretended otherwise.

The dark nobleman watched him tuck the papers into a saddlebag. "Blen," he said, "we serve the same master. I assume our king has chosen to employ you as his eyes in Lama. That is wise — there is always use for another view of things.

"I warn you, though, that there is much more happening than you could ever know. Stick to taking care of our embassy and keeping his majesty informed and, should you need help, remember that I am not your enemy. But do not, I warn you again, become involved in that which you do not understand."

"We call on thee, Lady of the Dark Moon!"

"We call on thee," repeated the circle of cloaked figures. Stone bowls were being passed from hand to hand, and each drank deeply.

"Bring the day when the sun is not reborn, when the new year comes not!"

"Bring the day that is eternal night," came the response. Their voices echoed from the dark cavern vault above them, invisible by the unsteady light of torches

In the middle of the assembly, on a dais hewn of the solid stone, stood one swathed all in black and holding a heavy, twisted staff. A faint sickly-green light played about its shaft.

"Sisters," she cried, "we have been tasked." There was a murmur that quickly died away. "A servant of the night came to me. As a bat did it come, to whisper of an enemy among us — an enemy of the dark!"

The murmur began again. This time it grew to become the howling of many voices, rising in a drug-driven frenzy.

"He is newly come to Castle Drolwym! We must slay him!" shrieked their leader over the cacophony of her coven.

"We will tear him apart!" one cried. "We will throw his tattered flesh to the four winds!"

"I will pluck his eyes from his head," promised another, "and make him look upon his own broken body!"

"And I will wear his manhood as a necklace!" cried one beside her, to the delight of her crazed companions.

Beneath her veil, their leader smiled.

4

On a hilltop, not so far away, stood another group of women. These women, despite the cold, were quite naked.

"Sisters," spoke she who led them, at the end of their rites, "rejoice with me. My son has returned."

"I'd best lock up my brother," joked one of the circle. The others laughed with her.

As did the handsome, middle-aged woman who stood at their center. "Yet he has brought serious news," she continued. "There is one with him who may need our protection. He has been marked for death by the Dark One."

"Oh, do you mean Donzalo?" asked a woman. "I've seen him around the keep. He's cute."

"If you think bears are cute. He looks like one of your step-sons, Lady Se," said another.

"So I have heard," replied their leader. "I have not yet set eyes on him. But if the boy needs our help and that of the Great Mother, we should be prepared.

"Now let us go someplace warm, put on some clothes, and drink wine!"

Borrago reached down to stroke the head of the half-grown dog lolling at his feet. The pup was, ostensibly, his grandson's yet it had chosen to follow the count about — and the count had not objected.

"Any word from your silent partner, Lector?" he asked the young man sitting across the table. Jobareth Nafal smiled faintly at the description of his supposed underling, Blen. Count Borrago had correctly surmised their actual, if secret, equal footing.

"No, my lord, which means he is probably on his way back here. Had he been detained he would have sent a message."

"But he himself can make as good time as any courier, having been one not long ago," spoke a third man who sat in the corner, his countenance partly concealed by shadow. Until then, Borrago's master of arms, Copago, had been a quiet but palpable presence.

"Well, I suppose we've done all we need on these papers." Borrago pushed the stack of documents aside. "Thank you for coming up, Nafal." He leaned back and regarded the young diplomat for a moment. "You will come for the Yule feast, of course."

"Certainly, sir. I would not miss it. Shall I bring my, uh, partner too?" Jobareth immediately wished he had not said that. It did not do to become overly familiar.

But the count laughed at his little jest. "By all means, my boy. Sir Blen is always welcome here." He reconsidered that. "Well, almost always. You and I have secrets to which he should not be privy, eh?"

The Sharshite immediately caught Borrago's intention. "There is news of Donzalo, my lord?"

"Indeed there is." The count took papers from a side table and laid them before him. "Two letters," he said, "one from my brother and one from Drolwym."

"Drolwym, my lord? I do not know the name."

"It is a hold in the Upper Cuddon. Guesare's father is lord there." Borrago picked up the letter. "The message is brief but it does say that both arrived there safely.

"Now this other letter — between it and what my man Corgos has reported, it would seem there have been some strange goings-on up the Abam."

"Is Sir Paren well, my lord? And Lady Thara?"

"Yes. Here, read for yourself." He passed the letter to Jobareth, who read through the message, written in Paren's own cramped scrawl.

"Strange goings-on for certain, sir." He looked up at the count. "All in all, it seems to have turned out well."

"Men and women were slain," interjected Copago. "That is never good."

Nafal nodded. "True, sir. Quite true."

"But it could have been far worse," said the count, "and there was much gallantry. I do believe that I shall knight our Corgos this Yule."

"He has requested that he be at your brother's keep that day," Copago said. "I hear he has a lady love there."

Boraggo threw back his head and laughed openly. "Well good for him. Let's dub him tomorrow and he can go to her as a knight!"

"Not all my brothers are fond of me. Nor of each other, for that matter."

"Is that so?" replied Donzalo, as they entered the crowded hall. "What of your sisters?"

"The one is far away, with her husband. Her, I get along with well enough. The other — well, there she is." He nodded toward a tall, stout woman of indeterminate age. "'Twould be better were I to let Ourru introduce you."

"She seems — formidable."

"Indeed. It is generally believed she poisoned her husband. Ah, here is Ourru." Guesare sighed. "And Mausare as well."

Mausare seemed a slightly smaller version of his brother, which made him still quite a large man. "Ho, Brothers!" came Ourru's greeting. "Donzalo, this is our brother Mausare. He's the runt of the family!' He guffawed at the sour look on Mausare's face. "Our women are about somewhere. By the way, Mausy's wife seems to think you're rather a handsome young fellow." He nudged his brother in the ribs with a massive elbow.

"Greetings, brother," said Guesare, and embraced the man, not with the enthusiasm of an Ourru, yet with a certain tenderness. "Is all well with you?"

"Well enough, Guesare." The man turned and took Donzalo's hand. "Greetings to you, young sir."

"Is anyone else here?" asked the minstrel.

Mausare answered. "Habidros is still with his free company, somewhere in the Siphic cities. To be honest, I'm not sure where Galaro is."

Guesare turned to Donzalo. "Galaro was the only one of us who chose to go into trade rather than fight or farm. Though I'm not convinced he quite understands the difference between trade and smuggling."

"I saw your sister a few minutes ago," Ourru suddenly stated.

"Nosana? We saw her too and avoided her." For once, all three brothers laughed together.

"Nay, I mean Jola."

Mausare seemed surprised and, perhaps, a bit dismayed. "It is rare for her to show up here." Noting Donzalo's puzzlement, he explained, in an almost too matter-of-fact a voice. "Jola is Guesare's half-sister by his mother. Our step-sister."

"Oh." Donzalo glanced at the minstrel, who was staring at the floor. There followed a moment of silence, decidedly of the awkward sort.

Then Ourru spoke. "Well, Cousin, someone must introduce you to Nosana and it would seem to fall to me. I'm the only one of us," he confided with a wink, "who isn't scared of her."

A group of children scurried across their pathway. Donzalo was surprised to see youngsters so much in evidence at Drolwym. Back at Castle Rosam, they rarely appeared at such gatherings.

Though Nosana was very tall, as women generally go, she did not seem so beside Ourru and Donzalo. Nosana resented that fact. She liked being the most imposing figure in a group.

She drew herself up as the pair approached. Nosana allowed her brother to hug her, but barely. "This is our kinsman Donzalo," said he. "Donzalo, this is my sister Nosana."

The woman stared at Donzalo a moment, as if uncertain of her best course. Then she smiled and embraced him. "Greetings, Cousin," she said, her voice all honey and wine. "We are most pleased to meet you."

Leaving Donazalo for a while to his siblings, Guesare crossed the hall to where his parents held court. Vantare was sitting quietly, seemingly bemused by the comings and goings of his guests. His son bowed to him but was barely acknowledged.

Guesare's mother beckoned him. "Your father is in one of his moods," she whispered as she embraced her son. "It is good to have you home."

"It is good to be home," he responded.

The Lady Se smiled. "For a while. You will grow restless, as always." She looked out into the crowded room. "But you have a charge, now, who requires your attention."

"He needs it less and less, Mother. Donzalo is becoming a rather capable young man. I think Nosana has her hooks in him at the moment but I'll bring him over to meet you, as soon as I can."

"Be wary of Nosana. I sense both lust and malevolence in her tonight."

"Would that I had your gifts!" Guesare exclaimed. "I can not read like that and certainly not from a distance."

"I've never heard of a man who could. You have your own abilities, my son, or you would not be here with me now."

"Lust, you say? Not for Donzalo?"

"Why not? He's a morsel I might not mind sampling myself." She laughed gaily at his expression. "Fear not, my Guesare, I will leave your friend be."

"There are too many people here and I know not friends from enemies," said the minstrel. "Maybe I should not have brought him to my home."

"You know you can trust me," Guesare's mother reminded him, "and your sister Jola, mad though she may be."

5

"They're little more than food for the swine," claimed the little innkeeper. "Why should I want these nags?"

Perdos sighed deeply. He had never enjoyed bargaining and always seemed to get the worst of it. But he knew horses well enough to place a proper value on these two — they were decent steeds. Certainly much better quality than their late owners.

"I'll not quibble," he said. "We both know they are good horses. Make a decent offer or I'll be off with them."

"Hmm." The man ran his hands over the animals, occasionally squinting or pursing his lips. Perdos suspected all of it was show. "Would you consider, say, two — no, let's make it three crowns for the pair of them."

"Let's not. Don't waste my time, man. I want to get over the river soon."

"Crossing the Weldar? Something over there you need? Or do you just feel safer on the other side?" The sly jest came close to the mark.

Perdos felt himself growing angry but then he considered the innkeeper's question. He leaned back against a fence rail and exhaled. "I'm not really sure," he said. "Damn it, I've no real reason to cross at all. I'm just looking for a place to spend the winter."

The man cocked his head at the knight. "This *is* an inn, you know. I have few enough guests when winter slows down traffic on the river. What do you say to four weeks lodging and meals in exchange for the horses?"

"Make it six," said Perdos, "and stabling for my own steed."

"You must include the saddles. Done? Very well. I'll show you your room."

Perdos sighed. He didn't know whether he had gotten the best of this deal but he was satisfied with it. And he was very tired.

It was raining in Celatas, a light, warm rain, little more than a mist. King Lareth did not mind it, welcomed it, after the cold winds and snows of the mountains. He and his entourage rode slowly through the cobblestone streets, climbing toward the royal keep.

Celatas was not an old city. Lareth's father, King Greneth, had chosen to build his capital on this spot when he took the throne. The name meant nothing more than 'Royal City.'

Unlike the old capital of Sharsh, which had lain near the coast, Greneth's city was placed well inland. A high rocky hill surmounted the city and the king's keep surmounted that hill. Far below was the wide River Chas, which flowed through the heart of the nation.

Lord Radal had once observed to the king that his citadel was much like that of the Rosam, the same defensible heights guarding a major river trade route. On giving it thought, Lareth realized that it made sense — similar needs would produce similar results. His city and keep were, however, far larger than anything in Lama. They were the capital of a great nation.

And that great nation made great demands on his time. There would be a flurry of celebrations and balls to mark his return and simply because it was that time of year. Then he must buckle down to the job of governing.

In the back of his mind, though, he was busy laying out his garden for the coming spring. He wished that Lomela could visit and see it. Why shouldn't she, yes, and his grandchildren too?

"Sire." He glanced at the squire by his side and then at the coming turn of the road.

"Yes, my boy," he said, "I've been day-dreaming. It's one of the few pleasures left a king."

"Mausare, like his father, is given to dark moods. We get along well enough, most of the time, and I think him a good man."

"That's recommendation enough for me," said Donzalo. "I like your mother. Is she really a priestess?"

"High Priestess of Rema."

The Earth Mother, thought Donzalo to himself. That's one of the really old deities. A Kamatian he might be, but a well-read one.

"I never saw your other sister."

"She was gone already," said Guesare. "It is rare for her to show herself at all. Jola spends more time in the company of the fay of the hills than she does humans."

The two were lounging before the fire in Donzalo's room, sorting out all that had transpired that evening. It was important to both that they understand what winds were blowing through this place.

"Mausare seemed troubled when her name was mentioned."

The minstrel gazed into the fire so long that Donzalo almost spoke again.

"He had an — entanglement with my sister," Guesare said at last. "Since they are not truly related by blood, there was no reason they shouldn't, after all. Except that it was bound to end badly.

"Jola is not an ordinary woman. She has abilities, as does my mother — or I, for that matter — but hers are much greater. They have driven her to madness."

"Is her father dead?" asked the young Laman.

"We do not know who her father was. She was conceived at one of the temple, um, celebrations, a couple years before the Lady Se married the thane." He shook his head and made an attempt at a smile. "Mother insists that the father was a god. Who knows? Maybe he was."

He fell silent again. Donzalo half-suspected he had fallen asleep.

"Beware my other sister," Guesare suddenly said. "She desires you. I think she may desire to kill you as well." He rose to his feet. "And on that shall I leave you to your sleep," he laughed, and passed out the door.

"Blen! We did not expect you so soon." Jobareth came forth from their lodgings to grip the hand of his associate. "Come on in."

"I felt an urgency to be back here," replied the knight, "so I rode courier-style." He gave the young diplomat a tired smile. "I am in great need of sleep."

"I would think so. At least you have a few days to rest before the Yule parties." Jobareth chuckled. "After them, you will need to rest again."

Blen nodded. He had little desire to exchange banter at any time, but certainly not right then. Bed was his desire, and sleep.

Yet the weary knight did not sleep when he lay down his head. Too much was going through his mind. What was expected of him? Was he to fear Lord Radal or to confide in him? And of just what had the councilor been warning him? Was Jobareth involved in some plot? Around and around the questions went and his legs ached and he could not find comfort.

As the morning sun brought Ros-town to life, slumber finally took him.

6

Nosana beheld her reflection in her mirror. She was proud of her mirror — it was of glass and the only one like it in the Cuddon, brought from the Siphic League by her husband at great expense and effort. Too bad, she thought, he didn't put enough effort into other things.

She was proud of her reflection, too. That she was a woman of appetites showed in her figure. But she was not unattractive, tall, erect, full-bosomed. Still young, too. Young enough.

Yes, she would have this Donzalo. And then, alas, she would have his life as well. A few drops of poison in his wine would do. It might be interesting to watch his death struggle. Two pleasures in one night, she laughed to herself.

Dropping her robe, Nosana beheld herself again and nodded. Shouldn't that be enough to get the young Laman into her bed? She shrugged. If not — well, there were potions.

It had been a good night, after all, and not marred by her fools of brothers. And little Guesare, despite their mutual hatred, had brought her quite a nice gift.

"I do not like this," the crown prince stated flatly, "not at all, sir. Allowing my brother to marry into that family cuts into my own claims to the throne."

"But it ties them to our dynasty," said Lareth. "Better Modareth than some ambitious nobleman." The king seated himself by a window, shuttered against the winter, and looked his son up and down. "I think you have nothing to fear from your little brother."

"Oh, certainly, Father. But marriages produce heirs." Both became silent for a moment before the younger man continued in more subdued voice. "Or it is to be wished that they will."

"There is plenty of time yet for that, Gawis. I have no doubt that you will give me a grandson." Lareth pulled his shawl closer about him. He should call the servants to build a bigger fire in here.

The prince brushed back his shock of stiff sandy-blond hair. Lareth knew it for a habit of his when at unease. Dressed in green again, he thought. Does he do that for the impression it makes or does he truly want to wear my colors?

"Sire," began Gawis, "I can only hope."

"It takes more than hope, boy." The king couldn't help making the jest.

Which his son ignored. "This marriage in itself is not so bad, I suppose, but it comes on the heels of Lomela's." He began slowly pacing before the fire. Giving himself time to think, thought Lareth. "That makes two ties to the family of Duke Paren."

"The bride is second cousin to Count Borrago," said the king. "That is not a bad thing, Gawis. Their families would make more likely rivals than allies."

"Hmm, yes, Father, I see that. The claim of one undercuts that of the other." Gawis frowned. "Would that I could recognize things like that. I doubt my ability to succeed you."

Lareth briefly felt himself likely to agree. "You'll learn, my son. More importantly," he continued, "you need proper advisers around you — not that circle of flatterers you think your friends."

The younger man nodded but the king did not know if he took his words to heart.

"Cursed cat!" Donzalo caught himself before he went tumbling down the stairs. "It's a wonder everyone in this castle doesn't have broken bones."

The offending feline purred innocently and rubbed against his leg. "You aren't in league with Lord Radal, are you?" he asked it. "Lying in ambush on these stairs, just waiting your chance to trip me up — why you even look like him in your black coat!"

From below him, came the unmistakable sound of a rebec. Guesare would not be hard to find this morning. The minstrel was seated on the floor, just outside the kitchens, surrounded by a circle of children.

"Ah, my little ones, here is my friend Donni. I must leave you now." The group turned around to stare at Donzalo.

"He's big!" said one of the boys.

"Not as big as my dad," claimed another. "He's the biggest man in the world! Right, Uncle Guessy?"

Guesare rose to his feet. "Your father is very large but he can't compare with the Stone Giants in the Lofty Mountains. Why, they use pine trees as toothpicks and have to be careful not to bump their heads on the sky when they stand up straight." He turned to Donzalo. "That's one of Ourru's boys."

"So, you have an whole other talent of which I knew nothing. You could be story-telling in the marketplace for the children's copper coins."

"I have done just that," said Guesare. "It is an honorable craft."

"Then I apologize for making light of it. I know many stories but I can not think of even one suited to children." Donzalo grew pensive, of a sudden. "My own son will soon see his first birthday. I would be there with him."

"And I'm sure you will be. Farewell, children. I'll play for you again when I can." The two stepped into the kitchen. It was late for breakfast and early for lunch, so the tables were mostly empty and the cooks and scullions were busy with cleaning and preparation.

"Speaking of bumping ones head, I need be careful in here," observed Donzalo, as he avoided a strand of sausages dangling from the ceiling beams.

"Can you bring us something, lass? Anything," said Guesare to a serving girl. "Tell me, Donzalo, in which temple would you prefer to stand your vigil? I know you're Kamatian, but that is not an option here."

"So what is? Thank you," Donzalo said as a bowl of bread and dried fruits was placed before them.

"Well, my father would probably recommend Jov. He is the chief of the gods, of course, so always a good choice.

"Mother, on the other hand, would say Rema, who is, after all, mother of Jov. Or grandmother, depending on which cult you follow. Sometimes both. I would recommend against that as her temples are quite open to the weather. Not at all a good idea at this time of year."

"Tell me," said the Laman, taking a sip from the tankard that had been handed him, "is there a temple of Diba? And what is this?" He sniffed at it.

"Diba, the Huntress? Yes, we have a shrine near here." Guesare drank deeply from his own tankard. "You've never had buttermilk before? Drink up, it's good for you. It will help you grow!"

Donzalo gave his companion a properly pained expression and sipped some more. He might like this stuff. Or maybe not.

"Why Diba?" asked Guesare.

"She's the one goddess whose worship lives on in Lama. Only among the peasants, who tend to lump her with the fairies and such. I always liked the stories they told of her and her wolf pack, hunting through the night for the demons who might harm children."

"You see, my friend, you do know stories for youngsters. You were only looking for them in the wrong memories."

Why couldn't any of the men she knew be like this Donzalo? wondered the Lady Fachalana. Between the dispatches — admittedly, not meant for her eyes but read none the less — sent to Lord Radal, the gossipy letters from Jobareth, and the reports of her personal spy, Maresta, she had learned quite a lot about him. And to think that her father was trying to kill the man!

Well, that wouldn't do.

Her father thought his secret papers well hidden and well guarded, but while he was far away in the mountains, she had looked through them and learned the reason — that Donzalo's son was prophesied to rule in Lama. If that were so, then who was to say who might be the mother? Fachalana could see herself beside such a man. Now that would be a proper stage for her!

Ha, she laughed to herself, am I to fall in love with someone of whom I have only read? Best to busy herself with her new theater and put such foolishness from her head.

The warm rain that had come yesterday was turning to light snow. Winter was never very bad here in Celatas and there would be a whirlwind of balls and feasting to entertain her for the next few days. But her boredom would return, Fachalana knew. She would soon thirst for adventure again.

7

"My Lady Nosana." Donzalo bowed toward the woman seated before him.

"Oh, you have accepted my invitation! Welcome, my young kinsman." She dismissed her serving girl with a quick glance from beneath her dark, arching brows. "Here, join me in some wine of Dor." She poured out the golden liquid into two goblets — goblets of fine Siphic glass.

The Cuddonian woman was dressed in a black gown, cut to display her ample breasts. Her raven hair lay loose upon her shoulders.

Donzalo could see the great vanity of this woman, the showing off of her expensive possessions, the mention of a rare wine, the self-conscious display of her own desirability. He had grown up with far more wealth, yet among a people who shunned ostentation.

Still, she was an imposing and, yes, attractive person. Her tendency to flesh did not conceal the firm jaw, the high cheekbones and strong straight nose, and certainly not the headstrong spirit that drove her. She's hardly much older than Guesare, he thought.

"I thank you, my lady," said Donzalo, evenly, politely, seating himself across the low table and taking the proffered glass. Nosana allowed her fingers to linger on his for a moment, before smiling and lifting her own goblet.

"To friendship," she toasted, "and all it might bring." There was a hunger in her voice and Donzalo began to feel an answering appetite within himself. It had been long since he had held a woman. It had been even longer since that last night with Lomela, the only woman to whom he had ever made love. Ah, that he could again, just once, be that simple boy who had loved a princess.

Nosana sensed his desires, or thought she did. She leaned back into the many-colored satin cushions that overflowed her divan and gave him a frank look. "You are quite a handsome fellow, aren't you? Some might think your nose too large but it suits the rest of you. I trust your largeness is uniform."

Donzalo felt briefly embarrassed, not for himself but for this woman. Such coyness suited her not. A mix of curiosity and boredom had drawn him here and, in honesty, he had come not completely opposed to the idea of a dalliance with her.

Now, though — she seemed silly, stupid, and almost certainly dangerous. But she remained physically desirable and, after all, no one had a claim on his fidelity. Not Lomela, not anymore. Not Posena, or whatever her name truly was. He recalled the little spy's fair face turned up to kiss him, when last they were together, and realized he wanted something other than what this woman before him offered.

He sighed deeply. "This is not to be, my Lady Nosana. I must leave." Her face immediately displayed her frustration, even anger, but she quickly hid that beneath a mask of sweetness and resignation.

"Then drink one more goblet of wine with me, at least. It will help ease my disappointment."

"I am worried for Donzalo. He accepted an invitation to attend Nosana in her rooms."

"Trust your friend," replied the priestess.

"I do but I certainly do not trust my sister," Guesare told his mother. "You are the one who sensed menace in her."

Lady Se put down her embroidery. It was a design made of mystic runes that the minstrel found quite confusing. "I always sense menace in Nosana. You think she means to do more than simply seduce him?"

"I don't know. Could she be allied with those who would do him harm?" Guesare sounded frustrated. "I did not bring him all the way here so it could be for nothing!"

"It will not be." She turned back to her needlework. "I have set one to guard him. Hmm, now which shade of red would work best here?"

Nosana smiled from her doorway as Donzalo walked, a bit unevenly, back to his own room. It would take but a short while for her potion to inflame him and then she would follow. It were best done in the boy's chamber, anyway, both her enjoyment of him and that which followed — his body in her rooms might have been difficult to explain.

She doffed her gown — no need for that now — and drew a loose robe about her naked body. That should be time enough, she told herself, as she stepped into the curving hallway. First side-passage and then — yes, here it is, door ajar. Nosana laughed softly. The boy's mind had not been on closing doors behind him, much less bolting them, by the time he got here. Nosana could have forced it with a minor magic, if need be, but she'd rather not have to bother.

But she would bolt it behind her and set a seal upon it as well. That done, she turned to where Donzalo stood in the darkened room. His breathing came to her ears deep and ragged. She threw aside her robe. "Come to me!" she demanded.

He stumbled forward, eager to have her. How beautiful he is, even so, mused Nosana. She'd best make the most of him. "Here," she said, placing his large strong hands where it pleased her.

"You will not," came a voice from behind her.

She spun around to see the door open, her seal as nothing. A tall woman, dark of skin but golden haired, stood there. "Your little spells are like cobwebs to me, Nosana, wiped away with a sweep of my hand." She looked at the confused young man and, shaking her head, turned back to Nosana with utter scorn.

"Do not try me. You know you can not. Now begone!" Nosana hesitated a moment, then ran from the room, quite quickly for so heavy a woman.

Donzalo stood bemused in the middle of the chamber. As the woman approached, he reached for her, tried to pull her close, bring his lips to hers. She gently pushed him away and smoothed her long white gown. "No, no, sweet boy. Sleep and I shall guard thee." She guided him gently to his bed and stayed there by his side, singing songs that seemed to hold all the dreams ever dreamed, until his fever left him and he found sleep.

Nosana fumed as she slipped back to her room. Her robe lay on Donzalo's floor and here she was skulking through the halls without a stitch on her. Such a fool she had been! She should have given him the poison right off instead of that love potion.

Ah, well. There was a guardsman who had looked on her with desire earlier. He could do for tonight. And there would be other nights to deal with Donzalo Rosam.

"I do not like both of us leaving the place unattended so long."

"You worry too much, friend Blen. Do you think I bothered to keep a close watch on the staff while you were gone?" Jobareth took the reins from the soldier who had brought his horse. "It is but a couple of days. Enjoy yourself"

Jobareth Nafal knew that was a tall order for his companion. Blen was a man who lived for his work.

Both mounted and began the ride up to Castle Rosam. "Know you any Yule carols, Lector?" asked Blen of a sudden.

"Now that may be the most unexpected question you have ever asked me, Sir Blen." He gave it a moment's thought. "I suppose I've heard most of the old songs, though I don't know if I could sing through a one of them. And some of those that have been written for the stage in recent years. Why do you ask — if I might ask?"

"It's been a long time since I've celebrated the season with anyone. I was still a boy when I left my home to join the army."

"Well, I don't think the count will call on you to serenade him. For that matter," continued Jobareth, "I doubt they sing the same carols here as back in Sharsh."

Blen nodded. "I heard singing in the street last night in Old Laman."

"Did you understand any of it? I know you've tried to picked up some of the old tongue."

"Only a word or two. I'm not sure the singers themselves knew what the words meant." The knight looked upwards. "Fine weather for the Yuletide."

Jobareth gazed up as well. "Indeed it is, Blen."

"Do you have memories of last night?" asked the Lady Se.

"I remember being in the Lady Nosana's rooms and, um, having some wine and, um, leaving. I don't think I — felt well?" Donzalo thought about it. He sat, somewhat subdued and seemingly somewhat puzzled, by her side. "No, I did not feel well at all. But I don't remember getting back to my room. Yet I must have because I woke in my bed this morning."

"Is that all?" She looked knowingly toward her son, seated on the other side of the room.

"In the night I thought I awoke and a beautiful golden haired goddess visited me. What a dream that was! She sang to me and I felt like — like I did when I was little and my mother was alive." Donzalo suddenly gave forth a great sob. "It seemed so real!"

"There, there, my Donni." Se put an arm around the young man. So large, so brave, yet sometimes still very much a boy inside, she thought. "It was no dream."

"Come over here, Guesare. I want to tell this tale to both of you." The minstrel came to sit on the other side of his mother. They looked alike in many ways. Surely her curling hair, now turning gray, had been of that same gold when she was young. That laughing mouth of Guesare, his sturdy artistic hands that plucked both rebec and recurved bow so well — those were of his mother. But something of his fathers broad, serious brow and compact frame were there too.

"Many years ago, over thirty now, I was only a girl of the temple, not yet a priestess, much less High Priestess. It was a night of the full moon, a night of celebration, a night of abandon. The sort of night when women young and old might seek love where they will.

"I have told you, Guesare, that Jola's father was a god. He was not though he seemed as one to me that night, when the stars and moon sang a baby into me, there in the shadows of the hills. He was a young nobleman of Sharsh, traveling through these hills. Tall, he was, and very dark, and I could feel the power within him.

"I had never known such a man before. I have never known such since. But I learned that he turned to the dark ways after leaving me. Such a waste." She shook her head.

Lady Se looked at Donzalo. "You know who her father was." Then, turning to Guesare, "And I suppose you do as well, now."

The two men remained silent, Donzalo appearing thoughtful, digesting all this, Guesare seeming simply stunned.

"Donzalo," continued the High Priestess, "it was Jola who visited you last night. I believe she saved your life." She sighed, seemingly both weary and relieved to have told her secret. "She and Nosana have been rivals since birth. They were born on the same night." Guesare looked up at that, surprised.

"I never knew that, Mother."

"Because I never told you. It was a night of celebration for me, a good birth, a healthy girl. Nosana's mother died in the birthing of her.

"And now, Donzalo, you must prepare for your vigil this night." The Lady Se, taking the young man's hand, continued in an even voice. "There may be strange things all about you, strange visions, strange voices. Do not mind them but hold to your vigil. Do not leave the temple and do not sleep.

"You have done well to choose Diba as your patroness and protector this night. I might call it destiny, though I would usually dismiss such claims as foolishness. My daughter Jola serves the Goddess Diba and, between the two of them, you should have all the protection you need."

8

Guesare was unusually subdued and Donzalo was not willing to intrude. The two walked quietly along the narrow dirt path; ahead of them was a small stone building.

"You don't have to do this," the minstrel said at last. "You can be knighted anytime. Your father could do it when we return, or your uncle."

They stood now at the entrance to the temple of Diba. It lay within eyesight of the keep, which rose behind them, the last light of sunset gleaming on its highest turrets. The two placed their burdens on the ground beside them — Donzalo's weapons and raiment for the morning, among them a new sword for his knighting.

Though it was not truly new, but one with which Mausare had gifted him, one he said only had once been given him. At the moment, the young man wore a simple white tunic.

"It needs to be now," stated Donzalo, with far more certainty than his companion felt. "As your mother said, it is destiny. Or did she say it wasn't destiny? The Lady Se can be confusing." He looked the shrine over. "It's pretty small, isn't it? You should do better by your goddesses!"

"Diba is a rather minor goddess here in the Cuddon. Her father Jov and mother Esefa get the big temples." Guesare went to the altar and lit the oil lamp that stood before it. It's light flickered on the close walls and the small alabaster statue of the goddess, standing with her bow over her shoulder and a wolf at her heel.

He looked at his young friend and then embraced him fiercely. "Be safe and well, my boy. I can not wait here inside with you. I would have kept watch outside but Mother says that is not at all a good idea tonight — anyone out here is likely to be torn to pieces. So stay inside!

"I will watch from the keep. And, yes, I shall say a prayer to Diba."

It was good to have a fighting man around the place, thought the innkeeper, in case of trouble. This one kept to himself, mostly, didn't bother the occasional traveler — they were few at this time of the year — and rarely complained. Oh, maybe he drank a bit too heavily at times but he was a quiet drunk.

"Need you anything, Sir Perdos?" he asked as the man entered his taproom.

The soldier shook his head. "I'm going to go out a while. I need to stretch my legs."

"Do not take too long. The wife is preparing a Yule-eve feast and we would gladly share it with you."

Perdos gave him a long, expressionless look, almost as if he did not understand the man's meaning. "Very well," he said at last. "I thank you." He stepped out into the cool, late-afternoon air.

The knight was finding he liked this small village on the river. It lay well south of Ros-town, outside of Rosam holdings altogether, so that was of no concern to him. A few houses, a landing, the little inn — that was all there was to the place. One of the lesser counts of Lama ruled around here, and with a light touch.

He strolled for a while, the wide flow to his left. There was no traffic on the river, only bits of flotsam slowly making their way down to Mor-paras. How many leagues up the Weldar was his home? It had been a very long time since Perdos had seen it, or his mother. Did she still live? It was just as well that he didn't know and would never see her again. He wouldn't want to tell her that her other son was dead.

Ah, poor Percos. Always a fighter and it had been his undoing. He remembered how the young scrapper had stood up to their father, when he could no longer stand to see him beat Mother. That was when the two of them had to take to the road and seek their fortunes elsewhere.

One thing he knew for sure was that Dad wasn't alive. He spat and turned back to his lodgings.

So, what fortunes had they found? Death in an unmarked grave for his brother, outlawry for him. Perdos was tired of his life but he had vowed revenge on the minstrel Guesare. Maybe when that was over —

He stood a minute or two outside the inn door. He could hear the innkeeper and his wife bustling about inside, singing snatches of Yuletide song to each other. Why not? he thought to himself and went in to greet them.

◆

Once, he thought he saw women in the darkness. Some danced. Some stood like statues. He wasn't sure, but one or two might have flown. Could they have? Some were naked and others wrapped in long cloaks.

Then there was a howling of wolves. That is a good thing, thought Donzalo. They are sacred to Diba. Perhaps her pack is out hunting demons. He smiled at that. To him, Diba and her pack was a childhood story.

Right then, though, he silently vowed that he would never again hunt a wolf.

None of it seemed real. That doesn't matter, he told himself. Real or not, he had been told to stay put and stay alert and that was what he would do.

Then more women. Some, he felt, were being rather lewd. Donzalo had had quite enough of that sort of thing the previous night so he paid them little heed. Oh, and was that — well, it might or might not have been Nosana. The figure disappeared into a veiled crowd.

Only to come out carrying the butchered body of a young man. For a moment, it seemed to wear his own face, and to cry out to him for succor. The women cast off their robes to attack the carcass with tooth and talon. One looked up, directly at him, and laughed soundlessly. Blood and entrails dripped from her mouth.

They are not in the temple with me, Donzalo told himself. Diba wouldn't allow that. Or Jola wouldn't. He remembered his golden woman, his dream woman, and fixed his thoughts on her. She would keep him safe.

Guesare stood before a high tower window, keeping watch. Once, he thought he saw lights flicker near the shrine of Diba but he was uncertain. After a time, his father came and stood silently beside him.

At last, the older man spoke. "There are things going on, aren't there? Things I don't know about."

"Yes, Father. But you —" He stopped.

"Go on, my son."

"You never wanted to hear of the misdeeds of your children. You called them mere family squabbles."

"They usually were, Guesare," responded the thane. "I know some of my offspring have done wrong. Great wrong. I know that Nosana probably murdered her husband."

"And almost killed Donzalo," said Lady Se, who had come up quietly to stand with them. "Jola found this in the robe she left behind in his room." She held out a small vial of purplish liquid. "I know this poison. It kills quickly but very painfully."

"She was in his room, eh? Well, I know she visits many men's rooms. That, I overlook." Vantare took the vial from his wife's hand. "But this —" He shook his head. "Ah, Nosana.

"What am I to do, wife? I think the girl has been cursed since the day of her birth."

"Do, nothing, my husband. We must watch and be ready, for more is certain to come and it is well we know who will bring it." She turned to peer from the window, drawing a soft red cloak close about her. "Our young Donzalo is being tested," said Se. "So far, he has proven worthy. I pray to the Great Mother that he will be found so tonight."

Wake up! He hadn't fallen asleep, had he? It was that music, that monotonous, continuous music. It was putting him into a daze. What wouldn't he give for a few more wolf howls!

And the mists. Now, he missed those lewd women and their contortions. These constant swirling clouds about him would drive him mad. As, no doubt, they were intended to do. Just when he thought he saw a figure taking form, moving through them, it would disappear again.

"Stay firm, Donzalo," a voice whispered in his ear. He liked the voice. It was a voice he remembered. He knew she wasn't really there, an illusion like all else he had experienced this night, but he did not mind. How better to fight illusion than with illusion?

"Remember yourself, you who defeated the Rupa, you who slew the Dogs of Asak, and do not fear."

He decided to answer aloud. "I do not feel so brave, this night." He waited a moment, then continued. "I do not feel so brave, many nights. I am often tired and I am often afraid."

"That, too, is part of being a hero," came the answer. Was that the voice of his dream? It seemed so, yet somehow unalike. "You have stayed alive. Remain so!" There was a liquid, golden laugh. "And remember you are not alone."

"Who are you?" he cried. A wind was starting to blow, clearing the mists from around him.

"I am Diba. But I speak through my priestess Jola." The voice paused a moment. Then, again came laughter, rich, deep, yet fully feminine. "Be good to my Jola. I think she likes thee."

There came a howling as of many wolves or perhaps it was only the winds, swirling through the shrine. Donzalo saw a faint light finding its way through the high windows. He went to the door. Yes, there was a rosy dawn spreading across the Cuddonian hills.

The golden-haired woman of his seeming dream stood outside the door. "You should be safe now, brave Donzalo. The new year is come."

9

The Yule is a time of cheer. It is a time, as well, to leave behind the past, to greet the promises of a new year. For Donzalo Rosam, the dawn of the Yule brought him before Vantare, Thane of Drolwym.

Guesare had come at dawn to escort him back to the keep, evincing little surprise at seeing his sister waiting with the young Laman. He had learned to be surprised by nothing Jola did. While he helped Guesare into his knightly raiment, she slipped away, not to be seen again that day.

Into the Great Hall in Keep Drolwym they strode. It was not that great a hall, really, and one of several scattered through that haphazard edifice, but it was so designated. There awaited the thane, the Lady Se, family, friends, kitchen maids, stable boys — pretty much anyone in the castle who cared to come. And since it was a holiday, that meant almost everyone.

The minstrel did note the absence of his other sister, Nosana. She had probably been up all night casting spells to counter those of Jola. Guesare did not doubt at all now that the woman had become an ally of Lord Radal.

Lord Radal — well, what his mother had told him of their liaison was still sinking in. The one thing of which he was sure was that he hated the man no less than before.

Donzalo went forward to stand before the thane, resplendent in white and gold. The young man was in white and gold, that is; the thane was wearing an old greenish kilt and an untucked shirt, but his wife had prevailed upon him to thrown an only slightly patched cloak on over them.

There was no kneeling here. That went against Cuddonian sensibilities. Following a brief recitation of vows, Donzalo handed his sword to Vantare, who had to reach up to tap the tall Laman on each shoulder with the blade, before handing it back. "I name thee knight," he said. "Sir Donzalo!"

The crowd didn't exactly roar but they applauded vigorously enough before going in search of their breakfasts. Some, it is to be suspected, even went back to bed, to rise later for this day of feasting and gifting and much drinking as the Yule log burned into the night.

Ansa, known to friends and theater-goers in the capital as Maresta and to some, elsewhere, as Posena, sat by herself on the day of the Yule. It came as no surprise to her that she was alone.

Fachalana would be at her father's house, no doubt, and probably at court later. She would have no time for her friend — friend only when she needed her, someone she permitted to address her familiarly but did not truly let into her circle. So, here she was in this empty theater. At least it was the best lodging she had ever had in Celatas.

Back in the Anian realm, her people didn't celebrate this day anyway. Oh, they marked the solstice with a religious observance but nothing more. But no one here knew she was truly Ani. They thought only that she played one on stage!

She found herself wandering about the building, wrapped in fur against the chill. Ansa had grown up wearing fur, on the high steppes. It would be good to see them again, to hug her spy-master brother and tell him she was done with this life.

And if she threw off this life, what couldn't she do? Where couldn't she go? There was one place she would like to go and it was not in the Anian Empire nor was the young man who lived there of her blood. She wondered where he was now, that tall Laman she had kissed once at Harvest Festival, before she fled into the night.

Nosana had made an appearance. It had been brief, and she had been surly and seemed very tired, but she took her place at the main table — she always assumed she belonged there and none was willing to tell her otherwise — where she picked at her high-heaped plate before pushing it aside and excusing herself.

"It is most unusual for Nosana to lose her appetite," whispered Mausare to Lanta, his wife, "but it certainly improves mine to see her leave."

The woman, who appeared about half his size, did not disagree. "Don't throw your pudding, deary," she said to the little girl seated between them. Their other four children were spread along the table on either side.

The toddler squirmed and then held out her arms. "Unca Donni!" she squealed.

"Sir Donzalo can't hold you right now," said her father. "Let him eat in peace."

"It's all right, kinsman Mausare. Lift her over to me. Oh, never mind." The little girl had slipped under the table and was climbing into his lap. "Here you go, my darling." He pulled her on up so she could stare triumphantly across the board at her parents.

"Have you any children at home?" asked Lanta.

Donzalo lied. "No ma'am." How could he explain his past with the Lady Lomela and how it had gotten him into all his difficulties? "I've yet to take a wife."

She looked to her husband. "It wouldn't be hard to find him one."

"Indeed not, my dear," Mausare laughed. "A younger son such as you could do worse than to find an heiress here in the Cuddon," he told Donzalo. "You are not, um, like our brother Guesare, are you?" He glanced toward the minstrel, seated beside his mother at the head table.

"Don't be silly, Mausare," said Lanta. "Didn't you hear about him and Nosana?"

The Cuddonian's eyes widened some at that. "No, I do not gossip in the halls with all the wives of Drolwym."

"Your loss, husband mine. But," she added, "there are some parts to the story you might not like anyway."

Donzalo felt himself reddening as the two off-handedly discussed his misadventure. "In truth," Lanta said, turning back to the young

Laman, "I am one of the priestesses of Rema. I heard most of the tale from the Lady Se."

"Then you probably know that I recall almost nothing of it," he answered.

"But you remember who saved you." She gave her husband a somewhat wary sideways glance. "She may well have saved you again, last night, with the aid of our circle."

Mausare grasped her meaning. "You are speaking of Jola." His wife only nodded.

"That was long ago, my Lanta, so long that it seems no more than a dream now." He shook his head. "And I do not remember whether it was a good dream or a bad one — only that I awakened from it," he concluded, speaking as much to himself as to his companions.

"We will return to our farm on the morrow, Donzalo. It lies not far away; visit if you can."

"Copago." The count motioned for his master of arms to approach. "You needn't be here. Go home to your family."

"Are you certain, sir? They do not expect me this early."

"Then surprise them, and kiss your pretty wife and daughter for me. And —" Borrago appeared uncertain as to whether he should continue. "And wish your mother well."

"That I will, my lord." He looked squarely at this man whom he knew to be his father and spoke frankly. Copago ever spoke frankly, or not at all. "She always wishes well for you.

"And I wish the blessing of the Yule on you and all your family, sir." With a slight bow to his liege, he turned and strode from the hall.

As he went to take his place at the high table, Borrago smiled to himself at the thought of this solid, serious man in the little cottage he called home, outside the castle walls and all the turmoil of the keep, with his girl on his knee and his loving wife beside him.

And, yes, his mother there too, long a widow for the second time. She had been a couple years older than he, the widow of one of his father's officers. Count Ros has seen to it that she was quickly married again when he learned she was bearing Borrago's child.

Ros's own widow, the Lady Vibola, was not with them today. Borrago feared that his mother's time was drawing to an end. Most of her days she spent in her own chambers, huddled by the fire and listening to the old tales and songs she loved so much.

Would that Donzalo were here! He always seemed to bring cheer to his grandmother. But the Lady Lomela, aye, and her friend, the diplomat Nafal, visited often with the old woman. He should find time, too, while there was time.

He reached down to feed a scrap of venison to the pup that lolled at his feet. "You spoil that dog, Father," said Bolos, seated, as was customary, to his right. Bolos was drinking some hot, dark liquid brewed of herbs. He had not touched wine for months.

"Well, your boy isn't here to spoil at the moment." He looked beyond his son to the very obviously pregnant Lady Lomela. "Though soon he will have even more competition."

"I caught the young rascal trying to get at the berries on the garlands, this morning. If he'd gotten into them, you might have had one less grandson."

"Do not say such things, husband, even in jest!" exclaimed Lomela.

"My apologies, wife," Bolos said, briefly taking her hand to kiss it.

"He is standing?" asked the count.

"Yes, Lord Borrago," answered the princess. "And tottering about as well."

"Hmm. Donzalo was an early walker. I am afraid you, my boy," he said to Bolos, "would not get off your fat behind until you were over a year in age."

"And, these days, it seems my brother has taken to outstripping me again. Is there any more news of him, sir?"

"No, only the one letter that said he arrived safely in the Cuddon. It is best that no messengers go back and forth that might be followed."

"Oh." Bolos gazed out over the crowd of Yule feasters. "Yes, that makes sense. Who knows who might be a spy here." His eyes rested on the two Sharshites, seated close by. Not being an official ambassador, Jobareth had no place at the high table.

"I trust Nafal, husband," Lomela asserted in a low voice. "Of his companion, Blen, I am not so sure."

Both noblemen nodded in agreement. They, as well, were suspicious of Sir Blen, that quiet shadow of the young diplomat.

"Well, that is not something to worry about on this day," said Count Borrago, raising his goblet. "Let us drink to the fellowship of the season. And also," he added, "to the health of my newest knight, Sir Corgos. May his Yule bring him all that for which he wishes!"

10

"You are learning to speak Krevod passingly well."

"I've not much else to occupy my time around here," said Donzalo. "It seems to have much in common with the Old Sharshic I've seen in books."

"They speak that tongue still in some of the remote villages of Sharsh. And yes, it is similar to our speech here."

A group of children waylaid the pair at the bottom of the stairs. "Sing us a song, Uncle Guessy," demanded their apparent leader. The minstrel sat himself down on the steps above them and took out his rebec. "Hold this, will you?" he asked the largest boy, handing him the leather bag. The youngsters formed a circle on the floor in front of him.

"I fear I did not have time to write a proper ode for you, Donni," he told the young man, looking up to where he stood just above him. "But there is this —" He strummed the instrument and began.

Donzalo's deeds are all the talk,
I hear he did wondrous things;
He took old Asak's dogs for a walk
And clipped the Rupa's wings!

Donzalo's deeds are wise and just,
And widely sung by the bards;
They say he is a man to trust,
Who never cheats at cards!

"My brother cheats," interjected a small girl.

"No I don't," the boy in question objected.

Donzalo's deeds make maidens swoon
And villains shake with fear;
He often visits the man in the moon,
Just to bring the old fellow a beer!

That brought shrieks of laughter from his audience.

Donzalo's deeds are known by all,
The lowly and the well bred;
And maybe if he weren't so tall
He wouldn't bump his head!

One little boy jumped up and held his head, staggering about saying, "Ow! Ow!" In a few seconds, two others had joined him.

"Sorry about all that, Donni, it's just something I threw off for the little ones," said Guesare, turning again to his companion. He was surprised to see the young Laman seated on the stairs, his eyes misting.

"You've a marvelous home, Guesare," he said. "I don't know why you ever leave it."

"Neither do I, my friend. At least I have the sense to come back." He rose to his feet. "So what's to do today? If you get bored enough, you *will* want to leave Drolwym."

"I'd like to ride in the countryside. It's fine weather and I've seen nothing of your father's lands."

"That could be dangerous. We should see what the thane thinks. Or, what my mother thinks, I suppose I should say. She'll have a better idea of the risks."

"You think there are those here who seek my life," Donzalo stated.

"I do," answered Guesare. "There had to be a reason you were assailed during your vigil and Mother seemed to know it would happen. And then," he continued, "Nosana might have normally only tried to seduce you, not murder you as well. Though I suspect she would have enjoyed doing both.

"Ah, boy, I tried to bring you to a place of safety and I seem to have made matters worse."

"Then let us speak with your parents and see what is to be done. And I — I would like to see your sister Jola again too. Is she ever about?"

"Friend Donzalo, if you are to see Jola, it will be when she wishes."

Radal was impressed. "You made your way through all my wardings. Did you even know they were there?"

"Wardings, Father?" Fachalana was puzzled. "I — I picked a lock and found your hiding places. What else was there?"

"No one should have found those 'hiding places.' No one except a very skilled student of the art." He sighed. "I might have know you had talent." He shook his had and looked at his daughter. "But you've never shown it. Twenty and two years years you are, and never an inkling!

"Why, I could barely discern that anything had been disturbed." He gave her a stern look. "It's not the first time you've done this, either, is it?"

The dark-haired young woman shrank from her father's glare. "No, sir."

"So what do I do with you, my girl?" She noted that his tone now showed more amusement — and perhaps even a bit of approval — than anger. This is an opportunity, she thought to herself.

"Make me your apprentice!"

Lord Radal was surprised. Moreover, he seemed truly appalled by the idea. "No! I will not have you as damned as I am." He turned away from her. "Do not enter my study again. And never speak to me of studying the art!"

"My only wish is for a blizzard so that you might be snowed in here."

"You would wear me out, my love. I might not survive!" protested Corgos. "And then you would be a widow all over again."

"I was better off a widow than married to my first husband." Tiana raised herself on one elbow. "But I have a much better one now, so I'll try not to kill him. Well, maybe I'll try a little." She rolled atop her new spouse and kissed him. "I'm glad we didn't wait, even if you do have to return to Castle Rosam."

"Mmm. I'm certain, my dear, that Sir Paren suggested we marry now just to be sure I came back. As if I could resist your allure, wed or not."

"Well spoken, my captain! We'll make a courtier of you yet."

"I will be well content to serve as Paren's new master of arms."

"Ah, then that is the only reason you married me?" she chided.

"I fear I have ruined my new career as a courtier already. I may end up being no more than your kept man."

"Well, I'll keep you for a while, sir. Now let's see you *earn* your keep!"

"This fine weather can not last much longer," remarked Guesare. "Why, I've even glimpsed patches of blue sky over the past few days!"

"I had heard that one never sees the sun in the Cuddon," Donzalo said.

"These hills are not always gray." Around them lay the colorless, rolling countryside. A flock of crows skimmed the brushy ridge-line, to disappear into the distance. Their caws might still be heard minutes later, across the still morning air.

And there were sheep. Many sheep. This land was not so steep and inhospitable as the Lower Cuddon they had traversed a few weeks earlier.

"Mausare's stead lies not far in that direction." The minstrel pointed toward what Donzalo thought was the north-west. It was hard to get ones bearings here. "He ran off while still a youngster to be a mercenary and came back with enough wealth to buy a quite sizable place.

"And up ahead, some, are the temples of Jov and Esefa. They are the largest shrines for leagues around and the hill on which they stand is considered neutral ground," Guesare told him. "So it becomes a favored meeting place for our cantankerous clans. None would dare break truce there."

"Where is your mother's temple? Or, I should say, Rema's."

"We passed it already. It is no more than ancient stones standing on a hilltop."

Donzalo stood in his saddle and looked about. "Ah, that high spot back there? Then I truly am glad that I made my vigil elsewhere!"

"It would have been colder but, perhaps, just as safe. I — I consider Rema my patroness and protector." The minstrel seemed a bit embarrassed to admit to the rustic Cuddonian beneath his worldly exterior.

"He chose well, brother mine."

"Jola! How do you do that?" Guesare turned to his companion. "She is ever creeping up and taking me unawares." He scowled, albeit good-naturedly, at the woman who stood beside his steed. "I think it was her favorite game when we were children."

"But it was so easy. You were always engrossed with yourself, even then."

Donzalo bowed to her from the saddle. "My greetings to you, Lady Jola."

"A good morning to thee, my brave new knight." She whistled lowly and an unsaddled stallion, all dappled of gray, came up. Jola vaulted easily onto its back.

"I would ride with thee a way."

She straddled her mount, not riding side-saddle as did most noblewomen, loose, unadorned white gown clinging to supple legs, her curling golden hair falling unbound to the small of her back.

For a few minutes, they traveled in silence, the siblings seeming to have nothing to say to each other, Donzalo unwilling to break in. Then Jola turned to her brother. "Mother finally spoke to thee of my sire."

"You knew?" asked Guesare.

"I have touched his mind from afar though he did not know it. Nor does he know I exist." Jola's voice remained steady, controlled. "It is a mind near-lost to darkness and despair. Only his great will has kept him from falling further.

"That is a brink on which I have stood myself."

"I know that, Sister. I have often feared for you."

"Yes, little brother, and I have known that." She turned, smiling, to Donzalo. "Near three years of age I have on him, yet Guesare has ever made himself my protector. He thought nothing of it to stand between me and his half-brothers, though they towered over him."

"It was more often my half-sisters. But they towered over me as well!"

The trio crossed over a ridge. Below them lay a farmhouse of good size, surrounded by a number of low, seemingly well-maintained out-buildings. Men and women could be seen working about the barns and sheep-pens. "Here is Mausare's cot. Do you wish to visit, Donzalo?"

Donzalo looked upon the scene with little interest, before turning his gaze to their companion.

"Go home, Brother," said Jola. "I shall tend to sweet Donzalo."

The minstrel looked into the dark, unwavering eyes of his sister and then to Donzalo. The younger man slowly nodded his assent. "Very well. I deem him safe in your protection. Safe *from* you, I am not so sure." And so saying, he turned and rode back toward Drolwym Keep.

11

Vanob recognized the two horses in the corral. Their owners had never showed up at their rendezvous. Could they be at this inn?

He'd best be cautious. They were the roughest of scoundrels and wouldn't hesitate to knife him if they felt it in their interest. The soldier slipped through the doorway and quickly looked about. "Perdos," he said.

The man he greeted glanced up from his tankard and put a hand to his sword. Vanob raised his own hands to show he meant no harm.

Perdos looked him over a moment and then waved him to the seat opposite his own. "Vanob, as I live. What brings you here?"

"The same as you, I would guess. Sojel disbanded our company and I'm at loose ends."

"Bring my guest some ale," Perdos called to the innkeeper.

"'Tis too late in the season for ale," the little man reminded him as he set a flagon down before Vanob. "But I've beer aplenty." He smiled at his new guest. "I have to keep telling him that."

"Aye, my own father brewed." He tasted of his beer as though it were a fine wine. "Pretty damned good, innkeeper."

"Thank you, sir. Will you be staying the night?"

Vanob looked slightly uncomfortable. "He is," said Perdos. "I'll foot the bill."

"That's good of you, friend," Vanob said, after their landlord walked away. "I've not had much profit lately. But you —" He wasn't sure he should continue but did anyway. "You seem to have found a couple of horses." He raised his eyebrows in an unspoken question.

"Yes, Van, I slew their owners and good riddance to them." He almost slammed his tankard down. "You and I, we're soldiers and there's good and bad that comes with that. But those two —" He shook his head. "Scum."

"Our comrades, none the less."

"I'd already left the company."

"Deserted, you mean."

Perdos disliked the accusation in this man's tone, though it was disguised as easy banter. "I owed them nothing. Nor Sojel. And not you."

"Very well, man. I was simply curious. It's naught to me." Vanob looked about him. His voice now became ingratiating. "So, a nice place. You staying the winter?" Perdos only nodded. "Maybe I could hang around here, too."

"As you will." The tall soldier rose to his feet. "I like to walk down by the river at this time of the day. Say, why don't you come with me and I'll show you the lay of the land. We can have some supper after."

"Sounds good," said Vanob. He smirked slightly as he followed his former comrade out the door. He might be able to milk this dummy all winter and then maybe even turn him in to Sojel when the company re-formed in the spring. The sergeant would reward him, wouldn't he?

An half-hour later, Perdos returned. "It seems my friend won't be staying after all," he told the innkeeper. "But he, um, sold me his horse."

And the bargaining, the knight congratulated himself, had gone very well.

Nosana had discovered this cave, far below the keep, when still a small girl, hiding from her father's moods and anger. She knew the thane hated her, had cast her aside, given the love that was her right to his young wife and her detested step-sister, so beautiful, and she so ugly and fat.

And he blamed her for her mother's death. "She was only the first I killed," she whispered to herself.

She had found another to love her, here in the darkness. Nosana had not been sure he was real. She was still not certain. Asak, this presence had named itself, and showed her things of which she could never have dreamed on her own. Could she have?

All around her, here, stood her coven. These were real. She had brought them to this place, taught them, made them hers. She was as a goddess when among them, a tall great goddess who would destroy all before her.

Ah, but two nights agone they had failed. She had failed. Throughout the darkness of the darkest of all nights, they had surrounded the little temple of Diba, contending with those who would oppose them. If the young supplicant had stepped out, left his protection, however briefly, the coven would have had him, torn him apart in a frenzy of lust and madness. Within, he had the protection of the Huntress and that they could not breech.

She did not like having to send a messenger of the night to the great sorcerer who set her this task, telling him of her failure. Twice, now, though there had been no need to mention the humiliation of her first attempt to destroy Donzalo.

"Sisters!" She cried, her voice harsh, awash with all the consuming hatred she contained. "The great battle is to come. Prepare yourselves to conquer or to go into the endless dark!"

"The dark! The dark!" came their response and Nosana, for a moment, forgot the pain of life.

"I saw the two of you above my home, this morning," said Mausare, "and Jola."

"Is that why you are visiting the keep, so soon after you left?" asked his half-brother. The three men sat before a smoldering peat fire in one of the common rooms.

Mausare nodded. "My step-sister frightens me and I fear for you, Donzalo. Her flame burns too brightly and I was near consumed by it."

"So you were," said Guesare. "I remember, though I was still a boy." Donzalo said nothing, but only listened to the two.

"Ah, I was young, too, Guesare, and she even younger. Children, truly, yet she so wise and I so foolish."

"I wanted to put a knife into you."

The big Cuddonian laughed. "I sometimes wanted to put a knife into myself."

Donzalo spoke at last. "Children?" was his only question.

"Aye, Donzalo, we were children. I was, what, sixteen, Guesare? And your sister two years the younger — just become a woman."

"It was a hard time for her, Brother. I know that now and lay no blame on you."

"Yes, she was only awakening to herself. But now, she is full of power. And so beautiful —

"She is dangerous, Donzalo. She does not mean to be but she might take the both of you into madness."

Guesare spoke. "You are susceptible, my brother, to such madness. It is in you, as it is in our father." He leaned forward to warm his hands at the fire. "Our Donzalo is one of the most level-headed fellows I've ever come across.

"Still, boy," he said to the Laman, "be careful. Might I ask how you and the Lady Jola passed your day? You need not tell me if you have no wish."

"We rode," said Donzalo. "We rode and spoke of many things." He leaned back, and continued as if remembering a dream. "She showed me how beautiful this land of yours is, from its rocky bones to the ever-changing skies above. I think I could stay here, Guesare. I truly think I could."

"My father is actually encouraging my theatrical projects now."

"Trying to keep you out of trouble, my lady?" teased Maresta.

Fachalana turned and looked squarely at the actress. "Yes, exactly. I fear I shall no longer be able to access his papers, now that he has found me out." She gave a quite theatrical shrug, extending her arms with studied grace. Maresta was used to such dramatic gestures from her friend and patroness; indeed, she quite expected them.

"But the increase in my allowance somewhat makes up for that."

"Then we can repair the dressing rooms. My quarters are terribly drafty."

"Yes, yes, of course. It is cold in here, isn't it? I'll give you the money to take care of it." She shifted the conversation away from the boredom of business. "My Jobareth is undertaking to write a play for me."

So he's *her* Jobareth? Maresta wondered if he knew that. "That is excellent news. Will you take the lead?"

"I'm not sure. Do you think I could play Oemse?"

"Hmm, she died in the story, didn't she?"

"I can die quite well," sniffed Fachalana, before laughing. "I know, I would ham it up horribly. And she doesn't even get to use a sword. I wonder if I could prevail upon Jobo to rewrite that bit of history."

12

There was a cottage. It was a simple cottage, a little sod-roofed house nestled in a hollow of the hills. There, one afternoon, Jola brought Donzalo.

They had ridden together often, these past few days, knowing such a time would come. It was as though they stood upon a shore and watched a great wave loom on the horizon, knowing it would rise up, engulf them, sweep them away.

"From a distance I saw thee, that evening Guesare brought thee down to the great hall. I think I loved thee then," the priestess confessed to him. "And it frightened me, so I ran away."

"I, frighten you, my lady?"

"Not you, sweet Donni. Love has not turned out well for me. Nay, nor for those I might love."

That was when he had first kissed her, leaning over from his saddle. She was not loath to meet his lips with hers.

And in her candle-lit cottage, in her great soft down bed, they first made love and her golden hair fell all about her golden body and upon Donzalo. He forgot all other women but this one, this goddess-touched beauty. It was simple: he loved.

How greatly might a man love?

No more greatly than a woman. At last, in this young hero, barely more than a boy, the priestess had found forgetfulness as well, forgetfulness of all other men, of a world in which she had found no peace, of a life of endless longing. It had been as though she had sought long for a home that never was, remembered only in dreams, and had now returned.

She wept, but did not let Donzalo see.

Later, as they lay together in her bower, scented of smoke and of herbs and of the pines that called to the winds of night, the intricately carved roof beams dim above them, Jola sang to him a song, a lullaby.

What shadow does a shadow cast?
How long does forever last?
Where sleeps the wind before it blows?
Where is love when it goes?

If I passed beyond the sea,
would you wait and watch for me?
If I crossed the mountains high,
would you pray for wings to fly?

Who am I without my name?
Are the gods or we to blame?
Why must dreams fade with the dawn?
Where is love once it is gone?

If I passed beyond the sea,
would you wait and watch for me?
If I crossed the mountains high,
would you pray for wings to fly?

Could a man count every star?
Why are all things as they are?
Do you love me when you sleep?
Answer these or silence keep.

"I love you always, asleep and awake, alive, dead. As for the other questions — they do not matter."

"No, they do not, my love," Jola had answered in the darkness, and wrapped her arms about him as she drifted into sleep.

Why should he not stay in this land, stay with this woman, be Uncle Donni to all the children of the keep? he wondered, lying there beside her. She was not that much older than he — a decade was nothing.

Ah, but their differences went far beyond age. She was wise, wise beyond any woman he had ever known. Would he ever be more than a boy beside her?

Donazalo could answer that riddle no more than he could those Jola had sung to him. And perhaps, as with them, it did not matter.

Nosana watched for her opportunity. It would come.

Another message had arrived from the great sorcerer Radal. She liked to say the name — Radal. It made her feel as if he were here.

She sometimes thought of that powerful, far-away man when she took pleasure. What would it be like to have such a lover? To feel contempt neither for her partner nor for herself?

Perhaps when she destroyed the boy — yes, and her cursed step-sister as well — he might reward her. She shivered at the thought that she might go to him, know his touch.

His missive had been short and pointed. Wait, it said. There will be a moment of weakness and she must be prepared to attack, she and all her circle. And then — ah, then would darkness triumph!

"My old friend Corgos returned today."

"Oh? And how is married life treating him?" asked Mistress Sima.

"Very well, it seems. It was about time he settled down, Mother."

"Not all men are as domestic as you, my son." The younger woman who sat by the fire, stirring a kettle, snickered. Copago winked at her.

"I think my mother means I am stodgy."

"You needn't tell me that," responded his wife. "The whole keep thinks you're stodgy." She rose from her low stool and smoothed her apron. "Yet we love you anyway."

"Humph. I prefer to think of myself as dependable."

"That you are," said Sima, "and always have been." The two women looked at each other and nodded in agreement. They understood the man in their life.

Copago looked fondly from the one to the other, his mother, slender almost to the point of being gaunt, his much rounder spouse, Janona. He was content to be here, to be with them and to serve his count — what else need a man?

Ah, the count. "Lord Borrago asked after you today. Again."

Mistress Sima smiled wanly. "Then give him my regards, boy. If he wants more, that is up to him."

Janona raised her eyebrows at her mother-in-law. Of course, she knew of her history with the count, that he was father to Copago, but Sima had never before shown interest in any renewal of their acquaintance.

"What can I say?" stated the older woman, shrugging. "Persistence pays."

"So, we shall send yet another envoy to Tod-ford, much good that it will do." Lareth tossed the sheaf of documents onto the floor beside his carven chair.

"As you will, my king. Better diplomats than troops — at least for now."

"Indeed," replied Lareth. "What of our other concern in Lama?"

"The boy is in the Cuddon, with his kin there."

"At Drolwym? You rode there once, didn't you, Radal?"

"Three decades ago, when your father had banished me. For a time, I rode many places." Some, not of this world, the mage remembered.

"He was certain you were a bad influence, even though your father had served him well."

"Yet remained a mercenary and an outsider until the day he fell in battle. I think, still, there are those here who think no differently of me." Radal gazed long into the blazing fire before them.

"Sharsh has been invaded too many times. The people fear all outsiders. Even," said the king, with the faintest of smiles, "those who were born here.

"Is there anything we can do about this Donzalo now? Is he beyond our reach?"

Radal turned to his king, the one man in the world he was willing to serve. "Not entirely, sire. We could try more assassins but at that distance they are even less likely to succeed than before. But I do have, ah, shall we say contacts at Drolwym. I fear that they be poor tools for the job." He thought of the pitiable woman who sent him messages from the Cuddon, at once obsequious and flirtatious. "Yet perhaps they might succeed where others have not.

"I wonder, though, if there is any point in all this. You know as well as I, Lareth, that prophecies, by their nature, can not be undone."

"I will not turn from my course, Radal. This threat will be destroyed if I have to ride into Lama myself at the head of my army."

"This changes things," Ansa wrote. "If F. no longer has access to her father's papers, she is of far less value to us. I wonder if there is any point in my remaining in Celatas.

"There is also the question of N. It is inevitable that he would see me and know me when he returns to the capital. From the looks he gave me when we met in Lama —" No, Ansa thought, don't mention the place. There was always the slight chance of interception and it did not do to name names. She blacked it out and continued. "— when we met before, I am sure he thought he already knew me from somewhere. I've no doubt he has seen me on the stage at some time."

Perhaps that was too much information, as well. Let's change that to "at the theater," she decided.

"Please tell me what I should do, my brother. Is it time I slip away from this role?"

She looked at the page before her and, for a moment, wondered if she might ask him for news about Donzalo. No, no, she told herself, she'd best not. The job was her concern now and when that was over, who knew?

Ansa would miss Celatas. She would miss the theater and she would even miss Fachalana.

"A," she signed and sealed the message, ready to hand off to the courier.

13

They were content. What more can one say, how better describe? For those few mid-winter weeks, Jola and Donzalo knew only each other, allowing the world beyond to go its way without them. But even love can not keep out the rest of life forever.

It began with a barking of dogs, distant, barely heard. Jola turned uneasily, sensing something amiss, a bad dream finding its way into her peaceful slumber. She felt Donzalo by her side and was comforted. Then the howling grew more loud and insistent, filling the dark night of a new moon.

The priestess sat up, instantly awake. "Donzalo!" She shook her young lover. "Awaken, Donzalo!"

He raised himself onto one elbow. "What is it, my love?"

"It is come. Prepare for the attack of darkness." Jola stood naked, facing the door, a long wand of silvery-white wood grasped firmly in her upraised hands. Silvery-white, too, was the light that slowly grew about her.

Donzalo leapt from the bed, taking up his long, heavy, straight blade, the sword with which he had been made knight. To his momentary surprise, he found that it was beginning to glow with that same silver light. There was no time to think about that now.

"Diba's people have warned us," said Jola. "Hear them all about us now!" The howling of wolves echoed through the night, yes, and the barking of every farm dog for a league around. "Whether they can aid us, I do not know.

"It will not do to be trapped here. Let us face them in the open." Donzalo stepped in front of her, sword ready, and passed first through the door. Jola smiled the briefest of smiles at his protectiveness — she should be the one protecting here.

The night was clear, the sky filled with the cold light of stars, the moon a darkened disk. A dusting of snow lay on the pines rising around them.

On an open rise stood cloaked figures and, in their middle, one taller who raised a heavy, twisted staff, a ghastly green light flickering about its shaft.

The lady Se awakened as well and knew the attack was upon them. Some of her circle were here in the keep, others scattered to their homes. All knew that this time would come and had kept watch.

She called to her serving girl. "Go, gather the others. The battle is begun!" The young woman, an attendant of Rema's temple herself, understood immediately and, wrapping herself in a gray cloak, hurried to fulfill her errand.

Se went quickly down the twisting stone corridor to her son's quarters, which lay near. She found him waiting and, with him, her husband.

The thane spoke. "They are being attacked, aren't they? Be not so surprised, wife, I do know what is going on about here at times." Vantare's voice became grave. "It is well that he has the Prince's sword."

"You recognized it?" asked Se.

"How could I not when he handed it to me at his knighting? It was wise of Mausare to give it to the boy.

"But he'll need more than one sword, won't he? Shall we gather men and ride, Guesare?"

Se shook her head. "You have no chance of breaking through the enchantments laid round them." To Guesare she said, "You, my son, might."

"Then I shall ride," said the minstrel and hastened away.

"And I shall follow, even if it be of no use."

As the thane went to assemble a troop, the lady made her way quickly to the castle gate. Many of her priestesses were gathered there already, silent and somber. "Should we go to the temple?" one asked.

"No," replied Se. "What we can do, we can do here. Follow me." She stepped out into the open field before the keep, doffing her garments as she went, so she might stand naked before the Great Mother.

The rest followed her and at cottages and farmhouses all about, women came forth to stand with them.

A cat as black as the blackest of hells, as black as night without stars or moon, its eyes a cold and insatiable green, seemed to tower behind Nosana, to somehow merge with her, to *be* her. Before her stood a great silver she-wolf, bristling in defense of Jola, but also rising from her. Each had been possessed by her goddess, each partook of the nature of one of these elemental forces that mortals named Diba the Archer or the Lady of the Dark Moon.

And if those goddesses existed on their own or were created and channeled by the powerful women who called upon them, even the wisest of sages can not truly say. Nor do the wisest believe it matters.

There were flesh-and-blood wolves there, as well, circling outside the enchanted arena in which the two sorceresses strove. And now, too, there were man-like figures slipping out of the darkness into the magelight, standing, watching. Others, thought Donzalo. Which side are they on?

On the horizon, he spied a faint, ruddy light, akin to the glow of a welcoming hearth, and knew instinctively that it was the work of the Lady Se and her goddess. Did it bring more strength to his Jola? He prayed that it would, prayed to a goddess he did not know in a land where he was a stranger.

The members of the dark coven were keening, crouching, contorting themselves, and the same sickly light that had emanated from their leader began to rise all about them. Fantastical shapes seemed to overlay them, creatures of another realm. Donzalo remembered well his last encounter with such, his battle against the hounds of Asak.

From the corner of his eye, he saw a horseman riding hard toward them, dismounting and rushing to the edge of the enchanted circle, only to be stopped by its magic. Guesare, he realized, come to my aid once again. But maybe he can't help this time. He turned his gaze back to the enemies before him.

Now he saw that each cloaked woman was opening the way for a creature, as solid a being as had been those hounds, yet somehow the coven seemed also linked to the monsters that came forth. And what monsters! Some were as bloated cats that yowled with the voices of the damned and others hideous rat-like beings. There were slugs that might be snakes and things with wings that should never fly. Donzalo held his sword, this strange sword he had been given, and waited for them.

A slender pale man — no, not quite a man — came forth from the gloom to stand by Guesare's side. Together, they raised their hands and where the power of one had not been enough, two began to make an impact. Slowly, a glowing fissure, a narrow door, opened before the pair and they forced their way through.

"The witches have called forth their familiars," said the stranger, in a high lilting voice. He stood as tall as the Cuddonian but was very lean and lightly made. His skin was the color of snow. Both drew their swords, Guesare briefly cursing himself for not taking the time to prepare his pistols.

All the while, a battle that could be sensed more than seen was raging between Jola and Nosana. To those that watched, it seemed that the great wolf and panther were locked in combat, each trying to reach and rend the others throat and the women beneath them appeared nebulous, hardly there, yet they were the ones truly battling. Deep in their magical trances, they stood unseeing, all attention focused upon their opponent.

But the men did not have the time to watch, for the beasts were upon them. More properly, perhaps, they were attempting to get past them, to attack Jola where she stood battling in her magical trance. Donzalo, by himself, would never have succeeded against them.

Three armed warriors was another matter, yet still the results were far from assured. These creatures were not easy to kill and would try to dodge past the men, no matter how wounded, entrails dragging behind them, as they sought to reach the priestess of Diba. The men hacked and stabbed and Donzalo occasionally kicked and stomped effectively with his long legs, preventing their advance. Each time one was finally slain, its mistress could be seen to slump and fall on the hill where they stood, not dead but clearly shaken.

Your power was never enough, Jola told her enemy, *even when the moon is hidden.*

If my servants reach you, it will not matter, came Nosana's reply, in a voice as harsh and ugly as her true spirit. The two women had been slowly moving toward each other, a step at a time, barely aware of it in their trance state.

A huge black rat, it's back covered with oozing ulcers, leapt upon Guesare and bit him deeply on the shoulder before rolling off him, skewered. As the minstrel fell, some winged thing hopped over him and reached Jola before they could halt it.

Only for a moment did it reach her before Donzalo's long sword cut it asunder, but it was enough. Jola was hurt, with a gash on her calf. Jola was distracted in a battle that needed all her focused will.

It seemed as if the monstrous cat locked its jaws on the wolf's throat and shook her. Jola sagged, reeled, before catching herself. For a moment, the wolf broke free of its enemy. How long could she survive, now, wounded?

Guesare had regained his feet but he was sorely hurt, the blood running from the deep puncture to his right shoulder. He would not be able to wield a sword much longer but he took a long dagger into his left hand, ready to fight on.

"Use the sword, mortal brother," the stranger said to Donzalo. "Only it can prevail against yon sorceress now. I will stand here with Guesare." He paused to aim a blow at one of their assailants. "Go!"

Donzalo rushed forward, swinging his sword wildly, scattering the familiars as he tried to reach Nosana. He could not, for that great black shadow, that monstrous panther, reached down and nonchalantly batted him away with a paw like a battering ram.

So, it's real, thought the Laman. Then it can be hurt.

Indeed, the avatars had become increasingly solid as their combat progressed, the magical combat manifesting itself physically and the two inextricably linked. Now Nosana-cat had again taken Jola-wolf by the throat and had her down. A desperate Donzalo, gathering all his strength, leapt upon the great beast's back, sword in hand, and stabbed deeply.

Maybe another sword would not have had the same effect. Maybe it would not have hurt a creature made of magic, a creature that was ultimately unreal. This sword that glowed with the silver light of Diba was another matter.

In a great convulsion, the panther threw him clear. Donzalo landed hard and was dazed but could see, above him, the two enemies, each locked on the others throat, neither willing to relinquish her grip. All around, the sorcerous wall that had enclosed them flickered, silver and green and flame and darkness contending.

And then it fell in a tumult of fire and the earth trembled. The familiars ran and were easily slain by the wolves who now rushed in and who hunted what remained of the coven over the hills until not one remained alive.

On the ground lay Donzalo as one dead. By him lay the two women.

Guesare and his companion approached them. "The boy is alive," said the Cuddonian, placing his hand on Donzalo's chest. "*She* is not." He looked toward the twisted corpse of Nosana.

The pale man held his ear close to Jola's heart. "She, too, is gone. Ah, Jola, how I loved thee!" He rose and took up the blade Donzalo had dropped.

"The sword has fulfilled its task," said the Prince. "I shall take it home now."

14

Lord Radal felt as if something had been ripped from him, a part of his soul he had not known existed.

And over the leagues, his mind suddenly sensed another that suffered the same anguish. It was a mind he remembered, that he knew, that he had touched and allowed to touch him. *Se,* he whispered.

Radal? She tried to hide herself from him but it was too late.

A daughter? We had a daughter? Ah, she was powerful!

Yes, and beautiful. I would not have had you corrupt her.

How? Through her eyes he saw all that had happened, saw his own minion destroy the shining, wonderful woman he and Se had created. Radal knew despair as never before.

And he saw Donzalo, and that it all hinged upon that cursed Laman. He broke their bond and walked swiftly to the library, where his daughter sat, practicing lines from some play. "Fachalana," he said, "come with me and learn."

"This land will no longer hold him," stated Se.

"No," agreed Guesare He stood by Donzalo's bed, his arm in a sling. "I could almost hate the lad right now, though I know none of this was his fault." He sighed. "I could hate myself for bringing him here."

"Sooner or later," said his mother, "Jola and her step-sister would have come to this. It was good that she found happiness first, even so briefly."

"Maybe brief happiness is the best kind," the minstrel mused, almost whispering, "before it fades.

"Anyway," he continued, attempting to sound less gloomy, "I'm glad he woke at last. He'll want to hear the news that came from his home."

"Do not think his mind is healed only because he awoke. It will take far longer to heal than those broken ribs he suffered. Or even," said Lady Se, "your mangled shoulder."

Guesare winced. He very much disliked being incapacitated, to be able to wield neither sword nor rebec.

"Many would not have survived such magic, so close. It will leave scars, albeit ones men can not see. And the death of his beloved will weigh heavily as well."

"I feared to tell him, but it was the first thing he asked. I think — I think he knew already the answer."

"He may have felt it in those last moments. As I did. That is a terrible thing." Se hung her head and wept for the first time since her daughter's death.

"I weep with you, my lady," came Donzalo's voice, low yet strong, from where he lay.

"And I," said Guesare simply.

In the hills had they laid her to rest, near the little cottage they had shared, so briefly. Donzalo stood by the grave of his beloved one morning, a morning when winter was making ready to give way to spring, and sang.

If I passed beyond the sea,
would you wait and watch for me?
If I crossed the mountains high,
would you pray for wings to fly?

Of Doors: the Fourth Tale

1

"What became of my sword?" asked Donzalo, of a sudden.

"It's true owner took it back," Guesare told him. "It was only lent to us for a time."

"The Other who fought along side us?"

"Yes. It is his sword. He is a prince of the Fay."

Donzalo considered this and nodded. "I had heard it called the Prince's Sword. So now I know why." He turned to gaze out the window again and then down at the paper he held. "I might as well go home," he said.

Though usually a man with a ready word, Guesare was not certain how to respond. "You are welcome to stay here as long as you will. Forever, should you wish."

"One place seems as good as another," said the young Laman with a shrug. "Or as bad."

All the joy has gone out of him, thought the minstrel.

Donzalo held up the paper. "You have read this?"

"Indeed I have, young friend. You have a new niece. It is good to have family," he stated.

The younger man smiled, but only slightly. "Yet you keep running away from yours." Then he turned the conversation back to where it had begun. "Why did this prince give the sword to — to whom, Mausare?"

"It was given to Jola. He told her it was meant for he who would be her champion. So she gave it to Mausare, not knowing who else." Guesare realized that was the first time he had spoken his sister's name to Donazalo since her death. "She offered it to me, first, but I was not eager to take possession of a magical blade and all the obligations that seemed to hew to it."

He was silent for a moment. "It seems to have gone where it belonged."

"Jola must have told him to give it to me. She saw too much of our destiny." He spoke with a bitterness Guesare had never heard from him before. "I am sick of the demands of destiny. All I wanted was peace and to love her."

Jobareth lied. "She is as beautiful as her mother," he told Lomela. The red-faced baby squalled and he gingerly handed her back to her nurse.

The Lady Lomela laughed. "She looks more like her father when he used to have too much to drink!"

The young diplomat thought that an accurate description but, being a diplomat, did not say so. "I am sure she will grow in beauty while I am gone. Indeed," he said, "she may be toddling about the place by then and charming all the little boys."

"That long?"

"Yes, my lady." The Sharshite sighed. "I must go all the way to the capital and then who knows how long it will take to return? I fear Lord Doufan is not one to hurry, either in preparation or in travel."

Lomela pursed her lips in annoyance at her father's bureaucracy. "Surely by mid-summer?"

"As good a guess as any." Jobareth had been waiting for the nurse to leave with the little girl. Now he broached another subject. "I hear there is news from the Cuddon."

"A long letter, written by Guesare himself. Here, I'll let you read it." She went to a small writing desk, made of unadorned oak, and retrieved a sheaf of papers. "The count let me keep it here."

Jobareth sat and read for a while. Then he went back to the first page and skimmed through the narrative again before speaking. "My heart goes out to Donzalo. To lose so much —" He shook his head, almost in tears at the tale he had read. Diplomat he might be by profession, but the poet was ever beneath the surface of young Nafal. Lomela recognized the emotions in her sentimental friend. She had wept herself on reading Guesare's missive.

"Someone will write back, I assume," said the diplomat, composing himself. "Will he be told of the Lady Vibola?"

"I think Donzalo is carrying enough with him right now. The news of his grandmother's death can wait until his return."

Perdos had come to like these people, though he knew the innkeeper would readily cheat him of his every penny. He had become comfortable here.

But spring was on the way and he must be on his, as well. Where to? Not far below this village lay a good-sized town where the River Tod joined the Weldar. That might be a good place to start, to catch up on news and rumors. Little of that had reached him here — most of what winter traffic there was on the river passed without stopping and the road and ferry brought few travelers.

"We will miss you, Sir Perdos," said the little innkeeper and his wife nodded in agreement. "You will always find welcome here."

"Aye, if I bring enough money. Or horses." The knight's gruffness could not conceal the affection he had come to feel for this couple.

"Horses are a good idea," agreed the innkeeper, "and we would never ask their origin." He winked at his wife.

Perdos laughed aloud. He had laughed more, these past two months, than he had in years. Maybe more than ever before in his life. "This would not be bad country to raise horses," he mused. "Maybe when I'm done with — with what I have to do, I'll come back and settle around here."

The pair shared a meaningful glance. They knew that Perdos had some unspoken quest that drove him.

What the innkeeper said then surprised both him and his wife. "We have no children, sir, and no heirs. If you wanted to buy into our inn, we would welcome you as a partner."

"Ha, you already have all my money!" Perdos mounted his steed, ready to set forth. "But it is a good offer and one I might think on. Farewell, now."

He turned his horse toward the river and the waiting ferry.

Every day, Donzalo rode to Jola's grave. He went nowhere else — the hills of the Cuddon no longer held any interest for him. Sometimes he saw her dappled gray horse running wild and the sight brought an odd mix of joy and pain to his heart, a heart that wanted to both remember and forget.

As he stood silently this morning, wrapped in the garment of thoughts he had woven for himself, a voice came, a lilting voice that he had heard but once, yet recognized. "I, too, miss her."

On a shadow-shrouded bench by the cottage, sat the Prince of the Fay, hardly to be seen in gray tunic and cloak. The eyes that regarded Donzalo from his white face were a misted pale indigo, the color of opals, beneath startlingly black brows.

"Come sit with me, Donzalo." The fay turned his gaze toward the overcast sky. "The sun does not love my people, even on days such as this."

The young knight took a seat beside him and looked out over the hills where so recently he had fought a great evil, both winning and losing, and then at his companion. A sword hung at the Other's hip, but the Laman could see it was shorter, lighter, than the one he had briefly possessed.

The prince noted his interest. "No, this is not the sword you wielded. It is not meant for one of my race nor do I think you will hold it again. The Moon Sword we name it. It is where it belongs now, until once more needed.

"Jola needed it. We knew that it would, in time, come to he who would be her champion. So it came to thee, young knight."

Donzalo considered, briefly, asking how the fay knew this. It doesn't matter, he told himself, and I've had enough of magic. He remained silent.

"She came broken to me," continued the prince, "little more than a child. And I, I who am near immortal, loved her." There seemed a great weariness in his voice, the weariness of uncounted ages.

"There is healing in Fairie, Donzalo, and rest. You too may come to us, if you wish."

2

Grippo had become a rare visitor to his brother's home. The duties of an acolyte had increased as he neared the time of his ordination. Less than four months remained before he would be made priest, on the most holy of days for Kamatians, the summer solstice.

And now there was Borrago. He liked the count well enough, but his presence in the cottage made him uncomfortable. It could not help bring images of his own departed father to his mind, his light-hearted, often irresponsible sire who had wed Sima at the request of Borrago's father, yet had come to love her dearly.

Brother Grippo told himself that he should remember him in his prayers more often. Yes, and light a lamp for him, now and again.

He rapped lightly on the door. A year ago, he would have simply gone in.

Janona, his brother's wife, opened the door to him. "Come in, boy! Why are you standing out here?" Grippo remembered when his grave, serious brother had courted this cheerful, even effusive, woman, the daughter of peasants who had come to serve in the castle kitchens. Copago could maintain with a straight face that he had married her for her cooking but the acolyte knew that her laughter had really won his brother over.

Only the family occupied the little common room tonight. "Mother," he said, embracing and kissing Sima. He then knelt to hug his little niece, who was tugging on his robe.

"Why, what has happened to your doll, my little lady?" he asked, looking at the mangled and barely recognizable object she clutched.

"King. Bad dog!" the girl replied and then laughed.

Ah, Borrago's constant companion. The count had named him King, saying he was the only king that would ever enter Keep Rosam.

"She loves the hound," said Copago, speaking for the first time, from where he stretched in a chair by the fireplace. "She and her dolly were playing keep-away with it."

Grippo wondered just how many times the count had visited there but was unwilling to ask. Nor did he think it was his business — Copago would see to their mother's well-being. The young acolyte had relinquished any rights to have a voice in his family when he had first taken vows.

"There is a flagon of beer on the table," said Janona. "Help yourself before your brother drinks it all." The plump woman, of a sudden, threw her arms around him. "It's good to have you here. You must come more often!"

Yes, I must, thought Grippo. And, Kamat willing, may this always be my home.

"The Prince's name? I do not know," admitted Guesare. "The Others do not give out their names to mortals. Certainly never to me, though I do believe he told Jola his true name.

"Yet I have known him since I was a boy. It was he set me on the path to becoming a minstrel."

"Do you still sing that dirge he taught you?" asked Ourru, freshly returned to the keep. The big man lolled on a couch that was new to his quarters. Both Donzalo and Guesare were a bit uncomfortable with that piece of furniture, recognizing it as one that had formerly occupied Nosana's apartment. Ourru did not care and wondered if he could get his late sister's mirror home safely.

"There was a song he taught me, yes, when I was a boy. And others since, but I think I know the one you mean." Guesare picked up his rebec and strummed across the strings. He wrinkled his nose at the result.

"It was good of you, brother," he said with a wink, "to come all this way to hear me play."

"It is far?" asked Donzalo.

"No more than a day's ride," shrugged Ourru, "and that's not hurrying. I like to get away from the cot to visit here now and again."

"He was his mother's heir, being the eldest, and has quite a nice farm to go home to," said Guesare. He turned a tuning peg, strummed again, and nodded.

Then he began a plaintive, yearning tune, almost chanted, to the accompaniment of slow strumming.

Legends they tell, where the dwarfs dwell,
of fires that well from the hearths of Hell.
There chains of gold were forged of old,
to bind, to hold, in caverns cold,
where the dwarfs dwell, where the dwarfs dwell.

In secret mines a captive pines;
and the runic lines form mystic signs
to tell her tale. A whisper, a wail,
all voices fail — doomed and pale
a captive pines, a captive pines.

In caverns deep the hours creep;
to wake from sleep means but to weep,
caught in this spell. Does a distant bell
their passing tell? Within her cell,
the hours creep, the hours creep.

The clamor, hark, in caverns dark;
an anvil spark, a dwarf-smith, stark,
to his tasks settles, he casts, he fettles
his magic metals, the crystal kettles
in caverns dark, in caverns dark.

What fate befell, where the dwarfs dwell?
The hammer's knell would rise and swell
on the fetid air, a song of despair
for the captive fair, beyond all care
where the dwarfs dwell, where the dwarfs dwell.

"That really should be sung to a harp," said Guesare, almost apologetically. "And not with a sore shoulder."

Donzalo had been staring at the floor, seemingly deep in thought. He raised his eyes to his companions now, and spoke. "I — am tempted to take this Prince's offer. To visit his fairie realm and see if it can bring me peace."

"Avoid the Perilous People," advised an earnest Ourru. "Peace can be found anywhere, if one gives it time."

Guesare slowly nodded. "Do not assume the Fay are good in any sense we know the word, Donzalo. They can be wise and kind, but also capricious and cruel. They will far too readily indulge their whims."

"Then they are not so unlike us, Cousin," replied Donzalo. "I am indeed tempted."

There was a tavern at Todmouth. Three taverns, to be exact, but only one that appears in our tale now. We shouldn't even mention the one on the other side of the Weldar.

Todmouth lay on high ground to the north of, of course, the mouth of the River Tod. To the south, lay swamp. Across the Weldar was a smaller town, where goods from up the Tod could be unloaded for transport eastward. Doing so was rarely practical, which explains why the town was small.

In that tavern, named *The Truculent Troll*, Perdos sat and nursed a beer, listening as he could to the gossip about him. At a table nearby was a group of men, traveling traders by the look of them, and their leader seemingly a large black-bearded fellow. Perdos caught snatches of their conversation, talk of deals both good and bad, of towns and ports and beaches where smugglers might land.

He knew of such men and the business they did in the south, where there was much disputed land and little enforcement of law. Up the Tod lay Count Orgelo's keep and, by all accounts, that nobleman had more than a passing acquaintance with such smugglers, allowing them to bring goods through his lands for a cut of their profits.

This endeared him neither to the Sharshites across the mountains nor the Anians who controlled Morparas, down at the mouth of the Weldar.

I'll learn no more here, thought Perdos, as it grew late. Might as well find a bed and move on in the morning. As he rose to leave, the big man motioned him over.

"My friends are all deserting me," he rumbled, "or falling asleep." He waved a ham of a hand toward two fellows drowsing, heads on the table. "Join me for a while. Then, you won't have to listen from afar!" His deep laugh seemed ready and natural, but Perdos suspected the man was accustomed to acting a part.

"Maybe I can provide you with some news, as well," he said. "Otherwise, I think you might not have invited me over."

"Probably so, sir," came the trader's reply, "though I welcome the company, anyway. I am called Galaro." He extended his hand.

The Laman took it as he sat down on the pine slab bench. "Perdos is my name, a knight from the north."

"Perdos?" The large man seemed a bit taken aback. "Late of Keep Rosam?"

The knight nodded cautiously. Was this man an enemy he had made somewhere along the road?

"Then you are the one trying to kill my little brother!" Galaro exclaimed, and then held up his broad hand. "Fear not, I've no great love for Guesare and he is quite capable of taking care of himself. I will not, however, wish you luck."

Perdos leaned back and squinted at the man. "He killed my brother. What makes you think I won't try to do the same to his?"

"He might thank you for the favor. We truly hated each other when young. Now," he said with a shrug, "we go our own ways.

"Besides, all my men are here and they would not take kindly to you slaying me. Or I hope they wouldn't!" He motioned to the barkeep for more beer. "Let's drink to that, eh?"

"As good a reason as any," replied Perdos.

Lareth knew something had changed. His friend and councilor had always been a reserved man, a man of secrets, but now Lord Radal seemed turned inward as never before, weighed down by some unspoken burden.

The king chose not to pry. It would do no good and there were other matters that needed his attention, and that of Radal as well.

"Borrago has grown cool toward us," stated the nobleman.

"Can we blame him? He certainly was able to deduce who was trying to assassinate his son."

"We might do better with his other son as count." Lord Radal spoke this flatly but his king caught the implications.

"It is not yet time to think of such things. We are still allies, officially, and he is a strong bulwark against Orgelo's ambitions." King Lareth rose from his plain high-backed chair and walked to the window. He thought he could catch a hint of the distant sea on this strong southwesterly wind, a wind that promised the coming of spring. "His heir, from all I've heard of my son-in-law, is weak."

"The easier we might control him, then. And if we could pin the deed on Orgelo, all the better." The courtier's voice remained matter-of-fact. "It would also mean less protection for the younger son."

"No, no, Radal." said Lareth, turning to his companion. "Let diplomacy have sway for now."

"Sometimes the best diplomacy comes on the blade of a sword."

"Ha, you quote my father to me!" The monarch looked at his old friend, so unchanged in most ways, tall, thin, his hair close-cropped, as always, and his beard shaven. Yet he was aging and new lines were etched into his dark, ascetic face.

"Let us speak of happier things. My son's wedding, for one — I trust the Lady Fachalana will attend." It was a royal command, rather than a question, but spoken as one friend to another.

"Of course, my liege."

"You have seemed to keep your daughter locked away, lately. She has scarcely been seen in society."

"She has been studying," Radal offered in explanation.

"Oh, a new role?"

"So to speak, my king."

There was a hill. It rose from the pine forest, but no tree grew upon it. Grass, withered at this season, covered its slopes and on the crest stood a great stone, stark against the gray sky of the Cuddon.

Donzalo sat his horse before the hill and thought. Did he do wrong to attack the cat-that-was-Nosana and set off a magical cataclysm? Did his actions at that nightmare battle lead to Jola's death?

And worse, had he ever any choice but to do so?

He urged his mount forward, slowly. It seemed skittish. Donzalo understood, feeling uneasy himself.

A door will open for you, the prince had told him.

And so it did, though if one did not look at it properly, it did not seem to be there at all. The young knight dismounted and led his steed on. A figure came forth to meet him; not the prince but another of his people, the same pale skin seeming all the more the color of new-fallen snow against his black armor.

"Welcome, Sir Donzalo. You may enter but your steed may not." He placed a white hand on the head of Donzalo's horse, which turned and trotted away. "It will return home on its own.

"Go forward, young knight, the prince awaits thee. I must stand guard here." Donzalo looked back at the way he had come. From this side, the gateway was large, bounded by stone pillars intricately carved with runic symbols, massive oaken doors drawn back. He gazed once more at the winter sky and turned to follow the passage into the hill.

3

In a small room, no more than a cell carved from the sandstone on which rested Mountain Keep, Sojel read his master's message. At last, he had received orders.

It was time to move east, though the Lord Radal himself must remain in the capital through the spring. Reform his troop and add to it if possible — there would be funds enough waiting for him in Oles — and do no more until further word reached him.

Sojel would have led his men into the heart of the Cuddon, had he been so ordered, but he would follow these instructions and wait.

Everything the soldier owned was in this room. It was all he needed, each item properly in its place and ready to hand. He began methodically to pack two worn leather saddlebags for his journey. It would be good to be on the move again, a leader of fighting men.

It would be good to ride with a sword at his hip and none to stop him from using it.

Blen shook his head. They were so slow!

He dismounted and walked to where the masons were taking yet another break. One of them made a laughing remark to the others in Old Laman, thinking he would not understand. Most of these were men from the countryside where that tongue was still sometimes spoken.

No point in letting them know I caught the meaning of that, the Sharshite told himself. It wasn't really an insult, anyway, just a mild jibe at his eagerness to keep construction moving. The 'impatient lover,' eh? He had to keep himself from smiling at the name.

Blen turned to thoughtfully appraise the rising foundations of the embassy. "It's going well," he said, evenly. "Fine work, men." That should befuddle them a bit, he thought.

"Thank you, sir," said the foreman, rising to his feet. "But it's damnably cold work."

"Better to get it done now, before the spring rains come," the knight reminded him. "It would be twice the job then." He looked over the site. "I see the rest of the stone has arrived."

The pinkish limestone blocks, much the same as those used in the walls of Castle Rosam, were stacked ready for use. They might come from the same quarry, thought Blen. I should find out where it is. Blen had a need to know things.

"Aye, sir. And we'd best get back to it." The man beckoned to his workers, who were decidedly loath to leave the comfort of their open fire.

Sir Blen smiled, knowing they would be back around it soon after he left. Oh well, the work was progressing, even if more slowly than he might prefer. He could have the carpenters in soon and walls and a roof would rise here. If Lord Doufan did not hurry too much, the place would be ready for him.

A tiny, hairless, naked woman came forward to take Donzalo's hand. "All we whom you call Others mourn the loss of your lady." The young Laman recognized her as a kobold. He had never seen a kobold but there were pictures in the books he had left behind him in Castle Rosam.

He had entered a great, cavernous hall. How could this fit inside the hill? wondered Donzalo. Stories said that such enchanted heights were but gateways to other worlds. It was not to be doubted that he had truly entered the realm of Fairie.

"We do indeed, my lady," spoke the prince, coming forward and bowing to the little goblin woman. "Sir Donzalo, this be a queen of the kobolds, come to offer her condolences.

"I welcome thee to my people's home." He turned to the kobold and exchanged a few words in a language the knight did not know. She looked up at Donzalo and nodded gravely in agreement.

"May your dreams bring all you seek, mortal knight," she said. "We shall help to watch over them." The kobold queen slipped away before he could respond, into the shadowed vastness of the cave.

"There was a great devotion to Jola among the little people," the prince told him, "the trolls, most particularly, but they are too shy to come here.

"Come, walk with me and I shall show thee what few humans have seen."

"Was that the language of the kobolds you spoke just then?" asked Donzalo.

"That it was. It is a serviceable tongue and one the People of the Sun could learn. Our language, the language of the Fay, has become exceedingly complex. Or languages, as we have many and use them as moved by need and mood."

"The People of the Sun — that is mortals such as I?"

The prince turned his pale eyes toward Donzalo. "Yes. Know that we only call your people mortal to forget that we, too, must die. To exist for millennia is nothing beside eternity.

"We — the fay, the kobolds, and our close kindred — are the People of the Air."

Donzalo told himself there must be peoples of earth and water as well, but did not question his host about it. There was too much else to see and learn here. Other fay moved about them now, some of whom looked on the knight with interest, others who did not seem to notice him at all, wrapped in whatever occupied their minds. They seemed careless of their modesty, apparently throwing on whatever clothing had caught their fancy or going quite nude.

All had the same snow-white color to them as the prince, but hair varied greatly. Donzalo suspected that some of the shades were the result of dye.

Great crystalline pillars joined ceiling and floor. Natural formations originally, the knight surmised, but artfully carved over uncounted years.

"You rule over all this, sir?" he asked his companion.

"No," replied the Prince of the Fay, "the Queen rules. I am but one of her consorts."

Before Jobareth Nafal rose the towers of Mountain Keep. One did not see them until almost upon the castle, hidden behind a spur of the Zadcelam. Above the fortress, one climbed to the pass into Sharsh.

The diplomat turned and looked behind him, toward the broad Laman plain, the river valley of the Weldar. One could see for leagues from here and further beyond, hidden in the blue mist of distance, lay County Rosam from which he had ridden.

"I'll welcome a bed, tonight," he remarked to his attendant, one of the soldiers that had accompanied Blen and himself to Lama the previous year.

"Yes, sir. Will we stay the one night only?"

"Most likely." Jobareth gave a thoughtful look to the young man, really no more than an overgrown boy. "I can pick up a new escort here if you would prefer to rest a couple days and head back to Ros-town. Or have you family in Sharsh you would like to see?" He wondered if Blen had given this lad any explicit orders.

The soldier seemed uncertain. "I've — no one back home, sir."

"But a sweetheart in Lama, no doubt." Why, the young fellow is blushing, noted the diplomat. "Then I shall let you get back to her embrace. But let us get up to the keep now, before it grows any colder."

They trotted forward. "I could use someone," Jobareth began, and then stopped to better organize the idea that had just come to him. "Yes, Pol, I could use someone to keep an eye on things back at the embassy while I am far away. Do you think you could do this?"

"Yes, Lector!" The boy's eagerness amused Nafal.

"Then we shall discuss it tonight, within yon walls. It is a long way to Celatas and it will be months before I can return to County Rosam with the ambassador. I will depend upon you, young sir, to keep me informed."

Jobareth Nafal smiled inwardly. What kind of diplomat did not employ a spy or two? It was time he had one.

4

Ansa held a letter from her brother, master of Anian spies. Use your discretion, as always, he told her, but it would be wise to leave Celatas.

It would indeed. Nor would Ansa mind putting putting the life of an agent behind her. Not at all.

The Lady Fachalana's friend, Jobareth, was on his way to the capital — the Jobareth who had seen her in Lama, who would know her for a spy. But Fachalana was the one reason she might remain.

Here she was, alone again in this theater. Ansa looked around the little dressing room she had reserved for her own use. Everything in it could be left behind and she could be on her way home in a matter of minutes, with nothing to tie up, no one to whom she had to say good bye.

Fachalana — she realized that she had come to think of her patroness as a friend and believed the lady felt the same toward her. Yes, she was self-centered and willful, but passionate and fiercely loyal as well. And Ansa was worried about her, for lately she seemed not the woman the Anian had come to know.

Jobareth Nafal was friend not only to Fachalana but to Donzalo. This she knew. Could she trust him with her secrets? Should she take the chance?

The decision must come soon.

"Dreams may be perilous here. Some never wake from them."

So said the Queen of the Fay to Donzalo. She sat upon a throne of obsidian and her long hair was as white as her skin. White, too, was the gown she wore, tied around with a ribbon of black silk. A wealth of diamonds was set in her diadem.

"Might dreams bring me peace, my lady?" asked the young knight.

"Peace, torment, life, death — who can say? We each make our own dreams. But you, I think," she said, appraising him with steady gray-green eyes, "have the strength in thee to dream what you will. Be sure to use it."

The queen turned to one of those around her and spoke in an odd, liquid language. The fay hurried away on whatever errand she had set him. Then she addressed Donzalo's companion in a quite different tongue, one of harsh music.

He answered in the same language and then spoke to the knight. "She asks if I have told thee one of my names. We rarely share them with your people.

"Jola was the only mortal to ever know my true, secret name. Be not offended, my friend, if I do not tell it to thee. You may call me Arsel. It is one name and it is mine."

"I am honored, Prince Arsel." Donzalo bowed to the fay.

The queen laughed at that, with a sound akin to the bubbling of water in mountain streams. "I have not heard you use that one in many years, my prince." To Donzalo she said, "The name means Wolf-friend in your language. Or something very like it."

The fay she had sent away a few moments earlier returned and gave his queen a slight bow. "I have ordered a chamber readied for our friend. He may rest there if he desires."

Prince Arsel bowed deeply and Donzalo felt it wise to imitate him, before following the fay from the throne room.

In the hall, he asked, "You are her husband?"

"One of three. It is more a ceremonial title than aught else, not that we haven't consummated it on a few occasions. Things do happen over a thousand years or two."

He who led them stopped and motioned toward a door, before turning and leaving without a word. "I think mortals make him uncomfortable," remarked the prince. "He, as most of my people, rarely leaves our realm.

"Here where there is neither night nor day, we lose track of the passage of our lives. That is why I choose to walk beneath the sky."

The room was simple but, as with much of what Donzalo had seen here, followed no rules on the shapes and angles of wall and ceiling. Or no rules he could discern, for the fay might see things with a different eye. It was comfortably furnished, even a bit opulently by puritanical Laman standards.

"I will have a meal brought to thee. Rest here a while," said the prince, "and we shall prepare for what comes."

Sir Jak sometimes missed the Bolos of old, the man who would buy a round for his retainers, aye, and drink it with them. With his sobriety, the young lord had also found a streak of the miserly within himself, not unlike his father.

As sergeant of Bolos's private guard, though, he could only approve of this more responsible master he served. A more cautious man he seemed, too, and at times a suspicious one, seeing plots where others did not.

Jak pushed back his hood to scratch at the top of his bald head. The night was mild and he did not need its warmth, only its concealment. He pulled it forward again, his face hidden in its shadow.

Keep an eye on my father, his master had told him. Bolos did not like his sire sneaking off to who-knew-where, unattended. Jak had quickly discovered that Count Borrago had one destination and one only, the cottage of his master of arms, Copago.

Had Jak, and Bolos as well, seen more clearly they would have bethought themselves of Mistress Sima's presence in that little house. But they saw only the count going off to conspire with his natural son. Between the competent master of arms on the one hand and his suddenly blossoming younger brother, Donzalo, on the other, Bolos felt his position threatened. He knew he had always been a disappointment to his father.

The burly guardsman yawned. Usually the count left Copago's cottage after an hour or two, but the time neared midnight and he had not appeared. Now the lights were being dimmed within.

Jak waited all that night.

A woman of the fay brought a tray to Donzalo. She stared at him for a few seconds and then, uninvited, sat herself down on his bed.

"You were Jola's love?" she asked.

The knight only nodded; it was not a subject he wished to discuss. He tasted one of the cakes she had set before him. There was a flavor of honey and some spice but, all-in-all, it seemed a bit bland.

The girl — woman? Who could tell with the ageless fay? — spoke on, with a little laugh. "I feared to bring thee such food as we might eat. The flavors we seek out in our need for novelty might well turn your stomach." She stood and came to where he sat in a low cushioned chair, all of purple and green silk. "These we bake to cleanse our palettes," the fay continued, picking up one of the little cakes.

"They are quite good, really,' replied Donzalo, and it was the truth, "but I could see becoming rapidly bored on such a diet."

She nibbled on the pastry she held. "Yes, they are good. I had forgotten how tasty they could be. So they become a new flavor for me!" The fay, whose hair was an improbable hue of red, looked down at him and smiled a smile, wistful and seeming to hold a deep sadness. "I had forgotten as well how tasty mortals might be. But you are not for me, young knight. Not now.

"The prince will be along soon to start thee upon a journey. Or perhaps not soon. Rest you until then." And so saying, she left.

"Guesare," came a voice at the minstrel's door. Framed there was a large, clean-shaven man in the garb of a soldier, a heavy sword hanging at his side.

"Habidros!" He practically bounded forward to embrace the man. "When did you return?"

Of all his half-brothers, Habidros was Guesare's favorite. He was the one who had been protective of him as a lad, when Galaro would torment him. Oh, Ourru was kind, but older and too often involved with other affairs to notice the bullying.

"I rode in late last night. They told me you were already abed." He shook his head at his brother. "You have the habits of an old man!"

"At times, I feel like one," said Guesare. "Have you breakfasted?"

"A meal awaits in the thane's rooms. Join us there and we can catch up." He turned and started toward their father's quarters, down the haphazard hallways of Drolwym Keep. Guesare quickly finished dressing and hurried after, not even taking time to comb his beard.

Both his mother and father waited in the antechamber where the thane usually conducted business, this morning the business being sausages and cakes and porridge with honey. Habidros had taken a seat across from them and was helping himself to generous servings. He had always gotten along well with his step-mother. And with food.

Guesare had suspected that the teen Habidros harbored something of a crush on the Lady Se. Perhaps that explained some of his protection. Don't be cynical, he told himself.

"I thought I was the one who sought adventure," the soldier said, between mouthfuls, "going off to fight the wars of the Siphic city-states. But it seems much has happened here of late."

"I told him the tale of our Donzalo last night," spoke Se. "I pray that the course he has chosen proves a wise one."

"Our kinsman seems a most capable young man," the thane opined. "We can only trust in him. Is there any more butter?"

"Here, Father," said Guesare, passing him a chipped crock. "Honey, too?" Vantare shook his head in reply, having already filled his mouth. "Well, Donzalo is capable, indeed, and quite level-headed. I am not sure those are the qualities one needs in the fairie realm."

Se nodded. "It a place more fit for poets and dreamers."

Vantare washed down his bread and butter with a gulp of cider and spoke. "There must be such a dreamer in him or he would not have loved your sister, nor she him." Se and Guesare nodded agreement to each other across the table. At times, the moody thane saw more than they realized.

"I hope to meet this level-headed dreamer," declared Habidros.

5

"If you wish, you may do no more than rest here for a while, enjoy our hospitality, and leave when you will. There are pleasures and diversions aplenty to be found in my realm." Tall and pale, the Queen of the Fay walked beside Donzalo. "I think you seek more."

"I — I know not what I seek, my lady."

"That is what you must learn here. Only then can you return to mortal lands to find it."

Arsel followed behind them, thinking his own thoughts, and speaking not.

"Once you pass through the doors of dream here, you may not turn aside. Destiny or death awaits." She stopped and met the young knight's eyes, thinking for a moment how their color was that of storms approaching over the hills. "Are you prepared for this?"

"Yes, my lady," averred Donzalo, "though I am not sure which I might prefer."

The queen slowly nodded. "This, I understand. I leave thee to our prince." She turned and disappeared down the crystalline hallway.

"Come," said the Prince Arsel, "and we shall begin." He led Donazalo a short way further down the passage and, drawing an intricate key from his robes, unlocked a door all of hammered silver, grown black with tarnish here and there.

"You may call this the Chamber of Dreams," said he. "It is as good a description as any, at least in your tongue."

"Did Jola sleep here?" asked the knight as they entered. The room was not large, or appeared so at first. After a few moments, Donzalo was not sure how far apart the oddly-slanted white walls stood.

"She did," replied the prince. "Sit before we make a start, Sir Donzalo, and hear my tale.

"It was some fifteen years ago, by your reckoning," he said, as Donzalo settled himself on the large bed central — or so it seemed at times — to the room. "In the hills of the Cuddon, where I sometimes wandered, too restless to remain in Fairie, came I upon a young woman, filled with great longing, great sadness, and very great power.

"And I could not help but love her. For fay and mortal to love is always perilous and more so for my people than for yours." Arsel shook his head and sighed deeply. "The People of the Sun fade away so soon.

"For some time, she seemed happy. As was I, who had seemed to feel nothing for centuries, but it was to last for no more than a few of your mortal seasons. There was that within Jola that needed more, to understand and to untangle the madness brought by her coming of age. She was both a woman and a being of great innate power, with none to guide her. Not I, not the Lady Se; we had neither the wisdom nor the strength.

"And so I brought her here to dream." The prince paused a while in thought. "Otherwise she might have been lost forever.

"Of what did she dream? She dreamed of the Huntress, I know, for she told me. She dreamed of her father; that she did not tell me but I surmised. The Sword of the Moon, too, was in her dream and so we gave it to her.

"Whatever she may have seen, she was no longer mine, after, but searched for the one she had dreamed. I see now that she dreamed thee and, aye, her death. Perhaps, it is not wise to know what one must seek, Donzalo. You may choose not to dream."

The knight responded simply, "I must, my lord."

"Very well," said Arsel. "You may see many things — no, you *will* see many things. You will be vulnerable to those who have power and knowledge of the arts, both dark and light. I will protect thee as I can and perhaps others, too, will be with thee."

The fay took up a cup of what seemed spiced mead.

"Drink of this, and sleep."

"The Chas is already at flood," observed one of Jobareth's traveling companions. They had just reached the banks of that great river, swollen by the rains and thaws of spring, turned red from the silt it carried.

Celatas lay nearly as far from Mountain Keep as did Castle Rosam, and the country was more rugged, yet he had made good time on the king's well-maintained roads. Much trade flowed through the pass guarded by that keep and it was increasing as winter faded. Assigned a young secretary of the diplomatic corps — a post he himself had filled not long ago — Jobareth had joined a caravan of merchants wending its way toward the Sharshite heartland.

Now the group was entering the northern end of the capital, where shops and inns had sprung up along the road in hopes of luring travelers on their way into the metropolis. At a distance, the diplomat could see the great bridge that Lareth had thrown up a few years earlier, the only one this far downriver.

"Flooded too, it seems, is the town," he answered. The way was crowded, bustling with travelers, vendors, soldiers, all about their business, and idlers with no apparent business at all.

"Here for the wedding," replied the merchant, "not that there wouldn't be crowds for the Spring Festival anyway."

Jobareth nodded, absentmindedly. The royal wedding — that would no doubt mean having to spend extra time in Celatas, as Doufan would be expected to attend. A year ago he would have welcomed the opportunity.

He reined in his steed. "I must part with you here, friends," said Nafal to his traveling companions. "May good fortune attend you." The secretary following, he turned toward the king's keep, high above the city, the farewells of the traders in his ears. He had enjoyed traveling with them, hearing their tales, sharing their wishes to be home again with loved ones.

King Lareth's castle was not his destination. Not yet. He stopped before an unassuming villa, the home of Lord Radal, set back from the wide cobblestone thoroughfare. One might not realize the house was there, among the many trees and flowering bushes, were not one look-ing for it. How many times had he passed through this little garden, just outside the tall double doors? There was the bench on which the Lady Fachalana had reposed, when last he spoke to her, before he was sent east.

Jobareth motioned his young aide toward it. "Wait for me here," he told him, and grasped the great bronze clapper.

He was admitted immediately.

"You may ride with us. Just promise not to try to kill my brother while I am around, for I would be bound to defend him."

"As far as I know, he is in your distant ancestral home," said Perdos to the large man busying himself with his steed nearby. "Well beyond my reach." He did not add 'for now.'

"Hmm, I did not know that," responded Galaro. "He will not stay. His wanderlust is as bad as mine.

"We travel north from here, keeping to this side of the river. There is a place," he confided, "a few leagues up from Ros-town where we can cross over quietly at night, and pay no taxes or fees."

"But perhaps a few bribes? I've seen how this sort of thing works from the opposite side of the road, so to speak." Perdos took a certain pride in the fact that he had never accepted such payoffs, not that he had ever been important enough.

"Oh, aye, that is ever a business expense in my line of work," the big Cuddonian admitted. "We may trade here and there along the way but intend to be at Ros-town for the Midsummer fair. You," he asked the Laman as he mounted up, "are not welcome there, are you?"

"No. But I intend to be elsewhere by then."

6

It seemed as though he were still in the room but it was, somehow, turned inside-out. Someone stood beside him. He sensed the presence but saw no one. Arsel, he thought to himself. Not really here with me but linked in some way.

There was a shifting, nebulous horizon. Silver light glowed in the distance, all around and above. Or did it come from below?

What do I seek here? he wondered. Over the course of the past year, Donzalo had grown increasingly confident, finding abilities within himself he had never known existed. That was all gone now, gone with Jola's death. What remained was self-doubt, a feeling that he had been only a child before, not seeing the world as it was, a world that held nothing for him.

All about him lay only the shimmering light and desolation. There was nothing here for him.

No, there, far away, an edifice of some sort. He felt himself moving toward it, swiftly, though he thought he had walked but a few steps. It was the temple of Diba where he had stood vigil, where Jola had been his protector and the goddess had spoken to him.

Did he hear the Huntress's golden laugh? How could he when there was no laughter within his own heart?

I shall go in, Donzalo decided, and watch as I did that night.

Fachalana could be infuriating. So apt a pupil at some times, so headstrong at others! Still, his lessons had gone well.

"Concentrate," urged Radal. "The other realms are always there but you must learn how to see them."

She was frustrated. Perhaps something to divert her mind for a moment would help.

"Let it go for now," he said to her. "Did you know your friend Nafal is back in the capital? He stopped here to report this afternoon."

"And didn't wait for me? Your diplomats should learn to be more diplomatic, Father!"

"He was in a hurry to see his family. Tell me, Fachalana, are you truly interested in that boy?" The Lord Radal had waited long for his daughter to wed and considered Jobareth Nafal a better choice than most. The fellow had promise.

The tall young woman shrugged. It was an elegant and dramatic shrug, the result of her dabbling in an acting career, and Radal recognized it as such.

"He is, well, a good sort, don't you think, Father?" She did not sound particularly enthusiastic.

"But not one to become passionate over, eh?" The councilor nodded in understanding. "You have known him all your life, Lana, and I think there would be no surprises there. He should rise high in the diplomatic service and with you at his side — who knows, he might even take my job!"

They laughed together over the thought but Fachalana knew that it might well be true.

"Let us try again. I will help you focus." Radal placed his long fingers, much the same color as the pecan-paneled walls about them, on his daughter's forehead. "Do you remember the words?" he asked.

She spoke the spell and he tried to help guide her thoughts. Suddenly, he sensed something else. Something that brought a knot of hatred into his heart.

He sensed Donzalo Rosam.

The knight stood before the temple doors, noting how they seemed of the same silver as those in the chamber in which he dreamed. Should I risk opening them? he now wondered. Would there be solace within or only more pain of remembrance?

The unseen companion at his side, the fay prince, offered no advice, only a reassuring presence.

Was there another here? He turned and saw a man taking form, a tall, black-robed man, and knew it was Lord Radal. Truly here or but a phantom? Did it make any difference in the land of dream? He had been warned that it was dangerous to walk this place.

There seemed to be another figure behind, shadowed, but somehow linked. A woman. She seemed — Donzalo gasped. No, not his Jola but so like her.

The sorcerer seemed suddenly to realize this second presence had followed him, was sharing his vision. With a word, he broke their connection and the woman was gone.

Then Radal turned his attention on the young Laman, raising his staff and beginning an incantation.

Prince Arsel saw the man, knew the man, and attempted to enter more fully into Donzalo's dream. It was dangerous he was aware, every bit as dangerous to him as to the young knight. His physical appearance began to take shape at Donzalo's side.

He knew as well that he was no match for this sorcerer in the realms of magic. No fay had the powers of the most gifted among the People of the Sun.

Donzalo seemed unable to move. Or perhaps unwilling.

"You must choose to act," the prince told him, once he stood solid — if aught might be called solid here — beside the knight.

"Why?" replied Donzalo. The wizard's spell seemed to be further sapping the lad, already seeming too sick at heart to resist. The fay attempted to block Radal's power as well as he might, to add to Donzalo's strength and will what he could.

"For Jola," said Arsel.

"Jola," said Donzalo. "Ah, my Jola. To what realm have you flown?" He turned his stricken gaze to the prince and asked, "Shall I join her?"

"Not in the hell to which yon mage will send thee!"

A fire seemed to light behind Donzalo's eyes. "Then I must not go," he whispered, perhaps to himself, perhaps to his lost love, and turned to throw open the temple doors.

There before the altar of Diba, surrounded by near-blinding silver light, stood the Sword of the Moon, the sword he had wielded the night he lost Jola. The young knight did not hesitate to step forward and grasp its hilt. As he came forth from the temple, blade in hand, the howling of wolves filled the sky.

Radal seemed shaken and, lowering his staff, broke off the spell. But rather than withdraw, the sorcerer pulled forth his own blade, a blade that flickered with unearthly green light, defying Donzalo to strike at him.

And strike he did, the silver blade destroying Lord Radal's weapon as though it were the tinsel of a toy sword. The mage cursed Donzalo, his face contorted by spite, before his form dissolved into nothingness.

What hatred drives this mortal? wondered Arsel.

Before them now stood a great silver wolf and Donzalo knew that it was, in a sense, Jola and, also, Diba. The golden voice of the goddess spoke to him.

"Beloved Donzalo, I will always be with thee, but you must seek your destiny elsewhere and in others."

And then, for a moment, he saw the form of Jola, her golden hair falling about her, before she and all dream faded.

7

Donzalo awoke to find himself not in the Chamber of Dreams but in the room the fay had first given him.

"You slept long," said the Queen of the Fay, who sat at his bedside. "Our prince has told us some of what happened but I would hear the story as your eyes saw it.

"First, we shall allow thee to bathe and eat. Come to us when ready." She rose to leave, but turned again to speak as she stood at the door. "You were touched by the shadow of Asak, the great despair. We are surprised that you live. And," she added with a small smile, "pleased."

The same fay woman attended Donzalo as before and the looks she gave him seemed to combine curiosity and respect. She showed even more respect and some astonishment after the prodigious meal he consumed. Thrice, she had to return for more cakes.

Then she led him to the queen's chamber where Arsel and, judging by their crowns, the other two princes listened to the tale he told.

"The Sword of the Moon entered into your dream," stated the queen, when he was done.

Donzalo immediately answered, "The blade served its purpose. It should remain here."

She nodded. "We have another trinket to take forth with thee." The queen stepped forward and pinned a silver brooch to his cloak, in the shape of a wolf. "When our Prince Arsel told of the Diba-wolf in your dream, we had this made for thee."

"This shall be my emblem, ever more," said the knight.

"There is some small magic in it," Arsel told him. "It might help you find what you now seek."

And what do I seek? wondered Donzalo. Was that woman in my dream a part of my destiny?

He spoke. "Perhaps I know what I seek no more than before. What I do know is that it is worth seeking."

Of Weddings: the Fifth Tale

1

A black cat lounged at the top of the stairs.

For a moment, and only a moment, Donzalo was taken aback, memories of a tragic night flooding into his mind. But this was no monster, only one of the many felines that roamed Castle Drolwym. He sat down there, on the top riser, and picked up the little creature.

"We might as well be friends," he told it, stroking its dark head. The cat showed no signs of disagreeing with the idea.

His friend Guesare ascended the stairs and took a seat beside him. He said nothing but was pleased with the change in the young knight. Donzalo had returned from Fairie no longer troubled by his great loss nor so wearied by his grief. It was not forgotten, of course; the minstrel realized that.

He realized as well that Donzalo had become a man and was no longer the boy he taken under his wing.

"I will miss your home," said Donzalo.

Guesare nodded. Nothing to keep you here anymore, he thought to himself. Not much to keep either of us. "We knew you would want to be traveling soon," he said aloud.

"Ah, Guesare, there is still a part of me that would like to stay. I think I have made peace with my memories and can again see what I loved about the Cuddon." He sighed. "Save for that one thing forever gone.

"Maybe I'll come back someday. We could be old men sitting together by the fire here, my friend. But my dream told me I have a destiny to find." He wondered for a moment if he should mention the woman he had briefly seen in his dream. Guesare might know who she was; the man was a spy, after all.

"Tell me," he began, "what you know of Lord Radal."

"I know very many things, Donni, and many of those quite unimportant."

"Well, does he have a wife?" Donzalo fervently hoped that the young woman was not married to the sorcerer, though he doubted it was so.

"His wife died many years ago. She was of a minor noble family in Sharsh." Guesare picked up the cat, which of a sudden had decided it preferred his lap. "I have heard that she was a beautiful woman and he was greatly devoted to her. If Radal has one virtue, it is his loyalty.

"They had a daughter, too, his only child." Guesare stopped. They knew now that there was another child, the Jola both had loved.

"Do you know her name?" Donzalo asked, as casually as possible. Too casually, no doubt, for the minstrel gave him a sharp look.

"I do not, but I hear she is an actress on the stage in Celatas, much to her father's chagrin."

Sojel sat in a tavern in Oles. He was not fond of the town. It was too tidy, too well policed by the smug burgess who ruled it.

Even the whores had to have licenses.

The man across the table was a banker. He was a big, hearty fellow, with a great soft gut, and Sojel was not fond of him either. He imagined himself spilling that gut onto the rush-covered floor.

"Are you certain, my man, that you wish to carry this sum with you? 'Twould be far safer in our vault."

Only by will power was Sojel able to keep himself from knifing the condescending fool. "It is needed elsewhere," was all he said.

"Very well. You will find it all there."

"But I'll count it anyway," the soldier growled in reply, and so did, taking his time. "Hmm, alright."

He looked up. The man was still there. "Need you something more?"

"Only to sign the receipt, sir." He slid the paper across the table to Sojel, who carefully made the letters of his name, and slid it back.

"Now let me drink in peace," he said. The banker hastened away, grateful to go back to his everyday business of bullying tradesmen and extorting widows.

On the morrow, Sojel would begin his journey south, down to the rendezvous point he had established when he had disbanded his troop in the autumn. Tonight, he might see about recruiting some of the fellows loitering about the place to increase their ranks. And then, maybe, pay the officially mandated price for a woman's company in Oles.

From her father's mood, Fachalana was sure that he had failed to harm the young Laman. Of that she was very glad.

And now she had seen him. Not really seen him, of course, but even her momentary glimpse in that dream world was something. Could it be a foretaste of a real meeting someday, maybe? He was most definitely handsome — despite that beard — and seemed troubled. She had seen the reason for that, too, in her father's unguarded mind before he broke their link.

Jola. She had had a sister and Donzalo had loved her.

Fachalana sat alone in the little garden by the front entry of her home, sorting through all the disjointed thoughts and memories that had flooded into her consciousness. Spring was coming and soon there would be flowers all about her here. There were many of the hibiscus her father loved or had once loved, the flowers he had planted for her mother years ago.

If Donzalo had loved Jola, could he not come to love her?

The thing, however, was to keep Father from killing him first.

"Your beard!" exclaimed Lanta.

"I approve," said Habidros, the only other clean-shaven man in the room.

Donzalo rubbed his strong, cleft chin. "If I'm headed back to Lama, I might as well look like myself and not some wild Cuddonian come down from the hills!"

Most of his relatives gathered there for the Feast of Spring laughed. They tended to be proud of their people's reputation in other lands.

Thane Vantare rose at his place and offered a toast. "May both your journey and your destination be to your liking." He emptied his cup and continued, "And remember you are always welcome here, Kinsman, for a day or for a lifetime."

"Aye," added a young man — a teen-aged boy, truly — seated nearby, "that goes when I am thane, too." Then, thinking maybe that statement was a bit of a gaffe, he said, "Though I wish my uncle a long tenure!" This cousin, Casurru by name and heir to Drolwym, had come to idolize Donzalo, somewhat to the Laman's discomfort.

"I thank you, all of you," said he. There were many things for which he could have expressed his gratitude to this family but there was no point in enumerating them. Donzalo realized that he felt more at home here than back in Castle Rosam and wondered, for neither the first time nor the last, if he might not find all he sought right here.

Guesare waved him to a seat at his table. This was a smaller hall, one lying next to the kitchens, that served for more intimate gatherings. This night, it was crowded with kin come not only to celebrate the holiday but to bid their guest farewell.

"The equinox is a rather solemn feast in Lama," Donzalo said to the minstrel, "preceded by fasting. We would be going to bed hungry on this Spring Feast eve."

"You more than make up for it at your May Festival," replied Guesare. "We barely mark that day, though it is sacred to the goddess Esefa."

"Does your mother celebrate it?" Donzalo helped himself from the steaming platters and bowls. The fare was heavy on root vegetables at this time of year, before the first fruits of the season. That and the ubiquitous mutton of the Cuddonian diet.

"I assume she does. She disappears with her circle and Jov only knows what they get up to!

"You should reach home well before May Festival. I know not when I shall find my way again to County Rosam." Guesare offered him a bowl of mashed turnips, which the Laman declined, as politely as he was able.

"Make certain that shoulder is healed first. You need be able to wield a sword before you travel."

"It gets better but far too slowly. There is still some stiffness," admitted the minstrel. "At least, I can play the rebec as well as ever. Or as poorly," he laughed.

"My roads and yours must diverge for a while, anyway. In the mean time, I do trust my brother Habidros to keep you safe on your journey."

"I am grateful for his offer, though a bit puzzled by it," Donzalo said. "We have only just met."

"He was between wars," Guesare told him, "and Habidros becomes easily bored. It is a failing we share. He welcomed the chance to see new lands." The Cuddonian leaned in close. "I did promise him payment from my Anian allies. My brother is a mercenary, after all.

"Which is not to say that he is in any way not to be trusted. I think he would have gone without the offer of money." Mostly because my mother asked, he said to himself. "He likes you, too."

"Well, that is to the good. 'Twould be a weary journey, otherwise!"

2

At another table, westward beyond Lama, beyond the mountains, Jobareth Nafal ate with his own family. The large dining room, its tall, arched windows opening to a view of the capital city below, only hinted of the family's wealth. It would not do to flaunt it and rouse the jealousy of the old nobility.

"I need to take some of this back with me," he said, swirling the wine in his goblet.

"You've come to the right place for it, my boy," replied his father, to laughter up and down the board. The Nafals knew wine, traded in wine, lived wine.

"Is the wine so bad in Lama?" his mother asked.

"Yes," said one of his older brothers, "how is the wine there?"

"I once had a white from the south I thought rather decent," broke in another.

"Mediocre, for the most part," opined the young diplomat. "Not particularly bad, not particularly good."

The elder Nafal considered that for a moment, absently stroking his neat pointed beard. "There's money to be made in mediocrity. Cheap but decent wine would find a market, if only it could be transported here more readily," said he.

Jobareth nodded his agreement. "If the southern passes were safer, it might be. But that is a job for the king and for my master."

"Then you must speak to Lord Radal about it as soon as possible," joked one of the brothers. "We shall hold you personally responsible for getting it done."

The young man had seen the Lord Radal again the previous day. He seemed haggard, worn, as if he had just come from some grueling contest. Their brief conversation was primarily of Lord Doufan. That nobleman seemed interested only in the royal wedding and not in the particulars of his upcoming ambassadorship.

"My master, as a rule, does not ask my advice," he dryly told his family.

"Then work on the daughter," suggested his mother, with an oh-so-innocent smile. She wants to play match-maker, thought Jobareth. It would be a good match, of course — for everyone but the couple.

He fell into banter, rather than acknowledge her implications. "That might prove a more difficult undertaking than the father." There were chuckles all around the table; they well knew the Lady Fachalana.

The royal wedding would be on the morrow, the equinox, the Feast of Spring. Maybe they could get down to business when that was done. In the mean time, Jobareth could enjoy this visit with his family, take in the theater.

Twice, he had missed Fachalana at her father's home but she had sent him an invitation to the premiere production at her theater. That, he did not intend to miss.

Count Borrago's renewed relationship with the widow Sima had become an open secret. Most thought it a most wonderful and interesting secret and readily shared it with their friends.

Lord Bolos was not inclined to agree. "My father is making a fool of himself," he told the hierophant, "and dishonoring the memory of my mother."

The high priest did not choose to mention that Bolos himself had never seen anything wrong with chasing after every woman who passed his way. But that was not really the same thing as this liaison.

He did, however, disconcert Borrago's heir further by letting him know that the count had spoken privately to him of marriage.

This served only to make Bolos the more suspicious of his half-brother. He had never had anything against Copago but neither had he ever much liked him. He would not have long remained master of arms were Bolos to become count.

But if Borrago were to marry Sima! Would Copago be legitimized? He would then be the oldest brother and could lay claim to Bolos's inheritance.

The king in Sharsh, father of his wife, grandfather of his own heir, would never permit that to happen. This Bolos knew for certain; all else remained far too uncertain.

At times like this, Bolos very much wanted a drink.

"Modareth and Carrana, in this year, the Twenty-ninth in the reign of Lareth, the One-thousand Three-hundred and Twenty-first since the Great Devastation, shall be legally joined in marriage." The Chief Scribe of Sharsh placed the marriage contract before them on his portable desk. "Sign your names, please."

They so did and the old man witnessed their signatures, before holding the paper up to the applause of the crowd.

At that point, the High Priest of Jov stepped forward to give his blessing. This, of course, was what everyone wanted to see, as it was far more theatrical than the signing of a legal document.

Prince Modareth drew himself up to his full height, which was not much. His shock of unruly black hair rose above him like a rooster's comb, surmounting a head that seemed too large for its body.

Scrawny, his brother called him but no one else dared.

The priest took the bride's hand and placed it in the groom's. To himself, he thought that it should be other way around. The Lady Carrana certainly out-sized her new husband in almost every respect, not that that was difficult.

"I shall be Modareth, at one with my husband," vowed Carrana.

"And I shall be Carrana, as one with my wife," responded Modareth.

"Then so shall it be and the blessings of the gods be on you," spoke the priest. He was pleased to see what seemed real affection between the two as Modareth kissed his bride. *Two misfits,* he thought, despite their noble blood. *It's good that they have found each other.*

King Lareth was pleased as well. Two wives had he buried and had loved each, in his way, but they had been political matches. Not that there was anything wrong with the politics here, but it was good to see his younger son happy.

If only the older one might be!

That older son, Prince Gawis, and he joined the procession behind the newlyweds, following them to the wedding feast. It was not that Gawis disliked the meek Mara, but his wife had given him only daughters.

Where is Mara? he wondered, looking into the crowd. Ah, there, with his three beloved granddaughters. Lareth did hope that his son would not make the mistake of putting her aside, once he was no longer there to forbid it. It would be unwise to divorce a daughter of the Partanacan emperor.

Dark the princess was, as dark as had been Radal's father, and, as royalty goes, a handsome woman. He waved toward them and saw Mara's smile as she bent to whisper to the girls. Telling them to wave to Grandfather, Lareth supposed. By then he had passed them and entered the great festively-striped pavilion erected for the wedding reception.

The king sighed. Politics would be the order for the rest of this day, a tedious afternoon of greetings and small talk with minor noblemen and functionaries. Duty called and Lareth, with forced smile, answered.

"Before you leave me for my brother, I ask one more service of you."

Count Borrago leaned forward, resting his elbows on his desk. Corgos's friend and commanding officer — Copago, the count's master of arms — stood gazing out the narrow window, seemingly uninterested in their conversation. Corgos knew better.

"One task or an hundred, my lord. I will serve as long as you desire."

Borrago glanced toward Copago and half-smiled. They had expected no less of the man.

"My son should soon be returning from the north. I know you rode in those lands before you served me here." There seemed to be a question implied so the knight nodded his head.

"Yes, sir, I did." He had no desire to speak further of his years as a wandering mercenary.

"Then what I ask of you, Sir Corgos, is to ride north and fetch Donzalo home."

The master of arms turned to them. "We can readily spare a half-dozen men or so. More, I fear, would attract too much attention to you."

Corgos looked from the one man to the other. "All the way to the Cuddon?"

"Most likely not," said the count. "We have reason to believe he is already on his way or soon will be."

Copago sat down beside his friend. "He may need protection." He shook his head. "We know not by what route he will travel nor how many his companions might be. That, wisely, has been kept secret.

"If he returns as he went, through the Cuddon, there is naught we can do, but if he chooses to ride through Lama, you may meet him on the road."

"Or," added the count, "if you do not, then ride on to Drolwym and learn what you can."

"I should take the Great Road, then, my lord?" asked Corgos.

"Yes. A party of armed men skulking on the back ways would raise suspicion."

Copago nodded his agreement. "You will pose as a mercenary band heading to the Siphic cities. We will provide you with the proper papers. Count Borrago's name on a document has weight anywhere in Lama."

"I should hope so!" laughed the nobleman.

"If Donzalo chooses to travel by back roads, then you may pass each other unknowingly. So be it," continued Sir Copago. "We can do only what we can do."

3

"We will ride with you a while," said Mausare, "a day or two, perhaps." Guesare sat his pony beside his half-brother.

"Welcome you are, Brothers." Habidros had four men at arms with him, doughty veterans from his father's garrison. The Cuddon was not always a peaceful place.

With his brothers and Donzalo, that made eight men riding westward from Keep Drolwym.

Or mostly westward, though their way sometimes trended north and at times Donzalo felt sure they were headed back the way they came. Silently and in single file, they traversed the fog-shrouded hills, following barely visible sheep paths, passing secluded huts. Were there shepherds within, huddled about their peat fires?

In the mists, he thought once he caught a glimpse of a gray dappled horse, disappearing across the moors.

Habidros halted of a sudden and held up a gauntleted hand. "Brothers," said he, "here we must decide. Do we continue this north by west course or turn aside to meet the Great Road south of Oles?"

The others bunched around him. "Turn, I say. It is safer to take the back roads," was the opinion of Guesare.

"We would attract less suspicion if we come to Oles by the Siphic Road before turning south," said Habidros. "They are used to seeing armed strangers pass through."

The men-at-arms all nodded their heads in agreement with this. Being Cuddonians, they would not allow themselves to be left out of the discussion.

Mausare spoke. "Donzalo should decide. This is his journey."

"Aye, that's true," agreed Habidros. "What say you, lad?"

"Which way is the shorter?" asked the Laman.

"We could save a day's travel by turning now," Guesare said, "despite being the rougher road."

"Maybe two," said one of the men at arms.

"Then turn we shall. Though," sighed Donzalo, "I would greatly liked to have seen Oles."

"It wouldn't have been safe to enter the city, anyway," Mausare told him. There were murmurs of agreement from the others.

"There is a road over — that way, isn't there?" asked Habidros, pointing toward a ridge to the left of the trail they had been following.

"Of sorts," said Guesare. He looked to the sky. "I do believe this fog is going to lift soon."

"If we see the sun it must mean that we are leaving the Cuddon," Donzalo replied. "Let's get going."

"You must tell me all about the wedding!"

"Oh, I shall," said the Lady Fachalana, "but first we must decide what to do about Jobareth Nafal. He will be coming to our opening tonight and he will want to come backstage."

"Let him," answered Ansa. "He might as well know what we have been up to."

"Indeed?" Fachalana arched her dark eyebrows. "I thought I was the reckless one!"

"Better to make him a friend and co-conspirator now than to forever worry about him discovering who I am. I have been thinking on this for some time." It will also provide a cover for my other, true mission as a spy, Ansa told herself.

"Hmm, I do suppose there is no reason Jobo shouldn't know. He will wonder about our motivation."

"Tell him straight out that you have a crush on Donzalo and make him jealous." Ansa attempted to say this seriously but then giggled.

As did Fachalana. Then she sighed. "Ah, Jobareth will never be jealous over me. His heart belongs to his princess."

Ansa fully recognized that her friend and patron was being dramatic. It might be true that Nafal would always adore the Lady Lomela, but neither had Fachalana any real interest in winning the man's love. Even if it was entirely possible that they might end up married to each other.

"All is set for tonight's performance," she said aloud. "Let us go to my dressing room and share some wine while you fill me in on every detail of the royal wedding. What did the bride wear? What did *you* wear?"

The Great Road paralleled the River Weldar, here closer, here winding into the countryside and through village and manor. From Morparas to Oles it ran and from there one might turn east toward the valley of the Siph or west to Mountain Keep and the mountained borders of Sharsh.

In the days of Anian rule had it been built, so men and materials might move efficiently east of the Weldar. There were other roads, on both sides of the river, but this was, indeed, the greatest of them, kept open and maintained by the noblemen though whose lands it passed. None would dare close it to traffic, anymore than they would the river itself.

As Donzalo and his party threaded their way down from the Cuddonian hills to find the highway and, further south, Sir Corgos prepared to ride toward them, others followed the lesser road along the western banks of the Weldar.

Far to the north, Sojel led forth the handful of men he had recruited in Oles. A pitiful bunch, he felt, but probably no worse than the usual riff-raff — as good as those who were to gather at their rendezvous point, anyway. He hoped Vanob would show up and help him whip these dregs into something resembling fighting men.

Neither king nor crown prince attended that night, but the royal newlyweds were in the audience. The bookish, retiring Modareth had never been known as a patron of the theater. It seemed his new wife intended to change that. Together they sat in their box, the prince nervously surveying the crowd. He did not much like being in public.

He toyed with the reading glass he always wore hung around his neck and turned to look fondly upon his spouse. She was no beauty, he knew, plump and large of bone, but he knew also that she adored him. Why, he truly did not know.

But Modareth accepted it and, so, chose to adore her as well.

There was a small window opening above the stage where one might look out upon the house. Ansa and Fachalana were doing just that.

"There is Nafal, front and center," said Ansa, "as you expected."

"Jobareth does love the theater, Maresta," answered Fachalana, for she still knew the Anian by that name. "I hope he enjoys this old warhorse we chose to present."

"It is a classic, my lady."

"So you keep telling me. I am glad our royal couple came. I've known Modareth since he was a toddler. Ha, I guess I was a toddler as well!"

"You are of an age?"

"Yes, as is Jobo. He somewhat took Modi under his wing when he first came to court." She sighed and Ansa sensed the true emotion behind it. "The three of us were inseparable for a time. We and," she added, "little Lomela when she came along."

The actress chose not to press further in that particular direction. "Did you know the Lady Carrana?"

Fachalana turned from their portal. "Not well. I probably treated her badly. She always seemed too — needy, I might say. Too eager to please.

"But she pleases Modareth and I am glad of that. Love is not to be cast aside, wherever we may find it."

Both women silently nodded agreement to that. And each pictured the same tall Laman in her mind.

4

"You should be able to pick up the Great Road by mid-morn tomorrow." Guesare stirred the campfire before him. "We will head back home at dawn."

Mausare nodded. "We will miss you, Brothers. Remember that Drolwym is your home, Habidros. And it can be yours, as well," he said, speaking directly to Donzalo.

"Who knows the future?" asked Habidros. "For now, we are but a little band of soldiers, traveling south to find employment. And when we are done play-acting and you fine fellows," he said, inclining his head toward the four men-at-arms, "make your way home, I may just stay and see what Lama has to offer.

"What say you, Donzalo? Might your father be hiring?"

"With a word from the right person, he might be," replied Donzalo with a wink to the man's brothers.

They camped beside a narrow dirt road, rutted by the wheels of farmers' carts. Around them rose the newly leafing trees, oaks and maples, still visible in the gloaming. The music of a stream in the valley below them could be distantly heard. Habidros chuckled and stood to stretch for a moment.

"Well, boy," said he, "mayhap you should consider a soldiering career yourself. There's little profit in a younger son staying at home."

"Not that you've ever shown much," remarked Guesare, with brotherly sarcasm.

"He has made plenty," said Mausare. "If he could but hold onto it!"

"Ah, yes, rub it in, Brother. Had I saved my coins I might have settled down with an even larger farm than yours." The big mercenary shrugged. "I would be very bored, I think."

Guesare spoke then, more seriously. "Our Donzalo, I think, is meant for bigger things."

For a few moments the men pondered this. Then one of the soldiers broke the silence. "We all know that. Donzalo is a man of destiny." His comrades nodded their agreement.

"That's what everyone back home says," averred another.

And what I have felt from the start, Guesare said to himself. Now all the world will be learning it.

Twice, Ansa had gone on stage only to take part in a crowd scene. Each time, she donned a dark wig and attempted to remain shadowed and unobtrusive. None the less, each time she wondered if Jobareth Nafal recognized her.

Her true role tonight had been that of stage manager. From start to finish, Ansa was the one who oversaw this production of 'King Nordoc.' It was an old play, and formal by modern standards, but she had pointed out to Fachalana that it segued neatly into the drama of Oemse that Nafal was supposedly writing — Oemse, of course, having been Nordoc's tragically slain first wife.

Now, they were drawing near the end of the final act. The heroic — and quite dead — Nordoc lay upon his bier, awaiting entombment. At least the ham couldn't overact anymore tonight. Fachalana came to center stage to declaim the closing lines. They were of a rather old-fashioned poetic style, but suited to the young noblewoman's delivery. Their very formality prevented her from emoting too strongly.

Where has gone the king?
Man no more is mighty;
silence spreads its shroud
where heroes sang of old.

Lizards doze upon
the walls of ruined cities;
the wells hold nests of snakes;
the wind rules realms of dust.

Victories forgotten,
sword beside him broken;
the king lies in his grave
and sleeps eternally.

Ansa actually felt moved as the funeral procession slowly exited the stage. Apparently, so did the audience for they applauded loudly and for a quite a long while after the curtain fell. She watched from the wings as the various actors went out to take their bows. Fachalana did so at least three times.

And then, quite surprisingly, her patroness took her by the arm and pulled her onto stage. Despite being a rather petite woman, Ansa was both lithe and well-trained and could easily have broken away. She chose not to.

"May I present the woman behind tonight's production," loudly announced Fachalana. "The talented and lovely Maresta, whom many of you have seen on stage before."

In the front row, Ansa could see Jobareth's eyes grow wide. On an impulse, she smiled and blew a kiss his way.

Fachalana could hardly keep from laughing and did so as soon as they reached the wings. "He will be back here soon," she said. "I have been asked to greet the royal couple and will attempt to take Jobareth with me. That will give you a few minutes."

A few minutes to make my escape, thought Ansa. It's not too late!

Jobareth Nafal had no choice but to be patient. Fachalana had, somehow, steered him over to the box where Prince Modareth and his bride waited. A single, seemingly bored attendant ushered them in and tactfully slipped away. Guarding the unassuming prince was neither an exciting nor a demanding duty.

In the mean time, all he could think of was the woman he had known as Posena. No wonder she had seemed familiar. He must have seen her a dozen times on stage!

Ah, but here was his old friend Modi. It been many years since they sat together in the king's gardens, reading passages to each other from favorite books and discussing the mystery that was girls. Then he had gone off to study, leaving his friend behind.

As shy as ever, the prince seemed unsure whether to hug him or shake his hand. Nafal, ever the diplomat, took the hand warmly and then pulled Modareth into a partial embrace. He wasn't sure how much of that was natural to him, now, and how much ingrained from years of training.

Fachalana had no hesitation in throwing her arms around the prince, and his wife as well. "It's like old times, Modi!" she exclaimed, beaming at the group. "How long has it been since we three were together?"

The young man shrugged, seemingly tongue-tied. His wife immediately jumped in, evincing a genuine interest in them and their history. Perhaps nothing she said was of great consequence but that did not matter.

I can see how this is a good pairing, thought Jobareth. He glanced at Fachalana from the corner of his eye to see her doing the same. Both smiled.

"Do come by sometime, won't you?" asked the young prince. "Either one or both." He looked towards his bride. "Th-that's alright with you, isn't it, my dear?" Modareth had largely outgrown his childhood stutter but it occasionally made itself known.

"Of course, husband mine."

Fachalana recognized that her characterization of Carrana as being eager to please was still quite valid. She would welcome any of her husband's friends and do her best to make them her friends. Perhaps it would do well to cultivate this warm, earthy woman.

"Then we will make our goodbyes. We should be getting home." The prince gave his wife a tender look. There was also a hunger in it that both Fachalana and Jobareth noted. Were they surprised? Perhaps, thinking they knew Modareth so well. They were also most certainly amused.

"They are newlyweds, after all," whispered Fachalana as they wound their way through the emptying theater.

"And, I would wager," answered Nafal, "both virgins up until yesterday."

"Hmm, yes, I suppose," murmured his companion. "I suppose." She spoke no more until they reached the backstage.

"I am saddened to hear of Lady Vibola's passing," said Ansa. "She was as fine a woman as any I have known. I didn't even mind," she added with a slight smile, "emptying her chamber pot. Well, not too much."

Nafal nodded. "I came to love the old woman," he said, "as did Lomela."

He took another sip of his spiced wine and looked at the two women across the table from him. Then he looked about the little room that served as Maresta's quarters and, apparently, her office as well. It seemed surprisingly spartan, from what he knew of women's bedrooms. She did not live here, he realized; she was only passing through. Was that the life of an actress?

"It seems that there was much I did not know about what happened a year ago. But I still do not understand why my master — your father, Fachalana — wants Donzalo dead."

"Oh, he does not know of the prophecy," Ansa nonchalantly remarked to her companion.

"So it would seem," agreed Fachalana.

Jobareth sighed. "I must resign myself to your whims, my ladies. Might I ask of this prophecy?"

"Our Lady Fachalana learned of it while rifling through her father's papers. She should tell the tale." Though I had already heard of it from my brother, Ansa added, to herself.

"This is a serious business, truly," said Fachalana, becoming instantly sober. She seemed to compose herself for a moment, straightening up her tall frame. Jobareth found himself watching how the light of the lamps fell on her finely chiseled features, her burnished skin. She is truly beautiful, he thought, isn't she?

"The Oracle at Cars made a pronouncement and it was this: that the son of Donzalo would rule in Lama." She was speaking in the measured cadences of the stage. Whether she consciously realized it or not, falling into the ways of the actor gave her the self-control she needed.

"So it is that King Lareth sees him as a threat and wishes him removed. As does my father, though I believe," Fachalana hesitated, albeit slightly, "that he has since found other reasons to hate Donzalo."

The young man let the information sink in for a moment before looking up at the pair. "May I tell Lomela of this?"

"Certainly," answered Fachalana. Ansa slowly nodded her acquiescence.

"Why not another conspirator?" she said with a shrug, though it went against all her instincts as a spy. She had already gone much further than she ever should have. "But as conspirators, we should make plans. We must meet again before you leave Celatas, Lector Nafal."

"Indeed, my ladies. Now, though, I had best be on my way." He rose and bowed to the pair.

"I will walk you out, Jobo," said Fachalana. As her friend went to the door, Ansa took the diplomat's arm, pulling him down to whisper in his ear.

"You and I also must speak again, when we can. There are other matters here — ones which concern our Fachalana."

Jobareth Nafal nodded and followed the Lady Fachalana into the corridor.

5

"I assume Nafal is your creature."

Radal was never certain whether Lord Doufan was obtuse or played games. The man was a sycophant and a sophist, but not to be underestimated.

And he seemed to be one of the few courtiers who evinced no fear of the powerful Lord Radal, adviser to the king and reputed sorcerer.

"These days," he replied, deciding to keep their exchange to small-talk, "I believe he is more my daughter's creature."

The man gave him a warm and, Radal suspected, entirely insincere smile. "There have been rumors of a match, my Lord Councilor. Might we expect another wedding soon?"

"Not if young Jobareth is off in Lama with you, my Lord Doufan. I must admit, I do have some hopes for an engagement announcement before you leave."

Doufan noted the 'some.' Apparently the match was far from assured. It would be better to change the subject.

"I hope we can be on the road east, soon. Even I grow weary of these endless parties and balls, Radal." He noted the nobleman's amusement at that statement. "Yes, my lord, I know this is, so to speak, my natural environment." He gestured, arms out, at the festive room in which they stood, surrounded by the elites of Celatas.

Lord Radal nodded. "So it is, Doufan. Let us hope you can be as effective a courtier in County Rosam." He looked seriously upon the man. "It seems you should be able to leave here on schedule. Understand that I expect Nafal to handle the everyday business of your embassy. Your duty is to make that as easy for him as possible."

"In other words, my lord, to be charming? It is my stock in trade."

Pol thought no one saw him slip his letter into the dispatch bag. That was all to the good, felt Blen, as he drew it forth. Best that the young fellow suspect nothing.

He had watched the soldier attempting to spy unobtrusively these last few weeks. Whose tool was he? Ah, the missive was addressed to Nafal. Sir Blen smiled benignly. So Jobareth had asked the boy to keep an eye on things for him. There was no harm in that.

He smoothed the sheet out on the desk before him. The message was short, printed out in large block letters.

Master Nafal, as orderd I write this to you. I have kept watch and all is good here in lama. The Count send a troope of men north. I think they be fetching his boy home. All the castle and the town are talking about Count Borrago and his lady love. There are wagers on the wedding date. I have taken midsummer and hope to win some.

The Princess is well and her son is too but the baby is sick a lot. She look worried when I see her at the keep last week. I watch Sir Blen too but he does not due much. Will keep my eyes open. Pol

Blen read through once more and, with a laugh, folded the letter and returned it to the bag.

The Great Road was broad here, and the river ran near at hand. Six men rode south. That they were fighting men, they made no attempt to conceal; the best deception, after all, is that which comes most close to the truth.

They did not hurry, these fighting men. That would attract unwelcome attention and, after all, there was no rush. This was, for the most part, a new country for them. Even Donzalo had never been so far north in his native Lama. So they enjoyed their journey, stopping often. There were plenty enough inns and taverns along the Great Road to take their interest and money.

But they chose to encamp rather than stay in those inns. That was easy enough along these stretches of the Weldar, where forest often grew down to the river's banks. Further south, perhaps, a secluded spot would be difficult to find.

On the second night along that road, Donzalo slept beneath the stars and dreamed a dream. It was an odd sort of dream. Someone was calling to him, he thought, from afar. It troubled him that he could not make out the words. Then the voice faded and he fell into deep slumber.

Fachalana was frustrated. She often was, these days. Her attempt at a spell, all on her own, to contact Donzalo's dream-self had not worked as she wished. She could not make herself heard, could not hear him, see him, as she wished.

Yet she had touched him, hadn't she? Was it a matter of practice or would she never have the skill? Little did she realize that her father, powerful sorcerer though he might be, would have been astounded at what she had accomplished.

As he would have been if he knew how much she had learned during their brief link in Donzalo's dreamworld.

Even if Fachalana realized how much she had managed, she still would have wanted more. Her mind, restless as ever, turned elsewhere. She thought of Jobareth and what he had said to her in the theater, of his casual comment on virgins.

Jobareth seemed to assume I wasn't one, she thought to herself. I'm almost tempted to marry him just to prove otherwise.

She sighed. Jobo treated her too much like a comrade. It had always been that way; even as children they had shared rough, boyish games and she the roughest of them all, their ringleader in mischief.

Fachalana liked Jobareth Nafal perhaps better than anyone in the world but knew she would never love him. She wanted something more, someone more, than the men she met here at court. For most of them, she felt contempt. Swaggering idiots!

Could she talk with Ansa about this? Fachalana's courage rarely failed her but the thought of baring herself to her self-possessed friend frightened her. How could she speak of her lack of experience to such a woman?

She seemed very tired. Was this how her father felt after working his magics? Fachalana had witnessed that often enough over the years. She would take a draught and try to sleep and perhaps, just perhaps, she would dream of Donzalo.

The band of smugglers had turned away from the river, trekking further west to avoid passing through the Rosam territories on this side of the Weldar. Count Borrago's tolls were notoriously high.

"These are the lands of Count Dordos," said Galaro to their traveling companion. Perdos was well aware of that fact, having been resident at Keep Rosam. Dordos ruled over a smaller, poorer county, west and north of Borragos's holdings. It was known that he disliked the Rosam. It was also known that he was in the pay of Sharsh.

Sharsh's couriers were allowed free passage of his lands, aye, and kept fresh horses stabled there, so the latter was not surprising. That other funds, for other purposes, came to Dordos from the king of Sharsh was uncertain but widely suspected.

"There is a spot on the river, north some ten leagues from Ros-town, where we will make our crossing. Dordos and his men will turn a blind eye for a small sum. Then," continued the burly Cuddonian, "we will wend north along the Great Road for a while, buying and selling."

"I should leave you when you cross," spoke the knight.

"I assumed as much," replied Galaro. "Where you are headed, I will not ask. Indeed, if it involves my brother, 'tis best I not know."

"Are you noting the band of men headed our way?" asked Perdos.

"I have been watching them for a while. We are well armed and seem matched in number. Still," he said, turning in his saddle and calling out to their troop. "Have your weapons ready, boys!"

"Always best to be prepared," said he to Perdos.

"Very true. But if they meant us mischief, they would not be riding so boldly," opined the Laman knight.

The other group of horsemen drew closer. Suddenly, Perdos hissed. He knew the man at their head.

"It is Sojel and his cutthroats. They are the ones who seek the death of your kinsman, Donzalo."

"I do not know this Donzalo and care little. Even less than for my brother. But you are under my protection and I do not break my oaths," Galaro stated.

He reined in his steed and held up a hand signaling his followers to do the same.

Sojel's troop also did the same, but bunched up in a much more disorderly fashion. Their sergeant sat his horse for a moment, staring at Perdos.

"Yon deserter belongs to me," he claimed, calmly, flatly, yet with readily evident menace.

"We are honest smugglers," replied the Cuddonian, "and want no trouble. But Sir Perdos is with us and remains with us."

Sojel assessed the group of hard, armed men before him and shrugged. "Very well. It is of no importance." He gave Perdos another long, malevolent look and then led his men past Galaro's party, headed south.

That party kept their hands on their sword hilts till all had disappeared down the road.

"There is a rendezvous point not far from here," said Perdos. "He will be gathering all his men there, I suspect. Far more than he had with him this day."

"Then," said Galaro, "it was Jov's own fortune that we met him this day and not some other."

6

"I, too, miss Lector Nafal and our discussions. There is none other here with his education."

"You two grew close after Donzalo left, didn't you, Brother Grippo?"

"Yes, my lady, though our respective duties and my studies left us ever less time for our talks."

"Oh, yes, your ordination is coming soon," said the Lady Lomela. "At mid-summer?"

Grippo smiled. "All ordinations are at mid-summer, my lady. That is the Kamatian way."

"And I am still a heathen at heart, by Laman standards, aren't I?" Lomela laughed aloud. "I fear I shall so remain, Brother."

"I would not have you change, my lady." Realizing how that sounded, Brother Grippo felt a sudden embarrassment.

Lomela noted this and spoke to him, quite seriously. "Do not be ashamed to be courtly, my friend. It will stand you well in times to come. Jobareth and I both expect that you will rise rapidly in the priestly ranks. Indeed," she continued, "we would not be surprised to see you hierophant here, someday."

"That is something I do not seek, my lady. I do not know if I wish to be a priest at all." He sighed deeply. "It was the only path to learning, in this land. Jobareth has opened my eyes to a greater world.

"Ah, well, I came here, ostensibly, to bless your daughter." He shook his head. "I sometimes doubt the efficacy of my prayers."

"I am sure that prayers are always heard by someone, somewhere, Grippo, if said in earnest. I hope you do not mind that I occasionally address mine to the Lady Esefa."

"That, my lady," answered the acolyte, "is between you and Kamat. And Esefa, too, I suppose," he added with a chuckle. "Let me see to the baby."

"She sleeps in her nurse's room." Lomela's eyes showed signs of tearing up. "I fear she will not live long, Brother Grippo. Please do pray for her, as hard as you can.

"And be sure to stop by here more often. This place has grown cheerless and we could use your company."

'King Nordoc' was scheduled to play through the rest of the month, so Ansa was at work each and every morning, attending to business, checking the receipts, making sure the sets were in order — all the details of running a theater and producing a show.

Fachalana appeared when she would. Her friend could not help but note that she often seemed distracted and sometimes quite exhausted. She was worried about Fachalana.

"I think you might use a break, Maresta," came a voice from behind her, as she watched her stagehands repair a painted backdrop. One or another of the cast had leaned too heavily against it last night. None was admitting to it.

"Lector. It is good that you stopped by." She turned away from the workers. "These may or may not keep busy if I leave, but I think it more important that we speak. Will you come to my room?"

In her dressing room and office, she busied herself with the making of tea. Her people were great drinkers of tea, back on the cold eastern steppes, and it was one luxury Ansa was willing to afford herself.

Jobareth sat watching her, waiting. What did he know of this woman? That she cared about Fachalana, he was certain, but there was so little more.

"Would you care for some, Lector Nafal?" she asked, pouring herself a cup. "No? You do not know what you are missing, you and your family with your constant wine drinking."

"Why do you not call me Jobareth? At least in private — I consider you a friend, now, and would have you do the same."

Ansa laughed. "Very well. But I shall not address you as Jobo!"

"Even the Lady Lomela does not use that name for me anymore. Only Lana." His tone became serious. "It is of her you wished to speak, is it not?"

She seated herself across from him and stated her concern outright. "Yes. Did you know she has become her father's apprentice?"

Jobareth slowly drew in a breath. "So that is why you were willing to risk revealing yourself to me." He nodded. "It explains many things. What can we do?"

"Be her friends. Try to guide away from harm, when able. I do not think there is anything more we can do here. Though," said Ansa, "perhaps if we could get her beyond her father's influence for a while, it would help."

"Beyond? Do you mean in Lama?"

"Yes, exactly. If you two were engaged, might she not visit you? And her friend, Princess Lomela, as well?"

The lector gave her a wry smile. "If either of us were actually willing to become engaged.

"Still, a visit might be arranged. The thing is to convince Fachalana that she wishes it. Then nothing will stop her!"

Already, Guesare was growing restless. His friend Donzalo, his brothers, all gone from Drolwym, he sat by himself, idly strumming his rebec.

"He will be leaving us again, soon," whispered the Lady Se to her husband.

"Did we ever doubt that?" asked the thane.

Oder had sent his friend a letter. It seemed that the Anian had a spy in the Sharshite capital and, although the details were kept vague, there was much of interest. It was more gossip than aught else, the minstrel realized. Oder would not be giving him serious information in this casual missive.

He had also named a place and time to meet, should Guesare choose to take to the road once more. Coded, naturally, but he understood it. He fiddled a moment with his tuning pegs. It would be good to exchange tunes with Oder again.

It would be good simply to be with Oder, to travel with him once more through the wide, ever-changing world. He knew Oder was not like him, not a man to fall passionately in love with person nor place. He knew he had two wives back in the empire and took casual lovers of either gender, when and where he would. The spy-master Oder was, and would remain, the one who could cast aside anyone and anything, without regret.

Perhaps he should ride to that meeting, a fortnight hence. Would not Drolwym be here when he chose to return? Guesare strummed again and thought on many things.

"Silence, my bullies! We don't want them hearing us all the way to Ros-town."

Perdos was impressed by the efficiency of this band. Already most of their goods had been ferried across the Weldar, quickly and quietly. This eastern shore was part of Count Dordos's land; on the far side lay Rosam holdings.

Their bribes — which Galaro claimed went up the ladder to Dordos himself — not only bought them passage but also provided false papers saying that all duties and levies had been paid. Those should get them across the northern border of County Rosam. Landing their freight on the eastern side of the river was the only part that might go wrong. They must not attract attention.

The knight had waited to the last, holding a baffled lantern for the smugglers, and uncertain whether he should actually cross over here with them. That it was not wise to remain on the same side of the river as Sojel, he felt sure, so when the time came he led his horse aboard the final barge. Galaro boarded aside him.

"You will leave us now, Sir Perdos?" rumbled the Cuddonian.

"Aye. I thank you for your company and for your protection." Perdos stared toward the far bank, still hidden in night. "May we meet again in friendship."

And on reaching the shore, he mounted his tall horse and rode into the darkness and away from his traveling companions.

7

"Lector Nafal."

Jobareth looked up from his list to see an attendant holding a diplomatic pouch.

"Ah, the latest dispatches. Thank you." He took it from the man and emptied its contents onto the big marble-topped table. All around the room were boxes and bales, being readied for the journey to Lama. These final preparations were keeping him busy, here in this wing of Lareth's palace.

But not so busy that he couldn't take time to sort through the dispatches — most could be passed on to the proper ministries or to Lord Radal. There was an official report from Blen. He quickly perused it and, finding nothing of great interest or import, added it to the stack of papers for the Lord Councilor's eyes.

No personal letters for him. He wished that Lomela had found time to write but knew she was busy as mother and wife these days, and not so gay since the passing of Lady Vibola. Then he came upon the note from Pol, his young spy.

Jobareth opened the letter and smiled at its message, before holding it to the candle to darken any invisible ink. Yes, there at the bottom.

I know Sir Blen is keeping an eye on me. Best he think me a fool. P

He was glad he had shown that trick to the boy while they had rested at Mountain Keep. Pol was proving more devious than he had hoped and, in this case, Blen seemed the fool.

Nafal looked back over the letter. Lomela's little girl was not well? He had not read that in any official correspondence, including Blen's. It was good to have young Pol at his service, if only to keep him up on matters others deemed trivial.

Now if only all his other plans went as well.

"These all seem in order," said the guard, handing back Galaro's papers after a cursory scan. "Did your stay in County Rosam go well?" He was not truly interested but his orders called for him to ask such of all travelers.

"Well enough," answered the Cuddonian. "Well enough. Tell me, sir, is there any news of trouble on the road, armed men or such?" The memory of Sojel's band was still fresh in his mind and Perdos's admonition that it would be growing.

"None. It has been quiet so far this spring and traffic is just starting to pick up along the Great Road. Hmm." He bethought himself for a moment. "There was a little band of soldiers came through here yesterday. Or was it?" He called to the guard on the other side of the border. "Which day did those mercenaries pass by?"

"Early yester-morn," replied the fellow. "A half-dozen of them, heading off to seek employment in the north."

"Yes. They seemed good solid men. Just the sort to have as traveling companions on some stretches of the road."

Probably well ahead of me, thought Galaro. Still, it might not hurt to take this guard's advice and try to catch up to them. "I thank you, sirs. Here is a little something for your trouble this morning," he said, handing each man a small gold coin and leading his caravan through the open border gate.

Word at last!

Sojel looked up from the newly-arrived message and out over his growing troop, wondering whether it was time to ride. If he waited, their number would surely increase, but not by much — most of the men had reported and those who had not, might never.

It was odd, though, that Vanob had not appeared.

He reread the paper in his hands. Rumor, it was, not solid intelligence. Still, a chance of catching the Rosam boy on the road was better than idling here.

He turned to the knot of men who stood near him, those he had made his lieutenants. He had little trust in them but they were the best of his mongrel pack. "Get the men ready to move," he commanded. "We are quitting this cesspool of Dordos."

"So, all is readied for our delegation to leave on the morrow?" asked Lord Radal.

The man well knew that it was, of course, realized Jobareth. The question was more a statement of fact. "It is, my lord," he answered.

"Very well." The dark nobleman sat, erect, impassive, for a moment, seeming to be more interested in the papers on his desk than the young man standing before him. Then he spoke again.

"Up until now you have been, officially, secretary to the embassy with rank of attache. That is to change." Jobareth tried to remain calm. Was he to lose his post?

"Our Lord Doufan will have his own long-time — and, I assume, trusted — secretary with him. You will need to keep an eye on the man, by the way. We have assigned you a secretary of your own — the young fellow who accompanied you here from Mountain Keep."

"He seemed competent," ventured Jobareth, breathing easier. He was not being sacked, apparently.

"And he admires you," replied the Lord Councilor. "I think he will do well enough, though green. It is to you to see he properly learns his duties."

"I will, my lord."

"I am sure that is true, Nafal. You have done well in Lama, so far." He leaned back in his chair. "Unofficially, you have been acting as our legate, with all the duties thereof but not the authority. We are changing that state of affairs.

"The king and I feel you should be legate in name, as well, still second-in-command to our ambassador, Lord Doufan, but with the authority to act in his name when he is not able." Radal smiled thinly. "Doufan chose not to object, though I doubt he likes it."

Lord Radal held out a document to his protege. "Here is your official appointment. Do not disappoint us, Jobareth."

"I thank you, my lord. Might I ask if Sir Blen's position will change?" It was a question best asked now, though he barely dared speak it.

"He will remain master of arms. He will also remain your equal in command, at the king's insistence." Though he allowed no pique to be evident in his voice, Jobareth was certain his master was unhappy about the situation.

Then he decided to broach another subject, most definitely even chancier. "I — I would speak to you of your daughter, sir."

This time, Radal showed actual surprise. "Do so," he commanded.

"My lord, the Lady Fachalana and I have discussed the possibility of marriage." That was certainly true, even if they had not done so seriously. He dove deeper into his semi-deception. "We both feel that, with me leaving for an indefinite period, we should not announce an engagement. That assumes, sir," he continued, attempting to play the hesitant suitor, "that you would approve."

"You know I would, my boy." The councilor paused a moment. "I would not have objected to an announcement at all. I suppose it is too late now, though."

"Perhaps, my lord, you could permit Fachalana to visit us in Lama. The Lady Lomela would greatly love to see her."

"As I recall it," said Radal, "Fachalana rather mistreated the princess when they were children. There were tears and skinned knees and her father's displeasure."

"Which, sir, Lomela and Fachalana remember as great adventures."

The nobleman laughed. "Fachalana sees everything as a great adventure." He gave the young man a stern look. "Be sure she does not lead you into too many.

"And we shall consider allowing her to travel. Now you had best go make your final good byes."

Bolos sat with pen in hand. He would trust this missive to no scribe; it was for his eyes only and for those of the king in Sharsh.

The king in Sharsh — not long ago, he had spoken against closer ties with his wife's father. That Lareth had been complicit in the attempts on his brother's life, Bolos had little doubt. But to whom else could he turn now?

He sat back and composed his thoughts. Best he simply tell all his suspicions, lay out each of his grievances to the king. Then, sealed against the prying of spies or diplomats, he would have his own man carry the letter to Sharsh.

Bolos put pen to paper and began writing.

8

"It is done," Jobareth told the two women. "I think he believed me completely."

"You are very much sticking your neck out, Jobo." Fachalana was quite uncertain about this whole scheme. "If our plan puts you in any danger, I *will* marry you. I promise you that."

"You two could do far worse than each other," observed Ansa. Looking into herself, she realized that she liked and admired them both. That was a dangerous thing for a spy.

Indeed, we could do worse, thought Fachalana. But the one reason she had fallen in with this scheme was for the chance to, at last, meet Donazalo Rosam. She would not tell these two that, naturally. What had started as a lark, when she sent Maresta to spy on her friends, had become a much more serious matter to her.

Another might have seen it as obsession.

And in his study, in his villa above the city, Lord Radal wondered if he might, somehow, use his daughter as a weapon against that same Donzalo.

The tedium of travel may lead to the wandering of the mind. Donzalo's mind wandered to thoughts of the daughter of Lord Radal.

He still did not know her name. He still wondered if he was meant to seek her. And his recent dream haunted him. He could not shake the feeling that it was connected to her, somehow.

Habidros wondered about his mood. He barely knew the young Laman, it was true, but he did know that the boy had been through much.

And all this talk about his 'destiny.' That would be a load for anyone. Especially if one believed it. The Cuddonian avoided such ideas, himself. It was enough to live and let the future take care of itself.

It always had.

He tried to distract the lad with tales of his exploits in the Siphic states. But it was not his battles that interested young Donzalo; no, it was the city-states themselves, their politics, their sciences. Habidros realized that he actually was not well-schooled on these subjects, despite the years spent fighting the states' wars.

"Is it true that there are no noblemen in the Siphics?" he asked.

Of this, Habidros knew some. "It varies from state to state," said he. "Almost all are republics of some sort, but in one the people will rule and in the next power is concentrated in a few noble families.

"It is true that those nobles keep a low profile and avoid ostentatious display. They fear the people would rise up if they flaunted their positions."

"That," said Donzalo, "may be so everywhere."

"Ha, I suppose it is. From what I have seen of Oles, it is much like the cities of the Siph. Except full of puritanical Lamans rather than the easy-going folk of the east."

"We are not like the burgess of Oles in our county." Donzalo had met and talked with many of them, come down to Ros-town for the fairs. "Though my father," added the young knight, with a laugh, "loves his profits every bit as much!"

The Weldar could not be crossed here. He must lead his men further to the north, well beyond the borders of County Rosam, to a morass of swamp and forest and few people. His troop was far too large to go unnoticed anywhere else. Two score they numbered now.

Sojel was not overly familiar with that area. A haunt of bandits and river pirates, he had heard, and the isolated huts of fishermen and hunters. Such should give him no trouble. More importantly, that lawless wilderness also harbored smugglers who would be of assistance in getting his men across. Already had he dispatched messengers to them.

He gave the order now to his lieutenants to move out. Each led a small band, five or six men, so that they might not attract undue attention, with orders to rejoin their comrades in two days.

Whether they would be behind Donzalo's party or ahead of it they would not know. It was not even certain that he was on the Great Road at all. Sojel could but muster his men on the eastern side and send out scouts to search up and down the highway.

And then, at last, perhaps he could act.

Make sure your bearings in what lands you roam:
The wisest man is he who travels far,
Yet keeps his eye upon a guiding star
That someday serves to show him his way home.

"That," said Lord Doufan, "has ever been my philosophy."

Jobareth Nafal recognized the passage, the work of an obscure poet from the previous century. The name of its author escaped him.

He was baffled by this man. The ambassador was full of such quotes and seemed to have a prodigious memory yet not a single original thought in him. At least none that he would share.

Certainly, there was much more to Doufan than he had been led to believe. More than the smooth courtier he appeared on the surface.

Would that the fellow rode, thought Jobareth. They would make far better time. But no, he insisted upon a horse-litter, all the way to Mountain Keep. Probably beyond, as well, on the road to Oles where they would take to the river, passing down the Weldar to County Rosam.

On further consideration, he decided that Lord Doufan was asserting himself. He could ride, no doubt, if he wished. It was his way of showing that he was not to be taken lightly, that he was still the head of this embassy. Jobareth had no intention of challenging that idea nor rising to any bait.

"It seems good advice, my lord," he said. "I have a star of my own." Let him think I speak of the Lady Fachalana, he told himself. It will remind him that I have also a powerful patron. "I shall ride forward and see if anyone knows how far it is to the next inn. My lord." He gave a respectful nod of his head and urged his horse ahead.

He could not remain here on the northern borders of County Rosam. There was too much chance of being recognized. Perdos decided to ride due east, up into the hill country and away from the larger villages.

All the way into the wild country that lay between Rosam lands and the Cuddon would he journey, and then swing back to the south, toward the River Abam and Sir Paren's keep. There, he knew the lay of the land. There, he could keep a watch on things and be prepared if the bard Guesare returned.

It would be a hard life, for a time, but he was willing to live on the move, hunting his dinner, sleeping in the open. It would be worth it and, after all, this countryside was a pleasant enough place in the summer.

Perdos bethought him of the inn where he had wintered. He should go back there when this was over, he told himself. Yes, he *would* go back.

9

"You know you can always tell your father you changed your mind, my lady. I dare say he would not be surprised."

"No, I suppose not," admitted the Lady Fachalana. "But it might do harm to Jobareth's career."

"You care greatly for your friend Nafal."

"Yes, Maresta, I do. Too much to marry him, I think." Both women sat a while in silence. "Has anyone ever proposed to you?" Fachalana asked, of a sudden. It seemed an awkward sort of question to her so she felt it best to simply blurt it out.

Ansa considered her answer. She could be more or less truthful if she left out a few details. "Yes, Lana, they have, back home when I was a girl in the countryside." That the countryside of which she spoke was in the heartland of the Anian Empire, she need not mention. "I knew I wanted more. At least before settling down to being wife and mother."

Fachalana hesitated for a moment and then spoke. "I have had more proposals than I can remember."

"Every popinjay in the court sees you as a path to higher position," Ansa observed. "None of them are worthy and you know it."

"Perhaps I should not have kept them all at arm's length." Fachalana sighed deeply. "Have I missed out on too much with my play-acting and self-absorption?"

There is much unspoken here, thought Ansa. Has Fachalana never been with a man? She thought back to the trysts of her teen years, the eager young Ani warriors she had known and loved, to some degree.

But Ansa had become quite the strait-laced young woman since entering her career in espionage. She had taken no lovers in Celatas, choosing to focus on her mission.

"When the right man comes, you will know and let him in," she said, half believing it and knowing it was what her friend would want to hear. "It will happen, my lady."

Perhaps for both of us, she added, to herself.

He knew the man. It had been half a year ago but he remembered this knight, leading his men to Sir Paren's manor while he and his mates waited in hiding for an order to attack. An order that did not come when the sergeant decided it was wiser to bide his time.

So what was he doing here on the Great Road, riding north with a handful of men? Surely it had something to do with their mission. Best he get back to Sojel and report.

He mounted up and headed toward the Weldar. The sergeant was a smart one, sending scouts across its stream before the main body of his men. Maybe all had come over the river by now and they could see some action, eh?

The going was difficult here, swampy and uneven, and the Road lay well away from the river, passing in and out of forest where no man lived. A good place for an ambush, he thought to himself. A very good place.

He waited beside the road. Another might not have seen him but Guesare was attuned to this land and to those who dwelt in it.

The Prince raised a hand in greeting. "You are leaving," he stated.

"Yes. As much as I love my homeland, I find that I can not abide here long." He swung himself down from his mount to stand beside the fay. "Is that Jola's horse?" he asked. The stallion, all dappled of gray, stood on the ridge opposite,

"He awaits Donzalo's return." The horse turned, silently, and disappeared over the hill.

"Donzalo and I shared a dream. I did not see and understand all that occurred, for it was his dream, not mine. He has told thee of it?"

"No, not a word," Guesare said.

"Then it is not my place to speak of these things. Perhaps your friend will, in time." The Prince's pale eyes met those of his mortal friend. "But of one thing I will speak.

"There was one there who, I believe, did not belong. Only for a brief moment did she enter our vision, but it was enough for us to sense her presence, and she ours.

"She was much like Jola. I think she must be her sister."

"Lord Radal's daughter? Ah, so that is why the boy was asking me about her!" Many small things came together to form a whole in the minstrel's mind.

The Other nodded. "Then he recognized the kinship as well. Perhaps this, too, is a part of his destiny. We do not know.

"This we of the fay do know: the woman is growing as a sorceress. We have felt her new-found but still undisciplined power from afar. It is very great, though it will never rival that of our Jola." The Prince paused for a moment, as both mortal and fay remembered their loss.

"Her name is Fachalana," he continued. "Do with this knowledge what you will. I know only that Donzalo is your friend. Care for him.

"I bid thee farewell and fortune upon your journey."

Habidros slid one long pistol from its holster. The other lay ready at hand on the other side of his saddle. "Those are fighting men headed our way. Be on the lookout, lads."

Shielding his eyes from the afternoon sun, Donzalo scanned the approaching group. Then he laughed and spurred his steed forward. "Captain Corgos!" he called out.

"Master Donzalo!" the soldier hailed him.

Habidros relaxed and slipped his gunne back into its sheath. He cantered up to the pair. "That would be Sir Donzalo now," said he, "and well deserving of it. You ride from Castle Rosam?"

"That we do, sir. I am Corgos." The knight held out his hand in greeting.

"Habidros, late of Drolwym," said the Cuddonian, taking it. "You have come to fetch our young friend home, I would assume."

"That would be so, Sir Habidros. 'Tis already late in the day. Let us encamp here and take council." It was rough country, and wild, lying at the northern edge of swamplands. Corgos swatted at a mosquito. "And let us build a good fire to keep these pests at bay. We passed through clouds of them this day!"

As the darkness of a spring evening fell upon them, the men of both parties circled a roaring fire. It was only in part a deterrent to the swarms of biting insects.

"I rode these lands when younger," said Sir Corgos. "Save in the cold of winter, such are always about.

"As are," he continued, "brigands. It is not a good section of the Road to travel without protection."

"It would seem well suited to ambushes," observed one of the Cuddonians, to nods of agreement all about.

"Well, with both our troops riding together, any bandits will likely choose to leave us alone," said Habidros, "but it is not such that concern us. Those who seek Donzalo's life may not be easily discouraged."

"You intend to ride south with us?" asked the Laman captain.

"We swore to accompany him home and we will do so."

"Then our lucky thirteen shall begin the journey to Castle Rosam in the morning," declared Corgos, slapping at his neck.

Sojel pondered his scout's report. Behind him, his men were mustering on the river bank, all safely across the Weldar. It had gone well, some small payments, some intimidation, and a pair of smugglers' skiffs were put at his disposal.

Those smugglers prepared now to row their boats home. At the sergeant's signal, a pair of his ruffians ran their swords into them and let the bodies slip into the dark Weldar's stream. Best no one be left behind to tell tales.

"Pull those skiffs up into the bushes and hide them, lads," he called. They might come in handy if they needed to cross back.

Sojel could think of but one reason this captain of Count Borrago should be riding north with a half-dozen men. He was going to fetch the boy back to his father.

And if he went, he must surely return. They could wait right here in this wild land and ambush them. A rare smile came to the man's face.

It was not a smile you would have wanted to see.

10

"You would treat with Orgelo?" Bolos asked of his father. He paced back and forth across the small tower room, obviously ill at ease with the idea.

"That I would," replied Count Borrago, "if only so Sharsh does not take us for granted. And do sit down, won't you?"

The younger Rosam plunked himself into one of the plain wooden chairs, pulling irritably at his short tunic where it had creased beneath his leg. He knew Sorsen, son of Count Orgelo, had ridden in earlier that day. Why had he not been informed of the visit?

Borrago noted the expression on his son's face. "County Arvaram is not our enemy, Bolos. Our rival, aye, and often opposing us on policy, but between us we keep the peace in Lama. That is a delicate balance and one we must take care not to upset.

"Anyway, Sir Sorsen's presence is not as his father's representative." Though we will most surely speak on matters of import, the count said to himself. "He has traveled here to do business in the town and comes to the keep only out of courtesy. And to discuss armor with our master of arms, undoubtedly," he added, chuckling.

The mention of Sir Copago did nothing to improve Bolos's mood. Indeed, it made him only more suspicious. Why should his father's bastard be spending time with the heir of Orgelo?

What if he sought his support in an attempt to usurp him?

Bolos told himself he had done well to write to the king in Sharsh.

"They come!"

What? So soon? He had barely brought his contingent to the road, much less had time to plan an ambush.

"Where?" Sojel asked the scout.

"Barely a league north of us when I saw them. Half that by now." The man climbed down from his lathered mount. "It looked to be a dozen men and the Rosam boy among them."

More than he had expected. Still, his forty should be be enough, with the element of surprise on their side. He quickly called his lieutenants to him, pointing out where he wanted them to position the men. No, not across the road from each other, idiots! Do you you want them shooting their own fellows?

Five men with matchlock muskets. Group them over there and let none reveal themselves until they had loosed a volley. Any man who showed himself prematurely would be flayed alive, yes, and his leader with him.

Then they waited but not for long. Indeed, they had barely concealed themselves when they heard the clopping hooves of approaching horses.

Two-by-two they rode, eyes wary and scanning the roadsides. A doughty group of men, thought Sojel, gripping his pistol. Not the sort to run from their duty. This may not be easy.

Then he blew his whistle and the muskets blazed.

Galaro knew this stretch of road. He had done business here more than once.

He knew also the dangers of it and warned his followers to keep a sharp lookout. Would that they had caught up to that band of soldiers that went before them!

He would not have minded the company of Sir Perdos, too, if that man had chosen to remain with them. The Laman knight might not be much of a talker but his sword arm would make up for it.

But the fellow was obsessed with his revenge. That his brother Guesare was disliked here and there, Galaro was not the least surprised. He had never gotten on well with him either. Oh, he should admit it, he had bullied him terribly when they were young. The Cuddonian regretted that, for the most part, but never let it bother him.

This was more, of course, than mere dislike. Guesare had slain the man's brother. A fair duel, Galaro had heard, so such hatred puzzled him a bit. It must go deeper.

He turned his attention back to the road. It was rather marshy here and too open on either side for concealment. There was thicker forest ahead, if he remembered aright.

Those traveling mercenaries had been more than a day ahead of him and had remained so, according to those he had asked along the way. A train of pack-horses could only move so fast.

He thought again of his brother and then of his ancestral home of Drolwym. It had been long since he had seen its haphazard towers rising from the hills of the Cuddon. Maybe he would go back someday.

Not this year. Too much business to attend during the summer. And who would want to winter in the Cuddon, with its fogs and chill winds?

Then, from not far ahead, came the sound of musket fire.

Lord Radal looked over the missive before handing it back to Lareth. "Do we take this seriously?" asked the king.

"We must," replied Radal, "even if his fears are baseless."

"Do your spies have anything to say of the situation? I know you have men in Lama that report only to you." If he did not trust so thoroughly in the loyalty of his friend and councilor, he might not be willing to countenance that.

"The reports are — conflicting. Different men read situations differently, depending on their own biases. I shall instruct our agents as to what occurrences and situations they should be alert." Lord Radal paused. When he spoke again, his voice seemed barely under his control, a rasping whisper. "I hope to have news — good news — shortly of our other concern with that family."

Lareth gazed long from the window before speaking. A mist of spring rain obscured the city below him.

"And if your minions fail you again?"

"Then, my king, I may just go there and tend to it personally."

11

One man had fallen in the first volley. Another was thrown from his stricken mount but rose to his feet, unharmed. The smoke and stench of gunpowder hung in the air.

Then the horsemen broke from their cover, charging the small band.

In the open, the seasoned soldiers could have withstood the attack of this rabble, aye, even outnumbered by more that three to one. Here, there was no room to maneuver, to mount a counterattack. It was man against man, sword against sword.

Sojel discharged his pistol and was pleased to see another man reel. Then he plunged into the battle, saber in hand. Straight toward Donzalo Rosam he rode.

Corgos drove his steed between the two. Blade rang on blade and then the foes were separated by the maelstrom of battle. "To me, men!" rang out the voice of Habidros. "Stand united!"

A half-dozen or more of the attackers lay dead or wounded, mostly fallen to pistol fire on their first charge. There would be no time to reload, now, on either side. The musketeers had left their weapons and entered the fray with drawn swords.

It is not only men who count in such a fight; horses matter as well. Donzalo's defenders had not only the better skills and weapons but also the superior mounts. Their heavier warhorses could push through the nags opposing them, allowing their riders to come together around their captains and the man they protected.

"Should we run for it?" gasped Corgos, hacking at an opponent.

"It's our best chance," came the reply from Habidros. "Go!"

The group urged their horses forward, hoping to break through and away from the attackers. Too many men, too many swords, slowed their progress. Another of the Cuddonian men at arms fell from his saddle to be trampled beneath the milling hooves.

Doufan was stretching his legs, walking alongside his litter for a few minutes. This meant the entire entourage must slow down to his pace.

I might as well dismount too, thought Jobareth. It felt good to be out of the saddle briefly, to work out his riding cramps. His horse, seemingly, appreciated the change as well.

"It's not much further, my girl," he told her. The Royal Road climbed through pine-clad foothills now and the pass at Mountain Keep lay but a couple days travel away. He should write some letters while they rested there, to his family, to Fachalana.

To Lomela, as well. Any message would reach her far sooner than he would personally. It would be slow progress through Lama with Lord Doufan, who wished to spend time with his fellow ambassador in Oles.

Jobareth Nafal recognized the importance of such a visit. The burgess who ruled that city would certainly wish to know what a new embassy in County Rosam might mean for them, to be reassured that no secret treaties were being planned between Sharsh and Count Borrago. Doufan was just the sort of man for the job.

I don't really have it in me to fill such a position, do I? he asked himself. I'll always do my best behind the scenes.

And that, after all, is where true power lies.

Galaro took in the situation with a glance. He and ten of his men had ridden hard up the road, leaving the remainder of the troop to guard their train.

Bandits, he assumed, attacking fellow travelers. There was no question as to the proper course of action — any outlaw band operating on the Great Road was a danger to him and to his own business. Drawing his pistol, he spurred forward, his fellows close on his heels.

As a battering ram shatters a dry-rotted door did they shatter Sojel's rag-tag force, driving deep into the heart of the battle. The ruffians who opposed them saw their sure victory become suddenly uncertain and had not the courage to stand, breaking and running in all directions. There were those who did not make it to the cover of the woods.

In fury, Sojel watched his green rabble disappear, before doing so himself.

"Well met, Brother!" came a voice from behind Galaro.

"Habi?" He wheeled his steed about to face his sibling, only a year younger than he and his companion on many a boyhood adventure. "Well met, indeed!" he roared.

Ansa nibbled her pen tip. She did that when she was not sure what to write.

Oh, now I have to sharpen it again, she told herself, and took a dainty but quite sharp knife to the quill's end.

"Dearest Brother," she started. Well, that's a good beginning anyway.

She had already sent ahead her usual report, mostly full of rumor and overheard bits of gossip. There had not really been much of import to send along in some time.

No, this was to be a more personal message.

"The big news," she wrote, "is that F. may cross the mountains later this year." Hmm, she thought, I'd better explain that better, and crossed it out.

What I should do is tell the whole story of Jobareth and Fachalana and the prince and everything else that has gone on around here. Yes, all of it.

And she put pen to paper and began writing.

12

"So you have been behind us all the way from Ros-town, Sir Galaro?" asked Corgos.

"More or less," replied the burly Cuddonian. Almost from Ros-town it had been. "We had hoped to catch up with you. It seems we did, at last!"

"You might as well have the horses and arms left behind," said Habidros. "I know you cherish your profits, Brother." There were several captured mounts, with their harness, and a number of dead whose bodies had been stripped of aught of value before being tossed into the swamp. Galaro's men went about that task quite efficiently.

"Ha, profits are in part what kept us from catching up, I reckon. We did have to stop and trade here and there along the way. Although," continued Galaro, "we intended to do most of our business further north."

"Why not ride back south with us now, sir?" Donzalo asked. "It is not long till May Festival and the Spring Fair."

"We had intended to be back in your father's lands for the Midsummer Fair, lad. I will speak of it with my fellows. Though I may lead them, we are a free company of traders and must vote on such decisions.

"Now, how stand you and your men? You have taken casualties, I can see." Galaro's men had come away from their charge largely unscathed.

"One of those who accompanied us from Drolwym lies dead and another sorely wounded," reported Habidros.

"Two of mine are slain, as well," Captain Corgos said. "The rest are all fit enough to ride, though several of us bear wounds." He held up his own bandaged arm. "We are fortunate we did not lose more."

"We would, I think, have lost all our lives were it not for Sir Galaro," observed Donzalo. "I regret that I am the cause of this."

"Ah, yes, Perdos told me these men sought your life." He noted that several present knew the name. "It is not my business as to why.

"Let us finish clearing things up here and then we can encamp down the road with the rest of my crew."

There was nothing to be done about it. His attack had failed and the boy would make it home before he could mount another. Best to break up his troop for now. What was left of it.

Fewer than a score had made it back to the banks of the Weldar. Some lay dead, Sojel knew, or wounded. Others would have fled, choosing their direction at random. Some of those might find their way back in time and some of them would choose not to.

He would get this bunch back across the river and disband, for now. Let them get south as they will and regroup later. Another handful boarded one of the skiffs and pushed out into the stream.

As for the sergeant himself, he would have to report all this and then await his master's instructions. Best he head straight for Mountain Keep.

A great bonfire lit up the camp. Some of Galaro's men had broken out instruments, flutes and hand drums and small lutes, and brightened the gathering the more.

"Your wounded man will need to be borne in a wagon," Galaro whispered to his brother. "I would not see a fellow Cuddonian, indeed, a retainer of our father, receive less than we can offer him. Whichever way my company goes, we will take him along."

"I thank you, Brother," replied Habidros. "I would truly welcome your company on the journey south. Perhaps your protection, too, if the need again arises. I have no doubt," he added, with a smile, "that the count's gratitude might prove profitable as well."

"It's unlikely you will be attacked again, don't you think? Your enemies have scattered and the Great Road grows safer as you ride toward Keep Rosam. But it would be good to ride together again."

He rose and gestured for his men to gather round him. They conferred for no more than a minute or two, with much nodding of heads and glances toward their guests. Then Galaro turned and spoke.

"We ride south with you, gentlemen. Let us be on our way in the morning."

Book III
The Sign of the Arrow

Of Daughters: the Sixth Tale

1

A town of tents had sprung up beside the Weldar, some garishly colored and some plain, striped tents and tents of solid hue and some seemingly sewn together of whatever material came to hand. The Spring Fair was in as full a bloom as the flowers that carpeted the surrounding hills, and would continue yet a fortnight, to conclude at the May Festival.

"This is nothing compared to the Summer Fair," Donzalo told his companions. "There will be twice this many, aye, and more than that."

"I have done business at Borrago's Summer Fair these past two years. There is none larger, at least that I know of," said Galaro.

His brother gazed out over the field in wonder. "In the Siphic states, they think Lama is a land of bumpkins, and backward in all things. They are, it seems, much misinformed. As," he continued, shaking his head, "am I."

"We shall do our best to remedy that, Sir Habidros," stated Corgos, titular Captain of this small troop, though all looked to young Donzalo as their true leader. "We had best get on to the keep. The sooner we can report to the count that Donzalo is safely home, the better."

"And the sooner to see your new wife again," jested one of the men at arms he had brought with him from Castle Rosam, to chuckles all around. Along the road south, Sir Corgos had made no attempt to hide his eagerness to again be with his bride.

Donzalo looked toward his home, perched on the heights above the town, the home he had left but two seasons ago. Those seasons seemed now like years. "Then let us finish this journey," he spoke, spurring his horse forward.

"So." Oder, Anian spy-master, pondered the story Guesare had told him, then raised his sky-blue eyes to regard the man who had been protege, friend, lover. "You are correct that it makes no difference, for now. Still, it would have been a fact worth knowing."

The minstrel shrugged. "And now you know it. When the child is older I am sure you will have all sorts of plots in place."

Oder shook his head. "Donzalo the father of his brother's heir — it is amusing, truly."

"It didn't amuse young Donzalo very much to be the target of assassins. Now you have the last piece of that particular puzzle."

The Anian paused, momentarily baffled by the reference. Jigsaw puzzles had not been part of life on the steppes where he had grown up nor of his experiences as a spy since.

But, being a spy, he was quick to catch the intended meaning behind words. "Yes. This needs be a secret known to a very few. Perhaps you did well to guard it.

"Now, all this you have learned of Radal's daughter — some I knew, some I did not. I was aware that Fachalana had become her father's apprentice, thanks to my spy in Celatas." He took a piece of paper into his hand. "I have her latest report here."

Guesare waited, expecting him to hand it over, but Oder chose not to and replaced it on the tavern table before him.

"Her?" asked the Cuddonian minstrel.

"Yes. I have my own little secrets, Guesare, and I think I will let you in on this one. Even if," he chided, "you were not as forthcoming as I might have wished about Donzalo."

Guesare chose to ignore his friend's accusation, knowing it not serious. He waited for Oder to continue.

"You have met my agent. You knew her as Posena." Oder smiled at the minstrel's reaction.

"She was your creature? I was much puzzled by her," he said, narrowing his eyes, "and the reasons for her presence at Castle Rosam."

"Those reasons were not mine, though I willingly approved her plan. She was there to further the plots of her friend and patroness, the Lady Fachalana. In Celatas, my young spy is known as the actress Maresta."

"This grows tangled," observed Guesare. "Who is the girl, truly?"

"Ah, I think Donzalo glimpsed something of her true identity. He is an observant one." Oder beckoned to the barmaid, gossiping at the door with a passer-by. "Two more tankards of that fine dark beer, girl."

The Anian watched with obvious appreciation as she went to fetch their brew. Guesare could not help but feel a twinge of jealousy.

It was a small tavern in a small town along the Siphic Road, and a favored haunt of the spy-master. Ostensibly, these rugged hills — the northern end of the Cuddon — that divided the valleys of the Weldar and Siph were a part of the Anian Empire. In practice, the Ani left the people here to rule themselves and were content to simply keep the road open.

Oder drank deeply. "There won't be much more of this brew until next spring. It's the main reason I chose this town for our rendezvous."

Guesare knew they were accustomed to seeing Anians here, making it useful as a meeting place, as well as being well-located for sending out spies into Lama and beyond. He remained silent — the man across the table from him enjoyed his little games of manipulation but the minstrel could choose not to play.

"The girl is, of course, of my people," spoke Oder. "Her name is Ansa." He paused to take another quaff from his tankard, then added in a low, matter-of-fact tone, "She is my sister.

"Donzalo may have recognized the kinship between us when we were traveling together. He suspected something — I could see it in his eyes."

The normally loquacious minstrel could think of nothing to say.

Oder knew well the odd mix of the complex and the simple that made up his friend. A momentary wistfulness filled him as he leaned back and regarded the minstrel, still a young man but no longer the boy he had taken under his wing. Then, such thoughts were quickly swept away in favor of the business at hand. "Your paths may well cross again. Possibly soon. You will be heading to County Rosam?"

Guesare nodded. "I should be there for Summer Feast." He gulped down the dark brew in his flagon. "Could we have some wine, now?"

"Whom do you serve, Captain Nordoc? Hmmm." Lady Fachalana looked up from the page she held. "Whom do *you* serve, Captain Nordoc?"

Ansa nodded her approval. "Yes, yes. An accusation, almost."

"Not that it matters," replied the tall young noblewoman. "I do not intend to play the role."

"Better you than I. You cut a far more heroic figure."

Fachalana smiled at her petite companion. "But you are the better actress, Maresta," she asserted, knowing the woman still by that name. Throwing the sheaf of papers onto the table, she took a seat. "The play is not finished enough to mount, anyway. We will not attempt it this season."

"Then we'd best choose another to finish out our spring. And try to get Lector Nafal to complete this one to our satisfaction."

Fachalana shifted her weight on the hard wooden chair. I should bring some cushions, she told herself. She had told herself this before yet never remembered to do it. "Jobareth is halfway to Lama by now. We need to sit down with him and work it out."

"Then, my lady," replied her friend, with a ghost of a smile, "all the more reason for us to go visit him there."

"Shall we take our company on the road, as do so many others in the summer?" Fachalana had actually been giving the idea some idle thought. All who could deserted Celatas during the hottest months and most theaters would close until autumn. It was a good time to tour.

"All the way to County Rosam?" asked Ansa. "I must warn you that Lama is dreadfully hot in the summer. It is not at all like touring in the uplands here." Mountain villages — especially those that lay near the summer homes of the aristocracy — were the preferred venue of most roving companies.

"Well, then just the two of us," decided Fachalana, "and whatever retinue on which my father insists."

"If he permits it, at all."

"He will, I think," said the noblewoman. Both suspected that Lord Radal had hidden reasons for allowing his daughter to visit Lama. Neither chose to voice her suspicion.

"What of 'The Purloined Pigeon' to close out the season?" said Fachalana, of a sudden.

"A comedy, my lady?"

"Yes, and you in the lead." She became emphatic — passions easily and quickly took hold of Fachalana. "It is more than time that you played such a role. We can not have you forever cast as the villain! But," she added, her smile signaling another change in mood, "you may need to dye that blond hair."

Ansa nodded. It would be nice to be the heroine, she told herself, if only in make-believe.

"Pol! What do you here?"

"Sir Blen sent me, Lector, to await you here at Mountain Keep and to accompany you on the way back." The young soldier laughed. "And to get me where I would not be nosing about, eh?"

A not too subtle message that he knew Pol was Jobareth's man, the diplomat told himself. They stood in one of the many passages that honeycombed the fortress, some built upon the mountain rock and some carved into it.

"You should address me now as Legate," he said to the boy. "Yes, I've been promoted. This is my secretary, Benawis. Him you call Lector."

He turned to his aide. "Pol, I suppose, could be considered my sergeant, had I any other soldiers in my troop." These two are nearly of an age, thought Jobareth. Benawis may have lived a year or two more but has had little experience of the world. I should treat them as equals and hope they do the same. "In fact, I officially confer that rank on you right now, Sergeant Pol.

"You should move to our quarters. We are searching for them now."

"I know where they are, sir. I moved into them when I arrived two days ago." Pol turned to lead the way up the corridor. "Is the new ambassador with you?"

Benawis looked both scandalized and amused by the soldier's informal manner. "He's been among Lamans too long," Jobareth whispered. "You'll have to become accustomed to it there. He's a good lad," he continued, "and you'll do well to make him a friend."

"Yes, Legate. I met him when you both arrived here from Lama."

"Oh." This Jobareth had not known. Some things must be beyond ones control and the first encounter of these two had been one of them. "Yes, Sergeant," he said more loudly, "the Lord Doufan has accompanied us. He is paying his respects to the reeve of the keep."

2

"The Lady Vibola passed quietly in her sleep," Doctor Heragos told Donzalo. He pulled his long robes up as they began to ascend the stairway. "Your grandmother did live long enough to see the new baby."

"The child is not well, I have been told."

"No, Sir Donzalo, she is not." The pair spoke no further until they reached Lady Lomela's door. It stood ajar.

"I suggested that the air be allowed to pass through her chambers. 'Tis healthier," whispered Heragos, "and more so now that the days grow hot."

A round face appeared in the opening. "I thought I heard someone out here," said Mistress Traspa, in a subdued voice. "Welcome home, Master Donzalo."

She pulled the door open to them.

Unexpectedly, not only Lomela sat in the room, this room that was once so familiar to Donzalo, but his brother, Bolos, as well. The latter rose to greet him.

"I heard you were back. You've been with Father?"

"Just coming from him. How are you, Brother?" The two briefly and, perhaps a bit stiffly, clasped hands. They had never in all their lives embraced.

"Well enough, Donni, well enough." The words seemed unconvincing to Donzalo. He noted that his sibling had lost more weight and had the appearance of a man worn by worries.

The young knight bowed toward Lomela, who had come to her husband's side. "Greetings to you, my lady."

"And to you, Donzalo. *Sir* Donzalo," she corrected herself. "We must remember your brother is now a knight," she told Bolos.

A sour expression passed across the older man's face; as quickly, it was replaced by an impassive one. He only nodded.

No one cares that he is, as well, thought Donzalo. He has no tales of derring-do to follow him about.

Heragos broke in. "Might I look in on the child, my lady?"

"Of course, Doctor. As you suggested, we are being certain she has fresh air." She went to the girl's crib, beneath a window opening to the courtyard below. The doctor followed and laid his hand on the baby's head and then on her chest. He put his ear to a hearing-trumpet and listened to her breathing. He pulled at the tuft of beard on his chin and shook his head.

"She seems no better, gentlefolk. I am sorry."

Bolos sighed and put an arm around his wife. He feels this deeply, thought Donzalo, a bit surprised to recognize the ache in his brother's heart and an answering empathy in his own. He has cleaned up his life and this has been his reward.

The knight remembered his own loss then, the emptiness within him where once his Jola had been. Without thinking, Donzalo put his hand to the silver brooch at his shoulder. It seemed to reassure him.

He made his subdued goodbyes and found his way to his own long-unoccupied quarters.

"We will not again attempt an ambush."

"That seems wise," came Lareth's dry response, "considering your record." The king turned his head toward a young woman seated in the corner, quietly embroidering. "Will you leave us, my dear? But do be sure to return later."

She departed in a rustling of blue satin.

Radal looked askance at his monarch. "A new mistress?" he asked.

"Only a dalliance. The Lady Lis will remain at my side until the day one or the other of us is buried." Lareth gave a wry laugh. "We might as well be married, were it not politically unwise."

The king's councilor did not comment. He knew his liege had never let his love for his wives or, now, his mistress, get in the way of his love for all other women.

"So the boy will be home again," mused Lareth, King of Sharsh. "I would assume you have agents there."

"Yes, sire." Lord Radal did not mention that he had been unable to place anyone in Keep Rosam itself. Observers in the town — or embassy — would have to do. "Security has grown tight there and Borrago has most certainly grown cool towards us."

"That is not surprising. But we have done what was needed."

"We have tried to do what was needed, my king," replied the dark noble, "and failed. Again and again, we have failed." Lareth noted the barely suppressed bitterness in the man. This was not at all like his old friend.

"We can not have the Rosam allying themselves with Count Orgelo and this wedding is a threat to all our plans," Radal continued. His vehemence was now unconcealed.

The king was taken aback. "You would have us move against Borrago?" Surely, the man would not think to act so rashly.

"Remove the father and his whelp stands unprotected." The sorcerer's tone softened as he went on. "You said, my lord, that you would yourself lead an army into Lama were it necessary."

"And it is not yet necessary, my friend." Had this become personal for Radal? wondered the king. "Watch and wait. You leave in the morning?"

"Yes, sire. I can watch and wait, as you say, more effectively from Mountain Keep."

Lareth nodded his agreement. Then, turning their conversation to a lighter matter, he said, "I understand your daughter will be joining you there."

"Yes, my liege, as soon as she closes her theater for the summer. If all seems well, she will travel on to visit your own daughter. And," added the nobleman with an increasingly rare smile, "the man I hope to be her future husband."

"Well, join me in a goblet of wine, Radal, and before you must leave we shall drink to all good futures." The king himself poured out their libations and handed the cup to his friend and one-time protege.

If he will not act, I shall, the Lord Radal told himself later as he walked purposefully away from the king's chambers.

And in those chambers, the king wondered if his life-long friend and councilor should be removed from his duties.

Perdos rested in the shade of a sandstone outcropping, as his horse grazed one of the meadows scattered through this forest of oaks and of tall hickories, and thought on the reasons he hated the bard Guesare. He had much time to think of such things as he skulked in the wilds above Castle Rosam, near the borders of the Cuddon. If he remained here long enough, surely the man would return and he would have his chance at him.

Until then, he would live the life of a hunter, on the move and on the watch.

Guesare had slain his brother, Percos, of course. That was bad enough, though admittedly a fair fight. It was how he had instigated the whole affair, tricking the boy into dueling with him.

That had been politics, Perdos now realized. The brothers' dealings with Sharsh and Lord Radal had been at the bottom of it. If only they had kept away from intrigue and the promise of easy money, and had re-mained honest — well, mostly honest — soldiers.

That was another sore spot. Thanks to Guesare he had been banned from County Rosam and lost his comfortable post in Sir Bolos's retinue. Here he was, now, a homeless wanderer in the hills.

But most of all it was his own arm that reminded him of his hatred. He lay awake nights, feeling the pain in his shattered shoulder, know-ing the only way to ever make it feel better would be to plunge a sword into the cocky Cuddonian.

Then, maybe, he could rest. I'll go back to that little inn, he told himself, when this is done. I'll settle down. I'll raise horses and take a wife and grow fat.

Perdos thought frequently of such things.

"Can you find me a cook, Marmoyo? Taking our meals at inns will no longer do when we move into the new embassy."

The Sharshites' agent pondered the request as though it were a question of great import. "Will you need more staff than just a cook, Sir Blen?" he inquired.

"I've already hired from the countryside locals. Every mason and carpenter who has worked on the place has relatives looking for a job. We need someone more sophisticated to prepare the ambassador's meals."

The Laman nodded knowingly. "You will be out of here soon, then?"

"Within the fortnight, Master Marmoyo, be the embassy finished or not. As promised." Blen rose from his chair, a signal for his visitor to do the same. "Have you made progress on my other request?" he asked.

"Indeed, sir, I have found several smaller houses that might do." He looked about the room. "The rent on this building is quite reasonable. You would not save much."

"It is too well known now as our residence. We desire a more private place where one of us can do business while in town, or stay over, if need be."

The two crossed the near-empty room to the doorway. "You can show me what you have found on the morrow. No, make that the day after. I must ride up to inspect the construction today and then on to Castle Rosam. Young Donzalo has returned and I should pay my respects."

"I bid you farewell then, sir," said the Laman, descending from the porch to the muddy streets of Ros-town.

Visiting the keep was not a task for which Blen cared. He would be happy to see Jobareth and the ambassador arrive so they could take over the work of diplomacy. For the last few months, all had fallen on the capable shoulders of the knight. Even those shoulders could grow tired.

Something was amiss here.

Indeed, Fachalana had felt something was amiss since she had risen that morning, knowing it was imperative that she visit her childhood friend, Prince Modareth and his new bride.

She had spent the previous evening trying to establish a link with her father, as he traveled toward the Mountain Keep. It had not gone well; Radal faded in and out of her trance-vision, their attempt at communication resulting only in disjointed and meaningless syllables.

It was she, though, who had been fading in and out. Fachalana knew this. She had not been able to hold to the link, to keep herself in that other place where they might meet. For that was how it worked, according to her father: their own physical being partially entered into other realms where they might come together.

All that talk of spirits and such was nonsense, he had told her. Wizardry meant learning to control ones passage into and through the myriad worlds other than our own, to be able to find what was needed in them — and to use it.

Fachalana had at last abandoned the attempt, knowing it was her own lack of discipline that caused her to drift away from her father's link. Her anger and frustration led to fitful, half-awake dreaming.

In the night, it seemed as if someone were speaking in another room. Not her father, a different voice, but with some of the same authority. A god? she wondered. She would like to meet a god someday.

Then she slept, but woke with the conviction that the prince was in danger.

She had been planning to say goodbye to Modi, anyway, before leaving Sharsh. Now Fachalana stood at the door of his dwelling, the small villa that he and Carrana had moved into following their wedding. It was really rather close to her father's home. She should have visited before.

Yes, something was amiss but this was not the foreboding she had felt earlier. Someone was clearing groaning on the other side of the door.

An unlocked door, the noblewoman found, when she placed her hand upon it. The red-lacquered slab swung open to reveal Modareth's single attendant and bodyguard spread prone on the floor, his blood flowing into the mortared joints between the tiles.

At that moment, Fachalana dearly wished she had brought her sword.

There was a dagger at the dying — probably dead, now — guard's waist. That would have to do. She slipped it from its sheath and hurried up the hallway.

3

Later, the Lady Fachalana realized that she had never hesitated. That fact quite astounded her when she thought upon it.

Up the passage she had gone, knife in hand, to face whatever danger threatened her friends. Yes, friends, for she now counted the Princess Carrana as such.

She heard a shriek, a quite blood-curdling shriek, and rushed toward the sound. Carrana? No, it had been the cook. The woman had apparently fainted and now lay upon the floor, pieces of a broken platter and an assortment of sweet cakes scattered about her.

Beyond her stood a man, a poniard in each hand, his back to Fachalana. And beyond him stood the royal couple. A late breakfast was spread on the table between them and the assassin.

Years of training — and much natural talent — had made Fachalana a skilled fencer. She could best most men with a dueling foil.

And that had not been enough for her so she had also studied the saber and the longsword and, yes, the dagger.

The man turned to face her with a sneer. His face seemed familiar but the noblewoman had no time to think of that.

She lunged into an immediate attack and almost had her man. He backed away in surprise — directly in front of where Carrana stood.

The portly princess promptly picked up a plate and smashed it over the man's head. It had not enough force to do him serious harm but it certainly did distract their attacker for a moment.

Fachalana lunged in again. The man parried with his right and almost brought the blade in his left through her guard. She would need be attentive of this two-handed assault.

From the corner of her eye, she saw Modareth hurrying his wife from the room. Good, they would be safe. And it was only right that he would think first of Carrana's life.

Back and forth, they attacked and parried. The assassin was skilled. As, after all, he should be, she told herself.

There was shouting. Modi calling for help, she guessed. There were always plenty enough good fellows about here, be they guardsmen or gardeners. They would run to the prince's aid.

The assassin realized this too. He lunged desperately, hoping either to overwhelm her or break by and make his escape. Fachalana saw the opening he left and felt the dagger in her hand and drove it to the hilt into the man's chest.

"Do you wish to stay in those same rooms, boy?" asked Borrago. "We could find a larger space for you."

Donzalo considered this quite unexpected question. "It is enough for me, Father. Even if I had more books," he answered.

"Once we marry, Dame Sima and I shall take your grandmother's former chambers." Borrago had insisted upon this title for his lady ever since announcing their engagement. She sat beside him now, as the three took lunch together in the count's tower apartment. "I'll keep my bachelor rooms here, however, for my everyday work.

"But, Donzalo, you need a retinue now. A man-servant, at least. There is no room for anyone but you in that cave of yours."

There came a rap at the door. "That should be Copago. I want his advice on this.

"Come in," he called.

The master of arms entered and nodded respectfully to each in turn. "My lord. Mother. Sir Donzalo."

"Sit, Copago, and fill a plate," said Borrago. "Be sure to have some of these ribs. The new cook is a master of sauces! I have suggested that my son have a retinue and intend to set an allowance upon him." He wiped his fingers after slipping a bone to the dog that lolled beneath the table and looked up at the man. "What think you?"

"I think, sir, that whatever sum you have in mind you should double." His mother laughed aloud at that. Borrago's stinginess was legendary.

The count knew this and chuckled as well. He took some pride in his reputation.

Sir Copago went on, more seriously now. "Much depends on what future we have planned for Donzalo. And what future Donzalo has planned for himself."

All three looked to the young knight. He sighed and began. "Sometimes, I think I would like nothing better than to go back to the Cuddon and live my life out there." Donzalo paused a moment, seemingly lost in memory, before adding, "Our kin would welcome me."

"But you are not yet ready for that, are you?" asked Copago. "I've been talking with Sir Habidros. He has a high opinion of you." Turning to Count Borrago, he continued. "If Donzalo were to have retainers, he could do well to start with Habidros."

"He seems a good man. Not one I would want in my garrison, but well suited to serve in such a role." The count looked straight and steadily at his son. "As competent as you have become, I still want you to have a bodyguard. Guesare may be gone but his brother seems a good stand-in.

"By the way," he said, turning to look at Copago, "what is the other brother up to?"

"He has pitched his tents at the fair, sir, and intends to remain until May Festival."

"Galaro has told me he will ride north then and return for the Summer Fair," spoke Donzalo. "The men of the Cuddon will ride with him on their way home."

"Then we must speak to this Habidros before he decides to ride off with them," said Count Borrago. "Try these fried cakes, Copago. I have never tasted such a mixture of spices!"

Lord Doufan's secretary was not a man of Sharsh. He had come from Lorj where he had been trained in that land's scribal tradition. Why he had chosen to come to Sharsh and serve Doufan, perhaps only he and that diplomat knew.

Jobareth Nafal certainly had no idea. Nor, he realized, did he know the man's name. It would seem silly to ask him at this point.

Yet it seemed equally silly to address him simply as 'Scribe,' in the manner of his master. He had avoided the man while they were in the Mountain Keep and now that they were again on the road there would be little interaction. That would probably change when they reached Oles and took river passage down to County Rosam.

And more so when they were settled into the embassy there.

The ambassador had again insisted on a horse litter for his transportation. The way here, however, was far easier going than had been the Royal Road up to the Keep. It sloped gently down into the broad valley of the Weldar, passing over rolling hills and on to the plain.

No one seemed to agree on the name of this highway. Some Sharshites insisted on calling it the Royal Road, maintaining that it was but an extension of that thoroughfare. Others chose to call it the Siphic Road. All agreed that was its name beyond Oles as it passed into the east.

Those who had traveled it the most seemed to settle on Oles Road and so did Jobareth come to refer to it.

He rode now by the side of Lord Doufan's litter. The secretary followed close behind, ready to his master's call, on a donkey. Jobareth understood that this was the traditional steed of a Lorjam scribe.

Where his own little retinue was, he had no idea.

"As you know, Nafal," spoke the ambassador, "Oles is a republic."

"Yes, my lord. As are many of the Siphic cities beyond it."

"True. It is a widespread disease."

"My Lord Doufan disapproves of democracy?" asked the young diplomat.

"Democracy is only the freedom to choose your master," replied Doufan, as ready as ever with an appropriate aphorism. "But these cities are mostly not democracies anyway."

"True indeed, sir. It is the wealthy who rule."

A genuine smile came to Doufan's normally bland countenance. "I am gladdened, Nafal, that I have not been saddled with a dolt on this mission. That would be far too tedious."

He returned to his subject. "Such wealthy men increasingly wield power in our own Sharsh. Your grandfather is one." He glanced up at the younger man. "And you will quite possibly rise to the highest of positions, yourself. I have heard some speak of you as Radal's heir."

Jobareth was unsure of how to respond.

"No, speak not," said Doufan. "Any words would be meaningless. Scribe! Come and read the dispatches to me now."

"You do not think I had aught to do with this, Father." It was half a question, half a statement.

"No, Gawis," replied the king. "Do sit down and cease your pacing." Just watching the boy was tiring him. The prince threw himself into one of the deeply cushioned chairs and, as quickly, slid forward to perch on its front edge.

"It's a bad business, sir. I don't know what to think."

"I think we owe much to the Lady Fachalana," said the third person in the room. Prince Gawis turned his eyes toward Lady Lis, who, until now, had been quietly reading. Gawis had no quarrels with the Lady. He did not remember his own mother and much preferred his father's current mistress to his late step-mother.

He had hated the mother of Modareth and Lomela, and was certain the emotion had been returned. Lis, the widow of some minor baron, had no agenda and she pleased his father. Would that he could do the same.

"That we do," agreed Lareth. "It was great good fortune that she chose that time to visit." *Or was it fortune?* the king wondered to himself. *There is almost certainly more to it.*

"It is true," he went on, "that the would-be assassin was traced to one of your circle, Gawis. What was his name?"

"The assassin or the employer, my lord?" asked Lis, with a little smile. "Lady Fachalana recognized the attacker as a bodyguard of one Godos.

"Yes, Godos. A scion of the Tasetha family." The Tasethas were wealthy merchants and owners of a considerable fleet.

"I am convinced he had no part — the lad has too much money and too little brain to involve himself. Still, I did suggest to his father that he board one of their ships and voyage elsewhere for a time."

"But some one of my supposed friends is surely involved."

"Surely, indeed." *The boy is showing some brains for once,* thought his father. "We can always assume that at least one or two of those in a prince's circle are in somebody's employ."

Lareth sighed deeply. "I do fear your father-in-law may have had a hand in this."

"The emperor? Oh, of course." Gawis's previous nerves were giving way to a growing numbness.

"The Partanacans would not like to see Modi sire an heir to challenge your daughters. And the emperor may fear you would be tempted to put aside his daughter in hopes of conceiving a son with some other woman."

The prince nodded. The idea had crossed his mind on occasion.

Lareth guessed as much. "That would be unwise," he said. "Partanaca is too powerful to make an enemy."

"It is hard to be a king, isn't it, Father?" came Gawis's near-whispered reply. "I think I begin to understand the motto on our crest."

"*The king is the servant of the people.* Your grandfather put it there for a reason."

4

Lareth's bridge across the Chas had become a favored meeting place for the citizens of Celatas. "I'll see you at King's Bridge," they would say, or "wait for me at the midspan." One could see most of the city from that wooden center span that lay between two great stone piers. One could see far up the broad river, and down as far as the bend below town.

It had also become Ansa's favored place to pass messages along. She had just handed off her last report to her brother. Soon, she and Fachalana should be on the road and out of contact.

Their two-week run of 'The Purloined Pigeon' would be quickly over. It had been easy enough to throw the show together at the last moment. Every actor knew the lines for at least one character in the old warhorse. Those actors would scatter now for the summer, off with touring troops or taking odd jobs around the city until the fall theater season.

She batted a stealthy hand away. The bridge had also become a favored spot for pickpockets and confidence men. "I'll cut it off next time," she whispered and let the would-be thief slip back into the crowd.

Ansa and Fachalana on the road — it sounds like a comedy, she thought, the sort one would fill with mishaps and misadventures. The leads would be two flighty and naïve women — old maids from the country, maybe — taking on the wide world, to roars from the crowd.

But these two women were neither flighty nor naïve. Well, maybe the Lady Fachalana could be on occasion. But she had shown herself to be more than Ansa had ever guessed she might be in her recent encounter with the assassin.

And some might consider them old maids, even. She smiled to herself at that.

Did slaying a man trouble her friend? she then wondered. Ansa had killed and knew it was not something to be done lightly and forgotten.

Ansa looked downriver, toward the docks and warehouses that lined its banks. Sea-going ships did not come this far upriver but the large riverboats were impressive enough. Someday, she would like to board one and go take a look at the sea.

"What news I received in the Cuddon did make passing mention of my father's interest in Dame Sima. Finding them engaged when I returned home was unexpected.

"As was," he added, "learning of my grandmother's passing."

"Nafal spent much time with her in her final days," said Sir Blen. "I regret that I really never came to know the Lady Vibola."

"Have you news of Jobareth?" Donzalo asked. "I know he corresponds with Lady Lomela but she has had no time for me."

"The latest rider brought word that he and the ambassador have left Mountain Keep on their journey here. Their diplomatic duties would call for them to arrive in time for the Summer Feast and the count's wedding."

"Seven weeks. That should be enough time, even coming down the river," observed the Laman.

"How like you the new quarters?" asked Blen. "I never saw your old ones but they were described to me."

Donazalo could imagine that description, probably couched in the colorful words of a certain minstrel. "There is more room, for certain. Room enough for Habidros, had he wished, but he preferred to lodge in the barracks, so it is only I and the man-servant that was forced upon me."

"You should have asked instead for a librarian."

"Indeed, yes! I am still in need of bookshelves." Donzalo gestured toward the stacked volumes around the room's perimeter. "It is nice," he added, "to have a window, even if only the one."

"And there is the famous mace," remarked Blen, fixing his eyes on said weapon, temporarily reposing on the mantle. "Yes, I know that story. Such have a way of leaking out."

"Probably through the mouth of Guesare," guessed Donzalo, "and well embellished in the telling."

"This Habidros you have taken on is his brother?"

"One of four half-brothers, and of them perhaps the most alike to Guesare." He gave the Sharshite a long look. "I have no doubt you already know all this and of his brother Galaro, as well."

"Ever direct, Sir Donzalo! I like that." He had been toying with his goblet and now raised it to take a sip. Blen had never been a heavy drinker. "And I hope to better understand you." He left his explanation at that.

"Maybe when I understand myself, I can help you," came Donzalo's wry response.

That answer, in itself, helps me, thought Blen. But there was much more to be learned of the plots and secrets that seemed to revolve around this affable young man, this unassuming hero.

"You mistrust me," he said aloud, "yet Jobareth Nafal and I serve the same master. I am no more your enemy than is he." Blen remembered that Lord Radal had once said much the same words to him. That thought momentarily disturbed him.

"That may be so," replied Donzalo, "but neither are you yet my friend."

The courier had come at great speed, with a letter directly from the hand of the king. Radal sat by the window in his high tower, the window that looked east toward Lama, and carefully broke the seal.

His henchman Sojel had been waiting when Lord Radal entered Mountain Keep. They had closeted long before he sent the sergeant on his way, to do his bidding and work his will in Lama.

He was gambling with his future, the sorcerer knew, going against the express orders of his king. Radal no longer cared; he wished only to drag Donzalo Rosam down to share in his own damnation.

Ah, but there was his daughter to consider. If only he could teach Fachalana enough, make her sufficiently strong to stand against the world as he had. He knew she had the ability but he could not give her the self-discipline she needed.

They had again made the attempt at a link when he had arrived. The girl was excited about something and that did not help. Radal did glean the fact that there had been an assassination or an attempt at one and that Fachalana was somehow involved. That weighed on him.

Until the courier brought this dispatch. He read it carefully, then read it again. One could rarely, if ever, say that the lord councilor showed delight in anything, but there could be no other description for the look that came to his dark face.

If only Fachalana could bring the skills and discipline she showed in swordplay to bear on her studies of sorcery! No, thought Radal, they are very different endeavors and therein lies the problem. One is about quick decisions and reading situations and the other about the slow and steady imposition of ones will. His daughter was not willing to focus long enough on one thing. She looked to the next challenge, the next riposte and parry.

We will speak on it when she arrives, he told himself. A fortnight or so? He had lost track of the day here.

And we must try to learn what brought her to the door of Modareth at that hour.

The keep of Sir Paren had changed little. Corgos saluted the guard who opened the gate to him.

"It is good to have you back, Captain."

"It is good to be back."

His wife would be waiting in their cottage behind the main hall but first he must report to Sir Paren. He wondered if he should mention the news he had heard of Perdos. Once again, that banished knight had come off in a favorable light.

Paren himself came to the door to greet him. "My brother sent word you would soon arrive. Here boy," he said, addressing a groom, "take the Captain's horse and be sure it receives a good rubdown." Sir Corgos alit from the saddle, somewhat stiffly from his three days travel, and bowed to the reeve. Also stiffly, as Paren duly noted.

"Come on in. I sent a page to tell Tiana you have arrived. You both dine with me and my lady tonight." He stepped back and looked the man over. "Yes, I know you are weary but I want to hear all the news. And then hear it again tomorrow, in more detail!"

It *was* good to be back.

Not one, but two bridges span the Weldar at Oles. The burgess of that town, with their love of regulation, decreed that one would serve eastbound traffic and the other, travelers to the west. This naturally confused visitors to the city who ofttimes found themselves needing to turn about and seek the other span.

"My credentials would let us pass no matter which bridge we chose," declared Lord Doufan. "Let us go to the wrong one so I may prove it."

Is this his idea of a jest? wondered Jobareth. It did seem in character for the man. Or perhaps he thought it a way to cow the ruling council of Oles before he ever met them.

"We will go by the proper bridge," said the the caravan-master, and so they did.

"Perhaps it is just as well," Doufan confided to his second-in-command. "If they didn't let us through it would have been most embarrassing." Jobareth Nafal could only nod in agreement and a bit of bewilderment.

The ambassador had abandoned his litter and, for the first time in this journey, sat astride a horse. Doufan knew how to project a proper image, when need be. "We must make three official visits," said he. "First to the council, then to the pontifex, and finally our own embassy here. But unofficially, it would be well to contact our diplomats first. See to it, Nafal, will you?"

Jobareth had already dispatched a man to the embassy but he said nothing of it. He did suspect that Doufan knew.

"The pontifex, sir? The other two I expected."

"Many Lamans consider the Pontifex of Oles to be the head of their religion. It is well to be friendly to him."

"In County Rosam, they mostly defer to their own hierophant — and the wishes of the count — even while giving lip service to the pontifex," Jobareth pointed out.

"We will be friendly to them as well, my boy, even if the southerners are considered to be somewhat schismatic up here."

The younger man shook his head. "Laman politics are bad enough but when we throw in their Kamatian religion, if exceeds understanding."

"That is why I make no effort to understand, Nafal. A smile and a polite word is often all that's needed." Jobareth did not believe him for a moment.

"It is to be noted," continued Lord Doufan, "that our friends in County Arvaram give their allegiance to the pontifex in Lorj, who has claim to being the first and original. Whether they believe he is the true head of their faith or merely wish to oppose the Rosam on yet another issue is anyone's guess."

"I would not be surprised to see my friend Grippo back in County Rosam rise to hierophant one day," said Jobareth, musing more than making a statement.

"A good friend to have then," replied Doufan. "But it is not wise to rely overmuch on such friends."

"Indeed, my lord, indeed."

They had passed into the center of Oles, where much was built of gray granite and the streets were well-paved with cobblestones. Jobareth thought he had never seen so clean a city.

"It is quite hideous, is it not?" asked Lord Doufan.

"Yes, I suppose it is, sir. I would not want to live here."

"Then pray to Jov that you are never named ambassador to Oles." Doufan winked at his younger companion. "The citizens are even worse.

"And this would be the City Hall, where we must greet the Council and, no doubt, an assortment of prominent burgess whom we shall promptly forget. Follow me, Nafal, and then decide if you truly want a life as a diplomat." The ambassador was still chuckling when they passed through the great bronze doors.

5

"Farewell, my brother," said Galaro. The two over-sized men, much alike aside from one being bearded and the other clean-shaven, embraced fiercely. "We shall meet again at Summer Feast — if you can bear to stay put that long!"

"I have been both leader and follower," said Habidros. "I can follow young Donzalo for at least a few weeks."

The Cuddonian trader swung up into his saddle. "Let's go, boys! We have a lot of road to follow before we return."

His brother stood a while in the center of the Great Road, watching the troop dwindle into the north. Then he mounted up and started back across Count Borrago's fair ground, already half-empty as more merchants packed up. Today was May Festival and the Spring Fair was at an end.

His young master was at some religious affair, at that open-air temple up above the town. He had noted it in passing, a typical Kamatian stoa. There were some of that religion in the Siphics and it seemed to be spreading.

Habidros was not a religious man. He did, however, carry an assortment of charms to keep him safe. In that, he was not unlike many another soldier.

He pulled out a small silver medal bearing the likeness of the goddess Esefa. This day was special to her; back home they would be wrapping her image in garlands of flowers. He sighed and felt momentarily homesick. Then he shook the reins and headed his steed toward Castle Rosam.

Neither Fachalana nor Ansa had ever taken the road to Mountain Keep. Lady Fachalana had simply never had reason to travel there. Ansa, as a spy, had followed more roundabout ways in and out of Sharsh.

"I feel as though I should whisper," said Fachalana, "amid all this beauty. It is like a great temple." She did not whisper but neither did she speak very loudly.

Ansa had seen wonders in her own travels, yet she was inclined to agree. "I fear the Murb does not appreciate it."

Murbalana was the sour middle-aged woman whom Radal had insisted accompany them as chaperon. It would not do for a young noblewoman such as the Lady Fachalana to travel alone. Murbalana complained a great deal, about the food, about the bumpy road, about her husband who had run off some twenty years before.

For the most part, she remained in one of the wagons, where she complained about having no one to complain to. At times, the fourth member of their party, a stolid man-servant to handle the luggage, rode with her. Being deaf, he did not mind the complaints but rather liked the fact that she was talking to him. He imagined that the Mistress Murbalana fancied him somewhat.

But the young women went horseback. Fachalana rode sidesaddle, as would any lady of breeding, and she did it well.

Ansa, feeling freed from her usual need for pretense, had donned Anian trousers and sat astride her mount. This, Murbalana considered the height of scandal. Were it not for her hair, still dyed black from her last role, none would mistake her for anything other than the Ani she was.

Indeed, Fachalana began to wonder if there were more to her friend than she had realized.

The way was growing ever steeper. A fellow traveler, a merchant who passed this way frequently, said they were but two days from the Keep. And then on to Lama!

Fachalana dreamed sometimes of Donzalo in these starry, pine-scented mountain nights. Perhaps Ansa did too.

A tiny coffin was consigned to the fire. A woman cried and a man put his arm around her shoulders. A priest spoke a few words of sympathy.

Donzalo watched from the small crowd of relatives. He knew of loss. But then, don't we all, sooner or later? Lomela did not need his presence right now. He would visit in a day or two and things would go on.

Brother Grippo passed by, in procession. Donzalo gave him an unacknowledged nod. Grippo would become a priest this year, wouldn't he?

He put his hand to the silver wolf that was ever present on his shoulder. Yes, we all know loss.

That night, for the first time in nearly a year, Bolos Rosam got drunk.

Two long, narrow, flat-bottomed vessels slid down the Weldar's stream. There had been three tedious days crammed with meetings in Oles, and Jobareth Nafal was relieved to at last see that city's docks fade from view.

Lord Doufan, seasoned diplomat that he was, seemed to thrive there. Jobareth had never seen a man so at ease in a crowded room, ever ready with the proper word or expression, soothing where soothing was needed, effortlessly inducing men to speak freely, even of things they should not.

He knew he had better watch himself or he might as easily fall under the ambassador's spell.

In the front of his boat, Pol and Benawis sat conversing. He had been too busy to notice that they had become friends since leaving Mountain Keep. What could the two have in common? Jobareth realized he knew almost nothing of his secretary's background. Most young, low-ranking diplomats came either from the minor nobility or the rising middle class.

Pol, of course, was of the peasantry. Wasn't he? The legate realized he didn't really know him very well either. The young fellow's accent suggested that he came from the north, perhaps even Arolin.

One of the men at arms had informed him that the pair spent most of their free time in Oles visiting the brothels. Jobareth could hardly censure that — he had on occasion frequented such establishments himself in his student days. Whores held little interest now for him.

Jobareth Nafal knew the one woman he wanted and he knew she would remain always beyond his reach. Yet in a few weeks he would be seeing her.

As well as the woman he could well end up marrying. It might be the only way to get the Lady Fachalana away from her father's influence. That would be a good thing, wouldn't it?

Jobareth felt sure he could convince himself it was.

6

Things would be different this time, Sojel assured himself.

He did not hurry as he rode south by circuitous ways but roughly paralleling the west bank of the Weldar. It would be necessary to reform his band when he reached his destination. Not so many now and just the best men.

It would not do to linger in Count Dordos's lands. They lay too close to County Rosam, too vulnerable to being spied upon. No, he would take the men south and cross the river a few at a time, here and there, so as not to arouse suspicion.

He wondered for a moment what had happened to his former second-in-command, Vanob. Sojel was not one to dwell on such things for long; still, it was odd that Van had never showed up.

He would have been a good man for the work at hand, thought Sojel. As it is, I may just have to do it all myself.

Sojel did rather like that idea.

"Your friend already knows most of your secrets, doesn't she? More of them, perhaps, than you realize."

Lord Radal had insisted that his daughter's companion accompany her to his chambers. This made Ansa understandably apprehensive. She had heard much of Fachalana's father yet had never met him.

What does he know? wondered Ansa. She felt suddenly trapped.

"Yes, Father," replied Fachalana, baffled — and intrigued — by the seeming tension between the two. "There is nothing we need hide from Maresta."

Radal looked long at the young spy and then shrugged. "I am sure whatever matters I would speak of here to you would sooner or later reach her ears. So stay, my lady."

The sorcerer had wondered about his daughter's comrade for some time. She did look Anian, didn't she?

He turned his gaze back to his daughter. "You are become the heroine of all Celatas. I have little doubt that the king will bestow some title on you, with income to match." He smiled thinly. "Perhaps I won't need to give you so large an allowance now."

Ansa managed a small smile as well. Lord Radal did not seem nearly so terrifying as his reputation had him.

She knew, however, not to be fooled.

"I am proud of you too, my dear," he told his daughter and truly meant it. "But a question remains: why did you go to Prince Modareth's house on that day and at that hour?"

"I — I had dreams, Father. I heard a voice, a far-away voice. I know not what it said but I awoke knowing Modi, I mean Prince Modareth, was in trouble.

"I *had* to go."

The Lord Councilor thought on this a moment. "That was the night we tried to speak to each other, wasn't it?"

"Yes, sir." Fachalana glanced toward her friend. "Maresta doesn't really know much about that. I suppose I may have, um, mentioned the idea in passing."

"The wizard-link is no secret, my girl, though most do not understand how it works." He fixed his eyes again upon the Anian. "And unless one has talent, it makes no difference how much one knows. This one," he said, giving a nod toward Ansa, "does not."

For which I give thanks, said Ansa to herself.

"So," the dark sorcerer continued, "I can guess what occurred."

"Was it a god?" asked his daughter. She still had hopes.

"Nay, Fachalana." Her father could not help laughing outright this time, nor could Ansa help joining him. "I believe it was another wizard, speaking to someone else. Someone who was arranging an assassination attempt.

"You must never have completely left your link and somehow ended up overhearing them. That," he said with sudden gravity, "takes great ability. I know of only two sorcerers, mighty mages, who have reputedly done so.

"Ah, if only you could harness such a talent and do it at will."

Ansa decided to speak up. Why not, after all? "Who, my lord, would have been planning such an attack?"

Radal shook his head. "There are too many possibilities. The link does not require great natural capability and many can enter it. You, too, will in time," he said to his daughter. "It is in you.

"There is much in you, Fachalana, and you have yet to discover it."

He rose and went to a narrow window. They had met in a lower room of Radal's tower, a tower only he and those he invited ever entered. Higher up were the chambers where he practiced his magics, where folks saw strange lights playing in the night.

This room held only an ordinary desk and chairs.

"Come to the window," said Lord Radal. "One can see Lama from here."

Fachalana peered through the opening. "It looks just like Sharsh," said she.

"That it does," replied her father. "I still have my reservations about allowing this. Take care, Fachalana, on the road and at Castle Rosam.

"And I charge you, Maresta, with keeping her from getting into trouble."

All three knew that might prove a difficult task.

Galaro stood in his stirrups and looked up the road. "I would recognize that rider anywhere," said he.

"An enemy or a friend?" asked the man who rode beside him. He cocked his head so he might regard his captain with his one good eye.

"A brother."

"Ah, then both."

"You must have brothers," remarked Galaro. He raised a hand in greeting as the horseman came nearer.

"Have you come to play us a song, Brother?" he roared.

"I might as well serenade the deaf!" came the answer. Then both men were off their steeds and, after only a moment's hesitation, embraced.

"Friends, it seems," remarked Galaro's companion.

"Nay, Guesare hates my guts. And with good reason!" He held his half-brother at arms' length and spoke. "I would hope you might forgive some of what I did to you as a lad."

"Some," agreed the minstrel.

"'Tis better than none," allowed Galaro, "nor do I expect you to forget what has been. Are you on your way to Castle Rosam?"

"That I am."

"You need not hurry. Your young friend is in good hands. Those of our brother Habidros, in fact." The burly trader turned to his train of followers. "There is a good spot to pitch our tents a half-league up the road," he called to them. "Let us do so.

"And I would that you stay with us tonight, Guesare. You may even play your rebec, if you don't mind the accompaniment of good Cuddonian bagpipes."

"I thought I had escaped those! But I will encamp with you this night, Brother," said the minstrel, vaulting onto his wiry pony.

Guesare admired the efficiency with which the troop set up their tents on a field bordering a middling-sized village. Potential buyers began to show up immediately.

"We will not do much business here," confided Galaro, "but there is no point in bypassing a sales opportunity. And, after all, we do need to stop and sleep somewhere.

"These necklaces come directly from Lorj," he said to a woman who was perusing his wares. Guesare doubted that the villager believed Galaro's sales pitch but, knowing him to be a smuggler, thought it might well be true.

As they relaxed by the fire that night, Guesare idly strumming his rebec, the brothers filled each other in on recent events.

"It seems I should thank you for saving Donzalo's life," said Guesare.

"Possibly. Habi and Sir Corgos are competent fighters, They might have gotten him to safety on their own." The two sat without speaking for a few minutes.

"Your old acquaintance Perdos rode with me a while in the spring," spoke Galaro of a sudden.

"I assume he still wishes me ill."

"Oh, indeed. One thing that seems most certain, though, is that he is not in league with those who wish to harm Donzalo."

He paused, composing his words. "But be careful of the man. We parted ways north of Ros-town and I suspect he yet lurks about those parts." He turned to Guesare. "Why don't you ride north with us? We will return to Count Borrago's lands for the Summer Fair."

"You fear for me on the road?" Guesare was surprised that his long-estranged brother would feel concern for him. Or maybe he thinks to make up for our past, he thought.

No, he could not postpone his return to Castle Rosam a month or more. Too much was coming together there and he needed to be in place before it did.

"I must decline, my brother. I shall see you at Summer Feast."

"I was once ambassador in Morparas, you know," remarked Lord Doufan for no particular reason, as they watched the fog-shrouded river banks slide by. Or no reason that Jobareth could discern. One could be sure of nothing with the ambassador.

At any rate, Jobareth did know this. He had learned all he could of the man before they left Sharsh.

"Is it like to Oles, sir?" he asked.

Doufan laughed loudly. "There are no two cities more unalike! Morparas is dirty and dangerous and disorganized. It was also the largest city I had ever seen. Larger than any in Sharsh, though no city in Lama proper rivals Celatas."

"I was told that Lanlaz dwarfs even Morparas." This he had heard from Guesare, the only man he personally knew — until he met Doufan's scribe — who had been to the isle of Lorj.

"Some say it is the largest city in the world." Doufan looked up as the boatswain approached.

"This be a dangerous stretch of the river, gentlemen," he said. "Best keep a watch out for pirates and such."

"As long as it is not one of my former wives, I shall feel safe," said Lord Doufan.

The man chuckled appropriately and went aft to speak to the other passengers on deck. Most chose to remain in the open air in this warm weather, rather than the stuffy cabin that sat midship. The increasing swarms of biting insects were beginning to change some minds.

They danced above the water, swarming in the misted golden light of morn. It was growing warmer. Donzalo came near to dozing off.

Then he spied a pair of skiffs, partly concealed in the willows overhanging the stream. They were filled with men.

"Guardsmen! To arms!"

Immediately, each man at arms rose in his place, hand to his sword, as did Jobareth. The ruffians in the boats stayed where they were and only glared at the travelers as they passed.

Doufan eyed him appraisingly. "You are a good man to have about in a crisis, Nafal. Have you ever considered a career in the military rather than diplomacy?"

"No, I'll not drink, Jak."

Bolos waited while the sergeant of his guard quaffed his tankard of ale. He found himself watching how the lamplight reflected from the man's bald head. Could I be losing my hair? he wondered. His father, the count, had been bald nearly as long as he could remember.

The stolid soldier wiped his beard on the back of his hand and looked at his master. "You shouldn't beat yourself up over it, sir, if I may say so. 'Twas only once."

Bolos nodded without speaking.

"And you've done well this past year," continued Sir Jak. "The boys are all pulling for you, sir."

"This past year has not done well by me." Jak recognized the self-pity in his employer's words but felt maybe the man had a right to it. It was not to him to judge, anyway.

"Is there anything I should know about?" asked Bolos, breaking the silence that had followed his plaint. Jak was relieved. Now they could get down to business.

"Not really, my lord. Your father still visits the house of Sir Copago more evenings than not. And when he does, he usually stays the night."

"What of my brother? Donzalo." Bolos did not want the man to think he meant his half-brother Copago or that he even acknowledged their kinship.

He had received a letter from the king's councilor, Lord Radal, stating that Sharsh had his interests in mind and warning him against the ambitions of Count Orgelo. This had served to strengthen the suspicions he already had.

Should he trust Radal? He still did not understand why he and the king had tried to kill his brother. But the message also suggested he keep an eye on Donzalo. It was not an accusation but it made Bolos wonder.

"He has kept to himself, sir, for the most part. I set a man to watch him but he finds little to report." The burly soldier chuckled. "It seems he spends the better part of his time sorting his library."

"Keep up the watch." Sir Bolos sighed. "Whatever is coming, we must be ready for it."

7

"Sharshite nobles may not haggle but it is expected in Lama," explained Ansa. She held up two fingers to the roadside fruit merchant. He nodded his agreement, handing over slices of melon in exchange for a pair of copper coins.

"All of us," she told the man. "Don't try to cheat me."

Their entourage had grown. Lord Radal had insisted that two guardsmen be added, making the group now six strong. Ansa had been glad of those two men at arms when they spied a band of men in the distance, cutting across their path. She breathed easier when the troop continued toward the south on whatever business it had.

"Mercenaries, I would wager, my lady," whispered one of the guards. Ansa nodded her agreement.

The purveyor of melons distributed his ware to all, the two soldiers on their horses, Murbalana and the man-servant in a two-wheeled cart. The deaf servant, known only as Doo — but who did not answer to any name — enjoyed being in charge of driving the wagon and was sure that Mistress Murbalana admired his skill.

She seemed to comment on it frequently.

They had turned from the Oles Road and now traveled south-easterly toward County Rosam. This was the route the couriers of Sharsh usually took.

"You were certainly right about Lama being hot," said Fachalana.

"Wait a month," replied her companion. Though she knew better than to wear an Ani costume in Lama, Ansa still straddled her mount. The Lady Fachalana noticed that it was not uncommon for women of the countryside to do so here.

She also continued to dye her hair.

Ansa daydreamed sometimes about meeting Donzalo again. Would he recognize her with her dark tresses, now cut shorter than when he had known her? Would the clothes of a gentlewoman rather than a serving maid fool him?

Would he remember her at all?

There was also the possibility that Borrago would have her thrown into a cell as a spy as soon as she set foot on his lands.

"How far to the next inn?" she asked the Laman.

"If you are not too picky, my lady, less than a league," replied the fellow.

To Fachalana, he looked a typical peasant of the land, slight, olive-skinned and dark haired. She had to admit that they all seemed much alike to her.

Her friend had taken charge of their little company. She knew Maresta was competent but this surprised her. Fachalana was accustomed to being the leader in any circle she entered.

The Lady Fachalana was more suspicious than ever that the actress was not all she seemed.

"I want you to remain in the keep for a while longer," said the King of Sharsh to his younger son, "and I want you to remain guarded."

Modareth nodded. He turned to his wife and took her hand. "Whatever you think best, Father." As soon as the two had seated themselves before the king's desk, Modareth had slid his chair close to that of his wife.

"Sire," spoke the Princess Carrana, somewhat hesitantly. "Do — do you think the Lady Fachalana might be named my lady-in-waiting?"

Lareth liked it immediately. "Yes, my dear, an excellent idea. It would give her an official position at the court — just what she needs when I make her a viscountess." He smiled at how the pair looked to each other at that. "You realize that she would no doubt be very lax in her duties."

"She has attended her duties very well, sir," said Modareth. "I would certainly not complain."

"Perhaps I should also name her your bodyguard," jested the king. "But you are correct, my boy. Fachalana has already served us as well as any person might. If she never lifted another finger for us, we would still be satisfied with her.

"Now, we must speak of you and your bride and who might seek to kill you."

"It is about the succession, isn't it, sir?"

"Almost certainly," said Lareth, "and, therefor, it shall continue to be a problem. Partanaca may be behind it. Or it may be some sycophant of your brother who thinks to better secure his place."

"You think the former, don't you Father?"

"Yes, Modi, I do." Why couldn't Gawis have half the brains of this one? wondered King Lareth. When it comes time, I hope the older brother has sense enough to lean on the younger.

"Would we be safer in the country, sir?" asked Carrana. She wasn't exactly dim-witted either, was she?

"Maybe. A well-defended keep somewhere might be ideal. Not too far from here, of course, and near a garrison."

He looked at the pair and was a bit surprised by the fondness he felt for them, fondness he had always seemed to reserve for Modareth's siblings. "For now, however, remain safe here in my fortress. And maybe make me a grandson so we can truly worry the Partanacans!"

The king laughed to see both blush so deeply.

"You have fallen in the world, Hendel of Pora."

The stout cook looked up at the mention of his name. "Thanks to you and your master." He nearly spat out his reply.

Sojel barked a derisive laugh. "No one forced Sharsh's silver into your hand."

Two of his henchmen stood behind him in the tavern doorway. They were the last that he needed to get across the river, here at Todmouth.

All the way down the Weldar, he had kept his men to their task, not allowing them to turn aside for plunder or sport, sending two or three across at a time, with orders to meet up later. Most should be waiting for him when he crossed.

"You know these scoundrels?" asked the woman behind the bar. She was not a young woman nor was she pleasant to look upon. But Mistress Oba owned this tavern and here she was a queen.

She had her own henchmen should any be unwilling to recognize her as such.

Hendel turned toward his employer. "I knew Sergeant Sojel when I worked upriver, ma'am. The other two are strangers to me." The cook retained the manners he had learned while serving aristocrats. It had stood him in good stead when he sought a job here.

And, as had others before her, Oba fell in love with his pastries. It was rumored that he was a confection she sometimes sampled as well.

"Humph. If you plan to drink, come in and stop dawdling at the door, boys. If you want food, Hendel is at your service. If you want more than food," she added with a wink, "the girls upstairs can accommodate you."

Hendel shuddered involuntarily at the thought of those 'girls.' They made Mistress Oba look a beauty in comparison.

Sojel and his men seated themselves at a stained and splintered table, the veteran of many a spilled beer and idler's knife. "Ale for us all," he ordered, "and tell the girls to expect us later."

"That I will, sir," said Oba, a smile splitting her leathery face. "That I will."

At this early hour, the cliffs below Keep Rosam stood yet in darkness and the sun hid behind its battlements. Guesare gazed upward at their silhouetted shapes for a little while, recalling his memories of the place. Perhaps, next to Drolwym, it was the place most like a home to him.

He recalled an old song of his homeland and spoke the words lowly to himself:

Travelers all, we wear
the dust of yesterday.
The rain will fall at last,
and gently wash away
each fragment of the past,
the long road's clinging clay.
Travelers all, we fare
yet upon our way.

Ever a traveler — was there any other life for him? He turned his mount toward the winding road up to the castle.

They still might not be counted friends, but Sir Blen and Sir Donzalo found themselves spending more time together. Where they spent much of this time was on the green between Castle Rosam's outer walls, exercising their knightly skills.

At times they were joined by Habidros the Cuddonian, now Donzalo's bodyguard. At others, Sir Copago joined them. His duties often had him elsewhere and Habidros did not like to rise early so, frequently, it was only the two. Blen would ride up from the new embassy at dawn — it was a much shorter trip than the one from town — and Donzalo would be there to greet him.

They fenced a great deal. Blen knew he lacked in this skill and that the lanky Laman had become a fine swordsman. He could learn from the boy and about the boy at once.

This morning, he was become somewhat miffed at that boy. With his long arms, Donzalo was choosing to play with him, reaching in and poking him here and there at will with his wooden practice sword. Blen hoped he would never have to face the lad in a real duel!

Suddenly, Donzalo dropped his guard and stared at something behind Blen.

"That would have been a great mistake in combat," came a voice. "Sir Blen would have skewered you properly.'

"Guesare!"

Blen turned to see the Cuddonian minstrel astride his pony and held up a hand in greeting. "Welcome back, Sir Guesare."

The man dismounted and took his hand. "It is good to see you, Sir Blen." But he embraced Donzalo as he would a brother.

"Habi should have come down with me," said Donzalo. "He has missed the opportunity to greet you in exchange for an extra hour of sleep."

"He probably considers it a fair bargain," remarked Guesare. "I hear he is now your man."

Donzalo nodded. "You are leaving, Blen?"

"Back to my duties, Donni," the knight replied, as he tied his gear to his horse's saddle. "Tomorrow?"

"I shall await you. And trounce you once again."

"Undoubtedly," laughed the Sharshite as he swung a leg over his steed and headed for the gates.

When did these two become friends? wondered Guesare, waiting while Donzalo gathered up his own gear.

8

The shores of the Weldar grew ever more populated. There were many villages now and farm fields that ran right down to the water's edge. This was the rich middle of the great river valley, and the counts who ruled it were wealthy men.

The wealthiest of these was Borrago, Count Rosam. They were only two days from Ros-town now, the boatswain told the Sharshites.

Sometimes the Great Road swung close to the river and they watched the traffic upon it, lone riders and men afoot, farmers' wains, bands of merchants. At first, more seemed to travel north, back the way they had come; now, traffic seemed more balanced, with many heading toward the south, toward County Rosam.

"They're starting to come back this way for the Summer Fair," said Pol.

Doufan seemed subdued as he surveyed the richness of the countryside they passed. "I never quite understood why the king attached such importance to this embassy," he confided to Nafal. "Now, I think I do."

"Lord Radal considers the Lamans dangerous," said Jobareth in return. He remembered when he had first come to Keep Rosam, as the dark sorcerer's aide.

"Lord Radal is frightened of many things."

"Indeed? He does not seem so."

"He puts on a good front but Radal is an empty man. Despair walks ever at his side and Death close behind." Lord Doufan smiled at his young compatriot's expression. "I rarely wax so poetic. That is your strength, isn't it, Jobareth Nafal?"

It was, thought Jobareth. How long had it been since he wrote anything?

He took a close look at the diplomat, the bland face, the thinning hair. It was so easy to dismiss such a man, to not see him at all.

"Ambassador," he said, "I wonder if Lord Radal might not consider you dangerous as well."

Both sat and watched the shore slide by.

"It is even wider than the Chas!" exclaimed Fachalana.

Ansa nodded absently. "The Siph is larger," she said. Then, thinking better of it, added, "Or so I have heard." There was no reason anyone here should know she had ever looked upon the mighty River Siph. Aye, and crossed it more than once.

Right now, they must cross this flow. She motioned for Doo to bring the cart up.

"There should be a ferry," said Ansa, surveying the town spread below them, most of it close to the river banks. The party stood atop a small hill. Across the Weldar they could see Ros-town proper and, above it, Borrago's keep.

Fachalana pointed. "Could that be it on the far side?"

"I believe so," replied the Anian, shielding her eyes from the morning sun. "The count only allows one ferry to operate. Of course, he owns it. If there were but one or two of us, we could find a boatman to take us across but I suppose we shall have to use the official transport." She had employed such boatmen on her previous visit to County Rosam.

"It may be on this side by the time we make it to the river. Let's head down."

Fachalana rode close to her friend and whispered, "From here on I had best play leader of our group. I know you do not want to call attention to yourself."

Ansa agreed. "I can fill the role of demure companion to a great lady. Our looks would make most think us such, anyway."

The Lady Fachalana laughed at that. "Shall I play my part with great haughtiness or am I the sort to treat my underlings well?"

"You have had a lifetime to practice the role, my lady. I think you will find the proper approach.

"Do you wish to present yourself immediately at the count's court?"

"Oh, no, Maresta. Let us find the embassy first. Do you think Jobo might be here yet?"

Their road had become a rutted street lined with shabby wooden structures, mostly warehouses from the look of them.

Ansa shrugged. "We shall find out, soon enough."

There was a capacious dock at the end of their way. Out on the river, the wide, flat-bottomed ferry was slowly steering toward them, oarsmen at a pair of sweeps on either side.

The heart of each beat a little quicker as it approached. Within these two accomplished women there remained yet a pair of impetuous, romantic girls, wondering what great adventure might await them here.

Doo wondered only if Mistress Murbalana would be seduced from his side by the sophisticated men of this city.

"It is hard to believe you met Galaro on the road yet you are both still alive."

"Our brother is now a leader of men. I think that changes one." Guesare looked about him. "I like your new digs, Donni."

Donzalo's quarters had more and more come to resemble his old ones. The biggest difference was the large table in the center of this room, overflowing with scraps of manuscript and bit and pieces of mechanical devices. The minstrel walked over and surveyed them. "Cannons, Donzalo?"

"He keeps talking about building a foundry," said Habidros. "'Tis not a bad idea, I think."

Guesare nodded. "Borrago needs more artillery here, whether he buy it or cast it himself. I believe he does not realize how quickly a bombard or two might level this keep."

"We should have emplacements on the river, too," declared Donzalo. "Then we would truly control it."

"You'll never convince the count of that. He's not even convinced his men should have muskets. Yes," continued Habidros, "I have noticed things in my short time here."

"You're the only true soldier of we three, Habi," said his brother. "Donzalo may have need of such, one of these days."

"Not if I end up as Uncle Paren's heir. I suspect Habidros would not want to spend the rest of his days serving a rural reeve."

"There are worse fates," opined Guesare. "But we both expect more for you."

Donzalo sighed deeply and, perhaps, with a note of exasperation. "Not the destiny thing again."

"We all have destinies, my boy. Mine is to starve if we don't get down to the kitchens."

"Whence came these horses?"

"Which ones, sir?" The little innkeeper looked up at Sojel and then at the knot of armed men behind him.

"That one. And that one over there."

"Oh." He had suspected the soldier meant those ones and also suspected this was not a good thing. "I bought them from a traveling knight. A Sir Perdos. I can give you a good deal on them." Would that he had managed to sell all of them already.

"Isn't that Vanob's mount?" asked one of the men. Sojel ignored him.

"Perdos, you say? Where is this Perdos now?"

"He crossed the river a season ago, having wintered with us. He seemed a good enough fellow."

"A traitor and a deserter is what he is. A murderer of his comrades too, it seems. And you harbored him." Sojel felt his anger as a fire rising within him. He did not tamp it down as he might usually but let his temper rage. He had been frustrated too much and too frequently lately.

He rode his horse into the little man, knocking him down. The innkeeper's wife ran shrieking from the doorway where she had been standing.

Sojel let his warhorse thoroughly trample the body beneath its steel-shod hooves. Before the now-widow could reach her husband's remains, he grasped her by her collar and threw her to the ground before his troop.

"You may have the woman," Sojel told his followers, already eagerly dismounting.

"Bring me a flame!" he shouted, and one of the bravos ran into the inn to return with a lit lantern. Sojel tossed it onto the thatched roof and saw that it readily caught fire.

Two lightly equipped guardsmen had come running up from their post at the ferry. On discovering the number and arms of their opponents they hesitated, then ran the opposite way. Sojel's men easily rode them down.

The sergeant sat in his saddle, satisfied, and watched the inn burn. "Get the horses," he ordered, "and let's be on our way."

9

The house was empty. They had been assured that the embassy was at this address.

An idler watched them a while from the shade of an awning across the street, before ambling over. "Looking for the Sharshites? They moved to their new place."

Fachalana sighed wearily. "Thank you, my good man," she said in her most refined tones, playing the role of great lady to the hilt. "Could you tell me where that is?"

The man looked at her slyly. "I could guide you."

Ansa whispered to her friend. "He means for a price." She knew Fachalana might not readily recognize that sort of thing.

The noblewoman said nothing but immediately urged her horse up the street. Ansa signaled for Doo to follow.

"We'll find someone else to point out the road," declared Fachalana.

Which they did and soon found themselves passing out of town and into the hilly countryside. "We could still take rooms in Ros-town," said Ansa. "It might be less bother."

"I don't want to waste any more time," replied her friend.

In town, they had learned that Jobareth Nafal and the new ambassador were not yet arrived. They heard quite a bit of news, in fact, on the ferry, at the docks. Lamans, like most folk the world around, enjoyed their gossip. So Ansa and Fachalana were well filled in on the goings-on at Keep Rosam.

They had to ask directions but one more time before they spied a large edifice, obviously still under construction, on a hill to the left of their road. The duo would have made far better time had they not needed to match their pace to that of the cart that followed them.

Murbalana could be heard voicing displeasure over something. They could not make out exactly what and remained as ignorant as the man seated by her.

The ugly, squarish, crenelated building stood in three stories of pinkish stone, the lowest being sunk partly into the ground. "It looks like a fortress," observed Ansa. Sir Blen had a hand in its design, no doubt. "Stay here," she called to the wagon and then held up her palm so Doo would actually know what she meant. The two women rode up the rise toward the embassy.

"I hope they plan to pave this eventually," remarked Fachalana. The ground was rough and rutted from the many wagons that had brought stone and timber up this hill.

"Why, it is Blen himself," whispered Ansa to her comrade, as a man stepped from the wide doorway opening into the basement floor and walked toward them.

"My greetings and welcome to you, Lady Fachalana," said he. "My man in town sent a message saying you had arrived. It came to my hand only moments before you yourself came to my door or I would have ridden down to escort you."

He looked quizzically at Ansa. "Posena?" he said, in sudden recognition. He turned back to the Sharshite noblewoman. "Do you know who this woman is?"

"Be not concerned about it, sir," she replied, slipping down from her mount. "Maresta came here before under my orders and as my agent."

Sir Blen considered her words for a moment. "That clears some things up, my lady," he calmly replied.

He has a cool head on him, thought Ansa. I like that. "Shall I have the cart come up, sir?"

Blen motioned to a pair of men who stood near. "Go fetch up the luggage and see to the servants. You, my ladies, must come in and throw off your road weariness. Maresta, you say?" he asked, helping the young woman dismount. "Is that how we should call you here?"

"Yes," Fachalana said. "Although I have long suspected that too is a made-up name for the stage."

Close to the truth, my friend, thought Ansa.

The knight tossed the reins to a waiting groom and escorted the duo up a wooden stairway — obviously temporary — to the second level and what was clearly intended to be the main entrance. A pair of heavy oak doors hung open.

"It looks better inside than out, my ladies," said Blen. "Would you like to go to your rooms first?"

"I'm starving," stated Fachalana.

Ansa laughed at her friend's directness. "As am I, Sir Blen."

"Then let us lunch together, " said Blen, "and you can tell me all about your trip.

"And maybe," he added, "something about this Maresta whom I knew as Posena the chambermaid."

Little Ros was shy of his very large 'Uncle' Donzalo. He had been far too young when last the man who was truly his father had seen or held him and there were no memories.

He hid behind his mother's chair.

"He walks very well for his age," remarked Guesare. The boy was not altogether sure about him either.

"I have heard that Donzalo was the same," replied Lady Lomela. She did not know that the minstrel was privy to the secret of Ros's paternity.

Guesare could see his friend's heart was breaking. Maybe he should never have returned to his home. Maybe a peaceful life in the Cuddon was the only destiny he needed.

Mistress Traspa picked up the toddler. "Nap time, my little lord," said she and carried him to his nursery.

A rap came at the door, to be answered by a chambermaid in Traspa's absence. She admitted a man in robes of white.

"Brother Grippo," said Lomela. "Come in and visit with us."

"Thank you, my lady." He held out a folded paper to her. "A message came from Sir Blen and I offered to deliver it to you."

The princess read the note quickly. "Fachalana is here!" she beamed. "At last! Oh, how I wish that Jobareth had already arrived."

Guesare and Donzalo exchanged thoughtful looks. The name Fachalana meant many things to them, different things to each.

"Is she coming here, my lady?" asked Donzalo.

"Tomorrow morning. Sir Blen will bring her up. Oh, you must meet her, Donni, and you too, Guesare." She laughed. "And Brother Grippo. All of you are always welcome here."

Grippo spoke. "I understand that she is — engaged to our friend Nafal?"

"No, not officially," replied Lomela. "But everyone expects it to be only a matter of time." Once again the other two men exchanged glances.

On their way back to Donzalo's rooms, Guesare warned, "Do not make the mistake of looking for Jola in this woman."

"I know not to, my friend. How do you feel about meeting a sister you never knew you had?"

"Stepsister," Guesare corrected him. "But I, too, must avoid seeing Jola in she who is her sister."

"Lord Radal's daughter is here, my lord," said Copago, entering the count's tower study.

Borrago turned to him. "At the castle?"

"No, sir. She is staying in the Sharshite embassy. Sir Blen asks to bring her by tomorrow morning."

"Hmm, what's her name again?"

"Fachalana, my lord. The Lady Fachalana."

"Of course, of course. I don't know how many times Lomela has mentioned it to me." The count shrugged. "Well, let her come."

"Sir." There was concern in his master of arms' voice.

"Speak."

"Her father did try to kill Donzalo. Should we let the two of them, well, be anywhere near each other?"

"You do not think she is an assassin?"

"No, though I have heard some surprising things about her, sir. You heard the story of her saving King Lareth's son from an attack?"

"That was this girl?" Borrago whistled. "I wish I had a better memory for names!" He thought a moment. "Tell Donzalo that I want his man Habidros with him at all times. Most times, anyway. And it wouldn't hurt if his brother Guesare tagged along."

Copago smiled. "That should keep the boy safe."

"We are never safe from women, my lad. Of that you may be sure."

"I should not go with you. Not until the Legate arrives."

"Oh, don't call him that, Maresta. He is our friend Jobareth. You could even address him as Jobo and get away with it."

"However I might name him, I want him there to vouch for me before I enter Borrago's keep. You may have prestige in Sharsh but the count does not know you. Nor does he have any love for your father."

"I suppose you are right," admitted Fachalana. "You are always the level-headed one of us." She smiled warmly at her friend. This trip had brought them closer than ever before, had let them become the true equals that true friends must be. "I envy you the extra time to rest while I must be once more on horseback. I don't know if I'll ever be able to sit properly again!"

With that, Fachalana bustled out the door, not to return until late in the day.

Ansa looked about the room for a moment, wondering if she should indeed return to her own and get some extra sleep. No, she was too on edge for that. She would like to see more of the embassy and the countryside that lay around it and she should check in on their traveling companions, too.

The Murb's little chamber was right down the hall, where Ansa and Fachalana could call on her at need. They had no need and no desire to do so, but had let the Sharshites put her where they wished. She rapped lightly on the door. If the woman were asleep, it would be unwise to wake her and provide yet another grievance.

No reply. But what was that thumping noise? She carefully pushed open the unlocked portal to glimpse Murbalana and Doo quite occupied with their own business. As quickly and as quietly as she could, she shut it, her expression hovering somewhere between a smile and a grimace.

Well, at least I need not worry about those two, she told herself. And though her rear end was as sore as Fachalana's, she thought maybe a ride would be a pleasant morning's diversion.

"Now you two must be our surrogates while we are gone," said Sir Paren. Corgos and Tiana stood respectfully, waiting for the reeve to mount up.

"Do hurry, my dear," called Lady Thara from one of two wagons. "We are going to travel slowly enough with all this baggage. Do you want to miss your own brother's wedding?"

A half-dozen men at arms sat their horses, waiting, and there were servants and drivers with the wains.

"Very well, my lady," Paren called back to her. "Expect us to be gone at least three weeks, maybe a month," he said. "He had told this to his master of arms several times already but thought it bore repeating. "With any luck, maybe we can bring Donni back with us."

"He is a fine young man," replied Captain Corgos. "I would gladly ride with him again."

"It is my hope that neither of you ever has to ride anywhere again," said Sir Paren, mounting up. "No further than my brother's keep, anyway."

He signaled his followers to form up their column and set off down the road toward Keep Rosam.

"Shall I address you as Lady Tiana for the next month?" teased Corgos.

"It wouldn't hurt," replied his bride.

10

That had gone well enough, thought the Lady Fachalana.

Borrago had been polite, if a bit brusque, and seemed to bear her no ill will. She was surprised at how short the man was, knowing of his tall son. Fachalana suspected that if she and the count stood side by side, her height would be the greater, and perhaps by more than just a bit.

So much for the official presentation. Now Sir Blen led the way to the Lady Lomela's apartments. The keep was not large by the standards of some she had seen in Sharsh and had a sense of the rustic about it. But it seemed spacious and probably was a comfortable enough place to dwell. It might not be her father's palace but the princess was not suffering here.

Would Donzalo be there? Their meeting would be complicated. This she knew.

And here they were. Ah, Lomela, it has been too long. Is that your little boy? And Traspa! Fachalana entered the room wordlessly and embraced her childhood friend.

There were tears in at least three sets of eyes.

"My ladies," spoke Blen. They turned to look at him, still standing in the doorway. "I will leave you for a little while but return later." Both knew he meant that he would bring guests with him.

There was much to talk about, once their tearful greeting was out of the way. The two sat on Lomela's divan and spoke of many things, Jobareth Nafal being high on the list.

Little Ros stood a while, silently regarding this stranger, and then climbed onto Fachalana's lap. She had never before had a child sit in her lap.

It was not unpleasant.

So it was that Sir Blen found them on his return. With him were three men, two quite large, one of a more ordinary size. From the rebec he carried, Fachalana recognized that the latter was a minstrel and therefor was able to put a name to him: Guesare.

Brother to Donzalo's slain love. A love who was also her own sister.

The two larger fellows looked rather alike, but she had no trouble knowing which was Donzalo. Had she not seen him often enough in dream? The other whispered something in the young knight's ear and then took up a station outside the door. A bodyguard, she surmised.

"Habi is taking his duties too seriously," said Donzalo. "He too is a kinsman but says he will stand guard outside."

Lomela rose from her place. Fachalana was uncertain what to do with the boy in her lap. She gingerly lifted him onto the cushions beside her and came to stand beside the princess.

"This is my old friend, the Lady Fachalana," Lomela said.

"Not old, you silly," broke in Fachalana. The men smiled, which had been her intention, and she smiled back. She knew how to act the role of flirtatious girl. It was a stock character of the stage.

"Very well, Fachalana," replied Lomela, with a laugh that overflowed with her happiness. There had been few such for a long time. "These are my dear friends Sir Guesare and Sir Donzalo. That is Habidros in the hallway. He is Guesare's brother."

"Half-brother, my lady," murmured the minstrel. His eyes were fixed on the Lady Fachalana. So like his dead sister, yet so different. And he could feel that she was filled with the same power. For good or for evil?

That he could not tell, yet he sensed no malice.

Donzalo stepped forward and kissed the lady's hand. He, too, saw much alike to Jola in this woman but it did not affect him in the same way. She was not Jola and that was that.

This did not mean that she was not entangled somehow in his own destiny, and he in hers.

"My Lady Fachalana," he said, being as courtly as he knew how. For Donzalo, that mostly meant trying to avoid serious blunders.

She was tall, like Jola, perhaps even taller, and had much the same burnished skin tone. But her hair fell in dark waves where his lost love's had been golden and curling. Her eyes, too, were dark and as piercing as any he had ever seen.

"Sir Donzalo," she replied in turn. "It is good to meet you — at last."

Both knew the meaning behind that, the fleeting glimpses they had of each other in dream.

Guesare came out of his reverie and stepped forward as well to greet the young noblewoman. "My lady." He could feel the latent ability in her when he took her hand. The minstrel was almost afraid to touch his lips to it.

And Fachalana, too, sensed something in Guesare. Until now, her father was the only man of magic she had ever known.

"It is nearing the luncheon hour," said the ever-practical Blen. "Shall I order something from the kitchens?"

"An excellent idea, sir," replied Lady Lomela. "Traspa, will you take Ros to his nursery? I'll have something brought up for the two of you, as well."

The plump servant disappeared into the next room, sleepy boy in her arms.

Blen, his powers of observation as strong as ever, could feel something going on. There was a sense of anticlimax in the room. They had met — what now?

Lomela and Habidros — whom they finally prevailed upon to join them — seemed oblivious to it. But the other three — ah! Something was there but they were choosing to hide it behind good manners and small talk. They were still feeling each other out.

What will happen, he wondered, when Nafal and Maresta are thrown into this mix? Blen would just have to wait and see.

The men dispersed after lunch, leaving Lomela and her friend to further catch up, Blen lingering at the keep until time came for him to escort the Lady Fachalana back to their embassy. With the daughter of Lord Radal, best he do that in person.

"Madin."

Borrago's secretary looked up from the papers he was transcribing. "Sir Bolos?"

"I understand the count received visitors this morning." Bolos added nothing to this. Was it a question?

"Yes, my lord," said the scribe. If his master's son intended to be sparing with his words, then so would he.

And Bolos was not so obtuse that he did not recognize it. He took one of the chairs by his father's desk and sprawled in it.

"So, the Lady Fachalana — what is she like?"

Madin put down his stylus and smiled at the lordling. "Tall, sir," he answered.

Bolos chuckled at that. "So I have heard! And dark, too, if you had a mind to add it." He had always liked Madin, with his mix of dignity and dry humor. It let him get away with remarks that might not have been tolerated from others. "Did the meeting go well?"

"Such as it was, my lord, yes. Their time together was brief and I think neither wished to be there. The Lady Fachalana seemed eager to see your wife."

"Hmm, yes, they are longtime friends, the Lady Lomela has told me."

"I must say, sir, that Sir Blen appeared far the most interested individual there. He seems to enjoy watching people interact." Madin chuckled softly. "I also watch people at times, my lord."

"You have the perfect seat for that arena," observed Bolos.

"That I do, my lord, but your father expects discretion from me."

"And I would expect it no less," Bolos Rosam responded. A good man, he thought to himself, and not one I should seek to compromise. He is more valuable as who he is. He rose.

"A good evening to you, Madin."

"And to you, sir."

Fachalana thought much and said little about her day. Donzalo was not disappointing, but neither did he seem as exciting as she imagined. He did come off a bit bookish and awkward.

But how can anyone live up to ones dreams? She would have to get to know him better.

She wanted to know Guesare better, too. She was intrigued by the thought that he was a sorcerer, though apparently a rather minor one, a dabbler in magics. As she sat thinking, her friend entered from her adjoining apartment.

"These rooms are comfortable enough," said Ansa. They were. They were large and the windows allowed plenty of air on these warm nights. The appointments were far too masculine and functional, but that could be remedied.

"If only the building were not so ugly. It's hard to believe that Jobareth had a part in its design."

"We must blame Sir Blen as well. The two were thinking more of defense than of aesthetics." She spoke jokingly to her friend. "If only you could cast a spell to knock it down so they would be forced to start over."

"An excellent idea," said the Lady Fachalana, rising from her cushioned stool.

Fachalana decided to ham it up. She visualized herself as a wise and powerful sorcerer, wrapped in robes of sable, writ all over in mystic runes.

"I call upon the Demons of Droga!" she declaimed in her best and most serious stage tones. Fachalana had no idea who the demons were nor even whether Droga was a place or a person, but had seen the name in one of her father's books."Hear me, O Demons, and bring down this hideous house!"

Suddenly, the floor trembled below them.

Ansa's eyes grew wide and Fachalana cried out, 'No! No! Never mind!"

Then she grew silent, thinking on what had just happened. "So that's how it works," she whispered. She looked to her friend. "I need to *act* the spells. I need to put on the role of magician as I would any on the stage."

Fachalana spoke louder now, and with assurance. "This is how I can find the discipline I need. This is how I will have control. This is the key, Maresta!"

Ansa was not sure whether joy or fear was the proper response.

There came a rapping at the door. The Anian opened it to Mistress Murbalana. "My ladies," said she, "Sir Blen asked me to tell you that the ambassador just arrived, and your friend with him.

"Did you feel that earthquake? We never had such in Sharsh!" She shook her head. "The ground stays where it should, back home."

Gawis did not love his wife.

Indeed, he rarely thought of her at all. Their marriage had been a matter of politics, their daughters more the result of diplomacy than intimacy.

Yet he did not dislike Mara and felt it his duty to occasionally spend time with her and in her bed.

"Husband?" she said, after he had performed his duty and turned to sleep.

"What, Mara?" The princess rarely initiated a conversation with him. She was an exceedingly quiet and unassuming woman and Gawis did not mind that.

She pulled the covers close about her and sat up in bed. That was not modesty — child of the hot southern isles, Mara often felt chilled in her adopted land.

"Do you think my father tried to have Modareth murdered?"

"It is possible." The prince sat up as well, but let the bedclothes fall from his pale, compact frame. "Whoever is responsible, it bothers me greatly that they chose one from my circle to attempt the deed."

He had forgotten that Mara was one person to whom he might unburden himself. They talked so little anymore.

"Perhaps, Gawis," she began, hesitance obvious in her voice. "Perhaps it is a new circle that you need."

She could see his smile by the flicker of the candles, the smile that had charmed her when first they were wed. "That, my lady, I think is better advice than any other I have received lately."

He looked upon his wife, still a comely woman, and felt it might be a good idea to do his duty a second time this night.

11

"Our Lord Radal's daughter is upstairs?"

"She is, my lord," answered Sir Blen. "Would you wish to speak to her this night?"

"Oh, no, of course not. Even if she is not abed, I should be." Lord Doufan took a cursory look about the embassy's reception room and continued. "You can give me the tour tomorrow, sir. I suppose I should go present my credentials to the count, as well." He sighed with exaggerated weariness.

Jobareth Nafal smiled behind the ambassador's back. He had come to know the man well on their journey — as well as one might know such an enigma.

"Nafal, I shall see you in the morning. You, as well, Sir Blen. Now lead me to my rooms," Doufan said, turning to the majordomo. "And do have a bite sent up, too, won't you?

As the diplomat and his guide disappeared down a hallway — his apartment being here on the central floor — Jobareth took Blen aside. "Is Fachalana's companion with her?" he asked.

"She is. You know her true identity?"

"I do. I should have recognized her before from her stage appearances in Celatas." He barely whispered his next question. "Has Donzalo seen her?"

"No, not yet. It will be most interesting when he does, won't it?"

"That it will, Blen."

Blue and argent were the banners of Count Orgelo. It was a deeper blue than that on the Coradean arms, but clearly meant to honor that heritage. County Arvaram prided itself on the unbroken descent of its rulers from men of Lorj, men who had never surrendered to the Anians but had withdrawn their forces into the mountains and continued to fight.

It was Orgelo himself who came to Borrago's wedding, leaving his son Sorsen to rule in his stead. Sorsen was much loved throughout

Lama, handsome, courtly and capable. He was also a bit of an ass, thought Orgelo, whose talents seemed better suited to battlefield and boudoir than to governing. But he loved his son.

On his way up the river, the count had heard rumors of roving bands terrorizing the countryside. Perhaps he should send his heir out to hunt them down once he returned to Tod-ford. It was the sort of thing Sorsen did well.

And his less powerful neighbors would not complain if his troops crossed their lands in pursuit. They expected Orgelo to keep the peace in their neighborhood.

Count Orgelo and his men had kept to the west of the Weldar all the way up to Ros-town, rather than crossing over to the Great Road. He felt more comfortable on what he considered his side of the river.

Now his men were boarding the ferry, under the watchful eye of Borrago's agent. The man seemed uncertain as to whether he should charge Orgelo for the crossing. He certainly did not intend to offer any payment, even if his entourage did require two trips across the Weldar.

This was, after all, an official visit.

Dawn. There was time to get his men encamped before he paid his respects to Borrago. The old dog, remarrying after all this time — it seemed politically dangerous. Couldn't he have just kept the woman his mistress?

Well, it would happen in ten days and what would come after, who knew?

Fachalana sat in the kitchens of the Sharshite embassy, thinking upon the previous evening and sipping hot barley-brew. Few were up and about this early, only a yawning scullery maid, a pair of grooms seeking their breakfast, a guardsman just off duty. They left her alone and that is what the Lady Fachalana wanted right then.

She realized that she had actually seen the Demons of Droga when she called upon them. She had entered, in part, into their realm.

It did not seem a place she would want to visit again. Had her father been there? Maybe she should try contacting him again, with her new found ability.

Or not. It would not hurt to keep it a secret for a while.

"A good morning to you, my Lady Fachalana."

"Why, Lord Doufan. I would have expected you to sleep in, sir."

"May I sit?" When she nodded assent he took a chair across the table from her. It was quite a new table and still held the scent of pine. "I wished to explore this place before the official tour." Doufan kept his silence for a long moment.

"Nafal is a good man. Are you going to marry him, my lady?"

The noblewoman laughed aloud at the bold question. "I do not know, sir, I do not know."

"I would advise against it." This was even bolder. Who was Doufan to offer such advice?

"Explain, sir," she ordered.

"It is obvious that neither of you truly wishes to wed." He looked at her, and receiving no rebuttal, continued. "I could tell that from the way Jobareth spoke on our trip here and now I can see it in your eyes."

"What we wish may not matter in the long run," murmured Fachalana.

"My lady, it is all that matters. Have you seen the boy since our arrival?"

"No, my Lord Doufan. Shall I assume he will be with you at Keep Rosam most of the day?"

The ambassador considered the question briefly. "Perhaps I could leave him here and let Sir Blen escort me. I fear he would not like that, being very scrupulous in his duties. Moreover," he added, "Nafal does think he needs to keep an eye on me."

He laughed. "And perhaps he does."

Guesare had none of the power of his late sister, nor did he equal even his mother in magic. Still, he had felt the turmoil last night and knew it was the work of Fachalana.

He rode alone now, down to the embassy so that he might speak with the two young women. Little had been sorted out during yesterday's pleasantries; it was time for serious discussion.

Along the way, just before the road turned down toward the river, he passed a party of men, Nafal, Blen, a pair of guardsmen, and one he assumed to be the new ambassador. He only raised a hand in greeting and passed them by, not stopping to be introduced. This Lord Doufan seemed so nondescript that the minstrel would have been hard put to describe him a minute later.

Someone else was coming up the road now, a slight figure astride a galloping pony. It was the Anian girl herself. She reined her mount in as she reached the Cuddonian.

"Greetings, Mistress Ansa," said he.

"So, you have been speaking to my brother," she replied. "Please do not use that name again here."

"I will not," promised Guesare. "The secret of who you truly are is safe." He paused for only a second. "I think Donzalo has figured it out on his own."

He gave her a long look. "I do not believe I like the dark hair."

"My disguise?" Ansa laughed gaily and tossed her darkened locks. "And here I thought it would fool everyone!"

"It will not fool Donni. You do intend to see him, don't you?"

"Should I, Sir Guesare?" She turned her horse around. "Ride with me back to the embassy."

He clucked at his pony and moved forward to ride at the girl's side. "There would be no sense in hiding now," he said. No reply was forthcoming.

A minute later, he spoke again. "Were you with the Lady Fachalana last night?"

Ansa turned to him immediately. Her look told him all he needed.

"So you were," said Guesare. "What magic was she attempting?"

"It was only intended in play. The lady was as shocked as I when the earth shook."

"Ah." Guesare rode on a bit further before speaking again. "Fachalana is a danger. To Donzalo, to you, to herself."

"She means no harm. Of this I am certain. She — she has a crush on Donzalo."

The minstrel looked on her in astonishment. "So that is what this is all about?" Then he began to laugh. "Oh, I should have seen it!

Guesare shook his head. "And Donni, ah, poor Donni, loved her sister." He had become of a sudden sober in his speech. "My sister."

He looked once more to Ansa, meeting her eyes. "Once, I think he may have loved you, too. Might you be the lady's rival?"

"I might," replied Ansa, "but I know not my course here."

She looks so like her brother, thought Guesare. Why did Donni see that and not I?

"The only proper course," said he, "is that which our heart sets us."

Blen had been up to Castle Rosam earlier, taking his morning exercise, and had confirmed that Borrago expected them. Sir Blen had become a surprisingly effective diplomat in Jobareth's absence.

It occurred to Jobareth, then, that Doufan and Blen were alike in many ways. He was not entirely willing to trust either.

"A luncheon, sir, is what the count suggested," Sir Blen was telling the ambassador, "preceded by a simple, family-only reception."

Lord Doufan nodded agreeably. He had made no discernible attempt to exercise his authority since arriving. The party was passing through the inner gate and into the courtyard before Borrago's hall.

Master of Arms Copago awaited them at its door. He and a pair of his men escorted the diplomats ceremoniously within.

There was Lomela. Jobareth could not go over and greet her right now, as he might have wished, as he might have done on most occasions. She stood at her husband's side as Doufan was introduced.

That he was charming her, as he did most, was obvious. And Bolos too.

Gruff Borrago, he suspected, would be more immune. An aide came to that man's side and whispered something in his ear. The count nodded in assent.

"Lord Orgelo has just arrived," he announced aloud. "He will join us shortly."

Nafal could not help notice the look of displeasure that crossed Bolos's face. Perhaps no one in the room missed it.

After a couple minutes, Count Borrago and the ambassador went aside to speak privately and the guests mingled more casually.

There was Donzalo, making his way toward him. And who was that large fellow who seemed his shadow? "*Legate* Nafal!" He exclaimed, emphasizing his new title. Jobareth was surprised that Donzalo embraced him. That was new.

"This is my kinsman and bodyguard Habidros," said the Laman, gesturing toward his tall companion. "He's Guesare's brother."

The two bowed wordlessly to each other. "Father insists that he accompany me everywhere. Not that either of us minds.

"So, Jobareth, how fare you these days?"

This was neither the time nor place to unburden himself to his young friend. "Well, enough, *Sir* Donzalo," he replied, echoing the emphasis on newly acquired title. "And glad to have fared back to my friends here at last." Does that sound hollow? he wondered. Have I become too much the diplomat?

He did not realize Donzalo was directing their way to Lady Lomela until they were almost before her.

"My lady," he said, and took her hand.

"At last! You certainly took your time, Jobareth Nafal." The Princess Lomela laughed with true pleasure. "Welcome back, my friend."

"Lunch," whispered Habidros in Donzalo's ear.

"Oh, we're being served," said the young Laman. "And there's Count Orgelo, arrived just in time for a free meal!" Lady Lomela's husband was already at the table and lost in his own thoughts, so Donzalo took her one arm and Jobareth, the other, and escorted her.

For a few moments, it seemed like the way things once were.

12

Guesare had parted from Ansa at the bottom of the embassy hill. Some other day, perhaps, he could meet with Radal's daughter. He had a better idea of motives, now, of Fachalana's, of Ansa's. Indeed, of his own.

Play-acting, eh? If the Sharshite noblewoman caused that much ruckus without intending, what could happen if she truly harnessed her abilities? She might not be the equal of Jola but she was not that far less.

The woman's whole life is acting, isn't it? he asked himself. She has cast herself as Donzalo's lover, his destiny. Might she actually be intended for that role?

Ansa seemed a practical person. She would not pursue Donzalo thoughtlessly, hopelessly. Maybe she needs to, thought Guesare. Maybe she needs to be less the spy, less like her scheming brother, and find her happiness.

Of course, there was also always the possibility that Radal was somehow using his daughter to get at Donzalo. It should never be forgotten that the sorcerer still wanted him dead.

Ahead of him lay Borrago's castle and many choices.

It was more than a week until the Summer Fair had its official start, yet tents and booths were already sprouting on Borrago's wide fairground.

"We'll need to secure a good spot," said Galaro's second. "It's none too soon."

"You pick a likely place or two and I'll go find the marshal to pay our fees. If Borrago has raised them again, I'll curse him even more loudly than the last time!"

"Aren't those some of Orgelo's men?" said the trader, peering at a group with his good eye.

"He or his son must have come for the wedding. That should bring in even larger crowds than usual. Ha, old Borrago should marry anew every year!"

He set off in search of the harried fellow who organized this fair with the help of far too few assistants. It was fortunate that the many merchants here did a good job of policing themselves through the month-long event.

The afternoon sun beat upon the tall Cuddonian. He could feel the perspiration dripping down his beard.

"Ho, Galaro!" one of the other merchants greeted him. "Which direction are you smuggling goods this season?"

"South to north," roared the trader in response, "but I'm about to switch it around!"

He continued across the grounds, skirting groups of men intent on erecting multi-hued pavilions, greeting rivals who were, for the most part, also friends. There stood a couple of the Rosam soldiers in their colors of green and sable. "Tell me, my bullies, be the marshal about?"

One pointed toward a small hill rising by the field, and a grayish tent upon it. "He's set up shop up there," said the fellow. "Says it's easier to keep an eye on all of you."

"An excellent idea. I thank you, sirs." And a good way to avoid our complaining, thought Galaro, if we have to go all the way over there and climb a hill each time.

When he finally reached the man, he found that the fees had, indeed, increased again. And he did curse Borrago most roundly.

"It is good, my lady, to have young Master Jobareth back."

Traspa had never gotten used to referring to Nafal as Lector. Would she ever learn to call him Legate?

"Yes, Traspa. It is too bad his duties kept him from remaining this afternoon. How I would love to sit and talk as once we did!"

"That ambassador can't keep him busy all the time, my lady. I'm sure we'll see more of the boy. Here, don't eat that!" The maid removed a bit of ribbon from young Ros's mouth. "Your mother needs it for her new dress."

The child took Mistress Traspa's admonition without complaint. He was a notably good-natured boy, albeit active and apt to get himself into places he should not be.

Lady Lomela found herself wandering out onto her little balcony. The sun shone fully upon it at this time of day. There was Guesare riding in. Where had he been?

She would not mind sitting and talking with the minstrel too. The princess remembered how he had pleased the late Lady Vibola with his songs and his tales, full of both adventure and amusement.

Yes, she must have Guesare and Donzalo visit, and Jobareth, when he could. Donzalo could even bring his bodyguard cousin along. The man could be interesting when he chose to speak, full of stories of his life as a mercenary.

Why not bring back all that Lady Vibola had, when she was the grand dame of this household? That role had fallen to Lomela now. Sima would never be a rival to her, nor seek to be, even when she became a countess next week.

Lady Lomela turned back into her sitting chamber, carefully closing the doors behind her. A breeze would have been welcome on this warm afternoon but little Ros could not be trusted. He would be out there as soon as their backs were turned. One could wager on that.

There was little else the lady was willing to wager on right then.

Pol had settled into the barracks of the new embassy, a spacious room on the basement level. His companion on their recent journey, the young diplomat Benawis, now resided in a small room two floors above him, ready at hand for his duties as secretary to the legate.

He knew Nafal did not want to show him any particular attention now they were back in County Rosam. Pol would be a more effective spy for his master that way.

Maybe he could show Benawis around Ros-town once things settled down a bit here. Something about the fellow gnawed at Pol. He had seemed too ready to befriend the young soldier. Pol, for his part, had been willing to act the naïve country boy when he was with him.

As he had been willing to act his friend. Pol was not sure he actually liked the secretary very much.

Night guard duty. He'd better grab a bite and get to his post.

"You may leave us, Lector"

Benawis bowed to his master and, with a perhaps slightly-too-long look at the two rather attractive young women in the room, exited.

None of the three had missed it. "My secretary appreciates feminine beauty," said Jobareth. "Or maybe just anything feminine."

Ansa laughed. Fachalana did not. "I dislike him," she stated.

Then she seemed to remember something. "The man visited Father," she said, "before you left with the ambassador." The noblewoman sniffed. "I did not like him then, either."

"Probably when he was being considered for this post," Jobareth surmised. But it was unusual for the great Lord Radal to be interviewing so minor a diplomat.

"Anyway, I hear that you visited the town this afternoon, while I was busy with my duties."

"I gave Lady Fachalana the complete tour," said Ansa, "ending up at the fairgrounds. They are only starting to fill up but it will a marvel when they do."

"We must visit again next week," Fachalana stated. "I should have brought more money with me!"

"And who would cart everything back to Sharsh?" asked her companion.

Jobareth smiled. "I can't help with cartage but this may prove a boon to your finances." He handed a dispatch to Fachalana.

Ansa brought her head in close so she could read it too. Wonder crept across her visage.

"A viscountess, Lana?"

"And a position at court. There will be an income attached to that. Maybe to the title as well." Jobareth chuckled. "Maybe I *should* marry you. For your money, you know."

"With your grandfather one of the wealthiest men in Sharsh?" replied Fachalana. " A thought came to her. "Why, I will officially have a higher title than my father." Lord Radal had always refused high rank, feeling he could work most effectively with no title other than lord.

King Lareth had reluctantly agreed, knowing that elevating his friend might cause ill feeling among the old nobility. Or perhaps, considering Radal's reputation, ill feeling among pretty much everyone.

"This will be interesting," continued the lady. "It doesn't have much bearing on what we do here in Lama though. I'll worry about it when we get home." Assuming I ever go home, she told herself. If her destiny were truly entwined with that of Donzalo, might she not remain here?

Suddenly, she laughed. "What will Lomela think of this? We must go visit her tomorrow, the three of us. Do find time for it, Jobo."

"I will, my ladies. I consider it another of my diplomatic duties."

"You see, my dear, we arrived in plenty of time."

Lady Thara nodded absentmindedly. "I should seek out Sima and see if she needs any help."

"She has Sir Copago's wife and the Lady Lomela and probably every other woman in the keep to assist her. Relax, wife of mine. Let's get to our rooms.

"Assuming my brother hasn't given them away to some other of his guests."

That brother had watched from his tower window as the little caravan entered the courtyard. He could talk to Paren in the morning. Let his stewards attend to him and Thara tonight.

He looked at the stack of documents on his desk and his secretary, Madin, waiting patiently, and the count sighed. Borrago would not be visiting his bride-to-be this night. So much to be done.

Would that Bolos could take some of this load. But he did not trust his heir's judgment nor did he care for his secretive ways since he had become a sober man. Maybe after the wedding he should send him out to visit their many allies scattered through Lama. That would give the boy something useful to do.

He took one more glimpse from the window and turned to his work.

13

No one had taken any notice of Ansa as they entered the castle. Why would they connect her with a serving girl who had spent a few weeks in Keep Rosam, nearly a year ago?

Lomela thought her familiar and then thought no more on it.

It was Mistress Traspa who knew her the moment she laid eyes on the girl. "Why, Posena! What has happened to your hair?"

And then immediately asked, "Does Master Donzalo know you are here?"

"Posena?" repeated the Lady Lomela, turning her gaze to the Anian. "Oh!"

"We know her as Maresta," said Fachalana. "She is my friend." She had to follow this by again telling the tale of Ansa's mission to Lama and her role in instigating it, with more detail than she had ever provided Jobareth.

Satisfied with the explanation, Traspa went to attend to her duties elsewhere. She had taken charge of young Ros, as she had of the boy's mother, and took the responsibility most seriously. But she still wondered if Donzalo knew that girl was here.

They spoke of many things, those four, through the morning and most of it was of little import. Eventually, the talk did turn to the young Laman knight.

"The ladies have explained to me why your father yearns for Donzalo's death," said Nafal. "Shall I tell it?" he asked them. The two women nodded an assent.

"The gist of it, Lomela, is that the king fears he poses a threat to Ros and his inheritance. The Oracle at Cars handed down a prophecy that the son of Donzalo will rule in Lama."

Lomela seemed very much taken aback at this news. None of the three had expected it to shake her so.

"His son?" she whispered. "His son." Then a half-smile played on her lips. "You have often seen his son here, Jobareth. He has played in your lap, Lana."

It was their turn to be astounded.

Suddenly, the princess was on her feet. "I must write my father and tell him this!"

"No," spoke Ansa. "A letter might be intercepted. What if your husband learned of it?" She has her wits about her, thought Jobareth. And knows her spy-craft as well, I would wager.

"Maresta is right," he said. "It would be far too dangerous. Such news would need be delivered to the king in person."

"I could tell him when we return," said Fachalana, reluctantly. She did not want to go back to Sharsh anytime soon and maybe not ever.

"What of your father?" asked Lady Lomela. "Could we tell him of this?"

"I do not think the prophecy drives him anymore. He has other reasons to hate Donzalo." Fachalana did not intend to speak of those things she had learned of her sister and of her death. "He might use this as a weapon.

"Why not come back to Sharsh with us for a visit?" she asked, with sudden inspiration. "You could tell your father yourself."

"He was sitting by the road, sir, as bold as can be."

"And you are sure it was this Perdos?" asked Captain Corgos.

"Aye, sir, though he looked like he'd been through some rough living and his beard lay on his chest."

I'll send out a patrol to check this, thought Sir Corgos. Best to be safe.

"All he wanted, as I said, sir, was the latest news from down at Keep Rosam." The man, a peddler who visited from time to time, continued. "And he did ask if there was a minstrel there. What with him being banished and all, I thought you should know."

"It is well done and I thank you. I know the ladies of the keep will want to see your wares and hear your gossip, so I'll leave you to them."

Still after that Guesare, is he? I can't fault him for that but I can't permit him to loiter on the roads either. Not on my watch.

There he stood, even taller than Ansa remembered, and no longer looking a boy.

"Donzalo," she whispered.

He strode across the room, paying no mind to the other three and spoke. "I ask again as I did when last I saw you: who are you, truly?"

She found herself uncertain as to her reply.

"Her name is Ansa," said the man standing in the doorway. "I am sorry, Ansa, but he should know the truth." Guesare turned his eyes toward the Lady Fachalana. "As should you, my lady."

"Oh, you mean that my friend is an Anian spy," Fachalana cooly replied. "I had figured that one out, though it did take me a while." She looked at the young woman seated beside her. "Ansa, is it? I like the name."

Donzalo turned to the minstrel. "She is related to Oder, isn't she?"

"He is my brother," said the girl.

Jobareth Nafal and the Princess Lomela were understandably confused by this exchange.

"You are Ani?" asked the diplomat.

Ansa nodded. "Born and raised on the high steppes, Legate."

"But she spoke truly when she said Lady Fachalana sent her here before," said Guesare. "Not that it might not have fitted well into some Anian scheme or another."

Donzalo stood in silence and pondered all of this. A few moments earlier he had been the least well informed person in this room.

Fachalana noticed his hand go to the silver brooch he wore ever at his shoulder, a brooch in the likeness of a wolf. Hadn't she glimpsed something like it in the dream world where she first saw Donzalo? It had been so brief, she was not sure now.

But she did sense that there was some sort of power in it. She had not recognized that two days ago.

"Then, Ansa," said the Laman knight, "since we have now been properly introduced, may I welcome you to Castle Rosam?"

"He's a man of habit," said the cloaked figure. "He comes down that pathway, if he comes at all, and he comes always by foot." He pointed out the route on the scrap of paper he held.

Sojel nodded. Was there more?

"And his dog is always with him."

Dogs could cause problems. "How about in the morning?"

"Back the same way. But his son sometimes walks with him."

The sergeant folded the crude map and stuck it in his belt. "Good enough. Our master will be pleased with your work." That was high praise from Sojel and, perhaps, unlike him. But he liked the fact that things were moving again and seemingly in the correct direction.

Both men disappeared into the dusk.

"You should not have come, Uncle, if you did not want to be put to work."

"It always seems to fall on you and me, boy, doesn't it?"

"Someone has to show them how things are properly done," replied Donzalo. He and Sir Paren had spent most of the day on the logistics of the upcoming wedding. It was a welcome break to the young man from the drama of the previous days. It was an opportunity to think on things while busying his hands.

They had worked late into the evening. It was only six days now — well, it would be, come morning — till the event and much was to be done.

"So we shall have the procession begin — here," said Paren, pushing a stake into the ground, "and then out the main gate."

"I still think it would be easier if we formed up outside the keep," opined Donzalo.

"We would never get them together out there. The more impatient would take off down the road before we got everyone else in line.

"At any rate, I think we are done for this day," Sir Paren said. "Let's get back to the hall and see if they held some supper for us."

"My lords! My lords!" A soldier was running toward them over the green.

"What is it man?" called Donzalo, holding his lantern high.

"The count has been slain!"

Of Exiles: the Seventh Tale

1

"It was the dog, sir. We heard him howling."

King strained at the end of a rope. "He didn't want to leave his master," claimed the soldier at the other end.

"Was there any sign of who was responsible?" asked Bolos, now Count Bolos. "Any sign at all?"

Another man at arms held out a bit of blue cloth. "We think the dog may have torn it from the assassin."

It was the blue of the Arvaram. Everyone there could see that.

Sir Copago thought finding the scrap overly convenient but held his tongue.

To his surprise, his half-brother did not. "It might be planted," said Bolos. "We will make no conclusions now."

The new count could see no reason why Orgelo would want to kill his father. All Borrago's recent actions had been favorable to their relationship.

He looked at Copago. The same could be said of that man. The marriage of Borrago and his mother could only help him.

Indeed, the man who stood most to gain was Bolos himself. That upset him. He was weary of intrigue and politics and all the worries that had surrounded him lately. He was weary of losing those he loved.

Could his father-in-law have a part in this? Could Bolos have brought it on with his own letters to the king?

"Bring the body to the hall," he ordered. Sir Copago motioned for the men to bear it forward. What was to be done with Sir Copago?

By Kamat! swore Bolos to himself. I opposed this wedding but I would not have had it become a funeral.

"With County Rosam in turmoil, I must urge you to leave for home as soon as possible."

Lord Doufan sat behind the largest desk Ansa had ever seen, flanked by Jobareth Nafal and Sir Blen. The ambassador's secretary sat inconspicuously in a corner.

"Have I time to say goodbye to Lady Lomela?" asked Fachalana, in a quite even, matter-of-fact voice. She's in role, thought Ansa. It really does help her control her emotions.

Nafal spoke. "I shall convey any messages for you, my ladies. Our Lord Doufan is right — you should be on the road immediately."

The ambassador nodded. "I will not order this," he said, "but I think it would be wise for Sir Blen to accompany you." This was news to Blen.

Doufan turned to him. "I can not think of anyone better qualified, sir, nor whom I would more trust with this mission. Moreover, I wish you to go straight to the king with my report on this situation."

Of course, a courier was already speeding westward with the news.

"Very well, sir," replied the knight. The request made sense to him and Blen was a very sensible man. He addressed the two women. "We will travel faster without your servants. They can follow later with one of the guardsmen. I and the other will ride with you."

"Best cross in a boat or two, rather than the ferry," said Jobareth. "Bolos may have closed cross-river traffic." Blen nodded agreement.

Ansa rose. "We can be ready in an hour," she said.

They were across the Weldar in two.

There came a knock on their cottage door, an almost timid knock. Janona opened it to the Lady Lomela, accompanied only by her ever-faithful maid, Traspa.

Lomela crossed the room at once to where Dame Sima sat with her son, the acolyte Grippo, and embraced the woman. They sat a while in silent, tearless grief.

Traspa, waiting by the door, could not hold her own tears. Janona gently escorted her to a seat at the table, where she sobbed quietly. The wife of Sir Copago then busied herself with the making of tea. One custom the Ani had left behind was the drinking of tea. Most Lamans did not know of its connection to the hated invaders of their land.

Those who did, ignored it.

They spoke for a time, Lomela and Sima, and their speech was inconsequential, full of remembrance and regret and condolence. Then the princess asked a question that was, indeed, of consequence.

"What now, Sima? Will you remain here?"

"Your husband may not permit that, my lady," came from Grippo, who had remained silent until that moment.

"He would not force you to leave! I would not permit it."

"No, my lady," said Sima, "he would not throw us out but he will most certainly discharge Copago from his service. How could we remain here, then?" She let her vision wander about the little cottage, so long her home. "All things end, don't they, Grippo?"

"Please don't ask me for sermons, Mother." He remained quiet for a moment, before saying, all in a rush, "I will not take my vows this year. My family is more important."

"No," objected Sima, "your brother can take care of us. You have worked long to become a priest."

"There may be little prospect for him as priest now in County Rosam," said Janona, bringing tea to the table. She poured out a cup for Traspa, who, being a good Sharshite, would have preferred wine. "Would you care for some, my lady?" she asked Lomela.

"Yes, thank you." The Lady Lomela turned back to mother and son. "Janona is right. Grippo's fortunes will ever be tied to those of his brother." She sipped politely from the cup handed her before setting it aside. "Waiting a year might be wise and, after all," added Lomela with a smile, "this family may need Grippo more right now than Kamat does."

The three Lamans nodded at that. They understood duty.

My mistress knows her Lamans, doesn't she? thought Traspa, who then spoke aloud. "My lady, we'd best get back."

"Yes, Traspa, we should." Lomela rose. "I suspect my husband will have much need of me in the days that come."

Jobareth Nafal was not pleased by the absence of his master of arms. Yes, it was important that Blen accompany the women back to Sharsh but the defense of the embassy was important as well. The other fighting men here were ordinary soldiers, not leaders nor tacticians.

"I do not expect trouble from the Lamans, my lord," he told the ambassador, once the travelers were on their road home, "but I would want to be prepared for the eventuality."

"They may suspect that Sharsh has a hand in this," stated Lord Doufan, and added, quite matter-of-factly, "I suspect it myself."

"The king would order this?" asked the younger man.

The ambassador sighed. "He is certainly capable of it." He considered that statement for a moment and then continued. "His councilor Radal would be more likely to order such an action. He has become used to having his way and acting independently.

"And he wants Donzalo," Doufan added, looking up to meet Nafal's eyes. "You know that."

"You know of the — prophecy, sir?"

"Lareth himself filled me in before we left Celatas. And who, sir," asked the ambassador, with arched brow, "filled you in?"

Jodareth smiled wanly. "The Lady Fachalana, my lord. She has been know to, ah, peruse her father's papers."

"I can believe it," said Lord Doufan. "I can very much believe it."

"How fares your mother?"

"She — copes, my lord."

"Please convey my condolences to her, Sir Copago. I extend them to you as well." Count Orgelo thought of his own wife of some thirty years, back in Tod-ford, and wondered, fleetingly, whether he could bear her loss. How much harder would it be to have happiness torn away from one, just as it was finally being given?

"I thank you, my lord," replied Copago, eying the men milling around them. "I should to my duties."

"You know, my boy, that those duties may soon be taken from you. Bolos has never loved you.

"Know, too, that there is always a place for you in my service. My son likes you, even if you have unhorsed him from time to time." Orgelo rubbed at his unshaven jaw. Though the count's long hair remained as black as in his youth, Copago could see that the whiskers were peppered with gray. "It would be good for him to have someone like you at his side."

"It seems soon to be considering it, my lord, but I thank you for the offer. For now, I remain the man of the Count Rosam, whoever that may be."

Orgelo nodded gravely as the knight returned to his post. A good man, yes, and the fact that he could just possibly claim his father's inheritance didn't hurt any.

It had become obvious that Sir Blen — and probably Jobareth too — had an emergency plan in place for just such an occasion. Blen had led them swiftly down less traveled roads to a house by the river. It was a shabby, slouching, low-built house near where the Abam joined the Weldar and the men there asked no questions. They were taken across in a barge with muffled oars.

The party traveled through the night and most of the next day before stopping at an inn. "We are in Count Dordos's lands now," the knight told them, "beyond any harm that might come from County Rosam."

Dordos was thoroughly dependent on his Sharshite paymasters and would not think of crossing them.

That evening, Fachalana attempted the link with her father. It came easier than ever before.

Fachalana.

She could sense his pleasure in this demonstration of her ability.

Count Borrago has been murdered, she told him.

Her father said nothing.

He knows this already, she thought. Is he behind it?

You are returning home? he asked.

Yes, Father. It seemed best.

Radal did not comment on that. *You have grown*, he said.

I am learning, Father.

That you are. We must talk on it when you reach here.

He seemed distracted by something or someone with him in his tower room.

Farewell, said Lord Radal and unilaterally broke their connection.

Well, certainly her father was a busy man. Walking into his mind was little different than walking into his office — he couldn't be expected to drop everything to talk to her!

Ansa was sitting on her bed in the room they shared, staring at her. "Where were you?" she asked.

"At Mountain Keep," answered Fachalana truthfully. She felt very tired, both from their journey and the strain of forming the link. I hope it gets easier with practice, she thought.

"And now I have returned and the only place I wish to be is asleep."

2

Radal had not known that Count Borrago was dead. This is not to say he did not expect the event.

Now he would expect a messenger, hastily bringing the news. Two, in fact, one from his own agent and one from the embassy. He turned back to the magic with which he had been occupied, here in his high tower, when Fachalana had made contact.

She had grown stronger. No, the girl had always been strong — she was learning to control her strength. Allowing her to travel, to be beyond his influence for a while, had brought unexpected rewards.

He did wish she had remained in County Rosam. Radal might still have been able to use her in some way to further his plans there.

A little sprite-like being spoke to him. It was not in the room nor was he with it, truly, but each had entered in some part into another world. When he did not wish to be troubled with forming a link such creatures as these were the best and least tiring way to send messages swiftly and secretly. The spirits of the winds would go by ways only known to them and speak the words with which they were charged.

Radal had many such messages to send. Things were moving now and he was the one who had provided the impetus, for better or worse. It had to be done, no matter what Lareth had ordered.

He smiled mirthlessly at his attempt to rationalize his own actions to himself. Mankind is but a flicker in the great darkness, he told himself. None of it matters.

Nothing but vengeance for the life of one daughter, the daughter he had not known, and the realization of the other's gifts.

"You do not blame Count Orgelo for this?"

Bolos looked at his uncle for a moment, as if not understanding the question. Then he spoke and his words were bitter.

"I blame Orgelo and I blame Copago and I blame even his mother. I blame the king in Sharsh and I blame his dog Radal. Most of all, I blame you, Donzalo. All the turmoil of this past year has been centered on you."

Sir Paren's eyes turned to the third man in the room, Donzalo Rosam.

"I would serve you how I can, Brother," was the only reply from the young knight.

"As I did your father," Paren reminded his nephew. "It is good to have someone to depend on."

"Stay or go. I do not care." Bolos turned to survey the courtyard from the narrow window. This was his office now, here in the tower where Borrago had so long resided.

"Why not come home with me, Donni? Aid me in the running of the estate," said Paren.

Bolos's words came cold. "I have not yet named him your heir."

Then he sighed and turned back to his family. "Ah, forgive me. You are welcome here, Donzalo, and I will continue the allowance our father set upon you." He shook his head. "But trouble follows you. It might serve both of us better were you elsewhere.

"I do have one great favor to ask of you, Uncle. Give me Sir Corgos as my new master of arms. No, I can not have Copago here any longer. I know he served my father well and I know that he is family. But I must and will have my own man.

"Jak would never do. He is loyal but not suited to the task."

"I will ask him on our return. He may not wish to leave the comfortable life he has found at my keep." I most certainly would not, added Sir Paren to himself.

"The count has discharged my brother, as expected. He will serve only until Summer Feast."

"Being who he is, he will serve faithfully to the last moment, eh?" asked Jobareth.

"Most certainly," replied Brother Grippo, "but Bolos has also set a somewhat generous sum of money on him to ease the departure. And perhaps to ease the count's conscience as well.

"He does not hate Copago, I think. He simply wants him gone."

Jobareth Nafal agreed with his assessment. The man was level-headed and a reliable source of information. Maybe he should be on his informal payroll.

"You still intend to forgo your ordination?" he asked.

Grippo only nodded.

Jobareth questioned further. "Where then?"

"Sir Paren has offered a place for our family at his keep. I will accompany them there and, perhaps, remain. Along with," he chuckled, "Donzalo's books."

"I heard that he was moving them all again. To his uncle's?"

"He thought it the safest place to store them. I do not think he intends to remain at Castle Rosam."

Nafal leaned forward to refill Grippo's goblet from a frosted pitcher. Chilled wine seemed unknown here in Lama and he had missed it, especially on hot nights such as these. Fortunately, there was a springhouse not far from this new town dwelling and they were quite willing to keep a cask or two cool for him.

From the high porch — it seemed every decent house in Ros-town had a high porch — he could see mist rising from the river. Beyond it, Sir Blen and the women must be well on their way home.

He would have to let Blen know he approved of this house he had taken for them.

"Your brother won't go to Sir Paren's keep, will he?"

"No, Legate. He has said not yea nor nay but he is giving serious thought to joining Count Orgelo's service."

Some mourners were gathered in the hall. Others stood outside the great doors, flung open to the clear morning air.

Borrago lay on his bier, his body wrapped in green silk. Beneath the silk, nothing, as it was believed that one should return to Kamat as one came. This was not so much a Kamatian belief as a Laman one, and in keeping with their tendency toward austerity.

The hierophant intoned a passage, known well to most of those in attendance.

As an arrow flies my soul,
into darkness, into night;
none whom I have left behind
sees the ending of its flight.

The mourners responded.

Flies to Kamat, ever watchful,
waiting in the realm of light.

Two acolytes raised censers above the late count's bier. Fragrant smoke floated toward the ceiling beams and the high priest continued.

As a comet through the sky,
burning with creation's flame;
as an arrow flies my soul,
without substance, without name.

Flies to Kamat, ever waiting,
to the one from whence we came.

The crowd murmured their answering prayer and began to fall into a column behind the cart bearing Count Borrago's mortal remains, passing in slow procession from the hall, through the courtyard and toward the gates of Castle Rosam.

"If we keep to this pace, we can reach Mountain Keep by the solstice," Sir Blen told his charges. "We are better than half-way there now."

"He seeks to train us as couriers," Ansa confided — albeit in a rather loud voice — to her companion.

"You, my lady," responded the knight, "need no training, I think."

Are these two flirting? wondered Lady Fachalana. She was too weary to give it much thought. Didn't her father have drugs that helped him carry on? She should ask him when they reach the keep.

Now that she had learned how to look into all the many worlds other than our own, she was having trouble keeping them out. Things and places and voices filled her dreams, when Fachalana was able to sleep at all.

Did Blen know that Ansa was Anian? She couldn't remember for sure — oh, right, only Jobareth and his circle at the Keep Rosam were in on it. Donzalo knew.

Donzalo. When would she see him again? *Would* she see him again? Her chance to know him had been torn from her as soon as she had reached for it. With the turmoil she and Ansa had left behind them, it seemed unlikely that they could again soon travel to Lama.

"I fear we may need to tie the lady in her saddle," Ansa whispered to Blen, as they rode on toward the marches of Sharsh.

3

The procession wound from the castle gates, following the markers Donzalo and Paren had set out for a very different ceremony, only three days earlier. The column turned not right, as most did, not toward the town nor toward the stoa where many of their Kamatian rites were held. Left they went, on a less-traveled, narrower road that gradually grew steeper.

Near the gates, it passed the cottage of Copago, that road, and then other cots until the ground grew too rocky for farmer or even shepherd. Below a craggy outcropping, jutting into the sky like an arrow aimed toward the heavens, they paused.

Paren motioned toward the two carts loaded with the required wood. Men came forward and began carrying the bundled staves up stairs roughly carved into the rock. Pine and oak was the wood; they would know how to lay it properly.

Bolos, Donzalo, Paren and Galaro each took a corner to bear the bier up to the high place — it had been realized that Galaro, if one did not acknowledge Copago, was the next closest relative to the late count in attendance. Bolos, of course, was not willing to acknowledge Copago.

But he did not forbid his attendance. Count Bolos had no ill will toward his half-brother. He wanted only to have nothing more to do with him and all the things of which he was a reminder.

He did, however, forbid the presence of the Sharshite diplomats at this ceremony, even his wife's friend Jobareth. The ambassador had been allowed to attend the funeral but Bolos would not have him here. Bolos wished he could have banned Count Orgelo, as well, but that would have been an unnecessary insult.

Bolos also wished briefly that his three fellow pallbearers were not all a head taller than he.

The pyre was ready by the time they finished their ascent. It was fitting that a man return to Kamat this way, by flame, here on a high place where his ashes might be scattered by the winds.

Carefully they placed the pallet atop the pile and stepped aside for the hierophant. That man was lighting his torch from the brazier they had carried along — getting a fire going could be a tricky job in these high windy spots. Then the high priest approached and wordlessly set the wood, now well soaked with oil, aflame.

He stepped back and made the sign of arrow, as did the rest of the mourners, both those on the crag and those waiting below, and turned to begin his descent.

"Come with me," ordered Sir Copago.

Donazalo had been occupied with the packing up of his varied belongings, but he followed the man without question. Copago had such an effect.

"Have you chosen new quarters?" asked the master of arms as Donzalo followed him down the hall.

"I thought I might take my old ones back."

"I have a better idea," said Copago and then said no more, leading onward.

The way led them past Donzalo's former rooms and then down a flight of stairs to the ground level. Only barracks and stables occupied this area, Donzalo knew. He also knew that the room before which they now stood was used for nothing but to store tack. Copago drew forth a ponderous key to open the heavy, iron-banded door.

"These were, long ago, the quarters of the Anian commanders when they held this keep," said the knight. "Before any of the rest of it was built." He carefully barred the door behind them.

"Your father —"

"Our father," interrupted Donzalo.

"Yes, our father, showed me a secret here. It is unknown to Bolos or anyone else alive. Now I will show it to you."

The room was somewhat narrow, though long. Donzalo suspected that it might once have been divided in two, as were his old quarters a floor above. Directly above? Possibly. Close, anyway. As in his former rooms, the far end was the castle wall itself, though at this level the stacked stone merged with the solid rock below it.

Copago was near that wall, busying himself with the moving of some of the detritus that had accumulated in this room. Much of it was overflow from the stables, old saddles, faded blankets, empty containers someone thought might be useful someday. He motioned the younger man over.

"Here," he said, and showed him a hidden latch. A panel opened, a narrow doorway to darkness. Donzalo held his lantern before him and looked within to spy a steep staircase, practically a ladder, cut into the stone that lay beneath Keep Rosam.

Copago chuckled. "I think you will fit, boy. Go on down."

Seeing he would need both hands free to negotiate his way, Donzalo grasped the bail of his lantern in his teeth and started down. Thankfully, the stairway was short and he was soon standing on a more or less level floor.

"It is easy going from here," said his guide, squeezing by him. They followed a cramped passageway — low enough that Donzalo could not stand upright — that slowly sloped downward, here and there broken by a stair or two. Within a minute, he could see light coming from ahead.

"I think this cave is natural," said Sir Copago, as they entered a larger space, "and the Anians carved out our passageway to it. Also," he added, with a nod toward a large rock around which sunlight filtered into the chamber, "they hid its entrance."

There was a narrow way, to the right and hidden from eyes below, where one might slip between the rock and the cliff face and step out onto a ledge. It was a very narrow ledge and Donzalo did not like standing there.

Copago pointed. "There is a way down here. See? Just follow the ledge. I have little doubt the Anians cut it into the cliff wall. It will carry you over to that spur and beyond it lies a wooded slope that is easy to negotiate.

"We wouldn't attempt that in daylight and risk being seen. I went down it once at night. And then back up, of course. If fact, we'd better get back inside now and take no chances."

Donzalo took a second to peer upward. The castle walls could not be seen from here. So they could not be seen from the castle walls.

"You may show this to my replacement, if you feel it wise. But," warned Copago, "I would tell no others."

"Are you bored, Brother?"

"That I am, Galaro," responded the minstrel Guesare. "This place has little to offer when its people are in mourning."

"They will throw off their somber garments and come pouring into the fair in two days. But that is not the real reason, is it? Being banned from Keep Rosam and your noble friends there is the root of this mood of yours.

"I know, too," added Galaro, "that you like to know what is going on. Why," he said with a wink, "one might think you a professional spy!"

"Please, Brother, say that not in public."

The big Cuddonian laughed outright. "This fairground is fairly riddled with spies. I am sure at least two in my company report to someone. Not my competitors, I hope."

"Nobos is in the employ of Count Orgelo," asserted Guesare. "I know him of old." He put his rebec aside and took up the flagon of ale by his side, first checking for flies afloat in the brew.

Galaro took a seat beside him in the shade of the tent fly. "Nobos, eh? Well, no harm in that. Old Orgelo is just keeping an eye on his investments."

"I may ride south with the count after Summer Feast," said Guesare quietly. "I and Sir Copago."

"Can't you wait until the fair ends? I intend to be here at least three weeks, four if it seems profitable." The trader waved to a passing acquaintance. "We could ride south together. There are things even you have never seen and I'm the man to show them to you!"

The minstrel looked out upon the bustling grounds. There were still late arrivals but the field overflowed with tents and stalls.

"It is too bad the tournament was canceled," he remarked. "I might have stayed for that."

"It wouldn't have been the same without Sir Copago here to win everything," mused Galaro. "Why even you might have had a chance."

Guesare smiled at the jest, while recognizing its truth.

"It is possible," he said, "that young Donzalo and Habidros will ride with us."

"Ah." Galaro understood immediately why Guesare would wish to accompany them. "Would they travel further?"

"Donzalo has relatives in that region — his mother's people. He thought perhaps to visit them. Beyond that, who knows?"

"You have a habit of traveling 'beyond that,' Brother. All the way to Lorj once, as I remember."

"It could be a good place to see again. If Donni is willing, perhaps we'll sail across the straits."

"I've crossed those straits on occasion myself, Guesare, but never journeyed far inland. But then," he added, "I wasn't exactly supposed to be there."

"Would it not be better than having him underfoot here or at your uncle's keep?" asked Count Orgelo. "While he stays with us he could visit your mother's family. We're related, you know, by marriage. Probably in other ways, too, if one goes back far enough."

"Their lands lie close to yours?" I should know this already, Bolos told himself.

"They border us on our north. It is a small county and not a rich one. The current count would be a nephew of your late mother. So, a cousin." Orgelo fixed his gaze on the younger man. "Has he not visited here?"

Bolos shrugged. "If I were told it was so, I would believe it. I fear I never paid much attention to such matters.

"Be that as it may. I know that Donzalo does not particularly wish to remain here. He has been storing away his belongings and has moved into a small room near the stables. He even let his manservant go." But not his bodyguard was the thought that came to both men's minds.

"He may be safer, too, in County Arvaram," said Orgelo. "We are not friendly with Sharsh there — of this I am certain you are aware."

Yes, let his brother be someone else's problem for a time, thought Bolos. "If Sir Donzalo wishes it, he has my permission." Whether Sharsh or the man seated beside him had a part in his father's death, he would be glad to have both Donzalo and Orgelo far away.

"Will you come to the Midsummer bonfire tomorrow night?" Bolos asked his guest. "I think it is time to return cheer to our land."

"I shall try but fault me not should I fall asleep." Orgelo rose. "I bid you good night and good fortune, Count Bolos."

"And I to you, Count Orgelo."

Bolos looked around his father's office — *his* office. He should have more space, he thought, and he would never sleep in that tiny room upstairs. Maybe he should take a look at the rooms Donzalo had just vacated. Why his brother had chosen new quarters in a stable storeroom neither he nor anyone else in the keep could fathom.

4

Lareth felt he should speak of this to his sons and no others, for now. Whom else might he trust?

"The count was a threat to us, wasn't he sir?" asked Gawis.

"His son might have been," said the younger brother, Modareth, "had the marriage happened."

Lareth slowly shook his head. "It is unlikely that Copago would have ever posed a threat. Had he, we would have moved against him later rather than chancing chaos now.

"I fear," he continued, "that our Lord Radal had a hand in this."

Gawis knew Radal only as a presence in his father's court, a man feared by many but of unquestioned loyalty. Modareth, as a friend of the lord councilor's daughter, had a very different and more personal view of him.

"S — Sir," he said, his childhood stutter returning to haunt him at such moments, "wasn't the Lady Fachalana at County Rosam at the time of the murder?"

Indeed she was, thought Lareth, and fresh from showing her talent with a dagger here in the capital. But the king could not see Fachalana as a cold-blooded assassin. "I would think it most unlikely that she was involved," he replied.

He did wonder, though, why Radal would let his daughter be there at that time. Assuming the count's death *was* the work of Radal — that was not yet established.

And there was that girl who accompanied the lady, what was her name? Maresta. He must learn what his spies knew of her.

But he likewise doubted the slender actress was any sort of assassin.

"You are princes," King Lareth said to his sons, "and princes need advisers they can trust in all matters. If we can not trust Lord Radal, to whom should we turn?"

"Carrana's father seems trustworthy," offered Modareth, adding with an impish smile, "Certainly more so than my brother's father-in-law."

Gawis reddened but Lareth laughed aloud. "I am heartened that you can joke about the attempt on your life, my son. But the baron, trustworthy or no, is not a man I would ask for advice." He could picture the stout nobleman, a fellow both coarse and good-hearted, whose greatest ambition was to spend time in his vegetable garden. He might ask him for advice on the growing of cabbages.

"What of the man you yourself sent to County Rosam, Father? Is Lord Doufan to be trusted?" asked Gawis.

"Were he not many and many leagues distant he would be with us now in this room. I would expect a fuller report from his hand soon." Lareth turned to the windows, flung open to the summer sky. "Had we any sense we would all be out of the heat of Celatas by this time of year. I leave immediately for Mountain Keep."

He spoke to his eldest son, once again garbed in the king's own personal colors of green and white. "You must govern here for me, Gawis.

"Modareth, it is time that you and Carrana found the safety of a country keep. I have given orders for a twenty-man to escort you into the mountains."

Ros, despite being a year younger, stood almost as tall as his cousin. However, he did not talk nearly so much.

King could not decide which child he preferred, bouncing from one to the other.

"You should take the dog with you," said the Lady Lomela. "I fear its presence irritates my husband."

"Then we shall remove many irritants all at a once, my lady," Dame Janona replied. "What a head of hair your young Ros is growing!"

The boy's hair was thick, wavy, a dark brown that seemed almost red. "It is much the color of my father's hair," Lomela remarked, "when he was young." Ros favored his grandfather in many ways; his size, however, spoke of his father.

"Were he a horse, I might call it chestnut," observed Sir Paren.

"Behave yourself, Husband," chided the Lady Thara. "And that includes no dancing about the bonfire. You are far too old and fat for that."

"And too drunk, as well." admitted the knight. "Tonight, I think, will be made of memories of midsummers past." Paren deeply grieved yet for his brother.

"But once upon a time, wife of mine, we might both have thrown off our clothes and danced all night," he reminded her, with a wink.

Lomela tried not to picture that in her mind. These Lamans, so strait-laced and yet so given to their revelries and festivals!

"Remember," she told her three adult companions, "that we wish to rise early to visit the fair. It will be your only chance before you leave." She looked about. "Is anyone else joining us?"

"My husband and his mother chose to busy themselves for coming journeys," said Janona, "As did Grippo. We will see them not tonight." She smiled. "My Copago is not one for frivolity anyway."

He isn't, is he? thought Lomela. No dancing naked for the sober master of arms. Donzalo is really a bit like that, too — nearly as reserved but not so brusque.

"Does anyone know if Donzalo is coming?" she asked aloud.

"Donni is spending the evening with his friends from the Cuddon down at the fairgrounds," replied Paren. "I think a part of him yearns to return to that land."

They stood on the wide green beyond Castle Rosam's outer walls. Some days found sheep grazing here; some mornings saw duelists at their deadly game. This evening, a great crowd from keep and countryside and even the town surrounded a tower of firewood, soon to be the midsummer bonfire.

There was music about them, and laughter, and many blankets laid out on the green where groups and couples shared food and drink. Vendors wound their way through the throng, offering nuts and wine and prani. They could hear the voice of Saj, master of hounds, rising over the noise of the crowd as he made announcements.

"I wish Fachalana could have stayed for this," said the Lady Lomela, mostly to herself.

"There are many things for which we might wish, my lady," replied Janona. "Many things, indeed."

Lomela nodded in agreement. Where was Bolos in all this crowd? The man seemed adrift after the dual blows of his father's and daughter's deaths.

The festivities of this night, and tomorrow's Summer Feast, might help. And then the new count could fall into the routine of governing and daily life and, perhaps, forgetfulness.

Lady Lomela smiled to herself. If only things could be that easy!

"Your blond roots are showing, Maresta. Will you dye again?" Fachalana knew to address her friend by that name here; ever the actress, she found it easy to slip into whatever play in which she found herself cast.

"My dye is with our luggage, far away. I think I will let it grow out." Ansa peered into her hand-mirror. "Maybe a hat until then?"

"Or a wig." Fachalana grew suddenly serious. "How soon do you think we can leave? I must speak with the king."

"Fear not, my lady. I spoke to Sir Blen before you awoke and he says King Lareth is on his way here.

"How do you feel this morning? You were barely with us when we arrived."

Fachalana's father, on seeing her condition the previous evening, had immediately prepared a draught for her. The young woman had slept long and soundly.

"As though I were made of lead," replied Fachalana, "but my mind has cleared."

"The Lord Radal was very concerned for you. He said that you might have been lost forever in whatever realms you walked in your dreams."

Ansa found there were tears in her eyes. "I would not want to lose you, Lana."

"I, my friend, would not have wished to remain in the places I visited. But I found a place where I could rest, a place all of silver." The place where she had first seen Donzalo. "I do not think I was supposed to be there but it became my sanctuary."

"Oh, Fachalana, give up these magics! Is it not enough to be both an admired actress and the best swordswoman in Celatas?"

"Those things are like the dye in your hair, Maresta. The real me will continue to show at the roots."

A cup of wine may make me jolly
But two can turn me melancholy,
And taking three is simple folly
For I'll fall asleep, by golly!

I'll have one for my stomach's sake,
Though several more seems a mistake;
Too many cupfuls surely make
Anybody's tummy ache!

"Aye, that's true," came a gruff voice from the darkness.

Good food is certainly a sign
To pour another cup of wine,
So bring enough when we may dine
To fill up yours and fill up mine!

Cups were lifted all around the campfire.

A cup of wine just might enhance
The mood that leads us to romance;

But sometimes we make an advance
When we shouldn't take the chance!

Guesare put down his rebec and raised his own goblet of wine in salute to his audience. There was much revelry that midsummer night, all through the grounds of the fair, as men — and, yes, more than a few women — relaxed and celebrated before their first chaotic day of selling on the morrow.

"Is that one of yours?" queried Galaro.

"Only in part, Brother. The words come from Donzalo's friend, Jobareth."

"The Nafal boy? I've done business with his family."

"From what he has told me, they would rather put you out of business," said Donzalo, "and establish safe trade routes in the south."

"And it will happen, one way or another. My guess is that the Coradeans will reoccupy at least some of their old holdings on the mainland and make life hard for an honest smuggler." Galaro thought a moment and continued. "But it's no ones land down on the south coasts now. Pirates and plunderers. Maybe some order would be a good thing."

Habidros slapped his scabbard. "I'd show them how to bring some order."

There were chuckles around the fire at that, and most of all from his two brothers. Galaro and Guesare, once enemies — or nearly so — had found that they had much in common and, in fact, liked each other. Both were amused by their brother's mix of bravado and naivety.

"It is the southern passes that more interest the Nafals," Donzalo pointed out. "Our friend Orgelo would want to have a say in that."

"We shall have a first-hand look at that part of the world soon," said Guesare, "and maybe more. Does anyone else here know a song? I'm tired of being the entertainment!"

"I need to stretch my legs and visit the latrine," spoke Donzalo, coming to his feet. "No, Habi, you don't have to come along." His bodyguard had risen to accompany him.

"I'd feel better if I did," he responded.

"As would I," added Guesare. "You still need protection, Donni, even here."

"I'll go with him," said Galaro. "I need to piss too. Watch out for the tent ropes," he warned Donzalo. "It's easy to trip over one in the dark."

Once they were beyond the fire's light, he added, "A couple of old mother hens. Need some time to yourself?"

"Ha, you are observant Sir Galaro. I don't get much privacy these days."

"With all the fires and folks wandering about here, it is probably as safe as walking a street in town. Maybe safer, for we traders take care of our own."

They did pass by many others in the night, some hurrying on errands, others seemingly strolling at random. Donzalo noted one tall vagabond with a great beard, who turned from them and slipped into the dark. He looked at his companion.

Galaro nodded. "Perdos. I would expect no trouble from him here."

"Looking for information, you would think?"

"Aye. It's a good place to find it."

"Then he'll have learned where we are headed, most likely."

"I'll tell Guesare about it later. He's in no danger now. The latrines are up ahead, to the left. It would have been quicker just to go piss in the river."

Donzalo's smile might not have been visible in the dark. "When you pack and leave they drain them into the Weldar anyway. Saves on having to dig new ones."

5

"My grandfather was born here. They changed the name to Grenethas in his honor."

Carrana nodded amiably. She knew this. What she wanted was to see their new home.

Modareth pointed toward a forested hill. "The chateau is up there." He had never visited but he had maps. "Greneth used it mostly as a hunting lodge after he took the crown."

"Does your father come here?"

"Not since he was young, he told me." He pointed again, up the single cobblestone street of what was called a city only out of politeness. "A few leagues up you would meet the old Southern Road and a few leagues more will take you to the Doram Pass. That is why there are garrisons nearby." Exactly how far a 'few leagues' was remained somewhat nebulous in the prince's mind.

"But we will have our own soldiers, won't we?"

"The twenty Father has sent with us and a small guard that always remains stationed here. Fear not, my love, even if we have no Lady Fachalana to protect us." He leaned down from his piebald stallion to kiss his wife, riding beside him in a horse litter.

The way up to their residence was short but steep. It was more fortified house than keep, though a low wall surrounded it, built of the rather soft limestone that underlay much of this country.

"That roof needs repair," Carrana whispered to the prince. "I'll wager it's worse inside."

"Then at least we shall keep busy this summer, my dear. Let's go see just what sort of job awaits us!"

Summer Feast was a festive occasion and Summer Fair was a festive place but Lomela was not in a festive mood. Her husband had fallen again into his old drunken ways last night.

She hardly blamed him. Life had dealt him heavy blows lately and a midsummer revelry was a good place to forget ones cares for a time.

This did not mean that she liked it in any way nor that it did not worry her.

Her party had left the keep early, eager to get the best deals at the fair. Only adults this time — Lomela and her faithful maid, Traspa, Janona and her mother-in-law, Sima, Sir Paren and his Thara, along with a couple of guardsmen to protect and to carry packages. On the road down they were met by Jobareth Nafal and, to the utter surprise of all, the ambassador Lord Doufan.

He rode with them as though he were but another old friend, smiling and making small jests. Before long, they felt an old friend was just what he was.

One advantage of being a countess was that the soldiers of ones husband could be expected to care for your horses while you wandered afoot. There were many such soldiers stationed about the Summer Fair.

Lesser personages had to entrust their mounts to the makeshift — and not inexpensive — corrals that sprang up near the fairgrounds.

They left their horses and entered the already bustling field. Fresh straw had been strewn between the pavilions, soon to be ground into the mud. This was yet another argument for an early arrival.

Nafal pointed to their left as they entered the grounds. "Galaro's booths are close — he arrived early and got a good spot. Donzalo may or may not be there."

But the ladies had already descended upon a jewelry stall in the opposite direction.

And Doufan was in earnest discussion with a vendor of crockery. "It appears that some of your wares have met with misfortune," said he, regarding a pile of shards behind the counter.

"Part of the cost of my business, m'lord," came the reply.

"Indeed," remarked the diplomat, "if things didn't break, there would be no potters." It was an old proverb and known to both men.

"Quite so, sir, though I prefer they break after I sell them!"

Lord Doufan turned to Nafal and whispered, "Cheap and crude, from somewhere upriver. Would that all his wares had not survived transit."

Jobareth nodded. "Yes, my lord. My family buys better just to ship our wine." There were markets that still preferred amphora to wooden cask.

"Ah, of course you would know something of pottery then. What is our group up to?"

The women had moved on to the next booth, followed by Sir Paren and the two soldiers.

"Cloth. I know they will take their time on that," said the younger man. "Shall we make our escape, my lord?"

"A most excellent idea, young sir. I assume someone sells refreshments in this metropolis of merchants."

"Come with me to my brother's pavilion and you may drink for free," said Guesare, coming up from behind them.

"Is Donzalo there?" asked Jobareth as they walked beside the Cuddonian.

"No, he went back to the keep to finish his packing. Sir Paren and all his company will depart early on the morrow and he must have his things ready for transport."

"You leave the same day, Sir Guesare?" asked the ambassador.

"Most likely. That depends on the whims of Count Orgelo."

"Orgelo is a man who bears watching," remarked Doufan, without further comment.

His companions needed none. They both thoroughly agreed.

Galaro was not one to deal in just one trade-good. A variety of items were spread through the tents and stalls occupied by his band, though different members of that band did have each his specialties. Galaro's own was weaponry.

"It is unfortunate," Lord Doufan said, "that the Lady Fachalana did not have the opportunity to view your wares."

"I feel unfortunate, sir," replied Galaro, "that I missed the opportunity to meet her. Tales of her exploits have reached my ears from several sources now.

Mayhap I can cross swords with her someday."

Guesare laughed loudly. "She would cut you to ribbons, Brother!" He had that on the best authority, that being the word of Ansa. "As would I, you know."

"I have little skill with the sword," stated Doufan. As oft, Jobareth had no idea whether the man's words were true. "But I do appreciate a fine gunne. Are these all you have?"

"All I have for sale, my lord. There is something here, however, that you might like to see."

He went to a chest near the rear of the tent and pulled forth a long slender object wrapped in rawhide and, within that, oiled cloth. Galaro held it out to them.

"A musket?" asked Jobareth.

"No, boy, a rifle," came Lord Doufan's correction, "and as pretty a one as ever I've seen." He carefully took it from the trader. "Siphic?"

Galaro nodded. "It has a wheel-lock to rival any that ever went into a pistol. And look here," he said, taking the weapon back. "It loads from the breech." The mechanism looked complicated but its use seemed simple — the ornate trigger guard became a crank that opened the weapon for loading.

"You already have a customer waiting for it?" asked Doufan. "A rather wealthy one, I would hazard."

"No, my lord," replied Galaro, "it is meant to be a gift." He handed it to Guesare. "For all that has ever passed between us, I wish this to be yours."

Another man might have protested; Guesare knew better and embraced his brother.

"Ah, customers," said Galaro, as Lomela and her party approached. The men — Sir Paren included — were already laden. "And a countess among them, if I am not mistaken. Welcome to our pavilion, Lady Lomela.

"Gentlemen," he continued, "why don't you leave your burdens here? I will have them sent up to the keep for you later."

"Your Galaro knows how to do business with the nobility," observed Doufan in a low voice. "He seems quite a remarkable man."

Jobareth smiled. "The whole family seems remarkable, my lord."

That was the last of it. What he wished to send with Sir Paren was crated and stowed in the wagons. What little he needed here was in his new quarters, where he would sleep tonight on a simple cot.

At first, that little room had seemed stifling. It was not overly hot, thanks to the thick castle wall and the rock floor, but too close and without ventilation, even if Donzalo left the massive door ajar. Then he bethought him of the secret passage that lay beneath the chamber. Opening the panel to it let in a stream of air to pass out through his door.

Probably bats, too, he thought. And it would not do to have the passage visible when his room was open to passers-by. Maybe he should just take a pallet down to the cave. It might be a most pleasant spot to sleep on a warm summer night.

Donzalo doubted that he would spend any more nights at Keep Rosam this summer. Where would his so-called destiny lead him? A memory of his Jola came to him, of the moments of contentment he had found in her cottage. His hand went to the wolf pin at his shoulder.

And what of the women who were now in his life? The Lady Fachalana intrigued him and, yes, attracted him. He would admit it. But all that, in itself, meant little.

There was Ansa. Had he fallen in love with her, nearly a year ago, before he found Jola? Could she ever regain that place in his heart now?

Or the first woman he had loved, with all the passion that comes of such a first love, his princess — Lomela. Had the fire died or did it only flicker low now? Might they burn bright again?

From the open doorway, Bolos watched his brother, rapt in his thoughts, unaware of his presence. Bolos wished Donzalo no harm but would be gladdened to see him ride away from County Rosam. He had concerns enough, already.

He spoke. "Greetings, Brother." He walked into the room and looked about. "I had considered moving my private quarters here. These are smaller, but you do have that window."

"I will miss the window," Donzalo allowed with a smile.

"You didn't have to abandon these rooms, Donni. We would have held them for you." Bolos shook his head. "Instead you choose quarters in the stables."

"I can be out of the way there, and ready to come or go quickly." He looked into Bolos's eyes and continued earnestly, "I doubt, my brother, that I shall ever truly live here again. Best I move."

"Well, these rooms will probably remain empty a while. I have decided to take grandmother's old apartment."

"Ah. As Father intended."

Bolos nodded. "I wish you nothing but good fortune on your journeys, Brother, and do expect you to return to us. Maybe you'll be willing to take decent rooms then!" He chuckled at his own remark."Be a good ambassador for us to our neighbors, eh? And know that I do intend to name you as Uncle Paren's heir. If that is what you want."

He suspected that it was not.

6

Copago watched the little train pass out through the gates, his wife, his daughter, his mother, aye, and even the dog, off with Sir Paren and Lady Thara to take up residence in their keep. His own commission at Castle Rosam had ended yesterday. There was no more to hold him here.

The captain of Count Orgelo's troop came and stood silently beside him. He knew no proper words but did know the knight's heart was breaking.

Turning to him, Sir Copago spoke in his accustomed calm and even voice. "Is it time to go, Captain?"

"Nay, sir, the count is not yet ready. I would hazard an hour or two."

Copago nodded. He looked at his comrade's breastplate and asked a question he had at times before considered asking. "Why do the men of Aravaram wear that black-painted hardware? Is it not hot on a sunny day?"

"Isn't all armor hot?" returned the fellow. "Sir Sorsen claims it prevents rust but I think he just likes the look of it."

"Yes, that is Sorsen, isn't it?" He looked again toward the gates but there was nothing to be seen. Even the dust of the road had settled. "I prefer a good shine on my armor. It is more military."

"And a better target for a musketeer," replied the captain.

"I see it rather as a deterrent," opined Copago.

"Ha, I can see why our Sorsen likes you, Sir Copago. The two of you might argue armaments all day!"

"I can think of worse pastimes."

"You have spoken with your father, my lady?"

"I have. And do not call me my lady when we fence. My master said all men become equals when they hold swords."

"Until they cross them. I have heard that one," replied Blen. "When we cross swords you very much become my better."

"There are many in your company," spoke Ansa, lounging against a wall while the two practiced swordsmanship. "Tell me, sir, how does she compare with Donzalo? I heard that you two exercised frequently."

"He is certainly far my superior. Let's stop and have some water." He dropped his point to the stone floor. "Whether he is better than Lady Fachalana, I am not qualified to judge."

Lady Fachalana glared at him for using her title.

"What? Shall I call you Lana as does Maresta?"

"Just Fachalana. It is not difficult, man."

Blen bowed to her. "Very well, Fachalana. I will say that Donzalo has a prodigious reach to his advantage."

Ansa had poured them tumblers of cold water, always readily available here in the mountains, as they approached her. "Fachalana has a pretty good reach herself," she remarked, handing them their drinks.

The lady laughed. "My father has warned me that I reach too far," she said. "But how else does one learn the length of ones arms?"

"An inch at a time," responded Sir Blen with great seriousness. "I must agree with the Lord Radal."

"And even one inch can give the advantage," added Ansa.

"Until someone else has an inch more," retorted Fachalana. She drank deeply and turned to Blen. "What do you intend to tell the king about Maresta?"

"Mostly the truth. That is, that she has served both you and the Princess Lomela with her actions. Is there more I should tell him?"

"Only what you know will serve quite well enough," Ansa said, "and we shall leave any secrets I might have out of it! Even so, it will not help my career one bit."

Blen would assume she meant on the stage; Fachalana recognized that she was referring to her life as a spy.

"Then find a nice boy and retire," suggested the Lady Fachalana. Maybe the one right in front of you, she said to herself.

Over the river before noon. That's not so bad, felt Guesare.

He and Habidros had been assigned a spot near the dusty rear of this column, ahead only of the baggage, while Donzalo and Sir Copago rode on either side of the count. The three seemed to have much to talk about.

He considered the thought that Orgelo regarded the two Cuddonians as baggage too. They would not be in his train were it not for Donzalo.

What the three men ahead were sharing were their remembrances of the late Count Borrago.

"The count was greatly pleased by the way Donzalo matured this past year. He very much loved this over-sized son of his."

"Of the three of us, you may have loved Father best," asserted Donzalo. "And he could never conceal his pride in you."

"Then, it would seem," Orgelo mused, "that the current count was his least favorite."

Neither was sure how to answer that. "No, that's all right," said their host, holding up a hand. "I know that Bolos long vexed his father with his drunkeness and sloth. He made strides in this past year as well, didn't he?"

"That he did, sir," allowed Copago.

"But he could and can still be thoroughly unpleasant, " added Donzalo. His half-brother had to nod in agreement. "He is my brother and I love him anyway."

"And I will truthfully admit that I do not," stated the former master of arms. "I will also say that I feel no anger toward him."

"That is a good start," said the count, "for your new life. I can not guarantee this, lad, but I would lay odds that Sorsen will name you his master of arms. If not, I can promise you a captaincy in my own troops."

"I thank you, my lord, again." They were making excellent time along the west banks of the Weldar. Here, the way was nearly as good as the Great Road on the other side of the river. "I have never traveled far south before."

"Nor have I," added Donzalo. "Father would not permit me to study in Morparas."

"With good reason," snorted Sir Copago. "A city of thieves and whores!"

Orgelo laughed loudly. "'Tis not so bad, my strait-laced friend. I do a fair amount of business in the city and you may have to travel there from time to time."

He turned his eyes toward Donzalo. "You are the more traveled, now, aren't you? All the way to the upper Cuddon, I've heard."

"Yes, my lord. I would have visited Oles as well, if my traveling companions had permitted."

"You missed little there. I visited when my father was count, on a mission of reconciliation to the pontifex. It ended not well."

"I've always found plenty to keep me busy at home," stated Copago. "Why seek trouble in other lands?"

Donzalo and the count exchanged expressions of amusement. "You, my boy," said Orgelo, "are far too much like your father."

"Thank you once more, my lord," said Copago, bowing from the saddle.

Perdos had shaved. Not just trimmed his lengthy beard back to its old accustomed length, but shorn it entirely. It was a break with the life he had been living — a symbolic gesture, of sorts, though he would never have thought of it in such terms. He just felt he should start afresh.

His face had not been without whiskers since he left the village of his birth, a little village north of Oles, near the Muram borders. He felt rather naked.

He had learned enough at the fair, back at Ros-town. Guesare would be traveling south on the west side of the river, with a sizable body of men. He would do the same on the east, by himself.

Surely, the minstrel had no intentions of staying at Tod-ford, at Count Orgelo's court. Sooner or later he would leave, quite possibly with his brother Galaro, when the trader came south again. Perdos had no quarrel with Galaro and had parted amiably with the man, but he would not let him come between him and Guesare. Hadn't he said they were unfriendly to each other, anyway?

South he rode. He might stop by the inn where he had wintered, had he the time. He had little enough money left to pay for even a drink, though.

Then, cross and head for Todmouth. News from upriver always found its way there and, too, Galaro was likely to pass through.

Perdos could think of no better plan and perhaps there was none.

Someone was shaking Blen awake. "Wha — who is there?" he demanded, groping for his dagger.

"Ssshhh! It's Fachalana."

"Lady Fachalana?" He realized he was quite naked, having always slept so. The knight wrapped himself in a sheet and rose to light a taper from the still-glowing coals on his hearth. Even in midsummer the nights were cool enough at Mountain Keep for a fire.

The lady was dressed for riding. "I need your help, Sir Blen," said she.

His placed his candle on the table and sat down on his bed. "Speak, my lady."

"I have just learned that the king is a day away on the road. I must speak to him before he arrives. It is an urgent message and for his ears only. Will you ride with me to meet him?"

The knight suddenly felt a great need to use his chamberpot. Ride with her? "What of, uh, Maresta?" he asked, as his mind became less cobwebbed.

"She will remain and cover for us. If you come not with me, I will ride alone."

"The king — yes, my lady, I will ride with you. Meet me in the stables in ten minutes."

Fachalana hurried away from Sir Blen's quarters, stimulated by thoughts of action. The sight of the handsome and not at all clothed young knight had also provided a certain stimulation of its own. The Lady Fachalana was in too great a rush to sort all that out right now.

7

Business was good. On this third day of the fair, the crowds had lessened — albeit, not by much — and now many traders were getting down to the business that truly brought most of them here, the exchange of goods that they would carry out into all corners of Lama, aye, and beyond, for resale.

That business could remain brisk through the entire month of Summer Fair, as new wares flowed in. There was always a question of whether to leave sooner and get a jump on the competition or remain longer and find new bargains.

"Captain." Sir Galaro looked up to see his second, his one good eye squinting into the morning sun. "The count is here."

Well, it was to be expected that Bolos would visit sooner or later. "On the grounds?"

"Still at the gates, getting his men and mounts sorted out. I reckon he'll be wandering through before long."

"Let's hope he isn't as stingy as his father was." Reports did not make Galaro optimistic about that. "I think I'll wander myself and go get a look at him." The burly Cuddonian rose and strolled toward the fairground entrance.

He didn't think he had seen the new count this year, save at Borrago's funeral. Had he? Anyway, Bolos had visited the fair the last couple years when Galaro did business there, so he was acquainted with the man. He had sold him some trinkets to give to one dalliance or another.

There he was, slimmer than he remembered him in years past. Less ostentatious, too, in an almost too subdued gray tunic. Around him, his men were resplendent in their green and black uniforms and burnished armor. He was hectoring one of them about something at the gate.

Then there was chaos.

It took a second for Galaro to realize what had happened, to see why Count Bolos's men suddenly surrounded him, swords turned outward. There in a gate post still quivered a crossbow bolt.

The Cuddonian realized later that he had heard the thud of its strike. He also realized he had acted instinctively but wisely by immediately turning and walking swiftly back to his pavilion. The scene of an assassination attempt was one place it would not do to linger.

This would probably ruin business for the rest of the day. Galaro suddenly wished he did not have an assortment of crossbows among his goods.

The girl had settled down some. That was good. She was out riding with Sir Blen, he had been told. He did not trust Blen in many regards but he was certainly a safe and trustworthy companion for his daughter.

Radal wondered if Fachalana's recent near-madness had left her stronger. There had been no evident relapse nor requests for more sleeping draughts.

Now, there were other concerns. He had known the king must come eventually. How would he deal with his liege when Lareth arrived? Time was short but he had already taken the next steps in his plans.

The king could not stop them. Even if Radal himself were dead, too many things had been set in motion. He must trust in them to play out the way he had intended, to fulfill his design.

And he must trust Fachalana now to find her own way. Only the gods knew if he would be able to guide her further and he would not ask them. Radal had little trust in gods.

Certainly not in any he had ever met.

He would do what he could when Lareth came. Perhaps he could even sway his king to his viewpoint. Even so, his old friend would never again trust him.

But Lareth would not have him executed nor, probably, even imprisoned. An exile, far from power, might more likely be his fate. Radal would not mind that.

Indeed, he would mind little so long as Donzalo Rosam ceased to exist.

Four soldiers rode forth from the head of the column. They did not like the look of these two travelers speeding toward them. One held up a hand, calling for them to halt.

"Who rides?" he demanded.

"Sir Blen and the Lady Fachalana. We bear an urgent message for the king," replied the knight.

The name of Fachalana was known to them. The soldiers looked at her with a great deal of interest. "Go inform the captain," said their leader to one of them. The man wheeled his steed and galloped back.

The captain, wearing the king's colors of argent and green, and a handful more of men reached them shortly. This officer knew the Lady Fachalana. "My lady," he said, bowing from the saddle, "what is this message?"

"It is for King Lareth's ears only," she replied, with a great deal of assumed authority. "Tell him. He will want to hear it."

The man hesitated only a second, then nodded. "Follow me," he ordered.

By that time the column of men and horses had reached them. The captain rode close to the king and spoke to him. Lareth shielded his eyes against the morning sun coming over the mountains and looked in the direction of Fachalana and Blen. Then he nodded and gave the man an order.

"Come with me," said the captain, when he returned to the pair. "The lady only," he added when Sir Blen started forward.

The king's men fell back to a discreet distance while the Lady Fachalana rode alongside their liege. Blen saw a look of astonishment cross his face. What secret message could she have been bearing?

Then the king looked toward him and asked a question. Fachalana shook her head and answered with a smile. Her smile was returned by the monarch. The knight quite rightly surmised that Lareth wanted to know if he were in on whatever secret the lady was conveying to him.

Then the king beckoned to him.

"I thank you, Sir Blen," said Lareth when the knight was beside him, "for once again serving well your king. Better than you know, this time, or perhaps ever will know."

"The Lady Fachalana asked and I acted, sir. Whatever service I may have performed was at her bidding."

Now that this so-important message had been delivered, Blen bethought himself of a question. "Should we hurry back to the Keep, sire, or ride on with you?"

The king turned his eyes to Fachalana. "What think you, my lady?"

"We should ride back immediately and swiftly. No one there knows we came to you nor should they." The king understood that she spoke of her father. Blen guessed something of the same.

"Then let us ride, my lady. We can be back hours before the king arrives. Maybe even in time for lunch!"

Blen had, of course, had no time for breakfast.

To Guesare's surprise, he had been asked to ride with Count Orgelo this day. The count was much interested in his travels, and their talk, more than once, turned to his brother Galaro.

He doubted that he told the man much of anything he didn't already know but he enjoyed telling his many tales. By the time they stopped for the evening, Guesare realized he had learned much himself, especially of his brother's exploits.

The men set up targets that night and held matches at archery. The minstrel let loose a few arrows with a borrowed longbow, but with no more than decent results. The recurved eastern bow was his weapon and he knew he could best any man here at its use from horseback.

The minstrel was amused that his brother Habidros proved a most wretched archer. "I've not touched a bow in years, " the man offered as excuse. "Give me a gunne," he growled, "and I'll show you a few things."

At the end it came down to Sir Copago and, to the surprise of Donzalo and the Cuddonians but none others there, Orgelo. The count had been a famed archer in his youth and still had the needed steady eye and hand. Eventually, he avenged his son's unhorsings at the hands of Copago.

"Sir Guesare," he called, "bring forth that rifle of which we have heard."

"I have not yet fired it, my lord, and know not its capabilities." He rummaged in one of the carts before drawing forth the carefully wrapped firearm.

Donzalo had heard of the weapon but not seen it. He found himself greatly fascinated by its mechanism once Guesare had it out and wiped down for action. There was great interest, as well, from Orgelo and his men.

The minstrel carefully loaded it and closed the breach, silently saying a prayer to the goddess Rema that it would remain closed as it was supposed to. Then he primed and spanned it, and took aim at one of the targets.

"Did I hit it?" he asked after the smoke cleared. A man who had run to the target pointed to a spot near its outer edge.

"May I?" asked Habidros, taking the rifle from his hands and a swab to its barrel. "It's rather a small bore, isn't it?" He prepared the weapon for firing, and then turned and walked twenty paces further from the target before taking aim.

This time a hole near the bullseye was pointed out. "It shoots well, Brother," remarked Sir Habidros, returning the rifle to its owner.

"You must have a scabbard made for it, my boy," insisted Lord Orgelo, "and a befitting one. Such a weapon should hang at your saddle, not be bundled away in a baggage cart."

"Indeed, my lord. And I think my brother needs to give me lessons in marksmanship!"

The reeve of Mountain Keep came forth to greet his king. This was the man entrusted with its everyday operation, who sent out patrols to keep the King's Pass clear and aid travelers at all times of the year.

He had much to tell his monarch but Lareth would not take the time. "Later. I must see Lord Radal. Accompany me, sir."

It was not yet dusk though the sun had dropped behind the mountains, cooling the air. Soon, the two stood before the ebony door of Radal's tower. "Await me," he said, and entered.

The king was immediate and straight-forward with his accusation. "You ordered the assassination of Borrago."

"I will not deny it, my lord," replied the sorcerer in an even voice. "I did what I believed necessary."

"Against my express orders. Radal, you know I can not have this. You may no longer serve as my lord councilor nor have you any other authority."

The dark nobleman bowed his head. "As expected, my king. Yet I would do it again," he added, with more vehemence.

"I know you would. But I tell you now that we will not again attempt to harm Donzalo Rosam. New information has come to me that changes our relationship with him completely."

"Might I know this secret, my lord?"

"No, Radal, you may not. I fear you would use it against him rather than as I wish. I am sorry it has come to this."

"What has come, has come. We must make the most of it," stated the sorcerer.

"So we must," answered King Lareth, turning to the door. "Pray to any gods you may have left that I can make something of this."

Once outside, Lareth issued orders to the reeve. "I wish you to set a guard at the Lord Radal's door, and make it a strong one. He is not to leave his tower.

"And have the Lady Fachalana and her companion come to my apartments for supper. Not Sir Blen, the girl."

He could speak with Blen later.

8

Who would profit from his death? That question pointed to a whole different group of suspects than had Borrago's assassination.

Surely Donzalo wouldn't be trying to clear a path to his title. Yet who else might want both him and his father dead? No, Bolos could not believe that.

Copago seemed an even less likely suspect.

But Donzalo's friend, the trader Galaro, was at the fairgrounds. With a selection of crossbows. He must have his agents keep an eye on the man.

Orgelo wouldn't mind having Donzalo as count, would he, or as regent for his nephew? The two had seemed altogether too friendly lately.

He hoped Sir Corgos would accept his offer of a position. Such a man was needed here. Jak was useless, save as sergeant to his personal guard.

Bolos took another sip from the flagon before him. There would be more flagons before the night was through, but no answers.

Ansa had been apprehensive when invited into Lord Radal's presence. The king of Sharsh made her even more so.

As soon as his young guests were seated at the table, one on his either hand, Lareth asked, "How much does your friend know, Lady Fachalana?"

"Everything, sire. She was my, um, liaison to your daughter last year."

The king laughed at that. "Your spy, you mean. I have learned much of Maresta lately. But not her origins." He gave Ansa a most disconcerting look. "That may remain your secret, if you wish."

"Th — thank you, my lord," she mumbled.

"Now, my dear, " he said, turning again to Fachalana, "you must have an official family name to go with your title."

"Sire, I would use that of my grandfather and vindicate his legacy."

"So, Lady Fachalana, the Viscountess Ildoram. I would be pleased to honor the memory of General Ildor." He gave her a long look, long in part because the servants were hovering close as they placed food and drink before them. He raised his filled goblet. "And I drink to his memory. How much do you know of the man?"

"My father never speaks of him, sir. I only know that he was a mercenary from Lorj who served King Greneth."

"Yes, from the south of the island and therefor with a Partanacan heritage. To be honest, I know not whether he served Coradean or Partanacan causes before he fled, nor know I why he fled. But he landed here and rose in my father's service. He married well, too, or so it seemed.

"You may not know that his wife, your grandmother, had gifts like your father's, and knew not how to harness them. As she grew madder and more dangerous, it weighed on Ildor and, I think, led him to become foolhardy. After he fell in battle, Radal cared for her but she, too, soon passed. Some whispered that she leaped from her tower window one night.

"My father saw the mother in the son. That is why he banished him." Lareth shook his head slowly. "Perhaps Greneth saw correctly. I fear for Radal's mind and soul."

His soul is long lost, Fachalana said to herself. I've known that, haven't I?

"You understand why I have placed him under guard, don't you?"

Fachalana had visited her father earlier and seen the guardsmen, but Radal would not speak of them to her.

"I believe so, my lord. What will become of my father?"

"When things are sorted out, retirement to his country estate. That is my hope, anyway."

"That is — kind of you, sir."

"I owe him much. As I do his daughter."

Back in the Anian court, the man would be garroted by now, thought Ansa. But she held her tongue and picked at the meal set before her. Was this chicken hiding beneath the sauce?

"Now I would ask another favor of his daughter. I have sent Prince Modareth and his bride to my father's old estate in Dor." The king raised his cup. "This wine comes from our vineyards there."

Ansa sniffed at the golden liquid in her goblet. She felt she would have preferred tea.

"My ladies, will you travel there and visit with them? It is not that distant a journey, though rugged if one follows roads near the mountains.

"Oh, and I shall send Sir Blen with you."

"Our luggage will never catch up with us at this rate, sir," said Lady Fachalana, "but we would be most willing to catch up with your son and the Lady Carrana.

She raised her cup. "To the journeys that come!"

There were only burnt ruins where the inn had once stood. Perdos stood mute, numb. Who had done this?

A man was walking toward him from the river. A somewhat stout man, a somewhat familiar man. Hendel. He remembered him from Keep Rosam.

The man did not seem to remember him, however. Perhaps his lack of beard could be credited for that. Or perhaps Hendel had simply never paid any attention to the soldier.

"Knew you the innkeepers, sir?" asked the man.

"I did," replied Perdos. "I would have counted them friends." He turned to Hendel. "What happened?"

"A band of marauders. Murdered them both, though perhaps not quickly enough." Hendel spat. "I curse the man who led them and I curse the fact that I know him. Sojel is his name, a mercenary out of Mura."

"Sojel," Perdos softly repeated to himself. "What brings you here, sir?"

"I left Todmouth a few days ago, growing, um, unhappy with my employment there. I am a cook," he offered. Perdos made no comment.

"My home town lies but a little upriver," said the man, gesturing in that general direction, "so I crossed here thinking to visit. Instead I found this. They murdered the guards down at the ferry too, I hear, and the current ones are very edgy. Even with their numbers doubled.

"Though I do mourn their loss of life, I recognized an opportunity and set up a little stall down close to Weldar where I might sell meat pies and such to passers-by."

Perdos nodded. "I may come down later to sample your wares. Could you leave me alone for a time?"

"Certainly, good sir," said the cook, with genuine sympathy, and headed back toward the ferry crossing.

When the man was well away, the knight picked his way through the burnt timbers to the great fireplace, standing yet. Might it still be here? he wondered.

He pulled out a stone. He had seen the innkeeper pull the same stone on occasion and made note of it. It had been the man's hiding place for his cash. Perdos had just enough honor to leave that be.

There was no point in that now, though, was there? Yes, there were the coins, tucked away in bags. Three bags, that crumbled at his touch. The heat must have done that, Perdos thought.

He filled his saddlebags with the loose money and headed toward the river and a meat pie.

The King's Pass was what Greneth had officially named it but most still called it the North Pass. Now Fachalana, Ansa, and Blen rode down from the pass toward Sharsh, accompanied by the four soldiers King Lareth had assigned them.

They would follow the Royal Road for some way and then turn left, southward, and follow roads that paralleled the ridges of the Zadcelam all the way to Dor.

Blen did not particularly like this plan of action. He would rather be back to Lama than accompanying these two girls. They seemed girls today, anyway, chattering gaily as they rode along. He knew they were two quite competent young women.

The knight liked them. It had been grudging at first and the knowledge that he was being shut out of many of their secrets did not help. But they had grown on him, even the sometimes difficult and undeniably dangerous Lady Fachalana.

Blen did not doubt for one moment that Ansa was quite dangerous as well, despite appearances.

Well, he had no orders to remain with them at Grenethas, only to get them there. It would be easy enough to cut back into Lama through the southern pass, the Doram Pass, the other major route through the mountains. That could be an interesting experience, too.

Lord Radal climbed to the highest chamber of his tower. One of his small messengers awaited him, bearing news from his agent at the Rosam embassy. It took little talent to deal with such messengers and that was what the boy had — a little talent.

The faked assassination attempt had gone off much as planned, though the intention had been to strike one of the soldiers, not a post. That did as well. Lareth could not put a halt to those plans by locking him in here; still, the sorcerer might operate more efficiently were he elsewhere.

Three nights ago had he called. To the Lofty Mountains had he called, beyond the mighty River Siph, beyond the plains of the Anians.

To the dragons had he called. He felt now the rush of wind that arose from mighty wings. He saw the eyes aglow in the darkness and smelt the stench of its fires. His steed had come and he would ride it.

Lord Radal fled on the wings of night.

Of Crossings: the Eighth Tale

1

Pol was not happy about this assignment. Was it Jobareth Nafal's idea to send him across Lama in the worst heat of summer?

Yes, probably.

And with that cart, it would take more than two weeks to reach the mountains. Mountain Keep would have been further but the roads to that destination were better.

He and the man at arms who accompanied him — a good Sharshite fellow and eager to be home — checked the map they had been given. They had followed the way they all knew well, the road by which he and the soldier and the two in the wagon had come into the heart of Lama, for some distance before turning due west toward the mountains and Doram Pass. Pol had been told there was a good road. It was rough, the red dirt rutted from traffic and summer downpours, but passable.

Murbalana was complaining again. "Did you put up with that all the way here?" he asked his companion.

"We did, Sergeant. Many a day I envied Doo his deafness." He had not told the man to address him as sergeant. That must have been Nafal's doing, too.

They had been all set to head off to Mountain Keep when the messenger came with this change of plan. Cross at the southern pass and find the ladies summering in Dor. Pol had heard of Dor but had never been there.

He was contemptuous of its wine, having been raised in Arolin where they produced the finest vintages in the world. Everyone he had ever known from his home province assured him it was so.

Pol looked toward the cloud-filled sky. There would be afternoon rains again. "I hope there are decent inns along this route," he muttered, "with decent wine."

His companion nodded his agreement.

"I ask this not for myself nor even for Lord Bolos, but for your friend Copago. He should have a worthy successor at his post."

"Would you order me to go, sir?"

"Never. It is for you and your wife to make this decision."

"Very well," said Sir Corgos, "I shall put it to Tiana." He leaned back in his chair. "I do like it here, Sir Paren."

"Lad, I have seen that you sometimes grow bored. There is little to challenge you in my keep," Paren observed. "I am sure your Tiana has seen it as well.

"You never speak of it but I know you have seen much of the world in your young life."

"Young? Sir, for a soldier I am already something of an old man. Older than Copago by half a decade." He sighed. "It was more than time to leave such a life."

"That it was. But you needn't bury yourself here in the backwoods. You know," the reeve continued, "Tiana might like life at Castle Rosam."

"Indeed, Sir Paren. But might that be a good thing or a bad one?"

"Why isn't the pass here used more?" asked Carrana. "It seems more convenient than going further north."

"I think," replied her husband, "it is because there isn't much of anything on the other side. The King's Pass is the gate to Oles and the Siphic cities beyond.

"Also, I hear it is a longer and rougher path. There are many ways through the mountains, in truth, but the others are not very practical for anyone but goats and smugglers."

"We should ride up and look at it some time, Modi."

"I fear it will only look like mountains. Besides," said the prince, "I am not certain you should be traveling at all."

"Pooh. It is nothing. My mother attended a ball the night before I was born."

"And danced with every man there. Yes, my dear, you have told me before." Modareth turned an ear toward the ceiling. "There is another leak somewhere. I can hear it dripping."

"I hope we can get them all fixed before the Lady Fachalana arrives."

"She wouldn't mind them, Carrana. Indeed, she might be inclined to get up on the roof and fix them herself." A courier had arrived only that morning, informing them of the viscountess' impending visit.

"I wonder about this Sir Blen who will accompany her. Her friend Maresta I know, of course."

"The actress?" asked Carrana. "I hope she isn't as wicked as her stage roles!"

"Oh no, my dear, she's quite a sweet, guileless girl and wouldn't hurt a fly, I am sure."

◆

Count Bolos paced back and forth in his wife's sitting room.

"So the Maresta who accompanied Lady Fachalana is one and the same as the Posena who came here as a spy?" asked Bolos. "Why was I not told — or my father?"

"It was unimportant, my husband. She was only here incognito at Fachalana's request."

"And I learn of it through gossip picked up by my agents. What am I to think when you keep such secrets from me?"

If only he knew what secrets I do keep, thought Lomela. "That I do not wish to bother you with trifles, sir."

"Humph. I have little trust in all these foreigners, be they from Sharsh or the Cuddon." He paused, abashed by his own poor choice of words. "Not all Sharshites, my lady. I do trust you.

"But I know not who else to trust and who to suspect. It must be admitted that the way this woman and your friend fled was most suspicious."

Princess Lomela diverted the subject. "A few days ago I might have told you not to trust my father. I have reason to suspect that might be changing."

"Indeed? Have you your own network of spies, my dear?"

"One might say that, Husband. I call them my friends in Sharsh who write to me with all the latest news. Those are the very best sorts of spies, for they do not know that they are." She smiled at the count. "You will hear this soon, anyway, but there has come a break between the king and Lord Radal. The sorcerer has been stripped of power."

"And you learned this from whom?"

"His daughter, Bolos. The Lady Fachalana."

Lord Doufan sat in a tavern near the Ros-town docks, nursing an ale and watching all that happened around him.

He became bored in the embassy. Indeed, there was little for him to do with the efficient legate tending to most of the necessary day-to-day diplomatic work.

The ambassador knew he could be of use at Castle Rosam but the count would not see him. The man seemed distrustful of all strangers, hiding behind walls built of stone and of wine.

Therefor, Doufan rode. Though he had chosen to give the impression otherwise on his trip here, the nobleman was quite comfortable on horseback. Sometimes he simply rode alone in the countryside, seeing what there was to see. At other times he would make his way down to Ros-town and visit one tavern or another, learning more of these Lamans among whom he must, for a while, live.

When he chose, he could be a popular fellow at those taverns, always ready with the right words and a bit of money. Often, as today, he chose to observe instead, keeping to himself.

"What word, Grandfather?" asked a young woman who sat down across from him. He did not mind that the whore saw him as an old man; it was the impression he intended to project.

And he *was* old enough to be her grandfather, after all.

"None you would care to hear, my dear," he replied. After a moment, she moved on.

It was probably dangerous to be in such places, not that he was in any way defenseless. He had all the training of a Sharshite noble in sword and dagger, and carried a well-concealed brace of pistols as well. Lord Doufan was not nearly so innocuous as he chose to appear.

This place, low-ceilinged and dark, was favored by stevedores and raftsmen. Rough men but honest, for the most part. He might be able to defend himself but he would not care to indulge in a fist-fight with one of these burly fellows.

Nafal, perhaps, saw into him — as far as he had let him, anyway. The boy was smart and an excellent administrator, but he would never be able to do what Doufan did. Yet he might well take Lord Radal's place one of these days while faceless diplomats such as the Lord Doufan were forgotten.

That was all to the good.

2

Across the wide Laman valley the dragon had flown, over the mighty Weldar and toward the high hills of the Cuddon. They would have passed near Castle Rosam but Radal could not see it in the dark.

There was a place, a small keep, in the rugged central highlands, east and some south of the River Abam, that the sorcerer knew. He knew it was empty for it had been occupied by the deceased and inept wizard Sabatare.

It would do as his new base of operations.

His mount was slowly descending toward the tower, practically a ruin, its great wings riding subtle winds that rose along the faces of the steep, scrub-covered hills. Radal could see the dragon clearly now in the morning light, seemingly a large beast at first glance but mostly all wing and slender, snake-like body. The big dragons did not fly; their bulk could not be supported by any wings.

He had paid dearly for this transport. What did that matter when he had already bartered away all that was Radal years ago? With his extinction would come peace and any torments before that were meaningless.

The sorcerer longed, these days, to fall into that great darkness.

He alit from the worm in an unkempt space before the crumbling walls. The beast eyed him for a few seconds — hungrily, perhaps? — before launching itself into the still morning air.

Radal thought of all he had left behind in Sharsh. He could never return now, not go into a quiet retirement, never have Fachalana's children playing about their grandfather, unaware of who he once had been. He must trust his daughter to find her way, to give him those grandchildren he would not see.

All this he did for her, now. He knew that Donzalo was entwined in her fate, as he had been in her sister's. Radal could not let the man live. He could not lose both Fachalana and Jola.

He would need a horse, wouldn't he? Radal turned toward the doors of Sabatare's keep — the magics that barred them were easily swept away — and went to do the things he must do.

He knew his old circle was not trustworthy. But where might Gawis find new advisers?

The bureaucrats aiding him with all the small details of governing in his father's absence were useful men, but not ones he would take into his confidence. He needed someone at his right hand, someone loyal to him only, as Lord Radal had so long served his father.

Yes, that was ending badly now but the dark nobleman had been faithful many years. It was madness that drove him these days, wasn't it? Not malice toward the king.

The sorcerer perhaps did not see it as betrayal at all.

Gawis toyed with a paperweight on his desk. It was dark green glass, blown at one of the shops right here in Celatas, in a fanciful fish shape. They did good work with glass here. Celatas could rival any city in that industry.

There was his brother. He knew Modareth was smart. But would he be loyal to his brother? The two had never been close — too much difference in age, not to mention temperament, in the siblings born to different mothers. He might ask the boy's advice but doubted he would ever trust him with his secrets.

It seemed the only one to whom he could unburden himself was his wife. Mara could be insightful; after all, she had grown up in the great imperial court of Partanaca and knew the ways of power. Even if she shunned them, herself.

He eyed the stack of papers before him. Why did they all need his signature? Prince Gawis took one from the top of the pile and began reading.

Ansa was eyeing a small harp placed on a table in the library.

"You play the harp, my lady?" asked Modareth. "It was my mother's instrument but I fear I have no skill on it myself."

She ran a finger across the strings. It was much out of tune. "My brother taught me, when I was a girl." Ansa looked up at the prince. "He is a minstrel, my lord."

For a few moments, she twisted the wooden tuning pins and then sang, in a high, clear voice.

Moon of silver, sun of gold,
I who was young now grow old.
Daylight dims, night grows cold,
Should I fear death, I who was bold?

Life is short, forever is long,
I tried to do right, often did wrong.
Will is weak, wine was strong,
I would forget the words to my song.

Moon of silver, queen of night,
I knew you once, grown full and bright,
And madly I danced, by your light,
But those who danced with me fled from sight.

Last fading stars, by dawn swept away,
I, as you, may no longer stay.
Yet you return, come end of day;
Where I might go, I can not say.

Every road walked, every tale told;
All I then loved I could not hold.
Sun of morning, spun of gold,
I who was young have grown old.

"I didn't know you could sing, Maresta!" exclaimed the Lady Fachalana.

"None of my roles ever called for it," she answered.

"Our Maresta surprises me anew each day," spoke Sir Blen, from a chair in the corner.

Prince Modareth rose from the divan where he rested with his wife. "I must have those words written down, Lady Maresta. Did your brother compose them?"

"I learned it of my brother, sir, but it is the work of the bard Guesare."

"Guesare? He is one of my sister's friends, is he not?"

How does her brother know Guesare? wondered Blen. This was a new bit of information for him, another peep into the tangle of secrets around the two women he had been accompanying.

Fachalana recognized all this as well. She is teasing poor Blen, she thought. He so wants to know who she is.

"He is, my lord. He and my brother have ridden together at times in Lama."

The Lady Fachalana could scarce keep herself from giggling. "I did not know of this place, Modi," she said. "It looks as if everyone else forgot it too."

"It is in great disrepair. I fear many of these books are ruined from the damp." Modareth swung an arm toward the volumes lining the walls.

Donzalo would love this place, Blen thought.

"Are you up to a late supper, gentlefolk?" asked Carrana. "I have had what clothes you brought cleaned and laid out in your rooms. Refresh yourselves and please join the prince and me in an hour, won't you?"

To Donzalo's disappointment, Orgelo and his men bypassed Todmouth, cutting westerly across the countryside toward their home. The young knight had wanted to see Ros-town's greatest rival on the central Weldar.

"It is not much, really," Guesare told him, "not half the size of your town."

So Donzalo had heard before. Though the Tod was a major tributary to the Weldar, and a far mightier flow than the Abam, there was simply not that much trade coming down its stream. Ros-town stood central to all of Lama, amid its richest farmlands.

It also interested him that Todmouth was a free city, ruled by a lord mayor. None of the surrounding counties had been able to agree as to which should control the place so they had chosen this solution. The mayor, however, was appointed by the counts — who took turns naming him — and not elected by the folk of Todmouth.

The party, in time, reached the northern banks of the Tod.

Orgelo pointed out landmarks to his young guest, who rode beside him again on the last leg of their journey. This was a political consideration — the count wanted Donzalo at his side when he entered his own keep, as a symbol of his goodwill toward the Rosam.

"It is but a short way now to my home," said he, "where there is, naturally, a ford across the Tod. It is the first place one may safely cross the river." A sensible spot to place a keep, thought Donzalo.

"Have you given thought to putting a bridge across, my lord?" he asked.

"Why, when one can wade?" said the count. The concept seemed without merit to him. He had heard that Donzalo liked to build things and put it down to that.

"Up that way," the count went on, pointing north-westerly, "lie the lands of your cousin Daboreth. 'Tis poor country, at least as farm land, though I visit sometimes for the hunting.

"I have sent him word of your coming. I've no doubt he will visit."

The land through which they passed was quite rolling and there were many gullies washed into the hillsides. Cattle grazed here and there. Donzalo thought of treatises upon scientific farming he had read.

He knew by now that Orgelo would turn a deaf ear to such ideas.

Unlike Castle Rosam perched on its cliffs, Keep Arvaram spread upon a low hill near the river. It looked larger than his home at first, but Donzalo realized it did not rise so high and that it somewhat merged into the village around it. He could not help thinking how quickly a few cannon might level such a place.

Perhaps Sir Copago could tighten things up around here. He would have the ear of Orgelo's heir.

The muddy flow of the Tod reached not even to their stirrups. "Is the water higher at other times of the year, my lord?" he asked.

"Yes, boy, but very rarely impassible." The count laughed. "We really do not need your bridge."

Radal flown from the keep. On the wings of a dragon, no less, if one believed the reports.

King Lareth was glad the Lady Fachalana had already been on the road when it happened. He did not need her further complicated in this matter. Let the girl go enjoy some time in the countryside.

For a moment, he wondered what all this might mean for her supposed union with Jobareth Nafal. Lareth did not believe for a moment that either really wanted to marry the other and now they had no reason.

But that was not of great concern right now. What plans did Radal have, wherever he might have gone? They would center on the Rosam boy, of course, but would have wider implications. He must inform Lord Doufan as well as was possible and put trust in that man's abilities.

Lareth remembered his last interview with the ambassador before he left Celatas and the words Doufan had spoken to him then. Radal serves the king, he had said, but I serve the kingdom. The king smiled briefly at the memory — it was so like the man.

Let him now serve well.

He looked out from the battlements toward Lama. How often before had he done so? He would need men on the ground there. Radal had a company at his service, the king knew, and that threat must be countered. He would send trusted soldiers, a few at a time, to muster in the lands of Count Dordos.

Perhaps it would not be amiss to send a few through Doram Pass as well, and Sir Blen with them. Yes, he must send word and soldiers to the knight.

And have more men mustered here at Mountain Keep. He might yet, as he had once told his lord councilor, ride into Lama himself at the head of an army. It might be the only way to put things right.

3

"I myself drove the dagger into the old man," boasted Sojel. It was unusual for the sergeant to brag but it was unusual as well for him to be so drunk.

"We're going to see some real action now, my boys," said he. "The master has come and is ready to unleash us." Sojel knew not that his master no longer wielded any power in Sharsh and perhaps he would not have cared. His loyalty was all to Radal the man.

"You should have hanged many times over, Sergeant," said one of his ruffians.

"That goes for all of us," muttered another.

"But we haven't yet, have we?" asked Sojel, his high cheekbones — evidence of his Muram heritage — catching the glare of the fire. "We are kings until the moment we mount that scaffold, answering to none but ourselves and Asak."

There came grunts of agreement from around the blaze.

"Will he come here?" asked one.

"I know not and it is not mine to ask. I sent a couple fellows and a horse to him." The mercenary snickered. "Vanob's old mount. It's a good piece of horseflesh."

He rose, only a tad unsteadily. "We ourselves must move our camp in the morning. Be ready." Sergeant Sojel staggered off to find his bed and dreamless sleep.

Fachalana found herself staring at her hostess. There was something about her, something she sensed.

"Carrana" she asked, a bit uncertainly, "are you with child?"

Ansa glanced quickly and sharply toward her friend, and then back to the princess.

The woman nodded an assent. "How did you know, Lana? Has Modi been telling our secrets?"

"No, I just — knew it somehow."

Carrana looked pleased and a little frightened. Ansa could not fault her for the second; Fachalana scared her now and again, as well. "Please let it go not further than we three. Modi does not want his father to know until we are safely back in the capital. He fears it would distract the king."

Ansa spoke up. "The prince has a head on his shoulders."

"When he chooses to use it," replied Carrana dryly. Fachalana laughed openly at the remark. That was very much the Modareth she had know all her life, bookish and full of knowledge, and often spectacularly impractical.

The Anian, not knowing him so well, did not laugh with her. "When are those boys getting back?" she asked.

"If they only tour the vineyard, in time for lunch," answered Carrana. "If they stop to sample its products, maybe never!"

Donzalo had only one room in the keep of Count Orgelo, but it was quite a large one. That seemed to be the norm here, in this rambling edifice.

"If we run out of space, we double and triple up," said the servant who had shown him to his quarters. "This way, we needn't build so many rooms."

Accordingly, the young knight told his bodyguard to move into the room with him. No one objected. They were rather a relaxed people here at Tod-ford.

Or a lazy people, said Habidros. The Cuddonian did not approve at all of their lax ways. "I could take this place with ten good men," he claimed, "and lose not a one of them."

To which Copago had replied, "They do not put much faith in fortifications. The soldiers of Count Orgelo are ready to ride quickly anywhere rather than hide behind walls."

Donzalo did not envy Sir Copago his task here. That knight was, indeed, immediately made master of arms for Sorsen's household. In that

Sir Sorsen rarely remained home, this meant Copago would do much traveling.

All knew that Sir Copago was very much a homebody. He might not soon send for his family when he must live in so unsettled a manner.

"Sir Donzalo," called Sorsen, as he came down to the great central hall on his second morning. It was higher than the hall at Castle Rosam, a full two stories with an arcade around the upper level, and built all of rough-hewn logs. "Come greet your cousin Daboreth."

"Hail, Cousin," said the man. Donzalo remembered the young count from a visit he had made to County Rosam. It had been for Ros's naming, near a year and a half ago, hadn't it?

"My greetings to you, Count Daboreth," said he. Despite his title, this cousin of his held sway over less land than Donzalo's own uncle.

Sir Sorsen stepped between them and wrapped an arm around each man's shoulders. Sorsen was of more than normal height, but still had to reach up a bit for Donzalo. "Come have some breakfast.

"Ho, you," he called to a passing servant. "Have food sent for we three. Eggs. Plenty of eggs. Come on, kinsmen."

Donzalo had never greatly cared for Sorsen's bluff persona — which he suspected was at least partly assumed — and could see that his cousin had similar feelings. But one must put up with things from ones host.

Sorsen released the two when a guardsman came hurrying up to him. After a brief, low conversation, he said, "My apologies, I must let you breakfast alone. There is word of bandits crossing our lands." He grabbed a large piece of beef from the plate of a man seated nearby and rushed out the doors, gnawing upon it.

"By bandits, he means smugglers who have not paid the proper bribes," remarked the count. "Shall we eat?"

Shortly, a boy from the kitchen came to them with three plates. When he saw there were only two men, he shrugged and left the third portion sitting on the table.

There were, indeed, plenty of eggs, along with the beef that seemed to appear at every meal in Keep Arvaram. The bread that accompanied them was, in Donzalo's opinion, heavy and of rather low quality.

That did not prevent him from starting on the absent Sorsen's plate when he had finished his own. Donzalo found that he had an appetite this morning.

His cousin watched for a while, clearly amused but polite. As Donzalo remembered, Daboreth was a somewhat retiring sort, not inclined to initiate a conversation. He was a bit that way himself, he had to admit.

"Are you staying long, Cousin?" he asked.

"Only a day or two," came the reply. "And you?"

"Haven't decided." They ate in silence a while longer.

"You would be welcome to visit my home," spoke Daboreth.

Donzalo nodded only, as a rather tough piece of steak was in his mouth at that moment. "I would be honored, Cousin," he responded, when able.

"Call me Dabbi. Everyone does."

"Donni." He looked at his cousin. "How soon can we get out of this place?"

Daboreth laughed, somewhat circumspectly at first and then more loudly, shaking his head. "As soon as possible," said he.

"It seems like an exchange of prisoners," joked Tiana. "You come here, I go there."

Tiana had a somewhat skewed sense of humor in Janona's view, but she could see her point.

"Do you truly think your husband will stay at Keep Rosam?" she asked.

"He blustered a great deal about only trying it out and insisted on me remaining here for now, but I have no doubt he will settle into the job. 'Twill keep him out of mischief until he calls for me." Tiana turned her eyes back to the knitting in her lap.

For just whom is she making those little boots? wondered Janona.

The third woman there said nothing. Sima mourned still in her heart for her lost Borrago and found it hard to be merry.

"Like my Copago, he is a man who feels called to his duty," said Janona quietly. She too was mourning a loss, even if only a temporary one.

"Does anyone know what Grippo is up to?" asked Sima of a sudden. "I've barely seen him."

Janona had an answer. "When not attempting to unpack and organize all of Donzalo's books, Grippo has been serving as secretary to Sir Paren."

The older woman nodded her head. "He could find worse employ."

"He will be ordained someday, Mother, I am sure of it. If not here, in some other county by some other hierophant."

"Not among those Arvaram heretics, I would hope!" objected Sima.

The other two looked at each other; both had heard Brother Grippo express sentiments that might be seen as favoring the Lorjam Pontifex.

"Certainly not, Dame Sima," said Tiana, "most certainly not."

Radal had been able to bring only one thing with him, other than the dagger at his belt, the clothes he wore, and the small grimoire he kept always on his person. That was the ebony cask which held his most powerful object of magic. All the way here, clinging to the back of the dragon, he had made certain not to let it slip from him.

There were many other things in his tower, back at Mountain Keep, that he might have wished to bring, but the sorcerer could do without them. He could raise magics enough, here in this dusty, crumbling keep.

And he would.

But for now, he was depending on his human agents. Sojel had sent him a satisfactory mount, should he need it, and a couple of men to do his bidding. Soon more messengers would be going back and forth between Lord Radal and the sergeant, as well as his various spies. Not all those messengers need be human.

Then, there was Fachalana.

He had tried to make contact with his daughter. She was blocking him and, moreover, disappearing into some place he seemed unable to follow. That took great power.

Radal sighed. So it must be. He would never see his Fachalana again in the flesh but he could still hope to speak to her once more. Just once more.

4

Fachalana would not permit her father to link with her. Not now, not as things were. When he pressed too strongly she would take refuge in her silver world. She did not want to speak with him. She feared to speak with him.

Had he remained in Mountain Keep, not gone forward with his madness, she might have been open to Lord Radal. But the news had, in time, reached here of his flight.

With it came Sir Blen's new orders. She would miss the knight, even if he were a bit stuffy. Ansa would miss him, too, she was sure.

She heard a creaking in the courtyard below, and voices. Who might that be? The soldiers on guard knew not to let anyone in.

Oh, it was Murbalana and Doo with their cart, and the other soldier who had accompanied them to Lama. Who was that fourth fellow? He did look familiar.

"My luggage!" she exclaimed. "Maresta! Our luggage has arrived!"

She rushed to the cart to find her travel chest, the one with all the drawers and the top that became a vanity. Fachalana greatly missed that chest and its contents.

Ansa followed more cooly, and greeted the tired travelers. "Pol, isn't it?" asked she, when the young man climbed down from his steed.

"Yes, ma'am. You — you remember me?"

"Why, Jobareth Nafal told me you were his chosen man. How could I forget that?"

Pol felt quite puffed up at that moment.

As well he should, having shepherded this group across the mountains on less than well-maintained and somewhat dangerous roads.

"Is Sir Blen here, my lady?" he asked. He thought he should be making a report to someone official.

"Off preparing for his own trip across the mountains," Ansa told him. "He might want to take you back with him."

"Not soon, I hope. I am very tired of going up and down, ma'am!"

Daboreth did not truly have a keep at all, only a manor-house surrounded by a wooden palisade. The pair of cousins, accompanied by Habidros and the single attendant the count had brought with him, left the home of Orgelo as early as manners permitted the day following their meeting. They had spent much of that day in conversation, as Count Orgelo seemed to have quite forgotten his guests.

Guesare chose to remain behind, saying only that a private matter must claim his attention. Donzalo surmised that private matter was the handsome young fellow who sat enthralled by the minstrel's playing the night before.

Let Guesare have his flings. There was no need to burden Dabbi with another guest, anyway.

"Much of my day here is spent with my herds," said the count, as he gave them a tour of his holdings. How old is he? wondered Donzalo. Thirty, maybe, and he knew he had been count nearly a decade. His father must have passed when he was young. But then, so had Donzalo's, hadn't he?

"Have you a wife to help you with all this, Cousin?" he asked.

"Not yet. Count Orgelo keeps throwing his eligible relatives at me when I visit but I have been able to dodge them so far."

"I could find you someone suitable back home in no time," said Habidros. "A man like you is appreciated in the Cuddon." He sniffed at the air. "What is that stench?" Donzalo could smell it too.

"Oh, there is much brimstone on my lands. Where it rises to the surface, it ruins the grazing."

Donzalo and his bodyguard exchanged a meaningful look. "Might we see some of it?" asked the young knight.

The count shrugged. "If you wish. It's not useful for much other than curing the mange."

Soon they were surveying a hillside streaked with the near-pure mineral. "A treasure!" exclaimed Habidros. Daboreth was completely baffled.

"Know you not, man, that brimstone is an essential ingredient of gunpowder?" asked Donzalo.

"The other necessary components are easier to come by," added Habidros. "Yon woodlands would provide charcoal and your cattle could be a ready source of saltpeter."

Donzalo continued. "Much of the brimstone we use now must need come from Lorj. I hear there are great mines in the north-west of the island."

"They are closest thing on earth to Asak's realm, says Guesare. He has viewed them," said Habidros, "or claims to have."

"Even with his customary exaggerations, I would not doubt it," replied Donzalo, who had read of those mines. He turned to his kinsman. "You are wealthier than you know, Dabbi. Far wealthier."

The nobleman stared at his young cousin. "What am I to do?"

"We can think of some things," replied Donzalo, with a wink to the Cuddonian. "Let us get back to your manor so we might discuss them."

Ros had again climbed to the top of the divan, standing perched there. He growled.

"He must be a tiger today, my lady," said Traspa. "I dare not get close to the boy for he will surely pounce on me."

"Ros! Get down from there." He only growled more loudly at his mother.

"He can be obstinate," observed the maid. "It is good that he is speaking some now but I wish that he knew other words than *no*."

"That is perhaps the best word a ruler can know," observed Count Bolos from the doorway.

"Husband, I did not know you were there." Lomela put aside her embroidery and went to kiss him on the cheek. She could smell the wine on his breath. "You do not visit here much anymore."

"I know, I know." Bolos shrugged. "And I've no good excuse." He held out his arms to his heir, who leaped into them with a great roar. The count dropped onto the couch with the boy in his lap.

"Our Corgos has decided to stay," be said, "and has sent for his wife. She will come down with my uncle when next he visits. What boy, you are a pick-pocket now?" He removed Ros's hands from the purse hanging at his belt. "Ha, he was able to untie the strings!"

"He is clever, my lord," offered Mistress Traspa.

"I know nothing of this Tiana he has married but I think the happiness of my master of arms depends upon the happiness of his wife. I would have her feel welcome here."

"She will live in the keep?" asked Lomela.

"Aye. No living outside the walls for Sir Corgos. The man likes to be close to his work." He put the boy down beside him. "I am going to put the both of them in my old rooms. Please do help her find her way about, won't you, my lady?"

"Most assuredly, my husband. It will be good to see new faces." Indeed, it would, she said to herself. This place has been dull lately.

Ros growled again and started to climb the back of the divan.

It was not proving to be as profitable a season as Galaro and his company had hoped. Many called for pulling out of the fair as soon as possible.

"Let's stick it out another week, boys," said the Cuddonian. "If things are no better, I'll be first to start packing up."

It was Bolos and his suspicions that was hurting everything. Yes, the death of old Borrago and the cancellation of the tourney had put a damper on the fair, but trade had been good enough until someone shot at the new count.

Now he was banishing traders for no reason and arresting honest travelers to be questioned up in the keep. That was no way to do business. Count Borrago had known that, despite his exorbitant fees and tariffs. They might grumble but the merchants could live with those, aye, and make a profit too.

If too many did decide to pull out of the Summer Fair, the whole thing might collapse. This was the hub for trade throughout central Lama, and much of what lay beyond. It was where merchants from all over bought their wholesale goods to carry far and wide.

"One more week," he told them again, "and we'll see."

5

"I had mused upon gunpowder production while at my uncle's keep," Donzalo told the man seated across the large round table from him. The table, like much of the furniture in Daboreth's home, was of pine brought down from the mountains. Indeed, as was much of Daboreth's home itself. "He certainly has enough trees to provide the charcoal and I have heard of brimstone deposits across the hills of the Cuddon in the lower Siph valley."

"Which is thoroughly in Anian hands," objected Habidros, seated to his left. "I'm not sure how they would feel about that plan."

"The Ani, as everyone else, like to make a profit, Habi. If it were worth their while, they would send their brimstone over the hills.

"But this is better."

"What of the saltpeter?" asked Daboreth.

"There are methods to extract it from the dung of your cattle," said Habidros. "You've plenty enough of that."

Donazalo spoke. "Back home, there are caves in the hills rising to the Cuddon. Those caves are full of bats and their droppings. That's the best source."

"Aye," agreed Habidros, "or at least the easiest to gather."

The fourth man at the table was the count's master of arms. Here, that title meant essentially foreman. The leathery fellow felt that firearms would never replace the bow and was cool to this entire discussion. The idea of profits, however, did keep him interested. His master, if not exactly impoverished, could use a better cash flow.

"So are we talking about making this gunpowder here or at County Rosam?" he asked.

"Here, I would think," said Donzalo. "My brother would not approve one of my projects right now."

He looked to his cousin. "It will take money to get started. And do not think of asking old Orgelo for it."

"No, Donni, when he was done there would be money nowhere but in his own pockets."

To the surprise of all, the man of arms made a most astute comment. "Sharsh might be interested. We are near the southern pass here and I'm sure they would like a source other than the Coradeans."

Habidros nodded in agreement. "They would buy just the brimstone. You wouldn't need make the powder here at all."

Donzalo did not like that idea, even while recognizing its merits. He so wanted to make gunpowder!

"More profit in making it in Lama and selling it in Lama,"he argued. "Why give it to Lareth for a few pennies?" Especially when it could be used in those cannons he had long imagined back in County Rosam.

Habidros took a gulp from his tankard. He didn't know how these Lamans could stand to drink this thin, warm ale. "This talk of the pass interests me. Is it much used?"

"Orgelo tries to discourage its use in various ways," asserted Count Daboreth. "It is to his advantage to have trade come around the mountains in the south so he can better control it. Still," he continued, "there is always some traffic."

"More in the winter, when the northern route is less attractive," added the master of arms.

"The way to it runs through the lands of my neighbor to the north and he is no friend of Orgelo," said Daboreth. "Not that he likes me much, either."

"It's just your misfortune to be stuck between them, boss," observed the count's master of arms.

"Well," said Donzalo, "we are not going to build a gunpowder factory tonight, nor even on the morrow. This will take much planning.

"But, Dabbi, it might not be a bad idea to start gathering brimstone that can be refined when the time comes."

"And maybe some cow patties as well," suggested Habidros. "The stench of one can cover the stink of the other!"

Pol sipped from his goblet. "It's passable, I suppose."

"Spoken like a true son of Arolin," laughed Sir Blen. "This wine of Dor is an acquired taste, I think."

"It's unrefined," Pol asserted. "Too sweet, too strong — too *everything*."

"We need the expert opinion of the legate. He made you a sergeant, eh?"

"I think it was somewhat in jest, sir."

"Even his jests have meaning. He is far more calculating than one might realize." And he recognized potential in this lad. "I grew up in the valley of the lower Chas and what wine we produce there is only sold in the local taverns.

"Have you family in Arolin?"

"All dead, sir, slain by marauding Muram soldiers."

"Ah." The two sat in silence for a while, in the shade of a great magnolia that grew just without the keep's low walls. I would have this cut down, thought Blen. There should be no cover for enemies to approach.

"I have a dilemma, Pol," said the knight. "I must cross into Lama with the men we are being sent, yet I do not like leaving the ladies here without a guardian. Not to mention the prince, himself.

"Might I trust you to remain here in my stead?"

"What would I know of such a commission, sir? Are there not soldiers stationed here?"

"That is what they are — soldiers. You have shown you can be more, lad." A slight smile came to Blen's face. "A fairly able spy, for one thing. It took me a while, but I have seen through your subterfuges, Pol. You had me underestimating you.

"So, be my spy here and keep an eye on those two."

The boy actually wanted to stay, didn't he? I think he will do well, and it is not that great a matter, after all.

"Now you must tell me of your journey here. Everything, so I may know what to expect across the mountains."

"Welcome back, my boy. How were things at Daboreth's?"

"Interesting, my lord — for a while." He had been gone, between travel and visit, a full week.

"Life can grow boring at his place. He's a good man. Needs a wife, though. I'll find him one he likes one of these days!" Count Orgelo gave his guest an appraising look. "Perhaps you could use a bride, too. Have you met my sister's daughter?"

Donzalo had seen the woman in question and thought she looked altogether too much like Sir Sorsen. "I am but a younger son, on the road and with little prospects at the moment," he said. "Perhaps someday."

The answer satisfied the count. "So, will you remain with us a while, Sir Donzalo?"

"I am not certain, my lord. Perhaps I should see what my friend Guesare wishes to do."

"Oh, the minstrel grew bored too and set off for Todmouth yesterday. Says he may await his brother there, or go meet him on the road."

"Hmm, I have wanted to see that town. Perhaps, sir, I shall ride down myself in a day or two."

"'Tis a mean place, Donzalo, full of filth and whores. I am sure you would much prefer the company of my niece."

They knew the boy had gone south with Count Orgelo. Beyond that, there was little intelligence.

He must send out scouting parties. Sojel wanted to be out himself, rather than sitting here awaiting orders. His second could do that.

The sergeant craved action. He would take a couple men and head toward Todmouth. He could set up a sort of headquarters there, where his spies in the region might report to him.

And Sojel might, perhaps, find things to divert himself in that town.

Best he make a wide swing around that little village, though, and cross somewhere else. Someone just might recognize him from his last visit there. It would have been dangerous to have a large body of men on the road after that — patrols always increased after such incidents.

But they also always forgot them, didn't they, sooner or later?

Summer Fair had limped along for another week, even regaining some of its vigor, but Galaro knew it was time to take to the road.

"We stuck it out for three weeks, men, and made our profits," he said to his assembled company. "Not the profits we might have liked but not so bad, either.

"So I put it to you: do we go or remain for the last week of the fair?"

"Let's pack it up," said one.

"Agreed."

"Aye, the road calls!"

Not one voice spoke to the contrary.

"Then we go, lads," announced the burly trader. "And good riddance to Ros-town until next year. May we find more profits then!"

"To profits!" came an answering voice, accompanied by cheers and the raising of many flagons. The men quickly dispersed and began the methodical and efficient loading of their wagons.

6

It was good to have money in his pockets but Perdos remained frugal. Maybe he could use it to rebuild the burned-out inn when he finished his business. That would be a fitting use for the innkeeper's cash.

Yes, he could see himself there, greeting customers from behind the bar. Why not Hendel in the kitchen? The cook would probably be interested in investing in a real inn rather than manning a stall by the river. And a wife by his side and maybe kids who would grow to help out around the place.

Stop daydreaming, he told himself, and pay attention to the work at hand. Sir Perdos doubted it would do much good to travel up the Tod in hope of learning anything. He did not know the country well enough and it was, moreover, mostly open countryside that offered little concealment for him. Best he stay here in town for a few days, take a room at *The Truculent Troll*, and listen to what gossip there might be.

He let his hand rest on the hilt of his long sword. Would he ever get to use it on Guesare?

And once he got that chore out of the way, he would very much like to bury it in the gut of Sojel.

The crossing was not difficult on horseback but Blen saw that it might not have been quite so simple for Pol and the cart he had escorted. The way was often narrow, often steep. Rock falls seemed commonplace and one must either try to get around them or attempt to move them.

It seemed that neither Sharsh nor Count Mussago on the Laman end was particularly interested in maintaining the road. He remembered Nafal talking about it, that the legate's family would like to see more trade pass through here. Blen was not sure he would want to transport wagon-loads of wine across Doram Pass.

Mussago knew to expect him and his troop of two twenties, and would give them safe passage. That money had exchanged hands, Sir

Blen had no doubt. They could encamp near his southern border and wait.

Blen's duty here was to keep an eye on Count Orgelo's movements, should trouble arise in Lama. Their host apparently was not fond of County Arvaram and its lord and just might add some of his own troops to those of Sharsh, if he felt the need.

They now descended into Lama. It was poor scrubby country here. Could there once have been forest covering these hills, long since cut and not replaced?

He looked to his map. There was a town at the confluence of the Tod and Weldar. It would not do to take a large body of men into such a place but he might send one or two to listen for any news.

He might even go himself.

This latest bit of news his spies had brought him intrigued Radal. It seemed that his daughter had ridden out to meet the king, without telling him, and imparted some great secret to Lareth.

King Lareth had told him he had new intelligence about Donzalo, a secret that changed everything, when he came to him later that day, hadn't he? Had that information come from Fachalana? If only he could speak to the girl!

The prophecy — it had spoken of Donzalo's son. Was there something there he should know? Did the boy have a bastard somewhere of whom they had been unaware?

No point in wondering. But this might be the reason Fachalana refused his link so steadfastly. She could be afraid of revealing too much.

There were ways he could force her but he did not wish to use them on his daughter. She was not strong enough to withstand him if he brought all his powers to bear but what might become of her own mind if he did so? No, he dare not take that path.

But he would destroy Donzalo. That had not changed.

"I intend to have all these songs in a book," said Prince Modareth. "I know a good printing house in Celatas."

"The one Jobareth uses?" asked Lady Fachalana.

The prince had been taking down every lay and ballad Ansa knew. The Anian knew quite a few, and that did not include the ones in her native language.

"Yes, that is the one, my lady."

Pol was never quite certain of his place here. He knew he was not part of this noble circle and did not try to be. But Blen had asked him to take his place and that meant keeping close to them. The foursome would have included him without thinking but allowed him his reticence.

So he usually stayed in corners or near doors, eyes open for anything he thought seemed dangerous. He was exceedingly meticulous in this.

"It is too bad we can not show the tunes somehow," spoke Carrana.

"Most, my lady," said Ansa, "are old and traditional melodies. Minstrels have been reusing them for centuries."

"Still, my wife is right," Modareth said. "There are ways of writing down the tunes but none of us here know them. My brother's wife," he continued, "can sit down with a piece of paper before her and play a tune from it, even one she has never heard before!"

"Our son must be taught to do that," said Carrana, taking her husband's hand.

"Or daughter, my dear," he replied. "You appear tired."

"Yes, Modi, I think I'd best to bed."

"I too, then. I bid you good night, my ladies."

As the royal couple departed the room, Ansa leaned close to Fachalana and whispered, "I think our Pol is rather cute, don't you?"

"I thought you liked Blen, " was the reply.

"May I not think they are both handsome men?" objected Ansa. "And Blen is far away now."

Such an attitude seemed frivolous to Fachalana.

Pol seemed to be alert to something, cocking an ear upward. "Are there more squirrels in the ceiling?" asked Ansa.

"I — do not think so, my lady." The young man turned and ran toward the stair.

Guesare rode beside the wide, muddy River Tod. Its course had run almost due south for some distance, before making a great loop back to the east to join the Weldar.

The Cuddonian could have followed a road that cut across that loop and would have carried him back to the river at its mouth, but he was in no hurry. Guesare wished to see the Tod in all its length, though it would add the better part of a day to his travel. Down here the soil was richer and farm fields lay on either side of the water.

Was this still part of Count Orgelo's land? He wasn't quite sure where it ended but knew it did not include Todmouth. The minstrel didn't remember any border guards along the way but they were lax about that sort of thing in the south. County Arvaram's borders were too long and Orgelo's soldiers too few to ever hope to seal them.

There were shanties along the road now, slums on the outskirts of Todmouth. A slatternly woman stood before one and beckoned to him. Guesare shook his head politely. Not my type, he laughed to himself.

As he remembered, there were three taverns in the town. Yes, and the one across the river. There was the *Troll*, of course. That was the best. Oba's place, down near the docks, was thoroughly disreputable and no place for him.

The Count's Cow lay a little further from the center of town, which meant it was both cheaper and quieter. The clientele, when he had visited before, tended to be working men from the country, drovers, teamsters. That should be his destination.

Such men were likely to have news for him. They were just the sort to buy him a drink for singing a sentimental song, too.

7

There was a shadow with a sword.

Pol was no great swordsman but he rushed the man, swinging his own blade. It caught the surprised would-be assassin on his left arm as he turned to flee. The young Arolinian threw himself at the man's legs and brought him to the floor.

By that time, Fachalana had caught up to him, a dainty dagger in her own hand, and, not far behind her, Ansa with a pair of guardsmen.

Once the two soldiers had taken charge of his captive, Pol said, "I heard a noise, his scabbard on the windowsill, I think, and then the sound of steel being drawn from the scabbard. That sound I would know anywhere."

The prince stood silhouetted in his doorway, the Princess Carrana behind him. He looked at Pol a moment and then held out his hand.

"Give me your sword, man," said he, "and kneel."

He tapped the young soldier on each shoulder, saying, "I name you Sir Pol, Knight of Sharsh," and handed back the weapon.

"From this time you must be ever at my side, Sir Pol." The prince smiled toward the girls. "I can not expect the Lady Fachalana to be my full-time bodyguard, after all."

"Pol has gifts, too," whispered Ansa to her friend, "and I still think he is cute."

"He must have come over the wall," said the captain when he came to make his report. He appeared quite perturbed that he had let an assassin nearly reach his royal charge. "Sir Blen was right. I need to take down all those trees."

"And double your guard, " said Fachalana. The man nodded in agreement.

Modareth glared at the soldier from beneath raven brows. The lady could see that the prince was seething, barely containing his anger. He had always had a temper and could be prone to outbursts. It is good that he is managing to control it, she thought.

How like his eyes are to his father's, she also thought, to no particular purpose.

"You must learn who the man is," demanded the prince. "Have you questioned him yet?"

"He says nothing — so far. He seems to be Muram."

Pol spat at the mention of that name but did not speak.

"I would guess him a hired sword," continued the captain. "He is unlikely to know anything beyond who handed him his blood money."

"That would be a start," Modareth said. "Let us hope it is not also an end."

Princess Mara looked her husband up and down.

"It is a good choice, my husband. No, an excellent choice."

"Once I wear them in public, there is no going back, you know. Our colors will be forever green and gold."

"They both honor your father and mark you your own man, Gawis. I think they are perfect." Mara did not add that she liked the way they went with his straw-colored hair.

"I hope he sees it that way."

"I hope he sees all the changes in you," she said. "You will be a great king, Husband."

"A king is only as great as those who stand with him. This I have learned lately and I think it may be the most important thing I might know."

He took his wife into his arms and kissed her brow. "Let us pray to Jov that it will be a time yet before I wear the crown."

Princess Mara did not pray to Jov, being a good Kamatian, but she shared her husband's sentiment.

How this mud sucked at his feet! Were the streets ever dry in Todmouth?

Guesare had dismounted and now led his pony up a backstreet. It would not do to let the steed hurt himself in this mire. He remembered this way as a shortcut to the inn, his destination.

"So, Sir Guesare. Well met!" Before him stood Lord Radal's right hand man, Sojel. He sensed more than saw the two ruffians who had moved into the street behind him.

The minstrel stepped away from his mount to give himself room to move. There was not time to reach the saddle and attempt to bolt out of this trap. They would have him down in the mud if he tried.

"Your overlarge charge is not with you? Still up at Orgelo's place I would guess." The sergeant sneered. "We can deal with him later.

"But you have been an hindrance to my master all along. He will thank me for removing you." Sojel, holding the heavy, curved blade he favored, began to circle to his left. Guesare knew the men behind him were moving too.

One rushed in and he turned to parry his attack, to be nearly overwhelmed by the other. And Sojel was circling, ready to strike when he saw an opening. That opening would inevitably come; Guesare could not fight three swordsmen. Especially not when this muck impeded his movement.

'Tis too bad none is here to commemorate my last battle, he told himself. I will attempt to make it a memorable one.

Or was there someone there?

Sojel had turned to face a newcomer. Guesare almost did not recognize the man for a moment, without his beard. Did he now face four opponents?

Then let this last battle be his best.

It seemed that life at Castle Rosam was starting to return to normal. Perhaps the presence of the new master of arms had something to do with it. The competent Corgos was straightening out much of the chaos of the past month.

Bolos, too, was beginning to settle down and again allowing visitors to the keep. Jobareth had not been there in weeks, not since the funeral.

It looked the same as he rode through the inner gate but it was not. A new count sat in Borrago's chair. Many of his old friends were gone, and some might never return.

But Lomela remained, his princess. Ultimately, did he really care about anything else here? His job as a diplomat was only a job, even if he rose to the top of the government some day. He lived still to serve her, as he had as a boy.

What a fool you are, Jobareth Nafal, he told himself. He wondered then if he should still marry the Lady Fachalana. Would there be any reason now?

But then again, why not?

A groom took his reins. He should present himself first to the count, even if this were not an official call. The old informality would not do, maybe never again.

Just where did Bolos have his offices now, anyway?

8

"Perdos?" Surprise and rancor mingled in Sojel's voice.

The tall knight had drawn his long, heavy sword, and faced mercenary and minstrel. But which man would he attack?

He saw the faces of the little innkeeper and his wife before him, and knew that Percos must wait for his vengeance. He would have understood. "Forgive me, Brother," murmured Sir Perdos and launched a fierce attack upon Sojel.

Guesare had no time for astonishment, as the other two were again upon him. Perhaps this pair he could deal with; they were not mean swordsmen but neither were they his equals.

Sojel was a skilled duelist, and a ferocious one, but he could not get inside the sweep of the long sword where he might do damage. He saw from the corner of his eye that one of his men was down, as he again caught the force of that blade on his own.

"Murderer!" hissed Perdos. He recognized that he hated the Muram more than any other man in the world, Guesare included. As much as his father. A great overhand swing batted the sword from Sojel's numbed hand. "Monster!" Another roundhouse half-severed the man's body. He lobbed the head from it before the torso hit the ground.

He looked about the street. The other two assailants lay dead and Guesare stood facing the knight, holding his sword defiantly before him, and bleeding from a great gash on his left shoulder.

Perdos looked at the wounded man. This was not how he wanted his revenge.

"Sir Guesare," he said, "we will not cross swords today. But the next time I see you I shall surely kill you."

Habidros shook his head. "We can not let you out of our sight, Brother!"

"You might well have been arrested if Sojel — or what was left of him — had not been recognized as an outlaw," added Donzalo. "And Count Orgelo's man here put in a good word for you."

"Is it true that this Perdos I've heard about rescued you?" asked Habidros.

"Without him I would have been lying dead in the mud, I have no doubts. But I do not understand it." The minstrel, an arm once again in sling, looked about the tavern's common room. "Where do we go from here?

"Orgelo could provide us passports if you would care to travel south. Or would you prefer to head back to your home, Donni?"

"Maybe both, in time, but for now, let's go enjoy the hospitality of Count Orgelo a bit longer and wait for Galaro to arrive."

"His niece will approve of that," observed Habidros.

Book IV
The Hand of the Sorcerer

Of Brothers: the Ninth Tale

1

First came the wild man, shooting sparks from both hands. "Make way! Make way!" he shouted. He lifted his thickly bearded face to the summer sky and howled.

All wrapped in the pelts of animals was he. "The hides protect him from his fireworks," whispered Donzalo to his companions. They seemed mostly those of coyotes.

Behind him came the procession, players of fife, beaters of drum, revelers of both genders and all ages.

This was all new to Habidros, who had seen no such spectacle either in the Siphic cities nor his Cuddonian homeland. His brothers, being more traveled, knew how Lamans celebrated the Feast of Plenty.

"They do this better at your home, Donni," said Guesare.

Galaro nodded agreement. "They haven't the money nor the people for it here. Tod-ford is no more than an overgrown village. Still," he continued, "there will be profits to be made this afternoon and, aye, all the night. I'd best back to my men."

Though Count Orgelo's seat was, indeed, little more than a village, folk from all over County Arvaram, as well as neighboring principalities, had gathered for the festival. Galaro and his band of merchants would do good business tonight and on the morrow.

As the Cuddonian trader exited, the Queen of Plenty entered. Two more wild men accompanied her, armed with great cudgels.

"It's Lenasha," said Habidros, smiling for no apparent reason.

"I've no doubt Orgelo arranged for her coronation," observed Guesare. "Now the question is, whom will she name as her King?" He gave Donzalo a sideways look. "I would suspect he hopes it to be you, Donni."

Count Orgelo's niece walked through the crowd, holding a crown of grape leaves in her large and rather calloused hands. Her gown was all of green and she herself wore a chaplet of wildflowers. Donzalo admitted to himself that the tall young woman, whom he was used to seeing in dusty riding outfits, looked very much a queen this day.

Right to their group she came. "I name you the King of Abundance — Sir Habidros!" she proclaimed, placing the crown on that knight's head.

Habidros only smiled all the more broadly, and perhaps, some would say, foolishly, as he accompanied his Queen to their thrones.

"You must learn to ride a horse properly. Many things may be done sidesaddle, but swinging a sword is not one of them."

Fachalana felt she just might be able to prove her friend wrong about that.

"I think I ride quite well this way," she sniffed, even while recognizing that Ansa was right — straddling her mount would be more practical, despite all her years of training otherwise.

"As well as anyone I've seen sitting sideways," agreed the Anian, "not that *that* counts for much."

"Shall I wear pants like you, Maresta?" asked Lady Fachalana, taking care to use her friend's pseudonym. "If I must ride like a man perhaps I should look like one as well!"

"Do I look like a man?" laughed her slender companion. "I suppose I might pass as a boy, on stage."

Fachalana glanced at the woman riding beside her. Since she had cropped her hair short to remove the dark-dyed ends, Ansa did appear rather boyish. "We shall have such a part written especially for you," she declared.

Then, a thought came to her. Fachalana was given to moments of inspiration, some of which actually made sense. "We could both pose as men if we chose to ride back into Lama. What better disguise?"

Ansa looked to her friend with surprise and then slowly nodded. "A most excellent idea, Lana. We may make a spy of you yet.

"But all the more reason to learn to ride astraddle. We shall fit you out with a proper saddle when we return to the stables."

This little patch of land, known as the Laman March, was the only place where the kingdom of Sharsh extended eastward beyond the mountains. Only four leagues was its width where it lay in the foothills below Mountain Keep, and twice that was its length.

Here Lareth was mustering a small army, a few hundred men, and a larger force at the keep, should they be needed. More might alarm the counts of Lama and might prove unwieldy if called upon to ride into the wide valley of the Weldar.

Nonetheless, men were also being mobilized on the other side of the mountains, in Sharsh, ready at both the King's Pass and that of Dor to invade in much larger numbers. King Lareth prayed to Jov and to any other gods that might be listening that such would be unnecessary.

Indeed, if all went well the men he had already sent secretly into Lama could be sufficient, the two-score Sir Blen had led into the south and twice that number the king had sent, a few at a time, to assemble in the lands of Count Dordos.

He rode now up into the mountains, returning to Mountain Keep. It could not be seen until one was almost upon it, hidden by a spur of the Zadcelam, around which wound the Royal Road. Lareth rode and pondered.

There had been another attempt on his son's life. Perhaps he should have ordered him back to the capital rather than only suggesting it. But then, the boy was probably as safe there at Grenethas, especially under the watchful eye of Lady Fachalana and her friends. He would have to learn more of this young fellow Pol — Sir Pol, now — who had stopped the latest would-be assassin.

Lareth sighed. He had been guilty of sending assassins to murder another man's son himself. Indeed, much of the current situation stemmed from those actions. To think that the boy he had wished dead was the father of the king's own grandson!

That his beloved daughter was an adulteress bothered him not one bit. The younger brother was obviously a much finer man than the husband with whom he and diplomacy had burdened her.

But it most definitely complicated things.

The nearby calls of a moorcock awakened Perdos. He was reminded of the clucking chickens in his family's yard, long ago. He should be feeding them or Father would be angry.

No, Father was dead these many years. The knight shook off the remainder of his sleep and rose. His blanket was wet with the fogs rising from the Weldar, close at hand.

Where now? Since his slaying of the mercenary Sojel, he had been uncertain of his course. Perdos had relieved himself of a great burden of hatred with that slaying.

Another might have said that Perdos had seen his father in the man he had killed. Perdos would have claimed that he just despised anyone who mistreated women. Be that as it may, he still sought vengeance on the minstrel Guesare.

That braying came from cormorants, didn't it? They sounded like a herd of asses. Too bad they weren't — donkeys could be turned into ready money. Perdos had found the presence of mind, following their clash, to gather the horses of Sojel and his two henchmen and use them to increase his supply of cash. There was a very practical businessman somewhere inside Sir Perdos.

He hated Guesare, yes, but it was not the same. He no longer desired simply to kill the man; no, he saw it now as a matter of honor, of vendetta, against an opponent he had come grudgingly to respect. Perdos would meet the Cuddonian fairly one of these days, sword against sword, and settle their quarrel. Sojel, he would have knifed from behind and felt no qualms.

Yet he was glad to have seen the man's face, before he severed head from body.

The Cuddonians were still up in County Arvaram. They wouldn't stay forever. He could linger here a while longer, pick up what news came along the road, and wait his chance.

"I had hoped she would name you, Donni," the count lamented. "Sir Habidros is a fine fellow but he is far too much like my son!"

"I think Habi wishes to leave my service and enter yours," said Donzalo.

"And Sir Copago wishes to do the opposite," replied Orgelo. "I am not opposed to the idea. Habidros is well suited to life in the saddle."

"As is your niece, my lord," remarked the young knight.

Orgelo rarely laughed aloud, as he did not like to show his missing teeth, victims of accident and of time, but now he did. "Indeed she is, my boy! I would have hoped for a higher match for her." He paused to glance meaningfully at Donzalo. "But if your cousin asks for Lenasha's hand — and she is willing — I think I would say yes."

"We should have suspected something as much time as those two spent riding together," observed Donzalo.

"What of her father?" he asked. Donzalo had heard nothing of her parents.

"Long dead." The count sighed. "He was, as you, a younger son of a count of Lama. Unlike you, he was a fool and wastrel and was murdered in a brothel. I am the girl's guardian.

"She has grown up here, learning more of horsemanship than of etiquette. Her mother," he added with a shrug, "devotes herself to religion.

"It appears the festivities of this night are winding down at last. I think I will to my bed."

"Dawn is as good a time as any, my lord," replied Donzalo.

2

His hound Sojel had served him well.

Now he was gone. So be it. The man had wrought his own undoing.

"What name has the second-in-command?" Radal asked the messenger.

"Dovolo, my lord," answered the man, a nondescript ruffian who carried a bad odor about with himself.

"Do you know if he can read?"

The man shook his head uncertainly. "Not mine to ask, sir."

Radal approved of such an attitude, in general. "Well, I'm sure somebody there can read my messages to him, even if he is unlettered. Whoever wrote this, perhaps." He held up the scrap of paper he had been holding.

The scoundrel seemed to have no answer to that. Radal shrugged and continued.

"You shall bear my message back to this Dovolo, confirming him as my new sergeant." Though he would now have to take more of a hand himself, the sorcerer recognized. "It will require some time. Go rest yourself." He turned from the man without further word and entered the ruined keep which served temporarily as his headquarters.

Who would have thought such a seeming fool as Perdos could be Sojel's bane? If Radal had known the knight were so capable he might not have thrown him aside, a tool that was no longer of use.

Perhaps the lesson here was to destroy such used tools, lest another pick them up.

Lord Radal wished he could pass such lessons on to the one person for whom he most cared now, his daughter Fachalana. He had begun to suspect that others protected her when she fled from his attempts at contact, shielded her from his link in some place he could not see. Did she guess that she had such guardians?

If he could discover who they were, he might be able to move against them. But there were other concerns requiring his attention now.

He might not be able to reach the mind of Fachalana but there was another, his spy in County Rosam, with whom he could form a link. The boy was of little talent but he would serve Radal's needs.

Benawis! he called.

What bow has set me to this futile flight,
Has sent me arcing to your armored heart?
Dare I trace the journey of that dart
To some willful archer of the night,

Some jokester god who, laughing, took his aim
At a mark no man might penetrate,
Leaving me to curse both love and fate?
No, I will myself take all the blame

And know I was a fool, as are men all,
For we choose to fly and, spent, must fall.

"The legate wrote that?" asked Sir Pol.

"It certainly sounds like him," opined Fachalana. She strongly suspected that the sentiments in the piece were directed toward their friend Lomela. He would always love his princess, even were he to wed the Lady Fachalana. "Is that his second book of poems, Modi?"

Prince Modareth nodded. "That it is, Lana. I fear my father is keeping him too busy to compose a third."

"Not to mention Fachalana giving him the task of writing a play for her," added Ansa.

"I have seen him at work on it, my ladies," Pol said, "pacing back and forth and reciting the lines he had written. Who is this Nordoc, anyway?"

"A king in Lorj, wasn't he?" hazarded Princess Carrana. "You are the scholar, Husband."

When no one else showed interest in taking on the subject, the prince sighed and spoke. Modareth was not greatly enamored of giving lectures.

"It was near eight centuries ago, on the Isle of Lorj, that Nordoc and Oemse lived. At that time, most of eastern Lorj was ruled by the Caram Empire."

"Cars was their capital, wasn't it?" asked Fachalana.

"Yes, but it was pronounced Caras then. The Lorjans have lately taken to dropping some of their vowels.

"Anyway, the Caram Emperors had been mighty and had also spread the Kamatian religion through their realm."

"Kamatianism drove their conquests, I have read," said Ansa.

Modareth nodded. "But the empire had grown weak and was torn by civil wars. That was when the northern provinces, subjugated lands which included the Coradean nation, rose up in rebellion. One of the growing powers that bordered the empire sent the mercenary captain Nordoc with his company to aid the uprising.

"Naturally, they hoped to bring the area under their sway in time or, at least, to discomfit and weaken the Caram without committing any of their own troops."

"Thus Oemse's Question," said Fachalana.

"Oh, I know that," piped up Carrana. *"And whom do you serve, Captain Nordoc?"*

There were smiles all around. "Yes, my wife. Nordoc stopped in one of the towns and asked them if they would continue to serve the Caram Empire. That is when the young rebel leader Oemse stepped forward and posed her famous question.

"And that is when Captain Nordoc decided to quit his paymasters and become his own man," Modareth concluded. Or so he thought.

"And became a king, sir?" asked Pol. 'King Nordoc' was the title of a well-known play, after all.

"Indeed. He grabbed a goodly portion of those northern provinces as his own and named his kingdom Oemsebe in honor of the woman who had shown him his destiny."

"And whom he loved," Fachalana added. "Nordoc married her but she was taken by the Caram troops and executed. That is the tragedy that Jobareth is writing."

"Tragic it might have been," was the prince's reply, "but it did not prevent Nordoc from taking several wives later on and fathering many unruly heirs.

"In time, Cel Oemsebe — which most called by its older name of the Northing Kingdom — was absorbed into the growing Coradean Empire."

He smiled benignly. "But the history of the Northing War is another lesson, children."

"Sir?" asked Pol. He seemed uncertain but went on. "Are there books I might read? That tell of these things?"

Modareth gestured toward the towering shelves that lined one side of the room. "I'll show you some, Sir Pol. We both may be doing more reading once the ladies are on the road."

"You are going to give us our passports, Modareth?" asked Fachalana.

"Yes, both the real ones and the false. I hope you two know what you are doing."

Pol had known nothing of this. "You are leaving, my ladies?"

Ansa answered. "We intend to sneak back into Lama and make sure Princess Lomela and Jobareth are safe and well." And Donzalo, too, she added to herself. "We needed passports both as ourselves and as, um, someone else." Of course, Ansa's legitimate passport would have her name as Maresta — few knew her true identity.

The young knight nodded. It was not his to question their motives. But he thought he should speak of another matter.

"I do not trust the legate's secretary, Benawis," he stated outright. "I would advise that you do not, as well."

"Count Daboreth looks much like your brother," remarked Galaro, "if your brother spent his days in the saddle."

Donzalo nodded absentmindedly. He had noted Daboreth's family resemblance. "Bolos does take after our mother's people." The young knight barely remembered his mother and, somewhere along the line, her loss had become mingled with that of his Jola.

"It will take the better part of two days to reach Dabbi's place. Are you certain you wish to come?"

"I want to see this brimstone. My men can sit here for a week. Business should be good enough." Galaro looked into his young companion's eyes. "And are you certain you will not come south with us then?"

"I think not," came the answer, yet Donzalo seemed uncertain.

He has no place to truly call a home now, thought Galaro. Why shouldn't he travel south with me, and Guesare, as well? There are many opportunities for a man such as he in the south.

"Here comes Orgelo," said Donzalo. Their host was flanked by Copago and Habidros.

"Greetings, my lord," said Galaro to Count Orgelo. "So, who is coming and who is staying?"

"I shall remain," spoke Habidros. "Sorry to leave you, Donni, but, well — you know why I stay. Between Guesare and Sir Copago and, yes, my oversize brother here, you will be well guarded."

Donzalo embraced his cousin and erstwhile bodyguard, whispering in his ear, "I expect an invitation to the wedding."

"Sir Habidros can teach my men much," Orgelo said. He turned to Copago. "It seems we were not able to become a home for you, my boy. I am sorry for that."

"My lord, I thank you for allowing me to serve for a while."

"Ah, Sir Copago, ever the steady one, aren't you? I know you did not enjoy riding with my son day after day." Orgelo smiled. "Even I could not take that much of him!"

He spoke then to Donzalo. "I am hearing unsettling things out of County Rosam. Be careful and know that we, too, are keeping an eye on happenings there. If need be, my men are ready to ride."

Guesare and Daboreth had strolled up to the small group. "Are *we* ready to ride?" asked the minstrel, in mock impatience.

"I believe we are," replied Sir Copago, and then added, allowing just a touch of wistfulness to enter his voice, "I wonder if the peaches are ripening back in County Rosam."

Count Mussago looked again at the message from Daboreth, his neighbor to the south. Borrago's son? He had no quarrels with County Rosam and didn't really care much, one way or the other, about Daboreth either. Certainly he would give them safe passage.

In fact, he should invite them to visit here. His secretary could write something for him to sign.

Mussago reached down and stroked the dog beside his chair. Mussago had a great love for dogs and was noted as a breeder. Indeed, he had given one to little Ros Rosam on his naming day. He wondered how it was doing these days. It should be fully grown by now, physically, even if still a playful puppy in many ways.

The count scratched at his chin with a plump hand. Those Sharshite soldiers he was letting camp on his land should know of this too. Didn't they have something to do with the Rosam? He must have the secretary send notice to Sir Blen, as well.

3

Benawis served Lord Radal.

But to serve Lord Radal was surely to serve himself. To serve himself was always the first goal of the young scholar.

Even before the lord councilor gave him this post as secretary to Nafal, Benawis had served. That day he had waited on a garden bench outside Radal's tall doors, the sorcerer had felt the young man's latent powers as his daydreams had, quite unconsciously, carried him into other worlds, recognized that he, untutored boy though he be, possessed talent.

He had learned from the great sorcerer. So what if he had not the natural gifts of a Radal? Any knowledge, any skill, could be used to further his own needs.

And all men had needs. Those who claimed that they did not put those needs foremost were liars. The gods, if they existed, would understand the appetites of men. Had they not provided the night so we might tend to them?

Radal had asked only of news at the keep, but Benawis sensed that he meant soon to act. Perhaps he would aid the dark lord with his schemes; perhaps he would not. It was widely known now that the man was out of favor.

It would depend on how he felt about it at the time — and where his own good lay.

His thoughts lingered for some time on Radal's daughter, the Lady Fachalana. She was a prize for which he might risk much, beautiful and full of power. Benawis knew without asking that the sorcerer would not hear of such a thing; indeed, it would be worth his life to suggest it.

It was good that Lord Radal had taught him to cloak his own power or she might have found him out. The time might come when Benawis would be able to use that power to take what he desired.

A man hung from the gibbet by the road.

"It is our would-be assassin," said Ansa, as calmly as possible. Ansa had seen more of death than she liked to admit but its presence shook her still. She hoped it always would.

Her companion briefly looked up at the hanged man and then quickly away, urging her horse forward. Lady Fachalana had her own memories of a death that haunted her at times.

"A Mur, they said. Do you think Mura had anything to do with this?"

"I would doubt it. What would the Muram emperor care who sat the throne of Sharsh?" asked the Anian. "Many Muram soldiers turned mercenary after your king's last war with them."

"Your people have warred with them too, haven't they?"

"Border skirmishes in the disputed territories north of Lama. We never pressed into the Muram homeland." Ansa was feeling more herself now that they were well past the gallows. "And since, we have withdrawn from that area altogether."

"I suspect our Pol has his portion of Muram blood, considering where he was born. It has not been long since Arolin was a part of their empire."

"Ha, do not say that to him!" warned Ansa. Both knew of his hatred of the Mura and the reasons for it. "He doesn't look it, anyway."

"You look rather Anian today," remarked Fachalana. "I do hope you intend to change out of those trousers before we reach the pass."

"And you need better conceal that pigtail," her friend replied. The noblewoman had pulled her long hair back into a tight braid that she had tucked into the collar of her leather jerkin. A voluminous beret did not completely hide it.

"A helmet will cover it," Fachalana said.

"We can't go armored all the time, even if it does best hide our forms."

The Sharshite looked her companion over. "You look every bit the boy you pretend to be. A rather fearsome boy, too, with that bow." Ansa wore a recurved bow of the eastern sort on her back.

"And your height is an asset to your deception," said Ansa. "You are taller than many a soldier we have seen on the road today."

"There are quite a few, aren't there? Something must be going on."

"No doubt, Lana, no doubt. But we can't expect the king to tell us everything."

That her father was behind this, the Lady Mara was most certain.

Or, more properly, the circle of powerful ministers who surrounded the emperor. They were the true rulers of Partanaca, the Imperial Council. It was they who had sent her to this marriage in Sharsh.

Not that she minded that. It was a good marriage as such political matches go. She and Prince Gawis were fond enough of each other, even if not in love.

Yet her marriage to the heir to the throne of Sharsh was at the root of this trouble. That same council, undoubtedly, had sent assassins against his younger brother.

She looked at that heir, seated in a comfortable chair in the corner of her chambers. He was pulling on his soft leather boots.

The beginnings of a beard, darker than his straw-colored thatch of hair, framed the boyish face. Gawis would look good with a beard, she thought. People might even take him more seriously.

"Your brother will come back to the capital, you think?"

Gawis looked up from his lacing. "Father did not order it. And it is still very hot here." He smiled at his wife. "Would that we could go to the mountains for a month."

He considered that thought for a moment. "You and the girls should get out of Celatas until the autumn. There are many villas in the hills that would welcome you."

"You know I love the heat of summer, Husband." Lady Mara was a child of the hot southern isles. "But it might be good for the children." She laughed at a sudden thought. "Your brother would be most surprised if we showed up at his door!"

Gawis laughed with her. "I should like to see his face."

"Perhaps I and the girls will go down to the shore for a time."

The prince nodded. The sea was in his wife's blood. It would do her good to stay a while by its side. "An excellent idea, my dear. Just remember me now and again, sweltering here and attending to my princely duties."

"Have you seen the mines of Lorj, Sir Galaro?"

"No, but I know those on Ussan." Ussan was the largest of the isles that lay between Lorj and the mainland. "If there be brimstone there and brimstone here, then it would not be surprising to find it in the lands that lie between, would it?"

"Orgelo's holdings, you mean?" asked Daboreth.

"Aye, and all the south-lands beyond County Arvaram. Though I have traversed that area many times and seen none."

"Let us hope Orgelo never sees any either," stated Donzalo, "or all this might be in vain."

The group gathered around the big table murmured their agreement.

"Have *we* seen enough?" asked Guesare. "Or need we spend more time looking at rocks?"

Sir Copago spoke. "We have seen quite enough. Now is the time for making plans."

"My plan shall be to ride back to Orgelo's in the morning, I and my man," said Galaro. "All I can do is wish you luck at this time. And thank my host for his hospitality," he added, with a nod toward Count Daboreth.

"It was my pleasure, Sir Galaro. Do bring those bagpipes your brother so maligns should you visit again."

"That I shall, my lord!"

"We should leave soon, as well, " said Copago. "What plans we intend for this brimstone we had best make now."

All eyes at the table turned toward Donzalo. Well, it was my idea, he told himself.

"The actual making of the gunpowder is easy enough — simply mix the proper ingredients in their proper proportions. A central location, perhaps near Ros-town or even Todmouth, might be best place to do that. The making of the ingredients will prove more difficult." The young knight paused so his comrades might speak. None did.

"Right here is our best source of brimstone. It can be refined and carted to whatever location we decide upon. It is not," he continued, "the ideal place for the rest of it, but could possibly serve."

"What forest remains in these parts is sparse," observed Copago. "The supply of charcoal would run short quickly."

"And fires are needed to burn and refine the brimstone, as well," said Donzalo. "Best the charcoal be made upriver, where wood is plentiful."

"We could always bring it down from the mountains."

"Yes, Dabbi, it would take a great deal of effort but that is an alternative."

The count nodded his agreement. He understood this.

"And then there is the saltpeter," said Sir Copago. "If Count Daboreth's cattle were more confined that might not be so difficult to obtain. But they are scattered across this sparse countryside."

"Yes," agreed Donzalo. "Again, it could be done here but it is not the most practical way. I would really like to get at those caves filled with bat droppings back home."

"That is not a statement I ever expected to hear from you, " said Guesare. "Nor any other man, for that matter."

"I have come to expect the unexpected about here, lately," laughed Daboreth. "To the unexpected!" he toasted, raising his cup.

"The unexpected!" came from all around the table.

"I think," Guesare then said, "that we should spend the next day or two helping our friend Daboreth and his men set up their refinery. It is simple enough a process." The minstrel was the only one of the group who had ever actually seen it done. "That accomplished, we can be on our way and leave further plans wait."

Donzalo nodded. He knew that they looked to him for decisions, even though he was the youngest and least experienced of them all.

"So, this Count Mussago wishes us to visit his keep?" he asked. "Is it far out of our way?"

"Hardly at all," replied Daboreth, "and he and Count Dordos control much of the road between Doram Pass and the Weldar. It would be good to have him as your friend.

"In fact, he invited me as well so I shall accompany you!"

4

"As anticipated, sir, the man knew nothing beyond the name of he who hired him." The captain looked up from his report. "Which was, of course, a false name."

"Of course," came Modareth's even reply.

"None the less, we were able to learn something of this paymaster. He used a different name at the inn here in town — um, yes, a Marin Sorgovam," he said, finding it on the page. "I have no doubt, my lord, that it is false as well."

The prince tried to contain himself — he had intended to remain stern and severe throughout this interview — but broke out in laughter.

"False indeed, Captain. Marin Sorgovam was an ancient emperor of the Coradeans."

"It would seem, my lord, that your enemy has a sense of humor." This came from the ever-present Sir Pol. Pol took his duties as bodyguard seriously, even to sleeping on the threshold of his prince's bedchamber.

"And some learning," said Modareth.

"Might it be intended as a taunt, sir?" asked the captain.

"It may well be. Though had I been slain, I do not know who might have appreciated it."

The man himself, enjoying his private joke, thought Pol. "Is there aught else on the fellow?" he asked.

"A general description only, Sir Pol." The captain slightly resented this young fellow who had become the prince's favorite and constant companion. He turned back to his master. "My lord, we have sent couriers to all the nearby towns to keep an eye out for him."

"An eye out for a nondescript man with a false name?" asked Pol.

The captain resented the knight more than slightly now. "Well, sir, we know that he always wore a long tunic — gray, most say — and that he turned up his nose at the local wine." With a chuckle, he added, "Everyone remembered that detail."

"Good enough," said Prince Modareth. "Thank you, Captain." That was a signal for the soldier to leave, which he did.

"Sir," said Pol, "do you think that might be the sorcerer of whom the Lady Fachalana told us?" They had heard Fachalana's tale of the dreams that brought her to both the prince's door and his rescue, and of her father's conjectures about them.

Modareth shrugged. "It is possible. Whoever the man is, he thinks himself most clever."

"Yes, my lord, the name. The belief in their own cleverness may trip such men up." Sir Pol stood silently for a few moments. "Are we going to head back to Celatas?"

Modareth rose from behind his desk and walked to the wide doors, open to the cool evening air. The gardens here looked far better than when he and Carrana had arrived, didn't they? "I think so, Pol. Maybe in a week or two. With my wife's pregnancy it would be best to travel sooner rather than later. You have never been to the capital, have you?"

"No, sir, I have not. I am not sure how I will fit into your household there."

"As you do here, if you wish. Or would you rather be back to soldiering, I am sure my father would appoint you to almost any post you desire."

"I've no great love of being a soldier, sir. I do wonder if I should be keeping an eye on the ladies. No one else is." He shook his head, remembering that Blen had asked him to watch over them. "Couldn't you have ordered them not to go?"

"Pol, once Fachalana has set her mind to something, no one can prevent her. She and Maresta will follow their own road for now.

"You took on their pair of servants as your personal retainers, didn't you? Best you let them know we're going to be on the road soon as well."

Lady Thara had listened patiently to her husband's reading of the letter. "What will Bolos think of all this?" she asked then.

"He may not like it but he can not object to me making Sir Copago my master of arms. After all," he pointed out, "I did give him my own when he asked for him."

Thara nodded. "We must send Corgos his wife soon, before travel becomes unwise." That Tiana was pregnant had become common knowledge.

"As soon as Copago is here to take charge, I shall go visit our nephew and convey the lady to her husband." Sir Paren placed the missive on the polished wooden table between them. It had been crafted right here at his manor from one of the great poplars, the tallest trees in the forests that lay about the estate. "I suspect that Donzalo and Guesare will also wish to accompany me."

"I hope that Donzalo chooses to return with you. He should cease his wandering." Thara knew her husband agreed with that thought. "I should inform Dame Janona of her husband's coming."

"There was a separate letter for her, from Sir Copago. She would know of it by now."

"And his mother as well, no doubt." Lady Thara seemed briefly miffed that she could not bear such happy news to her friends. Then she brightened. "At least I can tell Tiana!"

"Feel free to do so, Wife," said Paren. "Would that the news that comes out of Keep Rosam were as good."

By all accounts, Bolos had fallen back into his ways as a drunkard and everywhere saw plots against him. Maybe he could settle the man down. Whom might he trust if not his old uncle?

"And let us hope that our travelers do not tarry overmuch along the way."

"Jan and Saj we are," stated Ansa in a gruff tone. "Oh, you did that so well, Lana!"

"You'd best use my man-name from now on," warned Fachalana, "even in private. And," she added, "don't be impertinent toward your betters, boy."

"Oh, of course. I know my spy-craft, Sir Jan. Or is it stage-craft?"

"They feel much the same to me."

"I suppose they are," mused Ansa. She had practiced both long and knew how similar they could be. "A rider ahead."

"He seems to be sitting his horse and waiting."

Ansa knew immediately who it was that awaited them here on the road up to Doram Pass. Had his message not reached her at Grenethas, saying to watch for him?

But she would let him play this encounter as he wished and say nothing to her companion.

Fachalana raised a hand in greeting to the stranger. The face beneath the fur cap seemed vaguely familiar, but she knew she had never met this man.

"Hail, travelers!" called he.

"Greetings, sir," she responded, her voice as low as she could manage. Maybe it should have more gravel to it? "I be Sir Jan, a knight of Sharsh."

"Greetings to you, Sir Jan." The man then leered at Ansa, saying, "Your esquire is quite a pretty boy. Would you sell him to me?"

"What?" The astounded noblewoman put her hand to her sword hilt. Furthering her confusion, both the stranger and her companion burst into laughter.

"Let me introduce you to my brother Oder," said Ansa. Of her brother she asked, "Didn't we fool you at all?"

"How could I not recognize my own sister? Still," he said, looking the two over, "not bad at all. A rather ruffianly pair, I would say."

Fachalana did not like the idea that she looked a ruffian. That had not been been at all her intention! "Sir Oder, surely you recognize a gentleman when you see one," she said in haughty tones. All three shared in the laughter this time.

"If I might," said Oder, "I would suggest a hood and cowl, my lady. 'Tis a bit old-fashioned but many fighting men still wear them beneath their helms."

Ansa nodded her agreement. "You are right, Oder. It would hide many tell-tales."

"I've one in my bags, my ladies. Or gentlemen, if you prefer to remain in character. Jan and Saj, eh? Such common names may seem a wise choice but they can also arouse suspicions.

"There is a shelter back that way a bit where we might speak of many things." He gestured in the direction toward which they had been traveling. "Let us stop there a while."

The shelter was only a few minutes away, a shallow cave at the base of a cliff overhanging their road. There were no other travelers sharing it this early in the day.

"On the morrow, you should cross over the divide," said Oder, " and begin your descent toward Lama. The way is long and rough but not so steep as on this side."

"And where are you going, Sir Oder?" asked Fachalana.

"It's not polite to ask such things of a spy," warned Ansa.

"At worst, he will only lie to me," was her friend's retort. Ansa knew her brother was capable of far worse things than lying but spoke not.

"I shall not lie today, my lady," replied the spy-master, chewing on a bit of the bread and cheese they shared. "We are alarmed by some of the goings-on in Sharsh and, in particular, the attempts on the life of your friend, the prince. I will spend but a few days with my agents there so I may report."

"What does the Anian Empire care about Prince Modareth?"

"Little, in truth. It is the ambitions of Partanaca that concern us. That is all I have to say on that.

"But I will cross back into Lama soon, whether by Doram Pass or the secret ways I know. We may meet again, my ladies, as you go about whatever mission you have set yourself.

"Of course, it would not be polite to ask two so lovely spies about such things."

Radal was not sure when he had first heard the voice of Darkness, but it had come with forgiveness for all the thoughts, all the desires, his mother had told him were sins. They are nothing, said Darkness, and her voice was as soft winds of night.

She whispered to him that the gods were only little things and would perish as surely as men. Then only she in her primal majesty would remain. Naught else would matter.

The sorcerer had a small obsidian figure he had found as a boy, half-buried in the clay by the river. His father, the tall stern soldier, had told him it was only a chess piece someone had lost but he knew that it was *she*, come to him so he might worship.

That figurine resided now in distant Celatas, on a shelf in his study. Perhaps it had been but a lost gaming piece. Perhaps it had no power other than that he gave it.

Darkness, the goddess of that unhappy boy, Radal now knew as a manifestation of the Great Void in our world. The Void was indifferent to all existence. It did not even hate, being empty of all things. But Darkness hated, as had Radal.

He would serve her always and her father, Death — Asak, as the Kamatians named him, and the Ildin before them. Someday, soon probably, Asak would come and give him his gift of peace, of extinction. He would be with his goddess.

Until then he would serve her, though she asked nothing of men.

Radal remembered still the hymn the boy had composed in her honor, that he had intoned before his little obsidian idol.

Darkness, Asak's eldest child,
Lady of the Lifeless Lands,
on your carved ebon throne,
scatter Time's unnumbered sands.

Wisdom comes as nightmare runes,
written on the lids of eyes
that beheld you, vast and still,
ere stars rose in ancient skies.

All the children of the day,
generations raised in light,
shrink from the Abyss's gaze,
waste and wither in your sight.

Darkness, born of endless Void,
Goddess to the men of old,
reign as Queen of endless realms,
worlds where all things grow cold.

Radal smiled thinly at the memory and, with a sigh, turned to his work. He must soon act, and decisively. Then let things be as they would be, knowing that Darkness did not listen to prayers.

5

"Bolos has banished the boy's dog?" Count Mussago pursed his lips and shook his head. He looked as if he might have said many things about Bolos but had thought better of it.

Dogs had greeted them at the count's door. Many dogs. Most were white and of a uniform size and shape, not overly large and well-formed.

"King's brothers and sisters and cousins, I suspect," had been Sir Copago's observation.

Mussago's keep was an unkempt pile of stones well up in the foothills of the Zadcelam and overlooking the road from Doram Pass. The travelers could see it was well placed to control traffic through the mountains.

They had crossed a range of low scrubby hills to reach this county. Here the streams flowed easterly toward the Weldar. South of the hills, in Daboreth's lands, they ran to the Tod and Count Orgelo's dominion.

Donzalo reached a hand down to allow one of the canines to sniff at it. It approved of his scent. Count Mussago approved of anyone his dogs liked.

"If — King, you named him? — King has a good home, I suppose all is well," said the count. "King should also improve the bloodlines about Sir Paren's keep," he added with a chuckle.

"You style them warden dogs, my lord, don't you?" asked Sir Copago.

"Yes, my boy. Smaller than mastiffs but quicker, and large enough to watch and protect."

"There is mastiff in their lineage, I would wager," said Daboreth, "and maybe some of the local herding dogs?"

"You have a good eye, neighbor," replied the stout nobleman. "There are contributions from across the mountains, as well. Now, most of those that I am willing to sell go to Sharsh." The count had thrown a richly decorated if slightly threadbare caftan on over a rough costume any farmer might have worn. He prided himself on not minding dirt on his hands.

"I will, of course, give you letters to allow free use of the road. Dordos will honor them. Three smaller counties lie between my borders and his, and each would otherwise try to charge you tolls for passage.

"See to it, will you?" said Mussago, turning to an aide, "and then bring them to me to sign." To his guests, he said, "Orgelo's passports would not get you far in this neighborhood."

He looked squarely at Count Daboreth and stated, "You should visit here more often, Daboreth. Orgelo may not be the friend you think him."

"I've no illusions about Count Orgelo. But family and geography tie me to him."

"A better road between here and Count Daboreth's hold would help," observed Copago. "You might be surprised at what could come over it."

"Oh? I am forever hearing that I should pay more attention to my roads." The count spoke to an attendant who had entered the room. "Our lunch is ready?"

"Yes, my lord," answered the servant.

"Then let us repair to my dining room, gentlemen. My granddaughter will be there, Daboreth. You must make her acquaintance!"

Jobareth waited patiently.

Young Ros was, in most respects, a very well behaved boy but he detested nap-time. "Why do you bother?" asked the diplomat. "Let the lad have his toys if he does not want to sleep."

Both Lomela and Traspa clearly disapproved of this advice. "Boys his age need their naps," asserted the maid.

"Perhaps the legate could use one as well," said Lady Lomela, with a weary smile.

"Would that the siesta were the custom here as it is back in Sharsh," replied Jobareth. "The Laman summer truly is too hot to be out and about in the midday."

"Jobo!" called the tyke, holding his arms out to Nafal.

"I'll not come to your rescue today, young man," replied Jobareth. "It would bring the wrath of Mistress Traspa down upon me."

"You shall have to call her Dame Traspa soon," Lomela said. "The wedding is not that far away."

"If she remembers to call me Legate," responded he, with a slight bow toward Traspa. "Sir Jak is a lucky man."

"I think I am lucky, young sir," said Traspa, her voice quite earnest. "He is a good solid man."

"That he is," affirmed the princess. "He has served well in keeping my husband from harm's way."

"Not Sir Corgos?" asked Jobareth Nafal.

"Corgos is a soldier. He has not the temperament to play nurse-maid, I think." She smiled. "He is most definitely not Copago, taking a personal interest in everything in the keep."

Jobareth nodded. He had seen that the new master of arms seemed to prefer the chain of command.

"Shh," whispered Mistress Traspa. "The little lord has fallen asleep."

"Your brother is both minstrel and spy, isn't he?" asked Fachalana.

Ansa nodded. She was distracted by the view of the great Laman valley extending below them into a distant blue-gray haze. What might these lands hold for them in the days to come?

"Do you know any more of his songs?" persisted the Sharshite as they followed the winding, slowly descending trail. There had been no traffic since a line of pack-mules had passed them earlier in the morning.

"Some," she replied. "They tend to be about strife rather than love. Oder is a warrior at heart." Then she asked, of a sudden, "Did you know that Pol writes poems?"

"Truly? I must ask him to recite when next we see him."

"No need to wait. I can give you one right here."

Lady Fachalana was already aware that her friend possessed a prodigious memory for songs and plays. "How do you come to know it? Has our boy been writing love poems to you?" she asked with a laugh.

"None that I have seen," replied Ansa. "Which does not mean that they do not exist."

Does she hope they do? wondered Fachalana.

"I came upon him scribbling lines in the library," continued the Anian, "and he quite unabashedly asked my opinion of them." She began to recite, her voice clear and musical.

Never trust a poet —
he'll only tell you lies
and pretty bits of nonsense,
pretending to be wise.

The words have all been crafted
to bring tears to your eyes;
he'll beguile your hearts,
he'll seek to hear your sighs.

But, in time, he knows
whatever words he tries,
you'll turn the page and read
some other poet's lies.

"Our Pol is a bit of a cynic, isn't he?"

"I would say a sometimes-disappointed romantic, rather. And he was poking fun at Jobareth's work."

"Hmm, I can see that. It's not really all that good, is it?"

"Nor particularly original. But good enough and he composed it pretty much on the spot, in a minute or two. That would be a considerable gift for one who wrote for the stage rather than books." She was silent for a few moments. "Pol is very smart, you know."

"And ambitious," said Fachalana. "I wonder if Jobareth truly chose him as his man or if he chose Jobareth."

"Well, he is a prince's man now. Who knows where he will go from there?"

Many bodies of troops passed him on the road. This made Oder nervous.

Whatever reason there was for their presence was almost certainly more important than the affair he had been sent here to investigate. Of the assassination attempt, and what followed after, the news he had heard from his sister had proven more useful than the reports of his agents.

Ansa was valuable as a spy. Of that there was not the least doubt, and all the more so since she had become the friend of a prince. Yet the Anian spy-master would be happy to see her retire from this life of danger. She should go back to the empire and marry some young nobleman there. Plenty enough of them had vied for her hand before she chose to follow her brother's profession.

Here in Sharsh, he was passing himself off as a merchant out of Lama. His credentials were the finest that might be forged; that was no problem. But there seemed to be a suspicion of Lamans right now. Added to that was a general mistrust of strangers following the attempt on Prince Modareth's life. Oder believed he should leave Sharsh quickly and quietly.

There were ways other than the two great passes to cross the mountains. Longer ways, harder ways, but safer ones, perhaps. Best he get the news that Sharsh was massing troops on the Laman border to his superiors as soon as possible.

He turned his horse onto a little-traveled road that led into the high Zadcelam.

The Lady Mara dreamed.

She was in Xose, the city of her birth, and her girls were there with her. But she was no older than they, playing with them on the sand beaches she remembered so well. The water was warm there and the waves gentle. So different from the cold rough surf here on Sharsh's shores!

"Look at my castle," said her oldest daughter, standing over a marvelously sculpted sand edifice. And as she did, it grew larger and the gates opened to her. There was Gawis, waiting for her.

No, his face changed and became that of another, that of a younger man. "Where is my husband?" she asked of him. He only took her hand and led her into a high-vaulted hall. There stood scribe and priest, as they had at her wedding.

"Gawis," she whispered. "Gawis."

He was nowhere.

When the lady awoke she tried to remember the face of the man she was wedding. But it was gone, fled into the shadows of sleep.

Six men had ridden to Count Mussago's castle. Now three returned south and three rode eastward.

The three riding south also carried a puppy, Mussago's gift to his fellow nobleman. Daboreth thought he might well visit his neighbor — and his neighbor's granddaughter — again soon.

Donzalo, Copago and Guesare followed the highway that would carry them toward County Rosam. In Dordos's lands, it would meet with the road to King's Pass and then on to the river and Ros-town.

"Whoever told Mussago to pay more attention to his roads should tell him again," complained Sir Copago.

"Be thankful that we are on horseback," responded Guesare. "A wagon would find the going near impossible in places."

"Such as one filled with brimstone," Donzalo remarked.

"Aye. A train of pack-horses might be needed."

They had passed several such on the road, going in both directions. It seemed the preferred mode of transport.

"That's all well and good for merchants going through Doram Pass," said Donzalo, "but not so suited to our needs." They continued in silence. In places, there were small gullies across their path.

"Riders are coming," spoke Guesare. "Three, I believe." He undid the thong that secured his rifle in its tooled scabbard, presented to him by Habidros before they left Count Orgelo's keep. Much fine leatherwork was done in Tod-ford.

Naturally, Habi had not wished to be outshone by his brother Galaro, who had gifted the rifle in the first place.

That the men were soldiers was evident as they approached. Their leader's close helmet kept them from readily making out his features.

"Hail, Sir Donzalo!" called the man. "Have you come to give me more fencing lessons?"

"Blen? When did you grow that beard, man?"

"When I came over the mountains. I've enough to do without taking time to shave. Sir Guesare, Sir Copago! Greetings to you as well.

"Will you come visit me in my camp? 'Tis not far."

He turned his horse and started away, clearly expecting them to follow. Donzalo looked at his companions and then at the two armored soldiers, and shrugged. "Why not?" said he, and followed the Sharshite knight.

It was, indeed, not far, only a short distance off the road. "Another league or so," said Blen, pointing eastward, "and you would have left Mussago's lands. The count told me you were coming."

"Then you are here as his guests?" asked Guesare.

"One might so say. Think of it as Count Mussago doing a favor for King Lareth. Incidentally," he said, turning to Donzalo, "the king no longer desires your life."

"That is — fortunate," replied the young Laman.

"Not so fortunate is that Radal still wishes you dead, for whatever reasons he may have. I'm not sure even Lareth knows what those are."

Guesare and Donzalo glanced at each other. They knew well what lay behind the sorcerer's hatred. Blen could not help notice but said nothing.

"Sharsh is concerned about the situation at your home, Donzalo," continued Sir Blen. "That is why we are here. Your brother grows more erratic and Lord Radal is somewhere, plotting something. We must be ready if things fall apart in Lama."

"Perhaps you might stay with us tonight and fill me in on what is happening in County Arvaram. We do not know if Orgelo intends to get involved but it wouldn't hurt to know how the wind blows there."

"It blows eastward, Blen, sending me home."

So, his father would remain at Mountain Keep and he must remain here, attending to the duties of governing.

Gawis put down the letter. All the king would tell his son was that he was keeping an eye on Lama and could not leave. The prince knew his father had been moving troops to the border; their orders had come across his own desk.

As had a report of his sister-in-law's pregnancy. There had been no official announcement from Modareth and Carrana, but it was not something that could be hidden from their staff there at Grenethas. Now, the pair and their entourage were headed back to the capital. Maybe his brother could be of some help to him here.

He sighed and walked to the westward-facing window. Gawis missed his wife. This fact surprised him. Not long ago, he would have been distracted from such thoughts by his circle of hangers-on, by wine, by the many women who were always willing to be with him. It was good that she and the girls were out of Celatas for a while, down on the coast where the sea breezes kept summer heat at bay.

But he hoped she would return soon. Maybe Mara and he could even come up with an announcement to rival that of his brother. Gawis smiled at the thought. Why not? They had already produced three daughters.

His brother — he had best prepare for his arrival. There was still need to protect him from assassins. Perhaps the Lady Carrana as well, now, as she and the unborn child might also be targets. He would speak to the seneschal about setting up a guard, as well as preparing their quarters.

What if it is a boy? he wondered. It would be to his advantage if an assassin were successful. No, he would not wish such a thing.

Summer was fading. The astrologers would say that it was already over, now that the Festival of Abundance had passed and the equinox approached. Would they be harvesting the grapes in Arolin now? Cooler weather had already reached there but had not penetrated to the heartland of Sharsh.

Arolin. It would be wise to move some troops about there so the Mura wouldn't think Sharsh had all its attention focused on Lama. Father would approve of that, wouldn't he?

Yes. Gawis turned from his view of Celatas and the River Chas and far beyond those, hidden from him, the sea, and sat to write the order.

Sir Blen had bidden goodbye to his guests and watched them ride into the dawn. He guessed it would take them near a week to reach the Weldar, as they were not hurrying nor would they have a change of horses. In his courier days, he could have made the journey in well less than half that time.

Then they intended to cross the Weldar south of Ros-town and ford the Abam somewhere upstream, traveling on to the keep of Sir Paren. He hoped they were not underestimating the dangers of their journey.

Of course, Bolos would receive word from his border guards that his brother had returned, even if he did skirt Castle Rosam on his way. Most probably, Orgelo had sent him a message as well, saying to expect Donzalo.

Ten days, perhaps, for the entire trip. Much could happen in ten days. Perhaps he would use that time to ride down to Todmouth himself and hear what news there might be.

He could see a pair of riders coming down the road. A man and a boy, it appeared, perhaps a knight or man at arms and his attendant, for they were on fine horses and he could discern a glint of armor. For a moment, Blen considered waiting there and speaking with them.

No, better he get on to other, more urgent errands. He turned back toward his encampment and let them pass.

His spies told him the boy was on the move. Radal considered sending his men, all his men, out to intercept him and be done with it. Too rash, perhaps — if those men failed and were scattered or destroyed, there might never be another chance.

Still, he was as unprotected as he was ever likely to be. Donzalo and his companions were reportedly headed back to County Rosam. Yes, he would chance it.

Not Radal himself. Not now. There were other schemes he must be ready to put into action and that were best done here. Soon, though, he would leave this broken tower where once had dwelt the wizard Sabatare.

He went down to the entry, where the tall oaken doors stood ajar, and called one of the attendants lounging in the overgrown courtyard. "I shall have a message for your sergeant shortly. Be ready to carry it to him."

Pol attempted to show that he was not in awe.

Until now, the largest city he had known was Oles. It was as nothing beside Celatas.

As he had throughout their journey, he rode only half an horse's length behind his prince, ready to act if need be. With the twenty sturdy troopers accompanying them, it seemed unlikely that such a need would arise. Still, Pol saw that as no reason to be slack in his duties.

Here, Modareth should be well guarded in his father's keep, the young knight's constant presence no longer required. He would miss the prince's company and his learned talk. He would miss the library at Grenethas. He had learned a great deal reading there.

But surely there were many books here in Celatas. They *made* books here. Pol smiled to himself. If Jobareth Nafal could have books printed, why not he?

The young knight had never really intended a military career. He had joined the army when his family had all been slain in the war against the Mura. That conflict ended before he had a chance to see action and, a couple of years later, Pol had found himself in Lama.

That, he felt, was one of the most fortunate events in his life. Had it not led to all that had happened in this past year, when he had risen from an ordinary soldier to a knight and the personal bodyguard of a prince? Had it not made him a friend of the Viscountess Fachalana? Had Pol any great belief in the gods he might have thanked them.

Prince Modareth motioned to him to move alongside. "My lord?" he asked.

"I just wanted to point out the King's Bridge," said the prince, gesturing toward the left of their route. Pol did not even try to hide his wonder this time.

"Do we cross it, sir?" He was perhaps a little apprehensive of such an action.

"No, my father's keep is to our right, above the city. We should see it soon — yes, there it is." It towered on the heights, as much a crown as the one the king wore on his head. The hills below it were dotted with the manicured villas of the wealthy and aristocratic.

Pol thought it looked rather similar to Keep Rosam, though obviously larger.

"Keep close to me, Pol," said Modareth, "and don't let yourself be rattled." The prince, being of a shy disposition, knew the hazards of entering an unfamiliar situation.

And Pol, although of a brasher sort, recognized and was grateful for his young patron's concern.

7

"Who is this Prince Modareth?" asked the guard, looking over their papers.

Fachalana was exasperated but Ansa spoke before her companion could say something rash. "He is the younger son of King Lareth, good sir."

"Humph. Why have I never heard of him?"

Fachalana had regained her composure. She spoke in the low gravelly voice she had adopted. "Surely you have heard of his great vineyards in Dor? Their fame is widely sung. The Prince Modareth has produced his marvelous vintages there for many years."

The man had heard of the wine of Dor and that it had a good reputation. He was therefor willing to believe the rest. Ansa was almost willing to believe it herself.

"Very well," he said, handing back their passports. "Count Dordos is a friend of Sharsh. You have proper diplomatic papers and need not pay the toll."

"Thank you, sir," replied the disguised noblewoman in her heartiest tones. "Would that the guards at our last two border crossings had felt the same. Saj, do give our friend a little tip for his courtesy." Ansa doled out a couple coppers. She suspected that the man got a cut of the tolls so it did not hurt to alleviate his loss and perhaps buy some good will. Ansa was a little surprised that Fachalana had also recognized this. The lady was learning the ways of the world.

"Sir," she asked, "have there been other fighting men through here of late?"

"You consider yourself a fighting man, lad?" he laughed. "Three fellows passed late yesterday. I think they were in a hurry to reach the river and make a crossing under cover of night." He lowered his voice, as if letting them in on a secret. "I recognized one as Count Borrago's old master of arms. He would sometimes tour the border crossings. From the other side, you know."

"Ah, what was his name?" said Fachalana. "Copago, wasn't it?"

"Aye, sir. Know you the man?"

"I have seen him at Keep Rosam." Which was quite the truth. "A solid man."

"That he is. The new count has treated him poorly." The man looked up at them. "Go you to visit Count Bolos?"

"That, good sir, I am not at liberty to say. A good day to you. Come, Saj." Fachalana rode through the gate, followed by her faithful esquire.

He had wasted his time, waiting here by the river, while Guesare and his companions had traveled through the hills. A tinker who had of late visited County Arvaram brought Perdos that information.

"I must say," the man told him, "I was glad to see the minstrel's brother head south. It is hard to compete with his band of traders."

"And the other brother remains at Tod-ford?"

"Aye. It is rumored that he will marry the count's niece. That may provide an occasion to make some sales." The peddler squinted at Perdos from beneath a well-worn turban. "Is there anything I might interest you in today, sir?"

The knight glanced at his wares. "Pots and pans? No, not today but perhaps some day soon."

As the man's cart disappeared up the road, Perdos readied his horse and gear. It was time to ride north, back toward County Rosam. Where else might they be headed?

Back to where it all began. That would be the place to finally take his vengeance.

Dovolo was baffled. They had waited on the road, west of the river, for the Rosam boy and his companions to ride into town. The plan was to waylay them among the warehouses and sheds that lined the road down to the ferry. It was dangerous to act so close to Ros-town but, at the same time, the men could fade into the crowds usually found at the river's edge.

But their intended victims had never appeared. At last he sent some men up the road to look for them. There was no sign.

"They musta crossed somewheres else, Sergeant," opined one of his ruffians.

Then they must not be headed for Ros-town at all, thought Dovolo. Where? Unfortunately, the man, though a capable enough leader, did not really know the area nor much about the Rosam family.

Another of his men spoke up. "Maybe they went to Paren's place, up the Abam."

There were murmurs of agreement to that.

"In other words," said Dovolo, "had we stayed in our encampment, they might have come riding right past us."

He hoped Lord Radal had a sense of humor.

"I like the colors, my brother."

Prince Gawis laughed. "They make my life simpler. I need not think about what I shall put on each morning!"

"I have that problem no longer," replied Modareth. "Carrana feels it her duty to choose my wardrobe."

The elder prince nodded. He was not at all surprised that his brother's wife would so take charge. Modi tended to be impractical and absent-minded.

Or the Modi he remembered, at any rate. His brother seemed no longer quite the man he remembered. More mature, more aware of the world around him — perhaps twice escaping assassination attempts had that effect on one.

"I understand the Princess Carrana is with child."

"Yes. We will make an official announcement shortly. I did not want to distract Father with the news." Though he attempted to say all this as soberly as possible, his brother could see he was delighted by the thought of becoming a father.

Again Gawis laughed. "Do not think that he is unaware of it! Father would have received regular reports from your household. As did I," he added. Should I have told him that? wondered the prince.

"I must hire some spies of my own, I suppose," mused the younger man.

"Who is that fellow who follows you about? Is he the one who captured the assassin?" Sir Pol had accompanied his prince to Gawis's office and waited now outside the door.

"He is. Pol is his name and he is a bright lad if ever there were one. To be honest, Brother, I am not sure what to do with him now. Sir Pol is meant for better things than serving as my bodyguard, I am certain."

"Perhaps he could be one of those spies you say you need," suggested Gawis, meaning it mostly as jest.

Modareth thought it a most excellent idea.

The guard looked over their papers and then looked up at them. "Is the ambassador expecting you?"

"No, he is not," came the weary reply. "But you might inform Legate Nafal that I bear a message from the Lady Fachalana."

He considered this briefly. "Very well. Come on into the stables and rest while I send someone up." The pair dismounted and entered while a groom hurried up the stairs to find the legate.

Shortly, Jobareth himself came down. That he immediately saw through his life-long friend's disguise is no surprise. He said nothing of it in front of the soldiers and servants. "Sir Jan, welcome to our embassy. Come on up to my office and we shall discuss your message. Your attendant, too — what is your name, boy?"

"Saj, sir."

"Then come along, Saj. Take care of their horses and gear, will you?" he called to the group watching them. As soon as the trio passed out of their sight, they burst into laughter.

"Fachalana, it is good to see you," said Jobareth, embracing her. "You too, Ansa-Maresta-Posena-Saj!" He stepped back to look at the pair. "And what in the name of Jov are you up to?"

"We are but knights errant, seeking adventure," said Ansa, "and the welfare of our friends."

"Ah. Does that include me?"

"You know it does, Jobo," replied Lady Fachalana. "And Lomela and Donzalo and even Sir Blen."

"Well, come on up to my office and I shall have refreshments brought and you can tell me of your journey. And then we must decide what to do with you!"

Tell him of their journey they did, as well as their time in Sharsh. It was a long tale and a long journey and they were tired at the end.

"So then, we were approaching the river and saw a band of most vile ruffians," said Fachalana. "I did fear we might be attacked."

"As did I," said Ansa, "but they seemed to be hurrying off on some urgent errand. I led us down to a place where one can quietly hire a boat to cross the Weldar, if one knows the correct words."

"Being a spy has its advantages," observed Jobareth.

"And then we rode straight here," finished Fachalana, "Sir Jan and his esquire Saj."

"It will be impossible to keep your identities secret if you stay here at the embassy," said Jobareth. "And I should tell Lord Doufan about you."

"Don't tell your secretary. Neither we nor Sir Pol trust him," warned Ansa.

"I don't quite myself," replied the legate. "It will take a while for me to think of my young protege as the heroic Sir Pol!

"Well, I can quietly find you some quarters here for the night. If, in the morning, you feel you wish to continue to go incognito, I think I know just the place where you can stay."

◆

"I have avenged you," said Sir Perdos, standing by the two graves near the burnt-out inn, "as best I can." Would that he could have destroyed every man who had been part of this. Still, slaying their leader had provided a great deal of satisfaction. The rest would no doubt grace one gallows or another someday.

He looked toward the ruins, the blackened stones of the chimney still standing as a sort of monument to what had been. Perhaps the best he could do for the innkeeper and his wife now would be to rebuild what they had once created.

"Now, my own vengeance," said he. "Then shall I return." Perdos mounted and rode north.

8

So, Sir Copago had returned and was now his uncle's master of arms. Bolos deemed this suspicious. There had been many strange comings and goings lately.

Armed bodies of masterless men moving about. Two strange fighting men who had shown up at the Sharshite embassy and then disappeared again.

And his brother Donzalo. Why had he gone to Uncle Paren's rather than coming first here? He was far too friendly with Copago.

No, they would not be plotting against him. Nor would his uncle be party to any disloyalty.

There were rumors of Sharshite troops across the Weldar, on the lands of Count Dordos. Orgelo, too, seemed to prepare for some sort of action and had sent his son out, ostensibly to deal with outlaws. Might there be more to that?

He turned to his ever faithful sergeant, Jak. He was the one man in the world Bolos trusted completely. He must find a proper gift for the fellow's upcoming wedding.

For a moment, the count's gloom was dispelled. Who would have thought this middle-aged soldier, a bachelor all his life, would find love now? Somehow, it seemed fitting that the most trusted servants of his wife and himself should wed.

Perhaps it would make up in some way for the love that had never existed between Bolos and the Princess Lomela.

"Jak," said he, "have you seen Sir Corgos today?"

"He is inspecting the walls this morning, my lord."

A good man, Corgos. He was thankful to his uncle for graciously allowing the knight to change to his service. Perhaps letting Paren have Sir Copago was only fair.

He would not complain about it, but Count Bolos still did not like it.

"Let us ride out ourselves. I could use some air." It could help clear his head. Better than sitting here in his chambers with the temptation of wine close at hand. He should stop drinking, Bolos told himself. He had done it before.

Before his father died, and his daughter. Before threats had seemed to beset him on every side.

"I'll bring the horses around, sir," said Sir Jak.

"The word is that Donni is at his uncle Paren's and both will soon come here."

"Is Sir Copago there as well?" asked Ansa. "We were surprised to have news that he was riding before us on our journey, having heard that he was in the service of Count Orgelo."

"He left that service to become Paren's master of arms," Jobareth replied. "I know not why. I do know that Donzalo's former shadow, Habidros, took his place there in County Arvaram."

"I liked Habidros," said Ansa.

"Do you like every man you meet?" Fachalana asked. Ansa had never shown this side of herself when she was an actress back in Celatas.

Not your father, Ansa said to herself. "What was not to like about Sir Habidros? Handsome, bold, and very tall. Not unlike Donzalo."

But not Donzalo. That thought came to both women.

"Do you intend to continue your masquerade, my ladies? Even here, that may prove difficult." Jobareth had installed them in the modest house the Sharshite embassy rented in Ros-town. He had also informed the ambassador, Lord Doufan, of their presence.

Both were puzzled by the sudden appearance of the pair. "Use your own judgment, my boy," Doufan had told him, "but do keep me informed." That was not out of character for the diplomat.

"If we reveal our identities, the knowledge of it will be everywhere within a week. Even Sharsh."

Jobareth suspected that Doufan had already sent a message to King Lareth with just that information. He would have, were he in the same position. How the king might act, he had no idea.

"Then you will remain Jan and Saj? If you don't leave the house much you might get away with it." The old butler who kept this house for him would be discreet, even if he noticed anything odd about the guests.

"But that itself would be suspicious," Ansa pointed out, "and there wouldn't be much point in coming here if we do not intend to do anything, would there?"

"I am the problem," stated Fachalana. "Ansa could mask herself in many ways but I know that I do stand out with my height and coloring."

"Then Sir Jan remains your best disguise," replied her companion. "There is no point in throwing away an identity you have already established. And," she went on, "it will allow you to ride freely about the countryside."

"Unless Bolos or some zealous fellow who serves him wonders about this stranger and has him taken in for questioning," said Jobareth. "I think I shall ask Lord Doufan if I can issue you diplomatic credentials. If you seem attached to the embassy, there will be fewer questions.

"Enough now, of this. I shall call to have food and chilled wine brought up, and we shall enjoy this evening as old friends rather than conspirators."

"I would enjoy that, Jobo," said Lady Fachalana. "But first I ask one more thing of you: do not let Lomela know we are here."

Jobareth Nafal nodded his assent and rang for the butler.

No harm, one way or the other, thought Lord Radal. He had not ended Donzalo Rosam's life but neither had he lost any men. Things could move forward according to his plans.

It would have been good, though, to have brought it all to a close. The longer the young Laman lived, the more he might pose a threat to the future of Fachalana. Radal could not shake his conviction that their destinies were entwined.

It was enough that Donzalo's involvement had led to the death of one daughter, the daughter he had not known he had. For that alone did he hate him enough to wish his death. He would not chance the fate of the other.

He still had spies on the other side of the mountains and they reported that his daughter had disappeared from Sharsh. Radal suspected that she had reentered Lama. Distance meant little to his sorcery but mattered quite a lot in the physical world.

And his spy at the Sharshite embassy in County Rosam had heard that two strangers had appeared in the night, to closet with Legate Nafal and disappear again the next morning. Could the pair have been Fachalana and her friend, Maresta?

He could only tell the man to keep watch. Fortunately, his reports could come to the sorcerer more quickly than those of his other minions. Radal felt a certain distaste for the fellow; he sensed that he had no center to him, no feelings for anyone but himself and his own appetites. Benawis was not a man to trust.

On the other hand, he was rather pleased with how well the newly-made sergeant of his small company had performed. The man had been, of course, rightly fearful of Radal after Donzalo slipped by them. It was good to have ones followers feel a little fear. But he had done well in handling the situation and seemed to have a head on his shoulders. Dovolo would do.

Soon he might have the chance to prove himself further.

Sir Paren had chosen to take no chances on the road, remembering the events of the previous year, and had brought a number of doughty men at arms along with him, with Donzalo riding safely in their midst.

Also among them was Dame Tiana. The woman had refused a wagon, saying it would slow them, and rode as well. Paren hoped that was wise and chose the gentlest horse in his stables for her.

"Now, do you think we should expect your husband to be waiting at the outer gate for us?" he asked her as they neared Castle Rosam.

"He had better be," replied Tiana. "Or even better, meet us on the road."

"Then perhaps this approaching cloud of dust is he," said the knight.

Tiana smiled. She knew her Corgos.

The master of arms reined his steed in as he reached them. "I have been watching for you from the walls. Welcome to your new home, Wife!" He bowed toward the reeve. "Greetings, Sir Paren, and my thanks to you. My thanks for many things! Donzalo, my boy! Greetings to you as well."

Such exuberance was unusual for the man, but all there understood it.

Through the three gates of Keep Rosam they passed, between the great oaken doors of the outer wall, under the iron portcullis of the second, and finally beneath the arch in the thick inner walls, with its double gates. Into the broad courtyard they rode, its stone tower rising above them.

For Donzalo, this was a homecoming. Dame Tiana, however, had never seen so grand a place as her new abode. "Will we live there?" she asked her husband, looking toward the tower.

"No, wife of mine. We will have more comfortable apartments over, um, there," he said, pointing to a spot somewhere to the right of the stables. Sir Corgos had actually been residing in the tower, in Count Borrago's old quarters, and had paid little attention to the furnishing of his new rooms. "Ah, and there is the count. I must present you."

Bolos and his wife, the Lady Lomela, stood at the doorway of the Great Hall. *He looks alert today,* thought Corgos. *Thank Kamat for that.*

The count welcomed the knight's wife gravely and soberly. Quite literally soberly, he was glad to see. Then Lomela embraced her and led her off to wherever women went.

By then, Bolos was shaking the hands of his uncle and brother. They were welcome enough in Keep Rosam, it seemed and would find their ways here. It was best he got back to his own duties.

Well, first, he should look in on Tiana and make sure she had found her way to their new apartment. Corgos was not absolutely sure where that was, right then, but knew he would soon get used to going there. It had been a long time since Corgos had been part of a family, near twenty years as soldier and roving mercenary, as a man without a home.

This would be his home now that his wife — and, soon enough, a third — was here.

The ferry crossing lay well outside County Arvaram, but he who ruled here as count had readily granted Sorsen permission to cross his lands. What had happened at this little village had much to do with that.

He and Sir Habidros surveyed what remained of the burnt inn. "It does not seem the work of ordinary bandits," stated Sir Sorsen.

"No, my lord," replied Habidros. "I would guess a military company of some sort." He had seen too many such ruins as a mercenary and had taken part in a few such actions himself.

"Nothing to be learned here," said Sorsen, and turned his horse toward the river.

There they found the cook Hendel at his stall and heard much the same story from him that he had told Perdos a few weeks earlier. At the name of Sojel, the two leaders looked at each other knowingly.

"So, Sir Perdos has already brought our culprit to justice," spoke Habidros.

"Perdos, my lords? He was here and told me the innkeeper and his wife had been his friends. He seemed greatly moved by their deaths." Hendel had recognized the knight from his days at Castle Rosam, but had felt it best not to let Perdos know this. Both men had pasts of which they would rather not speak. "It is good that he took vengeance for them."

"Only on their leader. The company may still be about somewhere," observed Sir Sorsen. "What say you, Sir Habidros? Shall we go look for sign of them?"

"North or south?" asked the Cuddonian.

"North," replied Sorsen. "If these men rode with Sojel then they were in the pay of Lord Radal. They might be seeking our friend Donzalo."

"Then let us ride, sir! But if there be trouble, remember to let my pistoleers protect your hussars from danger. It would not do to let any of them be harmed unnecessarily."

"Ha, my lancers would overwhelm them before your men got off their first shot!"

The two rode north along the Great Road, their column behind them, and each hoping for the chance to prove the other wrong.

9

"There is someone at our door."

Fachalana came to the window and stuck her head out alongside Ansa's. "I don't think I know him," she said. But the gentleman *did* look familiar, didn't he?

The butler was opening the door to him. The old fellow seemed to know the man, whoever he was.

"We had best don our man-clothes," said Ansa.

"And slip out the back?" Fachalana asked.

"Maybe."

"No need to hide yourselves, my ladies," came a voice from the foot of the stairs. "I am quite harmless."

In sudden recognition, Fachalana stated, "That is Lord Doufan."

"And he has let the butler in on our secret," replied Ansa. There was both resignation and a certain peevishness to her voice.

"Did you really think he hadn't noticed by now? You put far too much trust in the efficacy of your disguises, my friend!"

True, thought Ansa. Even when she had first come to Lama, Donzalo had surmised something of her actual identity.

"We shall be right down, sir," Fachalana called. To Ansa she whispered, "I think we should dress as Jan and Saj anyway. Best we stay in character."

"It will confuse the butler," the Anian replied.

Doufan was dressed as he did when he prowled Ros-town incognito, looking more like an old soldier in worn buff-coat and breeches, a longsword dangling at his side. The aged servant held a wide-brimmed hat the ambassador had doffed.

"Ah, Sir Jan," said Lord Doufan as the pair descended. "And this must be your esquire Saj. I give you greetings, gentlemen."

Ansa noted the slight smile playing about the old butler's mouth. Well, Jobareth had said to trust in the man's discretion.

"Lord Doufan," Fachalana replied, giving the man a small and courteous bow. "What might we do for you this fine day?" She used her masculine voice. Fachalana had practiced it quite a lot now and thought she did it well.

"You might dine with me, if you do not mind going out in public. We might, so to speak, put your identities to test in a tavern. But mostly," he continued, "I came to bring you these." Doufan handed an apparently official document to each woman.

"So we are now diplomats?" asked Ansa.

"Indeed. Or, more properly, soldiers attached to the embassy. That should get you through most difficulties you might encounter." He then spoke more lowly, more seriously. "I know not why you are here and perhaps I should not be aiding you. Will you come with me and explain yourselves over ale and a meal? I have a craving for fowl today. They serve it fried here, you know."

"They seem to serve everything fried in Lama," responded Lady Fachalana. "We shall gladly share some chicken with you."

There was a tavern not far away and near the river. Lord Doufan had built a personal knowledge of all such establishments in Ros-town. The rich, heavy scent of fried fish and fowl hung in the air as they entered. Fachalana was not sure whether it enticed or revolted her, but she allowed Doufan to order fried fowl for both her and himself.

Ansa, however, who knew more of Laman cuisine, asked for catfish. Lord Doufan nodded approvingly of her taste.

As did Fachalana, after she picked a bit of it off her friend's plate. She liked it far better than the chicken on her own. Chickens should be roasted only, she decided, or made into soup.

A passing whore eyed her and then squinted at Ansa. That she had seen through their guises was Fachalana's immediate thought. Then she realized that the woman was only wondering if the 'boy' was too young. Doufan waved her away from their table, its dark wood saturated with the grease of thousands of meals, and began to speak in a low voice.

"You are concerned about your father's plans here, are you not, Jan?" Doufan was every bit as good an actor as these two and not one to break character — his or anyone else's. "Especially as they concern your friends."

Fachalana nodded. Then she realized something and whispered, "How shall we name you here, sir?"

The ambassador laughed. "Around here they have taken to calling me Old Dog. Ask not why for I am not sure! But 'tis as good a name as any."

Neither woman could quite see herself addressing the ambassador so. Doufan, recognizing this, added, "The young ladies tend to name me Grandfather. Why not use that?

"But, back to our subject. Why do you think you can be of any use here?" He looked at Ansa. "You, as a well-trained spy, might be of some assistance. Yes, I know much of your past. But you?" Doufan looked intently at Fachalana. "Excellence with a sword is all well and good but what else have you to offer?"

The two women looked at each other. "It is up to you," Ansa said to her friend. "Tell him if you will."

Lady Fachalana hesitated. Not even the king was aware of her secret, nor were most of her friends. She thought Donzalo might have an inkling, having known her sister.

Why should she speak of it to this courtier?

"I — share in my father's gifts, sir."

"Ah." The ambassador said no more for quite a long while. "He has trained you in their use?" he asked at last.

"Yes." She sighed deeply — it seemed almost a sob — and went on. "Right now, I hide from my father and fear to use what I have learned lest he find me."

"Do you fear you might be used as a weapon against us?"

"If he were able to read my secrets, yes." This was indeed Fachalana's greatest fear.

"But you might read his as well. Is this not so?"

"Yes. I suppose that is true."

The group sat in silence again. Ansa drank of her ale and then spoke. "I think this should be the end of our luncheon, Grandfather Dog. We all have much to think upon now."

"That we do," agreed Lord Doufan.

"How could the Anian officers live in such a hole?" Jobareth Nafal looked about Donzalo's quarters with unconcealed distaste.

"That baffled me too," said Donzalo, "until I realized there was no floor above this level in those days. See up there? Those are the frames where skylights once opened this room to the air.

"Anians like to see the sky. I suspect that they actually slept out of doors as much as possible."

"Leave it to you to come up with a sensible explanation," replied the diplomat. "You haven't much here. Will your books remain at your uncle's?"

"Yes, and most of my other belongings. If you wish to read from my library, you must visit Sir Paren's keep."

"It might be worth the ride. Three days, isn't it? I've never been up that way."

"If I settle in there, I do expect you to visit, Legate. Bolos has named me the official heir so I suppose it is where I should be." Donzalo sounded less than enthusiastic about the idea. "Now, there is something you should see.

"This is a thing I would not show Sir Corgos. The man is too loyal to his duties to be trusted with such a secret." The young knight went to a spot on the side wall, close to the stone walls of the castle itself that bounded the far end of the chamber. There he opened the hidden panel that revealed a secret passage.

The Sharshite eyed the opening and then his friend. "Now I understand why you chose these quarters."

"I know not if I shall long remain here and I wish you to be able to reach the Lady Lomela, should it become necessary. So I trust you and no other, Jobareth Nafal, with this." He started down the steep stairway hewn into the rock. "Come along."

"We should have one of these at the embassy," joked Jobareth, following his friend down a sloping tunnel.

"Oh, um, the rumor is that Blen had one put in while you were gone."

"Indeed? I must ask him about this when he returns!"

They entered the cave at the end of the passage.

"We are on the cliffs?" asked Nafal. Donzalo nodded and pointed toward the narrow opening in the rock. The legate peered through this doorway to the outside world.

"There is a ledge one can follow. Or so Copago claims; I have not attempted it."

"I do not blame you. And," continued Jobareth, "I hope you never need to."

It was unusual for Count Mussago to leave his keep in the hills. He was not young, and somewhat stout, nor had he ever been a man of action.

His eldest son accompanied him. He looked as much a farmer fresh from the fields as did his father. Perhaps he was.

"We received your news of Sorsen," said the count. "Do you intend to act?"

"My lord, I know not his plans. It would be rash to commit Sharsh at this time." Blen knew only that Orgelo's heir had led a company of men out of County Arvaram and was riding north on the Great Road. He claimed to do no more than search for outlaws.

"None need know Sharsh is involved if you ride under my colors. I intend to send a few men under the command of my boy here," he said, placing his gloved hand on the middle-aged man's shoulder, "to make an official visit to County Rosam. There is no reason your company could not ride along."

Blen nodded slowly. He must make a decision. Should he take his men across the river? "Very well, my lord. I must send messages to Sharsh about the action I have chosen."

"Of course." Mussago turned to his son.

"Let Sir Blen command," he told him, "and keep out of the way."

Could all Lama soon be thrown into conflict? Oder and his superiors were not unduly concerned about Sharsh's actions — they knew there were enough tensions among the counts to bring war to the entire region, with or without outside involvement.

The Anian spy had sent a complete report along as soon as he reached one of their stations in western Lama. It was high in the mountains, that station, a little cottage in the wild lands where no one ruled. A courier had left immediately but it would take weeks for his information to reach any maker of decisions.

Which meant he might need to make the decisions himself.

And why not? Oder might have been a general, had he chosen. But he preferred this life and it was where his natural talents lay. Moreover, he suspected that most of the battles of the Anian Empire in the years to come would be losing ones.

Lamans hated Anians. This was a given. None would openly ally themselves with the Empire. Yet, behind the scenes, who might say? There were those who loved neither Sharsh nor An Corade, the two great players in the valley of the Weldar. There were those desired only peace and stability and would welcome the continued Anian presence in Morparas, gateway to Lama.

If the Ani ever lost that city, their power in the west would be at an end. It could not be regained. How long before the Siphic territories would follow?

He could go there. Although Morparas was officially a free city under Anian protection, there was an imperial garrison stationed there. But couriers already rode to warn them of trouble. Oder would not be of much use.

No, he would head into the center of things here in Lama, County Rosam. His old comrade and protege Guesare would be there. Most likely, so would his sister and her sorcerous friend. Even if his presence there proved of no aid to the empire, he could see to Ansa's safety.

To Keep Rosam, then, where much of this current trouble had its beginning. Where better for it to end?

10

Guesare had felt it best to leave Sir Paren's party before they entered the Rosam fortress. Bolos might or might not have tolerated his presence but he would not like it. That could color his relationship with his brother.

So another must guard Donzalo for a while. He should be safe enough in the keep, under the watchful eye of Sir Corgos, now that the king of Sharsh no longer sought his life. Only the sorcerer Radal, driven by his madness, pursued the boy.

Guesare still hated that man, as he had a year and a half earlier when he had first attempted to take Donzalo's life. And nearly succeeded in taking his own, as well. He hoped, when the time came, he would be the one to run a blade through Lord Radal. Though an arrow or even a bullet would give great satisfaction. He should practice more with that new rifle of his.

He had considered visiting Jobareth down at the embassy. But for what purpose? Donzalo would no doubt tell the diplomat that Guesare was in the area. Better to just stay in town a while, play the wandering minstrel for tips and meals, watch and wait. Things would happen, in their time.

From his seat in a small tavern, the sort of clean and rather wholesome place he preferred — to the surprise of many — he saw a trio in the street, an older man and two slender young soldiers. The one, indeed, no more than a boy. What was so familiar about them?

As they passed, he knew. Guesare laughed long and loudly and no one there knew why.

The river could be dammed up here, thought Copago, and a waterwheel placed right over there.

"What are you mulling over now, my husband?" asked the woman by his side.

"Nothing of importance, my dear." Felled trees came down the Abam. A way for them to pass the dam would have to be provided. Timber provided much of the income of Sir Paren's estate.

King ran ahead of them, barking at one of the dark fox squirrels that were plentiful here where farmland met forest.

Janona had greatly missed the knight while he spent his season in the service of Orgelo. She had expected, eventually, to be called to join him in Country Arvaram. To have him return and abide here at this rural keep was far better. Such a life was suited to Sir Copago.

It suited her, too, and their little daughter and, for that matter, King. Janona had grown up a country girl.

Copago put his arm around her as they strolled along the banks of the wild Abam.

Guesare had followed the girls and the man who could only be Lord Doufan back to their house. They knew he was following them, of course, but neither they nor he acknowledged it.

Doufan left them at the door and continued down the unpaved street. After a moment's hesitation, the minstrel decided to follow. The ambassador stopped before a livery stable and beckoned toward his shadow.

"Is there aught you need to know before I ride, sir?" he asked when Guesare reached his side. The man's expression was bland, pleasant, and quite unreadable.

"I was but on a voyage of discovery, my lord, so to speak."

"Call me not lord here. I am a simple old soldier to these people."

Guesare nodded. "I did not know my friends had returned."

"Sir Jan and his esquire? They are attached to the Sharshite embassy." There was an unmistakable twinkle in Lord Doufan's eye. "You should perhaps visit them while they are in town. Or inquire of them at the embassy."

An invitation. "Maybe so, sir. I did mean to call on the legate one of these days."

"I've no doubt he would welcome you. However," the older man advised, "you might do well to call first upon the ambassador."

Doufan said no more but turned and entered the stable.

Some days were good for Bolos. On others, beset by fear and suspicion, he would fall. After, he hated himself for his weakness, wondering if there were any point in trying to be a better man.

There were many better men around him. Bolos felt, sometimes, like a boy in a room full of men. But he would have to depend on those men.

Rumors spoke of troops massing, or already on the move, all over Lama. Beyond, as well — Sharsh had moved men to its borders and the Coradeans and Ani were sure to follow that lead.

He must send word to all his captains, telling them to be watchful. Maybe he should ask his uncle for some of his troops, or conscript more young men of the countryside into his service.

That he could trust Sir Corgos to take care of any necessary actions here at the castle, he knew. Corgos was one of those better men. He seemed a happier man, too, now that his wife was here. The count found himself liking Dame Tiana, with her sharp, humorous observations. The Lady Lomela, it seemed, wasn't always sure what to make of Keep Rosam's newest resident.

Lomela. They had grow distant again, hadn't they? She spent more time with his brother, or that diplomat Nafal, than with him. For a moment, Bolos believed that maybe he hated his brother.

He should not be suspicious of Donzalo. The boy had never done him harm. Not intentionally.

Bolos sipped from his cup of barley-brew. It had grown lukewarm.

Donzalo was a knight now, a fighting man and a good one, by all reports. He should have a post if trouble came. No sense in wasting him up at their uncle's estate.

But either way, he would not mind having him out of the keep again.

There was talk of war on the streets of Celatas. It was inaccurate, mostly, and some of it might have been deemed reckless. The authorities attempted to keep that to a minimum.

People must be allowed to speak their minds. It makes them think that they are free. Lord Doufan had said that; Pol had paid close attention to things the experienced statesman might say as they had journeyed from Sharsh to County Rosam. It had been a long trip and there had been much idle time for listening.

He was right, thought Pol. Let them talk. Listen to them as if you were interested in their point of view and then do whatever you feel is best.

Young Sir Pol had spent much time lately exploring the capital city. It intrigued him, the shops, the temples, the great banking houses, and, most of all, the theaters, just now beginning to open for the new season. He had found the shuttered establishment of Lady Fachalana. There would be no actors on its stage this year.

Rumors abounded as to her whereabouts, as well as those of her father. Most were wildly mistaken.

Prince Modareth had asked him to do this, to wander Celatas and learn its ways, and then tell him of what he had learned. The prince himself had become retiring since his return to the capital and spent much time in his well-guarded apartments.

But there were visitors to those rooms. Princess Carrana made certain of that and she also made certain that Pol could be there to meet them. The Arolinian shopkeeper's son-turned-knight now knew many of the most important and powerful people in Sharsh. He had even been introduced to Jobareth Nafal's father, a wealthy dealer in wines, but made no mention of knowing his son. After all, he had been only an ordinary soldier in his service — why bring that up?

Tonight, he was to meet the crown prince. His wife, the Princess Mara, had returned days before from the seashore with their children, and Gawis was hosting a party to mark the occasion. Pol had glimpsed the princess once in the halls of King's Keep, a slender, dark woman, who, according to gossip, was as shy as his own master.

He supposed Carrana would also keep introducing him to young women. That was all well and good but Pol had no time for such right now. There were so many things he wanted to do here, so many directions he wished to travel.

For Pol, all things had now become possible.

11

It was the Fay. Radal had become certain of this. They were giving their aid to his daughter, probably without her even realizing it.

The sorcerer did not entirely disapprove of this. Fachalana needed stability right now as she wrestled with her growing power. They had helped to keep her from straying down those dark paths to madness.

But it served to hinder his own attempts to communicate, as they hid her from him, gave her some safe haven he could not find and enter.

Now he knew who his opponents were and he knew also how to defeat them. Fairie was not his equal. The People of the Air had never been given such power.

They would frustrate him no longer.

Lord Radal climbed to the top floor of the crumbling tower he had appropriated as his base. Here, he kept the ebony cask containing the one object of power he had been able to bring with him from Mountain Keep. He would need it.

And he would need all his strength. Radal would be attempting great magics.

"Lord Doufan has been expecting you."

Guesare followed the scribe down the hall. The man seemed familiar. As they paused at the door, he asked, "Do I know you sir?"

The man turned and answered with a smile. "We met years ago in Lanlaz, Sir Guesare. I believe you sat in on one of my classes. I believe you also never paid your tuition."

"Oh, the university. How came you to be Doufan's secretary? If the question be not too personal."

"It is not. I decided to see the world and attached myself to the best man I could find."

"That simple?"

"Indeed yes, sir. That simple. Lord Doufan wishes to speak privately to you so I shall remain here."

That simple and not that simple, thought the scribe as he stood in the hall. He would not have met Doufan if the diplomat had not visited Lorj. He had been intrigued by the man and, chances were, would never leave him. It was a better and more interesting life than teaching dolts the declension of Muram nouns, anyway.

The ambassador got directly to the point, after waving Guesare into a chair. He took one beside him, rather than placing his oversize desk between them.

"Did you know that Lady Fachalana has sorcerous powers?"

"Yes, my lord. I have known for some time of her gifts." Thanks to the Prince of the Fay and his people.

"One might ask whether the lady shares her father's gift or his curse. I only learned when we ate together yesterday." Doufan paused for a moment. "I was almost certain that you knew or I would not have said anything to you of it.

"Your mother has powers, has she not?"

This man knows too many things, thought Guesare. "She does, sir. As do I, in small part." He might as well admit to that. "Do you know the story of Donzalo's time with us in the Cuddon?"

"I have heard rumors. Would you give me the tale?"

And so the minstrel did what perhaps he did best, tell a story. It was the story of Donzalo and Jola, half-sister to Fachalana, and of their love. It was a story of sorcery and of loss.

When the tale ended, Doufan sat a while, staring into the cup he held. "So, not only Donzalo lost someone when Jola was slain, but also Radal," he said at last.

"We believe this is why he so hates Donzalo."

"Yet he brought it on himself by pursuing the boy. And no doubt hates himself equally."

Guesare deemed that quite likely. "It has driven him to madness."

"That is an occupational hazard with wizards, is it not?" asked the diplomat, not expecting an answer. "It must be watched for in Fachalana."

"Perhaps, as did Jola, she should dream a while in Fairie," said the Cuddonian. He would speak of that to Donzalo sometime. Donzalo should learn that Jola's sister shared in her abilities. That thought led him to another. "Do you think Jobareth should know of all this?"

"I would allow Lady Fachalana to inform her friend in her own time. Unless, of course, circumstances require it.

"For now, I do hope you visit them there in town, Sir Guesare. Move into our house if you wish. Someone really should keep an eye on that pair!"

There would be no point in taking the main road directly to Ros-town, passing through Count Dordos's domain. There were already Sharshite troops secretly there anyway, in wait, and Blen would not wish to compromise them by riding boldly through.

No, he and the men of Count Mussago would angle south of east and hope to meet Sorsen along the Great Road. The distance was nearly the same from here.

Two-score of his troopers rode with him and near another score of Mussago's men. Sir Blen knew that the count could put a far larger force in the field if need be but wisely would not commit troops at this time. They were investigating, not going to war — he hoped.

Mussago's son — who was named also Mussago — rode beside him. He was a taciturn fellow, lean where his father was fat, and darkened by the sun. "This road now will lead directly to the Weldar," he said, after a day spent following winding dusty trails. It looked a fair road.

"Where does it end in relation to Ros-town?" asked the Sharshite knight. His courier duties had never taken him into these lands.

The man pondered the question before drawling, "Maybe four or five leagues south. Maybe more."

That was closer than Blen might have wished but there was no more time to waste. "That would be in County Rosam, wouldn't it? There is a ferry there?"

Mussago the Younger nodded. "There is a ferry but the crossing lies just below the Rosam border. We won't have to cross Dordos's borders, either. That's what you wanted, isn't it?"

"Indeed it is. Thank you, sir." It would be more than five leagues if the crossing was below County Rosam. Blen suspected that the ferry was not large and would require several trips to transport all his men.

Even the one at Ros-town would probably take three.

"Let's ride, men," he called. "If we want to beat Sir Sorsen we need to move!"

Ride they did, through sunbaked hills of grass and scrub that gradually grew greener. In time, fields of corn and of beans lay on either side of their way, and they crossed small streams. The great River Weldar lay ahead.

Now, the burgess of Oles were voicing their concern.

Madin sat patiently while his master scrutinized the letter, brow furrowed, and then ran his hand through his lank hair. Count Bolos's hair was thinning, wasn't it?

The man would get his thoughts together soon and dictate something. It would be up to Madin to better order those thoughts on paper and present the count with a reply he might sign. At least he was remaining sober most of these days.

"They don't like what's happening, up in Oles," muttered Bolos, to no one in particular. "But they worry only about trade being disrupted.

"They would welcome the Anians back, I think, if they thought it good for business."

Perceptive, thought Madin. The count was not the fool some thought him.

"I might myself, rather than let Sharsh and the Coradeans divvy up our land. What good was it to marry the daughter of King Lareth if he is going to plot against me?" He looked to his secretary. "Pardon me, Madin. I speak unwisely.

"Let us compose a fitting reply to Oles, letting them know that all is under control here in County Rosam and denying all rumors. And perhaps asking them if they would commit to coming to our aid, if necessary."

It was not the butler who opened the door to Jobareth but the minstrel Guesare. Doufan had told him that the man might take up residence in their house.

"The young, um, gentlemen are upstairs, Legate. I sent the old man out to fetch some of your wine."

"I hope you have not been doing that too frequently," laughed Nafal. "I have little left of what I brought from Sharsh.

"So the ladies are maintaining their charade?"

"They are professionals," replied Guesare with complete seriousness. "They would not break character." He looked to the stairs. "Here come Jan and Saj now."

"You may call us by our own names tonight," said Fachalana as she came forward and embraced her friend. "We may dress the part of men but we shall not play them now."

"And lovely women you are, even so clad," replied the diplomat.

"Indeed, were I the sort to marry a woman, Ansa would be my first choice," declared Guesare.

"Only because I remind you of my brother," the Anian dryly replied.

The door creaked behind them as the old butler entered with a covered pitcher. "It's not your best stuff, sir," said he to Jobareth, with a smile, "but then, it's not your worst either. Shall I leave it?"

"Yes, please. I think we shall sit out on the porch on this warm evening."

"I'll bring some candles, sir." The man disappeared into his pantry.

"Things are slowing down in Ros-town," observed Guesare as they sat watching the stars slide down toward the Weldar. "There is another one of those Laman feast days coming, isn't there?"

"Autumn Feast," replied Jobareth, "when they mark the equinox. It is primarily a religious occasion here."

"But there are celebrations, too," Ansa said. "Dancing will most surely occur."

"Oh, the Lamans will dance anytime," observed Jobareth Nafal, "and then turn around and follow it with a solemn day of fasting."

"What good is a fast without also a feast?" asked Guesare. "Otherwise it is but self-denial for its own sake."

"Now you sound like our friend Grippo. Is the boy still up at Sir Paren's keep?" he asked Guesare.

"He is, and likely to remain now his brother has taken up residence," replied the minstrel.

"Too bad. He is wasted there."

Fachalana had been following this exchange with interest. She did not think she had ever fasted in her life. "What is the purpose of fasting? It seems an odd practice."

"Our abstinences should make us better appreciate our pleasures and help us recognize those things that are important to our lives." Ansa had spoken very quietly but very clearly.

Guesare nodded approvingly. "Now I wish to marry you all the more, my dear."

Fachalana laughed gaily. "You can add our Guesare to your list, right behind Blen and Pol." Then, she suddenly stiffened.

"No." Her long fingers were whitening where they gripped the arms of her chair.

"What is it, Lana?" exclaimed Ansa, going immediately to her side.

"It is — my father!"

And with that, the Lady Fachalana fell into a faint.

12

In Celatas, a man in a long gray tunic felt the disturbance. Lord Radal, he knew at once, and shuddered. He was no match for that man, perhaps the mightiest mage alive. "Wine," he called to the bar maid. Enough would dull his mind to what was happening in the other realms.

His own master would sense this too, he knew. There would be no contact between them this night.

And no need. Their plan was already laid and action ready to be taken.

The wizard could not help but think Radal had been somehow involved in stopping their first attempt at assassination. Had it not been his own daughter who interfered? How he could have known of it was, and would most likely remain, a mystery.

Nothing would stop them this time, not even that boy of a bodyguard.

He drank deeply of the cheap red vintage and called for more.

Guesare carried the limp form of Fachalana into the house and laid her upon a couch.

"I do not understand," said Jobareth Nafal. "What has Lord Radal to do with this?"

The minstrel turned to him. "Our Fachalana has inherited the powers of her father. He seeks to link her mind to his."

"She has long been able to block him," said Ansa, looking up from where she knelt by her friend's side. "She has struggled with her father many times and won.

"I do not know what has changed."

Fachalana. Speak to me.

No, Father. She looked for a way to escape. Where was her refuge, her silver land?

She felt it was near but she could not see it.

Your friends can not help you.

Friends? What friends? Someone had been aiding her, hadn't they? Fachalana realized of a sudden. *Help me!* she cried.

We can not. Your father has found us out. He has blocked our way. The voices seemed far off.

You must do it yourself. She heard no more.

A door, she thought. All I need is a door and my sanctuary will lie on the other side. The door is — there.

It was. She stepped through.

I can follow you now, my daughter. Do not run from me. There was hurt in his voice. Her father loved her, she knew, but she could not let him in. It was too dangerous.

On the silver plain she stood, the plain where she had first glimpsed Donzalo. But Radal had been there as well, that time. It was true that he could enter here. There were no longer any wards against him.

If she could only reach that far, gleaming building, find safety behind its tall silver doors. Fachalana knew she would be safe there. *Come,* said a voice, a beautiful golden woman's voice, *and I shall keep thee safe.*

Who are you? she called. She was trying to approach the temple yet it seemed to slip away from her, into the silver mists.

I am your sister Jola. I am the goddess Diba. You must find the strength to come to me and to be one with me, Fachalana. Then none may stand against thee.

I will try. She was nearing the doors now but a towering shadow, blacker than any night she had known, lay between her and the temple.

She could not pass it. Her father was too powerful.

I would not harm you, my child.

I know, Father. But she feared him, none the less, as she fell into the embrace of his mind.

Fachalana felt his astonishment as he read her secrets. And his emotions provided a door for her and she was able to follow them into Radal's own mind and read there.

You know my secrets now, Father, but I know yours.

Perhaps it was fair trade, for Fachalana now knew that Lord Radal would never again be able to do what he had done to her. She knew how to block his way.

With a word, she did, awakening in the little house in Ros-town.

"There is a body of men across the river," observed Habidros.

Sorsen turned his back to the dawn and peered into the distance. "Indeed there is. I can not make them out well from here." The son of Orgelo pulled a long metal cylinder from a leather tube that hung from his saddle. Sir Habidros had wondered about that odd holster.

"Perhaps my sighting tube will help." Sorsen put one end to his eye. "Ah, the colors are those of Count Mussago. The sun is catching them now."

The Cuddonian recognized the device, a simple tube with a black interior that helped the eye make out objects at a distance. He had seen them attached to rifles back in the Siphic states.

"I have heard," said Sir Sorsen, slipping the tube back into its scabbard, "that the Coradeans are now placing a glass lens at either end of these instruments and greatly increasing their efficacy."

"It is a large party, sir," said Habidros, more interested in matters at hand than what was being invented across the sea. "Larger than ours, I think."

"If they are Mussago's rabble, it hardly matters," replied Sorsen. "But that is not to dismiss them. It is odd that the count would send out so large a troop."

"The ferry is on our side, Sir Sorsen. Shall we go over and ask them their purpose?"

The leader of their company thought only a moment before making a decision. "You go, Sir Habidros, and take a couple men at arms with you. I shall remain here with our company." He slapped his comrade on the back. "I trust you to deal wisely. " Sorsen knew his second in command was more skillful in such things than he.

Four oarsmen steered the modest barge into the broad stream The current was somewhat sluggish at this time of year and they crossed without great effort. An hour later, the ferry made a return to the east side of the Weldar.

His two men stepped from the vessel but Habidros was not with them, a leathery stranger having accompanied them in his stead. One of the soldiers handed Sorsen a note.

Sir, it read, *we agreed to an exchange to show our mutual good will and faith. I will remain here and Count Mussago's son will ride with you.* Sorsen looked up. Yes, he did remember the man from one official visit or another. He read on. *Officially, the younger Mussago is on a state visit, accompanied by men of his household. However, many of those across the river are soldiers of Sharsh. I know their commander.*

We have agreed to progress in parallel to Ros-town, each on our side of the river, where one can keep the other in view. I did warn them that there might be a chance that you would need to turn aside and pursue bandits at some point. If so, Mussago is to wave the banner he carries.

Again he looked at his guest. A long cloth of white was wound over one shoulder and tied at his waist. "Very well, Sir Mussago," said Sorsen. "You might as well have the horse of Captain Habidros."

"Master Mussago," replied the nobleman. Mussago had a low opinion of knighthood and of honors in general.

"Benawis is a traitor! He serves my father." These were Fachalana's first words on awakening from her trance. It was morning, though it seemed to her that she had only been gone a few minutes.

"I will tend to him," growled Guesare.

"Now," said the noblewoman, "before he receives warning. Father can speak to him from a distance."

"He is a wizard? We must deal with him."

Jobareth was already scribbling a note. "Take this," he said, "it will explain your mission to the guards and Lord Doufan." Guesare gave it a cursory look and stuffed it into his belt pouch.

"I shall come with you," said Ansa. "Fachalana will be well taken care of."

Within two minutes they had armed and outfitted themselves and were out the door. Their horses were at the nearby livery stable — the pair should soon be riding for the embassy.

Ansa silently said a prayer to the Great Sky as she hurried away. She could not remember the last time she had prayed, and certainly not to the primal deity of her people. It was not a prayer for her friend; it was a prayer for vengeance.

"Jobo," whispered Fachalana. He came close and knelt by her. "I could not hide my secrets from my father. He wrested the knowledge of Ros's paternity from me."

"It does not matter, Lana. How could he use it?"

"I do not know. But I fear he will find a way."

13

Modareth and the Princess Carrana would attend the theater tomorrow night. It was at Carrana's insistence that they were going; the prince had no great interest in the stage and would have preferred that both stayed safely home.

So would Pol. He might no longer be Prince Modareth's constant companion but his protection was still his concern. Now, he stood in the shadows across the street from the theater. It was still early in the day and there was little traffic in this district of the city.

He was watching three men. Two seemed stagehands; they had slipped out of a side door minutes earlier to meet with the third, a fellow in a long gray tunic. That tunic aroused Pol's interest. He remembered the description of a suspicious man in Dor who had so dressed.

Not that this trio were not suspicious enough on their own. Why would they meet out here in the street? If their business were legitimate, they would have gone inside.

That was a little thing, true, but enough for Pol. He decided to follow the man after he left the pair at the theater. It was easy to remain unseen, even though the young knight had no training in spy-craft — the fellow seemed quite oblivious to his surroundings.

In a shabbier neighborhood, the man entered one of a row of houses and did not reappear, although his shadow waited nearly an hour. He must have rooms there, surmised Pol.

Pol had met men here in Celatas, ruthless men who served the king's interests and would gladly pay his suspect a visit. He would go see one of them today.

And tomorrow, he would be sure to keep an eye out for those other two at the theater.

Benawis knew that Radal cared not for him and that his usefulness to his master was at an end. Yet he had warned him. Come to me if you can, he had said.

Perhaps if he could make his way to the sorcerer lord he might serve still in some way. What else was there for him? His career in Sharsh's diplomatic corps was gone. Sharsh itself was gone; he could not go home.

Benawis believed in his own abilities. There was nothing he could not accomplish in this world of hapless fools, who existed only so he might use them. Wherever he might escape to, he would make a success of it. Maybe he would just turn his back on Radal and this whole situation and head down to Morparas. It was said to be a good place for a man such as himself.

He gathered together a few belongings and threw them into a bag. Before anyone here was aware of his betrayals he would slip out of the embassy and disappear.

There was a bustle below. Had the news reached here already? The secretary hurried down the back stairs and through a door into the stables.

A guard blocked his way. "We've orders to stop you, sir."

Benawis, without a moment's pause, slipped his dagger between the man's ribs. Good fortune — a horse, already saddled, stood ready to ride. A slender boy loitered near it, one of the stable-hands, no doubt.

He brandished his bloody blade. "Out of my way, boy, or you'll get the same!" Benawis turned to mount Guesare's horse, first tossing his bag across its back.

Wound about her waist, beneath her belt, Ansa carried a bow string. Any Ani bowman would have an extra ready at hand in this manner. Yet any would also know that it had a second purpose. With an economy born of practice, she slipped the string from its hiding place and around the man's neck.

A few moments later, Guesare and a pair of guardsmen burst through the door. He looked at the man on the floor, his wide dead eyes staring into the void, and then at Ansa.

"Did you not think my brother would train me in such things?" asked she.

"There is little pleasure in my life these days, Donni."

Donzalo said nothing. He knew how things were but he knew not how to comfort Lomela.

The princess attempted to lighten their conversation. "Ros is getting larger every day. He reminds me of someone."

"Best not say that around Bolos, my lady."

She nodded soberly. "He is jealous of you anyway."

"There is little I can do about that, Lomela. We are each who we are." He gave her a smile. "I can think of reasons I might be jealous of my brother."

"There is nothing there to be jealous of these days. I fear Bolos has grown to distrust me as he does everyone else. He is becoming a stranger to me.

"I feel all alone these days. I pray that you will not leave me, Donzalo. I pray to all my gods and even to yours."

He took her in his arms. He had loved her once, with all the fervor of a first love, but knew he did no longer. But Donzalo cared greatly still for the Lady Lomela.

"I may have no choice but to leave, my princess. But know that I will always return."

The head of King Lareth's secret police in Celatas was a small, rotund man named Gos. Whether he had a title to go with his name, none of his subordinates knew. It was a secret police, after all.

He stood before both the royal princes now. "Sir Pol was correct about the man," said he. "Most definitely a sorcerer and there were papers that clearly incriminated him." He shook his head. "A bit of an amateur, I must say."

"Is he Partanacan?" asked Gawis.

"No, my lord, he is a man of Sharsh. Recently recruited, most likely, for his, um, skills."

That sounded logical to Modareth. "You said there were accomplices?"

"Yes, sir. We have questioned him quite thoroughly and he gave up names. We will be watching for the two assassins at the theater. Perhaps, my lord," he hesitated slightly, then continued, "you should not attend."

"My wife would be terribly disappointed. But perhaps so." A question then occurred to the prince. "But how will you catch them if there is no one there for them to assassinate? Or attempt to assassinate, I should say!"

"Sir Pol has some thoughts on that, my lord," responded the little spy-master with a sly smile.

What could he do with his new knowledge? wondered Radal. That Donzalo was the father of Lomela's child was momentous, indeed, but would be near impossible to prove. It could most certainly provide the wedge he desired to drive between the brothers.

But there were ways to suggest it to Bolos. He could send dreams, after a fashion, to the man, images that would enter his sleep and haunt his days. Not if he were drunk, though; then his mind would not be receptive.

So the whole premise on which he and Lareth had originally plotted against Donzalo's life had been wrong. That had been the secret Fachalana had told the king.

Lord Radal briefly thought of his spy Benawis. Had the man escaped? He had little talent and was probably of no more use as a tool, but Radal had learned not to throw tools away.

He would prefer he not be questioned, as well.

Fachalana. He would never again be able to reach her as he had. The sorcerer marveled at his daughter's strength, her ability to read him as he had read her, when their minds had occupied the same space.

He hoped that what she had read of her father's soul would not be too much for her to bear. It was nearly too much for him. Too often, now, he saw doors open to him that he had hoped to keep closed. Too often, they beckoned him into ways from which he knew he could never return.

The Fay had not been able to aid Fachalana, but there had been some other, hadn't there? He had sensed it only but knew it had almost provided her with a refuge where he could not follow. And that other had seemed, in some way, familiar to him.

It was time to call all his men to him here at this tower. It was time to go destroy not only Donzalo but the man's world and those he loved.

14

The ride north was uneventful. Blen found his Cuddonian guest an entertaining companion on their journey; Sorsen did not have the same experience with the silent Mussago. Both troops, in time, found themselves on the outskirts of Rostown, those of Count Mussago and Sharsh on the west, the company from County Arvaram on the east. These latter stopped just below the mouth of the Abam to make their camp. To reach Ros-town itself, they would need go upstream a short distance to where a narrow bridge carried the Great Road across this lesser stream. Heavier traffic went further up yet to a place it might be forded.

"Make camp here," Sir Blen told his contingent, halting by an open field just south of the town. "I shall go across and see what the intentions of Sorsen and Mussago might be."

He, Habidros, and two men at arms — he felt it diplomatic to choose one each from his own troops and those of Mussago — took the ferry across the Weldar.

Mussago and Sorsen awaited them on the shore, having left the Arvaram men encamped.

"The first thing," said Sir Sorsen, once the group had repaired to a nearby tavern, "is to go pay a visit to the count. He surely did not expect our troops to arrive without notice. We have sent a man ahead to announce both myself and Master Mussago. Then," he said, "we must have a council about all of this."

"I'd best not accompany you to Borrago's, I mean Bolos's, keep," stated Blen. "He knows me as part of the Sharshite embassy, not a soldier in your father's service, Master Mussago." He gave a little bow to the man who gravely returned it.

"I am not sure how Count Bolos feels about me," said Habidros.

"Nor am I," said Sir Blen. "You might better return to your own camp." Sorsen nodded his agreement. "I shall ride with you a way, however, gentlemen. I should report to the ambassador before I take further action."

"I do not understand why these companies of men have suddenly appeared." Bolos ceased pacing and sank heavily into a chair. "Mussago and Sorsen, arriving separately but coming here together, both expressing vague concerns about rumors they have heard."

"Perhaps the rumors they have heard were about each other," suggested Lady Lomela.

"Indeed, my lady! I think they trust each other not at all." He turned toward his brother, standing on the other side of the room and seeming to idly look out the window. "You were recently at Orgelo's, Donzalo. Did you hear aught there?"

"Nothing much at Orgelo's. But Count Mussago seemed to have some concerns." He did not feel inclined to mention the presence of Sir Blen and Sharshite troops there.

"The two are rivals," observed Sir Corgos. "If one took action, the other was bound to do the same."

Bolos nodded. "Let us hope the process does not continue with every count in Lama."

All four thought on that for a little while.

Then Bolos again spoke. "I hear too of strange incidents at the Sharshite embassy. One of their diplomats murdered and a guardsman sorely wounded!

"On top of that, Sir Blen seems to have returned and is friendly with Sorsen and Mussago."

Sir Corgos replied, "The ambassador claims that the slain man was an assassin and that he wounded the guard. I have learned from some of the staff there that he was the secretary to the legate. I have also heard that he was most expertly garroted by someone."

"That is the Anian way," observed Donzalo. Both he and Lomela thought of their friend Ansa. Could one of her countrymen be here? Neither knew that the woman herself had returned.

"I would doubt that there are any Anians in the embassy," said Corgos, "but none of the servants seem to know just who did it."

"I am certain Lord Doufan knows," Lomela said. "And I am just as certain he will never tell you."

Pol of Arolin could scarce keep from laughing. He stood in the shadowed rear of the royal box, while two of Gos's men, in the guises of Prince Modareth and his wife Carrana, sat watching the play.

To his eyes, they looked ridiculous. For those in the darkened theater, the deception probably worked well enough.

Although his attention was directed elsewhere, he could not help occasionally hearing bits of dialog from the stage. *I could write better than that,* he thought.

There was a signal from the other side of the hall, a man draping a red cloak over the front of his box. Something was happening. His two companions had seen it as well and put their hands to the hilts of their daggers. They would use them only if absolutely necessary and attempt to keep up this charade. Those in the theater might never even realize anything had happened.

Pol stepped deeper into shadow. The assassins would know there was a guard in the box but there was no reason to make him easy to see. Slowly, stealthily, the door was opened and a pair, dressed as ordinary stagehands and brandishing short swords, entered. The knight hoped that Gos's minions were close behind these two — Pol had no desire to engage in a sword fight this evening.

He stepped boldly out before them, sword in hand, hoping to create a moment of confusion as their attention went from their intended victims to him. Their sword points wavered. It was time enough for several burly policemen to enter and lay hands on the pair and drag them away with minimum fuss.

Then Sir Pol took a chair and tried to enjoy the remainder of the play. However, he found far too many things to criticize.

"I still feel weak," complained Fachalana.

"A weak Fachalana is still stronger than most women," replied her friend Ansa. "Give it a day and you'll be out challenging men to duels."

"I hope so. I know my body will grow stronger. But there was so much darkness in his mind, Ansa. I do not know if I can contain it all."

The Anian did not know how to answer that. And found she did not need to for Jobareth Nafal and the minstrel Guesare came into the room.

"How is our Lady Fachalana?" asked the diplomat.

"She feels weak," responded Ansa, giving him a look that clearly said to ask no more.

Jobareth accordingly broached another subject. "I think it is time that Sir Jan and his esquire disappeared. Lord Doufan would like me to invite the Ladies Fachalana and Maresta to come and stay with us for a while."

"Won't it seem as though we suddenly appeared in County Rosam without crossing its borders?" asked Ansa.

"We can claim you were with Sir Blen's company. In the confusion of bringing some three-score men across the border, might not a pair of demure ladies have been overlooked?"

"It's plausible enough," agreed Guesare. "Blen will go along with it?"

"He suggested it once Lord Doufan told him of the ladies' presence here." Nafal gave the women a look that seemed filled with questions. "Sir Blen seems quite concerned about our ladies."

"We spent much time together," murmured Fachalana.

The butler entered with a tray and a pitcher of wine. "Thank you," said Jobareth. "Just leave it."

"A good man," commented Guesare and then suggested a quite different destination for the pair. "My ladies, why not accompany me to Sir Paren's? It would be a better place to rest and you would be far from the eyes of Bolos and his spies.

Ansa nodded. "In time, maybe. Are you leaving soon?"

"Sir Paren hasn't named a day but I think he will not wait much longer. He would like to be home for Autumn Feast."

"I think we should accept Lord Doufan's gracious invitation," said Lady Fachalana. "If we wish to go further in time, it is a good starting point." She sat up on the couch and continued, "And I would very much like to visit Lomela. It's time she knew we were here!"

There had been a camp here, a large one, and for quite some time. They had gone no more than a day or two ago.

A filthy bunch, too. There was no military discipline among them, thought Perdos. These were brigands. They might be the men who had followed Sojel.

Gone where? East, he could see. There was no point in following their trail; he was not concerned with them right now, though he would gladly see every man of them swinging from a gallows.

And down the road a good distance, another camp, a new one. He had seen them arrive and recognized the colors and insignia of Count Orgelo. He also recognized the tall Cuddonian who had ridden in soon after, another of Guesare's brothers.

As to the minstrel's whereabouts, he was uncertain. He had heard that he was being seen around town, plying his trade. Perdos was unwelcome in Ros-town or he might have simply found the man and challenged him. But if the town guards laid hands on him, he might never find another chance.

It was much too far to see the Rosam keep from here. He had spent some good times there, he and his brother. Perdos felt a momentary nostalgia.

Maybe Bolos would lift the ban on him, let him return from exile. His former employer had always treated him well.

Ah, but that was a time that would not return. Perdos had other dreams now and they did not include serving in a nobleman's guard. And first, he must settle matters with Guesare.

15

"My father told me to leave things to your discretion, Blen. But if you take an action that I feel we can not support, I will withdraw my men and my authority."

He's probably been working on that speech, thought Habidros. But it is a quite sensible statement to make.

"Certainly, Master Mussago. If I need to take drastic actions, I shall do so in the name of King Lareth, not your father."

That seemed to satisfy the man, who added no more to their debate.

Habidros himself had no voice at all in this council, other than to make suggestions. It was up to Blen and Sorsen to come to decisions here.

"We should remain in our current locations," Sorsen felt. "At another time, I might have encamped my men outside the walls of Keep Rosam but I fear that would make Bolos nervous."

"That it might," said Sir Blen. "So each of us would be separated from Ros-town by water. Although," he added, "you can cross yours more quickly."

"Then come over and join us," Habidros suggested.

Sorsen nodded approval. "It would reassure the count that we are not about to start a war in his front yard.

"And, after all, we are here for the same reason. We are concerned about what is going on here and the plans of certain — traitors." Sorsen had been fully filled in on the part of Lord Radal in the situation. This did not mean that he suddenly trusted Sharsh.

"Very well," agreed Blen. "I shall send our men over a few at a time." He gave a quick glance at Mussago. The man seemed to have no objections.

"By the way, Sir Sorsen, did you ever catch up to any of those outlaws?"

"We did not, Sir Blen. There are rumors that they have ridden east toward the Cuddon."

"Sir Paren should know if they are passing near his keep," said Habidros. "He may want to return with his company."

"I shall tell him when I visit the count tomorrow," Sorsen promised. "But he has a good master of arms up there to take care of things in his absence."

His men were on the march. They should reach him here on the edge of the Cuddon in a day or two.

Radal was weary. His struggle with his daughter had taken much from him but he had not rested. There was too much else to be dealt with, both in this world and others.

And magic always took its toll.

The sorcerer had been sending dreams to Count Bolos. These dreams were not fully formed but, rather, suggestions. The count's own mind would provide the details. He could not make Bolos believe things he did not already suspect, somewhere deep in his soul. Radal would feed those suspicions and fears, make them grow strong, make them a fever that consumed the man.

He had what he had read in Fachalana's mind to thank for the directions he turned those dreams.

By the time he moved westward with his followers, Count Bolos might be ready to welcome him as a friend — the only friend left in a world that had betrayed him.

He had found Lomela weeping. He did not know why she wept; there were too many possibilities these days. Donzalo simply took her into his arms and asked no questions.

So they were when his brother entered the room.

Bolos was quite obviously drunk. "Slut of Sharsh!" he snarled. "First going behind my back with your dandy Nafal and now my own brother."

The princess was taken aback. There was enough truth in what he had said to stun her into a momentary silence.

"There is nothing between the lady and myself," said Donzalo. "I only comforted her as a friend."

"Do not trust her, Donni," was the count's slurred response. He looked at his brother. "Why should I even trust you?"

"Bolos!" Lomela stepped forward and took her husband's arm. In his anger he shook her off and the Lady Lomela fell to the floor. He stared for a moment as Donzalo stooped to assist her in rising.

"Leave my wife alone. Leave her where she belongs." He slapped his brother fully across the face and turned with outstretched hand, as if he would do the same to his wife.

A massive fist met with Bolos's jaw.

"I am sorry, my brother," Donzalo said, helping Bolos to his feet.

Sir Corgos burst into the room, followed by a pair of guardsmen. An attendant had run to him as soon as it had seemed there might be trouble. He looked from the solicitous Donzalo to the count, rubbing his jaw.

"Place my brother under arrest," ordered Count Bolos.

"Arrest, my lord?" The master of arms was astounded.

"Yes, yes." Bolos seemed suddenly unsure of himself. "Confine him to his quarters. I'll think on how to deal with this later." He stared at his wife for a moment, without expression, and then stumbled from the room.

The young knight silently accompanied the older one down to his own rooms.

"I will not lock you in, Donzalo, but there will be guards outside your door. Do not try to get by them," warned Corgos.

"Certainly, Sir Corgos. You have my promise."

"And that is good enough for me, Sir Donzalo."

The young man sat a while in his room, pondering.

Why should he wait here? At best, his brother would banish him so he might as well do that himself. Everyone might be better off that way. Donzalo went to the hidden panel in his quarters.

I'd best make sure this is well concealed, he told himself, and dragged a chest close to the wall before entering. Then he pulled it against the wall from within the passage and slid the panel closed. Down to the cave in the cliffs he went, and out into the night.

In the darkness, he groped his way along the ledge, clinging to the cliff wall. Thank Kamat it is not raining, he said to himself.

His pathway widened and Donzalo saw trees ahead, scrubby pines rooted into a rubble of rock and sparse soil. On their far side, a gentler slope allowed him to descend — still with care — to the base of the cliffs.

He stood on the more level ground and looked up at the way he had come, the sheer black face of the cliffs more a shadow than a tangible object. Could he ever return as he had promised Lomela?

There was a man near him. He could barely make out his form by the light of the stars. Donzalo drew his sword — he had kept one in his chamber and had made sure to strap it on before leaving. "Who is there?" he asked.

"A good evening to you, Sir Donzalo," said Oder.

Of Dreams: the Tenth Tale

1

"Gone? How could this be?"

Sir Corgos shook his head. "I know not, my lord. The guard was outside his door and saw naught."

"They must have been bribed. You will question them and find who is behind this." Count Bolos glared at his master of arms, his frustration obvious.

Corgos did not believe his men had been corrupted. Not that they couldn't be but it would mean that someone in the keep had turned not only Donzalo's guards but also the soldiers at the gates into traitors in a matter of hours. That seemed unlikely, to say the least.

But he could find no other explanation.

Not one soul had seen Donzalo since the master of arms himself had closed his door on him. Questioning would do little good now; men must be sent out into town and countryside to search. He would dispatch a messenger to the captain of the garrison down in Ros-town to be on the lookout.

The count had his own personal network of spies, too. Sir Corgos knew this. Donzalo would have done well to travel quickly and far. Best the boy leave all this behind and find peace somewhere.

It would all settle down soon, anyway. Count Bolos had greater concerns than the whereabouts of his younger brother. Even if that younger brother did fell him with a blow to the jaw.

He probably didn't even hit him that hard, thought Corgos. If Donzalo had put his full force into his punch, Bolos might never have gotten up.

But when all this had blown over, one question would remain: how did the boy get out of his guarded quarters?

Sir Jan and his attendant Saj had gone across the river. Lady Fachalana and her companion Maresta had returned in the company of Sir Blen.

As they rode up to the embassy, Blen was intrigued to hear their tale of the successes of the young soldier he had left in his stead, back in Dor. "Sir Pol, it is? I knew the boy had potential but did not expect him to rise so quickly."

"Pol has been a most fortunate lad," opined Fachalana.

"It was not just luck that brought Pol here to his posting in Lama. I picked the men that came with us and he had already proven himself bright and dependable.

"And I chose to send him with Jobareth to Mountain Keep when he asked for a good man as an attendant. Though it seems to me," he mused, "that Pol seemed eager to volunteer for that duty."

"He saw an opportunity for advancement," said Ansa. "Nothing complicated there."

"Or maybe he was just sick of guard duty in Ros-town," Blen replied. "Either way, he was out to change his fortunes."

"I don't like this horse," complained Fachalana, "nor this saddle." Her knightly steed had remained behind at Mussago's camp and she was riding sidesaddle for the first time in weeks.

"I'll see about getting your own horse over to you in a while. To come riding back on Sir Jan's mount would have been suspicious."

"But I fear you must continue to ride sidesaddle," said Ansa. "It is expected of you."

Ansa boldly straddled her horse, as no one had any expectations at all about her.

"I hope to ride no mount for some time," sighed Fachalana, "other than a feather bed."

King Lareth held two letters, dated a few days apart. Both were from Lord Doufan and both concerned the Lady Fachalana.

He had been amused by the first, telling how the ladies had arrived incognito in County Rosam. Lareth tried to picture them accoutered as fighting men and found it not that difficult. He knew Fachalana well.

The second had been alarming. So the lady had inherited her father's abilities? This helped explain a number of small things about which he had wondered. It also told him that Lord Radal was still actively seeking to take the life of Donzalo Rosam.

Would it matter if he did? Yes, Donzalo was the father of Lomela's child, the child prophesied to rule in Lama, but it would not do for that paternity to be discovered. Kings must sometimes be cynical, he told himself.

But most of all, kings must not act rashly. He would let things play out as they would in Lama and take action only if necessary.

Bolos knew he had acted badly. The count truly wished that Donzalo had not fled, however he had accomplished it. They would have smoothed all this over when they had both cooled down in the morning.

He liked to think that he would have dealt leniently with his brother and sent him packing off to Uncle Paren's with orders to stay away a good long while.

The count rubbed at his sore jaw. Yes, he would sign an official order to just that effect. If Donzalo wished to return, then, he would need fear nothing. But one way or another, he did not want his brother here in the keep again.

He had been wrong to doubt his wife, hadn't he? Yet in his dreams, he saw her in Donzalo's arms, and their embrace was not innocent.

They were dreams. They meant nothing. He must apologize to Lomela. He had never laid hands on her so before. It was the wine that did it.

Bolos vowed to take never another drink while he lived and he did not. But he still had disturbing dreams.

"We of the Ani — those of us who are spies — know of that passage below Keep Rosam. We built it, after all."

"So I had assumed," said Donzalo, "I and Sir Copago."

"He showed it to you?"

The young Laman nodded. "And he had learned of it from our father. Who told him, I've no idea."

"Your grandfather, Count Ros. He learned of the way through bribery and used it to capture the keep. How did you think he came into possession of so formidable a fortress?" The Anian spy's tone was only very slightly sarcastic.

Donzalo ignored that. It was to be expected that the Ani would still find their expulsion from Lama a bit of a sore spot. "Then he gained a keep in much the same way his father lost Mountain Keep to King Greneth — treachery." He poked at the campfire for a few seconds. "That is one of those two-edged swords that appear in so many proverbs, isn't it?"

"I suppose it is, my friend," replied Oder, "or something similar. Have you any thoughts as to where you might go?" They sat now looking out over a valley of small farms, well to the northeast of Castle Rosam. Donzalo wasn't sure whether this area was part of his uncle's jurisdiction.

Donzalo shrugged. "My friend Daboreth would welcome me. Probably Orgelo would, too, but I am not sure I would want to be in his hands."

"Nor would I," agreed Oder, with a smile.

"I could head for yon hills." Donzalo nodded toward the east. "And return to the Cuddon. I suppose I could even go to Sharsh now that King Lareth no longer wants my blood."

"Ah, but for what purpose?"

"None, I suppose. I don't know that I have any purpose now."

"You have friends for whom you care. That, I think, should be your purpose." Oder, who had been staring into the fire, lifted his eyes. "Did you know that my sister was in County Rosam?"

"Ansa? Is she there at your bidding?"

"No. She and Lady Fachalana can create enough plots of their own, these days."

2

"I may follow you in a short time, Sir Paren, I and the ladies."

"You are always welcome in my home, Guesare, as are the Lady Fachalana and her companion. I know not why they would want to visit our quiet manor."

"Fachalana needs quiet for a time. If we come, I shall give you the whole story as to why." The minstrel spoke on, lowering his voice. "I have heard news of Donzalo. He is safely with a friend of mine."

"Then tell that friend to send the boy to me. Bolos is willing to forget the entire business if Donzalo remains at my keep."

They rode slowly along, Sir Paren's men following. Guesare had felt it wise not to enter Keep Rosam and had joined the reeve's group as they began their journey home. "I would feel better if the women had an escort to my estate. Perhaps I should leave some men with you."

"You need all of them with you, sir. I have heard the reports of lawless men across the Abam." Guesare remained silent for a while, then said, "Donni is concerned about the Lady Lomela."

"I think Bolos frightened himself. Oh, I have seen him like this before, seen him mistreat and slap servants since he was a boy. It has always been the result of drunkenness.

"Bolos is not a violent man when sober and he is trying very hard to stay sober."

"Drink only brings out who we truly are," was Guesare's opinion. "Give my greetings to all at your keep." He turned and rode back toward Ros-town.

One would not be incorrect to say that Radal was pleased by the news from Castle Rosam. It is possible that he even smiled. Donzalo was out in the open again and more vulnerable. The phantasms he had sent to haunt Bolos's sleep had proven effective.

He would continue to trouble the man's dreams, but it was now time for more than that — time to leave the Cuddon, to move his force closer to the keep and prepare to act directly. They would ride on the morrow.

As others, he was puzzled by Donzalo's escape. He knew it could not be magic, as gossip around Ros-town had it. Magic did not work that way. Were it so simple, Radal would not have needed to summon a dragon to carry him from Mountain Keep.

Yes, he had once sent the Hounds of Asak from one world to another to destroy young Donzalo but a part of them remained tethered to that other realm. They were never completely here, existing in two worlds at once. If the men of Castle Rosam should ever dig where they thought they had buried the beasts, they might be surprised to find no trace left.

The other news did not much move the sorcerer one way or another. Benawis had been killed trying to flee the embassy. Death was always a good way to tie up loose ends. The circumstances of that death did interest him. It suggested that there were unknown players in this game.

And he knew now that his daughter's friend Maresta — no, her name was Ansa — was an Anian spy. Radal had almost overlooked this bit of knowledge amid all the rest he had read in Fachalana's mind.

He should have paid more attention to that little girl.

"Bolos was actually quite happy to hear you were here. I believe he hopes it will cheer up his wife. He feels guilty enough that he would allow her pretty much anything at the moment.

"Moreover, it helped dispel any suspicions he had about my own arrival — I was simply escorting you from Sharsh and we rode here with Mussago's men for the protection they afforded."

"That does leave a few days unaccounted for," Ansa pointed out. "Where does he think we were between your arrival and ours?"

"Tired and resting in Mussago's tents," replied Blen. "It's believable enough."

"And now tired and resting in the embassy of Sharsh," said Lady Fachalana. "Bolos will think us extraordinarily exhausted." Fachalana was propped up on many pillows in her bed; Ansa sat at the foot of it while Blen occupied a chair nearby.

"Are you, my lady?" asked the knight. "Jobareth suggested that you had undergone some great trial."

"I'm not even sure how much you know, anymore, Sir Blen, we have kept so many secrets from so many people. You learned that we came to County Rosam in disguise, no?" She furrowed her brow momentarily. "Well, of course you did."

"Yes. Nafal filled me in on all that I had not learned already from the ambassador."

Fachalana turned her eyes toward her traveling companion. "Your secrets are yours to keep or to tell, Maresta."

"If you are going to tell all, then so shall I," decided the Anian. Fachalana nodded her assent to that.

"Sir Blen, most of our friends here already are aware of this, including Jobareth Nafal — my true name is Ansa and I am Ani. I am a spy. I am also the Lady Fachalana's loyal friend."

Blen raised his eyebrows. "I should be more surprised, I am sure." He turned to the viscountess. "Can you top that?"

"I am a sorceress," replied Fachalana. "Will that do?"

"I believe so, my lady." He looked at her long and thoughtfully. "I have seen what the practice of magic can do to your father. Is that what wearies you now?"

"In a way. I don't think I'm up to telling the story, Ansa. Why don't you?"

So Ansa did, recounting their entire tale from the time Blen had left them in Dor. Before she was half-done, the weary Fachalana had fallen asleep.

"It was not only the struggle with her father that so weakened her," Ansa finished, "but dealing with all his dark memories that are now within her. She finds herself drifting and dreaming, Blen, and I fear Fachalana may lose herself."

"And we would lose Fachalana," whispered Blen. "That can not happen."

"No. But what are we to do? What are we to do?"

"If you persist in saving my life, my father will have to award you some sort of title."

"Knighthood is sufficient, my lord," said Sir Pol. "I think having a title might be quite wearisome."

"It is," agreed Prince Modareth. "I would as soon be a lecturer at the university." This office of his might make one think him just such, thought Pol, with its untidy stacks of books and manuscripts.

"And I, sir, have given thought to turning my hand to the writing of a play."

"Our friend Gos would rather see you enter his service."

"Our Pol a policeman? Surely not," objected Princess Carrana.

"More a spy, my lady," said Pol. "I do think I could readily combine the two."

"You could," agreed Modareth, "But if you are to be a spy, I would prefer you were mine." He rushed on, as he tended to do when he felt awkward about something. "I need men I can trust around me. This is one thing the last year has taught me."

Carrana smiled. She thought she had taught her husband a few things since their marriage.

An idea came to her. "Couldn't we order Lady Fachalana's theater re-opened in her absence? Pol might run it for her until she returns."

"Hmm, I think Father would not object. He did order Lord Radal's villa sealed but this isn't the same."

Pol laughed. "I know nothing of operating a theater, my lord." Then, on giving it a moment's thought, he added, "I must admit, though, it would provide an excellent base of operations."

"It's better than letting it sit empty," decided the prince. "We can always hire someone to actually manage the theater, as Maresta did for Fachalana."

"Very well, my lord and lady, I am willing to try it. But you must come to my opening!"

"We would not miss it," promised Princess Carrana.

"We are not far now from where we first met," said Oder. As they had climbed into the the Cuddon, the forests had thinned and now the hills about them were, for the most part, barren of trees. They were still green at this time of year, and many flowers yet bloomed, golds and yel-lows spreading across the upland meadows.

"The weather is certainly better."

"I do not intend to linger sufficiently long in the Cuddon to see it change," replied the Anian. "I need only visit one of our houses here, to send messages and see if any await me."

"The business of spies," said Donzalo.

"Indeed. We spend more time sending letters back and forth than aught else." Oder smiled and spoke on. "I could have taken you and Guesare there that night, rather than camping in the cold and snow. But I would not have trusted you with its location, then."

"The Cuddonians do not mind your presence here?"

"Remember that the area still has allegiance to our empire. It is old, the agreement between the nobles of the Cuddon and we Ani — they give lip-service to the emperor as their overlord and we leave them alone, mostly, and promise to keep Lama from pressing upon their bor-ders."

Donzalo knew of that agreement. It had saved the Anians from spending resources on a costly invasion of these hills while they had swept west into Lama, Sharsh, and even Lorj. Since, the Cuddon had served as a useful buffer between them and Lama.

"We may rest there a short while," continued Oder. "Then I think it best to travel back toward your own home. Perhaps your uncle's keep should be our destination."

What might await him there? wondered Donzalo. Would he be welcome? He had half a mind to turn north to Drolwym rather than follow this spy with his own secret agenda.

But Oder was right. His friends were what gave purpose to his life now. If he had any destiny at all, it would be found there.

3

Dovolo rode beside his master. He had never before had occasion to interact personally with Lord Radal and did so with some trepidation. Yet the sorcerer seemed affable enough and willing to converse.

Radal, having closed himself in his tower for quite some time with none to speak to but a few most ignorant ruffians, was pleased to have a more intelligent companion at his side. He commented to him now and again on things they passed along the road.

The sergeant, emboldened, posed a question to Lord Radal. "Sir, is it true you rode here upon a dragon?"

"I did."

"Did it breathe fire, my lord?"

Radal was amused enough for a small smile, the first in many weary days. "A common misconception. The fire, in fact, comes from the other end of the beast."

"They —*fart* fire?" The man was incredulous.

"In a manner of speaking. It is not truly fire but a corrosive liquid, such as a skunk projects. Indeed, most knowledgeable natural philosophers believe the dragon to be a member of the weasel tribe."

Dovolo had come of a good family, though his own estate had greatly fallen, and had a bit of schooling. He did not find this idea unbelievable.

But, never having seen a dragon — even one of the small ones — he was not inclined to accept it unquestioningly either. Not that it mattered right now.

They would cross the Abam soon. That would be when they were most vulnerable, most likely to be spied. Then on to the camp Sojel had established deep in the forest the year before, somewhat to the north and west of Sir Paren's keep.

Dovolo had not been there at the ill-fated attempt to take that small fortress, not having yet joined this troop, but had heard of it from those who were. Did Lord Radal now have some idea of taking Keep Rosam? They would be within a hard two days ride of it.

Well, he had his long sword slung over his back and would use it when the order came. No sense in worrying about things until then.

He took a sideways look at the man beside him. Dressed, as ever, in black, the sorcerer was impossibly lean, almost skeletal, and had allowed his beard to grow since leaving Mountain Keep, starkly white against his dark, hollowed face. To the eyes of Dovolo, Lord Radal did not seem a well man.

Radal grew silent. This undertaking would soon end, one way or another. If he survived it, he knew he would not live long after. He was too spent, too dependent on the elixirs he brewed to keep himself going.

When all was done, Lareth might see that he still served his interests. Theirs had always been a single destiny, a fierce loyalty of one to the other. He had not forgotten that and neither, he was sure, had the king.

Before that, though, came his vengeance and the assurance of Fachalana's future. Nothing else truly mattered.

Ansa had come to County Rosam just after the Autumn Festival the previous year. She was not certain how it was celebrated here.

"This festival is, before all else," Jobareth Nafal told her, "a religious occasion. For Kamatians, who see the sun as a powerful symbol of their god, all the equinoxes and solstices are such.

"But it is also a celebration of the first fruits of the harvest. There will be a certain amount of dancing and drinking of cider."

"I hope we can get Lomela to dance," said Lady Fachalana.

"And you as well, Lana," Jobareth replied. "You seem much stronger."

"All I needed was a little rest." Fachalana did not mention that she now possessed the knowledge of certain drugs that her father had used. She had taken only a small dose; surely there had been no harm in that.

"I think it is time that Lomela knows about me. It seems everyone else in the world does!"

"Of our circle, only she and Donzalo are still in the dark. And who knows when we will see him again?" asked the diplomat.

"Guesare can send messages to him," said Ansa in a rather small voice. "He is with my brother." This was the first the others had heard of this.

"But," she continued, "I am fairly certain he already has some sense of your powers."

Yes, thought Fachalana, we saw each other in dream, on the silver plain. She could not seem to find that world again, though she had searched.

"Be that as it may," stated Nafal. "Count Bolos has made all of us welcome at the keep for this holiday. Yes, even me. Indeed, he asked me whether you might want to stay there for a time with his wife rather than live at the embassy."

"Why not?" said Fachalana. "I'll start packing."

Bolos had dreamed of the king. Lareth had stood over his body with bloody sword, while his daughter laughed in the arms of a faceless lover.

There was none to save him. He thought he saw familiar faces in the crowd that stood about, pointing and making jokes to one another. Orgelo? Copago? They might have been there.

A tall man, dark, no more than a shadow, whispered to him. *I can save you*, he said.

But Bolos was already dead, and soldiers looted and burned across his land.

He had dreamed too many such dreams lately. Doctor Heragos said they might be the result of his quitting of all drink, that the poisons were working their way out of him and the dreams might lessen in time. The count hoped so, fervently.

In his waking life, he could barely remember King Lareth. He had seen him only the once, when he had traveled to Mountain Keep to escort his bride home. Bolos could tell at the time that the man had a low opinion of him, that he felt his daughter was too good for him.

Maybe she was.

Not that it mattered now. They had done their duty, as should the children of power, and he had a healthy heir to show for it. Now he must try to preserve all that boy should someday inherit.

Bolos knew how fragile the balance was in Lama. It was not that long since his grandfather and the other counts had established it, having expelled the Ani. Who could expect it to last forever?

Who could expect it to last with enemies on all sides?

Jobareth decided to ask outright. "Did you have a secret way built in and out of the embassy?" The thought was on his mind since Donzalo's disappearance, which he felt certain had been through the passage he had seen.

Sir Blen chuckled. "Who whispered that rumor to you?"

"Donzalo, actually. Is there one or isn't there?"

"Yes and no, Legate. There is a passage of sorts but it is not at all secret. Follow."

He led Nafal to the hall outside the ambassador's rooms. "Do you know what lies directly beneath us?"

Jobareth thought a moment, laying out a floor plan in his mind. "The kitchens," he stated with some certainty.

"They are," agreed Blen. "After you had gone to fetch Lord Doufan here, I remembered the dumb waiters I had seen in Mountain Keep and had one added." He gestured toward a panel in the wall.

"I thought this was but a closet," Jobareth said. "Does it go up to the third floor?" Visions came to him of late meals being delivered to his room.

"It does. We were not keeping it secret. We have simply not used it yet.

"But there is a small secret about it ," he continued, opening the panel. "I decided that as long as it was here, there was no reason not to make it big enough for a man, if an emergency arose. See, there is a ladder, off there to the side." He pointed into the opening.

Jobareth inspected it, looking up and down the brick-walled shaft. "This could be handy. For both its purposes."

Blen shrugged. "The ambassador is not interested in using it. He prefers to go down to the kitchen to gossip with the cook when he wants a snack.

"Incidentally," he added, "it goes all the way to the roof. You may not have noticed that we have one chimney too many up there."

The legate made a mental note to look the next time he was outside. "I should speak to Lord Doufan. It might not be a bad idea for you to join me." He rapped at the ambassador's door, which was answered by his scribe. The man gave them a courteous nod of his head and ushered them in.

Doufan sat in a comfortable chair in a corner of his office, writing. "What can I do for you, gentlemen?" he asked, waving them toward nearby seats.

"My lord," began Jobareth, "the Lady Fachalana and Maresta are now settled in at Castle Rosam. I would expect them to stay for several days."

"Yes," said the ambassador. "And then what?"

"That is very much the question, sir. The ladies want to visit Sir Paren's keep in the company of Sir Guesare and I thought it might be wise were I to accompany them. If you can spare me, my lord."

"And if I permit them to go at all," responded Lord Doufan. "Sir Blen will have to ride away with those troops of his sooner or later. Would you leave me with neither of you here?"

"I think I can trust my second to lead our men back to Count Mussago's lands," said Blen. "Though, indeed, sooner or later I would have to go to them."

"Do you think Donzalo will show up at his uncle's?" asked Doufan.

"I think it is — possible," Jobareth said.

"I've not doubt the ladies think the same. I shall have to consider all this." He busied himself with the papers on his lapboard for a moment before speaking again to the two. "Are you attending the ball at the castle? I am quite looking forward to the evening."

"I am, of course, sir," replied Nafal. "And I shall be certain to drag Sir Blen along, no matter how much he may object!"

Perdos was, in a word, bored. It seemed that all he did was wait and, for the most part, wait alone.

He again considered riding boldly into Ros-town and standing outside the house where he knew Guesare was staying. Challenge him right there in the street and have done. But too much might go wrong and he would lose his chance forever.

Attempting to waylay him on the road would be just as risky, though he knew the minstrel sometimes rode alone up towards the castle. If it were further from town, maybe.

Perdos had ridden down to the soldiers' encampment south of the Abam one day. No one knew him there so he could gossip a while with those fellows, learn what was going on, enjoy some comradeship for an hour or two. Their number had swelled; apparently another group had joined them, one including a number of men from Sharsh.

They all seemed to get along together well enough and, like Perdos, were waiting. Their leaders seemed uncertain whether to stay or go.

"Sorsen is going to the ball up at the keep," one told him. "After that, maybe we'll ride home. We're going to have our own Autumn celebration here at the camp. Come on by and join us."

It was tempting, but Perdos knew he would be watching, not drinking, on the day of the equinox.

The line dividing life and death

is measured by a single breath.

Exhale what is and all that might,
a wisp to fade into the night.

When next we breathe, what unknown air
fills souls now past all mortal care?

That dark divide breaks ev'ry bond;
breathe deeply ere you cross beyond.

"And that, gentlefolk, is the final soliloquy," announced Pol, lowering his manuscript. There was a moment of silence before Prince Modareth began applauding. His wife quickly joined in, followed by the others in attendance.

They don't understand it, thought Sir Pol. It was ridiculous to think he could write something.

"Will you open your season with this, Sir Pol?" asked the Baroness Ysena.

"No, my lady, I think something from repertory would be a better choice."

"But you must present it later in the season," said Modareth. "We need something new and fresh." The portly Princess Carrana, hanging on her husband's arm, nodded in agreement.

"I shall attempt it, sir." Perhaps they didn't hate the play after all. "It will need rewriting, I am sure, before it is presentable."

The opening should be within the month. Word had been given out that Pol was a close friend of the viscountess, who had asked him to operate her theater in her absence. The whereabouts of the lady remained uncertain in the public's mind.

Actual permission for the opening came from Prince Gawis, who was acting in the name of the king in Celatas.

Ysena spoke again. "I think it is very — vigorous," was her opinion. "Very passionate." The noblewoman looked directly at the young playwright for a moment, before dropping her eyes.

Pol hoped her husband was not paying attention. But he only allowed the baroness to drag him to these salons so he might drink the prince's wine.

The other guests were already turning their attention to that wine and to the buffet the servants had quietly laid out while he read. Sir Pol smiled. No more should be expected of these nobles.

He would put more trust in the actors back at his theater. Lady Fachalana's theater, that is. Pol wondered what she and Maresta might think of his effort. He had Maresta in mind when he wrote the part of his leading lady.

He'd best find a plate before these highborn freeloaders ate everything.

4

"Can you then do all your father does?"

Fachalalana shook her head. "No more than one could duel a master having read a book on fencing. It would take much practice and great dedication." Leave it to Lomela to ask so practical a question, she thought.

Princess Lomela knew her friend was capable of the passion necessary to master any craft. Would she throw herself into the practice of magic or only dabble?

They were referring to the subject only obliquely, as the seamstress was there, making final adjustments to Lady Fachalana's dress. Nothing in Lomela's wardrobe — nor that of any other woman in the keep — had come close to fitting the noblewoman's lanky frame so a gown must be made up new.

"Where is Maresta this morning?" Again, the presence of the dressmaker meant she must use Ansa's pseudonym.

"Riding," replied Fachalana. "I did not know how much she likes to be on the back of a horse when we were still in Celatas."

"With Sir Blen?"

"Not today. Jobo came up. I do suspect that Guesare will join them outside the walls."

"They not only ride but plot," said Lomela. Fachalana knew that was true.

"We can do our own plotting here," she said, "and on more interesting topics. Do you think Blen likes Maresta?"

An unusual question for her friend, thought Lomela. "Likes her, yes. More than that? Who can tell with Blen. He is a book kept carefully closed." The princess did not add her suspicions as to whom she thought Sir Blen might more than like, even if the man did not admit it to himself.

"I think they would make a good couple," averred Fachalana. "Careful with those pins, Mistress!"

"Sorry, my lady," the woman murmured. She had been paying too much attention to their gossip.

"I like that color on you," the princess said. "Few can properly pull off red."

"Thank you, Lomela. I am partial to it. And know," she added with the smallest of smiles, a smile that seemed to mask an underlying sadness, "that I shall never take to wearing black."

The pair looked over the pile of stone before them, a somewhat squat, crumbling tower. From the Anian's spy-friendly house, which was, in fact, a small inn on the roadside, they had traveled south and somewhat westward to reach this spot.

"A minor sorcerer, Sabatare, dwelt here," said Oder. "You would not know him but he was involved in the attack on your uncle's keep."

"Where is he now?" asked Donzalo. It seemed that the wizard was no longer in residence.

"He was among the dead that day."

The Laman knight nodded. "There have been men here not too long ago." The littered courtyard gave evidence of that.

"I believe Lord Radal was staying here with only a small guard. Had we arrived a few days earlier, you and I might have been able to put an end to all of this." Oder obviously regretted the missed opportunity.

Slay Radal? Yes, he and the Anian might well have been able to turn the tables on the sorcerer and accomplish that. Donzalo spoke. "So where has the man gone?" His hand went to the silver wolf, pinned at his shoulder, and his thoughts to when he had last seen the sorcerer, while he had lain dreaming in Fairie.

"Who knows? It seems that he and a large company of men rode out." Oder pointed to tracks leading westward. "All we can do is follow. Let us rest ourselves and our horses here for the night."

"If we pass near the estate of Sir Paren, I would wish to visit."

"As you see fit, Sir Donzalo."

Ansa was not dissimilar to Dame Tiana in size, albeit somewhat more slender, and wore one of her altered dresses. Tiana had owned only one old gown when she arrived at Castle Rosam but had quickly remedied that. She had to dress her part as wife of the master of arms, after all.

Of course, all those gowns would need altering as Tiana grew more obviously pregnant but that showed little at this time.

While Fachalana lingered in their room that morning, Ansa had attended the religious rite, mostly from curiosity. It somewhat bored her but, as a member of the party that returned from the stoa, she had also partaken of a sumptuous late breakfast. Her comrade had missed out on this reward for virtue, even were it sham virtue.

The Sharshite diplomats showed up in the late afternoon, Lord Doufan and his two right-hand men. Or perhaps we could say that Blen was his left-hand man. Jobareth bore a letter for the Lady Fachalana.

"It's from Modareth!" she told Ansa, breaking the seal. "Lady Carrana is doing well and so is her pregnancy." She looked up. "What would she be, around six months?" Ansa nodded. That should be about right. "Oh, he has had our friend Pol open the theater in our absence. I am not sure how I feel about that!"

"Perhaps better than letting it sit empty."

"Maybe. Pol has also turned to playwriting. You have a rival, Jobo."

Jobareth seemed skeptical. "He's only a boy."

"No younger than our friend Donzalo," Ansa pointed out.

Fachalana smiled at the exchange. "I think Pol has a bit of a crush on you."

"I know he does," replied Ansa. "And I think he is also the sort to get over it without too much difficulty."

"Shall we go down to the hall, my ladies?" asked Blen, who had kept himself out of their conversation. "Allow me to be your escort, " he said, linking his arm with Lady Fachalana's. He had practiced this courtly move carefully.

An amused Jobareth and Ansa followed.

The ball was no great affair but it gave the chance for the wealthy families of Ros-town to mingle with the minor nobility of castle and countryside in a formal setting. Count Borrago had deemed that a good thing and Bolos saw no reason to change it.

Moreover, it gave them all a chance to attempt the latest dances from Sharsh. But, inevitably, the old traditional rounds and reels would prove the most popular. Some of these were similar to those Sir Blen had known as a boy, so he cautiously took part.

Lord Doufan, to the surprise of none who knew him, danced well with many women and charmed all. Months later, people still spoke of his turn with the Lady Lomela, she in a swirl of green satin, he wearing a tunic of deepest blue, in the calf-length cut recently become popular. But they might not have remembered his face.

"You are sitting this one out, my boy?" he asked Blen, who sipped wine punch at one of the tables that had been pushed against the wall to make room for dancing. Blen had doubts as to whether peaches should be added to a proper wine but the taste was not unpleasant.

"It is one of the new dances, sir. I do not know it."

"The ladies would gladly teach you," replied the ambassador. "I have given thought to their request to travel up to the keep of Sir Paren. Count Bolos," he nodded toward the man, stiffly going through the unfamiliar moves, "has no objections, though he can not imagine why they should wish to make such a journey. Moreover, one of his regular patrols of the Abam Road will leave in two days and he suggests they journey with them. So I do not object either." He looked out across the room. "Sir Sorsen seems to be enjoying himself. I assume he too will leave soon."

"Yes, my lord. Both our companies will move south in a few days. I could not say how far south, at this time, for the situation here continues to worry the both of us."

"As it does me." Doufan bowed to a passing woman and continued. "We still have troops across the river."

"In the lands of Count Dordos, yes. I do not know their orders."

"They will come if you or I call for them. Let us hope that does not become necessary."

Music started up, a lively tune led by the shawm. "You would know this dance," said Lord Doufan. "Don't leave all the ladies to me and Sorsen!"

"When we sleep, the walls between the worlds grow thin," the chaplain told Princess Mara. "We may glimpse things that are not of this earthly realm."

"Could Kamat send dreams?"

"All things come from Kamat, my daughter," responded the elderly priest. Having given the orthodox answer, he continued. "But there are those who can influence our dreamings. Demons. Powerful sorcerers. Do not put too much trust in those things you may dream."

Mara frowned. "But they can be true, can they not?" she asked.

"They tell more truth about our own minds than aught else. Worry and concern are likely the soil from which your dream grew." The old man took her hand into his own, his soft, dark fingers gently holding hers.

How long since he has used any tool more demanding than a pen? wondered Mara, her mind momentarily wandering from their discussion.

"Mara, I have served you since we left our home and I shall probably die in this foreign land. Know that I shall always watch over you and, with the help of Kamat, try to keep you safe. If there are more such dreams, come to me." The chaplain blessed her and made the sign of the arrow, which the princess dutifully returned.

The priest sat a while in the palace gardens, after the princess had left him. He loved the gardens, the flowers that reminded him of his far away land of birth. Had another touched her dreams? he wondered. Though he had long ago chosen to follow the ways of light, the priest knew something of magic. That was one reason he had been chosen to accompany Mara when she came to wed the crown prince of Sharsh.

And he had felt the disturbances of late, some of which he was certain originated from his own homeland. For Partanaca, now, he felt no loyalty; he served Kamat and Princess Mara, and would remain vigilant in that service.

5

The end of the market season in County Rosam came, more or less, with Autumn Feast. Trade would most certainly continue through the colder months — which were not so cold in this part of Lama — but diminish now along the Great Road and on the River Weldar.

Merchants and traders were winding their ways toward whatever winter quarters they preferred. Some would continue to ply their trade in the south, in Morparas and along the coast of the Minor Sea. Others had homes to which they might return, up and down and across the Weldar's great valley.

Sir Sorsen and his troop were also ready to depart, as was the mixed force of Sharshites and the men of Count Mussago that Blen had commanded. Only one tent remained unstruck at their camp. Within that tent, Sir Blen, Mussago the Younger, and Sorsen held their council.

"I would feel better about this were you accompanying us, Sir Blen," spoke Sorsen. "No offense intended to you or your leadership, Master Mussago," he added, bowing to that taciturn gentleman.

"None is taken. Leading soldiers is not my vocation."

Blen and Sorsen exchanged a quick glance. They knew that Mussago had the admiration and complete loyalty of his men, thanks to his fairness and willingness to work hard alongside them.

Moreover, he was as fine a horseman as either had ever seen. If Mussago did not so disdain knighthood he would long since have had his spurs.

"It seems you must need lead soldiers for a while, my friend," said Sir Blen. "I would not place my second in authority over you."

"I shall be losing my second for a time," spoke Sorsen.

"What? Is Sir Habidros not returning with you?"

"I have given him leave to accompany his friends to the keep of Sir Paren. It was agreeable to me," Orgelo's heir explained, "as I thought it might be wise to have eyes there."

Blen nodded in agreement. "Wise, indeed. That's it then. I'll stay here and you two ride slowly to the south, ready to return if need arises.

Let's drink to that and be on our ways." He raised his goblet, drained it, and stepped out into a mild autumn day.

In a few weeks he expected to ride south and rejoin this company, perhaps bringing Habidros with him. After that, who could know?

All around the perimeter of the embassy's low-pitched slate roof ran a narrow walkway, shielded by a crenelated wall. Jobareth Nafal peered out over that wall toward the Ros-town road, watching an approaching horseman.

Habidros. Now we can begin our journey, he thought. Jobareth looked down toward the great double stairway that led to the building's main entrance. Its construction should be finished by the time he returned and all that temporary wooden structure would be gone. The embassy would look the way he and Blen had intended, its front dominated by a stone arch that opened into the ground floor with stairs rising on either side to the second story.

Nafal would have no secretary on this trip. He had not taken on a new man since the death of the traitor, Benawis, writing his own dispatches and orders or depending on the fellow who served as Sir Blen's aide — a soldier, but capable enough with a pen. Someone in Sharsh would eventually think to send out a young diplomat to assist him.

Perhaps he could prevail upon Grippo to serve as his secretary while he was at Paren's keep. If possible, he would ask him to come back to the embassy and serve in a more permanent position. The acolyte was being wasted where he was. Grippo could never be officially named as his secretary but there were many other capacities in which he might be useful.

There was Guesare, greeting his brother. He had best go down to his chambers and prepare to ride.

Jobareth turned toward the roof, where rose Sir Blen's false chimney. The legate had examined it on learning of this not-quite-secret way into the embassy. The shaft was topped by a simple trap door, though equipped with a sturdy lock. Blen had presented him with a key. So far as he knew, only the pair and the ambassador held keys.

However, from the inside it was possible to open the hatch without a key. This made sense; the purpose of the lock was to keep intruders out of the embassy, not to prevent the use of the shaft as an escape route. The idea of descending into that dark hole, clinging to a vertical ladder, did not appeal to Jobareth at all, so he did not attempt it.

The stairs were a much better way. Jobareth Nafal opened a door inset into the roof — also requiring one of a restricted number of keys — and started down.

"Two men will suffice. Hold the rest here until I send word."

Dovolo nodded. "Yes, my lord. I have chosen a pair to accompany you." He gestured toward a couple of ruffians squatting by their horses. They looked to be casting dice.

"I shall send one back to you when I arrive at Keep Rosam. Start the men moving then. But," Radal continued, "if the second does not meet you with instructions before you reach me, it means that my plan has failed. Disband then and go your way, Sergeant."

My plan must not fail, the sorcerer told himself. For the sake of my king, for the sake of my daughter, I will succeed. Speaking no more, he mounted his steed and rode from camp.

His two attendants scrambled onto their horses, hastening to follow.

"Good luck to you, old man," Dovolo muttered. He turned to his second. "Get these sons of Asak on their feet. We're going to drill every day until our master calls for us."

"I think, Dame Tiana, that your husband does not much like me."

Tiana glanced toward Traspa, to see if aught might be read there, before answering. "Sir Jak, he does not like having a force of men in this keep who do not answer to him. When Bolos became count, his personal guard became redundant." That's a good word, thought Tiana. She had never had the opportunity to use such back at Paren's keep. Settling into a chair opposite her guests, she asked, "More tea, Mistress Traspa?"

Traspa held out her cup, once again wishing that Lamans would more frequently choose to offer their guests wine. She noted that Tiana both served and drank with her left hand. Left-handedness was discouraged back in Sharsh as being unlucky, but there seemed to be no stigma to it in this land.

Tiana smiled at the soldier. "I suspect you like to occasionally flaunt your status too."

Mistress Traspa laughed aloud. "Jak likes to do things the way he always has and does not take kindly to suggestions otherwise. That will change," she said with a wink to Tiana, "once we are married."

Sir Jak chose to remain silent on that subject. He looked about the room. These used to be the quarters of Bolos, who had chosen to live separately from his wife. And still did, for that matter, though he had taken a larger suite since becoming count. They had changed, that was certain — there was nothing left of Count Bolos in this room. Would Traspa change his quarters? Would she change him?

Which made him think of something else. "Traspa, where are we going to live? Not in one of our little rooms, surely?" he asked, not so surely.

"There are several unoccupied rooms available," Tiana told them. As wife of the master of arms, she had taken upon herself the duty of assigning quarters. No one had asked her to so do, but Dame Tiana did not mind that. "Donzalo's old chambers are still empty. Both of them."

"One is too grand," opined Traspa, "and the other is a dungeon." Jak nodded in agreement to her assessment.

"For your honeymoon, at least," Tiana said, the idea having just come to her, "you might use Copago's cottage. No one has resided there since his family left. And," she added, "I might just be able to convince my husband that it should be yours permanently." Actually, she thought, he would welcome the opportunity to have Jak outside the walls.

And Bolos would would not at all mind giving such a wedding gift to his most trusted man. Especially in that it would cost him nothing.

Traspa and Jak looked at each other. It was obvious that they liked the idea.

"So," continued Dame Tiana, "now that the festival is past and most of our guests have departed, we could have a wedding anytime." She raised an eyebrow and looked expectantly upon the couple.

"I'd do it right now if a priest were here," avowed Sir Jak. Mistress Traspa did not seem to have any objections to the idea.

"I think Countess Lomela will want a day or two of warning," laughed Tiana. "You are very important to her, Traspa." She turned to the knight. "As you are to the count, sir. I think he cares about you deeply, in his way.

"What say you to three days from now?" That would give her plenty of time to set things up. Tiana relished the thought of being able to take charge of such an event. She would prove that she had a role to play in Castle Rosam.

"Three days," agreed Traspa, and kissed her husband-to-be.

"I hope you do not mind traveling quickly," said the captain. He turned his eyes toward the Lady Fachalana, who did not appear well this morning, slumping wearily in the saddle. Fachalana did have her own horse back now, a tall bay stallion from Sharsh, and was choosing to sit astraddle, as she had on her journey into Lama.

Jobareth answered. His rank and gender marked him as apparent leader of the little group of travelers. He doubted that he could actually assert any sort of authority over any of them. "The sooner we arrive, sir, the better. We know that the patrols do not dawdle on their way."

The company was mixed. The ambassador had insisted that a pair of embassy guards be added to the party. Nafal felt it not a bad idea — who could know what might be needed once they parted ways with the count's men. These two men at arms and the five travelers, with the patrol of ten men and their captain, brought them to eighteen.

There were also several pack-horses, including a pair laden with the ladies' luggage.

"Then, sir, if we do not have to turn aside for any reason, we should have you all at Sir Paren's manor in three days. There is always the possibility that we will have to chase after outlaws or help a traveler in need or any of a dozen other things that may happen on the road." The captain smiled and attempted a nonchalant shrug. It did not suit him. "You would then have to wait on us. The count does not want you traveling on your own."

"Nor would we wish to," replied the legate. A sound, serious fellow, he thought. He knew the soldier had a good reputation.

Jobareth turned to his friends. "Are we ready?"

"An hour ago," said Guesare. "I would have been prepared even sooner if I hadn't need wait on this malingerer." He nodded toward his brother.

"I've more important things to do all day than strum a rebec," responded Habidros.

"Aye, get in an extra hour of sleep."

"'Twill make me fresher for the road," came the answer and both laughed.

The captain nodded. "Take a place behind my lead four," he ordered and wordlessly signaled for his men to ride.

It was a pleasant, cool day and Fachalana soon roused herself enough to converse gaily as they rode along. But by afternoon, she seemed worn and more so the following day.

6

"My brother seems to be enjoying your farce," said Modareth, looking toward the crown prince's box. "The Princess Mara too."

Pol nodded, somewhat absentmindedly. His attention was on the stage. "I had truly intended to present something from repertoire but this came rushing out."

A portly figure with preposterous mustachios strode onto the stage and bellowed out a song. On the balcony above him, an exaggeratedly homely maiden — obviously played by a middle-aged man — pantomimed her passion with the broadest of histrionics.

"I can think of more than one of our friends who might be the inspiration for this Baron Bumbiap," the prince whispered to his wife.

"And the two young female leads are obviously drawn from Fachalana and Maresta," came her reply. She glanced toward their youthful playwright. "Pol may need to be more cautious with his lampooning."

"Hmm, yes." It was like the impractical Modareth to not think of such things. As a prince of the realm, it was not something he would ever have need considered anyway. "I think 'Bumbiap' is a success," he spoke more loudly. "My congratulations to you, Sir Pol."

"Thank you, sir. If you will excuse me, I must be back to my players." Pol bowed toward Princess Carrana. "My lady." He turned and hurried from their box.

"I think it a success, too," said Carrana.

Prince Modareth looked again toward his older brother's box, directly across the hall, and remembered something. "Mara is with child," he announced.

"Hush, there is a song coming." They had, of course, heard the entire play read to them by young Pol so they knew what was next. The youthful hero of the comedy stepped forward.

I've given you my heart
to do with as you please,
to break beneath your heel
or heal its injuries.
And nothing more I'll ask
of you, no words save these:
remember how my love
came singing on the breeze.

Oft wounded in the past,
I'll not avoid love's dart
nor falter on a journey
I once feared to start.
This starry, vernal night,
though we be far apart,
remember how my love
came singing from the heart.

As the applause faded, Princess Carrana turned to her husband. "Mara is pregnant? Where did you hear that?"

"The most reliable of sources," Modareth replied with a grin. "My brother."

"That must please Gawis. I did not know he and his wife were still intimate."

"They seem to have grown closer, lately. Perhaps we have set them a good example." The prince winked at his wife. "Gawis will be more pleased if it turns out to be a boy."

"And maybe the threats against your life will be over."

"I fear they will never be over, wife. It is the fate of princes." He did not add, 'and of their wives.' But both thought it.

"It would be best, perhaps, if I did not come to your uncle's keep."

"You have nothing to fear from Sir Paren," responded Donzalo.

Oder shrugged. "Maybe so. I should make contact with our friend Guesare. Where he is right now, I do not know, but Ros-town would be a good place to start."

"Then travel from Paren's keep. It is less than three days hard ride from town and there might be news awaiting us."

"Very well. I must have a different name when we arrive. Tell all that I am a minstrel friend of Guesare." The Anian frowned in thought for a moment. "I shall be a Cuddonian. Call me Remare."

One who follows Rema, the earth goddess, thought Donzalo. Guesare's patroness. He smiled at the little jest in Oder's choice. "Then, Sir Remare, let us cross the river as did those before us."

Their tracking had brought them to this spot where Radal's men had gone over the Abam. In these highlands, the flow was not wide and there were many places it could be forded.

"Your uncle should know about these men," observed Oder. On the north side of the stream, they could see that the tracks led off into the wilderness, rather than turning south toward Paren's manor and Ros-town. "Later, perhaps, we can follow their trail again."

Donzalo nodded soberly. "They are passing far too near his keep. He may want to send out a patrol to investigate."

"'Twould be better than having we two stumble upon them. We'll leave it to Sir Paren." Oder eyed a narrow path to their left. "This, then, is our way. How far, do you reckon? Two days?"

"No more, I would think." The young Laman was not particularly familiar with this area, though he had passed through, going the opposite direction, a year earlier.

He urged his horse forward through an autumn forest of gold and red.

So, his old friend was marrying. Perdos considered Jak to be a friend, or, at least, not an enemy.

An enemy — he had only now learned that Guesare was gone, journeying with a group of travelers to the keep of Sir Paren. It would have done him little good to know this earlier, as the minstrel was in the company of soldiers and better protected than when he lingered in Ros-town. Should he follow?

Perhaps later. That company should arrive at their destination this day, the day of Jak's wedding. He had decided to stick around for that. Not that he would have been welcomed as a guest.

No, he would have undoubtedly been arrested on sight. But later, he had heard, the couple would be honeymooning at Copago's old cottage. Maybe he could drop by discreetly in a day or two and offer his congratulations. Jak wouldn't turn him in.

And he might have useful news.

Ah, this must be they leaving the castle. Perdos stood in his stirrups to get a better look at the wedding party proceeding from the outer gate. He dared not come any closer

Even the count was there. Bolos could be a good sort, he remembered. He always did right by me, Perdos told himself. Better than I did by him.

There were the newlyweds heading up the road in a flower-festooned donkey cart. The wedding party was dispersing and Perdos had best be on his way too. It would not do to lurk near the gates of Keep Rosam over long.

It was good that Jak had found someone. A good woman, too, this Traspa, as he recalled. The knight, perhaps, felt a moment of envy, a touch, even, of self-pity, before allowing himself a smile and turning his mount toward Ros-town.

I should have my father's books, thought Fachalana. There was much in them that might be useful.

Jobareth Nafal looked up from the papers he was holding. "You're awake. Feeling better, my lady?"

She nodded. "Where is Ansa?"

"Out exploring. Our friend is rather taken with this land. I must say, I find it pleasant myself."

There are spells in those books, she told herself. I need to know more. To her companion, she said, "I was very tired, Jobo. How long have I slept?"

"It is near noon now."

Fachalana recalled arriving around dusk. She must have gone to bed immediately but that she did not remember. "I'm hungry!"

"I shall send for something." Jobareth started to rise.

"No, no. I want to get up and get doing. Let me dress and we'll go find some lunch."

The diplomat chuckled. "Your luggage is already unpacked." He waved an arm toward an oaken wardrobe on the other side of the small, stone-walled room. "I'll be outside," he told her and took his leave.

Yes, I need spells, the young woman thought as she quickly slipped into a simple gown, brown with red accents, and suited to almost any occasion. Fachalana knew that the words of a spell had no power of their own. They served only to focus the mind on the task at hand. But focus was what most she required.

There was a young man waiting outside the door with Nafal. It took her a moment to put a name to him.

"Why, Brother Grippo! I almost didn't recognize you without your robes."

"I know not when I shall don those again, my lady." The former acolyte was clad in nondescript tunic and soft boots. "If ever," he added.

"My brother and his family are about to take lunch. Will you join us?"

"Gladly," she replied, taking his arm. Jobareth followed them down the narrow hallway. Fachalana looked about her. "Are we inside the keep?"

"Inside the walls, my lady, but not in the keep proper. This is one of the houses that surround it."

"Paren has chosen to add these rather than build a larger keep," said Jobareth, "as the numbers of those living at the manor have increased."

"Yes. There are more houses outside the walls, as well," Grippo said.

Not well suited for defense, thought Fachalana. It's more like a village than a castle.

The door to Copago's suite stood open. A little girl ran to greet them. "What is her name?" whispered the noblewoman.

"Ramapa," answered Grippo. "It's a Muramized variant of a very old Laman name."

Another scholar, she thought. I can't seem to get away from them. She knelt to say hello to the child. "How do you do, Mistress Ramapa?"

The girl looked to her uncle, who gave her an encouraging smile. "This is the Lady Fachalana, Ramapa."

"Hello, Fasalama." She turned and scurried back to her parents.

"Something smells quite good," said Fachalana, rising to her feet.

"Something always smells good in here," Grippo replied. "The one great advantage of not being made a priest is that I get to eat meat for another year."

"Come on in and have a seat," invited Dame Janona. "There is plenty of stew."

Sir Copago half-rose from his place to acknowledge them and then returned to his bowl. "You might or might not recognize what has gone into the pot," said he. "There is wild meat aplenty about these parts."

"I feel as hungry as a wild beast myself," answered Fachalana, taking a place at the long table. "And I think when I am done I shall have to return to my lair and sleep some more. Yes, Jobareth," she said, seeing the look of concern on his face, "our journey taxed me more than I realized. But I should be fine after a bit more rest."

And certain elixirs she had brought with her. That was all she needed, she was sure.

"Something is afoot at Keep Rosam. The count has ordered the gates closed and would not let me enter."

The ambassador sighed. "I regret already letting Nafal leave. Bolos trusts him more than he does either of us."

"His father did," said Sir Blen. "I am not so certain Count Bolos feels the same."

"Perhaps so. Whatever is happening, gossip is bound to reach our ears in time." Lord Doufan turned back to the cleaning of a pair of compact pistols laid out on his desk. Blen did not recall ever seeing the weapons before though he knew the man sometimes carried them concealed. "Keep yours open, Blen."

"Yes, my lord." He hesitated a moment, as though it might be best to leave the conversation there, but then chose to speak on. "The legate and his friends should have arrived at their destination yesterday."

Doufan did not look up from his task. "I have no doubt the Lady Fachalana will grow quickly bored up there in the country. I would expect them to return within the fortnight."

7

Sir Pol's play had been a great success, by all reports. Her husband had laughed uproariously during the performance but Princess Mara could not quite follow it. That was of no importance — she was often baffled by the ways of her adopted homeland.

The handsome young playwright and impresario had taken a bow at the end of the performance. Mara had seen him about the palace on occasion — he was, after all, a protege of her brother-in-law — but this night there had seemed something more familiar about him, as though he were a long-ago acquaintance, half-forgotten. Yet they had never even spoken, to Mara's recollection.

That night she had dreamed. Pol was in her dreams and her husband and they all spoke lines upon a stage. The words made no sense to Mara or, if they did, she forgot them upon awakening.

But she did remember Prince Gawis lying dead at the end of their scene.

Maybe her chaplain was correct. Maybe these dreams were but the result of worry and concern. Mara sighed. She had another concern now, a child on the way. May Kamat give her a son this time!

She would write to Sir Pol, she decided, congratulate him on his success, invite him to one of their parties. That would do no harm and Mara could learn more of the young knight.

Somehow, she felt she should.

A woman stepped out into the road, well ahead of them. Blond was her hair and her short gown was of white. A recurved bow hung from her shoulder; a white wolf followed at her heels.

"Diba," whispered Donzalo.

Oder looked sharply toward his companion and then back to the figure. "Nay, friend Donzalo, it is my sister."

"So it is," agreed the young knight, seemingly not the least embarrassed about his mistake. "So it is. Ansa — and that is King with her." He slipped from his saddle and raised a hand in greeting. "Ansa!"

She had looked so alike to the alabaster statue in the shrine of Diba, the site of his Yule Eve vigil less than a year before. That time seemed distant now, like a dream of his childhood. He touched the silver wolf pinned at his shoulder and momentarily lost himself in the memory.

Then he crouched to pet the dog that had come bounding to him.

"Greetings to you, Sir Donzalo," said the Anian girl, leisurely approaching the pair of travelers. "And to you, my brother. Guesare will be pleased to see both of you."

"He is here?" asked Oder, who had dismounted to stand beside Donzalo.

"He is, as is his brother Habidros. At the moment, they are off practicing marksmanship with Sir Guesare's rifle."

"I would assume the Lady Fachalana accompanied you?" said Donzalo.

"Yes, though most would say I accompanied her," Ansa replied. "Jobareth did so, as well. By the way," she continued, "name me Maresta here, not Ansa. Our friends may all know who I am but Sir Paren and his people do not."

Donzalo nodded. "Then, my Lady Maresta, allow me to introduce you to my friend, Sir Remare."

Ansa glanced at her brother and laughed. It was, perhaps, not a musical laugh but it was an honest one and a hearty one. "A Cuddonian, eh? The unshaven pair of you look like you just came down from the hills."

"We did," admitted Oder, rubbing his chin. "But I do not intend to maintain this part of my disguise."

"Come along, then," said Ansa. "We are near the manor."

The two joined her as she started up the trail, one on either side, leading their mounts. Donzalo watched her converse with her brother, catching up on all his news, and noted again how she looked like the goddess Diba. *She is a silver woman, as Jola was golden,* thought he.

Though most of Donzalo's logical mind scoffed at the idea, a part of him, a place deep within his wounded heart, could not help but take it as a sign.

◆

This fellow did not know Perdos and neither he nor Jak intended to change that. The sergeant had been calling him 'Dos, as in the old days, and they left it at that when he joined them.

"There he was at the gate, looking like an old beggar," said the soldier. "We had no idea who he was." He took a quaff of his beer. "Good stuff, Jak."

"Captain Corgos sent a keg down as a wedding present," Jak replied. "I think he would prefer to keep me here drinking it as long as possible. Here," he said, taking the man's tankard, "let me get you a refill. Do you need any, 'Dos? No?" He went to the barrel and filled his guest's cup, as well as his own.

"The wife is up visiting her princess. You'd think she would be happy to have a few days off but she believes they can't get by without her in the keep. So," said Jak, setting the beer down in front of his visitor, "it was Lord Radal. That was bold of the man."

Having had dealings in the past with Radal, Perdos did not feel overly surprised by such an action. Not that he truly knew the sorcerer — did anyone? — but he had seen enough of his ways.

He looked about the little cottage. This was where Borrago's bastard and his family lived, eh? Good riddance to them — he had never gotten on well with Copago. Perdos had dropped by an hour earlier, to the surprise of his old sergeant, and, with the Dame Traspa absent, the two sat and drank uninterrupted. Until this soldier showed up, bursting with news from the keep.

"The count let him in?" he asked.

"That he did," replied the man. "Had him taken to the tower. He'll keep him there until he decides what to do with him, I reckon."

"I'd send him straight back to his old master," declared Sir Jak. "Maybe minus his head."

But he doesn't trust the king of Sharsh, Perdos said to himself. Bolos is mistrustful of everyone these days.

Aloud, he said, "Could be he hopes to bargain with him."

"That's a dangerous game," replied Jak.

His companions nodded their agreement to this and drank of Jak's good beer.

"It was the king who was behind all this. I acted only on his orders."

Bolos half-believed the former lord councilor. He had no doubt that Lareth's hand had been in all that had happened. But he was not inclined to see Lord Radal as without guilt.

Sir Corgos remained silent. The count would have appreciated a word of advice now; he had to admit that Copago, as much as he may have disliked the man, would always have had something useful to say.

But he did appreciate his master of arms' solid presence. It was reassuring, as was that of the two guardsmen who accompanied him. Bolos would not have wanted to be alone with this sorcerer.

Why was he here? That was the foremost concern. But another question, one ultimately of more import to Bolos, lay behind it: had Radal been involved in his father's assassination?

He would not ask now but he would have the truth from this man.

"That does not make you blameless, sir," he said to the dark nobleman. "Why should I not send you back to Sharsh in bonds? For that matter, why should I not hang you from my walls?"

"Because I might be useful to you, my lord. Because you are surrounded by enemies who would throw down all you and your forebears have built." The sorcerer sighed. "My own master among them, I fear. I have fallen from favor for opposing him."

Corgos snorted. There was no obvious response from the impassive Radal, yet malice danced in his eyes. This captain could prove a stumbling-block to his plans.

"Hmmph." Bolos pondered a moment, before speaking to his master of arms. "See that he remains in the tower. Guards both above and below this floor." Turning back to the Sharshite, he stared at the man for a long moment. So old, he seemed, so frail. Yet dangerous, he was certain. Then, shaking his head, he left him.

At last. Lareth placed the dispatch on his desk and gazed out through the stone archways toward the east. At last, news of Radal.

But in Castle Rosam? That was baffling. It baffled his ambassador there, Lord Doufan, as well, but the man had made a formal complaint to the count, stating that Radal had fled from custody in Sharsh and requesting his return.

That was well. Bolos might even do as asked.

He should write the count himself. Yes, and at the same time, alert all the Sharshite companies in Lama to stand ready. Then, he would have to depend on the steady hands of Doufan and of Sir Blen to act when needed, to keep this from being the match that lit up all of Lama.

For a short while, Lareth listened to the steady beat of the kettle-drums, as his men marched and maneuvered outside the walls of the keep. Those drums were one good thing the Ani had brought with them to Sharsh.

"Take dictation," the king told his secretary, settling back into his chair. "We have much to do."

8

"This dance is so simple even Sir Blen would have no trouble with it."

"Do they ever go in the opposite direction?" asked Fachalana. It seemed that they had been circling to their left forever.

"Never," Jobareth replied, stepping sideways and then following with his right foot to bring his heels together. "This is how the Carole has been danced for centuries, or so Donzalo told me."

"If I knew any of these songs I would attempt to sing along." The Lady Fachalana giggled at a thought. "Were Modi here he would want to write them all down in a book."

Many of the circle of dancers were joining into the singing. Some of the tunes were faster, others slower, and the dancing followed their rhythm and that of an accompanying hand drum with the stamping of feet and the striking together of clogged heels.

"Our Maresta may well be committing them all to memory. Would you like to drop out for a while?"

Fachalana nodded. She looks strong enough today, thought Nafal, but there is no point in tempting things. The two left the circle, which was immediately closed again as the couples on either side linked hands.

"We should mount an entertainment," the noblewoman declared, sipping from a cup of cool cider her companion brought her. "Perhaps a read-through of your play, Jobo."

"I thought you considered it unfinished, my lady."

"It would help you to see its many weaknesses," she told him. Although Fachalana smiled, Jobareth Nafal knew she very much meant it. "You and I and Ansa and — who else? We should have another reader or two."

"Grippo, maybe? He is well lettered. In fact," he confided, "I have prevailed upon him to come back to Ros-town with me and serve as my secretary for a time."

"Yes, he would do. As actor, I mean. I've no idea how good a secretary he might be. I wonder if Remare can act." Though she knew the man as Ansa's brother, Fachalana would not reveal that identity.

Jobareth himself had recognized who the man truly was, but likewise chose to speak not of it. "Guesare's friend?" asked he. "I know not. He has not drawn much attention to himself since arriving. Now what is this?"

A messenger had discreetly entered the courtyard and handed a dispatch to Sir Paren, who gave it a quick perusal and then beckoned his nephew and his master of arms to join him. Following a moment's whispering, he waved Jobareth to him, as well.

Whether the reeve meant to include her or not, Fachalana decided to include herself.

"It is your father, my lady," Donzalo said to her. "He is in Castle Rosam." He turned to the legate. "We must leave at once!"

"Someone is in a great hurry behind us," remarked Master Mussago.

Sorsen held up a gauntleted hand, signaling their troop to halt. "Let's see who it is."

They sat their horses, watching the figure draw closer. The day was damp and cool, and a mist lay upon the road so they could not make out a face till the rider was nearly upon them.

"Why, 'tis Sir Blen!" exclaimed Sorsen. "I did not expect him so soon."

"Trouble, no doubt," opined his companion.

"No doubt," agreed the knight. "Or news, at least. We'll know soon."

"If it's important enough to ride after us, then it will take some time." Mussago stood in his stirrups and called to the men. "Make camp here.

"I'm going to get down and stretch my legs," he informed Sorsen.

For a moment, the son of Orgelo was annoyed that his ostensible second-in-command was issuing orders, but then he shrugged. "Good idea," he said, and dismounted as well.

Shortly, Blen was down from his mount and greeting the pair. "The news is straightforward enough," he told them. "Lord Radal is at Keep Rosam. We suspect his men are nearby."

Mussago spat. "We go back then?"

"No," replied Sir Sorsen. "Best to wait on developments and be ready."

"You two have the authority of your fathers to back you up," Blen said. "One of these minor counts should be willing to let you linger near the Rosam borders."

"Poised to return if needed." Sorsen turned to his fellow nobleman. "We should send swift couriers to both our sires with this news."

"Aye." The lean Laman sighed. "I hope something happens soon, one way or another. I would hate to miss being home for Harvest Feast."

Perdos did not care over much about the intrigues of Lord Radal and his presence at Castle Rosam, but did recognize that they would inevitably impact his own business. This, he thought, should send Guesare and his friends scurrying back.

He felt safer loitering about Ros-town these days. His banishment was old and forgotten news; no one paid attention to him, all too caught up in the goings-on at the keep. Wild rumors spread among the dock workers and the tradesmen who frequented these taverns. He listened to much but believed little.

An elderly man settled into the place opposite him. Perdos looked him up and down. A fighting man, once, he surmised, and of no importance to him. He turned his attention back to the plate of sausages and corn cakes before him.

"Sir Perdos, I assume?"

"How do you know me, sir?" His left hand sought the knife in his boot, even as he asked.

The old fellow chuckled. "There are many voices that whisper in my ear. One told me of an outlawed knight who lurked in Ros-town, waiting on his chance for vengeance."

He leaned forward and spoke more lowly. "I am Lord Doufan, but you may address me here as Old Dog. We might be of assistance to each other." He held up a hand to attract a passing serving-wench. "Bring us a couple beers, my dear."

Perdos again eyed the nondescript man before him. Doufan, eh? Not really so old, either. "Speak, Old Dog."

"I have heard of your recent exploits in Todmouth. You did the world a great favor there and crippled Radal in the process. That I personally appreciate."

"Radal is none of my concern and I care not one way nor the other for your appreciation." He drank deeply from his tankard. "But I do thank you for the beer."

"I can provide more than beer. Gold, for one thing.

"But you want the Cuddonian minstrel. I am aware of that." The Sharshite spoke as though he were confiding in an old friend. "I know Guesare and I like him. But he is a spy for the Ani and, therefor, not to be entirely trusted. Ah, you didn't know that, did you?"

"I did not. But I can't say I am surprised."

"It may or may not be to my advantage — Sharsh's advantage — if he lives. You might say I am neutral on the issue."

Perdos slowly nodded. This he understood. But to what was all of it leading?

"What I do need is another set of eyes, one known only to me and reporting only to me. You know the keep and many of the men there. That is useful.

"I can give you official papers, identifying you as attached to the embassy. You will be able to come and go more freely. Of course, someone might still recognize you but you have seemed willing to chance that. How are those sausages, by the way? I'm feeling a mite hungry."

"Middling," replied Sir Perdos. "They spice everything too heavily down here in the south."

"That they do," agreed the ambassador. "Think on my offer, sir. And if you think to accept it, meet me here tomorrow." He rose and left, but not without placing silver on the table that would more than cover both their tabs.

A sly old fox, thought Perdos, his naturally distrustful nature taking over. Still, a bit of money and a chance to get close to the minstrel was tempting. He would indeed think about it.

"It is much easier to be someone else when one has a well-written script, my lord."

Modareth nodded slowly. "I have enough trouble, Pol, remembering my own story, much less that of someone else."

"Then perhaps, sir, I should say it is also easier to be ones own self when properly prepared."

The prince smiled. "Maybe so!" He lifted his reading glass, the lens that ever dangled from a bit of black ribbon about his neck, to his eye and peered at the bottle he held. "Clever idea, putting wine into glass containers like this."

"Your brother has had a part in that. Prince Gawis has done much to foster the glass industry here in Celatas."

"And now he wishes to show off his success. Here he comes," he said. The crown prince approached slowly, acknowledging his guests as he crossed the crowded room.

On reaching them, he nodded casually to Pol, who bowed gracefully, and took Modareth's hand. "I see, my brother, that you have been examining the wine bottles," said he, attempting not to sound too obviously proud. "Only a few years ago we could not have produced glass strong enough for this."

"The coals of the earth permit this, do they not, your highness?"

"Indeed they do, Sir Pol, with the great heat of their fires," he answered, slightly raising an eyebrow in momentary surprise at the question, before resuming a proper princely demeanor. This young fellow is a bright one, isn't he? he asked himself. He must tell Mara to invite him again.

Gawis then looked his younger brother up and down. "Are these to be your colors?"

Modareth blushed and stammered out, "Ca — Carrana thought I should have my own." Then he laughed. "But I did not let her choose them!"

"No green," stated Prince Gawis. "I can understand that." Green was not only associated with the king and, now, himself, but also with Partanaca. After the recent assassination attempts, Modareth would naturally be sour on the color.

"Your argent and purple are the colors of Dor," he continued. "You no doubt intended that." And, therefor, also the colors of our grandfather, he noted to himself. "It would seem you have heard that Father intends to name you Duke of Dor." How did Modareth learn what they thought a well-kept secret? His brother was showing unexpected capabilities and the man at his side might have something to do with that.

Modareth sighed. "Am I to be stuck there, administering provincial bureaucrats?"

"Such duties attend your birth, my lord," Pol remarked. "The freest men are neither slaves nor kings."

"Ah, a proverb! You sound like Lord Doufan," laughed Prince Gawis.

"I consider that high praise, your highness," replied the young knight, with a bow.

He bowed as well to Princess Mara, who had come to stand wordlessly beside her husband. "My lady," murmured Pol and kissed the hand she extended.

"Mara, how are you?" asked Modareth, taking that hand into his own. "We see too little of you." His Carrana had frequently extended invitations to their sister-in-law, invitations that were politely declined. The shy prince, perhaps more than anyone else in their circle, could understand this.

"I do well, Modareth," she replied. "And now we do see each other, no?"

"Indeed, my lady, we come to you." Did that sound wrong? Modareth did not want it to seem he was chiding her. He looked about the room. Where had his wife gotten to? She was better at this sort of thing.

Recognizing his patron's discomfort, Pol intervened. "I think, sir, I would come as often as possible."

"You are always welcome, Sir Pol," said Gawis, "with or without my brother." He winked at Modareth. "We greatly enjoyed our evening at your theater."

"It remains the theater of the Viscountess Fachalana, your highness. I but mind the place till the lady returns. I am gladdened that you enjoyed our performance and I thank you for kind words — and for your invitation."

"We thank you, Sir Pol," Mara said. "I have not seen my husband laugh so in years." She went on, somewhat sheepishly. "But you must explain to me sometime what all of it meant. I fear there was much I did not understand!"

"With pleasure, my lady. But in return, you must play upon the dulcimer for us. Prince Modareth has spoken highly of your skill."

Said prince reddened. Perhaps Mara did as well, beneath the darkness of her countenance.

"She would be pleased to so do," averred Prince Gawis. "I have not heard you play in far too long a time, my dear," he said, turning to his wife.

The princess smiled. "Then, Husband, you should sit in on our daughters' lessons."

As the group chuckled over that, Mara took the opportunity to look more closely at the young playwright. Yes, he did seem so familiar and she thought now she knew why.

Could it be that Sir Pol was the man she had seen in her dreams?

"May Kamat be with you. I shall follow as soon as I may, with the ladies and Sir Habidros."

"Will it be safe for you, sir, and for your people here?" asked Guesare. "There is still an armed company somewhere in the wilds."

"My scouts have only now reported signs of Radal's men, moving southward toward Castle Rosam. It would seem," said Sir Paren, "that they have no interest in my keep. Sir Copago and a troop rides to follow them."

"Then let us ride too," spoke Donzalo, impatient with any delay. "It is time to bring all this to a close."

"That it is," Oder asserted firmly. Though he had remained quiet and unassuming throughout his stay, Paren had sensed that the supposed minstrel was a man used to issuing orders — and to having them followed.

"Legate," said he, holding up a packet to Jobareth. "I have written to your ambassador. Make certain Doufan receives these, will you? And he may share them with you should he choose."

Nafal took the papers, nodded his assent, and spurred his mount to catch up with his comrades, already riding ahead. The two Sharshite guardsmen who had accompanied him from the embassy fell in behind.

9

"Openly camp and offer no harm, he said."

Dovolo nodded. "And that is all?"

"Once you're settled, he wants you to go to the castle, alone. Let 'em know you're friendly." The soldier frowned into space, as if trying to remember if there was anything more. "They watched us when they let me in to talk, so they'll be expecting you, I reckon. If he can, the boss will get word to you one way or another about what's next."

"Refer to our master as Lord Radal," came Dovolo's curt reply. He *would* maintain discipline among this lot.

"Right, Sergeant. Sorry."

Dovolo nodded. "Good. Go get yourself some grub." He turned from the man in dismissal.

So he was supposed to go marching into Keep Rosam, eh? Well, if the old man could do it, so could he.

And this spot, a clearing in the woods no more than a half-day's ride from the castle, would do as their camp. Best he get the men organized and then follow Radal's orders. Whatever the consequences.

"I know you still seek the life of Donzalo. And I know why."

"And I know your secret," came Radal's reply.

Lomela shrugged. "It would do you no good to speak of it."

"Probably not." So like her father, he thought, more so than either of his sons. "Let us, then, speak of other things.

"You have seen my daughter recently. Is she well, my lady?"

The princess hesitated. "She — seems tired, sir." Her tone became accusatory. "That, I think, is in part your doing."

"Her doing, as well," sighed the nobleman. "She is at the embassy?"

"I think that knowledge is for Fachalana to divulge."

"But she will not speak to me, though she knows there is no longer any reason to fear revealing herself. I can see nothing of her mind. Neither can she see mine."

"What she fears, my lord, is the pain of such a conversation."

Radal went to the narrow window and peered out across the Castle Rosam's courtyard, where lay the long deep shadows of the battlements. It was nearing evening and would soon be dark. Yes, everything would soon be dark.

"Even your own shadow leaves you when you are in darkness," the sorcerer said, almost whispering, before turning back to Lomela. "Perhaps you should leave now as well, my lady."

"As you wish, Lord Radal."

Followed by one of the count's personal guardsmen who had waited outside the door, Lady Lomela descended the narrow curving way to the room where her husband and Sir Corgos sat. This had once been Borrago's office; now, the master of arms occupied it. The guard took up a post at the foot of the stairs.

"Could you find out what the man wants?" asked Count Bolos.

"He wants your brother's life. That I could have told you without speaking to him." The princess sat herself down on one of the hard chairs. Was that wine on the table? She could use some. No, just her husband's barley-water. "And you knew it already, did you not?"

"But why?" Bolos wondered. "Why does he so hate the lad?" He was clearly exasperated by all that was going on about him. "Ah, well, Donzalo is safely come to our uncle's manor, according to the latest word from Sir Paren. Best he stays there."

Lomela and Corgos exchanged a look before the captain spoke. "I fear, my lord, that he will not."

Mussago and Sorsen could manage matters without him. They were capable men. It was best that Blen return as quickly as possible to County Rosam.

It was likely that Jobareth would be returning too. Word would have reached Sir Paren's keep by now.

As for the others who had journeyed there, who could say? It might be best were the women to remain safely distant from Ros-town but

Blen doubted greatly that they would. Certainly not the headstrong Fachalana. She would not let herself be pushed to the side.

And Radal was her father. He had to keep that in mind.

The knight had never known anyone like the Lady Fachalana. He could picture her in his mind, remembering her as he had faced her in their fencing. Could one want for a better woman by ones side? But she was promised to Nafal, after all, and he himself was only a knight of no particular importance, a younger son of a minor baronet.

It had been nearly a decade since he had run away from his father's modest estate by the River Chas, yet it sometimes seemed no more than yesterday. He wondered if the salmon yet swam in the shadows of the willow-lined river banks. Of course they do, he told himself. They are not the ones who left.

So mused Sir Blen as he hurried north along the Great Road.

It was the company whose deserted camp he had come across south of the Abam. Of this Perdos was sure. There were not as many as had once followed the late Sojel, but they were undoubtedly the same men. The men who had murdered his friends.

This he did not say to Lord Doufan. He had taken the ambassador's papers and, aye, his gold as well. The man had asked the knight to first undertake this task for him, to scout out the disposition of Radal's troop.

"It was easy enough. There was a hill that gave me a clear vantage of the area. If that rabble had been any sort of soldiers, they would have had their own sentry up there." Perdos took a swig from his cup. Real perry like they made in the north — he hadn't had any in ages.

Another man might have guessed that the Sharshite had known this and ordered a keg. Perdos chose to enjoy the drink rather than question it.

"I was about to head back when I saw movement in the woods near the camp. Up high like I was I could tell it was a troop of soldiers and they meant those fellows no good.

"They must have tracked them from the east. I could see their captain had his riders stationed to charge the camp. Radal's men would have been slaughtered."

"And were they?" asked Doufan, as nonchalantly as if they were discussing the weeding of a garden.

"No, I'm sorry to say."

The ambassador only nodded and waited for Perdos to continue.

"Well, their leader and a couple men rode into camp, as boldly as you please, to tell them to surrender. I could recognize the fool even at that distance. It was Sir Copago."

"A fool indeed, but very like him not to attack without warning."

"That it is," admitted Sir Perdos. He might dislike the man but he respected him for his uncompromising sense of honor. "Anyway, one of those knaves sauntered right up and held out a piece of paper to him. The captain did not like what he read one bit. Threw it on the ground and wheeled his mount around."

Lord Doufan frowned. "I would hazard that the count had given them his permission to be there. What did our Copago then?"

"He led his men straight up the hill where I was watching, so I hurried away. If I were he, I'd be camped up there watching that bunch."

"As would I." Doufan looked out toward the river. There was little traffic, late on this autumn day. "I think we may leave them to Sir Copago for now. As for you, I have no assignment other than to keep your eyes open. Meet me here the day after tomorrow. You may," he continued, "sleep here if you wish. Those who abide in this house are discreet."

They were seated in a low ramshackle edifice near the mouth of the Abam, set on piles driven into the marshy ground.

"I think I prefer my bed on higher ground, sir," replied Perdos, "and in air less soggy."

"And in some spot unknown to me, as well," said Doufan.

"Aye, that too," agreed Perdos, emptying his cup.

"I intend to let you and your wife have that cottage as your own, once this trouble has passed, but for now I want you here in the keep."

"Thank you, sir," replied Jak. "We had honeymoon enough. I'm ready to serve."

As dependable as ever, thought Count Bolos. He spoke. "I don't know that I completely trust Corgos. To be honest, I don't know that I trust anyone other than you."

He was not going to mention it, but his master of arms had shown up in one of his nightmares. Those had not diminished, as he and Doctor Heragos had hoped, but had grown even more troubling.

"The captain is a good man," objected Sir Jak. "We might not always see eye to eye, you understand, but I don't question his loyalty."

"Maybe so." He sat a moment, brooding. He should ignore those dreams. As he should ignore Lord Radal's warnings of enemies on all sides.

Lies, all of it. The man was not his friend.

"I may need to use the cottage for other guests," said Bolos, turning their conversation elsewhere. "We'll see how that goes.

"In the meantime, a military company that apparently followed our Sharshite wizard is camped a half-day's march north of us. I gave them my permission but also sent someone to keep an eye on them. My scouts have told me that our former master of arms is camped nearby, also observing."

Hesitantly, knowing his master's dislike for the man, Jak spoke. "Co-pago is competent."

"I don't like Copago having contact with them. Nor do I want Sir Corgos conferring with him. The two were much too close when both served here.

"Lord Radal has agreed to order them here where we may watch them more closely. I want you to carry the message to their sergeant and see that they set up camp outside our walls." He held out a piece of parchment to the knight.

Is that wise? wondered Jak. He would prefer to have them further away, not nearer.

"Yes, my lord," he answered, taking the paper. "I'll start out right away."

10

The corpulent Gos slouched in his chair, behind a small and untidy desk. "Do not assume that there will be no further attempts at assassination," he warned.

"I do not. It is a constant in the lives of princes."

"Indeed," agreed the chief of Lareth's secret police. "You remain close to Modareth." It was neither a question nor an order, but a statement of fact.

"I do. I will attend one of his salons tomorrow evening. In fact," Pol continued, "his brother and the Princess Mara have for once accepted his invitation."

"I wouldn't expect anything to happen there."

"Perhaps not, sir," agreed the young Arolinian, "but then an enemy might take advantage of such expectations." He smiled wickedly and continued, "I certainly would."

"Not everyone has your imagination, Sir Pol," said Gos. "Thank Jov!"

"Lord Radal is my guest. I care not what your king wishes." The count tossed the document he was holding onto the table.

"Certainly, my lord, you are sovereign in your own lands. The king only asks this of you as one ruler to another — one *friend* to another," Doufan assured the count, "and from brotherly concern. The man is dangerous."

Bolos sighed wearily. "This I know, Lord Doufan. It is why he is confined in the tower where I can keep an eye on him."

"It has been shown, sir, that towers may not hold Radal."

"If the sorcerer does somehow flee then I am rid of him and no harm to me." The slightest and most fleeting of smiles appeared on the count's face. Then he spoke more seriously. "But he came here for a reason and I intend to find it out."

The two sat at a table in the Great Hall, empty now save for a sentry at the door. Count Bolos would allow no other, not his wife, not his master of arms. Nor did he show the ambassador any signs of hospitality, permitting him to come here and nowhere else in the keep.

At least he might have offered me a drink, thought Doufan. He's even more parsimonious than his father. Or maybe he just hopes I'll feel unwelcome and leave.

"Nafal has returned from your uncle's," said Lord Doufan.

"And my brother. I am aware what goes on in my county, sir." He shook his head. "I am sorry for my brusqueness, Doufan. This all revolves around Donzalo. This I know. I do not know why."

Should I tell him? wondered the ambassador. He wasn't sure he knew all the story himself.

"What else I know," continued Bolos, "is that Sorsen and Mussago have turned their men around and now lurk on my borders. I know also that your king has been massing troops. I will not turn Radal over to anyone under such circumstances."

He rose from the bench. "I have but one more thing to say, my Lord Doufan. If Donzalo is with you, warn him not to come here. There are too many dangers and, I fear, not only for him."

Count Bolos beckoned to the guard. "Escort the ambassador to the stables.

"I will call for you if I wish to speak again," he said to Doufan, and abruptly left the hall, leaving the letter from King Lareth lying where he had dropped it.

"Ride with me to Sorsen's camp," spoke Sir Blen. "It is little more than a day distant."

"It does you no good to sit here," added Guesare.

"I should go to the keep. That is why I came home." Donzalo looked toward the ceiling. "And I should be part of what is going on up there. Bolos is my brother."

In his office, a floor above them, Lord Doufan conferred with Jobareth Nafal and the Anian, Oder. Doufan, not surprisingly, had known

— or, at least, suspected — who the spy-master was truly and felt it wise to include him.

"A council with Sorsen and Mussago would also be important," responded Blen. "Your uncle and the ladies might be here by the time we return and then we can make further plans."

If nothing else, a journey south would be a way of diverting the young knight from his intention to ride into Castle Rosam, whether welcome or not. All their group had been agreed on this.

"Perhaps," agreed Donzalo. "Not that I trust Sorsen and his father to have the interests of my family at heart."

"Then all the better that you should keep an eye on them, lad," said the minstrel.

The young nobleman shrugged. "Very well. When do we leave?"

"I tell you, Captain, the count knows we are encamped here. We only await orders." Dovolo surveyed his camp from this vantage point. He would have thought to put a sentry up here were he not so busy running back and forth from Castle Rosam. It was a mistake to trust in his second to do things right.

"Your company has done plenty enough harm elsewhere for me to hang them all. I know they are the men who attacked my master's manor last year."

The sergeant slowly nodded. "That is true, Sir Copago, but I and many of the others were not with them at that time." He turned to face his companion. "Most of my men are common ruffians, I know. I have tried to bring some discipline to them since taking command."

He glanced toward Copago's well-ordered camp. Not enough discipline to ever take on this bunch, even with an advantage in numbers.

"See to it you have a document with the count's signature on it if you move your men," came Copago's curt reply. "If you do otherwise, we shall attack."

"Understood, Captain."

Sir Copago gazed out across the forested hills. The leaves were now past their peak autumn color and many were falling. He should be back at Paren's manor, attending to all the many tasks of the season. Land needed clearing so they could put in more orchard before spring, peaches and pecans, and there was that hillside that would serve well as a vineyard.

"Hold a minute," he called after Dovolo, who had begun descending the hill. "Riders come."

Three men had entered Copago's camp, soldiers clad in the green and sable of Rosam — the colors he had worn not so long ago. He recognized one as Sir Jak, sergeant of the count's personal guard, and raised a hand in greeting.

"Ho, Sir Copago," called the burly soldier, dismounting. "I've a message for the rabble down there." He nodded his head toward those below them.

"This is their headman, Dovolo." The fellow had returned to stand beside him and held out his hand to take the document Jak held. So he can read, thought Copago, as well as have the bearing of a gentleman. The man may once have been more than a leader of outlaws.

Dovolo perused the parchment and then handed it to Copago. "Here's the document you said I must have, sir. I'll go get my men ready to march."

Copago cursed and looked up at Jak. The soldier's stolid expression revealed nothing. "We will accompany you part way, Sir Jak. I don't like the idea of you three riding with these villains. But I must turn aside before we reach Keep Rosam."

"I will welcome your presence, Sir Copago. Sometimes —" The man hesitated. He had never been a friend of Copago. "Sometimes, I wish that you still served there."

Copago smiled thinly. "As do I, sometimes. And sometimes I am thankful that I do not."

"My duty is to follow the count, my lady, whatever I might think of his orders. I can not and will not do otherwise."

"But what, Sir Corgos, if those orders harm my husband? Should we not protect Count Bolos from bad counsel and evil influence?"

"That is not mine to question, madame, unless he asks for my opinion."

Lomela dropped wearily onto her divan. "It is good that you are loyal, sir. Know, however, that I fear what lies Lord Radal may be whispering in the count's ear."

The master of arms softened his voice. "My lady, do not believe that I feel differently. I would send the sorcerer back to your father if I could."

"I would send him to hell," came the princess' vehement reply, "where he could harm no one."

She looked up at the knight. "I must trust you to keep an eye on things, Sir Corgos. There is none other in this keep to whom I may turn." Even as she so spoke, she considered how she might bring her husband's faithful Sir Jak to her side or influence this man's wife, the Dame Tiana. But Lomela knew as well that she had planted seeds in his mind that might later yield a crop.

"I will serve as I can, Countess," responded the master of arms, "and attempt to keep you informed."

"I thank you, Sir Corgos. That is all I ask."

The old butler was gone. "Lord Doufan sent him off with a pension," said the new caretaker for the embassy's town house. "He felt that a younger man was needed."

The middle-aged fellow was unmistakably a retired soldier, possibly a former sergeant.

"Will it be just the two of you or will young Donzalo be coming as well?" asked he.

"Sir Donzalo is too recognizable to stay around town," replied Guesare. "He remains at the embassy."

The man chuckled. "Recognizable, indeed. I've known him since he was a boy and I served at the keep." He straightened up then, like the military man he was. "You may call me Ubos, good sirs. Sir Guesare and Sir Remare it is?"

"That is correct, Master Ubos," replied Guesare. "Tell me, man, is any of Nafal's good wine about? Remare and I could use a pitcher now, and whatever victuals you might happen to have in your kitchen."

"Certainly, sir," replied the butler and disappeared into his pantry.

"So, what have you been up to, my friend?" asked Guesare.

"Visiting my contacts here, writing dispatches — the usual stuff of a spy's life, Guesare. For once," he said, leaning forward and lowering his voice, "it seems that the empire and Sharsh have a common goal."

"Don't trust Doufan once this is over," warned the Cuddonian. "You know that of course."

"I don't trust him now," replied Oder. He leaned back again as Ubos entered with their wine. "I'll pour," he told him. "You go find us some food, won't you?"

Passing a goblet to Guesare, he continued. "I have become too well known here and, perhaps, everywhere. It is time to give up this life of espionage."

"Will I see you no more?" asked Guesare. He felt a sudden ache in his heart at the thought of losing the man who had been friend, mentor, and lover.

"Who is to say? Perhaps I'll become a diplomat and continue to pull the strings on our web of spies. Or maybe," he said, pausing to sip of his wine, "I shall retire to the family estates. I am a jarl of the empire, you know."

Guesare did not know. He realized he really knew very little of this Anian.

"Perhaps I, too, shall return home," he said, "and stay there this time."

11

"My father has sent you a gift, Sir Donzalo."

"Not another puppy, I hope," replied the young Rosam.

Mussago's lean, leathery face cracked into a genuine smile. "Nay, good sir," he laughed, motioning to a couple of his men to bring forth a small keg. He himself pried the lid off and tipped it so Donzalo might see the contents.

"Gunpowder!"

"That it is. The first to come from your kinsman Daboreth's brimstone. It seems that he and my father have gone into manufacture together." He noted the disappointment on the young man's face. "Be not wrathy toward them, Donzalo. It made good business sense for the counts to collaborate on this. And, moreover," he confided, "Daboreth is soon to be a member of our family. I have given permission for him to wed one of my daughters."

Donzalo shrugged in resignation. "Who am I to disapprove of a man in love?" he asked, and then looked quizzically at Mussago. "How came you to bless such a marriage when you have been far from your home?"

"I have met Daboreth from time to time and know him a good man. When my father approved their match, I readily agreed."

He probably approves anything Mussago the Elder suggests, thought Donzalo. But Dabbi was indeed a good man, and not unlike the one before him. "My congratulations, then," he said with a sincere smile. "We could use a great deal more of that gunpowder."

"We will make you a good price," replied Mussago.

"I must have my men scout County Arvaram for brimstone," mused Sir Sorsen, who had remained silent to that point. "Then we can give you a better price," he stated, but not without a broad wink.

"When all this has settled down, I may be competition for both of you," asserted Donzalo. "Right now, we have other matters to concern us."

"Indeed we do," Blen agreed. "I see the company here has grown."

"Yes," said Mussago. "Another dozen of my father's men came with the powder." He looked to the Sharshite, the man he considered the leader of their group — being quite unwilling to concede such a position to Sorsen, a representative of the rival Arvaram. "Is there nothing we can do but wait here?"

The troops were encamped just below the Rosam border. "I would we were in closer striking distance," added Sorsen. "Even riding hard, it is nearly a day's journey to Ros-town."

"Aye," Mussago said, "and a day more for us to get any news."

"There is a risk," said Sir Blen, "but we could send a man or two north each day to wait in Ros-town. You can provide passports and funds for their lodging, I would assume." He did not add that Sharshite soldiers were already passing from the lands of Count Dordos into County Rosam in just that fashion, and more were on their way across the mountain passes. "It could not be a large force but it would be useful to have men there."

Mussago looked to his fellow captain. "Too bad you are so well known, Sir Sorsen, or you might slip into town yourself."

"Not to mention those fine horses both of you ride," Blen reminded him. "I fear you two will have to remain."

"Well, that's all our business then, isn't it?" asked Donzalo. "What's to eat?"

Paren had not hurried. Haste could be left to those who went before him. The reeve's greatest concern had been to get the Lady Fachalana and her companion safely back to Ros-town. Then he would see what could be done for his nephew.

He gave a worried glance at the noblewoman, weary and seemingly dazed, as she rode along. At their somewhat leisurely pace, this journey had stretched to nearly five days. Fachalana soon tired.

"Will we go straight to the castle, sir?" asked Sir Habidros, who had moved up to ride beside him.

"No, I want to get the ladies to the embassy. Lord Doufan can put our small party up for the night." The only others who accompanied them were Master Grippo and a pair of guardsmen.

They passed by the turn toward Keep Rosam. He would take that road soon enough.

The soup here was good. Moreover, this little shop was close enough to the embassy's house that he could keep an eye on Guesare and his fellow minstrel, both holed up there. Not too closely, old Doufan had told him — he had a man on the inside for that.

Yes, the minstrel had returned. That was to the good, Perdos told himself, but with things as they were, it would be more difficult than ever to get at him.

He sipped some more of the savory broth from a wooden spoon. Plenty of garlic like they did it back home, and proper dumplings. He felt fortified against the coolness of this day.

There was no point in dawdling here. And they might notice him if he did. Maybe he should seek out Jak again. He'd heard the man had ridden north for the count and returned with Radal's band of ruffians, now camped outside the castle gates. The spot on which his brother had been slain, in fact. He scowled at the thought.

If it were left to him, he would have had a gallows waiting there for them.

Was something going on over there? No, it was only the caretaker off on an errand. Ubos. Perdos remembered him from the castle garrison. Hadn't he been minding the gates on the morning Percos died? He wasn't sure, now.

The knight drained the last from his bowl and set off down the streets of Ros-town.

Tiana knew there was no better time to get something from her husband than when both were snug in their bed.

Not because of their love-making — not that it hurt any — but because Corgos so fiercely loved this new settled and wedded life of his. When he held her, she became his whole world, a world that had never been his before, and he forgot the weight of his duties as soldier and captain.

She did not see this as wrong. Tiana was a practical and a realistic woman, and knew that it made sense to use ones advantages.

"Husband," said she, in the darkness, laying her head on his chest. "Our home seems to be in turmoil. Will it be safe for the child?"

She truly did fear for the safety of her family, now and future, and believed Corgos would share that concern. And she silently thanked Countess Lomela for speaking to her of these things.

His voice came hesitantly, even reluctantly. "I do not know, my love. The count seems to become ever more unreasonable."

"You could speak to him."

"I should have spoken my thoughts to him before. Now it may be too late." The regret in his voice surprised Dame Tiana.

"Do not blame yourself, husband!"

The master of arms sighed deeply. "In following what I saw as my duty I may have failed my liege. And now I fear to speak lest he come to mistrust me."

I believe he already does, he told himself. This he would not mention to Tiana. She had enough to worry her.

"All I can do," he continued, "is to try to protect Bolos from whatever comes. And if a storm is about to break, my love, it might be best if you were without this castle."

"No, husband," whispered Tiana, "I chose to love a soldier, knowing of his duties. Now I have my duties, too."

As such gatherings went, this was a small one. Even for his brother.

But Gawis thanked him for this. Mara should be comfortable with this little group. How long had it been since the two had attended such a salon together? Years, it must be.

There, not surprisingly, was Sir Pol. And the Baroness Ysena, all in gold satin, making eyes at the young knight. He had little doubt that her husband was busy at the buffet.

Once, a youthful Prince Gawis had been the object of Ysena's advances. He had dallied with her for a time, the baron ever unsuspecting. Had Pol cuckolded the old fellow as well?

The prince and his wife passed through the room, murmuring greetings, acknowledging bows, to where stood their host and hostess. The guests seemed to be forming a small crowd at one side of the room, across from the laden tables. My brother provides a good feed, thought Gawis. No wonder his salons are popular.

"Pol is about to read," Carrana informed them.

"From a play?" asked Princess Mara.

"He doesn't know yet, my lady. The boy seems to write these poems with no clear intention for them," said Modareth. "He may attach it to a production later."

Everyone, save a pair of servants at the buffet, turned to listen to Sir Pol.

"This is but a little song," said he, with a smile that was all boyish charm, "for one and all of the ladies present."

I'll hang the moon from a silver chain
to wear beside your heart,
And fashion ear rings of the rain
that drip in subtle art
Against the midnight of your hair
and dawning of your skin —
A glowing, flushing morning fair
with hints of flame within.

Princess Mara thought that he looked directly at her as he spoke, and perhaps he did. Or maybe he was looking at something behind her.

I'll set the sun in a ring of gold
to place upon your hand
And kiss your fingers, making bold
but making no demand;
No, only asking for your love,
that you be mine and stay
Each night of gem-starred sky above,
each jeweled golden day.

As he finished, he spoke loudly over the applause. "Stop that man! He has poisoned the prince's wine!" He pointed toward one of the servitors.

The fellow pulled forth a dagger and sprang toward Prince Modareth. His brother stood in the way. Gawis grappled with the assassin for a moment before the man broke free.

It was enough to keep him from reaching his target. Pol clouted the attacker behind the ear with the pommel of his poniard. He fell to the carpet, dazed.

There was a scream.

On the floor, a pool of red surrounding him, lay the crown prince.

12

Donzalo absently looked about the little common room. He had never been in this cottage when his half-brother and his family had occupied it.

Through the low windows, he could barely see the keep by evening's last light. He might keep an eye on it from here, for now, but he did intend to enter its gates and speak with his brother. Sooner or later, he must.

Bolos had requested that his Uncle Paren stay in this little house rather than Keep Rosam. Too dangerous, he had said, too much going on up there for guests right now.

"It's not so much me he wants to discourage from coming, boy," felt Paren, "as you and your friends. I'm sure he thinks you'll choose to settle in here with me, where he can keep a watch on you at arm's distance."

"And I intend to to keep a watch from closer up," Habidros said. "I may not be your official bodyguard anymore but with that sorcerer scheming up there," he explained, nodding in the direction of the castle, "and his men camped nearby, someone should be looking out for you."

No doubt his brother Guesare — and Oder, too — asked this of him, thought Donzalo. The Cuddonian would surely rather be down in Rostown with them.

"Are you planning to stay too?" he asked Grippo. "It might get a bit crowded with six of us in here." Paren's two guardsmen were bunking in the cottage as well.

"No, friend Donzalo. I am settled in the embassy as Legate Nafal's secretary and will come here only to bear messages." There was but a tinge of sadness in his voice. "This was my home for many years but that is no longer so. I would rather not be reminded of it."

"Are the ladies well?" Sir Paren asked of him. Fachalana's condition on their ride here had worried him.

"Seemingly, sir. Both are up and about, and the Lady Fachalana is eating enough for two. Practicing her swordsmanship, as well, on anyone foolish enough to fence with her."

Donzalo laughed. "Sir Blen, I think, will always be such a fool."

My dream, thought Mara. This was my dream.

Sentries had taken hold of the would-be assassin and Pol was now on his knees beside the prince. "He lives," he reported, holding a finger to his neck to feel the pulse. "Where — where is his wound?" the knight wondered, his hands seeking the source of the blood.

"Oooow," came Gawis's voice, low. "My head hurts!" He opened his eyes. "Modi! Is he safe?"

"I am, my brother, thanks to your defense," said Prince Modareth, who knelt on his other side. "Where are you hurt?"

Gawis held up his left arm. "He gashed my arm. And then I slipped in this damned wine and banged my head on the floor!"

Modareth sniffed at the red pool and then laughed aloud. "My brother bleeds a fine vintage!" He tore open the prince's sleeve. "It does not look too bad. Has anyone sent for a physician?"

"I have, husband," replied the Princess Carrana. "Give them some room!" she ordered their guests who had gathered round, dumbfounded by this turn in the evening's entertainments.

"We must make sure that the dagger was not poisoned," spoke Pol. He doubted it but there was always that chance.

Prince Gawis rose unsteadily to his feet, feeling gingerly at the back of his head. "I may bleed there, too," he said. "I shall most certainly have a great bump."

Princess Mara stood staring at her husband for a moment, before stepping forward to tearfully embrace him. "I feared you dead, my prince," she hoarsely whispered. "I feared you dead but you came back to me!"

He wrapped his uninjured arm about her. "What, would I leave before our child was born? I will not be cheated of that!" He tipped his head down to kiss her brow. That hurts! he thought, and let wife and brother lead him to a chair and the waiting doctor.

"Sir Paren wants me to stay here," Copago said. "He had left a message for me with Lady Thara." The master of arms clearly disapproved of his orders. "I should be the one riding to Castle Rosam, not he!"

"What could you do there?" asked the Dame Sima. "You know you are not welcome."

"In a crisis, fighting men are always welcome," he told his mother. "The count may need such."

"Then he should not have sent you away," asserted his wife, Janona, walking on his other side.

"The reeve will send word if he needs you," said Sima. "Paren is certainly capable of making his own decisions." She looked out across a newly-cleared field. "I'll miss the woods that were here."

"The cows won't. We needed more pasture."

"Your son is such a romantic," asserted Janona.

"Don't I know it," replied Sima. "As was his father." For a moment, memories of the late Count Borrago filled the minds of all three.

"I would do right by the legacy of my father," said Copago, at last. "Even if it means defending a brother who hates me."

"And one who loves you, I think," Janona said. "It is Donzalo who stands central to all of this."

"Aye," Sir Copago growled, "I will not abandon that overgrown boy."

"This seems far too familiar," said Sir Blen.

"Including the part where Fachalana ever bests you?" teased Ansa.

"That is to be expected, my lady." He looked the slender Anian up and down. "Have you ever fenced? Perhaps I should try crossing swords with you for a change!"

Fachalana laughed at the thought. "Our friend is no swordswoman. However, I would not wish to come across her in a darkened alley with a dagger in her hand."

Blen soberly nodded his agreement. He had seen what Ansa could do.

"Again, my, er, Fachalana?"

"No, Blen, I have tired." The tall noblewoman returned her blade to its scabbard. "It is my father. He is so near — I ever feel his presence. It wears on me."

"Does he try to speak to you?"

She shook her head. "He knows it would do no good."

He is always with her, inside, thought Blen. Being near the sorcerer must make it all the worse. Would she be freed of him were her father dead or would he live on in her soul?

"There is a place," she went on, speaking as if in a dream, "that I have seen. A place where I might escape all this. When we are done here," Fachalana said, her voice now more resolute, "perchance I might find it again."

Both Blen and Ansa sent silent prayers to their respective deities that such would be.

At times now, Bolos would go the tower alone and sit with Lord Radal, trying to solve the riddle of the man.

But it brought only more riddles. Despite the Sharshite's words, he knew he was no friend. What did he want?

And the dreams continued. Now, his brother was showing up in them more frequently and his presence was not a welcome one. Donzalo would never be the bloody usurper he saw in his nightmares.

And surely he shouldn't believe those visions of Lomela's infidelity with his brother.

No, it was simply all else that was weighing on him that caused these fantasies of the night. Radal was right to point out that Bolos's enemies were gathering.

"Who are my enemies?" he asked the man. "Can I trust anyone?"

"A wise ruler trusts none," replied the former lord councilor. "Do not trust me but weigh my words carefully for their truth."

Bolos thought silently on this a while before deciding there was no more to said on the subject. "Are you well, my lord?" he asked Radal. The man seemed frail, though no more now than when he had shown up at the gates of Keep Rosam. Reports were that he ate little and slept almost never.

"No, my Lord Bolos. I am dying." He smiled thinly at the count's reaction. "Not yet; there are things I must do before I leave this world."

"Where is Donzalo this morning?"

"He was here but a minute ago," replied one of the soldiers, "finishing up his breakfast."

"And quite a breakfast it was," said the other. "I think he stepped outside."

Habidros cursed himself for sleeping in. And he cursed the young Laman as a fool for taking a walk without his protection. Didn't he know Lord Radal's cutthroats were just down the road?

No breakfast for him. He hurried out the door to catch up with his charge.

Around the cottage he went to the small stable, overcrowded with the mounts of his companions. There, Donzalo was saddling his own.

"Where to, lad?" asked the Cuddonian.

"Home," came the reply. "It is time to speak with my brother."

It was bound to come to this, sooner or later, Habidros told himself. "I'll ride with you."

"Thank you, Habi. I doubt you will be permitted to enter."

"Then we shall part at the gate. Are you sure of this?"

"No," said Donzalo, leading his horse into the open yard. "But that makes no difference. Let's ride."

13

"Our foremost concern," said Lord Doufan, "is to protect the Lady Lomela and her son. Beyond that, the goals are flexible."

Jobareth Nafal was discouraged. "Can we truly have any effect on things here, my lord?" he asked the ambassador.

Doufan, to the surprise of neither Jobareth nor Blen, had a ready answer. "History is a runaway horse and most of the time all we can do is to hold on. But now and then, perhaps, we may find ourselves able to give a little tug on the reins and turn it, ever so slightly, in our desired direction."

"I think, sir, we are more likely to fall off and be trampled," said Sir Blen, half-jestingly. Such a quip from the reserved knight *was* a bit of a surprise.

"Indeed, my good sir," agreed the elder diplomat, "yet we must try to ride. That is why we three are met here in what amounts to a council of war. This is why we must discuss plans to defeat Radal."

He leaned against the front of his oversize desk, facing the two men as though he were a schoolmaster and asked a seemingly unrelated question of Jobareth. "Tell me, Nafal, what is the purpose of government?"

"Sir, my father would say it is to maintain and protect the roads."

Doufan chuckled. "That, indeed, sounds like him. But such are means, not ends."

"To see that everyone is treated fairly," suggested Blen, sounding at once earnest and uncertain.

His companions looked at each other with a certain incredulity and then began to laugh.

"The purpose of government is to help create and maintain a stable society," stated Lord Doufan. "All else serves that end.

"Now admittedly, Sir Blen, a fair government can, more often than not, best fulfill that task. But it can not let itself be a slave to such ideals."

"Nor to ideologies of any sort," said Jobareth. "I know that school of thought. I am not sure though, my lord, if I agree with it."

"It is not a popular philosophy at the universities," admitted the ambassador.

Blen, after a moment's thought, said, "It makes sense to me."

"You are a practical man. Nafal here is a poet and dreamer. As," he continued, "is our Lord Radal. Yes, Radal," he maintained, noting the doubtful expressions of his companions. "The man is the worst sort of romantic. He believes in power and all it can accomplish.

"The lord councilor has always been committed to the centralized power of his king. It goes beyond a personal loyalty to Lareth. It is his philosophy, even his creed, one might say."

"Power does have its uses," opined Jobareth.

"Yes, lad, it does. But too much power with one man or group is dangerous. I have always believed there should be a balance."

"Balance seems to be *your* philosophy of life, my lord," Blen quietly commented.

Doufan nodded in acknowledgment to his statement. "Balance and stability is what we must seek here in Lama, whatever our means might be."

He again addressed Nafal. "Legate," he said. Neither man recalled him ever using his subordinate's title previously. "I must ask you about your relationship to Lord Radal. He was your patron and his daughter is your supposed fiancée. Will this have any bearing on where your loyalties lie?"

"Our intended engagement was always a ruse, sir. There is no promise between Lady Fachalana and myself other than one of friendship."

Blen, although he gave no sign, was most interested to learn this.

"Moreover," continued Jobareth, "I long since pledged my loyalty to Princess Lomela over that of Radal."

"Very well. We need a way to contact the princess, and all those who dwell within the castle walls, since we have been shut out. Communication is key to any successful campaign."

"I know of one who might help us pass messages, sir," said Blen. "Sir Copago once told me of a certain laundress who visits regularly."

"She is readily bribed?"

"Better yet, my lord, she has a personal loyalty to the count and could easily be persuaded that we are trying to help him."

Should I tell what I know, what was entrusted to me by Donzalo? wondered Jobareth Nafal. How better to help him?

He spoke. "And I know of a secret way into the keep."

There would be no more from Jak. Count Bolos had shut the gates of his keep and none entered nor left, except on his direct order.

"You're a northerner, aren't you?" asked the woman who filled his bowl. Perdos nodded. From her accent, he recognized that she was as well.

"I have something here you might like," said she, setting a chipped earthenware plate before him.

He recognized the soft, garlicky cheese immediately, as much by its odor as its appearance. "Oulg! I haven't had any since I was a boy." Such memories it brought to him.

The woman laughed at his broad grin. "A northern boy, indeed!" she said, cutting him a generous slice. "I was afraid I would have to eat all of this myself as none here appreciate it. I am Rassana."

"You have none with whom to share it, Dame Rassana?"

"Mistress Rassana. My man left me and I have kept this shop as best I can on my own."

He leaned in close to her. "My name is Perdos but I ask you not to speak it loudly. There are those about who, um, do not wish me well."

"Very well, Master Perdos," she whispered in reply.

"Sir Perdos, actually." Why did he feel it necessary to impress her with his knighthood?.

She smiled. It was a very nice smile, he thought. "I shall call you Dorbi," she said. "That was my dog's name back in Flosa."

"Flosa? Why, I grew up only a few leagues from there. Over on the river."

Rassana cut two more slices of oulg, one for each. "You are watching that house over there."

Perdos nodded.

"Considering all the goings on in that place, I'm surprised more don't watch it."

"Maybe they do," laughed Perdos. "Maybe they're just better at it than I am."

"Well, Dorbi, feel free to watch from my counter anytime." She smiled again at him. "Anytime at all."

He could not leave now, not with how things stood in Lama. But these were serious events in the capital. His heir wounded while protecting his younger brother! That was not something Lareth might ever have dreamed of occurring.

Gawis should be here with him. It was never good to have two sons in the same town, much less the same room, and possibly lose both at once. Yes, he would send for the crown prince. Maybe he could learn something of ruling during this crisis.

And maybe his son could handle such a crisis himself the next time and let his old father take things easy in Celatas. The chill of Mountain Keep did not agree with him.

It would not do to be here in the dead of winter. Although the pass was rarely closed, it had been known to occur and then he would be cut off from his kingdom across the mountains.

Whatever was going to happen in Lama, it must happen soon.

"I like the countess well enough," said Aulla. "She knows my past and does not hold it against me. A true gentlewoman she is, not like some of those who grew up in these parts." The laundress looked at the cloak she held. "This is a fine puke, sir. Cuddonian?"

"The fabric is, Dame Aulla. The garment was cut in Celatas."

"Ah. 'Twill take special care." She looked up from the cloth. "So you wish to know of me and the count, do you?"

Lord Doufan nodded. "Only what you wish to tell me, madame, but the more I know, the better may I help the man."

She seemed satisfied with that answer. "Bolos danced the jig with me as a youth and left me with child." She nodded in the direction of a little girl, playing quietly with her doll amid the heaps of laundry. "He has since done well by us. Of course, I have a husband now and he is not too bad a sort. Lazy, but so it goes."

"Your own industry seems to make up for it."

Aulla laughed. "Aye, sir, and all the business of the castle being sent my way. I don't even have to get my own hands wet anymore!"

"And you, then, come and go in the keep as you will?"

"No one questions me, but I do have a regular schedule. I always attend to things personally up there."

The woman was short, broad of build and face. She seems quite ordinary, thought Doufan. He suspected that Aulla affected such a persona, even as did he.

"Then you will be able to pass messages to and from Countess Lomela and others." The ambassador made certain his voice expressed approval and, even, admiration. Subtle flattery was never a bad idea. "The count needs friends and I am sure we can consider you one of them. But know," he continued, "that we will not fail to reward you in other ways."

Aulla, after all, did not become a successful businesswoman purely on sentiment.

◆

"Do you remember Mother?" asked Bolos, of a sudden. It seemed an odd subject to bring up just then.

"I do, though I fear I would not know her face now."

"You were what, six, at the time she died? I remember how much you cried because you were not permitted to see her."

"It was the plague, wasn't it? No wonder Father didn't want me there."

"Nay, it was the grippe. It was widespread that year. Many died, some of them my friends." He paused for a moment, holding and then releasing old memories. "I was stricken too, but lived. If things had been but a bit different, you might be count now."

No, our father would would still be count, Donzalo said to himself. To Bolos he said, "Histories say that plagues broke the Ani ambitions in the west as much as any force of arms."

"You and your books." Bolos shook his head. "Are they all intact up at Uncle Paren's place?"

"They are." He let his gaze sweep the mostly empty suite he occupied, the one he had vacated a few months earlier. "I might as well have left them here. They would help me pass the time."

Bolos recognized the mild accusation. "I only hope to keep you safe here until we can get all this sorted out. You — you did right to give me that clout. I hold it not against you."

"But it was not necessary, Brother. I let anger move me."

"You acted like the fighting man you have become. You are no longer the boy you were not long ago."

I am very far from that boy, now, thought Donzalo.

"Lord Radal tells me I should distrust you, Donzalo," said the count. "I do not believe this. I can not believe this. But why is he your enemy?"

"Radal blames me for the death of one who was important to him." He stared at the floor for a moment, before raising his eyes to his brother. "But she was more important to me. I loved her, Bolos, and lost her to darkness."

"In the Cuddon?" He had heard rumors.

Donzalo only nodded his head slowly. Bolos saw his hand go the curious brooch he had ever worn this past year. It is best I ask no more, he told himself.

The younger man sighed and straightened himself up. "But know also that the sorcerer and his king saw me as a threat to you. That is what started all this."

So it goes back to Donzalo being a danger again, thought the count. There seemed no getting away from that.

And there seemed to be no true answers

"I won't keep you confined to this room," said Bolos, "though Lord Radal thinks you should be in the tower rather than he. Go where you will in the keep, as long as the guards accompany you." Keeping in mind Donzalo's mysterious disappearance from his previous captivity — another puzzle — the count had made certain that this brother was ever within sight of two guardsmen, even in his own rooms. "Visit Lomela. She would enjoy seeing you."

Then he frowned at a sudden thought. "Everywhere but the tower, Donzalo. I do not think you should be in the same room as Radal."

"We have had our differences, Sir Jak."

"Forget it, Corgos," said Jak. "None of it was all that important."

"No, it wasn't," agreed the master of arms. "Not compared to what is happening now."

He poured out more red wine for the both of them. Cheap stuff, thought Jak. Probably the sort of drink Sir Corgos became used to during his days as a mercenary. Himself, he'd rather have a beer.

"What can we do?" he asked. "Or maybe the question is what *should* we do?"

"I wish I knew. I don't want to go against the count."

"We may have to." Jak leaned forward and spoke earnestly. "Count Bolos is not only my liege — he is my friend. I have a duty there too."

"Yes, Jak, I know of your friendship," Corgos replied with the trace of a smile. "I suppose that was the cause of some of the friction between us. How long have you been with the man?"

"Since he's been a man," responded the burly knight, taking a gulp of his wine. "Count Borrago made me his bodyguard better'n ten years ago." Jak put a hand to the top of his bald head. "I even had hair back then. Some, anyway," he laughed.

"You know the count better than anyone, eh? Then you're best suited to keeping an eye on him."

Jak nodded. "And you're the fellow for organization. I know I'm not good at running things."

"I suspect that our wives and the countess may actually be running things," said Sir Corgos, raising his glass. "And I salute them."

14

Indeed, I should not be in the same room with Radal, thought Donzalo, for only one of us would leave it alive. He would not hesitate to put a blade into the man, given the opportunity.

The Donzalo of only a year ago would not have considered such a thing.

"Must you come in with me?" he asked his two guards.

"Those are the orders," one replied. The other nodded in agreement.

"Well, at least stay on the other side of the room so we can have a private conversation."

The two looked at each other. Clearly their orders were not specific about how close they should remain to their charge. "Very well, sir," said one. "But if you go into another room, we'll follow."

What would happen if I went out on Lomela's balcony? he wondered.

Dame Traspa opened the door to him and his companions. The pair of soldiers took up a station just inside.

"How is married life, my dear?" asked Donzalo, as he embraced the maid.

"Tolerably good, young sir," she responded, "though I miss the attention I used to get from the kitchen staff."

"You should flirt a little with them and make Sir Jak jealous," he told her. Lomela was rising from a seat beneath the window to greet him and, beside her, the master of arms' wife. Donzalo realized that he barely knew the woman.

"My lady." He took Lomela's hand but did not embrace her. He remembered the consequences when last he held the princess in his arms. "Dame Tiana." He gave her a small bow.

"Come sit with us, Donzalo," said the Lady Lomela. "You, too, Traspa. You are our best informant."

"Yes," agreed Tiana, turning to the maid. "Tell him what you were just saying to us about Radal."

"My Jak has heard that man whispering to the count that Corgos is untrustworthy and was the one who released you," said Traspa, as she settled on a low stool by their divan.

Tiana gave him a quizzical look. "We still wonder how you managed that, sir."

"I am afraid you must continue to do so, Dame Tiana. Secrets cease to be secrets when too many know them."

Donzalo has learned to talk like a statesman, thought Lomela. Perhaps to think like one, as well.

"We have a note for you," she said, handing him a folded paper. "There is a way to get messages in and out."

He opened it and quickly read. "In Nafal's hand but no doubt written by committee," he said with a smile. "Nothing of actual importance in it." He casually handed it back. "Best burn it after I leave. If I did so now it might make my two friends watching at the door suspicious."

"They report to my husband," Tiana said, "and he's in on this."

Donzalo nodded. "If only I could make my brother see the dangers of harboring that sorcerer, we would need not plot."

"I fear you are not the one who has his ear," responded Lomela, "nor am I."

"There are bad times coming, my lady," opined the Dame Traspa, shivering involuntarily at the thought. "I'm sure of it."

Tiana took her hand. "We can only do our best to be ready for them, my friend."

And hope we can survive the crisis, Lomela thought. She feared that not all those she loved would.

"Enough of conspiracy," she said, as gaily as she could. "Donni, you must tell me all about your time at Sir Paren's keep. And how fared the Lady Fachalana?"

Dorbi seemed a good name. Short for Dorbidros, maybe? Well, probably not short for anything if it was given to a dog.

Anyway, I'll use it, decided Perdos. It's better than 'Dos.'

He surveyed the camp before him. Not much going on there. Maybe the count had done well to have these men where he could keep watch on them.

Beyond them, down the road, lay the cottage where Sir Paren's group stayed. The knight wondered if he could ride by these men without anyone recognizing him. Not that he had any reason to. Paren and that brother of Guesare — what was his name? — could take care of themselves. Nor would they welcome Perdos to their lodging.

Maybe if he hung around here long enough, the minstrel would ride up here to visit. But it seemed unlikely; more likely they would make council down at the Sharshite embassy. There was too much going on around here, anyway, to seek a duel with the Cuddonian right now.

Best he wait until this current crisis ended, one way or another, and continue to serve the ambassador. If that man opposed Radal and his followers, then Perdos felt he had chosen the correct side.

And he would not mind at all hanging about Mistress Rassana's shop while attending to his duty.

The boy was so close, yet still beyond his reach.

Using magic against him was out of the question, at least for now. He could not be certain of its success and any great magic now would surely end his life. There was too little left of Lord Radal.

Better that Bolos be responsible for the deed or, failing that, one of his own men. He needed to get them inside the castle walls, one way or another.

To that end, he might manage some minor magics. Gates could be opened, guardsmen could sleep. Radal had noted the seals placed on the portals when he had entered the keep — the work of Guesare, he assumed. They were well enough done but would not withstand his mastery.

First, he must have Dovolo smuggle his ebony cask in to him. With the object of power it held at hand, he could better prepare for such work. He needed a staff, as well. Any stick would do. There was no potency to the rod itself; it only acted as means to further focus his strength.

Radal smiled. Surely Count Bolos would provide an old man a staff on which he might lean. He must speak to him of it the next time they met. Yes, of that and of many things, for imposing his will on the mind of Bolos was his true work here.

It was work that was going well.

"Thank you, Doo." Pol turned toward his manservant so that the fellow could read his lips. He then dismissed him with a few signs that he had learned. Who would have known that the deaf had their own language?

The young Arolinian had immediately recognized the usefulness of sign language to one who engaged in espionage. When he became more skilled, he intended to instruct a few chosen men in it.

He set the cup Doo had brought him on his desk and went to poke at the fire. Nights were becoming more than cool now, though he was told that winter was never that bad in Celatas. Certainly nothing like his native province in the north.

His thoughts turned to the Princess Mara and her reactions to the occurrences of a few evenings ago. It was as if it had all seemed familiar to her in some fashion, as if she were reliving the events.

As if she were an actor in one of his plays, he thought, and smiled at the idea.

The voice of Murbalana was raised outside the door, scolding someone. Murbalana provided excellent material for his writing. Pol did hope that she remained with the imperturbable Doo. Maybe even marry the man.

Mara. He should cultivate her. Oh, the prince too, of course. Wouldn't his parents, the simple shopkeepers, have been astounded by the heady company their son now kept?

For a moment, his heart became a lump in his chest as he remembered them, dead now half a decade. Then, an idea for the play on which he was working popped into his mind.

Pol went to his desk, took up his pen and began writing.

Fachalana practiced her magic. Yes, it tired her but how else was she to learn? If only she had books!

It was the link that she worked on, mostly. That she knew how to do, more or less, but she needed more experience, needed to make all of it as natural to her as wielding a sword. Her mind poked into many worlds, but not too deeply. Lady Fachalana had quickly learned caution.

Fortunately, it was not needed to enter those dangerous places to form the link. There were little empty worlds suited for such purposes, where two sorcerers might meet and speak. She had so spoken to several now, some of them lost, mad souls who did not understand their gift and had wandered into other worlds unintentionally. Without her father's hand to guide her, might she have been so?

Had that been the fate of her grandmother?

There had been those who, as had once her father, tried to take control of her. She was too strong for that now, too knowledgeable. Indeed, she could have overwhelmed any of them had she so chosen.

Daughter of Radal, came a voice, seemingly very far away.

It was like the voices she had heard when she fought against her father's power, the voices that said they could no longer protect her.

Are you the Fay? she asked.

I am of the Fay, came the answer, stronger now that she opened herself to this link. *I am Arsel.* The voice hesitated. *You are so much like your sister. But you are different, as well.*

He knew Jola, she thought. Could he hear her say that in her mind? If so, the fay did not reveal it.

You are ones who gave me shelter, said Fachalana. *I can no longer find that place.*

It is closed to thee now. When your trials are done, you may come to us and, perhaps, find it again.

Trials?

You must face the struggle that is to come, your battle against the Darkness. We will try but I fear we can not help thee in this. The fay was silent for long moments. Had he left her? *Donzalo holds that which may strengthen thee. Verily, it may be your salvation.*

What is that? she asked.

You will know it when the time comes. The voice of Arsel seemed filled with concern. *You are wearied. Rest and prepare yourself.*

And he was gone.

"Sir Paren says there have been reports of riders on our borders."

"Sorsen and his bunch? We know about them," said the count, putting down his spoon.

"No, my lord, this was a report from his master of arms." Corgos felt it best not to refer to the man by name. "Troops moving in the Cuddon."

"Cuddonians?" Bolos found the idea doubtful. Once, of course, bandits had raided from those hills but there had been peace for decades.

"Or Ani. Or both. Remember the thanes of the Cuddon recognize the Anian emperor as their overlord."

More enemies. They seek to surround me, Bolos told himself. "Surely the Ani would not invade Lama." He did not feel so sure.

"More likely, my husband, they are worried about the situation here," spoke the Countess Lomela. "If Sharsh or An Corade were to get involved, the empire might react."

Sir Corgos nodded in agreement. Lady Lomela grasped these matters better than any other in the keep.

"Indeed," she continued, "they might prove to be allies."

"What, against your father?"

"My loyalty now lies with County Rosam, Bolos. We have a son," Lomela reminded him. "I would think it unlikely that Ani troops would come into Lama. That would not keep them from using Cuddonian surrogates."

"Your brother has friends in the Cuddon," pointed out Sir Corgos.

"Hmm, yes." Bolos was uncertain whether that was a good thing or a bad one. "My own men report more Sharshite soldiers slipping over the mountains and finding their way to our borders. And Count Dordos is surely poised to take advantage of any turmoil. There are disputed lands he would wish to claim." Or even those not disputed.

"Altogether too many strange men loiter about the town as well, my lord," reported Corgos.

"I must depend on my captain there," said the count. On whom should he depend here? Corgos? Jak?

He turned to the lunch he was sharing with these two, here in the tower room that was once his father's office, now that of Sir Corgos. One floor above him, there was another. Was Lord Radal someone in whom he might ever trust? He must speak with him again later.

And he would take the man the new walking stick he had promised him.

15

Mussago was completely willing to sit and wait. This did not agree with Sorsen's temperament; he became impatient.

"If I take a different horse, I could slip into Ros-town," he told his fellow commander.

"You're still recognizable," said Mussago. "Not just your looks but your manner."

Sorsen sighed. He knew it was true. The nobleman poured himself more hot cider. The wind was cold today.

"What has your father to say?" asked his companion. A message had arrived minutes earlier. "I hope he is not sending more troops, for then my father would feel it necessary to do the same. I'd rather they were getting the harvest in."

"None now, Master Mussago," answered Sorsen, "but he has them on alert. He says the Coradeans are mobilizing too, moving more men to the mainland and to Sharsh's southern border."

"They would rather use your Arvaram troops here than send their own into Lama."

"Aye. I would not expect an invasion. But I should think my father will be concerned now about having Coradeans on his own border and be less likely to send any more men north."

Mussago nodded. "As my own worries about all the Sharshite men across the Doram Pass."

"I think perhaps," replied Sorsen, "that your father the count would not greatly mind his lands being a part of Sharsh."

"It might well be good for business," agreed Mussago.

Lord Radal opened his iron-bound cask. Within lay the skull of his long-dead master, a mighty object of power.

With this and the small grimoire he carried always upon his person, he could prepare great magics. Oh, and the staff, of course. The sorcerer would have preferred the familiar, heavy ebon rod he had of necessity left behind in Mountain Keep, but this stick provided by Count Bolos would do. Hickory, wasn't it?

Dovolo had done well, concealing the vessel between his legs and slipping it out even while a soldier stood guard in his chamber. Who would have thought to look up the man's kilt, especially in that he had come to the tower before without incident? Too bad he couldn't bring in a sword that way. Radal might need seek one in some other world.

Soon. The new moon might lend assistance to his strength — darkness was an ally both on the physical and mystic planes. There was much to plan before then, seals to set, seals to break.

"Give me strength for this final task, Lord Asak," he whispered, "and then you may take me."

A group of men crowded around Sir Blen, Lord Doufan among them.

"If the cuts are of proper depth," he explained, "the bombe will fly apart evenly when it explodes, throwing shards of metal in all directions." The knight held up the grenade he had been preparing.

"This is a talent I did not know you possessed," remarked the ambassador. "I might have expected it of Sir Copago or even our friend Donzalo."

Blen looked up at the man and smiled. "In truth, sir, I saw the design in papers young Donzalo had in his quarters."

"Oh, there is our laundress. I must speak to her of my tunics." Aulla's cart had drawn up to the wide, arched ground-floor entry to the embassy. "You wished to have words with Dame Aulla too, didn't you Sir Blen?"

"Yes, my lord. Carry on here, men."

"Do you think these bombes will prove useful?" asked Doufan, as the two walked to where the laundress and her hired man unloaded bundles of clean, folded garments. Most of the cart was taken up by the unwashed laundry of Keep Rosam, their previous stop.

"Who is to say, sir? Any weapon is only as good as the man who wields it."

"I could not have stated it any better, Sir Blen. Hail to you, Dame Aulla."

"Good morn to you, my lord. I'll have all your wash loaded up and be away in a nonce." She leaned close to the ambassador and whispered, "Your messages are in with your tunics, my lord."

He nodded and replied in a low voice, "I've none to pass the other way on this day." More loudly he said, "You must come up to my office on the morrow and we shall speak of our account."

"Understood, sir," she countered, with the ghost of a wink, and turned to her loading of dirty linens.

Jobareth felt as if he were a child listening to grownups when Oder and Lord Doufan conversed.

He suspected that his friends felt the same. The young diplomat glanced at Habidros and Guesare. They barely seemed to be paying attention.

Ubos silently refilled their cups.

Nafal had ridden down to Ros-town with the ambassador only an hour earlier, Habidros accompanying them as their only bodyguard. Doufan would have no others, thinking it would bring too much notice.

Now they spoke of things beyond Jobareth's knowledge, of diplomats and generals and goings-on in distant courts.

Of a sudden, Oder posed a quite unexpected question to Lord Doufan. "Have you been dallying with Dame Aulla?" The brothers certainly showed interest at that. Jobareth was rather taken aback by the suggestion.

The Sharshite shrugged and smiled amiably. "I have taken my pleasure there, yes. And, yes, before you scold me, I know the dangers in so mixing my secrets.

"Perhaps you should know also — especially you, Sir Guesare — that I have secret dealings with another."

"Perdos?" asked Oder. "We have seen him watching from the little food stall down the street. Though lately his eyes have been more on his hostess there than on us."

"I felt it wise to tie him to our cause rather than have him wandering masterless. Who knows what mischief he might have gotten into, left to his own devices?"

Guesare nodded, but seemed none too convinced.

There was a clatter in the street — most unusual in this neighborhood, at this hour. Someone had been riding hard and now hurried up the stairs. The steward went to the door to admit Sir Blen.

The knight paused a moment to catch his breath, and reported. "Radal's men are in the keep!"

It had been swift and bloodless. Mostly. One fool from the garrison had managed to be in the wrong place and had his throat slit as a result.

Now, he and his troop had a tenuous control of the keep. Or, at least, they had the count and none would dare act against them. If only this Corgos would give the boy up to them or Count Bolos would order it, they could be done with this business.

Dovolo had most of his men here at the tower, save for a few guarding the gates. It didn't hurt to have someone on watch, even if their chief concern was with those already within the keep. If any approached, they could send up an alarm.

Someone was opening the door to the Great Hall. Hadn't they all been told to stay within? Oh, it was that dolt, Jak. Lord Radal had made him their messenger boy.

It was fortunate that he had been the only one with the count when he and the men had taken the tower. Or maybe it was not fortune at all, but his master's planning. Had they not been sitting with the wizard, ready for the taking?

Well, that was beyond him. All he knew was that gates had been un-barred, men had slept or been locked in their quarters, and it had been easy entry for him and the boys.

And that this place was ripe for plundering. Maybe when Lord Radal finished with his own affairs he would turn them loose.

"Wake, Sorsen!"

The knight rolled over. Mussago? He was instantly alert. "The time has come?"

"It has. Radal has seized Keep Rosam and holds Bolos hostage."

Sorsen had slept in his tunic since encamping here, so he might be on horseback all the more quickly. "Leave the tents and luggage," he ordered, as he emerged from his pavilion. "We ride at once!"

In minutes, they were racing north. Mussago handed the message to his companion, that he might read it in the saddle. Behind them, the courier sped southward on a fresh horse with his news, to alert both their sires.

Sorsen gave it a quick look. "We are the closest. Even so, our friends may choose to act before we can arrive." It was late morning now; they could not hope to reach Ros-town before dawn.

"It is good that we sent some men ahead of us," stated Mussago.

"There are Sharshite soldiers across the Weldar, too. Sir Blen may call them to him."

"And in a few days, Lareth himself will be informed. Who knows how he might act?"

"All the more reason for us to handle it ourselves, and quickly." They rode on for a time, the only sound that of their horses' hooves.

Then spoke Sorsen again. "It will take too long, I fear, for Copago to respond. He would have been a good man to have beside us."

"Aye," agreed Mussago, "if we be not too late ourselves."

16

Radal had found a deck of cards in the room and had used it to fill his hours while held captive. It lay now on the table, no longer of any use to him.

Bolos noted it. "Is it so that one can read the future in the cards? Tell me of mine."

Radal regarded the man across the table for a moment, before taking up the deck. "Am I to be your fortune-teller, my lord?" The idea briefly brought a smile to his gaunt face. "The cards can not see the future, nor can I. What they do is provide us symbols, structure for our thoughts." He shuffled and laid out three cards between them, one above the other two.

"This is sometimes known as the ziggurat," said the sorcerer. "The two cards at the bottom speak of the forces in action and those in opposition. That atop them is a possible resolution." He looked up from the spread. "Only possible."

"Ziggurat? What means the word?"

"Some so name their temple mounds. The Kamatians of the south where they speak the Baxac languages." Radal returned to the cards. "We may not see the future but those with the proper gifts might glimpse into the timeless void where all things be. So works prophecy."

His long fingers touched the first card in the bottom row. "The Knight of Chalices. That might be your brother. And this," he said, pointing to that beside it, "the Ten of Blades." Radal considered the card for a brief while. "A card of disruption, perhaps, of plans gone awry."

No, he told himself, the Knight may not be Donzalo at all, but my long-time opponent, Guesare. I am this other, the old man, the troubled mind.

"Here at the top, the Ace of Torches." All too obviously my daughter, he thought, full of fire and promise. A promise of her survival? "A sign of success and new beginnings," he half-lied.

"Yours or mine?" asked the count, with enough sarcasm to surprise the sorcerer. He didn't know Bolos had it in him.

But he had already proven more difficult to manipulate than Lord Radal had expected.

There came a knock at the door. "Enter," called the Sharshite. Count Bolos turned in his chair to see who it was and then rose to embrace his sergeant and friend Maybe, thought Radal, I can turn the servant if the master remains difficult.

"Ah, the faithful Sir Jak," he said, with all the easy grace of a courtier. "Do sit and join us in our lunch."

"We must continue to work in secret," asserted Oder. "The Rosam captain here in town would not permit us to act nor would he willingly accept orders from a Sharshite. Nor," he continued, with a wry smile, "an Anian."

Sir Blen agreed, though he harbored many doubts about this spy who had joined their group. "He will do nothing for fear of harm coming to the count. And he is on alert for any activity. My lord" said he to Lord Doufan, "I have passed the word for our men to assemble here at the embassy."

"Tonight?" asked the ambassador.

"Tonight would be best. Donzalo's life is in danger every minute we wait, as are those of all in Castle Rosam." He turned to Jobareth Nafal. "We depend on you, sir. Only you know this secret way in."

Jobareth glanced at Oder. Did the mysterious Anian know of it? "Sir Copago holds this knowledge as well," he informed them. "If I meet mishap, turn to him."

"I fear he may arrive too late for it to matter," spoke Sir Paren. "It is a long way to my manor and a long ride back. Moreover, he may need tend to affairs there, if some of the rumors have it aright."

"Your master of arms need fear no threat from the east," Oder assured him. "Of this I am certain."

Having been told all his life to never trust the Ani, Paren was not at all assured.

"There can be no more messages to nor from the keep, so we may only guess at how things stand there. But," said Lord Doufan, "we must act. We must also ask, what of you, my ladies?" Doufan addressed the two young women who had remained silent throughout this council in his crowded office.

"I shall go where Lady Fachalana goes," Ansa firmly stated, "and nowhere else."

Fachalana voice came low, barely to be heard, yet still filled with determination. "And I must face my father."

"We will not turn you over, sir, no matter what."

"What if my husband orders it?" asked Countess Lomela. It was a question that need be answered.

Sir Corgos was reluctant to provide that answer. "I think, my lady, that if the count so does, then he is no longer competent."

One of the master of arms' lieutenants, standing at his elbow, nodded agreement. "He would have to be under that sorcerer's spell to order such a thing."

"Do it anyway," spoke Donzalo. "Radal's quarrel is with me."

"Oh, no, Master Donzalo. We could never give you to that evil man!" objected Traspa.

The young knight smiled at Lomela's faithful maid. "And I hope you need not. But be prepared if it comes to it. Ah, Sir Jak. How fares my brother?"

The beefy sergeant stood in the doorway, just returned from his visit to the tower.

"The same, Sir Donzalo." He shot an unfriendly look toward Corgos. Jak had most certainly heard their conversation. "Still unwilling to deal with the sorcerer."

"So we remain at stalemate." Donzalo thought of the secret passage he had once used to escape Castle Rosam. Why not take it again? They were all free to move about indoors so he could simply go down a flight of stairs, enter a room, and disappear.

No, he could not abandon those who were here, his brother, the Lady Lomela. But perhaps he should persuade Corgos to take the countess out that way.

"We still have our swords," he said, putting a hand to his own, "so things are not hopeless."

"Most of those in the keep are not fighting men but servants and family," Paren said. "It is little wonder that Corgos has not attempted to fight."

"Yet we shall. Are we being rash?" asked Ansa.

"We have no choice."

"Aye, there will come no better time," spoke Sir Blen. "All is readied. My men are gathering in twos and threes, prepared to come together at the gate when it is opened. Over a score and all soldiers of Sharsh whose foremost thought will be to rescue the princess." He looked to the others. "You understand that must be the goal of Lord Doufan and myself."

"And Doufan hides himself in the embassy, committing none of its men to our attack," complained the young woman.

"He can not afford to seem involved if things go awry. 'Tis bad enough that Nafal and I are."

Ansa shrugged and looked to her silent companion. Fachalana was rapt in her own thoughts and was adding nothing to their council. "Where has gone my brother?" she asked.

"Out scouting again," answered Sir Paren. "Sir Oder is certainly one who likes to leave little to chance." Paren suspected that he had been the last to have learned who the Anian was. Or who the woman with whom he spoke was, for that matter.

"Indeed so," agreed Ansa. Who knew where she and her companions fit into her brother's well-laid schemes?

Beside her, Lady Fachalana thought on the words of the Fay, Arsel, and his promise of something that would aid her in the struggle to come, something held by Donzalo. She would know it when the time came, had he promised. What was 'it?' Would it truly help her against all the power of her father? Could she face him at all?

She looked up at the others gathered here in this little cottage and asked, "How much longer must we wait?"

Jobareth Nafal led the way along the narrow ledge. It was, of necessity, a slow progress on this moonless night.

Behind him trailed some dozen men, most followers of Sorsen and Mussago who had secretly made their way north in recent days. These looked to the Cuddonian, Habidros, as their leader.

And the brother of Habidros, the minstrel Guesare, made up the last of their party.

Here was the entrance to the cave. "We can chance a lantern, now," said Nafal. Soon, the entire group was inside and began their ascent of the passage below Keep Rosam.

The panel. Where was the catch? Ah, there. He slowly slid it open and stepped through.

There was already a light within the room, and a man — a tall man. "So much for keeping this a secret," said Donzalo Rosam.

17

"There are two men on the wall," whispered Oder. "Whether more stand on the other side of the gate, who can know?"

"I hope to soon find out." Blen felt that any defenders would easily be overwhelmed by his well-trained soldiers, if not slain first by the band of infiltrators. There was, however, another consideration. "Might there be magic barring our way?" He had heard tales of such lately.

"Lady Fachalana sensed none. She feels that Radal would consider an attack here unlikely and not waste his strength by setting a seal." The Anian gazed toward the great oaken gates. "The lady dare not attempt any magic herself, for her father would surely recognize her presence."

"I trust that she will remain safely outside the walls with Sir Paren."

"I would not trust too much."

Behind them their men gathered, ready to rush forward when the gates were opened. A tall fighting man slipped in among them, his face hidden by his basinet, one shoulder rising slightly higher than the other.

"We heard that guards ever accompanied you," said Guesare.

"Corgos felt them no longer necessary. Not since Radal seized my brother. I was considering letting him in on this secret way, so he might smuggle out Lomela and the boy. But 'twould be a dangerous undertaking." He looked at the group of fighting men gathered in his former quarters. "Perhaps now, though, it could be a good idea."

"Let us go to her, you and I," said Jobareth, "and to Corgos, as well. These fellows here," he went on, with a nod toward his companions, "intend to open the gates to a larger force."

"Let's go," said Habidros to his men. "Are you with us, Guessy?"

"I would not miss it," said the minstrel. "Good luck to you, my friends."

"Need we avoid guardsmen?" asked Jobareth, once the party of soldiers had slipped out. "Radal's, I mean."

"None of them enter the living quarters. The sorcerer has chosen to keep most close to the tower. Come."

They ascended a stairway. "I suspect that everyone is still together in Lady Lomela's suite," said the young knight. "They were when I left them an hour past."

The door stood open. In a pair of chairs, Sir Jak and the master of arms conversed quietly. The Countess Lomela stood on her balcony, gazing toward the tower where Bolos was prisoner. "It seems the ladies have gone to their beds," remarked Donzalo as they entered.

"Jobareth! How came you here?"

Nafal glaced toward his young companion. "There is a secret way into the castle, my lady," said Donzalo, "which I once showed to our friend Nafal. We think perhaps you and your son should take it now."

"I will not desert my husband. But Sir Jak," she said, turning to the sergeant, "if things here go wrong, I must depend on you to carry Ros to safety. Do this for your count."

"I will, my lady," promised the soldier.

"Follow me," said Donzalo. "I shall show you the way you must take." And then, he thought, I must take a way of my own. "I shall depend on the legate and Sir Corgos to watch over you," he said to the countess and, bowing, departed.

Castles are intended to keep men out, not in. Their walls may not be easy to ascend but, if one thinks to bring a suitable length of rope, not difficult to go down.

So down the innermost wall of Keep Rosam went Guesare and the others, and then the second, as well, bypassing the gates and their guardians. Only one other sentry did they spy on the walls and slipped by him easily in the darkness, making their way to the outer fortifications. There, they crept along its lower stone walls, set atop an earthen berm, to the heavy oaken door. Two of Lord Radal's ruffians yawned atop the rampart.

They would open this gate to their compatriots outside. Yes, they could have brought ropes here as well and avoided the gates altogether, but it would have taken longer to bring them all up on a rope or two, and much increased the chance of discovery.

Moreover, if Sorsen and his troop showed up in time, the way would be open to them.

One man went down easily, throat slit without ever seeing his attacker. The other managed to let out a cry of terror before he joined him. Had anyone heard?

It seemed not. The bar was lifted, the gate swung open on its iron hinges.

"Come on in," invited Sir Habidros, beckoning to the waiting men at arms.

Now they needed to breach the other two entries.

Dovolo entered. "My lord," said he, "there is aught you should see." He nodded toward the narrow window.

Radal peered into the courtyard below. It was very dark but a pair of torches at the tower entrance allowed him to make out a tall figure, a man standing before the door to Castle Rosam's Great Hall. "Donzalo," he whispered. "At last."

Across that courtyard, Lomela and Jobareth Nafal stood on the lady's balcony. As the young knight stepped forward from the shadows, they spied him as well. "Captain Corgos," called Jobareth. "Donzalo is in the open! We must defend him."

The two men hurried down toward the courtyard, Corgos beckoning to a pair of guardsmen to join them as he went. "You should remain with the countess," he said to Jobareth as they reached the doors. "Watch over her and leave this to me and my men."

Nafal reluctantly agreed and turned about, as the three soldiers stepped out into the moonless night.

Lord Radal's attention must be on me, thought Donzalo, and only me. Not the men even now moving toward him in the darkness.

Above him, Radal saw Corgos and his men. "I must seal the doors over there so none others can interfere. It is but a minor magic." But an inconvenience, thought the sorcerer, as he sent his essence through roundabout ways to a place where he could touch each lock, bind it invisibly.

When satisfied with his craft, he turned to his sergeant and spoke. "The seals I have placed will hold for only a short time. We must finish our work before the garrison can break free.

"Go down and take them. But slay not the Rosam boy; he is mine."

There had not even been a guard posted at the second gate. Perhaps Radal had felt the heavy iron portcullis was impassable on its own. Even as it was being opened to Blen and his men, others had reentered the keep by the rope they had left dangling.

Before them in the courtyard, they saw conflict. Four men stood against a crowd of Radal's riff-raff.

"You get the remaining gate," said Guesare to his brother, "and I will aid yon fighters. You come with me," he told one of those who had scaled the wall behind them. The rest followed Habidros along the battlements.

Outnumbered greatly, Donzalo and his comrades were yet a match for their attackers. The first onslaught had left one lying dead before them, and the others had retreated to form a half-ring about the four. Backs quite literally to the wall, swords turned out, they waited.

"So much for sneaking in quietly and rescuing Bolos," sighed Guesare. He and his follower crashed into the rear of the pack without warning. Corgos rushed forward, sword swinging, the others but a step behind him. Radal's men were scattered.

But they were many against few. Ranks were reformed before the tower door. That door opened, to frame Dovolo holding a long dudgeon to the count's throat.

"Surrender," he hissed, "or I'll cut him ear to ear."

Donzalo and Sir Corgos immediately dropped their sword points to the cobbled pavement. The two guards followed their example. Guesare and his companion were not quite so willing to acquiesce.

And from the corner of his eye he could see the rest of his allies coming through the inner gate. It had not been well defended, if at all. Perhaps all this turmoil had drawn its guards away.

Of a sudden, Bolos broke free, in part, and struggled with the man who held him. The dagger flashed and Count Bolos, son of Count Borrago, fell slain in his ancestral home, slain in defense of his brother.

18

Radal slowly climbed to the top of the tower, ready to raise great magics.

Below him, battle raged. What was that he felt? Magic? It must be Guesare trying to lift the seals he had set. Not strong enough.

His staff and his cask were at hand. He must call on those he had never dared before, in this one last act of sorcery, the one that would end his life.

It was not the outcome he would have chosen but one he had ever known might come. And come was the time to raise a wall about himself and the one whom he intended to destroy, the one he hated, to cast him into the deepest of hells.

None could stop it now.

Now was battle fully joined.

Though numbers were near equal, the advantage was all to the better trained soldiers who attacked Radal's men. Still, the rabble might be difficult to root out of the defensive position they had taken among pens and outbuildings that lay between tower and castle wall. Moreover, their number included a handful of musketeers. Blen would not have his men charge those gunnes.

This is a good time to try out my bombes, thought the knight. Alas, though he threw the grenade as hard as he might, its glowing fuse a streak of orange through the night, it fell well short of the enemy.

"Would that I had a gunne right now," said Blen, "or even a catapult."

"I can give you the latter," said Donzalo, standing nearby. "Have you a lance or even a long stick?"

One of the men found an appropriate length of wood amid the rubble. Donzalo recognized it as a prop for an awning. "Excellent," said he, as he cut a notch a short distance from one end. "Now some leather and lacings." Quickly, he assembled what was unmistakably an oversize sling, which he laced to the end of the pole.

"Place your bombe in the pouch and light the fuse," he ordered, than swung the pole back and snapped it forward with all the force of his tall frame, launching the grenade.

It sailed far and landed amid their opponents. "It is a staff sling," Donzalo told them. "I played with them as a boy."

Habidros looked approvingly upon the results. "On the next one, we will charge."

And they did. It was all sword to sword now. Guesare found himself fighting beside a tall man, a man who seemed familiar.

He dryly commented, "Someday, we must stop helping each other fight our enemies and have our own duel."

Perdos laughed despite himself. Then he saw Dovolo bolt from the fray, hoping to escape a fight his men could not win. "He is mine!" cried he, and pursued the man, sword in hand.

The mercenary leader had clambered up a stairway to the top of the castle wall and now raced along the battlements toward the gate. If he could get beyond it, he might have a chance of disappearing into the night.

But there was no chance of eluding the man who chased him. Dovolo turned to fight, drawing his long sword from the scabbard he wore across his back, and waited.

"Whom do I face?" he asked of the close-helmed man approaching him, heavy blade in hand.

"I am Perdos. I am he who slew Sojel, as I shall slay you."

Dovolo laughed. "I should thank you for Sojel." He launched himself forward with a great overhand cut. Though a shorter man than Perdos, there was strength driving that lengthy blade. Perdos did not remember ever seeing a sword quite so long. Why, one could use it as a lance, he thought, as he parried the blow.

Within a few passes, he realized that the sergeant was an exceptional swordsman. How had the man ended up where he was?

Dovolo chuckled as he deflected a blow from Perdos and nearly brought his own blade through. "You will not beat me, Sir Perdos. Turn away from this fight and I shall as well. I seek only to go."

Allow this murderer of Count Bolos, one of the few man who had always treated him well, to escape? This filth who had ridden with Sojel and taken part in his crimes?

That long blade handicapped the man in close and, especially, down low. Perdos swept his own sword low, hoping the others would follow it. When he did, the knight lunged forward, smashing his shoulder into him, knocking him off balance, before he could bring the long sword up.

Damn! That's my bad shoulder, he thought, but it was worth it. An upward thrust, his blade into Dovolo's unarmored throat, and it was over.

It looked as though the fighting behind him was over too. Should he stay? There would be no duel with Guesare this night and he had done all he could.

As his erstwhile opponent had intended, he slipped out of the castle gate and into the night.

Ansa knew her strengths, and fighting battles was not one of them. She had accompanied Lady Fachalana as far as the inner gate — much against the wishes of Sir Paren — but urged her to go no further.

"The fighting is over," said Fachalana. "Come on."

Ansa followed reluctantly into the courtyard.

The minstrel Guesare approached them, blade in hand.

"Where is the castle garrison?" Fachalana asked. "I see only our men."

Guesare smiled inwardly at the 'our.' "Lord Radal's magic has sealed them all within their quarters."

"You can not force them? I heard you had skill in such things."

"These are physical seals," said Guesare. "The ones I placed here before were only to block others' use of magic. This sort requires far more power and are beyond my ability to break." He shrugged. "But it matters little, now, my lady. Your father's troop is defeated and the soldiers of the garrison are unneeded. It is the door to this tower that I must try to open."

Fachalana looked at the door before them and laughed. She could see where the minstrel had clumsily tried to undo the spell.

The lady had practice in unlocking what her father had locked. Had she not often, quite unknowingly, swept aside his seals so she might read his correspondence and books?

What were the proper words? No, not those ones, they were for shattering the door itself. Oh, why didn't she just reach in and — there, it was undone.

She smiled with satisfaction and pushed the door open.

And high above them, Lord Radal noted his daughter's success.

"Is it all over?" wondered Lomela.

"Only when Radal is in bonds, my lady," replied Sir Jak. "Best stay off your balcony until then."

The knight stared listlessly from the window. His master's body had been removed, at last. While the fight raged, none could reach it and he had stood here and kept watch over it.

He sighed. Jak blamed no one for what had happened and it was good that the count had gone down fighting, at the last a hero. If only he could have been at his side.

He could tell young Ros that his father was a brave man, when the boy got older.

Sir Jak looked toward the new widow. The Lady Lomela had done well by her husband, hadn't she? All things considered. If she did not grieve over-long, he would understand.

Traspa came to stand beside him. Jak put his arm about his wife and he wept.

Guesare bounded up the stairway that wound around the interior of the tower. Radal would surely not give up. He must stop him before he raised magics.

Had this night been success or failure? Yes, Lomela and the boy were safe, and that had been the first concern, but had the death of Bolos been too great a price? Others would have to sort that out.

And there still was very much a danger to Donzalo. The trap door that led to the top floor lay open. The minstrel remembered a council held up here once, a council where Bolos had suggested having nothing more to do with Sharsh. Maybe he had been right.

There stood the sorcerer, staff in one hand, sword in the other.

Guesare held his own blade before him. "Surrender, sir! It is over."

There came a mocking laugh. "It will be over when Donzalo Rosam lies dead." Radal raised his arms and a green light played about him. "Would you hope to best me in sorcery, minstrel?"

"Not if I can use my sword." *I could never match his magic,* he told himself, and strove to move forward. He was unable.

Well, thought Guesare, *it seems I can* not *use my sword, so I must need turn to magic. Might Fachalana be able to help me?* The minstrel had never had the gift of the link but attempted to reach out to her.

Standing in the yard below, she felt that touch. Should she turn her power against her own father? Could she help the Cuddonian at all? Fachalana still knew so little!

She did know that she would never be able to establish any sort of link with Guesare. His mind was not made for it. But she might seek to strengthen him, as he employed whatever enchantments he could.

All eyes in that courtyard were lifted to the contest above them, the two men facing each other atop the tower, harsh greenish light rising above the one, the other surrounded by a soft nebulous golden glow.

Guesare spoke a spell. Being a minstrel, words were his strength and the basis for any magic he might attempt.

Mother Rema, darkness confound!
Let Lord Radal now be bound!

Radal felt the invisible bonds placed upon him and shook them away. The fetters had been surprisingly strong. The words he then spoke were of no earthly language, nor can we report them without endangering the reader's soul.

The sorcerer did not bother with any elegance. It was power he unleashed upon Guesare, pure force. The minstrel staggered beneath its blow and attempted to retaliate. He felt another — Fachalana, he assumed — trying to lend him strength.

Lord Radal faltered only a moment before renewing his onslaught. It was hopeless to stand against him. Only steel would stop the man.

Guesare realized that the two had slowly been moving toward each other, step by step. Holding his sword before him, he tried only to withstand the wizard's onslaught long enough to reach him.

Then steel met steel. Radal was no mean swordsman; once, perhaps, he had even been Guesare's equal. He was old now, and worn.

But Guesare, too, was weakened, and the sorcerer continued to attack with both blade and magic. He was moving too slowly, the minstrel knew, missing his chances to get through Lord Radal's guard.

Back and forth across the rough timber floor they battled, the stars of a moonless night blazing above them. Surely others were climbing the stairs by now, thought Guesare, coming to his aid.

His fight, though, had been brief, far briefer than he realized. Men stood only at the bottom of the stairway now, beginning their ascent. Again, Guesare missed with a lunge, awkwardly staggering as the spells of Radal hampered him.

A sword slipped into his side, where his breastplate did not cover, and Sir Guesare slumped, gasping. A second blow ended him.

Far away, Lady Se of Drolwym knew she had lost another child.

Fachalana fell to her knees beneath the blow of Guesare's death. How much worse might it have been had they truly linked, both minds in the same space as once she had with her father? She did not think she could survive it.

Ansa knelt, placing her arm about her friend's shoulders. This was not over, she knew. Fachalana would face more, would need all her strength, before ended this night.

And beside them, Oder stood, his face betraying neither his anger nor his grief. Coolly, the Anian nocked an arrow and pulled back his bow.

19

Radal turned his face to the sky, arms outstretched, and called upon his god.

"Asak! I give myself to thee!"

A great dark form rose behind him, above him, from him. Like a web-winged dragon it was, but also some great horned demon-being.

An arrow, flying toward the sorcerer, fell harmlessly upon striking the walls of sickly-green light that surrounded him.

Oder swore, swore by the Great Sky itself. "It is as the shape of Asak, as I have seen him on the altars of his devotees!"

"How can we stand against him?" asked his sister, her voice barely audible.

He looked toward Lady Fachalana. "We must depend on his daughter. Only she can now save Donzalo."

And the walls of sorcery edged outward, threatening soon to enclose all of them within an enchanted circle.

Donzalo looked upward at that shape and remembered another night of the new moon and another battle. He stepped forward, ready to fight again.

Should she oppose her father? wondered Fachalana. Might she not join him, stand tall and powerful by his side?

No, came his voice, *you must not. I will not have you damned.*

Then must I fight you? She could not let him harm Donzalo, the man whose destiny she felt was entwined with her own.

But no, she did not love Donzalo, did she? No matter. She would protect him.

Do not stand between me and the Rosam. I do this for you.

He believes that, thought the noblewoman. He is lost to his hatred.

Again she attempted to speak to him, but now she touched only a vast void, icy and alien. Instinctively, Fachalana recoiled from that darkness. It was Asak, she knew, and no longer her father.

She saw the young Laman knight, who now stood closer to tower and wizard-wall than the others, turn to stare at her. Was he thinking of her sister?

"I shall protect you as I can, Sir Donzalo," she promised, even as the walls of sorcerous light engulfed him.

Habidros gasped and attempted to reach his friend. He could not pass, nor could any others who now stood outside that circle. "Blen led men into the tower," said he. "Only they might reach Radal now!"

Fachalana slowly shook her head. "No, they also are barred. Donzalo stands alone." She stretched out a hand toward the barrier, at once like a fire and a mist. It parted before her and she entered.

There was trouble up at the keep. Fighting, maybe. Captain Nidanem considered the report for only a moment before making his decision. Yes, his orders were to keep the town safe but he could not stand by if his count needed him.

"One company with me," he told his lieutenant. "You keep the other here on alert." Would that he had a cavalry squadron rather than men at arms. It would take an hour or more to march them to Castle Rosam. *It's all uphill*, he reminded himself. *Push them too hard and they'll be useless for fighting.*

As they set forth from their barracks near the ferry-crossing, Nidanem looked toward the keep, set high on its cliffs, and wondered about the greenish light playing above it.

Donzalo turned to see the sorcerer's daughter standing at his side. It seemed that great feathered golden wings spread above her, as had once a silver wolf stood over his beloved Jola. He thought of his brooch and his hand went to it.

You will know it when the time comes, had said Arsel. Fachalana recognized the power in the piece of jewelry, the trinket she had seen so often on Donzalo's shoulder, and knew it was that of which Arsel spoke. "Lend me the strength of my sister," she said.

The young knight pinned it to the jack-coat she wore. Did he see a wolf, shadowy, dim, along with the eagle that had taken form?

This is of my sanctuary, Fachalana realized, and she found herself able to draw on the power of that world of silvered horizons, of calm and of peace.

The Shadow-Asak loomed above them, a great black sword in its hand, greenish light flickering along its edges. Donzalo stood with his own blade ready.

Could eagle face dragon? Or, below them, could daughter withstand father — or that which was once her father? Both struggles were one, manifestations of their conflict.

How could he help? The physical Radal was high atop the tower, beyond his reach. Both avatars seemed without substance. That would change, Donzalo knew, and then would that dragon be of danger to him.

And then could he fight it, but he had doubts this ordinary sword he held would harm his enemy. At that moment he wished he held once more the Moon Sword.

That did not keep him from hacking upward at the misshapen, misty creature. It laughed at his attempt.

At least I might distract it, thought Donzalo.

Do not fight me, came a voice, a voice deeper, more melancholy, than Fachalana could ever have thought possible. So filled with despair!

Filled with emptiness, as Brother Grippo had once described Asak to their friend Jobareth.

Join with me! it demanded. *I shall make you mighty, a queen such as the world has never seen.*

No, said another, and she knew it to be what remained of her father. *Do not follow my path.*

Above her, eagle tore at dragon with beak and talon. Would that terrible sword strike her down?

Her strength was not enough.

Seek, said a liquid golden voice. *Seek that which the one beside you once held.*

Fachalana knew without asking that it was her sister, the Jola she had never known, and, yes, the goddess Diba who spoke. And she remembered the sword Donzalo had wielded against her father. She put her hand to the silver wolf above her heart and sought.

Across the silver plain her essence rushed, to the gleaming white temple. Its tall doors opened to her and she beheld the Sword of the Moon, the Prince's Sword.

It was not the sword Donzalo once held in this world, she knew, but a part of it that extended in some manner into that other, even as did sorcerers reach into different worlds. She stepped forward and took its hilt. Such power!

And in this world, the world where she faced what had been her father, she placed her hand upon Donzalo Rosam's sword arm, letting that power flow into him. A silver light played about his blade.

Did Lord Radal, what remained of him, also recognize that power? Did he feel the presence of the daughter he had lost, lending strength to the one that struggled?

Fachalana had let herself be distracted from the fight in this world while searching the other. The eagle was thrown down; she herself staggered before Asak's attack. Donzalo drove his weapon into the form of the ever more corporeal demon.

A hiss of anger and the great black sword swung, barely missing the knight as he threw himself back to avoid its sweep.

He could not long escape that blade. And Fachalana was reeling, barely holding on, but the eagle rose again to the attack on wings of golden fire.

Had Donzalo truly wounded their enemy? Around them, the wizard wall flickered and sparked, silver and green contending, shifting, beneath the dark sky.

"It is weakened! Perhaps now may our missiles penetrate the barrier," spoke Oder.

Habidros raised his brother's rifle to his shoulder and took aim. Did his bullet strike the sorcerer? He was not sure but it seemed that the figure flinched.

An arrow flew from Oder's recurved bow. Another followed, as the Cuddonian hurried to reload.

He looked up. "I'm sure he is hit," he said, as he spanned the clockwork firing mechanism of his weapon. Habidros primed the rifle and raised it to fire again.

Then he lowered it. The shadow demon above Radal had grown vast, hiding the stars. Its voice came as the inchoate howling of mountain winds, while its clawed hands tore at the great eagle that struggled in its grip.

There stood the sorcerer yet. Habidros took aim and fired, even as Oder released another shaft.

As a madman, Donzalo hewed at the creature that loomed above him, supporting the exhausted Lady Fachalana with his other arm. Weary though she was, she fought on. Both fought on.

Let my arrow fly true, prayed Oder, once more drawing his bow. Beside him, his sister Ansa said her own prayers for the two trapped behind the sorcerous wall, the two for whom she cared above all others.

Above them yet stood the sorcerer, Lord Radal, his staff in one hand, the other reaching toward the skies. A flame seemed to surround him, a green fire that burned coldly.

He faltered. All around, the wall of light was collapsing in a chaos of silver and green, of flame and darkness and tumult. The ground trembled.

Then Radal was falling, falling in fire, falling to his final ruin. Was he stricken or had he, at the last, chosen to leap?

And Fachalana was falling even as did her father.

Of Destiny: the Last Tale

1

Hooves thundered as a company of men rode to the outer gates of Castle Rosam. A hint of peach-colored light above the hills spoke of the coming dawn.

A troop in the Rosam colors stood guard at those gates. Their leader held up a hand. "Sir Sorsen! I was told you might show up, my lord."

Sorsen spoke to the man from horseback. "Captain Nidanem, isn't it? How fares it here?"

"It is all over, sir. I was told to let you and your men in." The officer turned toward the keep's entrance. "Open for them, lads," he called to the guards. Turning back, he said, "Best I let Captain Corgos give you all the news."

Sorsen and Mussago passed through the other two gates, their men behind them, and into the courtyard. There seemed to be a cleanup in progress, after whatever action the night had seen. They noted the bodies laid out on one side of the area.

Corgos stood speaking to Sir Paren as they oversaw the work. "Ho!" called Paren, upon spying them. "Too late for the fighting, sirs, but you might help us tidy up."

"What of Lord Radal?" asked Sorsen, dismounting.

"Dead, sir," spoke Sir Corgos. "As, alas, is the count."

"As well as Sir Guesare," added Paren.

"Ah, Guesare. He was a good man." *I may have to give the news to his brother Galaro next spring,* thought Orgelo's son.

"May Kamat grant them rest," said Mussago. Then, ever practical, he inquired, "Who governs County Rosam?"

Paren considered that question for a moment. "I suppose Countess Lomela and myself will have to act for little Ros. Perhaps Donzalo too, if he is willing. And," he went on, looking to the pair of southerners, "if there is no objection from the other counties."

"My father would agree with this, I am certain," responded Sorsen. "That is probably the only voice that matters." He glanced sideways at his companion. Mussago did not rise to the bait.

"But now you must tell us all of what happened here."

"Jobareth Nafal could do that. He is within with the Lady Lomela. But," asked Sir Paren, "could you first lend us some of your men to help out here? There are many dead to give to the fire."

That which had been Lord Radal, a twisted, charred remnant, had been wrapped in cloth of cotton. "I will see that he is returned to Sharsh, " Jobareth Nafal told the sorcerer's daughter. She gave no sign of having heard him.

She is damaged, thought Jobareth, and I know not whether it can be undone. Fachalana sat enrapt, barely acknowledging those about her.

Sir Blen, when able, stayed by her side. Ansa rarely left it.

Pinned to her gown was Donzalo's wolf brooch. "It should remain with her," said he. "It may lend her strength." He, of all those who cared for the lady, most knew that she needed it, that it might be the an-chor to keep her from drifting from them forever.

Donzalo also knew where she must go to find a cure, for she had whispered to him after their fight, and spoken no words since to any other.

"I must dream."

"I think, Countess Lomela, that I may soon be withdrawn as ambas-sador." Doufan nodded somewhat in the direction of Jobareth. "The legate here should do well enough without me."

Lomela also looked toward her lifelong friend. "Are you going to tell him, Jobareth?

"Sir," the young diplomat began, with a tone that held a certain defensiveness. "I intend to resign from the diplomatic corps and serve the countess."

"Ah! I fear our Blen will not appreciate once again being left in charge," chuckled Lord Doufan. "I shall not attempt to dissuade you from this. In truth, boy, I think it is an excellent decision. But don't tell your grandfather I so said!"

Jobareth appeared relieved. The boy values my approval, thought the ambassador. It will be good to have such a friend in Castle Rosam. He considered the young Lady Lomela for a moment. And perhaps in the countess' bed, he mentally added.

"Blen and I must travel before we do aught else," Jobareth stated. "We accompany Sir Donzalo."

"And the Anian, carrying Sir Gusare's remains to the Cuddon." Doufan nodded slowly. "You must both go?"

"It is not only Guesare we take but also Lady Fachalana," replied Jobareth. "Donzalo is certain it is the only remedy for her wounds."

Lord Doufan digested this information briefly. "We must do what we can for the lady. An unimaginable debt is owed her.

"I do not expect to leave immediately, Nafal. Indeed, I may well remain a season or three. Take your time."

But he had done what could be done in Lama and, sooner or later, he would leave. There was little left to accomplish here.

And Aulla's husband — a rather dangerous looking ruffian, thought Doufan — did not much approve of him swiving his wife.

"There is an empty keep I know in the Cuddon," spoke Donzalo, with a wink to Oder. "It might just be the place to take up residence one of these days."

The lad seemed little the worse for the fight he had just been in, bruised some in body, but undamaged in spirit. He mourned Guesare, of course, as did the Anian.

"First, though," he said, "we must take home our friend. And the Lady Fachalana, too, I believe should travel with us."

"When?" Oder saw little point in lingering longer in County Rosam. Though he did have his sister to consider — she might keep him longer.

"My brother's funeral is on the morrow. Then, perhaps." Another the boy would mourn, a brother who had followed their father into death.

Guesare's coffin awaited its journey to Drolwym, containing a body charred beyond any recognition. In those final minutes of Lord Radal's existence, all atop the tower had burned. There was a sizable hole through the floor up there. Paren would eventually see to its repair, assumed Donzalo. He had no great desire to take up such responsibilities here.

But he could see himself putting Sabatare's old keep to right. It was a good spot, and not that far from here. Yes, he could see himself there and he could see one standing beside him.

That was the sort of destiny of which he approved.

"Take care of my brother," said Habidros. "Someday, perhaps, I too shall ride back to Drolwym."

"Not if my cousin has aught to say about it," remarked Sorsen.

"Lenasha would like the Cuddon," Habidros responded, "and they appreciate such women there. She must meet my family eventually!"

"I could not see Thane Vantare ever traveling to County Arvaram," laughed Donzalo, "so I suppose it would be necessary to take your bride to him.

"Take care, my friend. And take care of that rifle." Guesare's gunne now hung in its richly worked scabbard from his brother's saddle. "It has done good work for us."

Habidros agreed. "I still insist that it was my bullet that ended Radal, and not the Anian's arrow!"

Donzalo was not convinced that it was either but, rather, the dark sorcerer's choice at the end not to allow his daughter's destruction. But who could ever say? He spoke not of it, nor ever again of that night.

"Then we bid all of Castle Rosam a farewell," said Sir Sorsen, turning his horse. The taciturn Mussago saluted them and both rode from the keep, their men following.

Habidros waved once more before disappearing through the arch of the gate.

"Do you think those two lordlings have become friends?" asked Donzalo of Sir Blen.

"We will know better when both become counts," Blen answered, shrugging. "They can afford to be friendly now."

2

"Sir Copago! Hail! Who are these who ride with you?"

"Friends of Donzalo I met on the road. We were both headed here." He dismounted to take the hand of Sir Corgos. "I hear that we are far too late for all that happened."

"Very true," said one master of arms to the other, "but you have come just soon enough that you did not miss Sir Donzalo's departure."

"Where is the boy?" asked a bear-like man who had come to stand beside them.

"Over in the stables, I think." Corgos tipped his head in that direction. "I can only assume that you are a brother of Galaro and Habidros."

"That I am, sir. I am Mausare."

"And I, Sir Corgos. What brought you all the way from the upper Cuddon?"

"My father sent me," the burly Cuddonian replied and started off in the direction the knight had indicated.

"They had some inkling of the trouble brewing here and the Thane of Drolwym had them ride." Copago looked toward the broad back of the man walking from them. "This Mausare has, like Habidros, been a captain of mercenaries so he was chosen to lead them. He seems a good fellow, though given to moods."

Corgos turned to regard the man, as well. "I think I shall accompany our Mausare. You can find lodgings on your own I am most certain, Sir Copago." He followed after the Cuddonian.

Donzalo was busied with the loading of a cart and saw not the man who approached him.

"Is this my brother?" asked Mausare in a quiet, even voice, looking upon the long box that was being carefully stowed.

"It is, Cousin," said Donzalo, embracing the man.

"It is good to see you, boy, despite the circumstances. And Oder!" The Anian had stepped forward from where he stood in shadow. "I've not beheld you in years." His smile came bitter-sweet. "I rejoice that there was a bard to chronicle Guesare's final battle."

"The events are still too close for me to compose a lay. In time."

"I understand this," said Mausare. He spoke again to Donzalo. "I have messages from Lady Se, but I suppose you can guess what is in them."

"She wishes me to bring the Lady Fachalana so the Fay might aid her, even as they did Jola."

"And as they did you."

Corgos had come up behind the Cuddonian. "Will you accompany Sir Donzalo and his party back to your homeland?"

"So do I intend," replied Mausare. "We were sent to fetch him."

"Then enjoy our hospitality for a day or two. We would not have you return weary to the road." He looked toward Oder and Donzalo. "You do not mind the delay, gentlemen?"

"Not I," replied the youthful knight. "Mausare and I have much catching up to which we must attend!"

There was a donkey cart on the street, laden with Mistress Rassana's modest belongings. I'll make that Dame Rassana soon, she told herself, and have Dorbi stand beside me before a priest. She did not think that would prove difficult.

"Ready?" asked Perdos.

"I always was," she answered.

The knight took a long look toward the Keep Rosam, standing above the city. It was time for a farewell to this place, maybe for good.

As he had said farewell to Bolos on the yesterday. He had attended the count's funeral and none had stayed him. Perdos shook the reins and the donkey started forward; his horse was tied behind and followed.

I'll need more horses at the inn, he thought. He had always felt that it would be good country for raising them, down-river where they were headed. Maybe good for raising a houseful of brats, too, Perdos mused, taking a look at the woman seated beside him.

And farewell to Sir Guesare. He no longer found it in himself to hate the man. Perhaps he hadn't for some time. Guesare had died a brave man and by another hand than his own. So be it and may his shade find rest.

Perhaps in some afterworld, the minstrel and his brother Percos could have another go at each other. Perdos smiled at that thought, as the cart followed the Great Road south and out of Ros-town.

"I suppose I needn't have called for you," Lareth told his son. "Things have settled down in Lama and now we can both go home, long before winter sets in."

"Sire, will Lomela be alright?" Gawis had never been close to his much younger sister but certainly wished her no ill. He seemed as restless as ever to his father, pacing back and forth. Maybe he just wants to get back to his wife, Lareth thought.

"Perhaps better than before. The loss of Count Bolos was no great blow to anyone, though I hear that he died well." The king gazed a while into the fire. "Lomela has competent friends to stand beside her. Jobareth Nafal, not the least of them."

"He is leaving our service, I hear."

"I always had doubts about that boy as a career diplomat. Far too independent." He thought of another too independent man who had served him and then banished that thought. "Lord Doufan will return to us soon," he went on. "We need him more here in Sharsh than they do in Lama. And there will be one with him, a Sir Blen, for whom I have expectations. You should make his acquaintance, Gawis."

The prince smirked. "I have thought of stealing Modareth's protege, Sir Pol, from him. He is also a man for whom one should have expectations."

"A talented lad, from all I have heard. I doubt he will want to serve Modi in Dor."

"Not with his successes in Celatas, sir."

"Should he continue those successes, he will not wish to serve anyone, my boy."

"We shall stop a while at your manor, Uncle, as it is on our way. Then, on up the road and into the Cuddon."

"Say hello to my mother," said Grippo, seated in the corner, where he had been dealing with a rather large pastry. He had resumed his robes of an acolyte and should receive his postponed priesthood this coming year. He was still not positive it was what he wanted.

"*Our* mother," corrected Copago, "and to my wife as well."

"We'll all see our loved ones soon," Sir Paren said, "There's little reason for us to remain much longer at Keep Rosam.

"Donni, are you sure it's a good idea to go into the hills at this time of year?"

"Another month and we might see some hard going." Donzalo thought back to his previous journey there. "I am assured it won't be bad now." His expression went from the light-hearted to the serious. "And I think the Lady Fachalana should wait no longer."

He rose, his head coming perilously close to the ceiling beams. "It's to bed for me. I want to get an early start."

3

It had been a rugged way, traveling up the backbone of the Cuddon, but the mild autumn weather had held.

"We missed Harvest Feast back home," Donzalo informed Sir Blen, who rode beside him.

"I wonder if I shall be in Lama when next it comes," replied the knight. "Our friend Jobareth, it seems, intends to remain permanently."

"I know not where I shall be in a year, either. Perhaps in this land through which we now ride."

Blen looked out across the colorless hills. "The Cuddon would not be my choice, Sir Donzalo. Lord Doufan has hinted that I shall accompany him to Sharsh when he returns. Perhaps I shall go down the River Chas a way and see if anything has changed."

Mausare came up to join them. "The turn is near," he said. Donzalo nodded and looked back to the cart where rode the Lady Fachalana. Ansa sat by her side as she had every day of this journey and, indeed, every day since her soul had been blasted.

Ahead lay Mausare's home, Guesare's home, but they would turn aside here.

They would have to tend to Fachalana before they beheld the haphazard towers of Drolwym Keep.

It was to be his tragedy, Sir Pol had told her. He had moved it up to mid-season, to make way for a different closer. Pol was secretive about that but rumor had it the closer would be Jobareth Nafal's long-delayed "Oemse."

It did not seem that Viscountess Fachalana would ever reclaim her theater and Nafal had apparently decided to remain in Lama. Mara did not know either very well.

She idly tapped out a tune on the dulcimer, one of the dances of Narcles. Did he still compose for her father's court? Mara put down her hammers and let her hands slide over the ornate instrument, its richly-hued mahogany sides carved with creatures of the sea. It was the most treasured of all the possessions she had brought with her from her home.

Mara had dreamed again of home, but it was a peaceful dream. The princess had walked beside the sea and another walked with her. Perhaps, she thought, it had been her father, that weak, indulgent man, or perhaps it had been some other. Mara had awakened suddenly, wondering, from that idyll.

The old priest had been right. These dreams were but phantoms of her own mind, embodiments of her fears, of her hopes. Gawis had awakened when she stirred and had held her in his arms until she returned to sleep.

Gawis had returned to her. That was all that mattered, she told herself. Gawis was returned and they would attend the theater this night. It was time that she readied herself.

Which gown would best conceal her ever more obvious pregnancy from the eyes of the crowd? That she was with child was common knowledge but there was no sense in displaying it — and it did show with Mara's slender body. Perhaps that stiff, heavily embroidered dress of cream-colored silk would do. Its rigidity had ever annoyed her but could be an asset tonight. And the weather was cool enough for an enveloping cape.

The princess smiled. She couldn't get away with that in her tropical homeland.

That homeland was the past. Sharsh was Mara's home now and, if Kamat were willing, she carried its future king within her.

Mara busied herself with thinking of names for that king as she dressed.

Before them stood the hill of the Fay. The Cuddonians had remained a distance back and only the six comrades approached its entrance.

Fachalana stood erect, turning her head slowly from side to side as if seeking. She senses what lies here, thought Donzalo.

He looked up to the overcast sky, the ever-shifting sky of the Cuddon, and then to the pine-clad hills. Did he spy a horse of dappled gray running there?

"The entrance is before us," he whispered to the others, "if you look properly."

There was one coming from it, his snow-white face framed by raven hair.

"Arsel. I greet you," spoke Donzalo, stepping forward.

"And I you, Donzalo. So destiny has led you back to us." The fay surveyed the group. "Only he who loves her may enter with the Lady Fachalana," stated the prince.

The eyes of Oder and Jobareth turned to Donzalo, but not those of Ansa. The young Laman slowly bowed his head toward Sir Blen.

"I am he," said the knight of Sharsh and, taking Fachalana's arm, followed Prince Arsel into the halls of the Fay.

Ansa sighed deeply. Donzalo put his arm around her and said, "Let us take Guesare home."

Afterword

I hope you have enjoyed the four books that make up the saga of *Donzalo's Destiny*. So concludes the story of young Donzalo and his friends, though we may revisit their world one day.

This fantasy novel is set in a place and time of its own, although it most closely resembles 16th Century Central Europe. The stories and characters, the world in which they "exist," arise from ideas I have played with for many years.

Incidentally, if one wishes to pronounce the names in this book, it is generally safe to treat them as one would Spanish — at least the names that come from the widely-spoken Muram language.

Stephen Brooke

Author and artist Stephen Brooke lives and works in an old farmhouse in the Florida Panhandle. All his books are available from Arachis Press, a small publisher dedicated to presenting meaningful literature for readers of all ages. Visit http://arachispress.com for our catalog.

9 781937 745370